D0842005

BEFORE
MY
TIME

BEFORE MY TIME

NICCOLÒ TUCCI

INTRODUCTION BY DORIS LESSING

MOYER BELL LIMITED

Mount Kisco, New York & London

Published by Moyer Bell Limited

Acknowledgment and thanks are due to *Encounter Magazine*,
London, in which the opening section of this book appeared.

LIBRARY OF CONGRESS
CATALOGING-IN-PUBLICATION DATA

Tucci, Niccolò, 1908–
    Before my time / Niccolò Tucci ; introduction by
    Doris Lessing.
        p.   cm.
    ISBN 1-55921-055-9 (pbk.) :
    I Title.
    PR9120.9.T82B44   1991
    823'.914—dc20   91-15356
                                               CIP

Printed in the United States of America
Distributed by Rizzoli International Publications, Inc.

This book is for Laura, also for Vieri and Bimba.

Had it not been for the absurdity of life and its unhappiness, this book would never have been written. I must therefore acknowledge first of all the absurdity of life and its unhappiness—best publishers on earth, best teachers and best friends.

But I had other friends and teachers to assist me as well, and a publisher who saw to it that my scribblings were edited, set in proof, bound and sold. We don't shed books the way we shed hair or skin or strange ideas. That is why I must mention all the people who worked with me and often for me. First and foremost Gaetano Salvemini, one of the greatest men my country gave the world in the last century, a man hated by everyone who had something to hide, and then loved by these same people the moment they learned from him that lies are limited and the truth endless. Salvemini will live long after his detractors have all drowned in self-pity and mental impotence.

During the last years of his life I used to entertain him with episodes from my family history and with the strange adventures of a man who, because of his honesty, had the whole world against him. Salvemini was very much taken by this character. He never understood that I was telling him his own life history.

"Finish these books, you fool!" he would say. Here is one. The others will soon follow.

Then I must thank Nicola Chiaromonte, a critic forty years younger than Salvemini but regarded by him with veneration.

Next in line Marguerite Caetani, who has done more for individual writers, for literature in general, and for the cause of better understanding among nations than any government or all of them combined.

Also, the Ford Foundation which enabled me, through generous financial help, to devote all my time to this and all those other books.

Florence Samuels was the first reader of the finished manuscript. She said the book was there. I took it to the publisher.

Bob Gottlieb, so much younger than myself, taught me to edit my own writing and even physically rescued this volume from destruction. Maria Leiper worked with him, also with me for six months, deciphering the manuscript and my corrections, debating all debatable points, then making me rewrite what had been left unclear, and then still trimming, editing, correcting, always with admirable endurance and most undeserved kindness.

INTRODUCTION

Through tumults of swirling snow and wind—a blizzard of Russian intensity—struggles a family group, adults with small children, appearing in glimpses to the reader's view during momentary weakenings of the storm, all huddled indomitably together against Fate and the weather, like exiles off on their long walk to Siberia . . . but wait, this is not Russia, this is Switzerland, though the family is Russian, and they are taking a walk for their health, but above all because, as Russians, they understand snow, its subtleties and its beauties—its essential qualities—as no one else in the world can do. If Switzerland is bourgeois and soulless, a mere spittoon of a country, then at least its snow is not. Like all Russians away from their *rodina*, their homeland, they are exiles from their best selves. Yet they live abroad from choice, and continue to do so, while forever deciding to leave at once for Moscow, or for almost anywhere. " . . . for she had dragged her unhappiness from town to town, from hotel to hotel, taking time from her major sorrows to note in passing that the cooking was horrible and none of the guests had enough wit to cheer her."

Niccolò Tucci is Italian. His father was the poor and idealistic doctor who fell in love instantly and fatally, a marriage of souls, with a daughter of this rich Russian family, and who spent his life thereafter captive to their whims and lunacies, knowing that somewhere along this destiny-ruled road he had sold out his best self. A contradiction, you are thinking: it doesn't add up? Not at all! Nothing less than a total impossibility rooted in the very nature of life would do in this family. *Before My Time* is a portrait of the family, but it has the quality of a novel, and as soon as you begin to read you forget it is a memoir, for the imagination of an artist has transformed memory into a work like Proust's: for *A La Recherche du Temps Perdu* should be called autobiography, if this book is; both are characters observed through a magnifying glass, the enormity of family life as a child experiences it, but distanced by the necessity to put oneself as far and fast as possible from its quicksand seductions. For ever and ever will the boy Marcel lie awake weeping till morning because his mother has forgotten to come and kiss him goodnight, and it is tolerable because the author Proust has shut the pain safely into his pages. And for ever will this family of stupendous Russians, all adept in sadomasochistic emotional torture, torment each other—but safely, in this memoir transmuted by the intensity of experience into a novel.

Often young writers write a certain kind of novel which is an act of self-definition, for their idea of themselves has been knocked askew or eroded by whatever it is they have suffered— and they have endured by observing, by learning the cool, ironical eye. In this case, the author has defined himself not by insisting on his own life, but that of his parents, and above all, that of the monstrous matriarch who stamped her image on them all.

She is of the same literary provenance as Chekhov's Lyuba Ranevsky and Irina Arkadin, but most of all Dostoevsky's prodigious grand dame in *The Gambler*, who tyrannises and bullies everyone, and then loses her entire fortune at the gambling table in one night's play and says Forgive me, Forgive me, as if she has mislaid a purse with a few roubles in it. (How did these terrible women, who drive themselves and everyone else crazy, who ruin themselves and everyone around them, come into existence? What permitted them?)

Mamachen, Grossgrandmutter, Grossgrand mamchen, or— seldom—just Madame, manipulates her children like puppets in orgies of emotional blackmail and self-flagellation, while she corresponds with Tolstoy, sharing with him her lofty thoughts (she knows he has got some of his best ideas from her) and allows her vast fortune to be stolen from her by a whole army of servants. Her particular victim, her alter ego, is Mary, the author's mother, she who was the other partner of the destined love. "She woke up and as she knew her husband detested tears in the morning (how uncivilised of him, how Italian, how peasantlike) she left her bed and in a great hurry took her tearful face like a *souffle' de fromage* right from the oven, to the exacting gourmet who liked tears hot and rich, made to order and plentiful; and in her mother's arms she cried and cried and cried. . . . The doctor found them together in tears and he was very angry. 'Cry as much as you like,' he said, 'since that seems to be a Russian sport. . . . But if you must, close the windows at least, it is freezing outside.'"

This is comedy with the abundant inventiveness—each climax of mad improbability topped by another—of Gogol's *Dead Souls*, which is its nearest literary relation. Gogol (on Pushkin's generous suggestion) sent his hero travelling around Russia in search of his gallery of grotesques, but why travel if what you need is at home, in your house, in your own memory?

Each member of this family is as wondrously distorted as the mysteriously suggestive shadows in a shadow-puppet play, or the wildly leaping shadows thrown by a draught-tormented candle: not only Mamachen, but Mary, her captive and jailor, and the "immoral" daughter Ludmilla, who finally turns her family against her at the moment when she crosses her legs and lights a cigarette, proof of the ultimate depravity, loss of virginity; and Pierre, the superior son in Moscow, who appears only at the end, at the matriarch's death. This is a scene of wonderful lunacy, each member of the family plotting how to cheat the others out of what is left of the mother's inheritance, while each hints that the others are mad, and broods secretly about the possibility of having them locked up. There is, in fact, a locked-up daughter, that common figure of the time (and not exactly known in ours) the girl who was never mad, but was found too "difficult" to be allowed to remain at large.

The servants who sponge off the family are the progenitors of scenes as richly comic, as close to farce, as any in Russian fiction. They manage with superb impertinence to make anyone who remonstrates with them feel guilty. This is usually the unfortunate doctor, who finds himself scolding them for wasting a few loaves of bread while whole fortunes stream past his face into their sticky fingers. (Thus they are enabled to complain that they are forced to eat stale bread out of the waste bin while ordering in meals cooked by a local gourmet chef—that is, for themselves, not for their masters.) So unpleasant do they make it for their employers that when they protest, their depredations are not only forgiven or glossed over but their salaries are doubled and trebled. (I keep thinking of Ostrovsky's play, "Too Clever by Half," that crescendo of comic impertinences that recently, at the Old Vic, in London, had whole audiences weeping with laughter.)

How is it possible that such a superb book has been overlooked in recent years? It is true that when it appeared in 1962 it was enthusiastically received. Since then, however, although a few continue to admire it and speak of it to each other and to friends, it mostly has been ignored. This is because it does not fit a category. Autobiography it may be, for the author insists it was all true; but we do not read *David Copperfield* because it was all "true." It may have an Italian author brought up in Italy, but it is a Russian novel if there ever was one. The Russians could claim it, and I believe they will. It is a modern novel, that is, set in the first part of this century—yet it has the atmosphere of the nineteenth—or of timelessness.

There are many readers who mourn the nineteenth century novel, its capaciousness, its pace, its scope, its ironies, the firmness of characterisation that is rooted in a world with neater moral boundaries. Those readers will find food and delight here.

I think *Before My Time* is one of the books, unjustly ignored, which come into their own when their time comes at last. This, I hope, is the time for this one. It is a great book, which will, I am sure, continue to gather lustre until it is set firmly on that special shelf side by side with the classics of world literature.

—Doris Lessing

BEFORE MY TIME

I

I WAS BORN BEFORE MY TIME. When my time came, the place
was occupied by someone else; all the good things of life
for which I was now fit had suddenly become unfit. It was always too early or too late. Too early to behave like a grown boy
and run ahead of the governess who wheeled my younger
brother through the park in his blue carriage, too late to sit in
that carriage looking like Queen Victoria and getting all the attention. Too early to have collected in my body at birth the
soul of my grandmother, too late to have known her and been
able to mourn her. Too early to be given injections of longev-
ity, which would be invented in the year 2000 along with space
travel, too late to have known the grand life of the Gay Nine-
ties, with gas lamps, horse-drawn carriages and private railroad
cars. Too early to be treated with deference, too late to be
treated with tenderness. Too early to be brought up in freedom, too late *not* to be brought up in freedom.

My education was a very strict one, yet it could no longer be
the strict Victorian, Prussian, militaristic education my mother
had received or the strict Jesuit education my father had received. My earliest ideals were all extremely worthy but somewhat contradictory: to be able to cry (proof of a tender heart),
to be able not to cry (proof of a manly heart), to be forever

7

grateful to my parents for benefits received (proof of humility),
to remember forever what I owed to myself (proof of independence), to leave Mother alone (proof of respect for other
people's independence), not to leave her alone (proof of respect for other people's feelings). They never clashed by ac-
cident, those worthy ideals; they came in twos and ran on the
same track in opposite directions. If I kept them both in sight,
having placed all of myself in both engines, I could only watch
them clash. If I kept only one in sight (the tender heart or the
strong character), my soul fled from the other and I was lost to
the love and esteem of my parents. "Extremist!" they would
say. "No sense of measure." To keep their love, their esteem
and my measure, I had the choice of either running against
myself or staying solidly rooted in mid-air and refusing to go
anywhere by any train. As an obedient son I ran against myself
and refused to go anywhere.

I was born a good child. Had I lost both of my parents at
the age of three or four, six at the most, I still might have become a good man. The trouble was I lost them when they had
already lost me. And yet I am devoted to their memory. They
tried their best—but perhaps not, because they did their worst.
I refuse to believe that their best was of such a low quality;
that would be like accusing them of inhumanity or stupidity.
Other interests kept them captive—here is a far more charitable view. They were caught unawares by their anatomy. They
were fit to have children, not to tend them. In other words,
they were like everybody else who casts upon his children some
of the evil left unused by his parents on the day of their death.
Hell is this side of life. The dead are punished over here for all
their sins. No need of devils with their forks and flames. Our
children are the devils, filial love is their instrument of torture.
Oh, how the dead must suffer when they see their nonsense
triumph! Two are the disadvantages of death: we are either
forgotten or remembered. If the hereafter clarifies our thoughts
(and they are too confused to be stored in eternity that way),

if our minds at least emerge in a better condition than our bodies, then the dead must begin to understand, they must open their eyes the very moment we are closing them on their sad faces, and they must watch the scene, not from on high, but from any point lower than the ceiling. They must begin to haunt us in full daylight, when ghosts are never feared and inner voices never heard, and they must cry and plead, "Forget us, oh, don't honor us, it hurts too much." To no avail.

My father was a doctor and descended from a set of dishes on which his face (half lion and half satyr) could be seen all in red with a wide-open mouth and two fiery eyes, flowers and naked women coming out of his skull, two cornucopias coming out of his ears, two cleft feet (obviously his own) on the two sides of his beard, and two identical sets of musical instruments (flutes, long trumpets, mandolins and bagpipes) tied to the ends of his long red mustache and plunged into an oval night all to themselves (they were painted on black). But ever since he had begun to study medicine, my father had (as he said) pulled all the nonsense out of his head and closed his skull, letting black hair grow over it. The cornucopias had been replaced with just one stethoscope which he kept in his pocket and used only to hear the answers of the microbes to his patients' coughing and counting. His skin had become pink with shades of yellow, and he kept his mouth shut or opened it only to talk and eat and pick his teeth with a gold toothpick in the form of a sword he used only when my mother was not watching. I never knew what had become of the musical instruments until one day I noticed them in a dark library in the house of an old gentleman who had become our friend, or, much rather, our clown: the Marchese Carlo Tempi of Rome, whose wife was more or less a friend of ours and whose father-in-law, a Mr. Schultz from Petersburg, was really our friend and also, in a way, our broker. But not all of the musical instruments were

9

there; the bagpipes and the trumpets were missing, and the black oval night was also gone. The only person who could know anything about them was obviously my father, and so the truth came out. He disclaimed all descent from those dishes; they were older than he, and, besides, English, and he came from southern Italy.

In 1913 my father invented diphtheria. I discovered this fact by listening behind the living-room door while he was talking to another doctor. I could not understand what need there was to invent another disease when there were so many already, but whatever he did was wise and good. He also invented on that same day the Italian word *insomma*, which I had never heard before. He seemed to enjoy using it, but, as the word was new, he tried it on to see how it would fit, and every time he did so there was a long, medical silence (the silence of injections, of pulse taking, of chart readings, in which silence a doctor waits for results), then the two men resumed their conversation. After another while, again my father used that word and again there was silence. I decided I would use it myself, and tried it with the maid in the kitchen, shouting, "*Insomma!*" Strangely enough, she knew it already, and yet my father had not moved from the living room. I ran back to my listening post and heard that Pope Pius X had just died. I wondered whether diphtheria had been tried on him while I was in the kitchen, and was curious to know how my father could have done it all so quickly. Then I heard that the Campanile of Venice had just fallen (nothing to do with diphtheria, but, all the same, how many things in such a short time!). "*Insomma,*" said my father, and the other doctor approved, then said he had to go, and I was sure he was going to spread diphtheria all over the town. "*Insomma,*" said the doctor before leaving, and my father wished him good luck.

Then there was a dispute between my sister and me. She said that before being born I had been dead for centuries and no one had ever noticed it. So I ran to my father and asked him.

"You never were," he said. "You were just born five years ago, and you will not die for another ninety-five years, I hope."

"Yes, but *before* I was born."

"You were unborn."

"Unborn and not dead?"

"Yes. You must be born to die."

I did not press the matter any further. I understood it as an order. You could not sit at table without washing your hands; just so, you were not allowed to die unless you were born. But in some remote countries, I thought, a boy could disobey his parents and die first. The idea seemed absurd, but fascinating all the same—if for no other reason, as a fantastic form of disobedience.

And so we spoke about a great many things, he and I, all a bit delicate, because they all converged upon the point of interest that could never be mentioned, namely death. A doctor was immune to disease, therefore a doctor could not die. As a matter of fact, my father spoke of death as a good thing, and besides he was *dirty with time*, the marks of death could not be washed out of his skin. His neck was full of irregular lines, and I asked myself why they should not have been made more calligraphic and parallel. He was beginning to have a double chin, a face within a face, or, rather, a new face behind a face, and the loose flesh under his chin swelled like a curtain in the wind, and the backs of his hands were shiny and brown with irregular spots (the dirt of time again); when they hung low the veins came out in knots ready to burst, and when he fell asleep after a meal, breathing through his open mouth, he was rehearsing for his death. To look now at a picture of my parents taken after the invention of diphtheria (my father was then forty-three, my mother thirty-five), they seem like adolescents—not a wrinkle in their faces, not a shade of awareness in their eyes.

But children are astronomers, they calculate the arrival of a comet long before it becomes visible: the decay of their parents is measured by their own freshness; that wrinkle which will scar their mother's mirror in ten years, like a sudden bad omen, has been their first toy when she was young.

The only guarantee that our parents were not going to die came to us from the fact that they could still give orders. Such phrases as "You heard me! What are you waiting for? Do you want to be spanked?" chased away every doubt as to their near-ing death. Speaking thus, they must have known they were still safe and strong. When, instead, they lost interest in our crimes and let us be, without trying to discover whether their orders had been duly carried out, we felt in this a loss of interest in the world, and the nearness of death.

I did not learn much about death that day. I still saw it as a low entrance to a cavern: people going that way must slowly bend in order not to bump their heads against the ceiling as they entered, and in spite of his age my father was still walking straight, thank God. But I learned a great deal about that past in which the world had been forced to do without me. There had been, long before I was born, earlier gods.

On my father's side I see shadows of peasants bent under olive trees, hardly distinguishable from the soil. Their actions are agricultural and seasonal more than moral or personal. Their anonymity, their silence, make me feel that down there in Apulia I descended from olive trees, fig trees and almond trees, also from oxen, goats and donkeys, and not dishes. That was a world of passivists, the real victims of God. A world of mourners too.

On my mother's side I see fir trees crash noisily under the ax, uncombing other fir trees in the forest; I see lumber yards, in-dustrial villages and smoke from factories; compasses, ledgers and shelves, binoculars and beards, bales and boxes on quaysides; gold-rimmed spectacles and banks, offices on black beaches with green seas and icebergs, offices on white beaches with blue seas and pyramids; and, at the center of it all, a quiet house with heavy curtains in a quiet street of Moscow. This was a world of activists with a religion of their own, even a trinity of their own: an Iron Will, a Sense of Duty to Mankind, and a Gigantic Self-Respect. Money in that world counted for nothing, or, much rather, it counted to become sinful afterward and was therefore treated with caution and contempt. It had the same function as mercury in the thermometer: it measured effort, worthiness, therefore honesty too. Left to itself outside the glass tube, it could never be mastered, it would break into smaller infinities which no fingers could pick up.

Closer to us in time were the later gods, known also as the dead. The last dead in our family were all in the respectable but somewhat distant category of grandparents—for us children, who either had not known them or could hardly remember them, far beyond reach of tears.

My Italian grandparents were no gods. They were human and buried. They had both died at the same time, or almost, and soon after the funerals my father had had to go back to medical school and obtain his degree, then come back home and look after his seven sisters and whatever was left of his estate. His dreams of academic work, teaching medicine as a form of philosophical discipline, were set aside, and he became a country doctor. In later years, if he spoke of his parents at all it was with reverence but without grief, and without mentioning their exceptional virtues or the wrongs they had suffered. They were gone from his memory like the smell of burnt candles and warm flowers, incense and disinfectant, from the room of the dead after the funeral. We had only one picture of them in the house, a two-seater picture; my grandfather, with whiskers that swelled his fat face considerably, seemed to emerge from the fog, as my father had done one rainy day peeping into a tearoom to see whether we were still seated there drinking our hot chocolate—his face had appeared suddenly from the fog blanketing the windowpane; we had seen him talk to us and we had talked to him, but he could neither hear us nor answer us. Of my grandmother I knew only that she had never had her picture taken in her lifetime, because her husband would have considered this a form of treason. In fact, in that one picture there she was already dead, and there was more fog around her than around him. Her head half hidden in white lace and sunken into a pillow, the whites of her eyes showing and her teeth showing, she seemed almost a skull. And yet those two asked nothing of us. They did not even want to know what we were doing when no one was looking at us. They did not even use their star to blink at us when we had told a lie. No death current if we touched their picture.

My Russian grandfather also was surprisingly harmless and contented with his old ration of tears. He had died when my mother was eleven. She had cried for a day, then left him for a Teddy bear we still have in the house; but even this toy, though more sacred than any of my grandfather's portraits, more sacred even than his marble bust, had a much smaller charge of sacredness than any of my grandmother's toys. There was a tragic reason for this fact.

When I opened my eyes to the world, the corpse of my grandmother was still rotting away about the house. The suffocating smells were neutralized with essences: sandalwood, tarnished silver, camphor oil, face powders, moth balls, jasmine, Russian leather, Chinese tea, Japanese lacquer, candied roses, burnt paper, incense, even boxes of unsmoked ancient cigars. But the smell of decay was stronger than all these. We had it in our cribs, we had it in our toys, we had it in our food, so we began to putrefy before we were allowed to grow. There was not a clean handkerchief, not a clean bedsheet, napkin, tablecloth or towel in the house, not a fork, not a knife, not a cup or a saucer, not a sheet of writing paper, not a book, that was not marked with her initials and cursed with her organic fall from that title of possession.

Walls were stained with her images, in brown on brown, in black on white, in oil, in tempera, in pastel, in miniature; always with that sad look demanding grief and worthiness; all examples to follow, taken from sacred moments of her life. Here she was standing in a personal pyramid of sealskin, topped by three layers of pearls, the protruding double chin, plus bulging cheeks, high cheekbones, frowning forehead, hair, and a small sealskin baby bonnet tied under her chin with ribbons (all of which items became symbols of virtue); there she came in a bust of white marble ("Be as pure as this marble" was the unspoken dictate to be read in that bust); farther down, under glass and in a heavy gilded frame with oak leaves and ribbons, almost two of her chins buried in sable, she seemed to imply that one must be as finely drawn and painted as that sable (and whoever was sableless was wrong); in the adjoining room, in a large photograph, she sat hugely in white lace under a lace umbrella in her victoria, against a glaring background of hotels, palm trees and balconies; then she came all in black, in a low sleigh pulled by black horses, with snow and black fir trees for a background; then, in another picture, she was seated alone at the head of a large banquet table, with a window behind her, so all one saw was a white tablecloth with dishes, glasses of all sizes, bottles, carafes and flowers, tending toward that dark shape of a goddess who did not seem at all tamed by those tributes. But her photographers went on trying their best to drag a smile out of that mass of international proteins. They took pictures of her on elephants in India, on camelback in Egypt, on the Pyramids, inside the Pyramids, under the Sphinx, amid the ruins of Pompeii (she did smile in that one, as if to imply, "See what I do to cities when they make me angry?"), and from each of those images there came a stream of sadness strong enough to ruin the most normal of children, let alone one like me who was already ruined by the mere fact of descending from her. The only picture in the house which seemed somewhat reassuring was that of her rich tomb in Berlin. She, of course, was not to be seen in it; a gravestone held her safely down, and a huge marble block with an overfed angel sitting on it had been added to the weight just in case. I, in my evil mind, saw her all wormy and frothing with cadaveric soap and still not smiling, but a look at that angel made me forget these shameful images at once. When I learned that she was not under that stone at the time the picture was taken, I was quite disappointed. That was only the picture of her former future tomb; it had been taken after her husband had been buried there—in fact, his name carried the dates of birth and death, and hers, carved under his, only the date of her birth.

That God might follow me through a thousand walls was bad enough, but then He was the Great, Merciful One, He forgave everything, and I was not his relative, I was just one out of billions and billions of children from all races and countries, and to follow them all required time even for Him. But the same omnipresence in a person like my grandmother, who had no use for anyone outside the strict family circle and who never forgave a son of forty if he smoked in her presence or got married in her absence, was a real danger. And though people are known to be bad, and nothing can be expected of them, grandchildren are not just people, and my grandmother had the right to expect the best of me as a bare minimum. That is why she blinked at me all the time from her personal star, when I passed in front of her portrait having just told a lie.

"Did you brush your teeth?" my mother asked me.

"Yes, I did."

"Can you swear?"

"Yes, I can."

"On your grandmother's grave?"

"No."

"Then you don't swear, you just simply confess that you have told me a lie. And last night too, and the night before, you always swore and you always knew these were lies. You have two oaths, a false one and a solid one taken on your grandmother's grave, but can you really believe that your grandmother doesn't know these things? Do you realize that every time you tell a lie you are spitting on her grave? How many times have you been spitting on her grave lately?"

Now, this was very confusing. At times I had brushed my teeth, at times I had only brushed the corner of the bathroom shelf with my toothbrush. Could I, with so much lying on my conscience already, volunteer to put under that heading also the rare occasions when I had told the truth? My mother kept insisting she wanted to know the exact number of lies I had told her. And as the choice was up to me, I first went through the comedy of a great deal of mind searching and soul searching, and then told her the smallest possible number of lies in order to save my soul from a new crime: that of killing my mother.

At the same time I realized that it was much too late for me to recapture my soul on its way to perdition, so I decided that I would at least never soil myself with the worst of all sins, namely ingratitude. I would always remember my debts of gratitude, always repay my benefactors a hundredfold for the smallest advantage or favor. Indeed, I went so far as to swear to myself that I would never profit by the benefits given me but for the purpose of praising my benefactors, and that even in the field of education I would never learn anything without learning and honoring my teacher's name and generosity first and foremost. This may sound a bit excessive until one thinks of the timidity of a child afraid of divine punishment or of adult reproach if he should dare forget that he must quote his father or his mother every time he remembers that the earth turns or that the sun goes up and down. "Who has told you these things? Where would you be if a loving father [or mother] had not worked very hard to learn them and to pass them on to you?"

Now, my parents were generous. They contented themselves with exacting that minimum of gratitude which all parents exact of their children for the fact that they feed them and clothe them instead of throwing them into the river as they well might if they so pleased, the child having no voice in the matter and no means of self-defense. And this is bad enough. But in the case of my grandmother my mother always came out with new evidence that the whole world should have thanked her for everything. Which evidence was given by her to my father in my presence, or even when I was not there, in a conversational tone, as if this were a social occasion and one of the two had come as a guest of the other for tea. I thus formed the belief that my mother went out of the house every night (my parents always stayed together in the daytime) to gather fresh details of the deeds of that wonderful person (my grandmother) whose untimely disappearance was still the object of universal grief. How could my mother otherwise have always had new things to recount that my father had never heard about? I knew from my own experiences in the world how difficult it was to have something new to tell, even for a few seconds. All my most interesting accounts of what I had experienced, heard or thought during a day came to an end after only a few minutes, even if I had recourse to a detailed description of what I had seen in shop windows, or of the animals I had seen at the zoo. Or the trees in the park. That my parents had not always known each other seemed a bit strange to me ("Good afternoon, sir." "Good afternoon, madame." And then: "Oh, you must be my wife if I am not mistaken?" "Right you are, and you must be my husband." "Right." "How are you, sir? "Very well, and you?" "Oh, very well indeed." "And how are the children?" "Oh, you mean our children?"

"Yes." "Very well, thank you, they are asleep in the next room.")

"Anything, anything, I would rather admit than lack of gratitude," continued my mother. "Theft, murder, are a thousand times preferable."

Then came the examples. She opened the *Revue des Deux Mondes* at random and found in it an article by a certain philosopher or a certain psychologist and almost at once exclaimed, "How strange! These are Mamachen's ideas! I remember so clearly when she suggested them to the man who has written this article! Isn't it awful that he should have taken such unfair advantage of her? Why not acknowledge that the ideas came from her?"

I remember her reading a book about Gladstone. She at once recalled how he had been staying at the same hotel as my grandmother in Lausanne, and how he had discussed all the major problems of the time with her, how she had given him advice, and how he had thanked her in a letter for her "most stimulating conversation and brilliant remarks." And now my mother recognized in Gladstone's life the pattern of her mother's own foreign policy for Great Britain.

"He could have told her he was going to use her ideas," she concluded. "What hypocrites, the British!"

(My father did somewhat the same sort of thing, but he attributed all the discoveries and ideas to Leonardo and other great Italians. When he read in the papers that for the first time in history a man-made iron bird had crossed the Alps, and that the French claimed credit for the flight, the pilot's name being Chavez, he said, "It should have been an Italian, and the plane should have carried the inscription 'This was made possible by the genius of Leonardo.'" Every time the telephone rang, he mentioned the fact that the telephone had been invented by an Italian, Meucci—not by Alexander Graham Bell, an American. Meucci was a Florentine, like Dante. And when he explained the pendulum to us he said, "Remember, Galileo's pendulum. Thanks to an Italian we can say it is now seven o'clock!" Luckily for us, neither Meucci nor Galileo nor Leonardo was our grandparent.)

Among the people who had been helped by my grandmother there was even Tolstoy, with whom there was a phonetic link: his wife and my grandmother had exactly the same name. And also an epistolary link, due to the fact that my grandmother had translated his essays into German. He too, who had thanked my grandmother for her thoughts on the Kingdom of God and everlasting peace, had then failed to let her know that he was going to develop these thoughts "so typical of her" in his new essays on both these subjects. Had she only known that a man she so worshiped had agreed with her views so completely, she might still be with us. These are the things that help you stay alive: the feeling that what one has given has been gratefully received. All the rest does not count.

But even more than the ideas she had given Tolstoy and (so I thought in my ignorance) Galileo and Voltaire, not to mention a number of psychiatrists of the French school, were all the precious friendships that people had established in her house with other people, forgetting that those were *her* friends, and that their fortunes, even at times their marriages, their children, were due to *her* generosity. How many people had grown rich and powerful because they had met someone with her help or at her house! And how many had profited by her advice! Madame Morosoff, to mention just one of them, the greatest steel industrialist in Russia at that time, had applied my grandmother's advice in an industrial crisis which had threatened to become a small revolution. Her thirty thousand workers (I am quoting from memory, I have carefully avoided checking these fragments of a child's recollections) had gone on strike. The director of the steel mills had been nailed into a barrel, rolled down to the river and drowned. Madame Morosoff had gone to the mills unaccompanied, faced her workers and asked them to stop all their nonsense. And they had stopped, hanging their heads in shame. The whole plan had been suggested by my grandmother, whose husband had at one time faced a crisis of the same type even though on an infinitely smaller scale (he had three hundred workers, and his were cotton mills), and it was my grandmother's advice which had prevailed on that occasion too.

How, with so many examples of ingratitude trumpeted into my ears all the time, could I help feeling as I felt? I decided that gratitude would become my life's career. For a day or so I kept this a great secret; then, as no one seemed to notice how grateful I was, and the ingratitude of others was beginning to irritate me, I decided to reveal it to the only person from whom it should have been kept secret, namely my mother. I even told her so: "Don't tell yourself, you must not know this, it is a great surprise for you." She was so grateful to me that she called me my grandmother's only worthy descendant, and I went to bed that evening feeling prouder than I can recall feeling on any other occasion in my life. Before going to bed I marched all through the house with my hands behind my back and my head high. I was aflame with imagination, I saw detailed scenes of my future life, in which scenes I, forgetful of injustice and slander and even of physical violence, insisted on being grateful to my enemies for a small act of kindness which they had done me years before and which they, but not I, had forgotten. And my grandmother blinked at me from the sky with such abundant tears of happiness that for the first time in the history of the universe, as I remarked triumphantly, it could be said that rain was falling from a star. This remark made me famous at once. But the next time I lost my temper my mother took unfair advantage of my confidence and ridiculed me in front of everybody.

"So, this is the knight in armor who defends his grandmother? The one who has sworn never to forget a benefit as long as he lives? Come and look at him, children," said she, calling my brothers to the scene. "Do you know who this is?"

And she revealed my secret, imitating my style and even my pronunciation, to conclude, in a violent diatribe against me, "Oh no. You a grateful person? You a champion of charity and justice? You, my boy, are the least grateful person in this world. You think only of yourself."

My humiliation reached a climax that suddenly transformed me into the very person whose description had wounded me so only a minute before. It was the very opposite of an act of rebellion. It was pure obedience. Confronted with such proofs of my hypocrisy, my selfishness, my cruelty, I became selfish, hypocritical, cruel. I recall this occasion because it was my funeral. My parents did not know that I was accompanying my character, crying behind him like a mourner. It was a form of maturation from superficial to deep sorrow. I, who until that day had always cried like a child for superficial reasons, was now crying so deep beneath the surface of the earth that no one could suspect the existence of that torrent of tears. My parents took it very badly; they saw only what they saw with their eyes, and it shocked them that I should not be playing the usual ham act of true love and repentance. So, to cure me of the devil that was in me, my father gave me a public spanking until I cried, "Enough, enough! I promise to be good!"

In the course of this ceremony, touched as he was by my cries, he beat me more and more strongly to punish himself at my expense, then told me so: "I am hurting myself more than I could ever hurt you," he said.

This was a bit too much, so, to regain my lost dignity, I decided to try to make everybody laugh. Trembling in every limb because I knew what would follow, I said, "Yes, but whose behind is red here? Yours or mine?" This time I was given the honor of a punishment in which he did not get the lion's share. Every blow was meant to hurt me and me alone.

"How is it possible?" he shouted at the top of his voice. "I suffer to punish him, I tell him so to have at least a bit of understanding from him, I almost apologize to him for performing my duty, and this is the result!"

This was my first experience of a heavy price paid for a brilliant remark. But this was not my style at all. In fact, I never had any relief from such performances. They were lies then and later, when I specialized in them at a price constantly heavier—not so much in punishment as in repentance. I despised myself thoroughly for behaving that way. Sensitive as I was, I reviewed the whole scene in my mind as I knelt in a corner afterward or (much later in life) as I went into a corner by myself because no one was close enough or bold enough (or cared enough) to punish me, and then I savored all the sadness of the episode. Also—and this is an important element in my confession—the episode became amusing only in its retelling. Which was all pure invention, even when the brilliant remark had been actually made, because my voice was always trembling with emotion, so that the brilliant words themselves were mostly inaudible. Thus, without at all possessing the stage presence of a clown, I earned for myself the useless (and unwanted) reputation of being one. No one was more ashamed than I after such a performance, and no one prouder when he heard it retold. So my father decided that he must break my character and eventually did, poor man, and he worked very hard to obtain such a wonderful result.

I must describe the whole process in full. The humiliation caused by that physical punishment and the loud declaration of my indignity left real physical traces all around me, more so than on my battered behind. I grew hungry for silence—not to rest in it myself, but to use it as cotton wool in which to muffle all the shrieks and the insults that others might have heard. I wanted to dry up every memory of what had just taken place in the house. I wanted time, not only silence, plenty of time to push everything away toward the dark well of the past in which guilt loses its sting. I hurried up the clock, and I spied on the faces of my parents, my brothers and the maids for signs of boredom and indifference, even after my claim to high ideals had been fully re-established. Those faces had been far too attentive before. They had relished my ruin, they had formed silent and negative opinions of me, and I wanted to know that these had been forgotten, too. Thus I began quite early to suspect that perhaps an ideal of gratitude placed on so high a level was not prudent, but, on the other hand, I could not artificially try to remember my past fallibility or accept the idea that it would soon present itself again. I really felt that I was not the same person who had sinned, and I had, for that naughty child of a minute before, the same contempt I had for last year's shoes and clothes and for their impotence to follow me in my growth. Promising to be a man five or ten minutes after having been a child was part of the technique of full forgiveness. Neither I nor my father believed much of these promises after a while, but we made them again all the same, he because he believed that this might have a good effect on me—"*Promissio boni viri est obligatio,*" he would say—and I because it seemed to me that he believed in them. There was no end to my ambition of saintliness and gratitude and peace, that infinite peace that comes only from the approval of the persons we love. But there remained a residue of shame, submissiveness and fear, which upset my relationship with everybody else. That is the reason I became closer to my father—I knew that he alone had completely forgiven me. The others had been too indifferent to have gone so far down and come back so far up to the surface again, tied to me like the devil to the damned.

Then I began to feel that violence was part of love, and that my father loved me more than he loved the others, because he had beaten me more. Thus, when any doubt arose in which I might have won my point by using my intelligence and my pursuasive powers in discussions with others, I preferred to force the issue deliberately and make way for the devil in me, because for one thing it was shorter than to carry on a discussion with my brothers or with a stupid maid, and secondly it was also shorter from the moral point of view. I knew that if my brothers or the maids made the slightest remark about my "well-known evil temper" I would hit them at once, feeling the unfairness of this blow, so why not hit immediately, why not repeat my well-known role of the boy possessed by the devil, in order to be able to sit quietly with my father, he and I alone like two grown persons, after the usual fall and resurrection? In other words, *the road that leads to peace through pain seemed far shorter and surer than the road through well-ordered conversation.* And also more rewarding—in the end I alone was worthy of his attention, while the others were excluded. They would stand on their own. If this was the beginning of masochism, it was for precise, logical reasons: to find an understanding, not to be left alone.

My mother never had any definite plans to transform me or to break me. She was simply using me, as she used everyone else, to bring herself as often as she possibly could to a crisis of tears, thus renewing the illusion that her mother had just died and that her feeling of loss was still undampened by the passage of time. She could not even think in terms of a moral education that would carry either me or any of my brothers toward a given future of our own from which she was excluded. She wanted to be a child together with her children, time being our common enemy. Independence and loneliness were to her the same evil. Whenever trouble was about to arise, she claimed it for herself to celebrate her solitude by asking me, "What would your grandmother say if she could see you now?" Then, instantly, without bothering to wait and see whether this question had struck the right chord in my heart (it always had a cheerful tone), she dealt the final blow: "I am glad she has died." After such a stupid remark made in bad faith, all she could do was cry and accuse me.

Frankly, I preferred my father's blows. If one must cry, he

gave me a lot to cry about, and quickly too. With her, instead, all I could do was to let her have the right of way and wait. I was emotionally exhausted, there was a feeling of great rest about me, a pleasant silence, a temptation to close my eyes and sleep, to which temptation I could never yield. I was on duty, like a guard in high uniform at an official ceremony. How dare I, who had heard such hard words about myself, I, forever condemned to infamy, I, who had made my mother cry, fall asleep like an angel and snore? But it was all so tiresome. If at least she would come to the point (I knew all the phases of the process by heart) at which she asked me, "Aren't you sorry for what you did? Don't you want to be good again?" But it took her so long to reach that point that, when she came to it, she herself was about to fall asleep, and we still had quite a way to go, a long detour through the forests of reproach and repentance; this was like the long way home in our afternoon walks, while my father's trail and punishment were like a brisk winter walk along the lake and back home by the short cut through the park. Because she always wanted to cry twice during these scenes, having embarked upon the painful trip through her own past, having recalled what she herself had done to her poor mother years before, how could she just forgive herself and forget all about it so easily? Only one person could forgive her, and that person, alas, was gone forever.

"Gone forever," she said, these being the verbal faucets to the fountains of tears. "Gone forever," and down they streamed, those tears. She cried so that it killed all filial affection, every trace of human pity in me. There remained only fear in the face of so much suffering. Also a great shame for her in front of me, because she became ugly, her nose red, the harmony of her face destroyed by strange muscular contractions, as if she were about to laugh. I felt like shouting "Stop it!" as one cries to an adult when he is about to scare a child by making faces at it.

Reconciliation and forgiveness came in those cases at one

26

millimeter from indifference, half a minute before supper, a walk or nightly rest.

"Let's not think of these things any more," she would say.

Thank God, I would think, and at once yawn.

But there remained Grossmama's holy objects: holy umbrellas, holy hat, holy fur coats, holy jewels, stationery, books and toys, everything she had owned—and that was everything we had, except for children's shoes and a couple of night pots in the nursery—and each of these sacred things could tell our grandmother how it had been touched or looked at. Our very secret thoughts could be revealed to her by these objects; they were spies, also amulets, they even had secret curative powers in a way, morally at least.

"I was just looking at Grossmama's things."

"I was playing with Grossmama's peacock, Grossmama's duck, Grossmama's turkey."

These were excellent reasons to be thought innocent and left alone. And if I happened to be roaming the house with evil plans in mind, or evil thoughts (nothing exceptional: a lie to tell or to conceal, or the rehearsal of a scene of liberation, imagining that my brothers had all died, I being the only survivor and my parents' only hope), I stayed carefully away from all those objects, without doing so deliberately; I was guided by an instinctive knowledge of the opportunity of certain associations, for I knew that a soul engaged in sin should not be exposed to those sources of virtue.

I was the fourth of a crop of five children, three born before my grandmother's health had begun to be seriously impaired (it had always been seriously impaired, she had always been sick, always on the point of dying, always wounded, battered to a pulp, pushed, carried, dragged to her grave by thankless children, but then also always healthy, alert, attached to life, an example of indomitable energy and wit to the very last moment of her life—one never knew what to believe, so one took everything as gospel truth and shining evidence of her perfection), three children born before her exceptional agony, as I had begun to say, but not free of putrefaction, either. Another corpse was still rotting away while my grandmother was alive: that of her father. When she finally died, taking with her, of course, all the perfection of the world, he automatically graduated to a heaven of evil, from which he looked down upon us in the glory of his sins.

No longer worthy of tears (he had had far too many), he was now a free target for laughter and abuse. But then even this abuse was of a sacred character. When my mother, describing her grandfather, said of him, "He was a thief, a scoundrel and a swine," this did not mean that we, his great-grandchildren, should be ashamed of him. Oh, no. These words were spoken with a nostalgic love of theft, arrogance, ignorance, avarice, vanity, murder, the whole list of the capital sins enriched with the latest additions in the field of criminal pathology, as if these and these alone had been our mother's guiding principles and her ideals. She delighted in telling the most horrible tales about him: He had slowly murdered his wife (this was not true at all, she had died of tuberculosis, so the best blow in his career had not been dealt by him but by the usual God). He had tried to bring up his four children to his own standards of stupidity and cruelty; they had deserted him and he had let them starve for years. His only daughter, my grandmother, who had married the husband he had chosen for her, eloped with a young man from a very poor family and asked for a divorce, which in those days, in a Lutheran family of the most solid banking bourgeoisie of Moscow, was regarded as a crime. She had finally married the young man and lived with him in great poverty until he had achieved success; in fact, he became richer than his father-in-law, and only then did the old man show lenience toward his daughter, but it was she now who refused to receive him in her house, so he did everything he could to ruin her husband. Even the only son who had stayed with him was forced in the end to leave, for he took special pleasure in hu-

miliating everyone. Only when people were completely destroyed, both morally and financially, did he seem satisfied for a
brief moment, and when they came to him begging for help
it was his joy to sneer at them and have them kicked out of the
house by his servants.

After these tales were told in front of his large portrait in
our living room, there remained in the air an aura of pride and
modesty, the same that follows great music: the pride that we
were able to understand it and be made humble by its beauty.
That a very special tone was needed for this litany of ancestral
abuse I came to realize the day I tried it on a guest, repeating
the same words I had heard from my mother many times. I was
stopped and sent to bed.

"One does not say these things."

"But you say them all the time."

"This is an entirely different matter."

And it was. Those were indeed my mother's ideals, even
though she herself would never have admitted it. By nature she
was reticent and timid, and my father's opinions usually became her own, so much so that when he said nothing she was
lost. But when she was in a bad mood, out they all came, the
hidden truths: "Nothing is achieved without cruelty, discipline,
order, efficiency; it is not what you do that may be judged immoral, but how you do it. You may be a murderer, but if you
do it well, openly and usefully, with a greater aim in mind, you
are forgiven—more than that, you are useful to society. Think
of Napoleon, think of Caesar, Alexander the Great. Did they
ever stop to hear whether other people wanted to be con-
quered or not? Did they change their itinerary to spare a small
tree or to avoid killing an ant? Straight ahead they went,
ants or no ants, trees or no trees."

Now, this requires first of all a great harshness with oneself.
My great-grandfather was the first one to suffer from his cruelty,
but he was cruel all the same, and for good reasons. He had
every right to exact from others the same kind of self-discipline

he exacted of himself. "Of course he was unscrupulous, but then look at the results. A genius in his business. Easily done, to slander someone who sacrificed and achieved something in his life. Who gave us the armchair in which we sit back and judge his actions?"

My father at this point became more and more violent against the old man. It was his only way of attacking his wife's mother without actually doing so. He attacked the man who had ruined her life in his lifetime and her character after his death.

My grandmother's exceptional virtues were the same as my great-grandfather's exceptional faults, and they boiled down to one: intolerance. Nothing was good enough for her. She had managed to detest every place in the world, she had dragged her unhappiness from town to town, from hotel to hotel, taking time from her major sorrows to note in passing that the cooking was horrible and that none of the guests had enough wit to cheer her. Not that she wanted to be cheered, God forbid, but were they supposed to know this? "No, no, they just don't have the wit even to try," she said. She herself had that wit, or so it seemed, but she had sacrificed enough to amuse others, let them now do their part.

She described Switzerland as "the spittoon." One could not breathe in it. I did not know what a spittoon was, I had never seen one, but I began to associate a spittoon in my mind with some sort of breathing aid; and whether Switzerland was or was not a spittoon, I could breathe in it very well and so could my mother and father and everybody else in the family. Yet my mother too now insisted that it was a spittoon, and that one could not breathe in it. She said so mostly during meals and with the windows closed. That is why I was so pleased when I saw her inhale the clean air of the mountains during our afternoon walks. At every breath she took I felt a bit more hopeful, I drew lines in half circles with the tip of my shoe in the dust, or kicked a pebble into the ditch, because I did not want to interrupt her in her breathing. She held her walking cane behind her back, horizontally in the hook of her arms, because that extended the breathing surface of the lungs, and she even praised the air, saying it was so clean. At times she would describe what she saw in the body of a mountain in front of her and find terms of comparison between that and the mountains of Norway, or the forests of Russia. And I, still with my eyes glued to the ground, and my heart full of hope, prayed silently, "Dear Lord, make Switzerland appear so big to her that she will never say one cannot breathe in it. Make it bigger, send more air to this place, and send it as far up as Grandmother, so she too will make peace with this country."

All in vain. As soon as we were back home and the slightest sign of life came from the "world," in a letter from Paris, or in the papers, again she would say, "One cannot breathe in this spittoon. Let's go to Paris immediately."

Another one of my grandmother's great achievements was the fact that she had spent something like five million rubles in the short space of fifteen years, without drawing any enjoyment from it. She had done this out of charity. To whom? Not, certainly, to the hotel owners, the waiters, the travel agents, the sleeping-car attendants, and the furniture movers of the places she visited. They were all vulgar, servile, ill-intentioned and well fed. She liked the poor in their classic garb and believed she could tell them as a drinker could tell a good wine from a mediocre one (not, indeed, from the cobwebs on the bottle, but from the bouquet, namely the look in the eye, the emaciated face, the sad but noble smile, the dignified behavior, etc.). She had been generous to the real poor, of course, but the bulk of her money had gone to the false ones. Who were, then, the recipients of her charity? Her children, who, by being deprived of a considerable inheritance, were forced back into that healthy character-forming status from which their father and other great self-made men had emerged: poverty.

"Let them not delude themselves," she said. "I know they are all hoping for my death, but on that day they will find nothing in the banks."

This evil thought, which replaced in her heart all such positive joys as could come to a normal person of wealth from the acquisition of objects of art or the experience of travel, was seen by us, her grandchildren, in a very noble light, as a supreme form of self-sacrifice and strength of character. Also as a proof of courage. She, whose heart was so tender, she who could cry if she only thought of the destitute, found enough strength to throw her children into the gutter, or almost, to prevent them from yielding to the soft, unmanly ways of great wealth. "Everyone must earn his own bread with the sweat of his brow. What my husband earned during a lifetime devoted only to hard work and to me he had already left to me long before dying, and not so that I might corrupt his children with it, but that I, in his company, could enjoy a well-earned rest after so many sufferings. Without him I have no joys left in life, but I feel that, for my children's sake, I should leave nothing to them."

Among her glories then was also counted her habit of traveling with her cook, her butler, her administrator, the packers and movers, the maids, and some of her furniture, namely her bed, her *chaise percée*, her cushions and the large portraits of her father, her mother and her husband, in heavy gilded frames, so that when she came to a hotel for two weeks it had all the appearances of a pageantry, the reconstruction of an epoch or the setting of a stage for a Wagnerian opera. The largest available living quarters in the largest available hotel were stripped bare of all furnishings and draperies, and for a day a crew of carpenters, cleaners and maids, under the authority of a hotel manager trained in the special idiosyncrasies of the well-known

Russian lady, drove nails into masonry and wood, and my mother had glimpses of their feverish work and inhaled the dust of plaster and of freshly sawed wood, while my grandmother, like an actress or an opera singer or a visiting sovereign expected not before a certain hour for the official reception, stayed shrouded in mystery, visiting churches and museums; and when her apartment was ready she would take refuge in it from a town or from a winter (or summer, or racing, or health) resort she had learned to detest the day of her arrival and for the remainder of her life. Her only problem was how to get out of it again and stand the torture of a trip from the hotel to the railroad station and the consequent trip to another place, where she might stop for only a few nights before reaching a final destination that was final in nothing but her intolerance of it.

She even built herself a house in Baden-Baden, which was as big as a hotel, but nowhere could she find peace or happiness. Her furniture took more fresh air and saw more of the world and its ways than she, who stayed indoors reading books she had brought with her, then summoned specialized teachers of languages, art history and political history who came to see her in her apartment and gave her a detailed account of the culture surrounding the hotel, while she listened attentively and took notes which had nothing to do with that culture or that language but a great deal with the person seated in front of her. Thus, at a fantastic price, she met quite a few characters and wrote quite a few humorous sketches describing them and even quoting them while they were busy teaching her their lessons. As for the countries where she lived, she often wrote of them approvingly in a few lines if on that day the sky had been as blue as expected, but woe to Rome, Naples, Sorrento, Genoa, Pegli, Venice or Lugano if they betrayed her expectations. Then Italy became a "geographic fraud," Switzerland a "spittoon."

II

To UNDERSTAND MY GRANDMOTHER'S UNHAPPINESS, of which I have so far given a very uncharitable picture, one should keep in mind a few facts that, taken in themselves, may appear a bit strange. Too early a widow and too late an orphan, she was also the childless mother of twelve orphans. According to the documents and to my recollections, she had six children of her own, but they sounded like twelve from what she said, they said, she wrote, they wrote—each with two faces, a white one and a black one, and not one of these faces the true one. They were like the great figures in our history books, of which one never knows what they actually did, but only what they did for or against the fatherland, the revolution, the Cause or the King—in the case of my uncles and aunts (and of my mother too), for or against their mother. So she had six "good" children and six "bad" ones, and no children at all. But, as she wanted children and they wanted a mother, all they did was exchange tentative definitions of their sonhood or daughter-hood on one side and of her motherhood on the other, like diplomats exchanging notes with a view to arriving at a *modus vivendi* between countries: "If you do this, you are my real son [or daughter]."

"No, I am your son [or daughter] only if I refuse to do this and do *that* instead."

In white and in black, Katia, the eldest, was insane. In white, it was the result of her brother Pierre's locking her up in an asylum against her will to rob her of her jewels and of twenty "famous miniatures" and also to prevent her from starting a new life by marrying a Polish pianist after she had fled to him from her bore of a husband in Moscow and taken refuge in a hotel in St. Petersburg. In black she was insane or even worse because she had always been wicked, she had always disobeyed her parents, and the climax of her wickedness had come when she not only broke up her marriage to that wonderful young "self-made man in the making," that brilliant German engineer who had been her father's choice as her husband and as his successor in the direction of the factory, but tried to rid herself of her husband by strangling him. Thus (still in black), if there existed any doubt as to Katia's insanity, there existed no doubt as to her criminal tendencies, for only a criminal daughter violates a sacred deathbed vow to her own father with the definite purpose of killing her mother, only a criminal wife tries to strangle her husband; the insane asylum, which was nothing but a beautiful rest home with all the comforts, in the outskirts of Berlin, was better than the criminal courts with a jail sentence and dishonor. And the whole story of the pianist was pure fantasy, perhaps a proof of mental derangement after all, not to say something worse. The Polish pianist had never even spoken to Katia, so he could not have told her, "Meet me in St. Petersburg at such-and-such hotel, I'll join you there and we'll elope together." There remained, of course, the fact of the jewels and the miniatures: her brother Pierre *was* a thief.

Thief or no thief, both in white and in black Pierre remained Peter the Great, and in this (white) he resembled his mother. He liked things great and wide and generous. When he went to the Hotel Plaza in New York, he took the entire floor to himself because he did not want to have strangers within reach of his room. Still in white, he was called a megalomaniac, while his mother was called a *"grande dame."* Too bad he did not have her gentleness of soul and her spirit of sacrifice and was instead (off-white) self-centered, greedy, though (white again) for good reasons, being as he was a great financial wizard, born to be a leader and to master situations, even if (black nearing) that instinct for command was at times accompanied by a (blackest of black) criminal instinct and also by a strange, incomprehensible pettiness, all the more incomprehensible in a man of his kind who (sudden white) had always been generous and extremely correct in his business. He had (still in white) married the daughter of a great German family with a tendency to madness and suicide. That was the reason Pierre (still in white) had found it difficult to stay with his wife and (sudden black) had abandoned her, (sudden white) quite understandably so, because he too had a right to have a life of his own, to (black) run after all the ballet dancers, of whom one, (white) an exceptional woman in a way, extremely beautiful and charming, had succeeded in giving him what his wife had been unable to give him, namely (unexpected black) all the vulgarity he needed, which his wife could not provide, being, as she was, much more distinguished than Pierre. However, it was a mystery how a man from such a good family, with two such distinguished parents as he had, could stoop so low and live with such a prostitute as Wally. Yet it must be owned (white again) that he had opened his own private bank in Moscow and was about to open one in London and one in New York. With all this (black) he had never given financial advice to his mother, although such advice (white) when it *had* come from him had always proven excellent.

Then there was Ivan, both in white and in black an imitator of his brother Pierre. Much better than his brother in every way (white), but also (black) much less intelligent, even though one may wonder at times (white) whether intelligence is of much use when applied to evil ends. Too bad indeed, because (black) Ivan's stupidity was at times very irksome. He neglected his mother; in this alone he was not different from Pierre, even though (white), all considered, he was still the only one not to neglect her. When he *did* neglect her, this happened only because that evil creature, his wife . . . Why evil? Well, (black) *should* a wife have such strength as to be able to prevent a loving son (white)—because there was no doubt, loving he *was*, he had been in the past at least—(black) so why should she, by the mere fact of her presence, prevent him or encourage him, for she actually *did* prevent him, (white) no, perhaps not, (black) in fact she encouraged him, prevented him, encouraged him, prevented him, envented him, precouraged him . . . (when white and black appear too frequently, here is what happens).

Now, this is where Mary comes in, but as Mary was the girl who later became my mother, we shall leave her for the last one on the list.

Instead of Mary we have Olga, the white sheep of the family, who seemed, by contrast with the others, an angel, neither hysterical nor melancholy, and for this reason she came in black, until she was blacked completely out of her mother's existence. No one took her too seriously, because she never took anyone too seriously and least of all herself. She stayed in her Swiss boarding school much longer than her studies required, and when she visited her mother she was patient and kind but never seemed affected by her mother's changing moods. Her attitude was that of an observer, which was regarded as a form of impertinence and a proof of stupidity. She married a young German industrialist who seemed acceptable and who for his part seemed to find everything acceptable: one more proof of stupidity and impertinence. And she was happy with him, which irked Mary and her mother very much.

After Olga we have Ludmilla, the black sheep of the family, except that she had something white about her, her resemblance to her mother, and an infernal temper, which at times was regarded as a virtue, at other times as a vice.

Mary instead, who always came in white except on two occasions that are the subject of this book, was the only child who had yielded completely to her mother's impositions. She was therefore the weakest of them all, and for this reason eager to appear strong. She was her mother's shadow and echo, her personal lieutenant and her spy. That is how she developed an urge to be thought independent—in order to believe it herself in the opinion of others. Exactly like her mother, she had two constant motivations for whatever she did: Supreme Sacrifice and Supreme Pleasure. She saw no contradiction in these terms; in fact, it was always the Supreme Sacrifice of Pleasure and the Supreme Pleasure of Sacrifice. Nothing on earth could please her or amuse her unless it was enjoyed in the company of her mother, but, when she stayed with her mother, nothing on earth was permitted her. Of course her mother did not deny her anything; on the contrary, they traveled together, they slept in the same room, they went together to the theater, to parties and to galleries; but as she shared these "pleasures" with her mother, so she shared her mother's widowhood, her mother's remorse for having been such a bad daughter, and even the diseases of her mother's old age (which later disappeared after her mother's death, when she grew up and became young, for which she never forgave herself).

Thus, as guardian to the guardian of an Eternal Sorrow, it was but natural that she should also share her mother's tyranny and begin to exercise it in her place. Unfortunately her first attempt, when she was sixteen, and was with my grandmother in Rome, was directed against the one person in her mother's household who exercised tyranny over her mother. And that was really the beginning of the series of subversive acts that resulted in Mary's changing from white to black for the first time.

My grandmother's entourage in Rome in 1890 (in the usual large suite in the usual large hotel), included her daughters' German ex-governess Fräulein Luther, her devoted old German butler Bernhard, and Monsieur Morin, her French cook.

Monsieur Morin approved of people who stimulated my grandmother's appetite and hated people who threatened it. He would become particularly incensed against anyone who interrupted her eating, whether in person or by mail. "Since she has such a good cook at her service and I have such a good eater at mine," he said to Mary one day, "why disturb her with your nonsense? Wait with your arguments. You can be unhappy at four o'clock, but you cannot eat lunch at four, especially if it was ready at one." He did not go so far as to ask for first reading rights on all incoming correspondence. ("It is none of my business to censor other people's letters." As if anyone had asked him to! "Besides, I am an old man, and at my age one does not care to learn such completely foreign languages as German and Russian, with which French has no link.") But he did ask that any letter in Russian be automatically withheld from my grandmother for a period not longer than a month, so that it could be given her together with the next letter contradicting it.

"What makes you think this might be the case?" asked Mary, who was quick to take offense.

"I beg your pardon, Miss Mary, I never said I thought this *might* be the case, I know it *is* the case with Russians. I happen to have served in some of the best Russian houses when I was young."

"And it is your opinion that we Russians are clowns, I take it."

"Clowns? Oh, no. I only wish you were. You would know how to live. The trouble with you is you are too serious, too sincere."

"And proud of it. There can be no limit to sincerity. We always say exactly what we think."

"And so do we, but then we *feel* the contrary, or we say that we feel and *think* the contrary. We never contradict ourselves as you do, because the contrary is always with us, as the

snail in the shell or the shell around the snail. You Russians
are too childish. You never allow anyone to come and discover what is inside you. There is nothing inside you that was
not blared to the four winds. Having said what you think, you
also think you feel what you have said, but you do not. This is
the reason your cooking is so appallingly bad. The truth is
crude, my friend; cooking is telling lies."

This was enough to horrify young Mary and make her wish
for someone to take action, either to rescue the old cook from
his own cynicism or to rescue her mother from his cooking.
"To think that you are eating things his hands have touched!
Please send him away! He is exploiting you! He does not care
whether you are happy or not. All he needs is an audience, a
guinea pig for his experiments! I hate that man!"

My grandmother was amused by the philosophy of her cook,
whose remarks of that day and many others I found faith-
fully quoted in her journals, and she was also touched by her
daughter's reactions. Both were useful to her; they made her
feel that her presence on earth was not in vain; but Mary felt
so sad to think that her mother might prefer eating well to
being loved by her children that she cried every time she saw
her mother eat.

And, to be sure, her mother made eating a theme, a symbol,
a whole language of jealousy between them. If Mary gave the
slightest sign of boredom, or expressed the desire to go out with
younger people or even to be left alone for an hour, her mother
concentrated on her dish as if the food were speaking in secret to her, saying wonderful things Mary might wish to hear
but never would; and as she chewed each mouthful slowly, she
went on smiling and nodding in acknowledgment of what
she had just heard, then gulped it down triumphantly as if the
secret were now sealed in her forever. She spoke only to send
messages of praise to Monsieur Morin, which messages were to
be relayed at once, either through Bernhard or through
Fräulein Luther; then, in a sudden tone of bitterness, she made

casual remarks about her health and the danger of overeating. Mary, a glutton herself, did not know what to do. If she decided to follow her mother's example, she would quickly be told, "So, I see, eating is the only interest in your life. *I* eat to drown my sorrow and to forget my solitude; you eat because you are a glutton and nothing but a glutton. So now even this pleasure is taken away from me! I cannot watch a young girl eat that way! It disgusts me!" And she would leave the table to retire to her room and cry. If Mary did *not* follow her mother's example, she would quickly be told, "So, I see, what your own mother finds good is not good enough for you! Why don't you eat?"

The only possible answer (which Mary was more than glad to give) was, "I cannot eat unless I am forgiven." To which the generous reply was, "What a silly little girl you are! I have never had the slightest grudge against you. Really, my child, you are too sensitive. What will become of you when I am gone? I must say I *had* noticed something in your behavior that seemed strange, and was of course upset, but you know me too well to imagine that I might ever ask the slightest question. I withdrew into myself, as I have always done, and only asked myself whether this was not all my fault. I am old, I am sick, a burden to the world and an impediment to you. Should I not make myself even more unobtrusive by dying?"

"Oh, no, Mamachen, please don't. What would I do without you?"

"Your brothers and your sisters would be happy if I died. The rule of the majority should be respected in these times of vulgarity."

"I don't care. I don't believe they would be happy, but I don't care. Forget them, think of me, I would die if you did. And please don't eat so much. It is not good for you."

This was a bit excessive. "If you think eating is a pleasure for me, you are entirely mistaken. I am eating too much, I confess, because, regardless of what you say, I feel I should eliminate

myself and am now slowly doing so in the way least likely to
bring scandal. Even in this my first and only thought is always for others. Were I to leap out the window, people would
say, 'Poor woman, the Lord only knows what her children
must have done to her.' While, if I kill myself with overeating,
all they can say is, 'Poor woman, she did not know any better.'
This is the reason I resent your saying to me that I should not
eat so much. But enough of this now. The modes and timing
of my suicide are my own private business. Let's speak of you
instead, my poor dear child! You were so anguished over
trifles, you have eaten nothing at all. You must be starving.
Come, let's eat now, this has made even me hungry again."

And they both ate abundantly, and if anything changed in
their relationship, making it necessary again that Mary be reminded of her guilt, there it was: "I have eaten too much to
keep you company. You did not notice it, I did. And I know
that tonight I should not eat at all, but I am going to eat three
times as much. Why should I go on living in this hateful world?
To keep *you* company? I much prefer to leave. Monsieur Morin
will see to that."

Another thing that humiliated Mary: She had always been
able to persuade her mother that a certain butler, cook, chambermaid, governess was to be dismissed. Even with Fräulein
Luther this had been the case; she was kept only as a nonentity.
What was, then, the strange power this man Monsieur Morin
wielded? It could not be his cooking. Mary knew in the secret
of her heart that her mother was far from a gourmet, who is
first of all a dispassionate character; she was a glutton—namely,
one who hates food but will eat anything out of despair and
eat nothing at all or just a crust of bread when there is hope
again. The explanation, as I find it in my grandmother's famous
"archives of characters," is that Monsieur Morin was a much
greater friend of men than of women. My grandmother, like
all Puritan women of the epoch, had not the faintest knowledge of that kind of philanthropy, but her feminine instinct

operated in spite of her ignorance and made her feel that here was someone she could trust. "Having him in the house is like having a glove that gives outer protection without imposing its own form on the hand. I cannot say I have a man under my roof. Bernhard is an old fool, Morin is a real man, but in the house he is like a woman. This is why I like the French: they can almost change their sex to be tactful."

Mary decided at this point that she must act, and act alone. She could expect no help from La Luther, and her own filial love was powerless. If only Pierre's filial love could be dragged out of his cold heart and made more evident! Pierre worshiped his mother, but he seemed so resentful, so fearful of exposing himself to a rebuttal. They were so much alike, those two. She must bring them together, she must communicate to Pierre her own anguish. Pierre would understand. He was her favorite brother, he had always been kinder to her than to anyone else in the family, so much so that he even allowed her to criticize him and advise him on how to rid himself of his excessive pride. Mary wrote him a long letter asking him to come to Rome at once. "I need your help before it is too late. We must free our poor mother from this criminal who is going to kill her with his cooking."

For a few days Mary had visions of her brother arriving unexpectedly and sobbing in his mother's lap, "Mamachen, please don't die!" And then she saw him standing huge, pale, distinguished, in his beautiful ugliness, with his Oriental face, his slanted eyes, and heard him tell the cook in his deep voice, "Out of here, you!"

But Pierre did not come. He wrote a letter, and it was by a sheer miracle that Mary was able to conceal it from her mother. He wrote very coldly that he was too busy to come to Italy, he devoted eight pages in his even, microscopic handwriting (so much like his mother's) to a minute description of his day at the office, the factory, the bank, the stock exchange, the club, using his two favorite English expressions, "nothing doing" and "time is money," and describing himself as a "business-man," concluding that, even in extreme cases such as his mother's death, he would find it impossible to leave Moscow. He then closed his letter saying that, to his knowledge, no one had ever been killed by a cook unless he was a glutton and a fool, having lost all control and self-respect. "You do speak of your mother as if she were a glutton and a fool."

Pierre's logic had always made the deepest impression upon Mary. He was right. What he said was so dignified it might have been written by their mother. What a pity she could not read such a powerful letter. How proud she would have been to be finally given a description of her son's crowded working day! She would have understood his hurried notes, his seeming lack of warmth. Oh, if Pierre could only write such a letter to his mother, she would go back to Russia at once, everything would be easier, and not only for her but for the entire family. What sense was there in traveling, in beauty, in sunshine, in antiquity, when her heart was not there and her eyes were full of darkness and tears? And now that such a letter had been actually written, word by word, sentence by sentence, with a logic that pounded like a hammer, it was she, Mary, who found herself forced by the very logic of those arguments to keep it from her mother! And the reason for this was so degrad-ing: to prevent her stupidity from being known and punished as it should be! Pierre was right, Pierre was a thousand times right, he had no knowledge of the facts except from Mary's own description, and his conclusion was contained in her prem-ises. Did she think that her mother was a glutton and a fool? Obviously so. Was her idea of filial love as a frenzy of remorse better than his? He saw it as a thing that cannot even be dis-cussed, like dignity, like self-respect.

Mary needed a friend. She went to Fräulein Luther.

The old governess was a tiny, foolish creature who still used baby talk even though all her former charges had outgrown childhood. The only difference was that now she applied her diminutives to inanimate objects—and not such objects as could stand being called "darling little," like a spoon, a table or a house. She spoke of "the darling little" Pyramids, Sphinx, elephant, "the darling little Great St. Bernard" and "the darling little Atlantic Ocean." If such horrors of linguistic distortion are possible in some languages and impossible in others, the person who is capable of them is indeed possible everywhere, though she is always defined as "impossible," because no one has the patience to find a better definition of her. The only spontaneous reaction aroused in us by her presence is a desire to kick her, but kicking such a person is like kicking a huge worm that will cling to the foot, filling the shoe with green, sugary blood, and die looking at us with sad eyes. Thus though all my grandmother's children, sons and daughters alike, spoke about "kicking Fräulein Luther in the face," this urge, especially when strong, expressed itself in a respect bordering on awe, almost a terror of provoking her to become even more pitiful than usual. Fräulein Luther was the only subject on which they all agreed, a beautiful subject, full of childhood recollections, a true catharsis of the soul, so much so that years later my father defined her as the *latrina verbalis* of the family. She knew she had this function and they knew that she knew it, one more reason to treat her with that caution which should have been hers and not theirs, she being an uninvited guest, almost a servant, and a useless one at that.

But Mary, needing a friend, forgot the need for caution and took her problem to Fräulein Luther. And La Luther submerged her with her nursery tenderness, "like honey into my slippers," to use Mary's expression. "Why, you were right, my child, you did the only thing you could do, and it is Pierre's fault if your letter has not awakened in him a spark of generosity, an impulse to come here and save his mother. Eight long pages to tell you he has no time to write! He knows he's wrong, or he would not waste all that time to tell you he has none. He wants to be forgiven, but also to be admired. He is still the same egotist, the same vain, stupid boy he always was. This is a horrible letter. Your mother should not read it. She would be horrified by him, not by you. Please never write to him again."

At this point Mary felt that she could not accept forgiveness from a stranger for what she had done to her mother in a letter to her brother. This was a family matter: she had sinned in the family, against the family, must atone in the family. So she decided to confess to Pierre, overcoming her shame and her resentment. She apologized first of all for giving, much against her will, such an entirely mistaken impression of their beloved mother, and, to exonerate her beyond all possibility of a doubt, she found herself inventing the strange lie that the cook had put drugs into their food, to extort money from her. And as soon as she saw her own lie verbally displayed in her own writing, friendly and relaxed like a family friend, she realized its impact, not negatively, as a stain on her conscience forever, but as something constructive, a new source of security and self-respect the existence of which she had never suspected before. In other words, she discovered the wonders of deceit as one may discover a gold mine. And when she spoke about it forty-four years later, showing me that letter, she still could not bring herself to admit plainly that she had been wrong.

First of all (this was her line of reasoning) here was a fact and no longer an impression. Pierre, as a hard businessman, was fond of facts and detested impressions. And besides, it was only an accentuation of certain truths that Pierre, less sensitive than Mary, could not have grasped with the mere help of intuition. More than a lie, this was a higher truth, or, rather, cooking. It is true that Monsieur Morin had never put any drugs into their food, but to Mary it was equally true that her mother was neither a fool nor a glutton. Therefore, if Monsieur Morin's cooking was able to corrupt her, this combination of his diabolical powers as a great cook and her exceptional sensitiveness to good cooking must be described, for reasons of brevity (or translated into a businessman's language), as the effect of drugging. Don't we speak of love potions in poetry? And of filters and treacherous venoms that are not in themselves treacherous or lethal? In other words, Mary was availing herself of poetic license in the everyday world, where that license should either be displayed or never used. She had just put it into a different pocket, and she was so proud of it, so immensely proud, even forty-four years later, that she deserved to be forgiven.

What brought her hate to a frenzy was that her mother did not even have the right to be sad any more. Whenever she refused to eat, Monsieur Morin, who was so sensitive when it came to his own feelings, showed no respect for her and took offense, as if all of her feelings were to be concentrated only on him. "If Madame has lost her taste for good cooking," he would say, "she can have her meals prepared by Fräulein Luther or Bernhard, they are equally skilled in the kitchen. Or, if she does not like their cooking, why not the table d'hôte of the hotel? People with no discrimination don't have to pay for an expensive cook."

And her mother, whose one thought in life was not to bring offense to others, was so crushed by these words that she apologized to him (which again goes to show how unjust were those who judged her haughty—who else would have humbled herself to a cook?) and said, "I am ever so sorry, Monsieur Morin, that my refusal to eat has been construed by you as a reflection on your cooking. I swear to you that I could never accustom myself to anyone else's cooking, and if I cannot eat at times this is because of the news I get from Russia. My children are so cruel to me; they either leave me without news for months or they write in such harsh terms that I lose not only my appetite but my desire to live." And upon saying so she cried. The humiliation was too great for her. Here she was taking a cook into her confidence against her own family!

He always replied with the same argument: "It is all Miss Mary's fault. I have told her many times not to show you the letters that come from Russia until the poison contained in each one can be given with the antidote contained in the next. To oppose our children's egotism we must arm ourselves with egotism—but this we can do only if we eat well."

"You are quite right, Monsieur Morin, but, to my great misfortune, that is the one thing I can never become—an egotist. No matter how much I may try, the thought of other people's good is always stronger in me than my own instinct of self-preservation. What can I do?"

"Don't ask me, madame, I only know that I can no longer do anything for you. I must leave this house at once."

"But please, Monsieur Morin, why do you have to leave in such a hurry? Of course I will eat. Don't I almost always do so?"

"Today you did not."

"But I promise I'll be good from now on. Give me another chance, stay on for another few months."

"I cannot take the risk, I would feel much too nervous."

"May I ask you to stay and double your salary?"

"That indeed I cannot allow you to do. Then your children in Russia will say that I am paid too much."

"Monsieur Morin, I beg your pardon. No one ever mentions money in our family. Besides, what I spend on myself is my own private business, no one would ever dare." After which, to punish him, she would say in a peremptory tone, "Your salary is doubled as of now, whether you like it or not."

"I do not, and I am not going to accept a double salary."

In the end he did not: it was a trebled salary he took.

Mary committed the mistake of recording this whole conversation in her letter to Pierre, not only to prove to him that Monseiur Morin dared make fun of her mother's most sacred feelings and got away with it, but also to speak to him in what she fancied was his own language, the hard language of business and money. Wasn't his motto "Time is money"? And what

a joy it was to be able to translate the idiosyncrasies and jeal-
ousies of a sixteen-year-old girl into strong, impressive figures!
This was her second great discovery of that day: the power of
money, almost greater than the power of lies. She felt like
Talleyrand, and she had to show her letter to Fräulein Luther,
also because she herself had no means to buy the necessary
postage stamps. And this time it was Fräulein Luther who took
up the defense of Pierre, while Mary slandered him.

"I don't think this is a good letter," said the governess, thus
resuming her disapproving tone of a school time long past.

Mary's heart sank and her resentment mounted. "Why isn't it
a good letter? What do you know about business letters?"

"I am an old woman, Mary, and you a little girl."

"But my brother is a banker, and he explained to me what
that implies. You have read his first letter."

"Yes, and I did not think that was such a good letter, either.
He was trying to impress you, just as you are now trying to impress him, but I don't think that he will be too favorably impressed upon discovering that his young sister speaks so cyni-
cally of money, criticizing her mother for squandering it."

"I am not criticizing my mother, I am only trying to protect
her, and besides, you don't know my brother. His time is
money, and his language is money, too."

"Of course, my child, of course you are right. Gertrud Luther
is no longer your governess, she is a silly old woman one keeps
in the house out of sheer pity. Of course. You know best."

"What shall I do, send it or not?"

"Why, of course you must send it, that is a very good letter,
even though I do not like it. This has nothing to do with its
merits. And Pierre by now is a grown-up man, whose every
minute is so precious that he has to see everything in terms of
money. You are right. Send it." And Fräulein Luther posted it
herself.

Pierre wrote back almost at once:

Before My Time

DEAR MARY,

I am greatly surprised that you should ask my help to prevent your mother (I cannot say my mother—owing to your good services she has become a stranger to me now) from spending her last pennies on the few pleasures left her, given her egotism and her lack of imagination. If, as you say (and I cannot believe it—this is all an invention of yours to make me forget what you said about her in your last letter), this French cook puts drugs into her food, how can you explain that you have not been poisoned by him yet, but have, rather, become more greedy than before? I must admit that you share your mother's greed, as you share her interests, her time, her bedroom and her money. I am forced to conclude that those strange drugs have a different effect on different people: some are made more generous by them, others less. I knew our mother's egotism, of which I have been the most outstanding victim; I did not know yours, and I must say that I find it infinitely more revolting than hers. In fact, this slow degeneracy of all her faculties, of which you have given such a priceless description in your last letter (everyone here has read it with delight), is almost touching, as it ends in a senile return of generosity, while the qualities you have suddenly developed make me wonder whether there has not also been some Jewish blood in the family from which you alone have benefited. This might not only explain your present qualities but also your great skill in converging upon yourself all of our mother's interests to the exclusion of your brothers and sisters, in view of the inheritance that will unquestionably be yours the moment this French cook completes his mission.

But leaving aside all such considerations which have no more than a speculative interest, as you insist on speaking in the language of a shopkeeper (I could hardly call you a businesswoman—you do belong in an inferior class), what can it cost you of your future inheritance to pay that cook two or even three times his original salary? He in return cuts her life down to a third, shortens her life, so in the end you can only be the winner. You complain a great deal in your last letter of the frightful ordeal of living with your mother, and we all feel very much for you; we remember her only too well. But none of us would have the patience to endure her irksome company for the sake of despoiling her after her death; you do, and this of course is the unpleasant side of the whole business. We can be of no help there. I personally do not know what wish to formulate for you, whether to hope for your mother's quick death or not. It so happens that, in spite of her successful efforts to estrange me from her affection, your mother has not succeeded as fully as I myself had so far believed. I still love her in a disinterested way. I would therefore wish for her that she may die rather soon. The company of vampires is not altogether the most pleasant for a lonely old woman with so much to repent about in life.

When you gather the fruit of your patient endeavors, may I suggest you keep in mind Fräulein Luther and Bernhard. No one here would pick them up if you left them in the street, as you probably will. And, last but not least, if this Monsieur Morin is still young, why don't you marry him? You would thus be recapturing all the money your mother has squandered on him.

Your loving brother,
PIERRE

Mary was so destroyed by this terrible letter that for a while, hours perhaps, she kept rereading the last words, the only hopeful ones, "Your loving brother, Pierre," and reasoning to herself that, if the rest of the letter was true, if she had once more been exposed (and not only to the extent of her lies; far, far beyond that, showing the profound rottenness of her whole nature), then those last words must be true, too, like the rest, and mean much more than they would in an ordinary letter, for how could Pierre, after what he had seen in her, still call himself her loving brother? He must really have meant it, so there was this good thing, this one anchor of salvation, and she must first of all thank him for not calling her some horrible name at the end of the letter, and then tell him with all the strength that was in her that to her knowledge she had never meant to do any of the evil things of which he was accusing her.

I swear to you [she wrote], *to all of you in Moscow, that I shall never accept anything from Mamachen, and that, if something terrible happened to her, I would go with her, too. Yes, I do confess that the story of the drugs was a lie, and I shall never do such a thing again. I did it only because I was unable to make you, Pierre, understand how grave the situation is, with this terrible cook here. Of course it was my fault, but I am such a poor writer, and then the notion that you are so busy and the fear that perhaps you might not read my letter made me invent that base lie, for which I wish to atone. Please forgive me and please write to Mamachen, she loves you so, she is profoundly unhappy because you are so cruel to her. All these misunderstandings would be solved if you came here and spoke to her, and saw her, and persuaded her to go back to Moscow, in spite of the sad memories that are awaiting her in the old house.*

Having written this letter, she felt pure again and light of heart and completely forgiven by Pierre.

But it was again Fräulein Luther who destroyed her brief happiness and threw her back into despair. "This is not a good letter at all," she said. "This is worse than the last one, in a way, because the last one was a mistake but it was not degrading. It deserved a mild reproach, but not this kind of insult. Read your brother's letter, please, and judge for yourself."

"But it was I who sinned, not you. I don't care what he says against me, as long as I know it is not true. Pierre flies into a temper just as easily as I do, we are very much alike. What do you know about our mutual feelings?"

"Nothing, my child, of course I know nothing at all, I am no longer your governess, I knew you only when you were still a child, and your feelings, of course, have changed since you are a grown girl. You are right, send that letter, by all means send it." And Fräulein Luther posted it herself.

Now began for Mary a real period of wavering and madness, insecurity and shame. After humiliating herself in front of Pierre and the whole family in Moscow with that third letter, she reread Pierre's letter, looking in it almost for an answer, or, if not for an answer, certainly for what might have justified hers, and was appalled by the childish vulgarity, the boastfulness, the greed, the total lack of generosity, which she had disliked always in her brother as a child, but had regarded recently as a thing of the past. Instead of which, here it was, as a permanent possession, an indelible part of his whole personality. She could not let him make such base accusations and even encourage him and accept them. She wrote a fourth and most violent letter, and this time she was sure that Fräulein Luther would approve of it, but she did not.

"I don't think this is such a good letter."

"But you would have liked it a week ago, this is exactly what you wanted me to write when I stupidly apologized to him for these crimes I never committed."

"Yes, you are right, but now it is too late. Now that you have taken a certain stand, stick to it. There is nothing worse than having two opinions. You can only have one."

"What shall I do, then?"

"Wait."

So Mary waited, and Pierre waited, too, and everything grew bigger, taller, deeper, wider: Mary's guilt, her mother's anguish, the cook's power, Fräulein Luther's wickedness and everybody's appetite. Which had by now become an intellectual appetite, a political party of appetite, which my father years

later described as *mangiarismo* or *bisognismo*, the belief in a
need that is not there and the gearing of everything to satisfy
it. They both ate, mother and daughter, like those poor alco-
holics who drink, overcoming their nausea with effort, to recapture their thirst in the next glass, where the devil has
hidden it. My grandmother was duty-bound to satisfy the cook,
who must approve the tone of her approval. And no question
of saying, "Just a little bit of this, it is *so* good." "Well, if it is
so good, then eat *so* much of it." For Mary the obligation was
completely reflective: she owed it to herself to be ready to eat
when the time came. Meals at regular hours are the only occu-
pation of the idle; if they don't eat at those hours it is almost
as if they approved of idleness in public, giving a bad example
to their servants, while at any other hour idleness is a personal
problem between the idlers and their conscience—it arouses
no scandal. Acceding to a meal is therefore also a ritual of confession and forgiveness; hope remains open that one may work
in the afternoon.

Mary felt this and went on feeling it for the rest of her life
with true religious fervor. She came humbly to the table, that
her sins of the morning might be forgiven. There alone she
felt the link with the deserving world of work, searching her
daily bread for the sweat of her brow, her venison for the long
hunting parties and for the hounds and horses, and the fresh
salads, the strawberries, the cream, for the walks through the
forests and the farmlands of home—things that no luxury, no
monument, no travel could replace, and that now seemed even
more removed since the beginning of her quarrels with Pierre.
Leaving the table after each meal, it seemed to her as if she
were abandoning her work and her bodily strength with it.
Weighted down by a strange weakness, with tremor in the
hands and unusually strong heartbeats which no doctor could
explain, she dragged herself back to the dining room and
cleaned up everything that was left on the table, basketfuls of
bread, butter, leftovers on the dishes and trays, and she sobbed

while she ate because this was like giving in to her great enemy.

Every day angry telegrams were sent by my grandmother to all of her children in Moscow (not to Katia, because Katia was already in her madhouse in Berlin; her mother's madness would have left her indifferent), and Fräulein Luther saw to it that not one of those telegrams was sent. But Mary paid for each of them in terms of shame and fear; Fräulein Luther never failed to express surprise at Pierre's silence, always in Mary's presence, wording it so that Mary might think this was going to be the moment, her sins would now be bared and she would have to atone for them:

"Yes, very strange that Pierre should not have written. Isn't it, Mary? And now, Mary, confess to your mother and clear your conscience once and for all, tell her that today's telegram has not been sent as yet and that it is your fault." Then, as she saw that Mary could not utter a word: "Well, all right, so it is for me to confess. And I want to clear Mary, she did not do it on purpose, she meant well. You see, madame, she thought she might write a letter to her brother and she made a draft of one, I read it, we discussed it at length, and so time passed, but I am going to send that telegram immediately." My grandmother was indignant that Mary should have written a letter without showing it to her first, and so Mary had to invent all sorts of lies to explain that this was only a plan, and that she would have shown it to her, and so on.

Or Fräulein Luther would stream into my grandmother's bedroom and say, "Madame, please do not punish Mary if she tells you what she has done."

"What has she done?"

"Oh, something terrible."

"What is it, Mary? Why do you blush?"

And Fräulein Luther would answer for her, "She has stained her white dress with China ink." Or "She has broken a glass." And it turned out each time to have been just a joke, a heavy German joke dictated by devotion and love. "How could my little Mary think that I, her loving Lutterchen, would tell on her?"

"Yes, but why did you have to scare me again?"

"Mary, my child, I too am only human. Being right is not enough for me. It is a meager satisfaction I have known in this house for twenty years, day in, day out. I want to be trusted. You say you trust me, but this is only because you are afraid of me, you know that I could harm you. I am an incorrigible person, my worst and only fault is that I love you so. But you despise me, I know you do."

And she cried bitterly, so Mary even had to console her and pretend that these charming little jokes of hers were the cleverest way of securing her love, devotion, gratitude and admiration. In her dreams then Mary strangled Fräulein Luther every night, but there was little satisfaction in this type of revenge, because in the same dream there arrived the police, in Russian uniform, who shaved Mary's head, chained her to a group of men and women, mostly Jews, with their heads clean-shaven, and sent her with them to Siberia. And her mother laughed and said, "I am pleased. He who tells lies can also kill and should be punished." Mary emerged from these dreams in such a state of agitation that after a few days (the postman still remaining sterile—he alone could have cured her) my grandmother found herself in open competition with her daughter: Mary's anguish was greater than her own. And when she saw Mary suffer more than she herself did, her first reaction was one of great anger. It was for her to suffer, not for Mary. In the presence of the god, how dare a simple priest feel the offense to the faith more than the god himself? There is no graver form of sacrilege than taking Christ's place on the Cross.

The violence of her mother's reaction caused Mary to lose consciousness, and she did not regain it for hours. How the old lady must have envied her, when one thinks that she had never succeeded in keeping up the comedy of her symptoms for more than an hour without letting herself be interrupted, even cheered at times, when taken by surprise! She who had paid her doctors the most fantastic sums without their declaring themselves alarmed or even baffled by her case! And here a stupid little girl of sixteen was so easily upset that she was suddenly a riddle to the medical profession. So, as soon as Mary regained her senses, the diatribe continued.

"And after all, my child, what is Pierre to you? A brother, yes, but look at me. He is my son, my oldest son, and if anyone here has a right to be upset or offended, it is I and not you. And look at me: I never lose my balance, never faint, never let the greatest sorrows (and I have had so many!) get the better of me. We owe it to ourselves to be in good health. What would become of you if I suddenly fainted because Pierre does not write? Let him stay out of our lives altogether, if that is what he wants. We are going to take a vacation, you and I, we are going to Naples, and Fräulein Luther will stay here. I don't like the influence she has over you. It is all her work, I know. She alone is to blame for your weakness. She treats me (and so do you) as if I were a sick old woman who cannot accept the simplest realities of life, namely that children grow up and must live a life of their own away from their mothers. Nonsense. Thank God I am an independent woman. I am much happier when I am alone than when I have my children with me. In fact, the only reason I have decided to take you along on my gypsy adventure is to shake you out of your morbid state of mind."

Having said this, she felt she had to go the whole way and inflict a deep humiliation upon Monsieur Morin and Fräulein Luther, not because she had any reason to suspect them or to punish them, but because, like all timid people, she could never move a finger without sufficient reasons to move a whole army. "We will show these two beasts that we can travel without cooks, without governesses, without anybody, like two real gypsies. They will never believe their eyes. But don't let them imagine they are dealing with a stupid woman. I have an iron hand when I want to. I shall appoint a personal administrator to look after my business while I am away, make payments, find me an apartment here in Rome and supervise the packing and moving. Monsieur Morin will stay in the kitchen and Fräulein Luther in the wardrobe, each one in his place."

Thus the first representative of Italy made his entry into their lives: the Avvocato Cavaliere Tegolani, who had connections everywhere, who could buy railroad tickets with the greatest of ease, overcoming the natural reluctance of the railroad officials to sell them, could obtain special reductions on anything he bought (except for postage stamps), could rent or purchase palaces or apartments for one fifth of the price asked, could get any cabbie in Rome to take him anywhere by the shortest, most direct route without having to pay five times the fare in tips; even the beggars made him a special price and still prayed for him instead of damning him and the dead in his family, as is the tradition in Rome. He was, in short, an exceptional person, a good family man, an exemplary father and, before that, a loving son who could never mention his mother's name without tears in his eyes. Besides this, lawyer Tegolani tended the sick, visited the jailed, fed the hungry, prayed for the damned, offered the other cheek and loved his neighbor more than himself, because himself he did not love too much: he exposed himself to drafts and foul weather, he let himself become sick without even granting himself an aspirin, he allowed himself only a few hours of sleep every week (a light sleep, ready forever to be broken that he might rise and bring aid to the needy), and he regarded himself as a poor Christian, a sinner, a lazy and stupid man. In this alone was his brother, a priest, superior to him, for Don Iginio, a teacher of water color and catechism for the young daughters of rich foreigners, took good care of himself. He too was given to good deeds, but obesity and asthma kept his pace a bit slow on the steep path of virtue. He had been given permission to teach all he knew of water color but nothing of religion to Mary, and it was to him that my grandmother went with her request for an administrator.

"The Avvocato Pio Tegolani," was Don Iginio's answer. "Why, of course, who else could better meet your requirements and take charge of these delicate and complex functions? Trustworthy? More than myself, I should say. Known to me? Like a brother. In fact, he *is* my brother; we both had the same father and mother, save that the Lord in His infinite wisdom did not see fit to distribute His gifts with His known impartiality in this case, for He gave me many organic impediments which are the cause of laziness and, ah, satanic temptations (dear Lord, what am I saying?), together with this gift for water color, which more often than not makes me neglect heaven for the sky which I praise with my painting, while He left me very poor in the wisdom of the world, in the handling of riches and even of a few pennies. In my brother's case, on the other hand, what generosity was shown by the Lord! How well he handles money, how he can make it come his way, and not, indeed, to use it for himself—only for the poor and for good deeds, of course, but I should say that his cleverness might well make the Jews envious. Therefore, dear lady, do trust him. Cunning and dishonesty melt away in his presence like the morning mist in sunshine. It is sufficient that he frown, no one dares harm his neighbor any more or even think of doing so. Your riches could not be in safer hands."

My grandmother was delighted. Never before had she heard such reassuring words, and it was good to hear things that usually go without saying. These Italians were wonderful, in spite of their religion and their laziness.

As for Mary, she could hardly believe her good luck. She had never seen her mother so active, cheerful, enterprising, independent and reasonable, and if Mary did not make a general confession of her most recent sins, it was only because Fräulein Luther begged her on her knees not to do such a thing.

III

THE TWO WOMEN left for Naples with the feeling that they had done something terrible, were surrounded by perils, had not a friend left in the world, had indeed left two corpses behind, that of Monsieur Morin and that of Fräulein Luther. During the trip Mary had to persuade her mother that perhaps this was not so, Monsieur Morin would understand and so would Fräulein Luther. But her mother was anguished and almost wanted to go back. Mary was not too strong herself, she was in fact more anguished than her mother. What changed their outlook on the future and the past was the great kindness of the train personnel: the whole train seemed aware of their problems; special instructions had been given from higher up (owing to Avvocato Tegolani's influence) to take good care of these two ladies in trouble. What dispelled the last clouds of gloom was the presence of Avvocato Tegolani himself at the station in Naples. He had taken an earlier train to make sure that the hotel in Naples would be made ready for them, and he promised to deal with the two victims in Rome so that they would not feel they were mistrusted or disliked. What a wonderful person he was!

"Now we can really be like two gypsies," said Mary's mother, after Tegolani was gone, not without having been duly reimbursed for his expenses and the loss of his valuable time.

Mary had been to Naples once before, but it had rained, she had hardly left her mother's room at the hotel, that room being her mother's room in Moscow, Baden-Baden, Pegli, Cairo, Ouchy or Rome, and, the curtains being drawn to abolish the view of a rainy Naples, she had never really known where she was, because they had left Naples before it had stopped raining. But now, oh, now it was a different matter altogether. Now the curtains were those of the hotel, even the cooking was that of the hotel, and there was sunshine, and Mount Vesuvius with the flames and the smoke, and the bay and the cheerful, sad, angry, mild voices of the permanent market place that is every street of that wonderful city; a whole world that came in through windows in a blinding way (the sea reflected on the white ceiling), in an intoxicating way (the smell of flowers, burnt coffee beans and salt water from the sea), and these things not only took away the shadows from around her mother's bed and armchair, but reduced everything to a ruin, as the sea did with the foundations of old fortresses and churches built on the stony beach. In the snapshots taken by Mary in those days, her mother, seated with closed eyes in the only bit of shadow still to be found in that room, appears drawn, small and even thin, resigned to a much greater power than hers, that of the sun.

To that first epoch belongs also the picture I mentioned before, of my grandmother in Pompeii, smiling, with the ruins behind her, all her own work because the city had kept her waiting or something.

The first week they did not wait for letters. They took long walks along the seashore, long rides along the gulf in those funny Neapolitan carriages that seem always on the verge of collapsing. They rode and rode and let themselves go to that *dolce far niente* which in those days was still a new expression and stood, as an experience, in such vivid contrast to the Puritan principle of hard work my grandmother still worshiped, that its enjoyment seemed to her as daring as a trip into space would be today.

They had no friends in Naples, in fact they knew not a soul there and were careful never to speak to other guests in the hotel and especially to stay away from Russians, the most impossible of strangers when met far from home. Instead, they tried to form an entirely new set of acquaintances among the pure, the simple of heart, the people: coachmen and their numerous families, and even beggars and their whole populations of interchangeable families. Smiling to one was enough to produce twenty on the spot; no one could tell where they came from, how they could suddenly materialize out of the air— and how could one not smile when greeted with a smile by such kind, lively, intelligent people as these Neapolitans? How could one, above all, not be touched by the sight of their appalling poverty, which they all bore with such dignity?

It soon became a problem, in terms not only of financing these smiles and those kind feelings, but also of traffic. The beggars of Naples made no special prices to the clients of expensive hotels, especially to foreigners who were so easily moved by their plight. Each tear became a promissory note, and until payment was made the creditors were not going to leave the sidewalk in front of the hotel. This would have been like doubting the sincerity of those tears, and they said so. "*Signora mia, signora bella, eccellenza,*" and other such flattering appellatives, "you are not going to tell us that your feelings are false, that you are a comedian, a person without honor? You have made us a promise, we have placed our confidence in you. Are you going to take it away from us now?"

She could not go back on her "promises," but neither could she recognize them as such, because they were not. And had she given them everything she owned, would this have helped?

. . . There they are, still crowding the sidewalk in front of the hotel and waiting for me. If I give them all I have, I shall be much poorer than they, as I don't know how to beg and am not enough of a liar. Besides, I have other habits they don't have, such as washing, living in solitude, eating with my own silver and crockery, not to mention the chaise percée, which is unknown to these barbarians. I would be all the poorer for having been richer. I would be a nuisance to them. Can I explain this to them? Would it be human? Would it be Christian?

There happened to be at that time in Naples, and at the same hotel, one of those fabulously rich maharajahs who had done worse than even she had, by encouraging impossible hopes in the poor; she had only smiled at them, listened politely to their troubles and given what she regarded as small sums, always trying not to be seen while she did this, to avoid humiliating the poor. The maharajah instead had almost summoned them to his side. My grandmother's description of this strange character is interesting.

Poverty and filth, the trailing, fighting crowds of the destitute who let themselves be trampled under their horses, are important to these people as the gold setting to the jewel, the walls and roof to the paintings and furniture; they seem unable to enjoy what they have unless it glitters in the light of envy. The ideal of work, this only true form of Christianity—earning one's daily bread, and other people's daily bread with it, so as to give not only dead money but live work—is absent from the rich as well as from the poor. This morning the maharajah threw coins out his window, and the most disgusting scene followed: human beings of all ages scrambling in the dirt for a coin. When they came back for more, he had them chased away by the hotel manager, who is a German, and who had tried to warn me against letting the poor come too close to the hotel!

Farther down on the same page, the German manager suddenly becomes a Swiss. Or was it a new manager she was accusing now? We shall never know the truth. But here is what she writes:

This idiot of a Swiss manager! Instead of trying to protect me against the poor, why doesn't he encourage me to study the social problems that have transformed this great, noble and intelligent people into a dirty mass of thieves, beggars and liars? They tell me Naples means Nea-polis, or New City. Before that it was called Partenope, a very prosperous Greek colony. Now, if these people have at a given moment in their history felt the need for a new city, they must not only have been strong and rich enough to build it, but also have felt the urge to do so; they must therefore have had the dignity that makes men wish to become other, better, more civilized than the beasts! And why have they become the teachers of dogs today? There is no other term to define them, for it is they who teach dogs how one should humiliate oneself in front of humans. What has happened to these people? I must *know!*

She sent for the Swiss (or German) hotel manager and asked him in a fit of indignation, "What has happened to these people?"

The manager bowed deeply, as he always did in front of money, and said, "They have left, madame. The way is clear."

"What do you mean, the way is clear? What way is clear? And is it? And if it is, how do *you* know, if I myself do not?"

This was a bit too much for the good man, so he explained, "If Madame will kindly trouble to look out that window, she will see that the way *is* clear. There is not a single beggar left in front of the hotel. We chased them away, all."

"Oh, I see. That is what you mean. To *know*, you look out the window. Very easy indeed. If that were only possible! I look into my conscience and see no clear way there. And it is not so easy for me. That is why I shall ask you for the last time: What happened to these people? Why are they what they are?"

The hotel owner tried to mumble some trite explanation, adding by way of apology that he had never exploited the poor, but, rather, had given them work, in fact the hotel personnel, hundreds of people, came from extremely poor families, they were well paid, well mannered, clean, dignified and a source of real pride to him, also because that had been his own work, his life mission in fact. In other words, he used with her the very arguments in favor of the dignity of work she was thinking of using with him, after having duly humiliated him. And he had not even taken offense at her violent words.

She did not know what to answer, she lacked the moral courage to acknowledge she had been very wrong (she would have done so, as Mary said years later, had he been a truly humble person, but he was not), so she attacked him with greater violence than ever, saying, "You are not answering my question. What I want to know is not how bad they are or how good you are or have been to them."

"Madame is perfectly right," said he, and again she felt she should apologize, and, not knowing how to do this without losing face completely, she went into a lengthy exposition on the virtues of the Neapolitans. She knew they must have had a sense of dignity; how had they lost it and at what period in their history? But the hotel owner had lost his patience and was quite determined now to make things very unpleasant for her so that she would decide to leave. She had been his best client for years, but this was too much.

"For this kind of information, madame, I advise that you do not come to me. I am not a learned man. You know, there are books, there are libraries, there are historians, there are even Socialists and anarchist agitators who have had to leave Russia, where the slightest remark against the government is punished with deportation to Siberia, so now these poor wretches are here, trying to wreck our country with our government's permission; they will give weapons to the destitute and you will see what they can do. As a matter of fact, with your disposition, this should please you very much. Why don't you ask them to teach you what they know? May I be excused, madame? With your permission." And he bowed out.

Mary burst into tears. "We cannot stay in this hotel where you are being insulted," she said.

But her mother was not of this opinion at all. "Of course," she said, "if Pierre had been with us, or if he had discussed these matters with me and given me his advice, this would never have happened. I would not have lost my temper and this man would never have lost his. But let it be so. My son abandons me to my fate, these people want me to be involved with the anarchists and either be killed by them or deported to Siberia. I am not the kind of woman who will recoil in the presence of danger. I shall do exactly what they challenge me to do."

How happy she must have been at that moment to discover that her daughter, at least, still took her seriously. "Mamachen, please don't go. If you go to the anarchists, I shall kill myself."

"Shame on you, to say such things! Suicide! Don't you know that suicide is the greatest form of cowardice? A woman must be strong, especially in a world of men where women are despised. Do you think it is a pleasure for me to go to these horrible people at the risk of being murdered or, in the best of cases, deported to Siberia? I do it because my dignity makes it imperative for me to do so. All I wanted was the truth, a very simple, historical truth I had the right to learn. They denied it to me; I had to accept their challenge. And you, you who could have been of help to me, you too can think of nothing but desertion. A normal daughter would have said, 'Allow me to come with you, I shall defend you.' "

"But I want to come with you, Mamachen. That is what I meant, you did not understand me properly. I said that if you are to die, I cannot live without you. But if you are determined to go, let's go this very minute."

"Oh no. I cannot take you with me. One does not take a beautiful young woman into that den of wild beasts, murderers, Italians!"

"Mamachen, please let me go."

"No."

They went on bickering like this for a while, but they did not even know where to go. And it was not until more than forty years later that Mary could understand that, far from being tragic, this situation was highly comical. It was my doing if she finally laughed at her own words, but only after she had cried again, as usual, and then cried a second time, because it was irreverent to laugh. I can almost see them, the two women lost in that hotel room, ready to meet with a most cruel destiny, the address of which was inscrutable as the destiny itself.

"And where will you go, Mamachen? Where?"

"I don't know, but I can easily find out." She rang the bell, and when the maid appeared she asked, "Where are all those criminal anarchists and social etcetera?" And when the maid said she knew nothing: "Ask the manager and bring me their address at once!"

The manager arrived again and said, very curtly, "Sorry, madame, but this is one piece of information we are not equipped to give our clients."

"I see, you are afraid; you are trying to prevent me from doing what you suggested I should do. But you'll be sorry. Oh, how I am going to laugh when I publish the whole story, the Truth. Never mind if I ruin myself, never mind. Who cares? But why am I saying these things to you? This is none of your business. From you I want only that address, and I want it right away."

"Madame should have a little patience, we are not trying to conceal it from her; we don't know it ourselves. All we can do is ask the police."

"Ask the police, ask the devil himself, but bring me that address at once! And also all the most subversive literature you can find. But be sure that I get the real thing, not just mild stuff for foreigners' consumption!" she said, as if she were ordering some very special wines. And before the poor man could leave the room, she wrote to Avvocato Tegolani complaining of the hotel management.

Thus for the impact on my grandmother's noble soul of the discovery that there had been a time when the beggars of Naples believed in the dignity of work. The next discovery was that the worthiest women of Naples had died, leaving a host of disconsolate husbands behind, all obese, very pale, and dressed in black. The first of these was one Cavaliere Gennaro Pollo, a high-ranking official of the police of Naples, who spent all his free hours in the hall of the Hotel Vesuvio, looking sadly at the foreigners who came and went, and thinking of the places he might have visited with his dear wife, had she not gone back to her Lord and Maker after only three years of married life, and without leaving children. Every morning at sunrise Cavaliere Pollo went to the cemetery to take flowers to his wife, then went to Mass and finally to the police headquarters where he spent his working hours. He ate alone, crying into his spaghetti, then went back to the office, where he slept with his head on his desk (he hated to be home alone), and in the evening, rather than sit with other men in one of the cafés of Naples, chatting pleasantly and winking at the women who passed by (and at times even finding one who winked back), he left the world as he entered the hall of the hotel, and found it almost soothing to be surrounded with the sounds of strange languages and the sights of strange peo-

ple whose facial play and movements of the hands or ways of
walking were as mysterious to him as the languages they
spoke.

To him the hotel manager went for advice in this emer-
gency, not knowing how to tame or send away the Russian
lady.

Gennaro Pollo listened to the story. He knew most of it, he
had seen her and highly disapproved of her ways with the beggars, and he was quite determined to have her arrested and to
denounce her to the Russian consulate, when a magic word
struck him in the manager's account: the word *widow*. "Don't
worry," he said. "Leave it to me, I know the case. In fact, I
know the person. More than that: we are closely related, she
and I."

He entered my grandmother's apartment, saying, "Madame, I
know you. We are closely related, you and I, through sorrow.
I am a widower. My saintly wife left this earth like an angel
long ago, and I still mourn her untimely departure. You, I am
told, have suffered the same loss. What can I do for you?"

"Nothing," said my grandmother very harshly, but not
only because of the tactless assumption that anyone else's
sorrow could be equal to hers. There was also real gratitude in
her reaction, even though no one would have known it. She
was so grateful that she had to be unpleasant. That was the
way she functioned. And she repeated, with less venom perhaps, what she had asked the manager to do for her. To quote
her own description of his answer:

*Cavaliere Pollo told me everything. He thanked me in the
name of his city for my interest in its poor population. He said
the population was not poor and was in no need of help from
foreigners. He said it was too noble to accept such help. He
said it was too ignoble to deserve it. He said the beggars were
comedians who hired children by the dozen to impress foreigners. He said they sold whatever decent clothing they received,*

because their rags were the tools of their trade. He said they had
hearts of gold, every one of them, and would give their most
precious possession to prove their friendship for those who were
kind to them. He said I should not try to have anything to do
with dubious elements such as the anarchists and Socialists,
first because such elements did not exist, but also because, if
they did, it would be a great mistake for me to go near them
since a foreign lady is never safe in certain parts of Naples and
besides I must never believe those foreigners who say a foreign
lady cannot safely visit those parts. Naples, he went on, is a
most ungrateful city, his salary being so low that it would make
anyone laugh in any civilized country. But he told me he knew
of a professor, a great intellect and a great heart, typically
Neapolitan in this, and like himself a widower, whose wife,
another angel, had been unjustly called back by the Lord because
she was much better off in heaven with the saints than on earth
with the scoundrels. This professor, he said, could tell me everything about Naples, he loves Naples, he sees only its shining
side and this is the only side the foreigners should know. In
any case, if it is of any use to me, the entire police force of
Naples is at my feet. What would I do with the police of
Naples? One never knows, he said. A most unreliable city, the
police can always come in handy. So now I have them at my
feet.

My grandmother must have relished this strange conversation more than anything else during that trip, because she un-
derlined each word twice; for all her acute sense of observation, however, she never noticed that her informant's contradictions were only a slight exaggeration of her own. But
perhaps that was exactly what she needed: a clown to portray
her own faults in safe disguise, so as to allow her mind to
function freely, leaving her body alone. Only the sight of a
much greater fool than we are can restore us at once to our lost
dignity. When we have that fool within us, greater than all the

fools around us, undescribed, unrecognized, then the mind cannot function and the body is not left alone. The pains of foolbirth are so acute that they tear us to shreds—we die that he, whom we detest, may live. Oh, the blessing of casting the first stone! "There, by the grace of God, go I, and let me show what I think of myself."

Jesus was a thousand times right, only he lacked a sense of the theater and of its curative effect. Certainly he who is without sin will not cast the first stone; he cannot feel offended and relieved at the same time by the sight of a person with whom he has nothing in common. Puzzlement is the most we can expect of him. As his curiosity is aroused, so is also his pity—without effort. And he deserves no admiration for the easy exercise of a feeling inaccessible to most. He is a stranger to the world, almost a god, unknowing and inhuman.

Here is what my grandmother had the courage to write in her journal on the following day:

Cavaliere Pollo came for lunch with the professor. I have never seen anyone eat with such greed as these two: wading through their soup, eating up their dead wives, and crying with their disgusting eyes while their disgusting mouths feasted on every bit of food they had finally stabbed in a wild hunt on the slippery dish. The professor is less of a widower than the Cavaliere, because he is much younger, but then one never can tell. He may still have a great career as a widower in front of him. His father was a widower for thirty years, he has been one only for three. It must be a national tradition, like that of the castrati for the soprano voices in the Vatican. These people lose their wives and go about the public stage of Naples singing their praises and crying. Young women should be able to recognize such men as are not fated to turn widowers, and marry only those, while avoiding the others.

Cavaliere Pollo speaks of his wife as a saint, and says he always addresses his prayers directly to her so that she will pray to San

Gennaro on the premises. "Much more effective," says he. "Who up there could refuse her a favor?" And the professor agrees. Which means that they both live like beggars: from prayer to prayer, always asking for charity, never earning their right to enjoy life. This is a very unhealthy state of mind. If their God is like this, he differs little from the maharajah; and he must be very suspicious of the hard-working, self-respecting men who would rather subdue their immoderate appetites than ask the Lord to assist them in their insane pursuit. Here I have found the root of Neapolitan begging. It is deposited in heaven.

A few pages of my grandmother's journal are devoted to a detailed description of how she discovered that she could offend the Cavaliere, namely by taking him seriously and asking him to explain every one of his countless conflicting opinions the very moment he expressed it and before he had time to make a fool of himself by stating the opposite of what he had just said. She pretended to be learning from him and to have no opinion of her own.

This did it. He had tears in his eyes as he asked her, "But why do you insist?"

"Because I am so much interested in what you say, and I love conversation."

"What have I done to you to be treated that way?" was all he found to say.

She saw in this the proof that conversation was so foreign to the Italian mind as to be mistaken for an insult, and she was right. Had she been only a little more versed in the history of Italian culture, she would have been pleased to discover that the poet Leopardi had said exactly the same thing half a century before.

But what happened on the following day so completely reversed the situation that it threw her into a state of pathological depression with grave consequences for herself and for Mary. Busy as she was anatomizing the Neapolitan mind in the person of Cavaliere Pollo, she had forgotten all her grudges against the hotel owner and his manager; she thought, in fact, that she had never done anything to antagonize them and was very much surprised when she saw Avvocato Tegolani arrive at the hotel in a state of the greatest alarm.

"Was it necessary to take me so much *à la lettre?*" she asked when she heard him quote her alarming message. "Luckily for me, the hotel manager and everybody else here is a civilized person, we can settle our little differences without anybody's help."

But she was greatly mistaken in this. The hotel manager, being less generous than she was (or probably less Russian), was not so quick to forget her quick moods. He forced upon her now a state of mind that she had been pleased to overcome, and this, too, seemed an imposition, an artificially contrived form of resentment. But there she was: her faithful lawyer had come to her rescue, expecting to find her in danger, in order not to feel that his trip had been pointless and his devotion silly. So he told her in private that she had been too generous with the two men.

"Let them not treat you as an eccentric foreigner," he said. "You were within your rights. Your questions were prompted by a highly commendable scientific interest in the social and historical causes of the poverty that has shocked you so much, and they deserved an honest answer. If there was a mistake on your part, it was only in your overestimation of these people's intelligence and culture. You are apt to believe that everyone else is up to your standards, but you should know by now that you are a great exception to the rule."

She could not deny it. Indeed, the Avvocato had understood her only too well, except for one mistake he made: he had brought along with him his brother, thinking this might be the right moment to complete the conversion of a soul which had been touched by grace but not yet by the Church. And together with the priest had come a complete reference

73

library on the subjects of poverty, immorality and idleness and the Catholic medicines recommended to cure them.

She dismissed the priest at once, and if she did not also dismiss the lawyer, this was a miracle for which the priest was not responsible.

"You don't exist for me," she said to the priest, "and you"— to the lawyer—"are not authorized to show my letters to your brother."

"Wasn't I right when I asked you not to come?" said the lawyer to the priest, by way of an indirect answer to her. And then, to her, "Nobody has seen your letter, madame. I never showed it to my brother. For us Catholics the thing is different. I showed it to my confessor, not to my brother. If my confessor showed it to my brother, that is none of my business."

"Are they not one and the same person?"

"They are, madame. But as a person my confessor is nobody. And my brother was wrong. We shall not give him absolution. And, to prove my good will, I shall now let you have all the Socialist, anarchist and Communist literature you asked for."

He did. And she was closeted for days with books she neither understood nor cared to understand.

Never, not even for a second, did she suspect that perhaps he had played a mean trick by letting her have exactly what she wanted. She copied hundreds of pages, entire issues of daily papers, mistaking the most obvious polemical arguments for scientific truths, and underlining twice, often three times, every line she had copied, then adding heavier vertical lines and exclamation marks all along the margins as if to summon —more than just call—her attention to those arguments; but as far as I know she never even looked at her notes again. Until one day she decided that the thing to study was not history or politics, but medicine, physiology and, above all, psychology, because, as she wrote in her last paragraph, "history is made by men, men have bodies, and these bodies have a specific physiology which obeys certain laws and which reflects itself in their psychology." But before she devoted her best efforts to these studies she had a brief social-hysterical period, which almost made it impossible for me to write this book fifty-two years after her death.

Here is a letter Mary wrote to darling Lutterchen in those days:

DARLING LUTTERCHEN,

I must write to you because you are the only person in the world who knows all my secrets and who can help me when I am in trouble. We lived through terrible days. The hotel owners in Naples almost had us killed by the Socialists or deported to Siberia! This all because they did not want Mamachen to discover the causes of the great moral degradation of this city. Now Mamachen is busy with a very serious study of this problem, which is all rather boring for me, I am ashamed to say, because I am too stupid. Whenever Mamachen asks me to dictate to her from the books she is studying, I fall asleep or overlook a line, making it necessary for her to rewrite a whole page.

The only good thing about this work is that she has no time to think of Pierre and never even asks whether there is a letter from Moscow. She sends me out alone or with Cavaliere Pollo and his archaeologist friend, and you will be amused to hear that the professor is in love with me. Can you imagine anything more absurd, a real archaeologist being in love with a stupid little girl like myself? Of course I don't believe it; he knows so much and talks so much and I never say anything at all—I just listen and learn, and that is why he thinks I know just as much as he does. But when he speaks about his love for me I find him so ridiculous that I cannot help laughing, and he says I should not laugh, because he is a widower. And not only is he a widower; he has arthritis (I confess I don't know what this is, probably a disease for widowers only) and a few other ailments that make it necessary for him to spare himself any, even

75

the slightest, heartache. It seems that I, being responsible for a very major heartache, should love him to atone for the fact that he loves me. I said to him I would never even dream of marrying a sick man, and he became extremely offensive. He said we Russian women were heartless, an Italian woman would do anything for love.

"So would we Russian women," said I, "but that love must be there in the first place, and in my case it is not."

"Too late to tell me that," he shouted, so that all the visitors to the museum (this was taking place in the National Gallery of Naples) turned back to look at us. "Too late! You, with your conduct, have led me to believe that we were engaged, now you are compromised, you must marry me. No other man will want you after you have been seen walking alone day after day with me!"

"Nonsense," I said, quite angrily, "I am not Italian in the first place, I don't live here, and besides, I don't care what people say. If my mother lets me go out alone, this means that she trusts me enough to know that I will not behave badly."

But he was so insulting that in the end I burst into tears, and he immediately changed tone, took my hand—and forgave me, saying this proved to him that I loved him, and he would wait even ten years for me to be ready for him!

Another argument of his I had forgotten to tell you about: he claimed I had ruined his reputation as a widower and as a man of honor, because he had been almost on the point of remarrying when I had come along. That, the lady being a very decent, rare, beautiful and rich girl, whose father is a very important man in town, I had ruined his chances for a rich marriage and his career, besides ruining his health and his honor.

Now, while he was trying to comfort me and tell me he had forgiven me, a young man came up from behind and put a hand upon his shoulder, greeting him with affection. It was someone I had seen before in that very museum when I had gone there with Mamachen. We were looking at a Greek amphora in a

76

glass case, and *I* noticed his face beyond the case. Every time he seemed to be looking at me, *I* promptly looked at the amphora instead, and every time he looked at the amphora *I* looked at him. The few times our eyes met, neither of us dared to smile, and when *I* was seated outside in a Victoria with Mamachen he appeared suddenly with a rose in his hand and gave it to me, then was gone. Mamachen had seen nothing. She asked me where the rose came from. *I* said a woman had just given it to me and *I* offered it to her. She was immensely touched by the kindness of the Neapolitan people and kept speaking about it as we drove back to the hotel, which made me feel quite uneasy, but it was too late for me to tell her the truth. So here is why *I* knew that young man, and when *I* noticed that the professor was determined not to introduce him to me, *I* stretched out my hand and said to him, "We know each other. Thank you for that rose."

You can imagine, Lutterchen, the face of the professor. *I* laughed so much that he said a few terrible words *I* could not even understand, and left. His friend was about to run after him and fight him, but *I* stopped him and he stayed because he could not very well leave me all alone there. He apologized to me and wanted to run after his friend and bring him back. *I* asked him again not to go, *I* assured him that there was nothing between me and the professor, and so we sat down and talked and talked.

Oh, Lutterchen darling, *I* have never had such a feeling in my life: to find myself completely in agreement with every word, every thought of his, as if we were one and the same person. He is a medical student, and he too, like myself, has decided to sacrifice his life for others. *I* have Mamachen to look after, he has seven younger sisters. Both his parents died a year ago and as soon as he becomes a doctor he will go back to his village and practice medicine there. He had great ambitions, he wanted to devote his life to science, but now he must give up these dreams. How *I* wish *I* could help him! *I* know he could become

77

a great scientist and discover all there still is to discover about the mystery of death and the immortality of the soul. And also about disease, of course. Oh, Lutterchen, there is so much to do in the world, and I know that with a person like him even I could do serious work and make some great discovery!

The only thing that upset our conversation was his fear of distressing his friend. I could not bring him to believe that I was not engaged to the professor. He too seemed to think that when a young woman goes to a museum with a man, she is engaged to marry him, and if she does not, then her honor is lost. So he kept speaking about the professor, lauding him, and advising me to go back to him because he is such a good man. He also kept apologizing for giving me that rose, and saying we should never meet again. I hope I shall see him again, however; I asked him and he almost promised he would walk in front of the hotel one of these mornings and wave goodbye to me. But he wanted to know whether I behaved like this "with all sorts of people," for in that case he would not come. But when he saw that I was very sad, he again "almost promised" to come. Oh, my dear, dear Lutterchen, I think your little Mary is beginning to know the pains of love.

The next morning the young man walked in front of the hotel; Mary saw him and asked her mother's permission to go out for a short walk. She obtained it and saw her friend, who again told her that they must never meet again, for the additional reason that she was so rich and he so poor, and that he could begin to respect her only if she really sacrificed herself for her mother and never walked with other men alone through the streets of a strange town.

"I shall live like a monk, you like a nun. This is our pact," he said. "Life is no pleasure. Giving up what we love is the highest form of love."

She wanted to say something, too, but was too moved and too disappointed to talk. Of course she agreed, of course self-sacrifice was the highest form of love; had she not always said so? But to hear herself reminded of it by the first man she loved (and the only one she ever would love) made her almost burst into tears.

When she went back to her mother's suite she heard voices in the sitting room. Cavaliere Pollo was speaking, his voice broken with emotion.

"I am sorry if I upset you with these revelations," he was saying, "but I felt duty-bound to warn you of your daughter's bad conduct, not only in the interest of my poor friend who is about to die, but also—even though to a lesser degree, given the grave condition of my friend—in the interest of your daughter's good name."

Mary's first impulse was to go in and tell the Cavaliere what she thought of his friend and then tell her mother the whole truth, emphasizing the fact that she had nothing to be ashamed of; but when she heard that the professor was dying, she saw the immensity of her crime and waited, trembling, for the worst to happen.

Then she heard her mother speak. "The only person in the world for whom my daughter must have a good reputation is her mother, and the only person who can destroy that reputation is my daughter herself, by telling me herself, as she certainly will, whether or not she had done something wrong. Neither spies nor intermediaries have ever had any place in my relations with my daughter. Therefore the denunciations of a stranger, even though he may control the police force of Naples, do not interest me in the slightest. As for your dying friend, I have never heard that the honor of a man may be impaired if a young woman is seen with him in the streets. This sounds neither virile nor logical. If the professor felt that because he was allowed to accompany my daughter to the museum she must be engaged to him, so much the worse for him. For us civilized people, this does not constitute a promise of marriage. If your friend has ruined his career or his chances to marry another girl, that is none of my business and I do not care. If he is gravely ill, I can send him a doctor at my expense, or I may even pay for him to take a trip and forget he ever met my daughter. If he should die, I shall pay for his funeral. More than this I cannot do. Goodbye."

Mary was utterly sincere when she entered the sitting room after the Cavaliere had left and flung herself into her mother's arms, thanking her for the confidence she had shown in her. Now that everything was clear she saw how right her young friend was in saying she must sacrifice and not think of herself but only of her mother. Oh, how she loved him now, and how certain she was that she would never leave her mother! Thus it seemed to her that, as her love was finished, the supreme sacrifice already accepted, it was not only useless but even honest not to mention it at all. "Mamachen, how can you think that I would ever marry anyone? How could I live without you?"

Thus all ended well—so well, in fact, that her mother decided to take a rest and leave for Sorrento. This time they would really live like two gypsies, taking along with them only twenty suitcases and five trunks, but no crockery, no table silver, and not even the *chaise percée*.

Those were perhaps the only days of happiness Mary's mother had known for a long time, idyllic days she never found again. Free from the nightmare of her gigantic work, happy at the thought that Mary was never going to leave her (she pretended to disapprove and kept asking, but only to hear Mary say again what she so liked to hear: "No, I shall never leave you"), she tried her best to make Mary's life a pleasant one. They took long walks together through wild, rocky regions overlooking the sea, dangerous regions they were advised to shun because of the brigands; and there Mary sat and painted landscapes while her mother, like a child, picked flowers and made crowns to put on Mary's head. They sat together in the green shadow of vine trees on the hotel terrace, and there Mary painted the village streets with the donkeys, the fishermen, the market place, while her mother wrote long letters, real essays on the beauty of the region, letters addressed to Mary, or wrote summaries of the books she had read to amuse Mary. She even began to write a novel on the widowers of Naples, namely Cavaliere Pollo and the professor. Then Mary was allowed to make friends with Beatrice, the daughter of the hotel owner, and Beatrice too was adopted by Mary's mother, so that Mary would not feel too lonely in the company of an old woman; but there were hours, walks and sessions in which Mary knew she must not see Beatrice, because her mother wanted her all to herself.

There were amusing incidents. The *chaise percée* was needed and they were going to send to Naples for it, when the hotel owner produced an old gentleman with a beautiful villa hidden among olive trees and a famous *chaise percée* which had been used by the last Queen of Naples and which he gladly lent to Mary's mother with the recommendation that she use it with care, for it was a historic relic. Every two or three days this gentleman inquired about his *chaise percée*, asking such embarrassing questions as "Is it not a real joy to sit on it? Don't you like the beautiful pattern of its porcelain?" He even dedicated a sonnet to Mary's eyes.

But Mary was unhappy. Never before had she known such unhappiness, her thoughts going back constantly to Naples and to her friend—whose features she thought she could recognize in almost every human shape she saw from a distance. All she wanted was to see him again and tell him that she had followed his advice and was resigned to living like a nun. She could not sleep at night and, as she had a room to herself, spent hours trying to write him a letter; but all she did was rewrite the first lines, which became more and more exalted with each new attempt and conveyed nothing but the feeling of her unhappiness over the sacrifice she had agreed to make for his sake only.

She knew nothing about him, not even his full name, let alone his address in Naples; and her new friend Beatrice was unable to help her. Then suddenly one afternoon when her mother was asleep, and she and Beatrice were sitting on the terrace, there he appeared, pacing the road in front of the hotel and casting fiery glances at all the windows.

Mary ran out of the hotel and spoke to him. That is, she said nothing at all, her emotion was too great and he gave her no time. And what he said was so confusing to her that she did not quite know how to take it, for the tone too was strange, almost resentful.

"Here," he said, "I have finally found you, and it has taken me some time. You did not have to flee from me. I am an honorable person and I never meant to harm you. And if I have come all the way out here from Naples, wasting a great deal of my most precious studying time, which I should have devoted to duty, and spending a great deal of money, this, I want you to note, is the best proof that I must love you in spite of everything. Of course I should not love you and I could never marry you. I have sacred obligations that I cannot betray and so have you. Besides, you are too rich and know nothing of life, and I, compared to you, was poor even when both my parents were alive, which means that now the difference between us is still greater than before. But I obeyed my strange urge to come and tell you all this in person, not only because I have reason to suspect that you would never be given my letters to read, but also and in the first place because I very much wanted to see you again. Goodbye. My train leaves in an hour, I cannot stay here any longer and what sense is there to it anyway? Life is no pleasure, and, as I said before, we must always renounce the very thing we love. Be virtuous and don't ever go out with a man unless you are ready to stay with him for the rest of your life." With these words he was gone.

When Mary staggered to her room she did not even notice that Beatrice was being questioned by her parents and that she and her friend were the object of their questioning.

She fell into a stupor. Now she knew he was gone, and nothing mattered any more. Her mother called her and it was with great difficulty that she rose from her chair and went into the next room. She made up a lie, fearing she might be asked why she looked so dejected; but she knew her explanation would not be a lie for long, because fever was already beginning to set in.

"Read this," said her mother, handing her a letter.

It was from Fräulein Luther, and it spoke of a dream she had had about a young man following Mary through a museum and many other things that corresponded to the truth, which Luther had set down to appear intuitive and make herself useful again. "My heart tells me Mary is in danger. I hesitated up to this day to tell about my dream because I know you think me a hysterical old maid, and then also because I know that Mary is above all suspicion. Forgive me, therefore, if I bother you with my silly dreams and insane fears."

"She is a fool," said Mary, "as usual."

"Is she? I thought so myself until an hour ago, and that is why I had decided not to show you this letter. But Beatrice has told her father certain things that ask for an explanation. You have seen this young man today, it seems."

Mary did not defend herself. "Yes," she said. "He came to say goodbye to me. Forever."

"What do you mean, forever?"

"Forever. Forever."

"Oh, I see. Then there was something. You had not told me the whole truth."

"There was nothing to tell. Nothing happened."

"Nothing happened? And the rose?"

"Yes."

"What do you mean by 'yes'? Did he give you that rose?"

"Yes."

"So. And you lied to your mother but told the truth to Luther, who is a stranger and, as you yourself call her, a fool. I, who am not a fool, receive your lies, am treated like a fool; she, who is one, is treated with respect, is told the truth."

Mary stood motionless, waiting for more.

"And that, of course, leaves you completely indifferent. The fact that I may have believed you and believed in my happiness is indifferent to you. Do you have any letters from him?"

"No."

"And do you expect me to believe you?"

"No."

"Then may I look at your desk?"

And Mary said, "Yes, of course. You will find nothing at all." She had been thinking only of his letters, which, to her regret, did not exist at all, and not of the many beginnings of her unfinished letter to him. But even had she thought of those, could she have answered, "No, you may not, my word should suffice"? Her word, alas, no longer sufficed.

It was only when her mother put her hands on her lettercase that she remembered what was in it and waited, coldly, for the end of the world. It came. Quietly, as her mother read, Mary saw it set in: her mother's face fell, old age descended and sealed around her mother an expression of bitterness which was never to leave her for the remainder of her days.

"So, it is sacrifice. For my sake only. Why not say you hate your mother? Why this hypocrisy?"

"Because it is true," said Mary.

"Do you still have the right to use the word *true*? What is 'true' to you—this, or what you said to me day after day, building my illusion only to destroy it better? Did you have to conceal your feeling from your mother? Liar, liar. Deep in your heart, liar, on every item, in every direction. You are the essence of treason. So you wrote everything to Luther, I suppose. Then you confided in Beatrice, corrupting a young girl purer than you. When her father, that excellent, honest, dear man, came to me with tears in his eyes, asking me to leave the hotel immediately because you had corrupted his daughter, I refused to believe him, I acted as proudly and stupidly as I had acted with that other honest man, Cavaliere Pollo, whose every word I now believe."

Mary threw herself at her mother's feet, sobbing. She was kicked in the teeth.

"Get up from there. No hysterical scenes, now. Face the consequences of your actions with dignity, the dignity any criminal has. Learn at least this from your colleagues. Even under torture they do not falter. Do the same. You are not being tortured. This can mean nothing to you. You have no shame, you have no *right* to shame. Be proud you have destroyed me. Laugh. Come on, girl, laugh, I say! Laugh!"

"I am going to die."

"Oh no. Oh no, you are not. If you died now, I could not even find consolation in the memory of the few happy days I spent with you in this place I loved so much until a few minutes ago. I have lost even the memory of a daughter. Yes, happy days that will never come back, when I wrote all those letters to you, those essays for you, that novel on the widowers of Naples. And you wrote this. . . . But I know now what I must do."

Mary hoped for a moment that her mother would hit her, but she did not. She left the room and came back, her arms loaded with papers and books. She put them on Mary's desk, sat down and began to tear every one of them to shreds, in a quiet rage, with a strength Mary had never imagined her to possess.

"Mamachen, what are you doing? Don't, please don't destroy your own work!"

"Away, you. Don't come near me."

Mary snatched her own letters from the desk and began to tear those, but was pushed away with violence and the torn bits of her unfinished letters were carefully pieced together and placed in their folder again.

"These must remain, these are the truth, while those must go, they are the lies, the lies of happiness, the sad fruits of illusion." And her mother went on tearing up everything while Mary looked on paralyzed by terror. That was, in fact, where Mary spent much of the rest of her life: in that room in Sorrento, standing in front of her mother and watching her destroy her own work. Until the day of her death, many, many years later, Mary could not hear the noise of paper torn, or bear the sight of a torn book, without crying convulsively for hours.

A high fever prevented her leaving the hotel. Her mother wanted to call an ambulance, but the hotel owner begged her to stay on and be lenient to Mary. "Forgive her, she is young, she did not know what she was doing. She is good."

"Good? Much evidence have I seen of that goodness."

"Unintelligent, yes; but good."

Mary refused to be cured, to take her medicines, but her mother, sitting day and night at her bedside, forced her to obey. "He who has done wrong must learn to accept goodness in return. All these comedies mean nothing. Had you not been found out, like a common criminal, you would have continued to deceive me without the slightest regret. God knows what you would have done in the next few days."

Luther arrived from Rome in the most cheerful disposition, thinking she would be praised for her great intuition and was much surprised when, upon entering Mary's bedroom, she was asked, before she could speak a word, "Where are Mary's letters?"

"Mary's letters? I don't know, I never received one, but how is my dear Mary?"

86

"None of your business. Where are her letters?"

Luther tried to catch Mary's eye, but Mary did not look at her.

"All right," said the old lady. "The two liars may consult with each other before they face an honest person." She left the room.

"What shall I tell her?" asked Luther.

"Anything. I don't care. You have already told her everything."

"I have not. I only spoke about a dream, to protect you, and you instead—"

"Tell her the truth!" shouted Mary.

When Luther came back to Mary's room she had red eyes and was still sobbing. Mary looked at her indifferently and waited for her mother to appear. Instead of her mother came the doctor. But unfortunately the fever was subsiding. Hours passed. Luther was still quietly sobbing to herself, and Mary, her eyes closed to avoid Luther's questions, was awaiting the next blow with her mother's return. Finally she got up, pushed Luther violently away and staggered into her mother's room —to find her reading all the letters she had received from Pierre in Rome. Mary was barefoot, and the only thing she thought of doing was to avoid the carpet so as to catch a cold on the marble floor. Her mother saw this, did not say a word. She was reading the same letter for the third time, Mary could not quite tell which of the three letters it was.

Finally her mother looked up from the letter and asked, "What is your program for tomorrow?"

Mary's eyes widened. This sounded so normal, so unangry, she could not bring herself to believe it.

"I asked you a question, Mary, did I not?"

"Yes."

"Then why did you not answer me?"

"I don't know."

"You don't know? Well, then I'll tell you: When liars cannot lie because they have been found out, they never know what to say. The truth is not for them. It does not interest them." Another long silence. "May I know, then, what surprise is in store for tomorrow?"

"None."

"Oh, I am disappointed. Why this refusal? What have I done to be treated that way? I was beginning to enjoy your constant show of fantastic lies, each better than the other, and now I must give up this pleasure all at once. It is a pity." No answer from Mary. "Don't you think it is a pity?"

"No."

"Oh, you do not? I do. Take your feet off that marble floor, you are not to catch pneumonia. Back to your room now. And write to your dear brother that if he wants to get rid of me quickly and at little expense, he should hire a couple of assassins to stab me during one of my solitary walks. Any Italian would do it for a modest sum, and in my case they would not even have to repent, because I am a Protestant; the Church would give the murderer complete absolution. Why not hire your medical student? He is so poor, this might be the beginning of his fortune. He could marry you after my death. So now write to your brother and show me the letter. I was hoping I would not have to pay for my own murder, but it seems rather difficult to avoid it. And besides, anything is preferable to slow death by deceit."

Mary had another crisis, but her mother would not yield to the temptation of the easy way out.

"Even this I must endure from you," she said, crying, as Mary cried at her feet. "The comedy of filial love. Your sorrow is not caused by the pain you have given me, but only by the fact that your schemes have been ruined. Of course it pains you to see me suffer, because in some strange way you must still love me. But it is not for me to help you. Go away."

From that day on and for more than a week she began to

apply the method of blackmailing her daughter by disappearing for not more than eight hours (a maximum of self-imposed boredom even for a person as enamored of herself as she was) in the "hope" that someone would murder her. She would go to the wildest regions of the coast, which were infested by brigands, besides being dangerous because the roads were steep and stony, landslides were frequent, and the sea battered the white rocks with a frightening roar straight down below. In vain did the hotel owner try to prevent her from doing such foolish things; she felt honor-bound to do them as they had already attracted his attention. Mary would spend hours of agony waiting for her mother's return and praying fervently in front of holy images or in the local Catholic church, for want of a Lutheran one. That was how she began to feel inclined toward the Catholic faith. Luther, formally dismissed from the household forever the very day of her arrival, was forced to stay on for a while at least, "until after the funeral," so that Mary would not be all alone to bear the shock of her mother's assassination. "I always think of others," said the old lady, "even when others think of me only to harm me or lie to me."

Beatrice had a difficult time trying to make friends again with Mary, because Mary would not see her—she was so paralyzed with shame, so full of self-contempt, that she regarded it as a just punishment to be left without friends in the world. But finally the goodness, the simplicity, the human warmth of Beatrice's family prevailed, and Mary became to them like an adopted child. Also, her mother slowly quieted down, because the nature of the place, even in its most savage spots, was idyllic and soothing. While waiting for her murderers, or for a chance to tumble into the sea from the top of the mountain, she felt well, happy, drunk with light, and she began to write long letters to the wind, her only friend: "Dear, honest wind, you who tell no lies . . ."

And when she came back to her enemies at the hotel, it was difficult for her to conceal her appetite. So Mary was forgiven. "What sacrifice would a mother not make for her children?"

Still, when they took their way back to Rome, it was not easy for Mary to see Naples again, thinking that *he* might still be there and she might see him. And not only because of this; also because her mother had to see Cavaliere Pollo, get all the facts from him, and make sure the young man would not be allowed to come near the hotel. Thus the police of Naples could be put to a good use for once.

I V

THE APARTMENT in Rome was beautiful. It was in the Via Gregoriana and it cost only ten times the price my grandmother, in her most extravagant moments, had expected to have to pay for it. Old furniture and paintings bought at staggering prices by Avvocato Tegolani had been placed in it in a very haphazard way, and my grandmother had to change all that, paying fantastic sums again for the slightest displacement of any object. But, apart from these trifles, all was well. Mary took up painting again, and also music; but more, even, than these two arts she took up eating, and soon became so fat that she could hardly move. Her mother could not have been more pleased, because not a single young man among those she so eagerly invited to the house seemed interested in Mary, and she noted down this fact in her usual big books with words of great contempt for the stupidity of those young men and words of praise for her dear child.

Two young men she feared, who were actually interested in Mary and often spoke to her at social gatherings, were the brothers Alberto and Carlo Tempi; but she found a strong ally in their step-grandmother, the Marchesa Mary Tempi, who frankly did not wish them to be husbands of decent girls, and said so. Not that the boys were bad. They were Italians; that sufficed.

Mary Tempi hated her husband and loved God, and these two feelings took up most of her time. She loved to hate her husband and hated to love God, said the usual evil tongues, because she took her God in larger doses than prescribed even by the Church doctors and emerged from her prayers and penances only to make her husband's life impossible. She was half English and half French, or so she said, but the evil tongues (and the well-intentioned ones, too, such as her husband) said that she was half Russian and half French, which made her furious. In her own version, she was the daughter of a Mr. Eberhard Schultz, an English banker living in Petersburg, and of his French housekeeper, pedigree unknown. In the evil tongues' version she was the daughter of a Russian grand duke and a Duchess d'Escarande, a nineteen-year-old French girl gone astray and exiled by her father, picked up by the grand duke in a night club in Moscow where she was singing, kicked out of his house, with child, and subsequently picked up by Mr. Schultz, who married her and adopted the child.

There were at least three elements of credibility to the second version: Mr. Schultz *was* the grand duke's personal broker, and no one knew how he had got himself into such closed strata of society, being himself a Jew and a very young man when he had gone to Russia. In fact (and this constituted the third element of credibility), Mr. Schultz was only seventeen years older than his daughter, and it was known that he had been a bit older than sixteen when he left London. It was further known that his late wife had made life very difficult for him and boasted everywhere that she had never had any physical contact with him. It was known, too, that her death had been a great relief to him. Also, there existed between father and daughter a strange relationship, which bordered on the tragic, as if they had both taken it upon themselves to sacrifice something important to something less important but stronger. That the daughter worshiped the father was clear, that the father was unduly severe with the daughter not less clear, and that he felt the urge to speak of her in the most tender terms as soon as she was out of sight more than just clear.

How she had come to marry Carlo Tempi, a notorious nonentity even by Roman standards, no one could understand, and she perhaps less than the others. Carlo Tempi was an elderly widower with grown children and grandchildren at the time she met him. He was not even beautiful: a shiny skull emerging from a crown of white hair like an Easter egg preserved in cotton wool; two purple spots, the eyes, framed with red branches of invisible trees; a huge red nose with purple branches connecting it with the rest of the face; a white mustache and a white pointed beard, often reddish with tomato sauce or wine; and a huge body that he moved with great effort, like an elephant. His way of speaking French, and the fantastic lies he told about himself, the Vatican, the kings and queens he had met in his life, had amused Mr. Schultz for a few evenings; Miss Schultz had probably thought that if she married such a man her father would spend many such evenings with her instead of always running away from her.

She had become a Catholic, had adopted the mentality of an elderly lady, had tried for a short while to educate her husband, then to re-educate his children and finally his grandchildren, growing disillusioned and stubborn and refusing her father's offer to arrange a divorce. She could admit no such desertion from her duties, and also she had never before experienced the joy of saying no to her dear father. For Mr. Schultz this had been a great blow; he had hoped she would marry a banker, certainly not an old glutton and clown.

With his wife's money Carlo Tempi bought himself the palatial country house Il Barone near Florence, a villa which had belonged to the *marchesi* Tempi until 1776. He also bought a smaller palace in Rome and gave large parties, boasting quite openly about his wife's imperial origins. How he had learned about them was a mystery to Mr. Schultz and to his daughter too. They suspected Miss Miller. Her erstwhile pupil wanted to dismiss her at once, but this the father would not let her do, and Miss Miller remained as the old man's personal secretary.

Mr. Schultz knew my grandmother very well, even though for years he had been on the side of her great enemy, her father, under whom he had had a sort of junior partnership in some financial company. He had admired the old man, as a meek and timid soul engaged in a heartless and arrogant activity like banking must perforce admire those who are by nature fitted for it; but, as a man who had suffered a great deal and always without sharing his sufferings with anyone, he felt attracted by cases of despair, and my grandmother was one.

Without telling her his troubles, he could listen to hers and tell her what he wished someone had told him in the past, namely that life is no pleasure and similar nonsense. People had always taken advantage of him, he had been forced by circumstances to expect nothing from life; now, in old age, he found it easy and even pleasant to act with detachment. This enabled him to extract from Pierre and his brother a few kind letters to their mother, and to prevent her from writing unkind answers. He encouraged his daughter, Mary Tempi, to make friends with young Mary, and this proved interesting for both. Mary Tempi overplayed the role of the old lady she was not, and young Mary believed her. Mary Tempi pretended to consider her husband a genius, and young Mary believed her. Mary Tempi spoke harshly about her husband's children and grandchildren, and young Mary believed her. Mary Tempi called young Mary "my daughter," and young Mary was full of veneration for her young mother. What real old mother believed, and God knows for what reason, was that Mary Tempi would be her best ally in her secret but violent fight against any possible husband who might shadow the horizon. She extolled Mary Tempi as her co-mother, banking, as usual,

94

on her own forthcoming death. "Remember, Mary, when I die, the one person on earth whose advice you must follow is the Marchesa Tempi."

Young Mary had her first shock of recognition when Carlo Tempi took her into his confidence, unasked, of course, and told her that his wife was still a virgin. Her second shock of recognition came when he asked her to go to bed with him. Mary, in her innocence, had never even thought that a man with white hair could be in love. As for his being a lecher, she had always imagined that such things could not exist in polite society but only among savages, criminals and beggars. God knows why beggars, but that was her opinion of the poor wretches. And here she found herself the unwilling possessor of a secret she could share neither with her old mother nor, for a stronger reason, with her young one. But she was so disturbed that she began to lose her appetite, with the immediate result that she grew slimmer and that Carlo Tempi's grandsons became rather obsessive. They would send flowers to her, wait for hours in front of her house just to greet her as she came out with her mother or with Luther, and manage to be always present by chance when Mary visited their step-grandmother. This, added to the fact that Mary ridiculed their grandfather and shunned him exactly as they did, gave her real mother reason for alarm.

"Mary, you must remember, Carlo Tempi may sound rather ridiculous at times, but he is a great gentleman and his wife worships him. Please be kind to him. When he asks you to accompany him on a tour of the Roman Campagna, don't refuse as you did the other day."

Mary did not reveal the truth to her mother, because she had not revealed it the first day and how could she explain such a reticence? Three long months of "dishonesty," as her mother would certainly call it. She accepted Carlo Tempi's invitation, but she insisted that he also invite a young painter, the only person she could think of at the moment, who happened to be visiting the studio of her art teacher when Carlo Tempi came to see her there. The old lecher was very reluctant at first, but, afraid as he was that she would give him away, he invited the young painter, and the three of them toured the Campagna in his carriage. Mary asked the young painter to stay close to her all the time, she found it easier to talk to him than to her mother, and the sense of security he gave her soon turned to affection, without any suspicion of love on her part. She never thought she could love anyone else after her first unhappy love.

What precipitated matters was her mother's behavior when Mary appeared one day, back from a ride on the Via Appia, in the company of the young man. Mary had been so curt with Carlo Tempi that he had left them before entering the house, and here she was, with a young man who had not been invited by her mother and whose family and origins were unknown even to her. How was she to introduce him and to explain why Carlo Tempi was not with them?

Her mother as usual took care of all that. She looked at the young man without answering his greeting and without taking the hand he was clumsily offering her, then asked Mary, "Who is this butcher? How dare you bring such scum into the house?" And she swept out of the room.

Mary followed her mother down the hall and answered in the loudest possible voice, "The butcher is a very good painter and a great friend of mine. You may soon have to accept him as my husband." She ran back to the "butcher," apologized to him and asked him politely to leave. But she was glad her words had reached him. So was he.

That same day, after a most violent scene, Mary was sent to the Marchesa Tempi under Luther's escort, with a letter in which the Marchesa was asked to tell Mary that she was murdering her mother. Obviously the old comedian was beginning to lose confidence in her own tricks, if she asked for assistance from the audience. What the Marchesa said to Mary was, "Don't let your mother do such things to you, or she may hate you in a few years for letting her. If this young painter is in love with you, and if he comes from a God-fearing family, marry him with or without your mother's consent, but before that become a Catholic. Your mother will protest at first, but when you have your first child she will forgive you."

Mary went back to her mother a changed person. She had so much to think of that she did not even notice her mother's letter on the table, which letter expressed the writer's hope of being murdered by brigands on the Via Appia that same day. When her mother came back, healthy, hungry and unmurdered, but expecting to find an anguished daughter at the door, she found her own letter unopened and, a few seconds later, in the drawing room, an impertinent daughter who was reading a book and eating chocolates and who said, "You look the picture of health, Mamachen. I envy you. The Via Appia must have been wonderful today."

"Wonderful? In my present state of mind? With the worries you give me?"

"My dear mother," said Mary, "there is no one on earth I respect more than you. For this reason let me tell you that there is no drama in all this."

And her mother's surprise was so great that she forgot the unopened letter and the insulting remark about her health. "Come here, my child," she said. "Give me a big kiss. I am so glad Mary Tempi has made you see the light."

And Mary said, "Yes, Mother, she did. She made me see that I must have my own life from now on. When I have a child, our relationship will be clearer and simpler."

Whereupon her mother tried to faint but could not, because she was too angry to lose consciousness. Mary noticed this, too, and said nothing. But half an hour later she was motherless and her mother childless. Mary went to her room,

97

where she fainted, and her mother went to hers, where she took her revenge knifing and biting venison and beef and eating up all by herself a whole dinner for six.

It may truly be said that if my grandmother ever felt hate for anyone it was for Mary after her inconceivable treason. She tried to see Marchesa Tempi, but the Marchesa, who had more flair than might have been expected in a woman of her limited experience, sent her father to see my grandmother and tell her that no help could be hoped for from that quarter. Mr. Schultz felt that, as he had been entrusted with the message, he could water it down to make it less painful. He therefore reported that his daughter had been too much upset to find anything to say, but, although he could not promise it, he thought she would soon explain everything by letter. My grandmother left Rome with all her furniture again and with Bernhard and Luther, but not with the cook, for the cook went to work for Carlo Tempi. This was a greater blow to her even than Mary's marriage—for Mary had quickly married.

Mr. Schultz told my grandmother he would do anything he could to help Mary in her absence.

"Mary?" she said. "Who is that? Your daughter?"

"No, yours!"

"Mine? I never had a daughter by that name. There must be some mistake."

She went to Baden-Baden, to build herself a castle on top of a hill and die there. Of which forthcoming death she gave a most moving report to her sons and daughters in a series of threatening letters, reinforced by angry telegrams. She summoned Ludmilla, the youngest, to come and stay with her (Ludmilla had been complaining in vain for two years of the horrors of life in a Swiss *pensionnat*), and Ludmilla came, glad to be able to displace her hated sister in her mother's heart; but after only a month in a hotel, despite the absorbing interest of the planning and building of her mother's burial place, she begged to be sent back to her *pensionnat* and was declared a traitress like her sister and as such counted among the dead, or, rather, the unborn.

After this the old lady went to see Katia in Berlin. There exists a most interesting account of that visit in a letter to Mary, written by Luther, who had now begun in secret to inform Mary of her mother's state and moves. Mary never answered these letters, but she kept them all. She wrote only to her mother, and her letters were read only by Luther, because her mother did not like to read letters from strangers. Mary, however, went on writing, and her letters became more and more desperate. Suddenly she received a reply written impulsively and in a very unfriendly tone, but she knew this to be a good sign: "Madame begs the letter writer to be informed that she is leaving Baden-Baden to visit her only daughter in the mental hospital in Berlin. Madame may be reached at the Hotel Adlon, but, given the sadness of the occasion, it is advisable not to disturb her."

The reunion with Katia was a strange one. Katia was the most beautiful of the daughters, and the one whose haggard look most resembled her mother's. They had one thing in common: Pierre had harmed them both, but in opposite ways— not thinking of his mother and thinking too much of his sister, not taking any help from his mother and taking too much away from his sister. So for a few minutes his name ("Pierre!" "Pierre?" "Pierre!") provided the most vivid exchange of a variety of thoughts between the two. But then began the complaints of the mother against the other children, and Katia grew more and more irritated.

"Don't talk to me about them. They have freedom. If you

complain that they want more of it, send them here, they will have none, you will be able to rejoice, like Pierre, who has taken all freedom away from me!"

"But you don't understand, Katia, they are insane—"

"Insane, you say? Insane? Dare you pronounce that word in here? Everyone is insane in here except for me. Learn from your darling son Pierre, put them in here, this will be the right place for the whole family, at least you will be able to keep them with you. We want you in here with us, understand? With us, not me with you in Baden-Baden because you have no other victim. Understand? What are you looking at with those strange eyes? Be careful, they might lock you up if you stare at me that way! You came here to be pitied? Doctor, take her away or lock her up, she is mad, she is utterly mad, she comes in here to be pitied by me! I could strangle the old egotist. Go away, you filthy beast, go away, prostitute, murderess, what do you want from me? Out of here or else in! And in for good!"

Her mother had to be carried out, and it was horrible for her not to be able to use the right word, which had lost all its negative meaning in there: "She is insane, insane!" The attendants took it as a redundant, rather childish, almost abnormal piece of information, which, if repeated, might tell more about her than about her sick daughter.

Mary was expecting a child, and the doctors were worried lest she lose it owing to her state of despair. Mary Tempi, who was about to retire to Tuscany for good, wrote my grandmother a short letter in which, rather curtly and without any friendly expression, she reminded her of her duties as a mother. As if nothing had happened during more than a year, my grandmother replied to the Marchesa that she had thought of coming back in a matter of days and was pleased that "someone at last" should have told her the truth. She sent a telegram to Mary announcing her return, left the Baden-Baden building project under the supervision of the architect, and descended again upon Rome, like Napoleon when he went to conquer Italy.

Mary's life with her first husband has remained a mystery. All her accounts were tainted by great bitterness, and bitterness engenders doubt more than curiosity, for it reveals more of the describer than of the people bitterly described. If those who want to ruin their enemies would remember to throw in one or two kind words for every ten unkind ones, they would of course be doing them a service but also a great disservice, for everything about them would then seem real, and it would be difficult for them to escape condemnation for their sins; while if the picture is painted only in black on black, no one recognizes a human trait in all that darkness.

The apartment in the Via Gregoriana being now rented, it became urgent to have another one in that same street or to persuade its new inhabitants to leave it, because Mary lived only a few steps away. In a matter of days the Avvocato was able to persuade the new inhabitants of the old apartment to go elsewhere, and, at the modest price of only twenty times its original price, which was already ten times its original price, my grandmother re-established her foothold on Rome and consented to meet her son-in-law. She hardly looked at him; she looked everywhere else and nodded grandly while he spoke, then noted in her journal: "I have not yet set eyes on him, but slowly will, for Mary's sake. It seems that Mary is not allowed to read Renan or Darwin. She is quite thin. He has painted her portrait in a gray hat. Not bad, but not original. He has a heavy Roman accent. He is half French, but his French is appallingly bad. However, it seems that his French mother speaks no French at all. I could not be less interested."

Happy as she was to see her daughter the first week, while she was still staying at a hotel, she became quite aloof again as soon as she was back in the old apartment. "I have perhaps forgiven her too early," she wrote the first day. "She should be made to realize what I have suffered all these months." Her first act of authority was to insist that Mary be seen by a doctor in Vienna. Mary's husband was discouraged from going with them. From Vienna they decided not to return to Rome, but to go straight to Baden-Baden, where one wing of the castle was ready and furnished, so that the child could be born in a civilized country, away from its Roman grandparents.

Mary was so happy to have been forgiven that she not only measured every word before speaking it, she said only such things as might be pleasing to her mother. Any sentence that did not contain an element of flattery or gratitude was apt to make her mother frown and become anguished. What does she mean by that? my grandmother would ask herself. Is this addressed to me? Does she need me to say such things? Would not any other listener do? What am I doing here, then? And she answered such questions as "Don't you like these flowers?" with other questions such as "Don't you have anything else to say? Is my presence such a burden to you? Would you not rather be with your new family, your new mother, your new father, in Rome?" And assuming that these were Mary's answers rather than her own questions, she would then draw conclusions such as "Why not say so before, if that is in the back of your mind? Do you think I could stand another blow such as you gave me the last time? Be frank, tell me now if you want me to leave, and let us have it over with before I get used to the idea of living. I was so happy with my plans for a dignified death away from everybody—why did I have to come back to the living, only to be punished again, a thousand times more cruelly this time?" Thus the tone of their conversation, which before Mary's marriage had usually been extremely high, amusing, interesting, was now monotonous, devoid of every element of intellectual interest and, above all, of laughter.

Mary knew that her mother was now passionately interested in psychiatry and all forms of psychology, but even there, when they began to read a book together, she would suddenly be asked, "Now tell me, since this too is part of the psychology of mental alienation: How could you lie to me so brazenly and for so long?"

"But I did not, Mamachen darling—"

"No 'Mamachen darling,' please. We are discussing a purely scientific question now. Answer my question and answer it honestly. That is all I want." (Mary could not even remember whether she had lied or for how long.)

The only way for her to avoid these strenuous questions was to surprise her mother with exaggerated manifestations of her gratitude; but then these too were dangerous, because her mother would soon say, "Be careful, don't promise too much. I remember a girl who said she would never marry, never leave her mother. Of course I did not believe her, I did my best to get her married, I introduced her to many young men, and she kept saying, 'No, Mamachen, how can you think that I would ever leave you?' But I suppose you are not interested in that fairy tale. It all happened so long ago, in quite another world."

So the next thing Mary hit upon was to tell her amusing little incidents about her brothers and sisters back in the days of their childhood; and when these were exhausted, she began to invent more, fashioning them according to the desires of her mother, who wanted only to hear terrible things about everyone but Mary and herself. And so Mary, who had dreamed of becoming a writer and inventing good things about imaginary people, found herself becoming a slanderer and inventing only bad things about real people, whom she otherwise loved very dearly—more so now, in a state of remorse, than before, in a state of innocence. Her mother loved this game. She became so excited with it that she asked for more and more tales all the time, and when Mary refused to provide them, accusations poured forth.

"You have told me lies, Mary, now confess and be honest for

once. You have done so to conceal your own hatred of me, have you not?"

"Of course not, Mamachen, how can you believe such a thing?"

"Tut tut tut tut, what do I hear? That ominous phrase, 'How can you believe such a thing?' Where did I hear it before, Mary? Can you tell me, where?"

And to persuade herself more than her mother, Mary would now repeat the old tales—true and false ones, who could tell them apart any more?—and each time they were picked from the bag they were polished and clarified, so that finally it was the artistic element that told the lie, not Mary.

"We will get even with those criminals, just wait and see," said her mother, and she kept questioning Mary until one thing came out which almost threatened to create a new crisis: Mary was still in love with her medical student. But she swore she knew nothing about him, not even his address. Slowly, more truths came out: The marriage was not working out very well, Mary hated the new world she had found herself tied to; she had nothing in common with it, and her husband was rude, he ate fried eggs every morning, and he smoked a pipe—three things that filled her with horror.

"Not another divorce in the family," said her mother quite sternly. "As for the rest, we will see to it that you don't spend too much time with your husband. But the world, and especially the family, should know nothing about this, or they will say it was my fault."

The child was born and named Konstantin Pierre Ivan Timofey Kyrill Vladimir, known from then on as Kostia. Luther became his governess, and his grandmother his real mother. Mary was just the donor. When his father came to see him, Luther disinfected the child's face where his father had kissed it, so as to ready him again for his grandmother's kisses.

There were already three other Kostias and two Vladimirs, one Ivan, one Igor, one Olga, and two Tatyanas among the grand-children she might have kissed and cared for; but she had never wanted to see any of them.

The child's first trip to Rome took months. First they stopped in Lucerne, then in Lausanne, then in Lugano, then in Pegli, and at long last in Rome, where the other grand-parents were allowed to see him, chaperoned, of course, by Luther, who disinfected him each time he was kissed. In his grandmother's home he was never disinfected, but simply photographed and looked at and discussed uninterruptedly day in day out, and this was very strange, because she had always had a distaste for children and never allowed them to be mentioned to her. Kostia was an exception, Kostia was not a child, he was an angel, an artist, a scientist, a banker, an in-dustrialist, an emperor, a genius, a god. And he would prove it, for he knew that his grandmother had said so and he was not the man to let her appear a liar in the eyes of the world.

Now travel was resumed grandly, with Mary's husband added to a troupe which proceeded (in hotel dining rooms, on promenades) in the following order: first came the grand-mother, then Luther with the child, then Mary, and, at the end, the husband. Whenever the husband began to find that a place was suitable for his work, his mother-in-law found it detestable and moved on to another place, where they stayed only until he had found that inspiring.

After only a short period of this, the husband found it more practical to stay behind in Rome and wait for the family's return. Of which return he read announcements in the papers, rarely in personal letters.

V

Ｓｅｖｅｎ ｙｅａｒｓ ｌａｔｅｒ, in 1902, the play *Resurrection*, by Tolstoy, was given in Rome. The occasion was solemn, especially for members of the Russian colony, and even more so for the members of the Tolstoy cult, to which both Mary and her mother belonged. How her mother could reconcile Tolstoy with her own ways might be a mystery for us who are examining her life, but it was not for her, because her views and Tolstoy's views coincided completely. And if her practice was divorced from her theory, this was, of course, the fault of those who did not understand her and whose lack of sincerity, of affection, of humility, made it impossible for her to be sincere, affectionate and humble, as she essentially was.

Mary's husband was away on a painting trip. These trips had become more and more frequent; they were paid for and encouraged by his wife and constituted a great joy for his mother-in-law. So the two ladies went to the theater. Before the play began, Mary amused her mother by making sharp comments about the people, the jewels, the dresses, and her mother would then look at the objects of Mary's attention through her own opera glasses to confirm Mary's impressions. Suddenly Mary stopped, her opera glasses fell down on somebody's head, there ensued a great deal of commotion with threats of lawsuits for damages (which Mary's mother promised to pay without any discussion the next day), and Mary, indifferent to all this, unable to explain how it had all come about, kept staring at the orchestra, from where a man was staring back at her.

The play began. Mary was moved by it, and her mother both moved and upset. She thought that Mary was not well and wondered about the cause of her behavior. "We must go out and have a breath of air," she said as soon as the first act was finished. They were about to leave, Mary looking pale and drawn and seeming to have some difficulty in walking, when there was a knock on the door of their box and the old lady said, "Come in."

In came a somber-looking young man with a huge, very sharp mustache and fiery eyes. He looked as if he intended to murder the two ladies at once. But this did not seem to be his intention, for he timidly asked whether he could present his compliments.

"And who are you?" asked Mary's mother defiantly. Mary sat motionless, her eyes fixed on the young man, who in the meantime mumbled his name; her mother understood only too well, but she too seemed in the grip of emotion and had to give herself a little time to decide on the course of action she must take. "Who is he?" she asked Mary.

Mary said nothing, but looked at him again, and he introduced himself again, this time very precisely, almost with too much energy.

"All right," said the old lady, "as you have come in anyway, sit down."

He hesitated for a while, obviously thinking that he could not accept such an insult, then decided to take it and sat down. There followed a great silence.

"I am in Rome," he said, with a strong southern accent;

then, not knowing what to say next, repeated, "I am in Rome tonight."

"We heard you the first time," said the old lady. Then, as if regretting her harshness, "So you are in Rome."

"Yes, I am in Rome. But I don't live in Rome."

"Where do you live?"

"If I told you the name of the place it would mean nothing to you. A savage place down south, far down south in Apulia. Southeast."

"I see. And is it far from Rome?"

"Oh, yes, quite."

"Very good. And when are you thinking of going back there?"

"Oh . . . I don't know. I should go back tomorrow."

"I think you should."

The young man became pale, his voice was broken with emotion as he said, "And how do you know I should?"

"You just said so yourself. Or did you not?"

"I did indeed, but I had not finished my sentence."

"Oh. You had not finished your sentence? And do you think we should hear the whole sentence?"

"I most certainly do. I never leave a thing unsaid. That would not be polite."

"Oh, and what does that mean? Are you a great specialist in matters of politeness?"

"I never try to impose it on others. That is none of my job. I am by profession a doctor, and even there if people don't follow my prescriptions I don't waste any time persuading them. Everyone has the right to choose his own doom. But, to go back to my unfinished sentence, I may go back tomorrow and I may not."

"Oh, I see. Do you have business in Rome?"

"None."

"And you do have, I take it, at home."

"Yes. Urgent business, too."

"It is a pity to neglect your urgent business back home and linger here where, as you say, you have no business."

"I like this city, and I may never see it again. We people from the south do not travel too much, we consider it a waste of time, and it is one, indeed. So, as I am here now, why not stay one more day?"

"Why not? There are so many monuments to see."

"Yes."

"Museums."

"Yes."

"The Via Appia."

"I know the Via Appia and I don't like it."

"Oh, you don't like it. What do you find there that is objectionable to your taste?"

"The Roman ruins."

"Why don't you like the Roman ruins?"

"I prefer Greek ruins."

"Do you know Greece?"

"I have never left my country. I cannot travel as I wish. I am too poor."

"Then how do you know that Greek ruins are better?"

"Because I have studied them. And because all of Rome—its culture, monuments and, of course, ruins—is inferior to corresponding elements in Greece."

"Quite an opinion to have."

"Yes."

"Especially as it is not based on experience."

"Motion by train does not give experience. Standing still, reading and meditating do. That experience I have."

"Very modest of you."

He blushed. "Sorry," he said. "I forgot to add: modestly speaking."

"Well, so now you have added it. Is everything all right?"

"Everything what?"

"Everything all right, I said."

"No, of course not. I don't know what this means."

"Never mind. And so you are going to have quite a day to-morrow seeing monuments you do not like."

"Yes."

"Well, if you have a little spare time between looking at horrors, I suggest that you come and have tea with us. We live at Via Gregoriana forty-two. Four o'clock sharp. Good evening and thank you for your visit."

He jumped up from his chair and said, "You said . . . you said I should come and have tea?"

"If you care to do so, yes. That is what I said."

"Thank you very much for the honor, but . . . why tea?"

"Because that is what we Russians drink at four in the afternoon."

"As a cure?"

"A cure? No, as a matter of habit."

"But I am very well, I don't need tea."

"You may have coffee if you prefer."

"Oh, I . . . don't want to disturb you."

"You mean to say you are not coming?"

"No, no, of course I am. But . . . don't trouble yourself to make coffee for me."

"I shall not make it. My cook will, or the child's governess."

"Oh." He frowned. "Oh. And . . . whose child's governess?"

"My daughter's child's governess."

"Oh. Oh. Then . . . perhaps I had better not come."

"Why?"

"I don't want to create a . . . disturbance."

"You are creating no disturbance, or, rather, you will create none tomorrow but you are creating one now. The play is beginning again, people are hushing us."

"I am sorry. Then you say I may really come?"

"I said so. Yours is the last word. I never insist, I am like you with your patients. Goodbye."

During the whole conversation Mary had sat as if *she* were the intruder, the stranger, almost the enemy, and those two the old friends meeting again after years. She could not sleep all night, and the next day she could not wait. She prayed all day that he would decide to come. And when he came, Bernhard called her and said would she please receive the guest, her mother had a headache and wished to be excused.

He had never been in such an opulent house before. She found him standing in awe in front of her mother's marble bust, and then jumping like a cat when he felt the leaves of a palm tree touch his ear; he had not seen the palm tree. When he saw her come in, he looked in every direction, like a frightened animal, and asked in a whisper, "Where is your husband?"

"He is away on a trip," she said.

"Away on a trip? I see. But . . . will the butler tell him I was here?"

"The butler? My mother's butler? And even if he did, what of it?"

"Yes, what of it. Easily said. Is this . . . honest?"

"What?"

"That I should come here?"

"Who knocked on the door of my box last night?"

"I did. I swear to you I did. No one else was with me."

"I believe you. But if that was honest, so is this."

"Yes, but your mother—is she alive?"

"Dear Lord, why say such a thing? Of course she is alive, thank God. You saw her last night."

"That's what I thought, but who is this?" He pointed to the marble bust.

"This is she."

"You mean to say she is alive and has in her own house her own future memorial monument? How strange."

"But this is not a future memorial monument. It is a bust by the German sculptor Cauer. And that there is a bust of my late father."

"Oh. I see. But he is dead."

"Yes, he has been dead for years."

"But . . . he is not buried here."

"Of course not. In Berlin."

"I see. So you have two busts, one here and one in Berlin."

"No, only this one here. In Berlin we have a tombstone with that monument there on top of it." And she pointed to a photograph of the tomb in Berlin.

He looked at it, said, "I see. A very big, expensive monument. One wonders if it was necessary to throw away all that good money which might have gone for better purposes."

She was touched to tears by this remark, even though it seemed almost in bad taste. He was moved, too, but went on speaking. "I don't mean to be offensive, but the cult of the dead, as the Italian poet Foscolo (who, by the way, was born in Greece) so well puts it, does not require all this display of masonry and opulence." And he began to quote: " 'In the shadow of the cypress trees and inside the funeral urns, comforted by the mourner's tears, is the sleep of the dead perhaps less hard?' "

Mary had never heard the poem before and had little interest in quotations. She was much too bewitched by the presence of the quoter, and baffled by his strange reactions.

"So," he said, interrupting himself almost with anger, "so you are happily married, that was of course to be expected, best wishes to you and what else can I say? Nothing, I suppose."

"But I am not," she said.

"Not? Are you not married? Don't you have a child?"

"Yes, but I am not happily married."

He seemed unpleasantly surprised. "And you are telling me in your husband's house that you are not happily married?"

"This is not my husband's house, it is my mother's house."

"Oh, I see. So you have left your husband."

"No, I have not."

"But you don't live with him."

"Yes, I do, in the Via Sistina, near here."

"And you dare say such a thing to a stranger like myself?"

"You are not a stranger to me. You never were. You have always . . . been with me."

"Oh. I hope . . ." A long silence.

"You hope what?"

"I don't know how to put it."

"Say it anyway."

"I . . . hope . . . you realize the gravity of this statement."

"Gravity? Yes, if you will, but to me it is natural and cheerful. It was grave as long as I could not speak about it to you. But now that you are here, nothing is grave any more."

He seemed still very doubtful. "I hope . . ." He hesitated again, then brought it out: "I hope I am the only person in the world who ever heard these words from you."

"What do you mean?" she asked, becoming furious.

"I apologize." He seemed quite pleased. "I see, I see—this is a healthy reaction."

"But how could you think—"

"I did not. But I was frightened, and one must always be careful. It is better to believe too little than too much."

She was beside herself. "Do you have such a low opinion of me?"

"No, of course not, but you never can tell. I am invited here by your own mother, she lets me talk to you and refuses to appear—admit that this is all very strange. I don't know you, after all, and I met you under the strangest circumstances."

Mary became very depressed and very offended.

113

"Do you want me to leave?" he asked.

"No," she said curtly. "Stay. And tell me about yourself. Of course you are not married. You . . . knew better."

There was another long silence, then he said, "But I am married."

"You are?"

"Yes."

She began to sob quietly. "And of course you have children."

"No, I have none."

"But you are happily married."

"No, I am not."

"You . . . are not?"

"Absolutely not."

"And you . . . remember?"

"What?"

"Me?"

"Madame," he said, sinking on his knees, "how could I forget?"

There was a long silence now during which they both looked at the doors, the various doors in the distance, and then at each other, without daring to make the next move. Finally she said, "Then there is no obstacle. Let us each get a divorce and . . . marry."

He remained speechless for a moment. "A divorce?" he said then. "But that is impossible."

"Why? Are you a devout Catholic?"

"Not in the slightest. I am an active anticlericalist, a liberal, a freethinker and a materialist."

"Then there is no obstacle at all. We can get divorces and be married."

"Divorce—but do you realize what that means?"

"Yes, my mother was divorced, one of my brothers may get a divorce, my sister was divorced, so I can be divorced, too. My mother does not want me to, but she will have to accept it. I am determined."

"But . . . what will people say?"

"About you? Do you care?"

"No. About you."

"I do not care. The only person in the world whose opinion can have any weight is you. Would you despise me if I got a divorce?"

"No," he said, but he seemed frightened all the same. "I would not want my seven sisters to think badly of you. . . ."

"They will not, once they see us together."

"And then, of course, there is also my wife."

"Do you love her?"

"No, not a bit. I hate her. I let my uncles persuade me to marry her because they thought it a good match for me, but she has ruined me financially, she is a fool."

"Why, then, there is no problem."

"No, of course not. But I will have to tell her."

"That, yes. I am afraid you will. But I can do it for you if you don't have the courage."

"Oh, no, I can do it myself. Only—a divorce . . . What a terrible thing. And it must cost a fortune."

"Leave it to me. I have the money."

"Never. I could not accept being bought by a woman."

"Nonsense. This is a loan. You and I will work together, you will make great discoveries and I will help you, I will help you do the things you mentioned to me once in Naples, so many years ago. Wait," she said suddenly. "Don't leave until I come back. I have promised my mother never again to tell her a lie. I shall tell her the truth this very moment, and if she does not like it I shall leave the house with you."

Before he could say anything she was gone. The few minutes he waited were full of horror for him. He was anxious to leave, he did not know what he would do if she thought she could leave with him at once. He was in Rome officially, with a commission of politicians and representatives of his whole region, to plead with the government for an appropriation on behalf of the thirsty population of Apulia and its dying agriculture. He had hardly any money of his own, how could he appear with a young woman like Mary who had no idea of life or of her legal duties as a married woman? Yet to escape at this point would have meant losing the only thing he cared for in life. So he stayed and prayed—"Dear Lord, make the whole thing impossible."

"Mamachen," said Mary, "I have something to tell you."

"No, Mary, you have nothing to tell me."

"Oh, yes, Mamachen, I have."

"Be quiet, Mary, you have not. I forbid you to speak."

"But I must speak—"

"No, you must not. I must speak first."

"Very well."

A long silence, then the mother said, "It is I who am speaking, not you. And it is who am saying to you that you . . ."

"That I . . . ?"

"Be patient, Mary. You—yes, you—will get a divorce and marry that man. Anyone who can answer me as he did last night deserves not only my respect but my daughter as well."

They left by night, like thieves, Mary, her mother, her child, Luther, Bernhard and a maid. The furniture was to be sent to Geneva, where a villa had been bought, sight unseen, by telegraphic order, and a lawyer, the greatest divorce lawyer in Europe at that time, had been retained for the two cases. The future husband would join them in Geneva.

He was by nature not talkative and seemed bored when brilliant conversation was "exploding and puffing and sizzling," as he described it, like green kindling in the fireplace, with much smoke in the eyes, much noise and little of any consequence, namely no reliable, good fire. Mary felt she was confronted with a new person every day, while in reality it was she who changed. He stayed always the same. He had never been abroad, he had never spoken French, although he had a silent knowledge of the language which was in many ways more accurate, more solid than even the old lady's French, which she had learned from superficial people, such as nurse-maids and tutors, for superficial purposes. It was with a certain irritation that she learned a few structural elements of the language from her future son-in-law in a most appalling accent, but he seemed not to notice that his pedantry had such an effect. It was Mary who noticed it and suffered, anticipating her mother's irritation and keeping it alive in herself long after her mother had overcome her first feeling and become grateful to him for the lesson.

Thus the relationship between her husband-to-be and her mother was simpler, easier and far more conversational than hers with him. And when they both laughed at her fears that he might hurt her mother with his crudeness, she became anguished and felt lonely—so much so that she fancied herself already abandoned by him, saw him pursuing another woman with her mother's consent and help. The further thought, This is my punishment for what I did to her, strengthened these vague apprehensions and transformed them into elements of fact. She *knew* it was this way, no one could fool her. And, as if by a miracle, her mother became eloquent on the subject of jealousy and its ruinous character. She even wrote an essay for Mary's information and guidance, and it was a good essay, said the doctor.

But these things could not fill his life or repay him for his lost sense of stability and duty.

They had barely arrived in Geneva when the old lady decided that the house she had bought sight unseen was not the house she would have wanted, so she decided to sell it again, and when told that it would be a difficult house to sell, she bought another immediately, regardless of the price and of the

loss on the first house. In view of the dangers they were facing
(scandals, trial for abduction of child and desertion of husband, etc.), money matters were of secondary importance.

This all seemed utter nonsense to the doctor. What had the
purchase of a new house to do with these matters? Was she
not using them as an excuse to act foolishly? Why waste all
that money? He expressed these thoughts to Mary in secret,
and Mary had a crisis. Her first and only thought was, He is
bored, he regrets he has come, he does not love me any more.
And indeed he did look bored.

"Tell me the truth: You regret you have come. I forced
you, yes, you would never have thought of a divorce had I
not forced you."

"It is true that you gave me the idea, but I take full responsibility for my acts."

"Oh, that is the way you express it? Then you do regret it,
and it is only out of pride that you stay on. It would seem too
foolish for you to go back."

"Nonsense, that has nothing to do with the fact that I find
this waste of money, this continuous agitation, very bad. Bad
for your mother, bad for you, bad for your child, and of course
bad for me too. My whole village could live for a year on
what your mother spent in this first week here in Geneva."

"But, darling, it is her money, she is spending it to please
me, to help us."

"No, she is not. And she is not even spending it to please
herself. She spends it mostly on things she does not like, houses
she has not seen and refuses to inhabit the moment she sees
them, hotels she despises and leaves the next day. This is not
spending it on your pleasures, but on your displeasures only."

"But, darling, we cannot criticize her. Whatever she does
with it, it is still her money, my father left it to her."

"That is no reason to throw it away as she does."

"But, darling, you are speaking like Pierre."

"Who is Pierre? If he speaks that way, I must meet him and tell him I entirely agree."

"But, darling, this is a terrible thing to say. Pierre is my brother, but he is a criminal."

"Why? What has he done?"

"He . . . he . . . Oh, I cannot even begin to tell you. Lots of things. He refuses to write to his mother."

"That does not make him a criminal. Perhaps he has his reasons."

"But, darling, please, you cannot speak that way in this house. He has no reasons at all. He is a beast, a criminal, he drags his mother to her grave."

"This has never been a crime."

"What do you mean?"

"It is simply a way of speaking, but it specifies nothing. If you told me he kills little children in the street or he squanders his father's hard-won capital and by doing these things is dragging his mother to her grave, I would agree with you. But you cannot expect me to condemn him on a figure of speech used to express the subjective impressions of your mother."

"But then you hate her, you side with her enemies. How can you?"

"I have never hated her. In fact, I like her very much; but I find her spending habits absurd, not to say outright offensive to the poor."

"We never speak of money. She is too noble to give it any attention at all. She despises money."

"No, she does not. She may despise people and use money to show her contempt, but if she despised money she would not have any."

"She is in fact spending it all because she feels that her children must earn their own money, as their father did."

"That is no proof that she despises money—rather, that she despises her children and loves money."

"Why do you say these things to me? Do you want me to hate my mother the very moment she is giving up everything to help us two with our divorces?"

"No, I don't want you to hate her in the future, as you certainly will if you let her spend her money so foolishly."

"You say these things only because you hate me and you want me to die. Tell me so—rather, kill me, no one will punish you."

And she had another crisis which could not possibly escape her mother's attention and so she chose to confide in her mother completely, not, indeed, out of sincerity (and she herself was not aware of the finer motives), but to arouse her mother's pity before her wrath could be aroused by any cold-blooded observation the doctor might make. And of course to scare him, too, so that he would not talk. Instead of which he felt duty-bound to repeat his criticism to the old lady in the daughter's presence. No shock could have been greater for Mary than the way her mother took it.

The old lady said quietly, "I am glad someone is thoughtful enough to tell me. No one cares what I do with my money, no one notices even that I don't spend it to amuse myself but only to find greater disappointment in each new thing I try. Here at least is a man who understands me and knows what I must suffer every day. Thank you, my friend. Tell me what to do from now on and I promise to obey you. I am so tired of being on my own, with not a soul to advise me or criticize me and stop me!"

This was a new responsibility for the doctor to take upon himself, and it weighed on him infinitely more than the much lesser financial responsibilities he had just shirked in his own village, where to be a mayor, as he was, meant to open one's arms and look at the ceiling for help from on high and repeat this unconstructive gesture twenty, fifty times a day—namely, at each single question that came up—because there simply was not a cent for anything useful, urgent or constructive, most monies having already been spent far in advance for such unworthy purposes as buying fireworks for the feast of the local patron saint (the largest item in the budget, and one over which the most starved mothers of twenty sick children would not yield for anything in the world) or such miserable, sad purposes as paying a pension to the former garbage collector who had lost his leg, purchasing second-rate medicines for the destitute, and repairing a leak in the roof of the school building. How often had he not paid for these items out of his own pocket, much against the will of his wife, whom he had bitterly criticized (and rightly so, he continued to think from afar) for her habits of luxury, the hats and dresses she ordered from Turin and wore in the midst of dejection and poverty, to mark her higher social status and enjoy the feeling of being envied. How he had hated her for that, and how different was Mary, of course; but in what a different world his wife had been, and how microscopic all that world seemed as seen from the heights of these budgets, these mad expenditures out of which no one derived any pleasure, except of course for the thieves like Avvocato Tegolani, the cook, the hotel managers, the servants and the shopkeepers whose bills he found in the old lady's drawer!

Back home in his village his conscience had been clear, though saddened by the great sacrifice of his teaching ambitions. However, this sacrifice was more than justified by the poverty, the ignorance, and the ill will of his townsfolk (he alone could do something about it, he had felt with youthful pride). Here his conscience was not clear. He could not possibly resume his scientific career without first practicing in hospitals and publishing some acceptable monograph, then getting his professorship; and these things were not for him—he was a foreigner in Geneva, the language barrier was difficult to overcome, he was unknown, with not a friend to counsel him, in a world whose obstacles rose in front of him at every step. And thus he felt somnolent, so much so that his only desire was to go to bed and sleep, and especially not to be asked by Mary, "Why are you so silent? Don't you love me any more? Do you regret the great step?"

To escape from these questions he took up his new task as her mother's comptroller very seriously, but there he felt somewhat ridiculous. He, who had never even seen a thousand-lira bill, let alone rubles, francs and marks, bonds and stocks, checkbooks and checks, was now surrounded by a mass of them, all dead, all boring, all certifying only to the total inadequacy and irresponsibility of their owner and handler. He could not help translating every new figure he saw, marked down casually in books or written out in bills, into his own financial language, mumbling to himself all the time, This equals a water system for the village, this road repair to the station, this medical supplies for our nonexistent pharmacy, this balancing of last year's budget, and this little nonsense here would, distributed to the poor in the square, make everybody mad with joy for weeks on end, it would buy food and clothing and what not. And then, of course, he thought of his sisters: the one who was a hypochondriac and who always said he alone knew what medicines she needed (nonsense, he gave her water and bicarbonate), the one who was still hoping for a husband, the one who had one and could not hope for his death even though this would have been the solution of her troubles, and the one who wanted to become a nun and lived like a nun to sacrifice for her sisters, her nephews and nieces, and the village at large. How far away they seemed, completely unaware of this gold into which he was dipping his hands with no permission to do anything worthy or intelligent with it! A thought kept haunting him: At first I could not study because I was too poor, and now I cannot study because I am too rich.

He tried to resell the first villa, and it made him lose his bearings completely. He discovered that the old lady had been cheated in the most blatant way, but he could not argue in a language he barely knew, and the old lady was too indifferent (too noble?) to discuss money matters with lower people such as the Swiss. "Let's *do* something with the villa, at least," he kept saying, and in his dreams he saw it house all the destitute in his village, he imagined it a hospital, a school, even a private dwelling for himself and his future family; but of course he had to be cautious when he spoke of these matters, lest Mary think him interested in money. The old lady did not, she knew better, but she was immensely amused by his sullen moods when they were caused "by such trifles." So he found a new task for himself: to teach Kostia about the classics, become his private tutor. This gave him unexpected joys, because the boy was very intelligent and sensitive, and, besides, he was a male. Back home also he had always been surrounded with women, but they were first dependent, frightened and subdued, then poor. Moreover, he had always escaped from them several times a day to seek the company of his friends. As a matter of fact, Kostia's friendship meant more to him than the friendships he had lost. Mary felt proud of his interest in the boy; indeed, it was the safest haven for him, because even the old lady did not dare interrupt them when they were busy studying together. And every proof of the boy's progress was a proof to him of his usefulness and his dignity as a scholar.

This new idyl was unpleasantly interrupted by the arrival of the first shipment of furniture from Rome. Why had the Avvocato shipped only an infinitesimal quantity of what was in the house? The old lady could not possibly understand, because the same number of freight cars had been used as were filled up last time, and now they were almost empty. Could they have been opened and ransacked on the way? The doctor had to go to the railroad station in the company of Luther, because his French was still inadequate and his anger made it even more so, but it was found that the seals had been opened only upon arrival, in the presence of a qualified Swiss inspector, so the theft must have been made in Rome.

"Impossible," said the old lady angrily when she heard this.

"Tegolani is a gentleman, I cannot doubt his honesty, he has been in my service for years. I refuse to hurt his feelings with a question of this kind."

"But he is the only one who can provide you with information on the matter. You don't want to lose your best paintings, your carpets, and all your silver and crockery."

"Of course not, but that is why I have entrusted everything to a man like Tegolani."

She finally agreed to write him a letter, which began with a formal and universal clearing for him. "I know you cannot be called responsible for whatever losses I may have suffered in this first shipment of the furniture and other belongings from my house in Rome," she wrote, "and I repeat here that my trust in you is boundless. Having said this, may I bother you to find out for me who is to be blamed for this partial shipment, and where the rest of my furniture is." The answer soon came back saying that he had shipped everything and there was nothing left in Rome.

When the old lady read this letter, she said, "Of course, you cannot trust the Swiss. They are all robbers. The inspector must have been in league with thieves. I am certain that my belongings are here in Geneva."

The doctor lost his patience and said, "This is impossible. It would be impossible even in Naples, let alone here."

"But, my dear, that is exactly what the Swiss always count on—the reputation for honesty they have built for themselves so that they can steal and get away with it."

"May I insist that it is far more likely to have been a thief in Rome, perhaps your trusted Avvocato himself, whose astronomic bills have already shocked me in the past few days. I did not bring up the matter, because it was none of my business and also because you seemed to trust him and I am completely in the dark as to prices for apartments in Rome. But I think it will be far better for me to go to Rome and look into this matter myself."

124

"You? To Rome? To be murdered? Never. I need you here, Mary would die if you left, we cannot let you go. If necessary, I shall go there myself."

"You cannot go, because you may be arrested for abduction of a child. The Italian laws are extremely severe in these matters, while they are less strict with a man who deserts his wife."

He was not allowed to go, but the old lady wrote a letter to Cavaliere Pollo, much to the doctor's surprise, and asked him to please look into this matter. Cavaliere Pollo went to Rome immediately at his own expense and wrote that an auction was being held at the apartment in the Via Gregoriana, in the old lady's name. Precious rugs, paintings, furniture, table silver, gold goblets, old crystal table services, china, even ancient jewels were on display, and everybody in Rome was talking about the sale.

When the old lady heard this she fell sick with rage. A severe case of jaundice kept her in bed for weeks, and the doctor tried to handle the matter without further upsetting her. Mary was also out of her wits, and the divorce lawyer, who was busy enough with the preparation of the double divorce case, could do nothing about it. He wrote to a lawyer in Rome, and the answer soon came back that the auction had been ordered by the old lady herself through her representative, the lawyer Tegolani, who had full power of attorney in the lady's own handwriting. What could they do? Nothing at all but try and buy their belongings again at the auction. Again Cavaliere Pollo was asked to give his help, and he did. He went to the auction with a list of the things he was supposed to purchase at all costs, bid the most fantastic prices, and was able to get only a few of the items wanted at thirty or forty times their original value, because there were other bidders who turned out to be agents for Tegolani himself. With the help of the police he was able to discover this fact and went to Tegolani to threaten him. Tegolani answered calmly that he was acting on orders from the old lady herself, as proven by her signed statement giving him her power of attorney. It was with tears of rage that Pollo wrote this to the old lady, reproaching her most bitterly for not having trusted him instead, because he would never have done such a thing—a widower with a saintly woman watching his every action from the heavens could not act badly even if he wanted to.

His letter brought the greatest consternation to the family assembled in Geneva. Every moment brought the discovery of a new painful offense when precious personal belongings were found missing from the freight cars that arrived. Beautiful Russian icons, gold watches that had belonged to Mary's father and grandfather, earrings, fur coats, even sheets and towels were missing. The doctor could not bear it. He wrote a long letter to Tegolani asking him to give account of his theft and to return at least the things that had a special personal value for the old lady and her daughter. The reply soon arrived, and it was very insulting. He was asked whether, as the young lady's lover, he felt he had any right to call others to task; secondly, he was informed that the auction had brought in far less than expected—in fact, it had brought so little that an additional payment was expected to cover a long list of items enclosed in the letter. If payment did not come immediately, "Miss Mary —or is she to be called by her married name still?—should be informed that her son will soon be returned to his father, by legal or other means." The letter ended with regards and best wishes for a most successful divorce.

"This time," said the doctor, "no one is going to stop me. I must get even with that swine. If I don't defend the honor of the woman I love, I don't deserve to live."

Avvocato Tegolani must have known what was coming, because a number of unsigned threatening letters arrived almost immediately afterward, all of them posted in Rome. In view of these, Mary, her mother and the lawyer finally prevailed on the doctor not to leave; but it was a great blow to his pride, and many of the mistakes made by him dozens of years later were still a belated attempt to leave on that day. But beyond having a destructive effect on his pride, this episode upset his entire system of values and shattered his ideals in many other ways. He began to acquire a sense of possessiveness, especially for the things that had been lost through Avvocato Tegolani's theft. He who had never owned anything and was now a participant in the wealth of that family (Mary was then expecting a child) felt that in the interest of his children he must put an end to these extravagant habits. At the same time he was ashamed of becoming a parasite and decided to earn fantastic sums of money through his profession, like many other doctors whom he had despised until that day.

He announced his intentions to his future mother-in-law, but his start was not brilliant. Wherever he was called to assist a sick person, he felt that the house in which he himself lived was richer, so he charged nothing at all, or very little, for his services. His name soon became known among Italian immigrants, seasonal workers who lived sparingly on one tenth of the little they earned as masons, bricklayers or railroad workers, sending the bulk of their earnings to their families in Italy. He became their friend, their doctor and their benefactor, which increased Mary's admiration for him and made her want to help him in his philanthropic endeavors. But she frightened the poor away with her own shyness; she was too typically a member of the moneyed class to know how to behave, what to say and what not to say. And she had fits of mad jealousy when she noticed that her "husband" was annoyed by her presence when he was with those uneducated people, with whom he seemed to be perfectly at ease—in fact, he laughed and talked with them as he had never done at home. So she decided suddenly one day that they must leave Geneva and settle down in Lugano, where Italian was the official language, so that he could begin to work in the Italian hospital there.

Again they left their house long before they could sell it, and before buying one in Lugano they took over a whole floor of the Grand Hotel there. This sudden move almost cost them the friendship and the services of their lawyer, who had made all the arrangements to keep them well protected from possible kidnapers and criminals and could not very well do the same thing in Lugano. Besides, in Geneva certain technicalities in the divorce case would have been easier to solve. Now everything had to be started again on a new basis.

VI

Lugano was then and still is today a small town, much less important than Geneva, and less prosperous, especially as far as its Italian population was concerned, and the Italian hospital was very modest. In her usual overgenerous way, the old lady would have been quite willing to buy the hospital and make a present of it to her future son-in-law, or build a new one, add to it, endow it, do anything he might want; but he stopped her and said he wanted nothing. It seemed wrong enough that he should live like a king in the most opulent hotel and go to work for nothing in the poor quarters of the town, while the few other local doctors lived modestly and tried hard to make a living. Unfortunately there was no solution to this; the old lady had never lived in a small town, let alone in an apartment in a small town, and she needed a staff of at least twelve.

Meanwhile the divorce arrangements had finally been completed, and he and his future wife went to Budapest for a while to establish residence there and came back married by Hungarian law. Now their first child was about to be born, and the doctor was anxious to leave the Grand Hotel and settle down with his new family in a small apartment. But again there were problems, because the old lady could not be left alone, and, as she was still paying for everything, Mary did not have the right to express her own will. Besides, Mary would never have wanted to leave her mother. At the same time she wanted to see her husband happy and to help him in his work. They had no friends, the old lady did not want to meet anybody, both she and Mary were more and more terrorized by the threatening letters that continued to arrive from Rome and from Apulia. The old lady paid any sum that was asked, and thus she encouraged the threats until they became unbearable. At the same time they provided a subject for conversation and prevented Mary, her mother and her husband from realizing that their situation was an unpleasant one. With the arrival of the first child, a girl, Mary quieted down for a while, and her husband began to work on the old lady, to persuade her that the life she was leading was meaningless and that there was no point in hating everybody as she did. He found her more than willing to take his advice, so much so that she immediately made peace with her brother, who lived in Paris, and invited him and his wife to come to Switzerland for the christening of her granddaughter Sonia.

For that festive occasion the doctor consented to be outfitted from head to foot at his wife's expense. He had, up to that day, kept at least his sartorial independence, which expressed itself rather typically in what the old lady had described in her books as "the battle dress of doom." She did not know that the battle dress of doom was the symbol of poverty. As death could not possibly be eliminated from their lives and every human being has at one time or another someone to mourn, and the duties connected with the dead cannot possibly be shirked, so it is life and the duties connected with festive celebrations of life that are sacrificed. Only the very rich have more than one suit to wear, and so they can affect gray and brown, colors which, in men's suits in all the southern Mediterranean countries, are almost symbolic of heraldic distinction. The poor always wear black.

Mary was not very maternal by instinct—she resembled her

mother in this—and the little she had had of that instinct had been crushed to make room for her mother's late awakening of the same on the occasion of Kostia's birth. Sonia was therefore her first child, but, again like her mother, she had little use for women, of no matter what age. Mary was so infatuated with her second husband that she had eyes only for him, not for that little monster in the crib. The child's christening, therefore, was postponed until the doctor could appear all dressed up for the occasion. Even Aunt Lydia and Uncle Jules were asked to postpone their trip to Switzerland, because Mary did not want them to see the doctor in his poorly tailored black clothes. It was with a sad smile and many bitter-sweet tears that the old lady consented to this whim. How proud she too had been when her husband had been able to afford his first new clothes (for which, however, he had paid himself), and how she too had kept her eyes glued on him, following him in every movement he made, regardless of who was speaking to her.

Less understanding were the expected guests in Paris, who could not see the reason for the delay.

"What does this mean?" said Uncle Jules to his wife after he had received his sister's telegram. "The Lord only knows what she is up to; probably she has regretted her first impulse to make peace with us and is trying to find a plausible reason for not having us there."

"Perhaps the child is ill," said his wife. "Let us send *them* a telegram."

They sent a telegram asking for news of the little girl, and the answer soon came that the little girl was in perfect health, thank God. Perplexity had now been transferred from Paris to Lugano.

"What can this mean?" the old lady had asked when she received the telegram. "The Lord only knows what they are up to; probably they have regretted their first impulse and are now trying to find a plausible reason for not coming."

131

"No," said the doctor, "they are simply surprised at the delay. It is unheard of that a child should not be christened the day it is born, or one day later at the most."

"Why?" asked the old lady.

"Because if it should die without the sacrament of baptism, it could not go to heaven."

"But I thought you were not a believer in these superstitious practices."

"I am not, you are right, but this is the tradition. Others believe in it."

It was the first, though very slight, disappointment the old lady experienced in her dealings with her son-in-law. She could not understand his reverence for whatever was connected with rituals, when he was very intolerant of other people's true beliefs, and she commented about it in her books. "When are they serious and when are they not? You never catch these atheistic Catholics; they always put their contradictions into different pockets."

But the person least willing to accept excuses for the delay was the bishop, who had been very much surprised when the doctor had come to him, hypocritically polite and subdued, to ask whether he would baptize his daughter. The whole story of the double divorce had been told to the bishop by one of his parishioners, the Countess Etruscoli di Torretrusca, self-appointed guardian of the town's morals; and if he did not blast his opinion in the doctor's face at once, it was only because he did not want to lose one more soul for the dubious advantage of trying to recapture another one, namely that of the guilty father, or even two, including that of the equally guilty mother. When he was told that the ceremony of baptism was to be postponed, he asked, "What does this mean?" And thought, Perhaps they have regretted their first impulse to make peace with the Church and are now trying to find a good excuse to get out of it easily. He mentioned the incident to the countess, who promised to look into the matter and let him know what those heathen were doing.

The doctor in the meantime had begun to regret having said yes to the idea of a tailor. Raised, up to the age of sixteen, to become a priest, he had retained in spite of his rebellion a strong attachment to the idea of austerity, and his view of the world was still very much that of a priest. He was now doing the wrong thing, he had been doing it since the age of sixteen, more and more so, with graver instances of weakness and sin all the time. Why also become vain now? And wasteful? His happiness in love had already cost such a fantastic sum of money and such suffering to so many; should he now let himself go in an orgy of self-complacency?

"All right," he said to his wife, "you had your way, now I am going to have mine. I'll find the tailor and the material. After all, this is going to be my suit and I must be completely satisfied with it before anyone else is."

"Yes," said Mary, "but you promised that you would let Mamachen pay for everything."

"As if she were not paying for everything already. Of course she will—if there is any actual expenditure."

How the brilliant idea (his first since he had left home) came to him he did not know; he did not have it as he left the room, only a strong determination to go out and do something about his old suit, the one he was wearing. Could he have it cleaned and made to look new, with a few minor changes? As he hesitated between taking the lift and walking downstairs he suddenly remembered that the lift boy, into whose hand he had so often pressed a large Swiss coin that belonged to his wife, was the son of an Italian immigrant he had treated recently (for no fee, of course) and that the patient had told him he was a tailor.

"Tell your father I want to see him at once," he said to the lift boy.

"I cannot leave my job," said the boy, "but I can tell him tonight when I go home."

"No, I must see him now. Never mind, I shall go to his house."

And the doctor took a long walk to reach the poorest part of town, where the old man lived.

"What can you do with this?" he asked, showing his suit and its various weak spots, which were many.

"Nothing," said the old man. "This suit was badly cut to begin with. Without meaning to offend you, I had noticed it before when you came here to examine me and I lay sick in bed. Even then I thought it very strange that a rich gentleman like you should have such a bad tailor."

"What do you mean?" asked the doctor resentfully. "The tailor who made this is a very respectable man, he worked for my grandfather and my father before working for me, he has fitted five bishops and a number of *monsignori,* no one ever complained of his work."

"That confirms my suspicion. He must be good at fitting clergymen, not men."

"Never mind. What do you think can be done to make this suit appear a bit more elegant?"

"Nothing, nothing at all."

"Not even turn it inside out?"

"Perhaps that could be done, but I would not touch it."

"Why?"

"Because when you turn a poorly tailored suit inside out it does not change it into a good suit. And besides, it will show that the suit has been worn on the other side of the material."

"How do you know these things?"

"Doctor, how do you know about the insides of people? Training and experience. The same with me."

"And if I ask you to do this for me?"

"I will say no. I would not want to be paid for this job."

"That is a different matter," said the doctor, who thought of what he had already done for the tailor's insides, and of all the large tips he had given the tailor's son.

"Look, Doctor," said the tailor, "you are a rich man and live at the best hotel in town. I don't believe it would be fair to you if you were seen wearing an old suit turned inside out. However, there is a very good tailor in town who is also an Italian and who has no clients yet because he is poor and has no one to work for him. If you go to him . . ."

"I will," said the doctor, "but only after I have seen what this suit looks like turned inside out."

The tailor finally agreed to give it a try, and the doctor left, somewhat worried over the promise he had made; but he hoped, in case he himself did not now need a new suit, to have one made for Kostia there. He ran back to the hotel in a state of great elation, having decided to wear an old summer suit for the few days his only winter suit was at the tailor's.

"Darling," he said to his wife as he entered the room where she was watching the wet nurse feed Sonia, "you will have a very elegant husband and it will not cost you a cent. You and I have, each in his way, paid already for the tailor's work—I by helping him get well, and you by giving large, undeserved sums of money to his son. Wait and see."

Brigida, the wet nurse, who was a very simple peasant woman from the mountains above Lugano, did not quite understand such words from a rich man—or, rather, she understood them too well. Arguments of economy are the only ones that the poor understand, they constitute almost the whole language of the poor, who have no words of wonder for the beauties of nature. Brigida had never seen a gold coin until she had come to the hotel and been given a huge sum of gold, all in one piece, by the doctor himself on the occasion of Sonia's birth, so she thought that the doctor was perhaps the richest man in the world—and now she heard him speak to his wife as her own husband would have spoken to her on a similar occasion, and she felt ashamed that she had accepted so much money from him.

Mary had run after her husband, who had gone to his own room in search of something. She was anguished again. She had never seen him so excited, and as she entered the room she heard him say aloud to himself, "But perhaps the summer one would be even better."

"What are you doing?" she asked.

"Where is my summer suit?"

"What summer suit?"

"You know. The one you liked so much."

"I liked so much? What suit could that have been but the one you are wearing?"

"Come, you remember it very well, help me find it, Giovanna."

"Giovanna?" she cried, and she slumped into a chair to give way to her sobs. "Giovanna he calls me!"

He was so upset himself he did not even notice what he had said, calling his second wife by his first wife's name. What upset him was the discovery that he had left his best suit back home, his only extravagant (that is, gray) suit.

"If I could only go back and fetch it now," Mary heard him say to himself, and as he remembered one thing he had left behind many others now presented themselves to his memory—his books, his microscope, his diplomas, the senseless little bits of adolescent life crystallized into notebooks and objects of no value that constitute (exactly for this reason) the foundations of adulthood, the ground we tread upon.

"Suitcase and blanket," had been his words, and they became proverbial for the rest of his life. "Suitcase and blanket —yes, my children, that is all I had with me when I left home. . . ." "Suitcase and blanket, your honor, that was all I could take when I left home, everything else having gone to pay the debts that my first wife had made with women's tailors and dressmakers in Turin. . . ." "Suitcase and blanket, my dear cousin Crocifisso, that was all I took with me, after I had distributed whatever land I still possessed to my dear sisters. . . ."

But at that moment, with Mary crying desperately and refusing to be consoled, suitcase and blanket seemed far too little to him. How he still wished he could go back, just to pick up his summer suit so that he could have something to wear while the tailor turned his one winter suit inside out. Why should Mary be so blind to these reasons?

"Mary, please, I beseech you, how can you be so stupid?"

"I am not being stupid now. I was stupid before, when I believed in your love."

All right, he said to himself, as this cannot be avoided, let's buy the cloth and go to a good tailor.

He had promised Mary that they would pick out the cloth together, he had already accepted from her the money he would produce from his pocket (there had been some discussion again, because she wanted the cloth delivered to the hotel, while he preferred to pretend they did not live at that hotel so as not to tempt the salesclerk to raise the price), and he was pacing the nursery while Mary was getting ready for her first shopping expedition with her husband. She had never shopped with her first husband, and she realized in this seemingly unimportant detail that she had never really loved her first husband, while she loved this one so much that she was certain something would make her lose him. One could not be so happy in life.

But how long it took Mary to get dressed! He walked and walked in ample circles, and each time he passed in front of Brigida, who was holding a bottle above Sonia's monstrous little face, he thought, How tempting for the Lord, to punish me for my atheism, for indulging my vanity, for divorcing my wife, for abandoning my sisters and my patients, and for keeping this child out of His divine grace. If He only existed, what reason would He have for not killing this child this very moment?"

Brigida, her black kerchief tied over her head, was staring at him with her fierce peasant eyes and thinking a great deal about him. She felt a link with him, she knew that he was in trouble. So she placed the bottle on the table, then with her bony hand made a wide sign of the cross. This frightened the doctor. He stopped and looked at her sternly.

Sonia had begun to cry, so it took Brigida a little time before she could speak. "If you have no money, take back that gold piece you gave me when this child was born. You must not throw your money away like that, you see what happens when you do: you don't even have enough to buy yourself a new suit. Your wife is right, you cannot wear this one you have on. If you let me go back to my place it will take me no time to bring you the money—one day to walk home and one day to walk back here. Can you wait two more days?"

"Yes, yes," said Mary obediently as she walked arm in arm with her husband to the Grand Magasin Milliet et Werner, the only *grand magasin* in Lugano.

"So you understand what I mean," said the doctor, who was not at all sure she did.

And Mary again, her thoughts miles away from whatever he had been saying: "Yes, yes, of course I do." She was so happy that she had paid no attention at all to his words, only (and too much so as usual) to the sound. And how she loved to obey him, no matter what he said. This was in fact the root of the whole trouble between them. She always thought this should suffice; he should feel happy that she loved to obey him, rather than insist on the details of her obedience.

"So you have understood, you definitely have," he repeated by way of conclusion.

"Yes, my love, I have."

And they both let themselves enjoy that great privilege so rarely given in life: the feeling that each has his way and that it corresponds exactly with the other person's way, after an argument in which the other person's way has been shattered and replaced with one's own way.

He had said, "We shall buy one of those ready-made suits that we saw the other day in the windows, and the rest of the money we will spend to buy a present for Brigida. She deserves it, she is a most extraordinary person. In fact, she reminds me very much of my own mother."

Mary had retained of all this only the latter part, "we shall buy a present for Brigida." As for the first part, she had instantly dismissed it as unworkable and forgotten it completely, thinking only that she must make a great show of her veneration for Brigida.

But the moment they entered the shop and he asked for the ready-made suits in the window she lost her patience and said, "No, you promised you would buy the material and have a suit made for you by a tailor."

"But, Mary, that was before we discussed it on our way here and you agreed that I should buy a ready-made suit and use the rest of the money—"

"For a present for Brigida, I know. But I never agreed that you dress up to look like a Swiss."

"But, Mary, please—"

"I said and I repeat that you cannot be fitted by the Swiss."

This was the first of her many violent clashes with that peace-loving, law-abiding, healthy, prosperous and beautiful country her husband had already begun to like more than his own.

"What is wrong with the Swiss?" asked the salesclerk, highly indignant.

"They are not built like my husband. Their ready-made suits will not fit him."

This was enough for the doctor to prove to her that she was wrong, and he bought himself a dark suit that she was forced to agree to—holding back her tears with difficulty and only until they were alone again, at which moment she cried like a child and could not be stopped.

"All right," said the doctor at this point. "I have a brilliant idea: I shall go to a very good tailor and have him make the necessary alterations, and I promise that if his work does not satisfy you I shall let you buy the cloth, and the tailor will make me a new suit."

This proposal seemed satisfactory, and the doctor finally went to see the tailor recommended to him by the father of the lift boy. The young man did not know what to do and was rather reluctant to cut into a new suit which to him seemed the last word in perfection. This alone won him the doctor's full confidence.

"You are a very honest man," the doctor said, "and your honesty must be rewarded. I agree with your view, but you know how stubborn women can be. I cannot possibly go back to the hotel without having some alteration in the suit. My wife says that the collar is too wide. If you don't know how to make it a bit narrower, I shall give you a helping hand. After all, as a surgeon, I know something about cutting, and the cuts I am used to making could easily be fatal, so I am certainly more cautious than you."

They worked together and, alas, when the jacket was put together again they sweated for hours and could not make it look right. Fnally, after days of work, the job was finished and the jacket had an entirely new defect: it made an ugly wrinkle on the left shoulder which could be corrected only if the doctor pretended he was some sort of cripple with one shoulder higher than the other.

"Look," he said to the tailor, "that is no problem. I personally don't care if there's a wrinkle. As long as it does not fall apart, a jacket is a jacket. It keeps me warm and covers my shirt and breeches, what else can I ask? As for my wife, I can pretend for a few days that I have a stiff neck, and when the christening is over I can slowly unstiffen my neck and she will notice nothing. How many times in my student days did I not walk like a cripple in order to prevent a hole in my sock from popping out of my shoe? You have done a wonderful piece of work and you will be duly rewarded."

He went home and expected his wife to be impressed with his new suit, but she had eyes only for his deformity.

"What has happened to you, darling?"

"Nothing, just a stiff neck."

"How terrible, you must go to bed immediately and stay in bed until you recover."

"Nonsense, a stiff neck is not cured by staying in bed."

"Oh yes it is. Doctors are incapable of looking after themselves, this is known. Go to bed, we will telegraph our doctor in Vienna, he is the only one who can take care of stiff necks."

They made such a fuss over it, she and her mother, that he had to give in and declare himself suddenly cured, but when he tried to put on his old suit there was another scene and this time the sad truth became known and he was ordered back to the tailor's, with the added demand for two more suits to be made at once.

"No civilized human being can live with one suit only," said Mary.

"What do you mean? I can name you a hundred among the most civilized human beings who did not even have one to wear. Socrates, who had nothing but his nightshirt; Jesus Christ, who was half naked! Diogenes, the wisest of them all, perhaps, dressed in a wooden barrel, which served him both as suit and house. . . ."

And he went on explaining his theories, or, rather, inventing them, becoming conscious of them as he spoke, and deriving more strength for his beliefs every time he touched the ground again, the sacred classical ground. How could she argue against Christ, Socrates and Diogenes? Civilization was economy, simplicity, the accent put on inner values only, not on waste, catering to vanity, excessive respect for appearances.

"And, besides, I do have another suit. Someday I must get back my summer suit from home. They may take my olive groves, my almond groves, my cattle and my houses, even my books, but what right do they have to take my suit? That was my own, I had only begun to wear it, it was the suit I was wearing when I went to Sorrento almost ten years ago, so it even has that historic-sentimental value for me." And to console his disconsolate wife he concluded, "We will recapture it, Mary, we will. Don't cry."

This made her laugh, and the sun shone again on their marriage.

"Thank God you are a reasonable wife, Mary. With the money we save on useless suits for me, we will take a trip to Greece. I gladly accept it as your present to celebrate the birth of our first child. A trip to Greece—think of it, Mary, the origins of all that is good and civilized in the world. All right, now smile and be patient. I shall be back in a matter of minutes. You see, this wrinkle is easily corrected. Tailoring, after all, is very much like surgery, I am beginning to develop a scientific interest in it." And he ran to his tailor's with ideas, great ideas.

"A simple thing?" said the young tailor. "That is what you think. You know nothing about tailoring, Doctor."

"What do you mean? Tailoring, my young friend, is nothing but surgery on dead cloth."

"Well," said the tailor, "if you are so rich that you can afford to ruin a perfectly good suit, as you already have, for the pleasure of playing your little games, go ahead. I am not paying for the dead cloth anyway."

"This, young man, is not the right attitude. Don't be discouraged, let me guide you and together we will complete this work. People will be amazed. They will ask me who made this suit, and of course I will give them your name, and so there will be some use to my meeting all those rich people. It will be your career, my friend, you will become known as a great tailor, so now let's get to work and don't be such a pessimist!"

They worked together all day long, and when the work was finished the same wrinkle had now gone from one shoulder to the other. In vain did the doctor try to brush it away with his hand, only another stiff neck affecting the other shoulder could cure it. The tailor was all in favor of it this time.

"You had one stiff neck," he said. "Why not another?"

But the doctor said no. "Under no conditions will I have another stiff neck. My wife is quite capable of calling a doctor from Vienna to cure me. Let's correct this mistake."

"No, sir," said the tailor. "You do it alone this time. I am sick of this suit, I have lost interest."

"But your career?"

"I don't care. And I cannot work with you. It is your fault. If you had not advised me the first time, I would have done a good job."

"How do you know?"

"I know, because I know my job, and you do not. What if I said that surgery is tailoring on living cloth?"

"But it is, my friend, it is."

"Yes, but what if I tried it without learning the trade? Eh?"

The doctor was speechless, and the tailor, seeing his enemy defeated, gave him the last blow: "Did you ever learn the first thing about my trade? Why should you know what you have never studied?"

This hit the doctor like a blow over the head. He had been standing in front of the mirror, angered by that wrinkle that would not yield to his manipulations, and his whole body was bent in humiliation now.

"All right," he said. "I have nothing to answer. I was wrong. I must pay for my mistake."

"Wait a moment," cried the tailor, suddenly stopping him from taking off his jacket.

"Why? What is this now? Let me take off this jacket, put on the old one and go home."

"But no, Doctor, see? It's gone!"

"What is gone?"

"The wrinkle, the wrinkle—it's gone! Gone!"

"How? Where?"

"I'll show you. Stand here as you stood before, looking very sad. Yes, this way—no, sadder, do as I tell you, don't pay any attention to the mirror. Don't look until I tell you. Just try to look sad. Bend your head—a little more, the whole back more bent . . ."

"But this is very bad for the lungs. It is a most unhygienic posture. It is, in fact, what brings about tuberculosis."

"Never mind, you are not going to get tuberculosis if you stand like this for a minute."

"Right," said the doctor, who again was surprised by the forceful logic of this uncultivated young man. He did as he was told and lo! the wrinkle was gone. It immediately came back as he straightened himself in an outburst of joy.

"No, no, no," said the tailor, "don't be happy about it or it will come back at once."

He was right. The doctor smiled. "I like this," he said. "It is almost a sign from on high. God, of course, does not exist, but divine justice exists in terms of punishment for our pride. I sinned against you by imagining that I could also be a tailor because I am a surgeon. This was an act of stupid pride and it deserved punishment. Here I have it: the mistake will be corrected by my correcting my own inner mistake and looking (or rather being) full of contrition. The Greeks were right, you know. They were right, and the Christian tradition took over from them. This idea of reward, the watchful Fates—"

"Don't talk so much, Doctor, and just go on looking sad. If you talk you become happy again and the wrinkle jumps back on you. See?"

"How true! It jumps back like an evil bird. Do you know

the myth of Prometheus and the eagle eating out his liver because he had stolen the fire from Olympus?"

"I don't know it, Doctor, and don't tell it to me. The moment you say something, the wrinkle is back."

"How incorrigible I am. Intellectual pride indeed is—"

"Shut up, Doctor, I say. Just be unhappy!"

The doctor did, but could not help commenting in a whisper, "How much wisdom in these simple words." Then aloud, like a child: "And, of course, if I keep a bad posture for a few hours, this will not be habit-forming and neither can it affect my lungs in a matter of hours or even days. And besides, after a while, when Mary is told this, she will not let me keep a bad posture on account of my looks and at the expense of my health. She will accept the wrinkle in the end." Again he straightened his back, and the wrinkle promptly sat on his shoulder again. "Never mind," he said this time, "never mind. I just had a good thought and felt pride in it."

"Doctor!" shouted the tailor. "Now, Doctor, it is a miracle!"

"What?"

"Puff your chest as you did now, and the wrinkle is gone again!"

He tried it and it worked. "But that is wonderful," he said, "that is truly allegorical: Be either truly humble or truly proud, as you can rightly be when you have a good thought, as I had now. Because pride, my dear man, is not always reprehensible, or, rather, not reprehensible per se, and in this the Jesuit fathers are wrong. In fact, they too are proud, but of what are they proud? Of their humility, but their humility in front of arbitrarily chosen superiors, which is wrong, because only in front of God (whether one believes in Him or not, God may well represent the idea of perfection, something the Greeks of course—"

"Shut up again for a moment, Doctor, I just want to see whether we cannot fix this by undoing the jacket again."

"Oh no. I would not let you this time. God knows what

other wrinkles might be visited upon us if we did. Let us be truly humble and thank God for allowing us to escape at so modest a price."

It was not too hard for him to look humble and dejected as he went back to the hotel, because he was truly apprehensive of Mary's reaction. "Look at this," he said, and he paraded in front of her.

"It seems perfect," she said, and he almost straightened up, but remembered to keep this for a future occasion. "Yes," she said, "it looks perfect, absolutely perfect." She was pleased to be able to approve of his work. "But you don't seem to like it," she soon added with tears in her voice. "Or, rather, you don't care whether I like it or not."

"Oh, I do," he answered, still without straightening his back or changing his expression, lest the Fates punish him and send the wrinkle back.

"You don't, you don't. As if I did not know you. There you stand like one punished by God, the epitome of unhappiness, of hate, of utter disgust. You don't love me any more, I feel it. There must be another woman. Tell me the truth. Something happened while you were away. Where were you all those hours?"

He was annoyed and felt it would have been human to change his expression and his posture with it; but could he get all the way to the other extreme without seeming to sneer at her? So he kept looking at the mirror in order to control his every movement and said, "At the tailor's, of course, where else could I have been?"

"It is I who am asking you. But you don't care. You don't even lose your patience any more, as you did until yesterday when I asked you such questions. Oh yes, I know, I need not ask, I know, I feel, there *is* another woman. In fact, all you care for is your own image, now that you have a suit that fits. You have suddenly developed a strange vanity you did not have when you left the house this morning. Tell me whether this is not so."

"Nonsense, Mary," he answered, without looking at her, because he felt he could not without losing control of his posture.

"And you say it in that tone, without even looking at me. I know, this is the end, the end!"

She threw herself upon the bed to cry, and he said clumsily, "Wait for me, I'll be back, I just want to show this to your mother." And he hastened to his mother-in-law's rooms, a thing he had never done before, to ask for her approval of his suit. If I get her approval for the proud posture, he thought, I can go back and take care of Mary and she won't notice anything; as a matter of fact, I can change into my other suit. He was glad he had brought it home with him from the tailor's. Proud and hurried, he knocked on the door of the old lady's sitting room and found her at her desk, writing as usual.

"Do you like this?" he asked, parading in front of her with a protruding chest, in a posture most unusual for him.

"I do," she said, a bit surprised. "But . . . I don't know. Do you like it?"

"Oh, very much."

"Does Mary like it?"

"Very much indeed. Very much."

"Where is she? Why did she send you here alone?"

"She is in her room. I'll go there myself now, if I may."

This seemed all rather inexplicable to her. She called Luther and asked her to call Mary.

"Never mind," said the doctor, who seemed in a hurry to leave. "I will call her myself. You do approve, don't you?"

"I don't know," she said now, becoming suddenly suspicious. "You look so . . . German in it. Or is it that you have another stiff neck?"

"Another stiff neck?" he answered, blushing, and still parading as if he were presenting arms to a national monument.

147

Mary appeared at this point and froze him into silence. She had been waiting for him to come and console her, but curiosity had been stronger even than her despair. She had been wondering what he might be doing at her mother's for so long. And here he stood, happy as a little boy, while she was crying all alone in their room. He felt immense pity for her, a desire to throw himself at her feet and ask her to forgive him. But he could not; he could neither explain nor leave his boastful posture except for the other one, and he at once assumed it: his back bent, his face falling, all his happiness gone.

"I am going to leave you two alone," said the old lady, nervously pushing her chair from her desk and making the first effort to lift her weight on her fat arms. "Luther, help me, let's go."

"No, no," cried Mary, throwing herself dramatically into her arms, "don't leave me alone, you too. It's finished, it's finished," she kept repeating between sobs, "I know it's finished. Tell me the truth. . . . Don't leave me alone!"

"Oh, Mary," said the doctor, "don't behave like a child now. What is finished? One cannot even try a new suit on without your making a Greek tragedy of it. What will your mother think?" And giving up all posture, monumental or tragic, he went to her and put a hand on her forehead.

The old lady felt relieved and said, patting Mary on the back, "Your mother thinks that what your husband needs is a good English tailor. We'll get him one, we'll ask Mr. Gladstone, if he is not dead, who his tailor is."

"Yes," said Mary, wiping her tears and laughing as she looked at her husband. "See? It's back." And she pointed to the wrinkle on his shoulder.

"On the other shoulder," he said timidly, but was not allowed to continue.

"I don't care on what shoulder it is, your tailor is no good, we'll make a present of this suit to the lift boy, it's good enough for him."

One glance at the two women made him realize that his battle was lost. Dejectedly he walked out of the room, looking sidewise at his image in the mirror all along the large corridor and the staircase, and in his present mood the suit seemed so perfect, and so natural on him.

Mary walked silently behind him, trying her best not to look proud, but she was.

And here he was, changed by miraculous charms into a puppet, a social fetus in its prenatal days, undergoing the strangest transformations from paper skin to cloth-and-canvas skin without arms and a collar, and from there by degrees into a gentleman, a husband and a relative with various possibilities according to the occasion and the environment. He could become a nephew, a cousin and a brother-in-law, even an uncle—though in his first stages of unclehood—and, of course, the most important thing of all, a father holding his child and being photographed to be framed in silver, in red leather, in purple velvet, in pink silk, according to the place where he was to be exposed: the grand piano (leaning backward and reflecting the window and a bit of crystal lamp in the middle of the room), the writing desk, the mantlepiece or the pink dressing table in his wife's boudoir. All of the secret mothers inhabiting the blood of pregnant women, changing cells into threads and weaving human cloth to reproduce the model they are given, were represented in his case by cutters and their various assistants of the great London house of Huntsman and Sons—who were also fitting Edward VII, so that the doctor found himself to be a brother-in-cloth to the King of England.

He no longer had the right to suggest anything, nor would he have tried if he could have, because any delay in the execution of the work meant another few days for the whole crew at the Grand Hotel. Of course, he was not paying for all this, but it hurt all the same, and all he could do was take the least possible space, time and material. He made himself available at any moment for fittings, lifted his arms promptly, even when he had not been asked to do so, and tried to hold his stomach in so as to need less material. He knew very well this was rather ridiculous, because he was very thin anyway, and what could a few inches more or less represent in his case? But it made him feel better, it was at least his own muffled *vox populi* against the tyrant, a small part all his own in this comedy in which he represented an inanimate object.

Thirty-two suits, not one! Winter suits, summer suits, spring suits and autumn suits ("But what am I?" he asked. "A living calendar?"), morning, afternoon and evening suits, suits for all kinds of activities and states of mind: suits to smoke in, suits to smile in, suits to sob in, suits to yawn in, suits to feel undressed in, suits to be completely naked in! He had never seen a *robe de chambre* before. And then overcoats, light ones and heavy ones, even one lined with mink. "What is the use of having all this precious rabbit skin inside," he asked, "if nobody can see it?"

He was beginning to understand, however, that Mary's insistence on sartorial perfection was not only a way for her to dress up her idol, but also a way of warning others that he had come to take his place in their society, that he did not despise the things they loved and was not in their midst as an intruder. Memories of his own better days came back to him while he touched the material of his new social skin—the days when his father had worn homespun from the wool of his own sheep. This, more than anything else, broke his inner resistance to the pleasures of vanity. He, who had left the priesthood at the age of sixteen to become a freethinker, stopped being a priest only when Huntsman found the right uniform for his happiness on earth.

"Mary, I am dressed for generations! This is wonderful! We can afford to have thirty-one children now, provided they are all boys: each one will have at least one suit to wear. And look at the material, please! Feel it: real sheep's wool, such as the ancients must have worn in Greece—the kings, obviously, for the kings of the world still do today, and probably (who knows?) even the gods when they mixed with the mortals in Troy, in Athens, in Mycenae, in Thebes."

VII

THE CHRISTENING WAS A SUCCESS, even if Pierre refused to attend it. Uncle Jules and his wife were greatly impressed with the poise, the nobility, the elegance of Mary's second husband; in fact, their reconciliation with her mother was made possible mainly by his presence. They were the first to remark (and to report to Moscow) that he would certainly become another Dr. Curie very soon, that Mary would be the new Madame Curie; she was so much in love with him that one could not even talk to her; she would answer absent-mindedly without seeing who had been speaking to her and without bothering to look; she had eyes only for her husband, and whatever he said was gospel for her. She had become so slender that they had not even recognized her at first and were now proud that so great a beauty should belong to their family; she seemed taller than before, she was regal and poised, she ate virtually nothing and her eyes had grown wide and hallucinated under the spell of love. If these were the results of a divorce, they were in favor of it. More surprising than this, her mother too seemed to be entirely changed, and for the better, since her daughter's new marriage. No decision was made by her without consulting her son-in-law first, and if he made any opposition she gave in to him at once.

They all went back to Paris together, where Uncle Jules called his physician and asked what could be done to give this great Italian doctor a chance to contribute to French medicine. "I don't feel that Italy deserves him at all. Imagine, he had to flee his country, leaving everything behind, even his summer clothes, all of this only because he divorced his wife! Now, when a country does this to a scientist, no wonder that it loses its best talent. Galileo Galilei, I am told, was the last of them to work for Italy. When they tried to prevent him from looking at the sky, because the sky belonged to the Pope, he stopped inventing things (the pendulum he had already invented, so it was too late to withdraw it from the Pope; I wish he had), and Italy remained without inventions. What can we do for my new nephew, a fugitive from Italian persecution?"

The physician, who had the reputation of a genius among rich Russians in Paris, might have been described as a general specialist, for he treated every subject as if he alone had the last word on it, having spent every minute of his life in an intense study of that particular branch of medical science. His name was Aristide Malachier, for which name he had suffered a great deal during his student years, withstanding the onslaught of his colleagues' hilarity by banning all hilarity from his own life forever. He was brisk, energetic, even brilliant, but never let his smile get out of muscular control, so he laughed with his eyes, and then only in approval of other people's approval of his brilliant remarks (on serious subjects only). When these were technically too brilliant for the wits of his audience, he knew he could rely on other people's self-protecting vanity to make them laugh without reason rather than ask, with reason, what he had meant by his cryptic remark. He took home from the hospital (and into the world as well) all that medical language which so easily allows the most ignorant men to present themselves in the guise of great scientists, especially in those places where scientists are not needed, such as drawing rooms, concert halls and theater lobbies. There again he realized that these verbal defenses were priceless, for they not only kept him from the elementary duty of making sense, but appeared as generous concessions on his part; everyone felt that being addressed as a neurologist, a surgeon, a pathologist by so universal a mind was a great honor, and all they could think of was how to avoid exposing their own ignorance in their replies.

He also affected a certain sartorial distinction which was too pronounced in its austerity: he appeared ridiculous because he tried too hard to appear serious. As Mary's mother wrote about him in her books, "His frock coat holds him in so tight an embrace that if one of his buttons breaks loose it will shoot like a bullet into a bystander's body and kill him. He looks to me as if he had been guillotined and his head were now standing on the tip of his beard, which is implanted behind that tiny pearl in the center of his necktie. How any man can fear him as a rival is beyond me."

Well, Mary's husband did, because he felt inferior to Dr. Malachier in many ways, even though he despised him. First of all, he himself was not used to such grandiloquence—his own use of medical terminology was a form of respect for medical science and solicitude for the feelings of those whose relatives were ill. And also Dr. Malachier was the first "man" he had met since his divorce and remarriage. Not that Uncle Jules was not a man, but he was a rich man, a Russian, and a relative now. As for the doctors in Lugano, they were men, but so foreign to his world that they had difficulty in understanding it. With Dr. Malachier he felt that the embarrassment should have been on the other's side and not on his; Malachier was quite obviously charging Uncle Jules beyond all decency for nonexistent ailments and had instantly taken his younger colleague into the secret without actually articulating it, letting it be understood that they were both engaged in milking these rich cows but that it was *"pour la science, mon ami*," meaning *pour* themselves, so that even the sacred name of science became soiled.

What am I doing here? he kept asking himself. What am I now but the husband of a rich wife?

This, more than anything else, was at the root of his jealousy, an emotion that was new to him. Moreover, he felt an infinite pity for Mary, because the husband she believed she had did not exist at all, and this pity was soon followed by fear that she would discover the sad truth and stop loving him.

Meanwhile, Malachier had discovered that Mary would do anything to help her husband in his work, and he had begun to plot with her, so to speak, against her husband's lack of self-confidence. Mary had taken to the game with the enthusiasm of a convert, or, rather, the frenzy of a young married woman in love. Malachier was her spiritual director in her fight to rescue her husband from the last remnants of his Mediterranean pessimism, the mental venom of "down there."

"Darling, Malachier is so worried about you. He says it is a crime that you don't do more for yourself."

"Malachier? What right has he to say such things? Let him mind his own business and leave me alone."

"But, darling, he believes in you, and he knows. You should take an example from him. Where would he be if he had had your attitude? He would never have become the great scientist he is."

"Oh, he wouldn't? And he is one, of course."

"But, darling, he most certainly is, he is a very great man. Uncle Jules says so, too."

"Oh, does he really? Because your uncle is a doctor, of course."

"A doctor? He doesn't have to be a doctor. Why all this animosity as soon as someone wants to help you? My uncle loves you so, it is he who found Malachier for you, he who first got him interested in you, for my sake, and you have to insinuate— I know! It is because you regret you married me and you haven't the courage to say so, and must take refuge in all the false reasons you can find. Admit for once that you still love Giovanna, that you hate us because we are rich, that you miss your helpless southern wretches from down there, admit it and be honest with yourself, rather than find all these weak excuses."

"Nonsense, if you want me to be honest I'll tell you frankly that I think Malachier is a swindler, that he enjoys no great standing among his colleagues, and that he cheats you all and you don't notice it. He is a kind of Tegolani of the medical profession."

"There comes the true motive out of you! Your native stinginess! Anyone who takes money seems dishonest to you. You have such an obsession about money that you let your family and your wife rob you of everything you owned, rather than lift one finger in defense of your rights. And now you criticize others for earning what they feel they deserve. You slander them, and you insult my uncle as if he were spending your money and not his. We are his guests, he has done everything he could to help you, and here is your gratitude. But no, that is already a crime in your eyes. You long to be a beggar, and anyone who is not destitute and completely nega-tivisitic about life is in your eyes a fool. Malachier says that the Catholic Church has left deep traces in your character."

"Oh, he does, does he? You have spoken a great deal about me. And may I know when these intimate conversations have taken place?"

"When you were at the hospital yesterday."

"Oh, so, when I go to the hospital because Malachier has made an appointment for me to meet one of his disciples— who, by the way, treated me very coldly because I had been recommended to him by Malachier—he comes here and has intimate conversation with you, about me. How generous of him. And how thoughtful of you."

"I beg your pardon. Malachier is a perfect gentleman and a most trusted friend. I am not going to let you slander him. He came here because Uncle Jules's laryngitis had become very bad again. He saw me and asked me about you and we had a few minutes of conversation about you, yes, about you, and he cares for you more than you yourself do, that is all I have to say to you."

They suspended hostilities to go down to dinner, Mary feeling upset but still proud of her beautiful husband, who seemed even more handsome with that frown on his face. She thought the frown came from a feeling of shame at the stupidity of his remarks, but there was more than just shame in him. Under the cloth that made of him a brother-in-Huntsman to Queen Victoria and King Edward VII, the little brother of the poor was slowly being reborn. Mary was right, and Malachier was probably right, too: deep traces had been left upon him by the Catholic Church, and he hated the rich only because they were rich. And if Malachier was not a great scientist, he at least was a doctor who practiced his profession and was capable of earning the full confidence of many people and the strange admiration of a young married woman.

What do I know about her feelings, anyway? he thought. Her first husband must have felt just as secure as I have felt, and she secretly thought of leaving him. I have a daughter by her, but he had a son. What she did before can be done much more easily the second time. And it is clear that now she has a greater admiration for Malachier than she has for me. Besides, I deserved this. God exists, and what I have done cannot go unpunished.

"Ah, here comes my young friend Mary," said Malachier when they entered the dining room, where the others were getting ready to sit down. "May I call you by your first name? After all, I am an old friend of your family, I am almost old enough to be your father, and your uncle has given me permission to adopt you." Then, seeing her husband's face, he hastened to add, "Of course I am adopting you both. I only wish your husband did not look at me as if I meant to eat him up alive."

Jealous people are often slow to recognize their failing in others. To Mary, her husband seemed cold and aloof as they found their places at the dinner table. It would have been a relief to her to know that it was jealousy that motivated his seeming aloofness, but, she herself being incredibly jealous of him always, it did not occur to her that she was inspiring that emotion in him now. Her husband was acting aloof, therefore he must be losing interest in her.

She looked at him and smiled pleadingly, inviting him to smile with her. "We are both very grateful to you," she said to Malachier. "I was telling my husband that I wished he had a bit of your enthusiasm."

"Oh, but he has something infinitely more precious than that," said Malachier. "He has genius, and I do not. I must have enthusiasm, I must be carried away by it, so as not to notice that there is no ground for such enthusiasm."

At this point there was a chorus of protests from everyone except Mary's husband and her mother. "We are all full of admiration for you," said Uncle Jules, "my nephew included, and we refuse to listen to such nonsense."

"Please smile, don't look so bored," whispered Mary to her husband, and he tried to comply, but the smile that appeared on his face was much worse than any look of boredom—it exposed the rift that had remained concealed, however badly so, until that moment. Mary, with her better social training, repressed her tears and engaged Malachier in a very active discussion on matters of medicine. And when dinner was over she tried to drag him as far from her husband as possible to avert an argument between them; but her husband saw in this the final evidence that his marriage was over, that Mary was leaving him for this fool whom she thought a genius, just as she had left her first husband for him.

When a person who is not particularly well versed in the graces of worldly conversation sulks in the presence of others, his mood can ruin the conversation and enjoyment of everyone else. Uncle Jules, who saw this about to happen in his drawing room, called his new nephew to him and pretended to be anxious to know—in great confidence—what he, as a foreigner and a member of the family, thought of French medicine after his first few visits to the hospital. But the young doctor seemed vague and his answers were not too encouraging.

"I think it is wonderful to see how Dr. Malachier admires Mary," Jules said, thinking probably that he was doing some good by extolling his niece's virtues at a moment when her husband was displeased with her for God knew what trifle. "Mary is a wonderful person, everyone is fascinated by her. And with her you can do great things. The girl is a born scientist, you know. Tell me, have you started your research work with Malachier's assistant? I so envy you for having the genius that no one in our family has. My father, as you may have heard, was a great builder, but he was never fortunate enough to help anyone do something in the field of science, and that was his greatest ambition. He was very strict with us all, and I'm afraid we criticized him for his harshness. We all regarded everything we had as if it were our right to have it, and we never proved our worthiness in any way."

So it runs in the family, said the doctor to himself, and he went on listening with bent head to the words of his new uncle, as if he were hearing the details of a fatal disease which he alone could recognize as such. It runs in the family and they thought they could buy me as the genius they needed. Now that Mary is beginning to be disappointed in me because she has found someone else, another "genius" like myself, only worse, as I am not a faker, they will let her divorce me and will help her get married to this new "genius," Malachier. But at least I will see to it that my child stays with me. . . . And this brought with it many more images of inevitable tragedy.

Just then his mother-in-law, who could not bear sadness in others, beckoned him to her and asked, "What is the matter? What is troubling you?"

The doctor was so touched by her question that he saw a glimpse of hope again. He had not thought the old lady could still care for him, once she had decided in favor of Malachier as her new son-in-law.

He began with a face-saving lie. "I am disappointed in Mary's lack of judgment," he said. "To regard Malachier as a great man seems to me the height of stupidity." He hesitated a moment, feeling the gravity of what he had just said, and not realizing how clever he had been, because the old lady instantly took his remark as a great compliment to her intelligence.

"My view precisely," she said. "I too had noticed something in him I did not like. Especially as a scientist," she added.

"As a scientist?" he asked, becoming very attentive, as he could not do much about following Mary's conversation with Malachier in the far corner of the room. "Tell me, what is it you dislike in him?"

"Everything," said the old lady. "He is immodest, while appearing excessively modest. He talks to us as if we were all scientists, and he knows very well we are not, but he also knows our weaknesses, and in this alone he acts like a scientist: he cultivates them, he encourages them, and he gets away with the most trite nonsense because we are not in a position to judge. A man who does that is not apt to bring greater seriousness to his scientific work."

"That was exactly what I found wrong in him," said the doctor with the greatest enthusiasm, smiling again. "I don't know why I did not mention this to you earlier. You could have spoken to Mary. I never can, because when I say the slightest thing about Malachier she declares I am trying to destroy all her plans for my career, she flies into a temper, she cries."

It was with a strange joy that the doctor made these intimate revelations—he who had always been so reserved about his private life. He was commemorating his past happiness, speaking about a legendary time when Mary was still so much concentrated on him. And the old lady listened with an ever greater pleasure. Since Mary's new marriage, she had lost the habit of tyrannizing over her, and here the occasion to do so was offered her by the very person who had stood in her way. What an unhoped-for chance!

"Mary is very stupid at times," she said with delight.

"I am afraid you are right," he replied. And he knew he had one ally at least. This second divorce would not be such an easy affair for Mary as her first one had been. Her closest relative would almost certainly be against her. So when he saw Mary and Malachier leave their corner of the room and come smiling to him, he thought bitterly, They have decided that was a bit too much. They have nothing else to tell each other for today, he asked her whether she was happy and she said, "No, let's get married, you and I," and she must also have said something to the effect that she could obtain her mother's consent very easily. But we shall see. . . .

In one thing only he had been right. They had spoken at length and they had realized that it *was* perhaps a bit too much; and since they had exhausted their main subject, there was no reason for them not to join the rest of the company at this point.

Mary was very happy. She had such confidence in Malachier. He had said to her, "Leave it to me. If you want your husband to overcome that inner resistance to success and that hating of the rich, you must follow my advice and do exactly what I tell you. Your husband is still very much of a child, he has that spontaneity you find only among the primitives—and, of course, among geniuses. And he is both. But we can help him. He must settle down in Paris, he must work in the hospitals here, do his research here, under my guidance but with your help, not mine. I shall stay in the background, I will direct you and you will persuade him to do what he would never do if I told him. Have confidence in me. And now let's keep this our great secret and join the rest of the company."

This was the reason for Mary's beaming face as she came toward her husband and her mother.

How naïve of her, thought her husband, to believe that I will fall for this. Her first husband did, of course, but I will not. There is a faint chance that they were not talking about their future, but it is better to be overcautious than overconfident. Let her prove to me that she has not been speaking about me, if she can, which I doubt. But until then, I shall be as reserved with her as she is with me. And while thinking those things he looked straight into her eyes with an air of reproach, and neither looked at Malachier nor seemed to notice his presence.

"What is it?" asked Mary, plunged into misery again.

"Nothing," he said in a whisper, and, to suggest to her that she must not lose her dignity, he walked out of the room, displaying his.

She ran after him, grabbed him by the arm and pleaded, "You cannot do this to me, in everybody's presence!"

"Please, Mary," he said calmly, "do not make scenes."

"And what have you been doing all this time?" she cried in so loud and desperate a voice that everybody heard her.

"I have kept my control and said nothing at all."

"Nothing at all, you call that? Nothing at all?" And she ran upstairs in tears.

Everyone had become aware of what was going on, and there was an awkward silence in the drawing room. But the old lady was unperturbed.

"Mary is always a bit excessive," she said, and she too made a display of her dignity as she left the room and followed her daughter upstairs.

"Yes, Mary, I understand, I was young, too, don't forget, and I was eager to help my husband, and he was my second husband, so there are many similarities between your situation today and mine so many years ago, many, a great, great many similarities, except for one: you have a mother to advise you and to help you, and I had none. But I succeeded in helping my husband. Oh, yes, here is another great difference between our two cases: we were poor, my family was all against me, yours is helping you, financially and otherwise."

"I know, Mamachen, I know, and I am grateful to you and to my uncle, but it was he who told Malachier to help us, and I assure you, Mamachen, I can swear to you that Malachier has no designs on me. What an absurd idea. Did my husband think that? I cannot believe it. First of all, he is not jealous at all. He does not love me, I know it, or he would not have treated me the way he treated me today and then walked away from me. He hates me because he feels that I have stood in the way of his career. Malachier made this all very clear to me."

"Will you stop quoting Malachier all the time as the source of all wisdom? Really, Mary, I too am beginning to worry. The man has bewitched you."

"Nonsense! I—"

"What was that word you just spoke?"

"Please, Mamachen, forgive me, I did not mean it, I said 'Nonsense' because it seemed so absurd, but I did not mean to insult you."

"You were speaking to me, if I am not mistaken, Mary, and that 'Nonsense' was aimed at me."

"Oh, nons— I am sorry, Mamachen, I am terribly sorry, but you see, this is so absurd, Malachier is a wonderful person and a real friend. And how could you have so little faith in me?"

"Mary, you did it once, you may easily do it a second time. The charm of genius . . ."

"Mamachen, you ought to be ashamed of yourself! I can't speak to you any more."

Mary made a dart toward the door, not quite intending to leave, because she was afraid of hurting her mother—and also because she was more than determined to settle down in Paris and see her husband start on his scientific work in the hospitals, under Malachier's guidance.

Her mother said nothing, waiting for her to come back on her own. She did. And she apologized. And of course her apology was not accepted for some time. When it finally was, the old lady said, "I realize that the situation is different this time, but a young woman who is known to have made a mistake once in her lifetime is regarded by certain men as an immoral woman, one who may easily be tempted into doing anything. You should impress not only others with your seriousness, but your husband first and foremost."

Mary became furious again. "If that is what he thinks of me, then I don't see how I can believe in his love! Love is based on respect. Oh, I should have known that everything was going to be ruined!" And she had one of her fits of sobbing.

After they had both cried abundantly together, the discussion was resumed at exactly the same point where they had left it.

"Just a moment," said the old lady. "Just a moment. You ought to trust your husband. He knows best. You should also remember that he comes from a very uncivilized part of the world, and that for him to have accepted the idea of divorcing his own wife is a proof of great courage. Don't overtax that courage by asking him to accept as a close friend, and a close friend of yours more than of his, a man he does not trust. That might be fatal to your marriage."

"Mamachen, please, let me take care of that. I can swear in the face of the world that Malachier has no designs on me and that I could not find him more ridiculous and less appealing as a man. The only reason I have trusted him and will continue to trust him is that I know he believes in my husband. I know that if we settle down in Paris it will be the beginning of a real academic career for us, and besides, Uncle Jules has the greatest faith in Malachier."

"Mary, let me tell you one thing: Your uncle is an excellent man and I love him very dearly, but as for his judgment . . ."

"But, Mamachen, please, think of the practical side of the situation. Even if Malachier is not a genius, even if he is a bit stupid, what does that matter? He offers us a most wonderful chance. Why don't you persuade my husband that we should stay? He has such faith in you."

"Oh no. I never stick my nose into other people's business, and you know it."

There was a sulking silence on Mary's side.

"Mary?" said her mother, as if to shake her daughter out of a dream. "Mary? Did you hear me?"

"Yes, Mother."

"Why do you have to say 'Mother' and not 'Mamachen'?"

"Yes, Mamachen."

"Is my child a good child?"

"Yes, Mamachen, she is."

That same evening the old lady wrote in her diary: "No. I don't have to regret this decision, because I am sure that the doctors in Baden-Baden are infinitely better than those in Paris; he can begin his career in Germany with much better chances than he could in France. German science is more solid than French science. And we have a house in Baden-Baden, which is also to be taken into consideration. If I bought or built a house in Paris, he would most certainly protest, and he would be right. So it is not that I prefer Baden-Baden to Paris, but that it is better for *them*." Which thought completely cleared her conscience.

It was a moment of great happiness for Mary when she finally realized that her husband had actually been jealous of Malachier, and she gladly gave in to him, becoming cold to Malachier and dropping all her plans to settle in Paris. She

and her husband had two or three ideal weeks visiting museums, going to the theater, holding hands like two children and
admiring each other and themselves in every mirror and shop
window. Malachier was disappointed when he learned of their
decision to leave the city, and so were Uncle Jules and Aunt
Lydia, but the sight of the young couple's happiness was the
best argument in favor of whatever decision they might make.

Only two persons were beginning to worry, and these were
the two victors, Mary's mother and her husband. Mary's mother
because she soon realized that leaving Paris did not mean going
to Baden-Baden, but just going back to Lugano, and Mary's
husband (who had insisted on going back to Lugano) because
he realized that Mary had been right: Malachier was no rival to
fear, and his offer had been nothing to take lightly. Too late.
So he carried this grudge against himself deep in his heart.
And in spite of the expectation of seeing Kostia and Sonia
again, the thought of leaving Paris pained him in many ways:
Paris was stimulating. Paris was making a man of the world of
him, and he knew how much he needed its civilizing influence. And, most of all, Paris would have meant much for
his work. As a result of his misgivings, the doctor became much
more dependent on his wife and began to respect her intuition to the extent of losing his self-confidence.

The return to Lugano made things worse. His former wife
was suing him, and his sisters were suing him; Tegolani was
suing the old lady and asking for fantastic sums of money in
payment of nonexistent damages, unsigned letters full of insults
and obscenities arrived every day, the few people they knew
cut them dead in the street or in the lobby of the hotel when
they met—and even though they did not care for the company of others, there is a difference between being reserved
and being rejected. Mary was expecting another child. She lived
in terror, yet the lawyers advised against leaving Switzerland,
and her husband was unable to reach any decision. All he did

was repeat every day that Mary had been right and reproach her for his decision to leave Paris.

"You were not sincere enough, Mary. That idea of the plot with Malachier—that was what made me jealous. Had you been more outspoken with me . . ."

"How can you say such a thing? More outspoken with you? But I told you in every possible way that Malachier was a good man, and you always said he was a swindler. From the very first day."

"And I was right, his fame is greatly exaggerated, highly undeserved, but think only what we missed. What a chance that was! Who cares if he was a swindler or not?"

"But this is what I always said to you, if you remember, these very words."

"Yes, Mary, this is exactly what you said. I am a fool. And I do not deserve a wife like you."

"Oh, don't say that. You will see—give me time. You and I together will do great things and astonish the world. We will discover new things, fight disease, perhaps even tear the veil that shrouds death from our eyes."

But he preferred dwelling on all the things he might have done if he had taken advantage of the wonderful opportunity Malachier had offered him, and regretting his lost chances. And thus Malachier's figure grew to such proportions that he became the symbol of paradise lost. ·

VIII

ALL RIGHT, I will," said the bishop of Lugano, "but remember, Doctor, I will not accept any delay this time. You worried me greatly when your daughter was born, and the Lord was merciful enough to allow the child to live or we would both have on our consciences the eternal condemnation of an infant to Limbo—you for base reasons of vanity, and I for my unforgivable carelessness."

"What do you mean?" asked the doctor.

The bishop replied, looking straight into his eyes, "I mean that you delayed your daughter's baptism until you had your clothes made by a London tailor. We know that. I knew it then, I knew everything about you. Not that you interest me, mark, or that your rich mother-in-law interests me, with her antireligious 'philosophical' studies. The world is full of such people today, even of people like yourself—young men trained for the priesthood and gone astray. But in this case I had to know what was going on in that hotel, because I was part of it, too, more so than both you and your wife, for I have charge of souls, and you only of bodies—and in this case, the begetting of them, too."

"All right," said the doctor, "there will be no baptism. I am a freethinker anyway."

"Oh, no," said the bishop, "you cannot say that. You are not a freethinker or you would not have come here."

"I came only because my wife insisted, and because, I don't know, a remnant of tradition . . ."

"I don't care what brought you here, to me it is only one thing, and I pray that you realize it, too. You are lucky, my friend, luckier than you think or deserve, to have these remnants of tradition to guide you where your wisdom does not. But let's not talk about such matters now. The time is not ripe. Set a date for this christening, and keep it, because I will."

The former student for the priesthood made a great effort not to kiss the bishop's ring and not to kneel in front of him.

"Why should he be so rigid?" he said to himself as he went out of the bishop's residence and looked at the mountains, the lake and the red roofs of the city. "It *is* nothing but a remnant in me of an ancient tradition. Does he want me to lose even that? Well, it's a boy anyway, thank God." And before walking down the steps that lead to the city from the heights of the cathedral he crossed his heart and kissed his thumbnail.

He decided not to tell Mary, who was already upset enough by all the enmity that came through the mail. And in order to still his sense of inadequacy for not having told the bishop exactly what he thought, he allowed his natural liking for the bishop as a person to grow stronger until it became a real form of affection and, as such, could be used to justify his weakness.

"Poor man, I like him very much in spite of what he is," he said to his mother-in-law, without telling her his reasons for disliking him.

"Very good," said his mother-in-law, who at any other moment would have smiled and said, "I still cannot understand how one may like a narrow-minded person like that," but was too preoccupied now. "I am so glad you like him," she said, "because then it will be no problem for you to ask him to postpone the ceremony."

"Sorry, but that is the one thing I will not do."

"But we must do it. Pierre writes that he cannot be here before the end of January, when he goes to Monte Carlo. Pierre is a busy man, it is a miracle that he agreed to come, you wanted him to come, not I, not Mary, and I believe you did the right thing, although I am surprised that he agreed to come at all. But we cannot ask him also to change his plans in order to do us a favor."

"Well, this means that we will have to find another godfather for the boy. And another godmother too, for I imagine that his wife cannot come, either."

The old lady was suddenly on the verge of tears. It had never occurred to her that someone might say no to her. This man had practically done so, on more than one occasion, but using a great deal of diplomacy and persuading her, rather, to say no to herself; and now, all of a sudden, this firm no in the name of a religion in which he himself did not believe. "But what can we say to Pierre?"

"We can send him a telegram and say that if he cannot be here by tomorrow we will find someone else."

The old lady said nothing. Remembering how skeptical she had been about the possibility of seeing Pierre again, and how quickly his answer had come, and what a kind answer it was, she thought that perhaps this young man in front of her could do anything and get away with it, and she answered, "Very well, I shall send Pierre a telegram."

The doctor felt his self-respect coming back to him. Here he was acting like a man, accepting no one's impositions, and refusing as a godfather for his first son the very man he had secretly courted in his thoughts. Pierre had always represented to him a great, mysterious power, his true rival in a way, because he knew that Pierre's disapproval could easily destroy him in Mary's eyes. And also, deep down in his heart, there lingered the old fear of disaster: he had a strange feeling that the old lady's money would never come to his children, and thus he took precautions by tying Pierre to his son and assuring the child's future. He believed that divine justice was going to punish him for abandoning his wife and his duties, and now, with all those threats coming in almost every day, he was sure that someone from "down there" would knife him in the back as he walked along the promenade with Mary. Perhaps Mary too would be killed, and then who would look after the children? Uncle Jules would take Kostia and Sonia, Pierre would take the boy. And now this last part of his plan was being upset by his own decision, for he felt very sure that Pierre would not be able to arrive next day.

He walked out of the hotel to the telegraph office, where he did something else that made him proud of himself. He telegraphed one of his sisters and asked her to come at once and be the child's godmother, and her husband to be the godfather. It was like asking his family to forgive him; more than that, it was like assuming he had been forgiven and agreeing to pay whatever they had asked him to pay through their lawyer. A telegram implies much more by its character of urgency than it could ever say. One sends telegrams only where many letters have been sent. After this, he went back to the hotel to give Mary the good news and to rejoice in the sight of his first true descendant.

Mary was with Brigida, showing the little boy to Sonia, but Sonia did not seem to be paying attention to him.

"Look, this is a boy," Mary was saying. "Your brother, your little brother." The last two words were pronounced slowly enough for Sonia to become conscious of them, if not to repeat them. Sonia frowned like a deaf old lady and clung to her nurse.

"She is afraid of him," said the father, "but she had better not be, because he is the only man who is going to defend her honor when she grows up."

"What do you mean?" asked Mary. "He is only a baby, and she needs no one to defend her. She has herself, that is enough."

"Oh no it isn't," said the father. "A woman needs a brother to defend her. I have been told that I burst into tears when my first sister was shown to me, and that when they asked me why, I said, 'Because if anyone dares touch her, I will kill him.' I cannot remember the episode, but the feeling I do remember, for I had it again very strongly when my other sisters were born." Then he turned to Brigida and said, "Seven of them, you know."

"That must have kept you very busy," said Brigida, and Mary laughed, but he did not.

"Why busy?" he asked. "The honor of my sisters is not to be discussed. They are all honest women. Some have already had more than ten children. One of them, who is childless, will be here tomorrow."

"Tomorrow?" asked Mary. "Why did you keep this a secret? When did you learn about it?"

"I didn't," he said, "I— Wait a moment! How stupid of me, of course she cannot be here tomorrow. It takes five days by the fastest trains—and she would never take one of those."

"Thank God," said Mary. "So we will have time to see how Pierre reacts. I wouldn't want your sister to be confronted with a sneering Pierre. You never can tell. Pierre is arriving tonight, I am already nervous about it."

"Oh, but he is not arriving. I had forgotten to tell you."

"He is not? And how do you know?"

"Ask your mother. He wrote he could not come until January. We sent him a telegram to thank him and to say that we could not wait with the christening."

"What? Why can't we wait? We waited months with Sonia's christening."

"Yes, but that was a mistake."

"What's all the hurry? Superstition again? And how could you imagine that your sister would get here by tomorrow?"

"I did not think about that. I am sorry."

"Nothing to be sorry about. I am greatly relieved. I prefer

to have your sister and her husband rather than Pierre. One never knows what mood he will be in. Let's postpone the whole thing until they get here. Very simple."

"That is what you say. How many complications, and how much easier it would have been had we remained in Paris."

Mary laughed. This was a compliment to her. "No problem," she said. "We'll send a messenger to the bishop and ask him not to come tomorrow but wait for us to set a new date."

"Impossible."

"Why?"

"Because it is not done."

"We have done it before."

"Never again."

"But what is it? Are you no longer a positivist?"

"Nonsense. Of course I am. But the bishop was very angry with me."

"What right has he to be angry? The child is ours, and he can consider himself very lucky that we have it christened at all. As a matter of fact, why don't we make the boy a Protestant? I hear there is a very nice minister here."

"Never."

"As you say. Then what do you plan to do?"

"Find two deputy godparents and have the christening tomorrow."

"Never. I don't accept the bishop's conditions. We shall wait until your sister arrives, or the boy can stay a heathen and it will be the bishop's fault. And he'd better look out, for he can be excommunicated any time for losing a soul out of sheer stubbornness. I can write to people in Rome—"

"Mary, what nonsense is that? You, a very bad Catholic, can scare a bishop and have him excommunicated for refusing to delay a christening? And through whom are you going to do all that? Who is your great personal agent in the Vatican? Tegolani, I suppose. Come, now."

Mary saw that she must give up her pretty plan to have the

bishop excommunicated, but she still did not see how they could find godparents for the child.

"Well?" she asked in anguish, as her husband paced the room with his hands behind his back. "Well? Who are our friends?"

He sighed, tortured his mustache and replied, "Our real friends? One, and we failed—or, rather, I failed—to heed his advice."

"All right, who is he?"

"Malachier, and I only regret I did not do what you had so clearly seen I should."

This pleased Mary very much, but it did not solve their problem. She was sitting at her desk, pencil in hand, with a white sheet of paper in front of her, and not a single name came to her mind. Suddenly through the open door she saw Brigida in the next room and knew—that was their friend. Brigida bore a certain resemblance to her husband's mother, he had told her so several times, and this would be like a tribute to her memory.

She called Brigida, embraced her and said, "Brigida, I have decided to have you as our son's godmother."

The poor woman did not understand and was very much embarrassed.

"Yes, yes, you, my son's godmother. Tomorrow," said Mary, speaking like an illiterate in order to be better understood.

"Mary," said her husband, "Mary, please!"

"No, no, let me tell her. I can do it very well, I must be the one to tell her, the idea is mine." And then to Brigida, "We are sisters now, you and I, real sisters. Give me a kiss."

Brigida disentangled herself, crying. She was frightened.

Mary asked, "Why are you crying? Don't you want to be my son's godmother? You too—because of the divorce?"

The doctor intervened. He took Brigida out of the room and told her that everything would be all right, then closed the door and said to Mary, very reproachfully, "Thank God she did not take you seriously."

"Why say that? Don't you want her as your son's godmother? Doesn't she look like your mother?"

"Yes, but there is a difference. My mother was not a peasant woman. She was a lady."

"But isn't Brigida a lady, too? A great lady? And wasn't your mother a peasant woman, too?"

"In a manner of speaking we landowners are closer to the farmers than to you city people, but still there is a difference, and Brigida is an illiterate shepherdess, don't forget. It would be most embarrassing for her to become the child's godmother. And besides, who would be the godfather?"

"I do not understand. I thought I was doing you a favor. Didn't you say you had a real veneration for Brigida?"

"Of course, but certain things are not done."

"How strange. But now I cannot take back my word."

"She never thought you meant it, I can assure you of that."

"And I can assure you I did. Let me make it clear to her too."

"You could not have had a better idea," said the old lady to Mary. "Read this telegram and laugh." It was from Moscow. Pierre had changed his plans and asked for a delay of only three days. "That proud German wife of his will have the shock of her life when she arrives here and finds that she is not to be the child's godmother after all. And think of Pierre, having to walk arm in arm with an illiterate shepherdess from the Swiss mountains!"

Mary was beginning to waver. She did not want this family reunion to be an occasion for the resumption of a family feud that might last for another ten years. She was very fond of Pierre, and also anxious to be forgiven for all the things she had done against him. To impose such a difficult situation upon him, the one time he came back in a friendly disposition, seemed unjust. The shock she had experienced when her husband had refused Brigida was not forgotten. For the first time in her life she plotted knowingly against her mother in the quiet belief that she was doing the right thing. And the plot was all hers.

"I have found the solution," she said proudly to her husband. "You will go to the bishop, but not to ask him for a delay, just for a godfather, as we have no friends in this town. Be frank with him."

How wonderful it is to be able to be honest, said the doctor to himself as he climbed the white steps leading from a dark street behind his hotel to the cathedral. But he was somewhat apprehensive as he asked to be announced to the bishop, so he said to the priest who received him, "Would you please ask His Excellency for a brief interview, but don't forget to tell him that this is not to postpone the date of my son's christening. It is for another reason."

"Couldn't you tell me?" asked the priest. "His Excellency is very busy, several people have come from Milan to see him, and I find here on his schedule an unexpected meeting with the teachers of our schools in Canton Ticino. As a matter of fact, I believe he won't be able to baptize your child, he will in all probability ask me to represent him, so you can explain your difficulties to me and I shall gladly help you."

The doctor was quite taken aback. He disliked this particular priest, who reminded him of his teachers in the seminary, and the mere thought of having the child baptized by him aroused his old anticlericalism.

"I must have the bishop," he said. "He promised he would baptize my son. It was he who baptized my daughter, less than a year ago, and I want my first son baptized by the same man who baptized my daughter." He said this pleadingly, but the priest seemed to stiffen.

"I told you the bishop is busy," he said. "He himself asked me to look into this matter. If I am not mistaken, you are not even a Catholic."

"Of course I am."

"Oh, are you?"

"Yes, I was even a student for the priesthood at one time."

"Is that so? Are you not the doctor who lives at the Grand Hotel?"

"I am."

"In sin?"

"What was that again?"

"In sin, I said."

The doctor felt the blood rush to the back of his neck and found it very difficult to master his anger. He said nothing, gulped down his venom, and looked at the priest with an air of defiant despair.

"There are many good Catholics who would deserve to have their children christened by the bishop," the priest went on, "and they accept any priest the bishop assigns for the occasion. You, who are not in the Church, must have the bishop. Why?" And he looked at the doctor with quiet severity.

The effect was immediate. That teacher from the doctor's schooldays looked at him now, and the atheist father of two children felt guilty and said, "I understand. I only wanted to see the bishop because he was so kind to me and with him I felt I could speak about many of my problems."

"Very well," said the priest. "Let me ask him if he has time for you."

The doctor did not know what to do at this point, he did not even know whether he still wanted to see the bishop. His last words, which had come so mechanically to him before he could think, sounded false and debasing. He felt as if his whole revolt against the Church had been useless—a mere physical resemblance between this priest here and one of his teachers had trapped him and destroyed him again.

When the bishop came in, he was still savoring his self-contempt and wishing he had never come to the cathedral.

"What a joy, but what a joy to see our good friend again,"

said the bishop, grabbing the doctor's hand and patting it like a small loaf of bread before putting it into the oven. "Why, it is touching to hear that our friend wanted to see us," he said, using the plural as if he were the Pope himself. "What can we do for you, dear Doctor?"

"Not much," said the doctor. "What can anyone do for anyone else? We all commit our errors, we all follow our consciences, more or less badly."

"Oh, no, no, no, my son, that is where you are mistaken. Everyone can do plenty for everyone else, and especially a shepherd of souls. My dear colleague, doctor of bodies, why don't you leave your soul to me when it is sick? Be as modest as I, who will come to you any time if my body is not well, trusting your knowledge and obeying your orders. Imagine if I were to be as proud as you are and said to my flock, 'When you have an upset stomach come to me. As a doctor of souls I can cure you with prayers.' Would you not consider this an insult to your science?"

"Yes," said the doctor, "but I have great respect for my colleagues. I don't ever attempt to cure souls, I would never invade your hospital—"

"What a word, what a word to use—'invade.' You have come to my hospital as a patient, my friend, and I am glad to see you here. Tell me, what is it now?"

"Oh, nothing, I just wanted to ask you for a godfather. We have no one we may really call our friend in this town. We asked our nurse to be the godmother, but we have no godfather. That is, we do, my brother-in-law is coming all the way from Moscow with his wife, but he will not arrive until two days after the christening."

"That is no problem at all, we can wait for his arrival. You must not take me too seriously. In fact, I meant to apologize for my unkind behavior the other day. Why do you have to ask a nurse when you have your own family who come from so far away for this happy occasion? If I say we can wait, we can.

Don't be more of a priest than the priest. I am the doctor here. Goodbye, my son, and remember me to the child's mother, please."

It was not until the doctor had almost reached the hotel that the unkindness of the bishop's last words became clear to him. It is a fact, he said to himself, one can never trust a priest. Why did he have to say that? Why not "Remember me to your wife"? Always ready to stab you in the back. They hold your hand, speak of the lost sheep and then . . . Had I been the bishop, I would have said, "Who are we, the clergy, to cast the first stone? Your first marriage, my son, was forced upon you by one of us. He prevailed upon you for reasons which have nothing to do with religion. And anyway, what is the point in making things harder for you, now that you have two children and a wife to protect?"

Thus imagining himself a most excellent bishop, the doctor justified his weakness and forgot his humiliation.

Pierre did not want just a room for himself and his wife at the hotel, as the doctor had assumed when he made the reservation. He had to have the entire third floor (the second was no longer available, because his mother lived there): one room for himself and his wife, the rest to insure his privacy. He hated to meet strangers in a corridor.

When the doctor was told this, he was both shocked and pleased—shocked as a man of the world, for whom this immoderate use of wealth was a sign of vulgarity, pleased as the father of a child who might partake of that wealth if he were to become an orphan.

The mental picture the doctor had had of Pierre was one of wickedness and pettiness, two abstract elements that did not help him much to imagine the bearer of such faults. Pierre's huge frame and deep voice upset his judgment. He no longer knew what he thought of him, all he knew was that Pierre and his wife, Mary and her mother, were all giants, and all had voices like the trumpets of doom, while he was alone, a church mouse frightened by the silence preceding a solemn Te Deum, then again by the infernal ado of the Te Deum itself.

The very quality of their family ties was far beyond his understanding. They, whose voices were always so loud, spoke in whispers today, manifested their joy with tearful silences instead of the shrieks and embraces that he regarded as typical for such occasions. This was a funeral, not a family reunion. When he was introduced, he instinctively opened his arms to embrace and kiss his new relatives, but was met with firm handshakes and sad smiles. Then the tone changed and there was a church organ bursting into the deepest notes of the Russian language. It resounded in the windowpanes, the chandeliers, the very bodies of those present. Mary's voice then became shrill, her mother's voice blared forth in a hammering laughter. This, he was told later, was just small talk of the most cordial type—brief comments on the trip, the weather and the family in Moscow.

Pierre's wife withdrew from the reunion at this point and asked her new brother-in-law to take her to the children. Kostia, all dressed up in black velvet with a starched collar and starched cuffs, was waiting like a soldier at the orders of his superior (Luther) to parade before his sovereigns. His new aunt kissed him on the forehead with great dignity, then spoke to him in German, while the doctor and Luther waited for the results of this great interview. Then came the turn of the two younger children, and the new aunt became slightly more affectionate, but no less artificial. The doctor could not stand it any more and went out of the room.

In the foyer he caught sight of Mary caressing Pierre's sable-lined black overcoat, his top hat and the white gloves he had left on a chair. The maid came to take the things away and Mary said to her, "No, leave them here."

She had not seen her husband. She went on touching the hat, the coat, the gloves, and smiling to herself. This was in fact the image she had seen in Rome at the time she had written that first letter to Pierre eleven years before: a fur-lined coat, a top hat and white gloves. Her husband understood more about her from that scene than he had in all the years he had known her. He knew now that her stories about Pierre were false even when they were true, and also that she must find it difficult to be married to a man with whom she had so little in common.

At dinner little Kostia was fascinated by the sight of his uncle, who looked so much like both his mother and his grandmother. Pierre's nose was immense and somewhat flattened on his face, and yet it was like theirs. He was pale, as they were, and yet he looked Oriental and they did not. Kostia felt the atmosphere of strife between this man whom he now admired so much and those two women who were everything in his life. Certain words that seemed kind the moment they were spoken suddenly appeared to have been charged with bitterness.

"You never sent me a picture of your children," said Kostia's grandmother, speaking to Pierre and his wife, Dodo. "Tell me about them."

Kostia expected his uncle and aunt to apologize and produce a picture of their children. He was anxious to see it, too, and to hear all about his Russian cousins.

"We have no picture of our children with us," said Dodo. Then, turning to Pierre: "Do you have one, by chance?"

"No, I haven't," said Pierre. "I never knew Mamachen would want one."

"How can you say such a thing?" asked the old lady reproachfully, but with a loving smile.

"Had you wanted to see them, you could have come to see them when they were born or at any time later."

"I was never invited."

"That is true," answered Dodo for her husband. "We knew you would not come."

"How can you say that, Dodo?"

And Dodo answered kindly and sadly, "Yes, Mamachen, how can I? Because it is the truth."

Kostia saw his grandmother blush with embarrassment. "It is not," she said.

"Oh," said Dodo. "Then we must be mistaken. Pierre, we are mistaken."

"You are," said the old lady, blinking nervously as she tried to smile, and playing with a fork. She soon began to mark the tablecloth with that fork. How many times Pierre and Mary had been punished in their earliest years for doing such a thing. Kostia too had been punished only a few weeks before by Luther, and his grandmother had not intervened as she usually did. Now he was on the same level with his grandmother, his mother, his uncle and Luther: all embarrassed and unable to express themselves. Dodo instead seemed amused, and the doctor looked on like a complete stranger.

The doctor was surprised that Mary did not come to her mother's assistance. The old lady had tears in her eyes. So he rose from his seat (another great infraction of the rules of the house), holding his large napkin in his hand like a waiter, went to his mother-in-law and, patting her hand, said, "What reason is there to be upset by silly things like these? We are all here, all happy and in good health, thank God. You are not afraid of long trips. Take a train to Moscow next week and meet your other grandchildren." And he took the fork away from her, saying, "Forgive me, but I come from a poor family. I never saw such precious linen in my life, it pains my heart to

see it cut for silly reasons." Then, noticing the terror on everyone's face, he added, still speaking to her, "It is not for you, of
course, that I am saying this, it's for Kostia. Children are like
monkeys, they imitate their elders, especially when they see
them do something wrong."

The old lady smiled, took the doctor's hand and pressed it
warmly between hers. At that moment, they all felt, he was
the head of the family. Pierre and his wife, who spoke not a
word of Italian, were the strangers in the house.

The child was named Filippo after his paternal grandfather,
Pierre after his uncle, Addolorato after his aunt and godmother
—because the doctor's sister and her husband had arrived two
days after Pierre—and Leonardo after his father.

Gennaro, Addolorata's husband, had never been in a non-
Apulian house, as he said to apologize for his behavior. He
had studied agriculture in Venice many, a great many, years
before, he was almost an old man, and in the three years he
had lived in Venice he had never set foot in a Venetian house,
to avoid temptation.

"Venetian women are beautiful," he said, "but I stuck to the
proverb that says, 'Wife and oxen from your province.' If my
Apulian wife tries to deceive me, I shall know it at once from
the tone of her voice or other signs that I may easily detect.
With a foreign woman, I might be deceived in the maze of
foreignness that is her nature."

His wife was a female version of the doctor, as Pierre was a
masculine version of Mary. The doctor's fine features were re-
produced roughly on his sister and looked extremely unfemi-
nine mounted over her bosom and displayed under a tray
bearing a dead pheasant still pierced by the arrows that had
killed it and half buried in roses. She was carrying that hat
like an amphora—steady as on a table, with her strong body
moving in careful waves under it and her eyes glued to its rim

and wondering, What does it look like to those who can see it?

"I know that look," wrote the old lady in her journal after more than a year of complete silence;

it is the look of peasant boys as they carry the statue of the Madonna, or peasant girls as they go to First Communion with a hairdo of roses and veils. Yet here is a woman who has more than I ever had or will have. She continues to serve, as they all do; their holidays are marked in the symbols they carry: statues of saints and gods, relics of martyrs, even, at times, whole tombs, with the body concealed by a small garden. We Protestants, who do not believe in rituals, find it extremely difficult to celebrate; no one knows we are happy, and in fact we are not. They don't have to be happy themselves. Their gods are happy, it is their holiday, they walk the streets and to them goes the envy of the crowds.

And a few pages later:

I can see now why these people could not accept Brigida. Two or three generations at the most separate them from the soil. Their elders tilled the soil, these watch it from their windows, making sure that their peasants till it well. Their elders never wasted their time reading and writing. What they received in payment for their work could not be recorded in books—it did not last long enough to be given such honors. Addolorata's eyes are full of objects, household utensils and crockery of gods: incense burners and oil lamps, embroidered altar cloths and candlesticks. Her brother's eyes are full of words; I see it now, because I see the difference between his eyes and hers. Whatever glimpses there still are of the soil or of utensils in his eyes are already transformed by the notion of money: he calculates, he does not know. His blood remembers and his mind counts. But when he sits behind his desk, surrounded by his books, he is at home. When his sister is seen against the bookshelf, she is away from home. And when she speaks about her brother's knowledge, proud as she is, one has the clear impression that she is at the same time agonizing over it. Only if he becomes rich or very famous will she forgive him. Knowledge is often an excuse for laziness—that is the main reason for their hatred of priests and their respect for cardinals and popes.

That hat of Addolorata's, the only straw hat with roses seen in Lugano during that cold November season, made her famous in the hotel and in town. She wore it proudly. And her husband, Gennaro, walked constantly behind her with a knotty stick in his right hand, to make sure that no man ever looked at her disrespectfully. He was sure that his wife, with that hat on, was dangerously attractive; he did not want people to think that she was wearing it to attract attention.

Gennaro was almost as tall as Pierre. His bald head was pale, while his forehead and the rest of his face was sunburned. He had a pointed beard and a mustache fiercer and larger than the doctor's. His was white, and his voice was the voice of a peasant; rusty and barking. "Lower that eye," he would shout to his wife when he saw men approaching. And he stared at the men, holding his stick with both hands, ready to hit them if they too did not lower their eyes instantly. He never parted with that stick. "For dogs and priests," he would say, battering the floor with it. His natural anticlericalism, which was irksome enough to his obedient wife, was stressed as a proof of his siding with Mary and against his legal sister-in-law. He could not just approve of other people's choices, he had to intervene and declare war on all their enemies.

"You cannot let her live," he said to Mary, after having said this of Mary to the other woman for a number of years. "Ever since I have met you I know: divorce is a good thing, and whoever stands in your way must die. I pray God every day for the death of that woman. And mark it, I don't usually pester the Lord with all sorts of petty things I want for my-self. I don't believe in Him the way the priests do; I have my own brand of religion, which is better than theirs, because in the first place it is masculine. When I go to the Lord, I tell him what to do after having weighed all the pros and cons in terms of justice. And if He does not want to help me, that's all right. I can wait. He will see things my way after a while, I know. At the beginning, I must say, I was against you, because I did not know you. Now that I know you (and I swear to the Lord that my thoughts are all pure), I accept you as a sister, and I want that other woman to get out!"

He kissed the old lady, he kissed Pierre, Dodo and Mary, then told his wife to do the same, and finally opened his suit-case on the sitting-room carpet and produced fresh cheese, jars of tomato sauce prepared by his wife, and a few bottles of "the best oil in the world." From another suitcase he produced hard biscuit of two qualities, salted and sweet, along with al-monds and dried figs, aromatic herbs and large leaves of to-bacco. Then he took off his jacket, rolled up his sleeves and showed his muscles.

"What can I do for you?" he asked Mary. "If you have any enemies in this town, just let me know where they live."

The restraint needed by the family to cope with these new relatives became reciprocal restraint, and the result was love, or the appearance of love. They vied with one another in an effort to be kind to the guests, they made an easy show of superiority, they aroused each other's jealousy and everyone was happy. They were happier, however, after Pierre and his wife had gone back to Russia.

Addolorata was the first one to ask questions. "Why must these people be bored? Life is so beautiful, and they themselves are so beautiful, what is it that makes life sad for them?"

"They have too high a concept of their importance, that is the whole trouble," said the old lady. "As a matter of fact, I am not going to Moscow. My only grandchildren are here."

186

And like all self-indulging people, she was the first one to be moved by her own generosity. But after a few minutes she began to realize that she was also the only one. The others were not moved. They were shocked, worried or unhappy. Addolorata and her husband were shocked, the doctor was worried, Mary and Kostia were unhappy.

"This is not right," said Addolorata.

"Of course it is not right," added her husband. "Parents have a duty to be just to their children. Even if they hate some of them and love others, they must hide both love and hate and present an even face which is a mixture of potential hate and watchful love. And I for one believe that you are doing a great deal of harm to Mary and her children by showering all your love upon them and taking it away from Pierre, Dodo and their children. You sow the seeds of strife between these children of yours. Of course, you are free to do what you please with your money, but are you sure that you will leave enough to Mary to repay her for the loss of a brother like Pierre? The way you spend your money gives me reason to fear that the day you die (and may it be only in a hundred years from now), there will be nothing left. And who will help Mary? Not Pierre. He can say to her, 'Dear sister, you received all the favors, your children were loved while mine were hated, now fare for yourself and leave me alone.' "

No one knew how to take this. Everyone's secret thoughts were out. And truth, when spoken, can no longer become an inner guiding light, the object of a policy, a secret medicine to be given in small doses. It is a paralyzing light, it accuses, it shames, and the result of its appearance is that those whose inner light it was must pretend not to want it, while those who were blind to it are offended but for some strange reason are eager to accept it in full.

The old lady was horrified. She stood like a criminal whose crimes have been exposed. There was a long silence, which was finally broken by the doctor.

"You are wrong, Gennaro," he said. "No one on earth is more impartial in her love of her children than our friend here. I am surprised that you could fail to notice this during the days you have spent here. It should be obvious to everyone. Besides, Mary would never dream of going to her brother for help. She has a husband who can take care of her. I am shocked."

"Don't be so proud," said Gennaro, thumping the carpet with the steel tip of his stick. "Don't tempt the fates into reminding you that you are but a frail human being. See what happened to your father's fortune and to yours. Today you are well and prosperous, tomorrow you might be hit by a crippling disease or be killed by unknown criminals upon orders from your first wife, and in either case Mary would need help. That is the whole purpose of providing your children with godparents, and if the godparents are rich, so much the better for your children. Addolorata is rich and has no children, but she has thirteen godchildren already, all of them her nephews and nieces, of whom there are twenty-four already, if we don't count the seventeen who died, and your dear sisters are still capable of putting thirty more children into the world. Now, with Pierre as a partner in the care of your child, and Addolorata to advise you on how to keep Pierre interested in him . . ."

"How can you be such a materialist?" asked Mary.

"He is perfectly right," said her mother.

"I am glad you recognize it," said Gennaro to her.

"Oh, yes, I do," said the old lady. "Do you think I have not always known it? I have always harmed my children, even with my love. One is alone in the world, alone and damned."

"Mamachen, don't speak that way!" cried Mary, throwing herself into her mother's arms. "I don't want anything from anyone, I only want my mother's love. I spit on money!"

"You are wrong," said her mother, in tears. "Money is sacred."

188

"Right," said Gennaro. "Money is sacred. I have heard the comments of these waiters and waitresses in the hotel; they think you are a crazy old woman and they rob you most shamelessly. If I had anything to say here, I would put an end to this. I have visited the kitchens, I know how much meals should cost. I have visited the markets too. I produce food, I should know. It is a scandal. Why don't you buy yourself a house that you can leave to someone when you die? You have two sets of servants here, those of the hotel and your own, and neither does a bit of work for you, but all are paid, and paid much too well. And how about that woman Luther? Does Mary need a governess at her age? The children have a nurse and a maid to themselves, this woman is a parasite and a spy. Get rid of her. I am saying this to help you, because I love you. We should be frank with each other. We have interests in common."

He went on thumping the carpet with his stick and leaving deep marks on it. No one dared speak a word now. He cleared his throat with a noise that horrified everyone and asked, "Is there a spittoon here?"

His wife pushed her elbow into his side to admonish him, and he took out his handkerchief, spread it open on his face and spat into it, then wiped his face, his neck, and the inside of his starched collar. "I am sweating like a pig," he said. "Too hot in here. God knows how much you spend in coal. With your permission, I shall take off my jacket."

"Please do," said the old lady, but his jacket was already being folded and placed, like a baby, in his lap.

"These stains of perspiration won't come out," he said. "Damned bastard of a tailor. He overcharged me when he heard I was going to visit rich relatives. But I'll get even with him yet." And this time he made holes in the carpet, rehearsing his revenge.

IX

MARCH 1908. A large house on a hill, all window frames and friezes, chiaroscuro with snow. On balconies, lampposts with icicles. Winding roads, terraces and grottoes carved out of the slopes into a large park, now all in white slipcovers, a museum of trees, well spaced and framed with boxwood, the fir trees resting deep in snow, the snow-repellent cypresses grouped together in shadows. Lemon trees wrapped in rags and protected by straw roofs. The city invisible, the lake almost invisible, the mountains in gray pencil, and the top of the distant belfry looking like a strange object in their own garden.

It was still snowing heavily, but fresh flowers with the sweetness of spring arrived by train from Italy and were distributed to the different floors, in different vases, on mantelpieces, tables, dressers, window sills.

Mary was arranging the flowers in her mother's sitting room, she was cutting the stems, trimming the greens and looking very much concerned, as if the very vase in front of her might solve her problems. Every few minutes she would stop and put an ear to her mother's bedroom door. A snoring rattle: an excellent sign, she thought, perhaps her mother would be better today; and she went back to her work, dedicating a bit more of her care to the flowers, now that she knew she could do nothing for her mother.

Ever since the beginning of her mother's long sickness, Mary had felt a greater calm, less anguish, therefore a greater happiness. The forms of things suddenly seemed to emerge from what before had been a fog in front of her eyes. She had taken to painting again, to drawing, and to long contemplations of happiness—that is, of silence in a beautiful setting, either inside the house or in the park.

The children were outside, playing. Kostia had built a sleigh, working for weeks in the carpenter shop near the wine cellar and the stables. The carpenter had given him only a few instructions on how to use the tools, and the boy had done everything himself. He had painted the sleigh red, blue and white, the colors of the Russian flag, and, impersonating Saint Nicholas—red tunic, white beard and all—had given it to his sister and brother for Christmas. To Mary and her mother this impersonation had been his official assumption into the world of grown persons. They had both cried because he had left a childhood illusion behind, but the boy and his stepfather had laughed, because they believed in scientific truth. So did Mary, but for herself only, not for her children. Now, watching them outside in the snow with that sleigh, she herself could almost believe there really was a Saint Nicholas with his reindeer and his sack of toys. Sonia and Filippo looked like two Russian icons, their red faces almost brown and their fur caps and coats giving off reflections of silver, while Kostia looked like a Russian hero in his beautiful officer's uniform, a present from Mr. Schultz.

Kostia shouted his orders to imaginary armies hidden in the white air, roared like ten thousand soldiers, thundered like a battery of guns, interrupted himself only to shout new orders and thus have an excuse for making more noise. After this, having looked at the battlefield with imaginary field glasses, he became a horse and pulled the sleigh all the way from the gate up to the house entrance, where he freed the St. Bernard dog, Tasso, from his chain and sent him into battle. But as Tasso

seemed unwilling to fight, Kostia now played the role he had
tried to assign to his dog, which was that of not one but five
thousand lions obeying their general and killing off all his
enemies. Then he charged with the sleigh, and the two
children rode behind him, laughing and rolling in the snow.

How much better for them not to have a stupid governess
who would forbid them to play this game, thought Mary. That
was the one concession she had won from her mother since
Luther had left three years before: permission to have the
children brought up directly by their parents. She now opened
the window to take part at least vocally in the game. She
could not run in the snow—she was expecting another child,
and this was a particularly difficult pregnancy.

The hissing noise of snowfall, which she had always likened
to a prayer from invisible angels for silence in the world,
brought her own childhood back to her. It also gave her
strength; the heavy scent of flowers and the dry heat of the
house had made her sick and sleepy.

"What are my little birds doing in the snow?" she asked.

"Come, Mama, come and play with us," they yelled.

"I can't," she said.

"Oh, please come," said Kostia. "I must show you how I
fight off ten thousand enemies with my new uniform."

She could not answer them; their shrieks drowned out her
words, and Tasso barked.

"I can't," she kept saying, "I can't. You know, Kostia, that
I can't."

"Children!" said Kostia to the children. "Don't act like
children. Mama cannot come; she is waiting for the stork."

Sonia and Filippo became pensive and began looking for
the stork, but the snow fell into their eyes. They rubbed them,
then tried again.

The scene was too beautiful not to be recorded.

"Wait," cried Mary, "I can come and take a picture of you.

Kostia, don't let them move, keep them just as they are this moment, will you?"

She closed the window, rang for the maid, asked for her snow boots, listened again carefully for noises from her mother's bedroom, then put on her cap, her gloves, took the camera and went out. Kostia was holding the two children with both hands in the position they had been in before, and Mary took several pictures.

"Why don't you come and try my sleigh?" asked Kostia.

"What a stupid idea," she said. "You know I can't."

"Please, Mama," he said. "I will go to your room, and if the stork comes I will ask him not to leave until you have come back. Or perhaps I can receive the new baby?"

"Look, Grossmamachen," said Kostia, entering his grandmother's bedroom with the snapshots he had just finished developing. "They are still wet, so you must not touch them, but look, I'll show you. This here is Sonia on the sleigh, this is Filippo and here am I. We were looking up to see if the stork was coming before Mama could go back upstairs."

She looked, she was amused, she asked to have the three snapshots framed and placed on her night table where she could always see them. Then she let Sonia and Filippo come and play on her bed, and Mary sat in a corner, feeling envious of her children who dared what she had never dared. Even now she was full of apologies every time she sat down in her mother's room.

Later her mother asked for pen and ink and wrote a long letter to Pierre, and one to Ivan and even one to Olga.

"This summer," she announced, "we are all going to Moscow."

Mary burst into tears. That had been her fondest dream since she was eleven years old, the last time she had been there.

193

"Why does this make you sad?" asked her mother, smiling. The smile made Mary's sobs more violent. She had never cried without seeing her mother cry, too. There was something abnormal now about her mother's cheerfulness. Could it mean that she was going to die?

"Come come, Mary, don't behave like a child. No one has died, why should you cry?"

Now Mary knew that her mother was about to die. Never before had she forgotten to mourn either her father or her husband. And today they were left without mention.

"Mary, listen to me," said her mother. "We will ask everyone to come for the christening of the new child. And then we will all go to Russia together."

Ludmilla was to be the godmother. She arrived suspicious and resentful, a few weeks before the child was born.

At once Mary, upon seeing her sister suspicious and resentful, became suspicious and resentful of her. She had other reasons too: Ludmilla was young, slim, elegant, carefree; Ludmilla found the doctor charming and flirted with him openly, and the doctor committed the mistake of expressing his admiration for her. Mary conceived such a hatred of her sister that she magnified every word of Ludmilla's into something solemn and forbidding that would make her mother and Ludmilla freeze into silence.

"What were you saying when I came in?"

"Nothing important. Ludmilla was telling me about her friends in Germany."

"Why can't she tell me too?"

"She will. Ludmilla, tell Mary about your friends."

But Ludmilla could not bring herself to speak. Mary's eyes were upon her, this was a repetition of the worst days of her childhood. And Mary left the room in tears, feeling that everybody was against her. What better evidence than this embar-

rassment of Ludmilla's? She now hated the child she was bearing, and when her husband gave her a sedative she knew it was
to keep her out of the way. She had to be persuaded every
time to accept sedatives, then she tried to fight off their effect
in order to be able to discover Ludmilla and her husband in a
compromising situation. She never did, and this made her unhappy. It was like a conspiracy to do nothing together. Reality
was no longer reality, it was one more trick of the devil. Her
suspicion was the only reality she knew.

"Tell me the truth, you love Ludmilla."

"No, darling, I do not, I swear to you."

"But you like her."

"Yes, very much."

"Oh, very much, you said."

"Well, why not? She is your sister, after all."

" 'After all' is right. *Before* being my sister she is Ludmilla,
she is younger than I, more amusing, less boring, she makes
you laugh and I do not. These are positive facts. That she is
my sister does not show on her person, in her wit, or in your
feelings. At the most, it is a negative factor, an impediment. So
when you say you like her because she is my sister, you are saying the opposite of what you think: you dislike her perhaps
because she is my sister, but you like her because she is herself.
Try to deny it if you can."

He could not. Confronted with the violence of her logical
reasoning, he became mute and confused.

"I see, I see. Enough of this. Go away, leave me alone, I
want to die."

"But, darling, don't you see that you are harming yourself?
In your condition you should be quiet and serene."

"I should, when everything around me takes away that
serenity I once had? I hate this child, and so do you."

"Mary, how can you speak that way? Why curse God's
blessings? You should be ashamed of yourself."

"I am not."

In reality she was. And she was punishing herself. But he had no psychology, because he had no such devils in his world. So at this point he treated her as one would treat a patient or a child. "Let me give you an injection." Or "If you are not ashamed, then I am ashamed for you." In both cases he left her to her nonsense, namely her tantrums and her suicidal thoughts.

The godfather was to be the doctor's cousin, Crocifisso. When he arrived, his clownish appearance became a momentary cause of amusement even for Mary. She was able to laugh at him, and thus to take part in the laughter of others. Crocifisso was fat, short and self-conscious. His voice was rather shrill, his movements soft, his nails manicured like those of a woman. It was obvious, from just looking at him, that he had never worked with his hands, and that the lower part of his head was more active than the upper. He could submit more beefsteak to the grinding power of his teeth than anyone Mary had ever seen before, and while eating he constantly complained that his digestion was not good, adding, however, that he took good care of his intestines in the evening, by taking a physic and eating very little. "In the evening a couple of sliced tomatoes with just a drop of oil, no vinegar, a slice of cheese, a couple of figs (fresh in season, dry out of season), and a small glass of red wine to get the poisonous substances out of my gums. That is Crocifisso in the evening."

These rules, however, seemed not to be valid while he was in Lugano waiting for the delivery of his godchild. And he said so. "Here, as a great exception, I allow myself to indulge. After all, I am going to become a godfather, this does not happen very often in life. Besides, you have such a good cook that it would be a crime for me not to take full advantage of this rare opportunity."

Had Crocifisso come forward with his marriage proposal on the first day, Ludmilla would have said no without even thinking. She was simply not in love, and not trying to escape into marriage. For the first time in her life she had everything she wanted: her mother's love, a home—in which she was surrounded by the objects and furniture she had known in her only other period of happiness, early childhood when her father was still alive—and children. Mary's three children worshiped her, they were constantly with her, after her, in front of her or at her side; when she lay down out of exhaustion, they sat on her. One of the maids, Brigida's daughter Adalgisa, was in charge of them now, but she did not know how to assert her authority and often resorted to slapping. Ludmilla, however, could get them to do anything she wanted just by asking.

This happy period lasted only a few days, until Mary made her mother conscious that she was being partial to Ludmilla, made the children conscious that they were traitors, made Ludmilla herself conscious of a rare chance she had to get even with her sister and have some fun too. Mary's jealousy revealed the doctor as a person to Ludmilla. (She had never before laid eyes on him.)

The first time Mary made a scene the doctor simply did what any loving husband would on similar occasions: he proved his faithfulness by being openly impolite to the other woman. He acted with complete lack of psychology, as does anyone who lets his jealous partner dictate the pattern of his actions. Ludmilla asked her mother what she had done to be treated unkindly by the doctor. Her mother asked the doctor and the doctor replied there was nothing, just Mary's jealousy. The mother chose the wrong way out by denying the existence of the emotion. But Ludmilla caught him warning the children not to play too much with her.

"Can't you leave your aunt alone? She does not want you to be constantly with her."

Sonia was in despair. She ran to Ludmilla in tears. "Why don't you like us? What have we done to you? We love you. You are the most beautiful aunt we ever had."

At this point Ludmilla too had her own fit of Muscovite sincerity, which functioned in spite of her "typical deviousness," as Mary used to define it. She found the doctor in the hall and said, "I have to speak to you." Then, as soon as they were in the library together, she closed the door and asked him point blank, "What have I done to you?"

"You? To me? Nothing, of course."

"Then why must you tell your children not to play with me?"

"This is pure fantasy."

"It cannot be their fantasy. They came to me in tears and told me you had warned them to stay away from my room because I did not like them."

"I did that?" And the doctor grew pale. Never before had he been caught in such a net of lies.

"Yes, you did. But even if you are a hypocrite, your children are sincere. It is difficult to train children in lies, let me warn you. I am surprised that you should not know these simple rules of psychology. But let's skip the psychology. There is more. Why are you unkind to me? I am not going to stay in your house one more day, if you want to know the truth. I thought I was my mother's guest, but obviously I am not. I am your guest and you are chasing me away. I'll leave, but not without having this out with you. What have I done to be treated so rudely?"

"Rudely?" The doctor was stammering. "I have treated you rudely? But this is pure fantasy."

"Yes, like the rest. All pure fantasy. Do you really believe me so innocent as not to understand certain symptoms? What is it? Mary's jealousy?"

"Nonsense. How can you say such a thing?"

"Never mind how I can say it. I can say it with my mouth,

in five languages if you want, even in yours, as you can see. My accent is not good, but my words are clear enough. And I want a clear answer. Is it Mary's old jealousy coming out even on this occasion? Does she fear for her husband? Have I given any sign of trying to snatch you away from her?"

"Nonsense, Ludmilla, I can swear to you that Mary is not jealous. She loves you."

"We know that. I have known her longer than you. She is my sister."

"But I swear to you, this is pure imagination."

"All right, and I believe you. Then it is you who dislike me, for some reason."

"I? How could I?"

"That is beside the point. In my modest opinion you can and I know it. Why? This is my only question. What have I done to you that you must drive me out of your house, out of my mother's house, and tell your children that I don't want them to play in my room?"

At this point she began to sob, and the doctor took her in his arms.

"Leave me alone, you don't like me, I know."

"But I do like you, Ludmilla, I swear I do."

"You have not answered my question. Who is it that hates me in this house; you or my sister? Or both?"

"No one, Ludmilla."

"All right. This is Italian sincerity. I shall never hear the truth. I am leaving. I was so happy here, I loved your children so, and now where shall I go?"

"You will stay here, we want you to become our child's godmother and to live here with your mother. This is her house, we are her guests."

But Ludmilla sobbed so that she had to be consoled, and finally a big kiss on each cheek confirmed that all was pure imagination. Even the kiss. Even the fact that the Russians kiss on the mouth. All pure imagination. One more kiss to confirm it, then another and another. And finally someone knocked at the door, but went away when they didn't answer.

"Was that the maid?"

"Who knows?" answered the doctor in a state of great anguish. "But let's not stay here another minute."

"No, I cannot leave the room with my hair mussed and with tears on my cheeks. You sit there, away from me, and talk to me. Try to speak about something that interests you. It will give you greater poise in case someone comes in again."

The doctor was not used to such coolness, any more than he was used to kissing his wife's sister while his wife was expecting a baby—or at any other time, for that matter. He had to cope with three new feelings he had never had before: the joy of adventure, the horror of sin, and fear of being caught. Plus a fourth, the last one being jealousy. An absurd, sudden jealousy. How could this woman be so hot and so cool at the same time, and remember what to do for an alibi in case someone came in, one second after having been in his arms? And was she pure? (Later, new feelings branched out from this question: Was his wife pure? Was he as blind to her as he had been to Ludmilla? Was this a new mystery behind the Russian soul?)

"Has this . . . ever happened to you before?" he asked.

"Of course not."

"I mean . . . being kissed?"

"Of course it has, what do you think I am?"

"So I was not the first one."

"Thank God, I should say, or what would I do now?"

"What do you mean by that?" His senses were aflame, and his Puritan mind too.

"Nothing, nothing. You still owe me an answer to that question."

"There is no answer to that question. No one dislikes you here. I least of all."

"I am beginning to believe you," she said, laughing, and he was even more shocked.

"Now, look, Ludmilla," he said, "we are friends, are we not?"

"Perhaps too friendly for our own good," she said, laughing again.

But he was determined to stay serious. "We are brother and sister, are we not?"

"You mean we had better try to stay so."

"Yes, that is what I mean. I am very worried."

"Never mind. I don't think it was Mary who knocked. The only thing for you to do now is to be very quiet. Or can you tell a good lie?"

"I was not thinking of that," he said. "Or, rather, I was, but there is something else too that worries me. You said this was not the first time. Promise me it will be the last one."

"Of course it will be. Even if my sister is not generous with me, I am not going to do this to her in her own house, and in her present condition."

"I know, Ludmilla, I know. But I mean, let this be the last time with others too. I want you to reform."

"To reform? I am not a bad woman."

"You have been kissed."

"Thank you for telling me. My memory is not so bad as all that." She laughed again.

"I mean by other men! Were they . . . married?"

"I don't remember."

"What? Have you had so many?"

"No, not so many, but three, five, perhaps seven, yes, seven."

"Seven? At your age?"

"I am nearly twenty-eight, my dear."

"Seven men have kissed you? And you don't even remember whether they were married or not?"

"One was—no, two were."

"Did they . . . do anything else to you?"

"Of course not, what do you think I am?"

"Not bad, but a silly woman, forgive me for saying so. A woman in great danger," he said, getting up from his chair and coming toward her.

"If you stay where you are I am not in great danger," she said, laughing again.

"I mean it seriously, Ludmilla, I am your only adviser and confidant in life. Do your brothers know you have been kissed?"

"My brothers? They have other business to attend to, industries and banks, and families of their own. Why should they waste their time with these trifles?"

"Trifles, you call them? That is what they are not, my dear Ludmilla. The honor of a woman is sacred, and easily lost, too. Let me tell you a fairy tale by the Venetian writer Gaspare Gozzi that applies to your case. It tells how Fire, Water and Honor became friends and went out into the world together. 'How are we going to find one another again if we lose ourselves?' asked Honor. 'Easily done,' answered Fire. 'Wherever there is smoke, there you will find me.' 'And wherever there is fog, or there are certain plants, there you can find me,' said Water. 'I envy you,' said Honor, 'for if I ever get lost, no one can find me again.' Do you see, Ludmilla, the moral implications of this fairy tale?"

"No," said Ludmilla, "I do not."

"You don't? Well, you had better get married very soon, as long as no one knows you have been kissed."

"And do as I please afterward?"

"Oh, no. Your husband will see to it that you do not. But you'd better not tell him about your past. I hate to give you such cynical advice, but, since I am your brother, I must."

"Very well, my dear brother. I like you even better now that I discover what a big child you are. Tell me, are all Italians so childish?"

"Ludmilla, don't be a child yourself. Remember the fairy tale I just told you."

"Thank you, my dear brother."

She was about to leave the room, but he stopped her. "One more question. It is my turn now to ask you: Are all Russian women like that?"

"You mean, women without honor?"

"I mean honorable but dangerously careless and too independent."

"No, there are also stupid women in Russia, as anywhere else on earth."

"Stupid, you call that? Let me ask you another question now, but swear you will tell me the truth."

"Of course I will."

"On your honor."

"But if you say I have lost mine?"

"Don't be silly. On your honor. Or, if you prefer, on your father's grave."

"My father's grave is in Berlin. How can I take an oath on it in Switzerland?"

"Ludmilla, this is not a joke. You can swear on his grave no matter where you are."

"All right, I swear. Out with your question now."

"Ludmilla . . ." And there was a long silence.

"I am waiting."

"Yes. Hm . . . Ludmilla, tell me the truth, without any regard for my happiness."

"What is it? Do you want to know whether I love you? Almost, I must say. More and more so as your childish charm reveals itself to me in full. But don't be afraid, I'll never do something hurtful to my sister. I am not the corrupt woman you think I am."

"I know you are not, and I am not the corrupt man you think I am. I was not going to ask you such a question, which in itself would be as sinful as the . . . act. Sin begins in our mind and finds its way into the world through our limbs."

"Great words. Is this another one of your fairy tales?"

"Ludmilla, be serious now. The question I was going to ask you and will ask you if you don't make a joke of everything that is sacred in life is this: Ah . . . hum . . . How shall I put it?"

"I don't know. Just put it. We cannot sit here forever or they will wonder where we are."

"Right. Ah . . . Ludmilla, tell me truthfully now, has . . ."

"Has what? Who? Where? Come on, out with it."

"Has—has Mary ever been kissed?"

"Well, my dear, you are her husband, you should know."

"I mean—before?"

Ludmilla burst into wild laughter. "Dear Lord, don't you know she was married for eight years before marrying you? Don't you have her first husband's child among your own children?"

"I mean before that."

"Before that? Before that? I don't know. She was eleven when I last lived in the same house with her."

"I see."

"So you will never know, my poor Othello. Never, never."

"I see." He was gloomy.

She rose from her chair, came toward him, pulled him up from his chair and said, laughing, "Trust Mary! She is not a dishonorable person like myself. She never lost her honor. She never lost her mother's love, she never lost anything. She found two husbands—two, I say, not one. And if she keeps the second one, she may well thank her dishonorable little sister, you can tell her that from me." And before he could find an expression for his anger, she had stamped a long kiss on his mouth. "There. Let this be our last one. And now, poise and a lot of dishonorable lies!"

His trembling hand was on the doorknob when she stopped him again. "I will flirt with your cousin Crocifisso today and tomorrow and in the days to come, and don't make scenes about it. I will be doing this to help Mary. And to help you.

It won't be easy. Enough. Come, a postscript for you." And she kissed him again, but the doorknob turned and someone pushed the door open.

"Here she is," shouted Sonia, "here she is!" And she threw herself into Aunt Ludmilla's arms.

"How is my child?" asked the doctor as he entered the room where Mary was resting in the dark.

"Ask your conscience how I am, don't ask me," was the toneless, desperate answer she gave him.

He said nothing. His conscience was answering him loudly enough for all time to come. He knew that his marriage was finished, that God (in whom he did not believe) would punish him by letting Mary and the child die together, in a matter of days, hours perhaps. Mary, meanwhile, was waiting for his answer. She sobbed quietly, she expected him to console her, but he felt he had no right to now.

"You spend hours with Ludmilla, but when your pregnant wife calls you and looks for you *all over the house*, you are nowhere to be found."

A faint glimpse of hope reached him, far down in hell, and gave him enough strength to ask, "You looked for me?"

"Of course I did."

"Where did you look for me?"

"Ah, you want to make sure I did not find you. How I know you by now!" She wiped away her tears, rose from her bed and, almost piercing his eyes with an accusing finger, shouted at the top of her voice, "I know! I know! You don't have to tell me—you were in the library with her! That is where Sonia found you."

The doctor felt that the moment had come for him to confess everything, and, before leaving the family and the house forever, he must not only confess but also explain to her that it was all her fault.

205

"Listen to me now, listen well, before you see me for the last time—"

She looked at him with terror in her eyes and stammered, "No, no, please forgive me, I shall never do it again. Never, never . . ." She sank on her knees and lost consciousness.

In the hour that followed, the doctor, sitting next to his wife's bed, feeling her pulse and caressing her hand while she rested peacefully and smiled every now and then, her eyelids half closed, knew the depths of contrition, regretting his untimely words more than his sin. He also reconstructed that sin in all its detail and realized that Sonia could not have seen anything, because when the door opened he and Ludmilla were not kissing. The last kiss, thank God, was a failure, it had been interrupted before coming to life. He was now duly horrified by Ludmilla and very, very faithful to his wife. She is a saint, he kept telling himself, and I am a damned fool and a swine. Never again. What had filled him with gratitude and admiration was that she should have asked him to forgive her. She had understood everything, she had answered his accusing confession before it could be made. She knew that one mistake is meaningless, and that suspicion is the seed of sin. If one meaningless kiss put an end to her jealousy, blessed be that kiss! he kept telling himself. What would become of Ludmilla now? Would Mary ask her to leave? Perhaps not, but in any case she must leave that same day, perhaps without seeing her sister again.

Mary opened her eyes and said, "I am completely rested now. Let me get up."

"No, you will not."

Her expression became anguished again. "Have you forgiven me? Will you stay?"

"What do you mean? I have nothing to forgive, nothing at all. On the contrary."

"So you will not leave your wife and children, you don't hate me?"

"What nonsense! How could I?"

"And you don't hate this child?"

"How can you speak that way? Tell me, how can you?"

"Why not? I have ruined your life with my jealousy—you have had enough of me, and you are right."

"Nonsense, my child. It is true that you have too much imagination, but that can be corrected. You can learn to control yourself. It is not difficult."

"With your help it is not. And you will help me, won't you?"

"That is my mission in life. As it is yours to help me."

"We will do great things together."

"We will. But only if you stop being jealous. Promise?"

"Promise."

At that moment Adalgisa knocked. "Miss Ludmilla would like to come in and see the Signora," she said.

"One moment," said the doctor. "Wait outside." He closed the door and asked Mary, "Do you want to see her?"

"Who, Ludmilla?"

"Yes."

"I don't think so." Then, to give a first show of her courage, she said, "Tell her so yourself. Be kind to her, don't hurt her feelings."

"Very well."

He left the room, bowing to his wife like a butler. He was still much too oppressed by shame.

"How did it go?" asked Ludmilla, and then, without waiting for his answer: "Smoothly, I hope."

"What do you mean by that word?"

"Nothing, nothing," she said in a hurry. "Was she angry?"

"Your sister is a saintly woman. You don't know her at all."

"All right, all right, but tell me, please, don't keep me waiting. You did not tell her the whole thing, I hope."

Her language hurt him. "I did not have to," he said.

"What do you mean? She couldn't have known it. Or was it she . . . ?"

"Do I have to remind you that, as a result of our—our lingering there in that room (and the fault was all mine and I am ashamed of it), someone caught us there?"

"Sonia cannot have seen a thing."

"Even so, Mary has more intuition than that."

"Did she ask you specific questions? Did you discuss it with her? Did you admit anything? I must know."

"I did not have to discuss anything or admit anything. She knows and she has finally understood that it was all her fault. Had she not been unkind to you because she was jealous, her jealousy would have found no ground to thrive upon. As simple as all that."

"I don't care how simple it is, I want to know: How much does she know, how much have you told her and what is her state of mind now? Does she want me to leave?"

"She knows everything and she did not have to ask me in order to draw her conclusions. She knows my fault, she is aware of her own. She did not say she wanted you to leave, but I personally think you should."

"Just a moment," said Ludmilla, who was about to cry. "Quite apart from the fact that this is still my mother's house and not Mary's or yours, and that I have not seen my mother in a friendly disposition since I was seven years of age, I believe it would be bad for me to leave like a thief when I have nothing to reproach myself for. What I will decide to do is my own problem. I refuse to discuss it before I know exactly what you told Mary."

"Nothing."

"Are you quite sure?"

"I am, but I am equally sure that she knows everything. And as soon as she is better, in a few days perhaps, or after the child is born, I shall make a complete confession to her."

"Yes, and make her unhappy for the rest of her life, and ruin my relationship with her forever. A nice result. You have become more Russian than a Russian. Let me take care of this." She made for the door.

"You are not going to see her now," he said, taking her by the arm.

"Don't touch me, please, I know what I must do."

"You are not going to see her now."

"All right, I heard you, I am not going to see her now, but as soon as she lets me."

"What will you tell her?"

"Everything."

He became apprehensive. "What do you mean?"

"Exactly what you yourself mean when you say she knows everything."

"There is a difference between knowing by intuition and hearing crude facts."

"Glad you told me. And you really believe that I would endanger my future relationship with my own sister and with my mother, and would make my sister unhappy for the rest of her life, just for the dubious pleasure of being truthful to myself? What does that mean, to be truthful to yourself? Let's not exaggerate matters. You consider me a prostitute—"

"Ludmilla, please—such words—"

"All right, a lost woman, because I have been kissed without being married to every man I kissed. I consider myself a normal person. You regard a kiss I gave you as a catastrophe, a reason to abandon your family, to divorce your wife. Well, I do not. And I am not going to give my sister any more food for her jealousy, to use your own expression. I shall simply deny everything."

"Ludmilla, you cannot do that."

"I can and I will. And I would still continue to deny everything if she had seen me with her own eyes. I would say, 'You are crazy,' and she would *have* to believe me."

What shocked the doctor was the use of such a word as *prostitute*. He regarded Ludmilla now as a dangerous influence on Mary, even asked himself whether he would have married Mary had he known Ludmilla before. As for his own moment of weakness, he regretted it less now that he knew how little such things meant to Ludmilla. And as this atmosphere of sin in which he saw her wallow made her all the more desirable, he found a safe refuge against temptation in a loud condemnation of her ways and her character, which found a willing audience and a generous echo in Mary. He was pleased when he realized that Mary knew nothing. Yet, lucky as he was, he did not feel he owed Ludmilla any gratitude. She had saved him from the pitfall of specific confessions, but she had saved herself too, and, besides, she had lied to his wife. Should he congratulate her on this fact?

"You are quite right, Mary," he said, "when you judge Ludmilla severely. She is a wonderful person in many ways, fresh, amusing, full of imagination, but, God forbid, what an egotist, what a cold, calculating mind, and how she would do anything to go on staying here!"

Mary accepted these words as good news. Not only was her husband aware of Ludmilla's wicked nature, he was horrified by it.

"You know, Mary my love, this may sound terrible, but if I had met Ludmilla when I first met you, I would never have married you."

"You mean it?"

"I do. How could I have believed that a person like Ludmilla might have a sister like you?"

Mary had an impulse of hate at the mere thought of such a possibility. "Now that I think of it," she said, "we pretty nearly had her in Naples during that very period. Think of the danger our love just barely escaped. Oh, there is something in her that always stands in my way. I have always felt it. Her standards are not my standards. She does not care about philosophy, psychology or music, she cares only about Ludmilla and Ludmilla's pleasure, and the world can go hang, provided Ludmilla has her way."

"Yes, I am sure you are right. That explains many things."

"What things?"

"Oh, attitudes, things much too vague to be pinned down. They result in an atmosphere that I would almost call unclean, were I not fond of her as a person."

"Fond of her? I know what you mean, but beware of her charms! As a matter of fact, I am beginning to fear that Mamachen is completely taken in by Ludmilla's comedy. The trouble with Mamachen, as with me, is that we are both a bit stupid."

"I would not use such a strong word," said the doctor, clearing his throat and feeling very principled, "but it is true. Innocence, we might call it—the divine innocence of the pure, who are intelligent but are not clever, thank God."

X

WHEN COUSIN CROCIFISSO made his proposal, Ludmilla said yes although she disliked him very much. She needed kindness at that moment and Crocifisso was kind, while everybody else, and especially her brother-in-law, was at best indifferent. Even her mother was indifferent. Mary had won her back, and the doctor had influenced her and made her suspicious of Ludmilla again. Ludmilla had no real grudge against the doctor. He is so blind, so insensitive, so much of a man, she kept saying to herself all the time.

What Ludmilla did not know was that the task of persuading Crocifisso had not been an easy one.

"Is she immaculate?" he had asked, and the doctor had sworn that she was.

"How do you know? The standards of these people are different from ours—that is what everybody told me before I came here. There have been three divorces in the family, and I am in no position to judge of the merits of the other three cases. Your case was different. Mary was divorcing a bad man to marry one from our family, and no matter how imprudent she was, she did well—people like us are rare in the world. But how about those other divorces in this family? And how about Ludmilla's character? She has already shown a certain readiness to listen to me, even to hold my hand, and I at times wonder, if I said to her, 'Let's walk into the garden together at night,' would she accept or would she slap me in the face as she should? A man must keep his head before committing himself for life. To be worthy of an honorable man, a woman must first of all reject him. If she does not, it is exactly as if she undressed the moment you asked her to become your wife. That readiness to say yes is a symptom of dangerous sensuousness. I for one cannot respect a woman who does not refuse herself to me."

"I agree with you," said the doctor, "but I can assure you that Ludmilla is absolutely pure. If she shows greater confidence than it would be appropriate for her to show, this comes only from the fact that she has our word regarding your respectability and your honorable intentions."

Crocifisso became somber. "How could you know I was likely to marry her? You gave her my word before I did. And how could she, as an honorable girl, take your word instead of mine? I had not given you such a mandate, I only asked you in a general way to sound her out on the state of her heart and to tell me confidentially how much she would get for a dowry. You refused to answer the last question, and you merely said you would ask her whether her heart belongs to another."

"Yes, I did, and that is all I did. But I also expressed the wish that she and you would be united in matrimony. Is there anything wrong with that?"

"Of course not. But I am worried, and I would like time to consult with my feelings."

"Take all the time you need."

"It looks as if she is anxious to yield to me only in order to forget someone else."

"Nonsense. But I can find out for you."

"And you swear that you will give me a full, truthful report?"

"Why always swear to this and to that?"

"Aha, you don't want to swear!"

"No, no, I will. I have nothing against it. But do you think I would wish you to marry a woman unworthy of your mother's memory? Your mother was my mother's first cousin. If I say to you, 'This is the woman for you,' you can only conclude that this is the woman for you. I say now, this is the woman for you. Does that suffice?"

"It does," said Crocifisso; and, kissing his dear cousin on the mouth, as cousins should be kissed, he added, "I am in love with your sister-in-law, a double bond unites us, and a much closer one will unite our children."

The old lady was allowed to leave her bed for a few hours to meet her future son-in-law. Everyone loved the new couple, and the old lady promised to give her daughter a spectacular wedding as soon as Mary's child was born.

Ludmilla was no less dramatic than Mary, but while Mary had found that drama yielded good results, Ludmilla had found that it did not. In her case it was comedy. Turning everything into a joke at once cured her of her craving for things and gave her, if not great satisfaction, at least little ones with great amusement still attached to them. Which, as consolation, was not bad. This time she had turned her incipient first love into a joke by accepting that ridiculous man for a husband, and no one laughed more than she did during the whole engagement party. Even the children had never laughed so much. Ludmilla played with them, made funny faces, spanked them in public, and thus gave them a criterion for amusement for the rest of their lives. The only one to be left out of the game was Crocifisso, who was preoccupied with his dignity and who tried to assert himself by saying jokingly, "Now, Ludmilla, that will do. Excessive laughter is not dignified."

As all clowns know from experience, it is far easier to play the clown on stage than at a social gathering. Ludmilla felt that the children were about to be tired, and she tried to dismiss them before they could lose interest in her stunts.

"Enough, children, leave me alone now."

She noticed a cold glance in Mary's eyes that told her more about her standing with the rest of the audience than any secret conversation she might have overheard.

What am I doing here? she asked herself. What am I doing in the world? No one loves me, no one needs me, my worst enemy has taken everything from me, even the things I never had.

"Children," said the doctor, "go to bed now. Say goodbye to your aunt and to your new uncle and go to bed."

"To your grandmother first," said Mary, with a sweet voice that made everyone suddenly look at her. The curtain had indeed fallen on the clown. Mournfully Kostia, Sonia and Filippo said good night to their grandmother, then to their mother and father, then to Ludmilla, but while Kostia, who was old enough to know, kept his restraint, Sonia and Filippo clung to her with such fondness that tears came into her eyes and began to stream down her cheeks.

"What is this now?" asked her mother severely, and Mary, extremely embarrassed, repeated her question: "Ludmilla, what is this?"

"Nothing," said Ludmilla angrily, wiping her eyes and trying to look cheerful. "Absolutely nothing."

Sonia and Filippo were looking at her, and it was clear that they too were about to cry. Kostia instead kept his eyes glued to the floor.

Ludmilla giggled again like a clown. "May I put them to bed?" she asked.

"I don't think so," said Mary, concerned. "They will never go to sleep. They are already too excited."

"Why don't you let her?" said the doctor, and Ludmilla said, with complete cheerfulness, "Yes, Mary, why don't you?"

There was a quick exchange of significant glances between

Mary and her mother, then Mary said, "Yes, of course, your aunt and your uncle will take you to bed, children. But promise you will let them go after one minute. Otherwise I will not come and kiss you good night afterward."

Sonia and Filippo nodded, and now Ludmilla said, "Let's go." But when her fiancé rose from his chair, she said to him, "You stay here."

"Why?" asked Mary.

"I don't want him," said Ludmilla. "He is not their uncle yet. These are my children tonight." And with a joyful giggle she rose from her chair and left the room, holding the younger children by the hand.

The next morning Ludmilla was called to her mother's bedroom, and she knew what this meant: a boring trial, then a few hypocritical questions concerning her plans for the future— "Ludmilla, how do you envisage your future if this is the state of your mind? You cannot always be excused just because your stunts are amusing. People like clowns for an hour or so at the circus, not in everyday life."

Instead of which, she found her mother leaning against a white cushion, pale, absent-minded, and playing with a large white leather box placed on her stomach. Ludmilla knew that leather box; it had belonged to her grandmother, then it had gone to her Uncle Jules in Paris—one of her grandfather's tricks to spite his daughter even after his death, in his will— and finally it had come to her mother through the kind and generous efforts of Aunt Lydia. Now that the box stood there in the hands of its owner, the hands were pale and their grip was soft. The box itself went up and down with the sick woman's breath, like a boat moored near the quayside.

"Good morning, Mamachen."

"Good morning, Ludmilla, my child."

216

"How are you, Mamachen?"

"Very well, Ludmilla dear. Before I forget, I have to tell you something."

"Yes, Mamachen?"

"Ludmilla, how do you envisage your future?"

"I—I don't know, Mamachen."

"You must know. When do you think you would want to get married?"

"As soon as you say so, Mamachen."

"Well, I think it will be preferable if you get married after Mary's child is born, so that Mary can be present at your wedding."

"As you say, Mamachen."

"But as you will be the godmother, I think you should have a nice present for the boy."

"I suppose so, Mamachen, but how do you know it will be a boy?"

"I know it. I have already seen him in my dreams two or three times. He even talked to me."

"And what did he tell you?"

"I cannot remember, but it was something anguishing. Don't tell Mary for the moment."

Now the old lady opened the leather box, and out came a gold watch.

"This belonged to my grandfather. My father gave it to me to spite Jules, then ordered me to return it to him when I left my first husband. I never did. I should have given it to Jules, but this was the only present I had ever received from my father. Jules hated me for that. Too late to give it to him now, but what am I to do with it? If I give it to one of my children, all the others will hate me. So you give it to your godchild. And here is something else for you."

Her hand fumbled in the box; out came two large emerald earrings and an emerald necklace—things known by her children to exist, which knowledge, highly explosive in terms of future peace, was kept a great secret, like the atom bombs by the future defenders of mankind.

Ludmilla approached the jewels like a cat which by instinct tries to steal even the food it is given with love.

"Try them on."

She tried them on, tried on facial expressions and approaches to the mirror, and made the discovery that, in all the situations of life invoked by her, those drops of green along her cheeks and that green line on her soft neck were more important than the situation they were framing. Anger, joy, boredom, a clear or dirty conscience were but occasions to exhibit those emeralds. She was beginning to understand why God had made the world. What matter if she hated Crocifisso? She would have taken Bernhard the butler for a husband in order to wear jewels like those, so why not Crocifisso the clown?

Mary came in, heavy with child, and Ludmilla made a new discovery: hate in the mirror, all over the mirror, not only on Mary's face behind her. And how becoming—hate in green.

"Now try on these."

And out of the same box came a diamond necklace, one of diamonds and rubies, one sapphires and coral, one gray pearls—all with their earrings. Ludmilla's happiness blinked for one more moment in her eyes, then died. She now felt nothing but doubt. Again every situation of her life was framed in necklaces and earrings; she panted like a dog in an effort to choose among them. Her preference was for emeralds, but she found them less becoming than sapphires, diamonds and rubies. What further complicated her choice was the fact that there were parures of diamonds, of rubies and of emeralds, but not of sapphires. She would have liked to know the actual money value of the different jewels before making her choice, but did not dare reveal her thoughts. Mary was watching her with a strange, secret, calculating look.

"They are so beautiful," said Ludmilla, picking up the emeralds again as if trying to sell them to herself. "So very, very beautiful." Then, putting them near the other four necklaces, she added in a sad whisper, "Smaller. How strange."

"Yes," said Mary, without quite knowing what she should praise aloud and what in silence.

"Smaller," said their mother, "but very, very precious. Historical too—it appears in a sixteenth-century French portrait."

"Hm-hm . . . hmmmm," murmured Ludmilla, green necklace in one hand, white one in the other. She was trying to weigh them. Mary looked on, a blank expression on her face.

Their mother was now fumbling in the box again. "I still have a set you never saw," she said. "A parure of gold and diamonds, a Florentine Renaissance piece, with earrings and necklace. But where are they?"

She began to think, while her two daughters became very attentive.

"Let's see. They are not in here. In Italy? I believe not. In Cairo? Or in the safe-deposit box in Berlin? Somewhere, I recall, in a bank, and I believe without a name, and no way therefore of getting them again. Oh, well . . ."

"Too bad if you cannot remember where they are," said Ludmilla dreamily.

"Yes," said Mary. "Antique jewels, too. And you—you cannot remember where they are?"

"Try to remember," said Ludmilla in a very soft voice. Then, seeing that her sister seemed tired, she said, "Mary, sit down here, it is bad for you to stand up for too long."

"Thank you, my dear," said Mary, with true love in her voice. "You are very kind." But she did not sit down.

"Yes," said their mother, "I believe I was foolish enough to leave no name or anything. Or did I ask someone to deposit them for me? Anyway, this is all unimportant. How little they belong to us, these objects! We die and go to a safe place, they remain in this box, they neither suffer nor enjoy themselves."

"And you cannot remember where they are?" asked Ludmilla.

But her mother was still lost in her thoughts. "To think that people often fight over the possession of stones! I hope you never will, Mary and Ludmilla."

"Of course not," they both said.

"Let me see if I can still remember where I left them, since you ask me."

She closed her eyes, there was great silence in the room, then she opened her eyes again and they seemed very big.

"How strange," she said, "I have a pain in here. . . ." Her hands began to shake. She looked at them and said, "I cannot see my hands—where are they? Oh, my God . . ."

The violence of the stroke made her lift her knees, and the box fell, with all the jewels rolling down on the floor, under the bed, all the way to the other end of the room, while Mary and Ludmilla shrieked for help.

They called their mother like lost children, hating themselves for having asked her such an ugly last question, about jewels. They did not want those jewels now, all they wanted was their mother; they were frightened by the prospect of a future without guidance and without safety from their own greed. Those hands were their only possession, those hands their mother had left in the dark while she was seeing the first glimpse of true light.

Twenty-four hours later she was still very weak, but beginning to recover, and proud that this had been a real collapse. Mary stayed with her, and Ludmilla was in charge of the children.

"Aunt Ludmilla, play with us."

"Aunt Ludmilla, look at me, don't I act like you when I do this?"

"No, Aunt Ludmilla, look at me first, I'm more like you."

They played in the garden, and they played in the house, until it was time for lunch and she took them to the nursery. In the hall they met Uncle Crocifisso, and Ludmilla gasped, "Dear Lord, I had forgotten all about you!"

Poor Crocifisso had not forgotten about her. He had been wondering all night what to do with her. He knew nothing about her morals except what the doctor had told him, he knew nothing about her dowry. Could he afford to arrive in Naples with a wife who had no respect for him? He had been engaged to Ludmilla for forty-eight hours, and there had been not the slightest emotion on her part, not a kind word between them, not a moment of privacy. He now decided to conduct his own investigation. If in the course of the next day she did not change, he would break off the engagement, or at least threaten to do so.

An occasion presented itself almost immediately. The doctor came downstairs and said he had important matters to discuss with Mary and her mother. Would Ludmilla have lunch with her future husband? Ludmilla was not too charmed. She kept thinking of the two necklaces and knew that Mary was plotting against her. But there was little she could do. Not for the first time in her life, she realized she was very much alone.

When she saw Crocifisso seated across the table from her and imagined her future life as an unending repetition of this, minus the comforts of that house and the presence of the children she loved and their father, she knew she must break her engagement. But still she could not bring herself to be rude to this man, whom she had already mistreated for two days. She felt sincerely sorry for him, more so even than for herself. This all showed in her smile, which he took as the first symptom of love.

"I can see from the way you look at me," he said, "that you know how much I love you."

Against her will, she blushed with pleasure. She had restrained herself too much in the last days; these words now caught her unawares. All the forbidden images of her brother-in-law began to burn inside her. She was helpless. This too showed in her smile, and Crocifisso took her hand. She withdrew it. He looked so desperate that she almost decided to give it back to him; then she thought it wiser not to encourage him.

But he had seen in this withdrawal the final proof of her innocence. If she is so withdrawn with me, he thought, this means that she would be ten thousand times more withdrawn with a stranger.

"You are pure," he said, choking with emotion.

She laughed, sadly. "I? Pure? Nonsense, I am the devil incarnate."

"Don't speak that way. You know this is not true."

"How little you know me!" Her voice was so sad that it made him suspicious.

"If there is anything that weighs upon your conscience," he said, "remember, I am the only person in the world to whom you owe a full confession of your sins. Don't be afraid to talk and don't keep me in this horrible doubt any longer. You see what I am suffering. Please be human, and, above all, be honest."

She had heard nothing, having become absorbed again in her great problem: Should she accept the emeralds or wait? Then she realized that he was expecting an answer and she could not give just any silly reply. Neither could she ask him to repeat his question. So she thought she might strike a middle course by looking tenderly into his eyes and playing coy while uncoyly calculating her chances and risks in very unsentimental matters.

He did not like that comedy, and he knew it was comedy. He began to observe her closely, and again she noticed nothing. She was now smiling tenderly at her mirror, smiling at emeralds and diamonds, then looking worriedly at rubies and sapphires, then wondering at unknown other jewels, then sneering at Mary, looking with terror at her mother's dying eyes, closing her eyes in shame, shaking all over with remorse, then smiling tenderly again at the mirror. During this time Crocifisso was seeing more and more men, all making love to her, and orgies, drinking, gambling and divorcing—what a sewer of perdition! Still, he thought, I must get a full confession from her. Let my cousin divorce and marry a divorced woman, his conception of purity, his standards of judgment shall never be mine!

So what was the next step? Act with diplomacy—pretend he was as cynical as they.

"Darling," he said, like a man of the world, "don't think of them, don't let *their* memory sadden your beautiful eyes. Do as I do: dismiss *them* from your mind. I know what you are thinking, I know everything, I have divining powers. But look at me—am I worried? Not a bit. Come, have confidence in me, I am your friend."

This was the first time anyone had guessed Ludmilla's thoughts and spoken to her so directly. She was no longer alone in the world. Perhaps this man might really be a friend to her, not like Günther, the German scholar and poet she had met while at school in Lausanne, who accepted anything but being treated normally, as a friend. In an impulse of gratitude, she touched Crocifisso on the tip of the nose and said, with a devilish smile, "A nice nose has my new friend, he who can read my sinful thoughts!"

All of his thick Mediterranean blood rushed to his face. He could not tell shame and sexual excitement apart. He was sorry for his cousin, who had married one of these women. That gesture, and those words, and that lascivious smile! Typical of the prostitute! And how happy she seemed, to have found a man who would accept her past without asking any questions! This promised to be interesting. He was no fool, to let such an occasion pass him by. But he would leave her an envelope with money and an insulting note, after a night of orgies. And hand it to his cousin, for her. What a revenge, and what a lesson for the cousin!

Ludmilla was admiring him now. She had never seen his face so alive and intelligent. Too bad, she thought. If I had more courage, and if this did not mean giving in to Mary's scheme, I could even learn to love him. But not this way, with those jewels lying somewhere in hiding, and Mary happy to get rid of me! Oh no, little Ludmilla is not so easily dismissed! And again she touched his nose.

"You are not ugly at all," she said. "I think we might become very good friends, if we stayed clear of marriage. For a certain time at least," she added, not to give him the bad news all at once. "And now tell me, did you really know what I was thinking, or were you only saying so? When you say 'they,' and 'don't think of *them*,' what do you have in mind?"

"You want to know too much and give nothing in exchange. Is your conscience clear? *They* might even be a *he*."

She blushed, thinking, This is the person who opened the library door that day. And to avoid further questioning she laughed and touched his nose again.

He had never had a woman, except for prostitutes in cheap Neapolitan bordellos, but he had heard a great deal about the celebrated Parisian cocottes who ruined millionaires with their mania for jewels. "I think," he said, with what he imagined to be the cold glance of a vicious millionaire, "that you must like emeralds."

"Emeralds?" she said. "You frighten me, you *are* a mind reader! Yes, I love emeralds, I could sell my soul for emeralds, but I don't know whether they really are my stones. My skin is too greenish for emeralds; perhaps rubies, diamonds or sapphires would look better on me. Wait for me here, I'll let you be the judge."

She knew that her request would sound untimely, but she was glad to have a good excuse for entering her mother's room. Her mother might be asleep, or listening to Mary's lies against her.

Nothing of the sort. There she sat, the great patient, with the same jewel box on her stomach, and Mary on the same bed, wearing *her* emeralds and admiring herself in a hand mirror.

"Why didn't you call me?" asked Ludmilla.

"You were with your fiancé," said Mary. "In your place I would have been extremely annoyed if anyone had interrupted me while I was with my future husband and told me to come see some stupid stones."

"What future husband do you have in mind when you say this—your first one or your second one?"

Mary threw the mirror down; it broke on the floor. Then she looked at her mother and was sorry. The old lady did not speak.

Ludmilla apologized for Mary. "I am so sorry, Mamachen. It was my fault. I should never have said such a thing."

Mary burst into tears.

"Mary, don't upset me now," said her mother. Then to Ludmilla: "You were wrong to say such a thing to your sister. This whole thing frightens me."

She gasped for air. Ludmilla and Mary looked at her, and when they saw that she was well enough to speak, they expected to hear the usual phrase, "You are killing your mother." It did not come—and for the first time they believed it. No doctor could tell them their mother was not dying.

"Ludmilla, Mary, listen to me. I don't want you to fight over these silly stones or those I mentioned yesterday that are God knows where—you probably know, Mary."

"No, Mamachen, I do not. What were they like?"

"I told you yesterday, don't ask me to repeat it now. Ludmilla, my child, if you want to show the emeralds or the diamonds to your fiancé, go ahead; here they are. And tell me which ones you would rather have."

"May I?" asked Ludmilla, and Mary sneered.

Crocifisso had reached his conclusions like a policeman who has had plenty of time to study the documents in a criminal case and in whose mind the various elements have come to a synthesis, exactly as in an artist's mind. When Ludmilla came downstairs again, her case was stated, her sentence final. He was going to use her for his pleasure and for the moral satisfaction of giving her a lesson. But when he saw the jewels and heard of the fabulous necklaces to be inherited later, he found himself confronted with a true moral problem. This was a woman from a different world. There comes a point at which wealth transforms a woman into a man. To marry so much money is like becoming a prince consort, the honor is so great that honor itself, the supreme standard of male supremacy, no longer counts. Crocifisso decided that he must not let the occasion escape him. He stopped behaving like a jealous Italian and affected great liberality of views, and Ludmilla found him so understanding that she spoke to him honestly.

"I have no intention of marrying you, but we can stay good friends."

"Of course," he said, knowing this to mean lovers, as he had heard was the habit of speaking among elegant people in Paris.

Ludmilla was relieved to have found it so easy, after imagining unpleasant explanations, and she conceived a real affection for him now.

"It is so good to have a friend," she said. "I don't feel ready for marriage yet, even though I would like to have children."

"Of course," he said, "the prejudices of the petty bourgeoisie would stand in your way there."

She looked at him with surprise. He was more of a free-thinker than even her intellectual friends in Germany and Switzerland.

"I like to talk with you," she said. "There are so many problems I want to discuss, problems concerning the place of woman in society, her freedom . . ."

"In my opinion," he said, "women must have complete freedom."

"That is what I think, but it is difficult to explain such matters to people like my mother and Mary."

"They are both very old-fashioned."

"You must be very intelligent," Ludmilla said, "to understand everything so well."

"I am not intelligent, but I am a man of the world."

"I like you very, very much," she said. "You know, perhaps someday I may decide to marry you."

"Well, that is very nice. But let's not talk about it now."

"I am so grateful," she said. "I cannot tell you how grateful I am."

"Grateful? For what?"

"For understanding that I must have my freedom."

She clung to his arm; they took a walk through the park. She kissed him passionately and he drew his conclusions without saying a word.

"Let us not reveal our secret to the others for the moment," she said. "They would never understand. We will keep postponing our marriage and then say one nice day that we don't feel like getting married."

"Excellent idea," he said.

That same afternoon Crocifisso decided to give up his career at home and establish his headquarters in Paris with his mistress. What would become of him he did not know. His only thought was to avoid living with a mistress in a small town in Italy where she would want to meet his mother and where his friends would consider him a pimp. Also where they might

try to take liberties with her, and succeed. He wrote letters to
his family—one to his mother, describing the splendor of the
house where he lived, one to the president of the university
where he taught, announcing his resignation and his decision
to live in Paris. No further explanation given. After dinner he
hoped to make plans with Ludmilla for the night (since she
was a free woman, why not take advantage of her at once?),
but she gave him no chance to speak to her in private.

"I *must* speak to you," he whispered to her the first moment
he found her not surrounded by the children.

"Not now."

"Why?"

"I must put the children to bed, then I want to see my
mother. She said I could come up to her room for a while."

"But . . . later," he said.

"Later? Oh, later I imagine I'll be too tired to sit and talk.
Tomorrow, at breakfast."

"Where?"

"Here in the dining room."

So, this cold-blooded Russian prostitute was more independent than he had thought. After she had asked him to sleep
with her, and kissed him, she thought she could dismiss him
the first night, because she must stay with her mother! But
this was Messalina, not simply a cocotte! And I, he thought,
I who have ruined my career, cutting all bridges with the past,
giving in to her without asking for any guarantee, I find myself
a slave in her hands.

The thought was unbearable. Through a whole night of
torments his mind wandered from one image to the next. He
asked himself whether his cousin knew of Ludmilla's ways. He
must. Why, then, had he assured him that Ludmilla was immaculate? Could he have an interest in getting her married
off as soon as possible? These thoughts, while filling Crocifisso
with bitterness, also excited his senses. Nothing is more con-
ducive to love-making than the suspicion of being cheated. It

was three in the morning when he decided to take action and left his room.

He walked on tiptoe, stopped to listen to all possible noises —hearing nothing but his heartbeat—and found Ludmilla's door unlocked. He turned the doorknob slowly and entered the room. She was not there. The bed had not been slept in. So that was the true reason for her reticence—she was in someone else's room.

He recalled hearing that Mary slept in her mother's bedroom. He thought of going to his cousin's room and surprising the lovers. He had a right to do so; Ludmilla was still officially his future wife. Now he saw why she wanted their plan to be kept secret from Mary and her mother. "The cheap whore!" he kept saying. He walked as far as his cousin's door and put his hand on the knob, but it made a noise, and from inside the room he heard a moan. He withdrew in a hurry, ran down the hall and went back to his room. Now the dog began to bark loudly. He heard noises and voices, then silence again.

In the few hours between then and breakfast he rehearsed his next meeting with Ludmilla so many times that when he finally saw her he had difficulty in keeping his eyes open. What made him keep them open was a headache more than a feeling of wounded honor.

Ludmilla came in from the hall, yawning and pale, with circles under her eyes.

"Good morning," she said. "Oh, I am so tired."

He grabbed a fruit knife from the table, twisted it, broke it and placed it on the table again, much to Ludmilla's surprise. Bernhard came in and asked whether they wanted coffee or tea, and how they would like their eggs. To his own great surprise, he heard himself say, "Coffee, fried eggs, toast, marmalade." Bernhard took the broken knife away, and Ludmilla looked at Crocifisso, somewhat concerned.

"What has happened?" she asked him. "Are you not feeling well?"

He stared at her with hate, until his wounded honor was completely awake again.

"Have I done something wrong?"

"Did you sleep well?" he asked in a very quiet tone.

"No, very little."

"Of course not. You were not in your room."

"How do you know?"

"You thought you could get away with it. I am not like all those other friends of yours."

"What do you mean? What is all this? When did you come into my room?"

"At three."

"But how dare you? Imagine if anyone had seen you! Why did you come?"

"You answer first. Why were you not in your room?"

Her eyes widened, she gathered energy, became a fury. "What right have you to ask? We are not even engaged any more."

"That does not mean that you have the right to betray me."

"Betray you? What was that? How dare you use such words with me? And I thought that we were friends!"

"Where did you spend the night?"

"None of your business."

They were interrupted by the arrival of the children. Filippo looked tired. He went straight to his aunt and buried his head in her lap. She put her hands on it and said, smiling at Sonia, who was now standing near her, "You were very nasty not to let your aunt sleep. Next time your brother is ill, you will stay quiet or I will never again spend the night with you. Understand?"

"Yes, Aunt Ludmilla."

Breakfast was served in silence. Ludmilla passed butter and marmalade to Crocifisso without lifting her eyes from the tablecloth, indifferent to the fact that he ate nothing.

The doctor came in, sat down and said, "Good morning. Did you all hear the dog at about three? Someone was in the hall, I don't know who. Ah, what a night. How are you?" he asked Filippo. "Feeling any better?"

The child nodded and came to his father for a kiss.

"And how are you?" the doctor asked his cousin.

"He is leaving today," said Ludmilla, without looking at him.

"Leaving today?" asked the doctor. "For where? And why?"

"Ask him," said Ludmilla sternly.

"I don't know anything about it," said Crocifisso, pale.

"I do," said Ludmilla, "and you can always trust my word. I am well informed. He is leaving today for Naples or wherever it is that he lives, and—that is all."

Crocifisso cleared his throat. "There has been a misunderstanding. I would like to explain it to Ludmilla."

"No explanations needed, thank you."

"Look, children," said the doctor, "stop this nonsense. He is not leaving today, on the eve of the event." Then he turned to the children and said, "Come out with me, we'll take a walk." He left the room with the children.

"All right," said Ludmilla now. "As your cousin insists, let's have this useless explanation. How dare you come to my room at night?"

"But I thought . . . after what was said yesterday . . ."

"I know. You thought I was a prostitute because I kissed you. I had a strange suspicion when I did so, but I was much too jealous of my happiness to let even the slightest doubt cast a shadow upon it. I had found a real friend, or so I thought, and you mistook that word to mean something quite different."

"Your words, your ways, were clear," he said.

"Were they?" she asked. "So let this be clear, too." And she slapped him so violently that he fell from his chair. "You have never met a respectable woman in your life and never will,"

231

she said. "Your cows down there are to be trusted only as long as they have their policemen to watch them. Not so with us barbarians," she said.

He sank onto his knees. "I love you," he said. "Please forgive me."

"I do not love you, and that's the main reason for my not wanting to marry you."

He looked at her with surprise, then smiled. "But that is no reason at all. Love comes later. I will marry you anyway."

"Thank you so much for the information, but I will not marry you." She waited for him to get up, then, when he did not, said, "Get up from there, don't make yourself more ridiculous than you are already."

He stood up and then asked, timidly, "Will you . . . tell . . . the others?"

"Of course not," she said. "The blame is all on me. I broke the engagement because I am a prostitute, and you, as your name so well puts it, are a crucified image of virtue. Were it not for your cousin," she added, "the only man from your part of the world I respect, even the children would be told this incredible tale. So you may thank him if you are allowed to keep your reputation intact. But be it understood that you are not to spend another day in this house."

She pushed herself away from the table with both hands, rose from her chair and ran out into the garden.

"Can one hope to get something out of you?" asked the doctor, who had spent the last hour in his cousin's room while Crocifisso was sobbing like a child. "Is that the only reason she rejected you—because she does not love you?"

"Yes."

"But love is not necessary in the beginning. Rare are the women who love the men they are supposed to marry. Love comes afterward; it is learned, like many other things a respectable woman has no way of learning beforehand."

"That is what I said to her," answered Crocifisso, almost cheered by this argument. "Do you think there is any hope?"

"We will see. With women there is always hope—and they are hopeless by definition."

He went from Crocifisso to Ludmilla's room and found her on her bed, in tears.

"Ludmilla, my child, come and make peace with your fiancé. He is crying in one room, you in another. I am busy upstairs, the child is about to be born, and this is the help I get from you."

Ludmilla wiped her eyes and said, "I am sorry. I shall be upstairs in a minute to help you."

"I don't want you upstairs. I want you to be reconciled with my cousin."

"That is the only thing I cannot do."

"But what has he done to you?"

"Nothing. I don't love him, I told him so, I lost my patience. He is right, I am wrong, let's stop talking about it."

"Ludmilla," said her mother for the fifth time, "this decision of yours is not serious. You cannot stay here forever. You must think of your future."

"Yes, Mother."

"Why do you have to say 'Mother' to me in that harsh tone?"

"I did not mean it."

"Will you marry this man?"

"No."

"Leave me alone."

Ludmilla had barely left her mother's bedside when the phrase came, as in the old days: "You are killing your mother."

"That's all right," she said, without actually meaning it, although she knew it really was all right.

"Ludmilla!" cried her mother. "Ludmilla! Ludmilla, my child!"

Ludmilla stopped and stood still. She let these cries hit the back of her head, which could show no reaction, while her eyes were looking pleadingly at the door and her whole face was distorted by tears. But she did not turn back. She knew she could not explain, she also knew she could not do her mother the favor chosen as supreme proof of filial love. She knew so many things with not a soul to help her carry the big weight of that knowledge. Now she must not go back, not show her face, and, above all, never apologize. Again she felt very much alone.

She walked downstairs, stopping at every step to look into the void below and think, Should I jump? Tears fell on the red velvet banister and on the black-and-white marble chessboard below. She was trying to find all the possible reasons not to jump. There were none if the jump was sure to be fatal. But she felt, If I should land on white, I would remain a cripple for the rest of my life, so I must jump on black or nothing. After ten steps she foresaw broken legs or hips, a month in bed, then the forced marriage to that fool. I had better cry, she thought, and she tried to aim her tears at the intersections between squares, so as to make a black-and-white rose. Tasso the dog paused lazily on the chessboard; a tear fell on his nose. He lapped it up and looked at Ludmilla for more. She now began to cry for her true friend the dog. The thought of yesterday, with the great, joyful notion, "I have a friend who will let me stay here instead of taking me to a strange country to live with him," wounded her each time it made its way into her mind. I am alone, she thought; I shall forever be alone, I want my mother, she hates me, I even want my sister and she hates me, I want her husband and her children, I am not going to take them and no one will thank me for this.

Here they came; she saw the children's heads and was going to withdraw when they took over. She played with them in the garden. They picked lilies of the valley together "for the stork," which was expected in a room above the library. But they picked some for their grandmother too, and when it came to taking them to her, Ludmilla burst into tears again; she could not go.

Lunchtime came; Ludmilla did not want to eat lunch. She went to her room and pretended to be ill, felt ill in fact, for she knew she could not continue to be her mother's guest after what she had done; her presence was not wanted in the house. But she could not pack her suitcase, could do nothing at all. She sobbed aloud. Everyone in the house could hear her.

"I have had enough of this," said the doctor, coming into her room. "We have done everything we could for you. If anything was my fault, please tell me so, insult me, hit me, but stop crying. Tell me what my cousin did that was wrong. Let's discuss it together like civilized human beings."

"I am sorry. You are right, I should not cry. It upsets everybody here, I am a fool." And she went to the washstand to wipe her face.

"Ludmilla," he said, taking her by the hand, "come and have lunch. I am eating alone, I want to speak to you."

Ludmilla followed him, but she prepared herself to irritate him as much as she could, because she knew her weakness: the last person who spoke was always right and she never found anything to say at the moment; later, too late for her own good, all the best arguments were hers. But they had barely sat at the table when the doctor was called upstairs. Mary was beginning to feel pains.

"May I come with you?" asked Ludmilla.

"Wait here."

He was gone for a long time. When he appeared again he said Mary was asleep, and he sounded evasive on the subject of her going upstairs.

"You could still go and see your mother."

"Did she ask for me?"

"No, but I know that you still have a chance. Not tomorrow."

"Why not tomorrow?"

"She may have lost her patience."

"What does she want me to do?"

"What we all want you to do. Act like a woman. Either be reconciled with him or tell us what happened between you."

She was about to talk, but the doctor was called upstairs again and she remained with the first of many thousands of words dead on her lips. There was no time. A new life was about to enter, the play was changing, old characters were suddenly becoming less important; why should she claim any attention for her problems when she herself found them ridiculous? The easiest solution was shaped for her by the turn of events. She remained out of the mainstream, a lesser country road which the newly built road pushes out of the way.

XI

I AM GOING TO LEAVE all by myself and nobody will care. . . .
It was night, and the doctor still had not come back to talk
to her. Ludmilla had spent the rest of the day with the children, but now even they, eager to see the stork, had stopped
calling for her.

. . . They will all wonder where I am, whether I had any
money, but I will be gone and no one will find me.

She knew this was a childish mood, so, while indulging it,
she asked herself a few practical questions: Where could I go?
Back to Moscow, to Pierre? Never again. Back to Luther's?
Better dead. What then?

She suddenly remembered her friend Günther, who had followed her silently all the way to Lugano just to be near her,
without ever trying to see her, waiting only for a chance to be
useful to her.

Why should I have forgotten him? Here is my only friend.
What would I do without him?

She knew where he was staying: in a small inn not far from
the villa. Hatless and coatless, she went out into the cold
night, walked down the garden path and opened the gate. And
the first person she saw was Günther.

"Ludmilla, what are you doing here?"

"And you, Günther? Günther! Oh, dear Günther, help me, Günther, I have no home to go to, I must leave, I want to stay with you, I want to marry you!"

She could not see his face in the dark, but she felt his arm tremble, and as he drew close to her to embrace her she could hear the violent heartbeat that shook him. She felt sorry for him but at the same time safe, because she knew that she could trust this man. She took his head between her hands and kissed him on the eyes, on the mouth, planting her kisses anywhere on that dark outline against the starlit April sky, and he looked lovable, he looked Italian, he looked like her brother-in-law. Even the shock of his Germanic voice did little to destroy her illusion. The things he said brought back a bit, but only a bit, of the infinite boredom that was typical of him, and caused her to withdraw for a moment.

"Is this the fallible being known as Ludmilla, or is it the Eternal Goddess of Youth and Beauty called Ludmilla that has spoken to me and kissed me in this southern night?"

The use of such expressions as *"das bedingte Wesen"* and *"in dieser südlichen Nacht"* froze all her sentimental weakness and appealed to the clown in her. These were words from a poem of his she had read with delight to another friend of hers, a very amusing German industrialist who also had besieged her for a while, then had lifted his siege to follow another woman. Günther did not seem at all anxious to hear whether it was the conditioned human being or the Eternal Goddess that had asked him to marry her. He was trying to quote from his poem (what better occasion than this?), but his emotion was too great, and he could not remember his own lines. She let him stutter over those lines for a while, and he became so upset that he began to cry.

"What a terrible thing," he sobbed, "to be affected by poetic impotence on such an occasion! And to think that I had never dared hope I could someday recite my verses to you, to you alone, in the presence of the stars. Here the gods make this possible for me, and I cannot remember my own poem!"

Ludmilla squeezed his hand with love and whispered into his ear, "*Ach, Du, poetische Gestalt . . .*"

"Ludmilla!" he cried. "Ludmilla, is it possible? You never even acknowledged that poem in your letters, I was resigned to the notion of my total unsuccess, in fact I hesitated for a moment before reciting it tonight, and here I find that you remember it, you have learned it by heart."

Ludmilla smiled in the dark. Is it possible, she thought, that the most decent men should always tempt you into doing awful things to them? She squeezed his hand. "Günther, I feel so unworthy in your presence."

"Ach! It is for me to feel unworthy. I am the humble archaeologist, I try to reconstruct the greatness of antiquity, you *are* antiquity in all its splendor!"

She laughed aloud this time. "Nice compliment. I thought I was young, in spite of my age! No man has ever likened me to antiquity."

"I am so sorry," he said. "I have made a foo poe."

Ludmilla could not restrain her laughter, and it became so loud that Tasso began to bark and a window was opened in the villa. She hid her face in Günther's jacket to stifle her laughter, and what made her stop was the smell of stale perspiration that it exuded.

"Poor angel," she said. "You don't know French, you should not use French expressions. *Faux pas* it is, not *foo poe*, my love. I know you meant antiquity in a flattering sense."

"I truly did," he said, nodding so that some stars were uncovered and then again obliterated by the quick movements of his head. "You are not bound by the earthy obligations which burden the rest of us mortals. Your logic is not in the *Folgerichtigkeit* that ties every premise to every conclusion in the minds of normal people, but, rather, the coincidence of your being with eternity itself! Your caprice is divine, your will supreme! You owe me no apologies; it is, rather, I who owe you an apology. You are the Mountain of Eternal Youth, and I have tried to climb it with my dirty boots! Oh, I wish I had wings, to stay suspended in the air over you like the Libellula watching a flower with its thousand eyes!"

He seemed to have forgotten that she had asked to marry him. All he could think of was his altruistic love and his poems. And I, she thought, I who believed that this was what he wanted—will I ever find a man who thinks of me and not only of himself? Yes, I have found one, and of course he belongs to Mary. . . . She made an effort to go on with her plan.

"You know," she said, "I am in great danger. My family wants me to marry a man I don't love, or to go back to school. You must help me."

"I will help you. With me you are in no danger. My love will be poured day and night upon your being, like the sweetest of Greek honeys. My love is so great that the sheer contemplation of it will take up most of your time. You can mirror yourself in my words, and this will cause them to become clearer all the time. We will travel together. We will go to Italy and Greece. Don't worry."

Although taken aback by these words, which again reflected nothing but Günther's infinite interest in himself, Ludmilla was tempted by the idea of seeing the world with so knowing a guide. Even the thought of being mirrored in his words, ridiculous though it seemed, suddenly took on a new light. Was this not similar to what Mary was doing with her husband? And would it not be nice to have her great man, too, and be responsible for some great future work of his? She kissed Günther again, and this was the moment when she saw a black shadow in front of her, and two blinding lights behind it: her mother's car slowly making its way out of the garden. She quickly disentangled herself, and when the shadow came to her and stopped she said to the chauffeur, "You may go. I will be back in a few minutes."

Then she saw Günther in that light; he was wearing his dirty *Lederhosen*, his legs were hairy and blond, his eyeglasses foggy with fingerprints, his face was cloudy with freckles and his jacket full of patches.

"How are we to get married?" she asked him. "I have no money. Do you have any?"

"My mother has some for you, and I have always more than I need."

"Yes, but where shall we go from here, and when?"

"In the course of the morning I will come for you. We will go to my mother's place near Ludwigshafen. I am going to buy the train tickets now at the station. We will travel third class —you travel just as fast and far on a hard bench as on red velvet cushions. Besides, the people you meet in first class are hardly worth traveling with. We will tell your proud family that they can do nothing for us, because we have ourselves, our future and the whole world of poetry in front of us."

"Of course," she said, just to say something, and was gone past the car into the dark regions of wealth and no poetry.

The enormity of her step became at once apparent to her: Günther, his leather trousers, his poetry, his books and a third-class ticket to the most horrible industrial part of Germany. She knew Günther. His love poems were bad, but his articles were good—she had never been able to understand them. His force of character was immense; he would never allow the family to give her a penny. Not only could he read instead of eating, not only could he tell on sight, from among many Greek vases, which was the important one, or distinguish early Luini altar triptychs from later ones, but he could tell that the flowers had blossomed in the fields and remain utterly unmoved by the stench of his shoes, his *Lederhosen* and the rancid salami in his rucksack, or the kitchen utensils he had rinsed in the sacred waters of Delphi or the blond Tiber, perhaps even the River Styx, but never in plain water and soap.

I cannot do this to myself, she thought; he may well be a genius, more so than Mary's husband, but what a difference between the two!

She looked at her brother-in-law's dear image in the dark as she mounted the steps leading to the main entrance, and the evocation was so vivid that there he seemed to stand, in front of her, waiting for her. She knew this was not so, until she heard his voice:

"Where have you been?"

"What is it, Mary, pains?" The doctor knew that Ludmilla had been about to speak the truth just now at the lunch table, and he resented this second interruption.

"No. I want you to talk to me."

"I was talking to Ludmilla, trying to persuade her to change her decision."

"Go back, go and talk to your dear Ludmilla if that gives you pleasure."

"It does not, I don't care to hear her problems."

"That is not true. You do care very much. After what Ludmilla said to Mamachen this morning, any normal person would have given her up. Not you. If you took the trouble only to inform her that if she does not see fit to apologize, she should at least have enough dignity not to stay in her mother's house . . . But I do not imagine that this was the theme of your conversation. In fact, I know it was not. You told me so yourself: you were trying to persuade her to reconsider. I am told she has been playing with the children all morning. Picking flowers for me—there they are. But she did not have the courage to bring them to me herself. She sends the children to me with her gifts. My own children. And then you too. Everyone is a toy in her hands—you a spiritual toy, as befits your nature. And I am nailed here to my bed, with this child you must already hate."

"Mary, I forgive you only because you are not in your right mind at this moment."

Mary sat up, her face monstrous with pain. "A woman in my state knows many things," she said, "has many threads to God and with the world. I know there is danger for me as long as Ludmilla exists. I know she is better than I, prettier, more clever, less sincere—and men like her for that reason."

"Nonsense. Who are these men? There are men and men. If men prefer her for that reason, then I am not a man. I like sincerity. I could kill a woman for not being sincere."

"Tell me one thing," said Mary. "Only one thing—but swear first, on this child that is about to be born, swear that you will tell me the truth."

"I do."

"Did you ever come to this room with Ludmilla?"

"Never."

"Swear?"

"Yes, of course. I swear to you I never even knew this room existed. As you remember, we discovered it only a few days ago."

"And you know that this door here, under that tapestry, leads to the library. One of the shelves just opens like a door."

"Yes, I know."

"And you can swear that you have never been here with Ludmilla?"

"Yes, I can."

She pondered for a moment. "There is a mystery in all this."

"What mystery?"

"Do you remember the day you were in the library with Ludmilla?"

"Yes, I remember."

"Well, you were not in the library. You had been in the library, but you were not there when I sent Adalgisa to look for you."

"I don't remember."

"But I do. Adalgisa is not the kind of person who would tell lies. I trust her. And you swore you were not up here."

"I do, again and again."

"Very well, then, I feel better. You have never told me a lie."

"No, I have not."

And he had not. But he knew that divine justice functions even when no one is watching us from above. A lie mechanically poisons the future, stains the light of the sun, ties the soul to a secret, leaves the unspeakable lying about in the torrent of speech, and it will grow and hurt like kidney stones. It is, in fact, a kidney stone. As a doctor he knew: I am most ill with falsehood and may die. After a pause he thought, And if it killed the child instead? Am I not trying to choose my punishment and to suspend my sentence the moment I pronounce it? Divine justice may kill an innocent woman or a child for the lie of a man.

Then he made a great discovery: it is not divine justice that kills; it is the love of a liar that kills, because a polluted source cannot give unpolluted water. And he thought, I should leave Mary and the children to save them from my sickness. Leave them and stop loving them. But even that is no solution; she would die of despair if I left her. The sinner either kills without knowing it or inflicts sufferings knowingly. No way out of the machine of divine justice. Then why don't I confess? But her jealousy is pathological, she is a Punished Person, I could only make things worse. So there is even this: Confession becomes dangerous because the world is full of slaves, any form of confession would appear like fresh punishment, confirm them in their native unworthiness. All I can do is take her hand and be patient with her.

He took her hand and was patient with her.

It was hours later when Adalgisa came in, hesitantly.

"What is it?" asked Mary.

Adalgisa looked at the doctor.

"What is it?" asked Mary again, and Adalgisa said, "Nothing, madame."

"I know," said Mary, sitting up. "My mother is dying. Oh, my God, why don't you tell me? I will get up and go."

"No, madame, don't move. She is all right. It's Miss Ludmilla."

"Miss Ludmilla? What of her?"

"She has left."

"She has left?" Mary sneered. "So she has left. Thank God."

The doctor looked at her in silence, he did not dare look at Adalgisa.

"Yes, madame, she has left, but we don't know where she has gone. She left without her things, without a coat, without a hat."

"Did she? Never mind, she will be back. This is Ludmilla. At a moment like this, she *would* demand attention." Then Mary looked at her husband. "You are worried," she said.

"No, I am not."

"You are. And you should be. This is very strange."

"No, it is not. You said so yourself. She will be back."

"Yes, but when? It is almost dark. Where has she gone?"

"Don't ask me, Mary. I know no more about it than you do, in fact much less. You know her habits. In any case let's wait."

"Of course nothing can have happened to her. Ludmilla needs two hats for an afternoon stroll through the garden. If she were to drown herself, she would first order three tentative suicide outfits to match the color of the lake, then call the whole thing a failure and accuse the tailor because he ruined her suicide. 'I almost died of shame,' she would say." She tried to laugh, but Adalgisa's face brought her back to reality. "Did you look for her everywhere?"

"Yes, madame, everywhere, with her fiancé. He is very upset."

"I'll go and talk to him," said the doctor, and he went downstairs.

Crocifisso was giving himself the consolation of the selfimpotent, letting the servants guess that it was he who had caused all the trouble, that if Ludmilla had done something foolish it was because of him. This was all accomplished by unfinished phrases spoken as if to himself, imprudently, aloud, in a state of complete unawareness of whoever might be present—and practically the whole household staff was present: Brigida, Bernhard, the Italian cook, the German chambermaid, Frieda, and the chauffeur. This was taking place in the kitchen.

"Let's hope she has not harmed herself. . . . I should have known it, poor Ludmilla, the blow was too severe for her. . . . How careful one must be with women."

The doctor stared at the scene for a moment, then called his cousin rather curtly: "Come here, I must speak to you."

The confrontation took place in the next room. "Are you completely insane, to speak that way in the presence of the servants? Whatever reasons Ludmilla had for leaving—and we don't know whether she has not just gone for a walk—it is our duty to protect her good name."

"But I swear to you, my concern was so great, it is only out of love that I—"

"Never mind. I don't want you to mention her name in the kitchen."

"But this is a misunderstanding, I swear to you. Let me explain—"

"I have no time for you now."

As the hours passed, it became clear to the doctor that Ludmilla must leave, for her own good more than for his, and leave at any price except the price of marriage to that indiscreet cousin of his. Yes, but where would she go? Who would give her the love and devotion, the standing, the children she craved?

He was sitting near Mary's bed again. She was asleep. How beautiful she was and how good it was to remember her as she had been back in the days when conversation between them had been varied and interesting, not mainly a constant repetition that he had not betrayed her, or that he did not love this or that woman, governess, hospital nurse or kitchenmaid. How long ago was that?

Where is that Mary now? he asked himself. She will never come back. Who will console me? Who will help me tell the children that their mother is dead? Ludmilla alone can do that. And Ludmilla will be kind to her sister's memory. How easy it would have been for Mary to be as happy as she was fortunate, had she only loved herself more and believed in her own attractions.

He realized that he was mourning her already. He went to the window and listened to the noises of the night: a train leaving the station, puffing loudly under the iron arch, then faintly out in the open; Tasso howling at unseen dogs from the kitchen, and distant dogs howling back at him, unseen; the unseen clock inside the belfry of the cathedral, nine o'clock, an hour late for dinner. All these sounds hitting the window-pane like flies. His silence was respected, like that of a tomb. Is this the way the dead receive our tears when we visit their vaults?

Someone laughed on the road beyond the garden gate. That was Ludmilla's voice. He opened the window, heard her again, but faintly this time, then a man's voice, then hers again.

He turned his head. Mary was still sound asleep. He left the room, called the chauffeur and told him to go out with the car, but slowly, so that he would see Ludmilla and she could see him. He knew this was as bad as what his cousin had just done in the kitchen, but he was burning with jealousy. Nothing else mattered any more. And when he saw her climb the steps to the entrance all his concern over her happiness was gone. The love policeman rose in him and made him ask, "Where have you been?"

Ludmilla decided at once that the first thing to do was to sound unafraid and test the ground with a first truthful answer, before daring a lie that might prove slippery.

"Out with a friend," she said

"A friend? Who is he?"

"Günther."

"Never heard of him. Have you made his acquaintance tonight?"

"Oh, no. I have known him for years."

"Ah. One of your . . . friends."

"It is not at all what you think. Günther is safe."

"Married?"

"No. He would not marry anyone but me."

"You never mentioned him to me."

"I never mentioned him to you because I hardly ever mentioned him to myself."

"What do you mean? Be serious, now. You had us all worried to death. Do you think that was fair? And then you turn up, fresh as a rose, hatless, happy, unconcerned, as if these things were normal for a young unmarried woman from a good family. Who is this Günther? Where does he live? When did you arrange to meet him in the street? Why did you have to see him secretly? Why not here in the house?"

"Günther is a much better person than your cousin, or you, for that matter. He would never ask questions. I did not know I was going to meet him tonight, but I had planned to go to his inn and see him there. He had written to me, but he never dared bother me, he never would. I could spend a whole night with him in his room and still nothing would happen. He worships me and he trusts me. And that was what I needed today, when I left in despair not knowing whether I was going to drown myself or throw myself in front of a train at the station. I needed someone I could talk to, and found him. Günther walks all around the park every night, I swear I did not know this until now, and I was touched to tears. So I talked to him, I did not even give him the time to say what he always says when he sees me: that he wants to marry me. I asked him to marry me and to take me away from here. So now you know the truth. He will come here tomorrow and you shall meet him."

"I see."

"I hope you realize that I am being very sincere with you. Exceptionally so."

"Yes, yes, I have no right to ask any questions, since you are independent and wish to lead your own life." He was sorry to find himself speaking this way. He had meant it kindly, but was saying it unkindly.

Ludmilla looked at him and asked, very slowly, "And what else could I do? You have a wife and children, you cannot solve my problem for me."

"I am afraid that is so," he said, and this upset her. There was a moment of hesitancy on both sides. She hoped to hear him tell her to come to her senses and marry Crocifisso, and he was trying to decide whether or not to tell her exactly that.

"Eat something," he said.

"Have you had dinner?"

"No," he said. "I am not hungry."

"Neither am I. How is Mary?"

"Nothing new."

"May I see her?"

"Better not. Good night."

249

"Good night."

He walked upstairs; she looked after him like a dog that has been ordered not to move.

Why did I have to talk that way? Why make it sound so definite, when I know that it is not? Only to see the effect in his eyes, and what have I obtained? I've lost his friendship, hurt his feelings, reminded him of his duties, and given him a chance to get rid of me without remorse. If I married his cousin, he would still be duty-bound to assist me and to forgive me if I did not stay married, because it was his fault. Here the fault is all mine, I dug my own grave, he will never be haunted by my ghost. And if I betray Günther, as I will because that is what Günther wants, no forgiveness from here, no help, no feeling of responsibility, nothing. A few more hours now, then everything is gone. Love will descend upon me like Greek honey from Olympus. Love and statues, love and antiquity, love and *Lederhosen.* And a third-class ticket to Ludwigshafen. Bought already, for all I know; the train may leave at seven, these archaeologists are early risers. Our days will be long and our evenings short. And who will be our friends? The neighbors of the Genius, and more geniuses like him, more *Lederhosen,* more books, more quotations. Dear Lord!"

She was still standing where the doctor had last seen her. Now she became aware of a strange similarity between the two men, Günther and her brother-in-law. Both early risers, both devoted to antiquity and knowledge, both extreme Puritans, except that Mary's husband was not serious. His principles of purity were only a police measure to make sure that others would not take away his women. Sinning with him was all right. Here at least was a man in the full glory of his vices, his greed, his injustice (she had no other evidence of this but his looks, his elegance and his vitality), while Günther was a complete professor and a hater of all good things, especially of women.

His contempt for the world began beneath his skin; he did not
know that legs should not be naked, that a man should not
become offensive through his smells. And what a guarantee for
that wicked Italian with that coating of marital hypocrisy, to
know that the woman he craved was in the hands of one so incapable of competing with him.

And did I have to do this to myself? she thought. Was it not
all rather impulsive? She began to rehearse the Right Solution,
like all those who have missed it: When he asked me where I
had been, I should have looked as embarrassed as I was, and
used the truth to tell him my lie, saying, "I felt unwanted
here, you were trying to force me into doing a thing I could
not do, so I went out in despair and met a man I knew but did
not like. In a moment of madness I asked him to marry me,
but I now realize I could never leave this house. Help me. Despise me. Tell me I should kill myself, as I can only ruin your
happiness and harm my sister." Then faint. And not a shade of
insincerity in all this. It would have solved my problems by
making them his problems. He could never have chased me out
of the house, or tolerated that my mother do so, and I could
have enjoyed a rest, sleeping off all my worries in my comfortable bed, and after a few days of rest there would have been
a new situation, a new life in the house, and nothing wrong
with me except for the state of my health. After all, this is
what Mary must have done to get him, or she would never have
succeeded in alienating such a man from his wife and his
church and his environment.

Why was I such a fool? And why should I ruin myself to help
Mary keep her husband and rob me of my jewels? Who will
thank me if I do this? No one. Go and sacrifice your own happiness to others, they will never know you have done it, and
should you remind them of it they will laugh in your face!
"What? Ludmilla has helped me keep my husband? Nonsense!
He hates her, he has contempt for her! Look what she has done
to poor Günther! She first bullied him into marrying her, then

left him. Oh no. My husband does not even allow me to see Ludmilla, lest I be soiled by her presence. He does not want the children to remember she exists."

These clear visions hit the mark. "Is that so?" she said in a loud voice. "Then let me show you something. . . ." Yes, but what? It was late for that perfect solution. So she resumed her wishful-thinking post-mortem and saw herself answering his question in a different style: "Where have I been? Out with another man, a man I trust, and he too wants to marry me, but I prefer to do what you have ordered me to do, even though I dislike it." What a burden on him. How she could play the comedy, again telling the truth and being natural: utter disgust at the mere sight of Crocifisso, a show of patience, eyes cast to the ground, a faint voice, a pale face, eating nothing at table, growing thin (she could never resolve to do that, but if there was a reason, what a joy to stay slim and keep everyone worried!), and then, at the last moment, asking Crocifisso to postpone the date of the wedding. Crocifisso would do it. . . . This made her think of him as her possible ally in the present situation.

He is not the same person he was when I rejected him. My first mistake with him was also due to an excess of honesty on my part. I am indeed too good, there is no getting away from this. I should learn from my mother and from Mary. Also, my mother played the game of obedience at first: she married the man her father wanted her to marry, then left him almost immediately. And in due course of time she got her jewels and everything. And she killed off her second husband, as Mary is going to kill hers. Her helping him in his scientific work is utter nonsense, as was my mother's helping her second husband with his work. She was a pest to him from the day they were married. This is the reason she and Mary are so close. They are alike. I descend from my father alone!

With a sneer, "Ludmilla's sneer," her most precious possession, her identity, her pennant, she decided on a new course of action, which would differ from her mother's and Mary's in a most satisfactory way, because it had none of their hypocrisy and their heavy taste for melodrama; her drama would be light in construction, based on good comedy, on real feelings, generous as she always was, altruistic and modern—that is, French, not Germanic and not Russian: She would obey and then delay, and in due course of time something would happen, not necessarily the worst thing. She might even end by liking Crocifisso better than his cousin, or she might meet another man. Then her mother would die—why not think of this too in true French manner?—and the jewels would be distributed in Ludmilla's presence; while, if she left with Günther now, one thing was sure: she would never see either the emeralds or any of the other jewels.

The first thing to do now is to calm Günther, she decided. I can write him a beautiful letter, a love letter, my first to him, the letter he always asked for and never received; and as he will never receive anything else, I must be generous on paper. This will inflame his mind, fill his time and tame his passion.

It was not difficult for her to be spontaneous. She could thank him for leaving her to her comfortable bed, to the children she so loved, and to the man she was not to love openly. And she could write her letter on two levels, using for the first time the counterpoint of words which, when they rise to the level of poetry, shed love in all directions, because no one can be their sole recipient. And he to whom they happen to be addressed, when he is a jealous Italian, does not dare ask how much they are addressed to him. Günther, through the things he pretended to love, such as poetry and knowledge, loved himself only; he would bow to this image of himself and ask for nothing else.

To think that people call him modest, she said to herself, because he never tries to improve on his own image in the mirror with physiognomic tricks, a curled mustache, a silk necktie, a well-tailored suit! Thinking now of the doctor by way of comparison, she knew that she could never write so freely to him. He knows himself too well to accept so high a tribute, she thought. It would frighten him, make him jealous at once, more so than the admission of treason, and he would be quite right, because love *is* a light shed in every direction, filling the world, warming anyone who comes along, knowing no faces, no places and no names.

She was in such a state of grace that she spoke to herself as she walked through the rooms—entrance hall, dining room, music room, drawing room, a smaller drawing room known as the card room, the billiard room and her mother's writing room. She did not want to write her letter in that room. She took some monogrammed writing paper and envelopes, finding nothing less personal to use, chose a penholder out of the many that stood there in a glass filled with gunshot, lifted the heavy inkstand and took them all to the dining room. On the way she pronounced the doctor's name aloud with love, closing her eyes. She never realized that she was not alone in the room, and when she turned, thinking she had heard a noise, she saw nothing and heard nothing. Reassured, she reached the dining room, placed her equipment on the white table-cloth and began to write:

GÜNTHER,

Don't come today, be patient if you love me. You have been patient for so many years, don't let this last delay discourage you, and please do not despair—you have nothing to fear, you have my love as no one else will ever have it, but if you came today things would become extremely difficult for me, so difficult in fact that I might even have to give you up. But please, do not abandon me, and have faith in my words. You are my only friend on earth, I need you terribly, but above all I need your understanding, your discretion and your letters. If

254

you doubted my love and stopped writing to me, I would die. But I shall have to be contented only with your dear letters for a while, let us hope not for long.

These people here are not easy to handle. My mother is quite ill, she may die any moment; when she saw me coming back last night she had a very bad attack. As for my sister, all she can think of is her own happiness, and her husband insists that I marry his cousin. I may have to give in, or pretend to give in, only in order to gain time. We shall win in the end, I know it, but the slightest act of imprudence on your part might be fatal to my mother's health and to my freedom. For less than this my eldest sister was interned, as you well know, and she may never leave the insane asylum. If the same thing happened to me, I too would lose my mind and be unable to persuade the doctors of my sanity. So please, let me handle this terrible situation in my way. I am alone, but if you write, if you assist me with your poetry, and above all with your work, this will give me the strength to continue and to win our great battle. Please go to Greece without me. I shall be with you anyway, as you are here with me this very moment, right here next to me, in front of me. Your dear image surrounds me, guards me, gives me strength.

Please do not demur, please obey my instructions, and be happy. Think how fortunate you are to have finally awakened in me that flame of love you had been praying for since we first met, five years ago. You rescued me from suicide last night. But if you want me to live, you must still rescue me from spiritual death, namely from remorse. I want to know that you are not despairing and unable to work. Before I give birth to your children, let me feel that I have given birth to your genius. You said last night you could never achieve your monumental work without me. Now you must show me that you can.

I love you I love you I love you I love you immensely.

LUDMILLA

255

She reread this letter and had that same feeling one has after finishing a year in school: Never again these books, let's think of something pleasant now. She folded the letter, put it into an envelope, wrote Günther's name and address and decided at the last moment not to seal it, in order to be able to read it again in the morning before sending it by hand to his inn. Then she thought of Crocifisso. How funny he had looked, kneeling in front of her and thanking her for slapping him in the face.

How stupid of me, how unforgivable, she thought. I had the solution right there, this whole thing with Günther would never have happened. What a waste of time and energy, and what dangers—all because I am too honest. Poor Crocifisso, he must be spending another night of hell, all alone in his room. He does not know how fortunate he is. If I could only spare him this last torture.

The thought, nonexistent to that very moment (Crocifisso could have died at her feet, she would not have bothered to look at him), became unbearable. Ludmilla was very accessible to feelings of compassion. She would have given anything to be able to speak to him, not only in order to lessen his sufferings but also to find out how much he now knew about Günther.

How difficult it is to please everyone, she thought.

She decided that the best thing to do was to write him a letter. Just a short note, to tell him . . . Yes, what? She scribbled a first note in Italian which said: "Your friend Ludmilla wishes to be forgiven." Then carefully she wrote another one, which said:

I am sorry I was so cruel to you, but you had hurt my feelings. I had believed in you so completely, had been so overjoyed to discover in you my only and truest friend, that when I saw that you had misunderstood my motives I was profoundly disappointed. No loss that I had suffered in my life, not even the death of my father, affected me so deeply. Let us become friends again. *I need you, I need your advice, and someday per-haps, when I have grown more sure of myself, I may even decide to marry you. You might find this assuming on my part, but I don't care if I expose myself to a refusal. I want to be sincere with you because I need your friendship and your constant advice. My life in this family is not an easy one, as you may well . . .*

She heard a noise outside that froze her into terror. She looked at the large window which served also as a door and wondered why the outside shutters had been left open. It was dangerous. She remembered Mary telling her that thieves had tried to break in through that window twice, and now she expected to see faces in the dark. She could not look at those two rectangular black spots, and could not look away from them, either. Distant noises came to her with a faint reassuring message: a train puffing, a boat whistle on the lake—but so far, so far away, beyond all possibilities of theft and even murder. She bent her head, to concentrate only on the solid table, the white light, the objects that had seemed so familiar a minute before, and with a great effort she scribbled a third note to Crocifisso:

Please don't be jealous of the man who was with me last night. He is an old friend, but he is very safe, extremely safe from the sentimental point of view, because his ugliness is simply appalling. Wait until you see him.

This seemed a bit disrespectful to Günther. She put down the pen and decided that the only thing to do was to knock on Crocifisso's door, enter, kiss him good night and say the things that seemed so coarse on paper, then go to bed. She was beginning to collect her various notes before destroying them when she heard steps outside, cautious steps. And finally the handle turned, the door opened, and she closed her eyes, emitting a faint moan. It was exactly as in a dream—she wanted to yell and could not. And what she saw gave her the vision of approaching death: Crocifisso, advancing toward her with the face of a murderer, pale, uncombed, his hands crisp on his necktie, ready to strangle her.

He stopped halfway to look at her—with love, it seemed to her. He smiled. "Have I scared you?" he asked.

She nodded, still unable to speak. Then, after a pause, now completely herself again: "How are you?" And finally, herself plus the clown Ludmilla again: "I am glad to see you."

He stood there, still with that smile on his face, and said nothing.

"Glad to see you," she repeated, and her voice was beginning to quiver.

"Are you?"

"Yes, I—I am. In fact, I was writing to you."

"To me? Ah, to me. Let's see." He advanced slowly toward the table. She put an elbow over the letter to Günther.

"I want to see all of my letters, not only these," he said, picking up eagerly the ones she was shuffling toward him like a pack of cards for a new game. His hands were trembling.

"That's all there is," she said, almost leaning over the table with her bosom to make her gesture seem natural.

"Under that arm there—lift it, please," he said.

"Oh, that," she said, as if speaking of an absent person. "That is nothing. That is written in German."

"Not all things written in German are nothing, my dear young lady," he said, sneering. "Some things written in German might prove even more interesting than those written in Italian, you know. Besides, you forget that at the time I was about to marry you I had taken German lessons and was already beginning to master the language. So, German or no German, that letter comes to me now, young lady, and you had better lift your arm before I make you lift it, understand?"

She understood only too well and was determined to defend her letter.

"It is not addressed to you," she said. "One does not read letters addressed to other people."

"How kind of you to teach me manners, young lady. I too may have something to contribute to your education very soon, sooner than you expect. Give me that letter."

"All right," she said, still leaning on the table, "but first you must read these. I shall translate this one to you, after you have read all of the others and heard my explanation of what happened tonight. Not before."

"But after all these things have taken place you will, won't you?"

"Of course I will. You will probably not care to hear what it was. Let me tell you one thing: You know what I was about to do when you came in and frightened me so? I was about to come to your room."

"To my room?" he said, growing unsteady.

"To your room. To give you the good news and tell you not to worry any more."

"Oh. I see." He was very serious now, and much paler than before. "I see. You were coming to my room. Just like this. Very well." And he stepped forward, his two hands aimed at her head like two pincers. "But you are coming to my room anyway. You and the letter."

She withdrew in a hurry, almost stumbled over the chair as it fell backward, and made for the wall, with her letter under her left arm, pressed now against her side.

"You are coming to my room. You said so yourself. This time you are."

"No," she said, "please no. Let's talk here. They might hear us, see us—"

"Who cares? Haven't you been heard and seen before in

this house, in this garden, in the street where you belong? What difference does it make to you? You have no honor. Neither have I at this point."

He came to her like a dead mass, pressed her against the wall, bit her neck, then began to tear at her clothing.

"Help!" she cried. "Help—"

Her cries were suffocated by his hand. She could not breathe. Her body jumped like something shapeless thrown up by a volcano, while Crocifisso held his hand on her face. Someone else screamed, another murder attempt seemed to be taking place upstairs. The whole house came alive. Crocifisso ran out before anyone could see him, and Ludmilla stumbled to the floor, retching and moaning.

She did not faint. She managed to get out of the room and drag herself through the halls and then upstairs, while those terrible cries were still resounding. She reached her room and fainted there, where nobody could see her.

XII

❦

WHEN SHE CAME TO, the cries had died down, it was daytime, she felt rested, a bit cold, a bit sore on the neck and the breasts, but otherwise extremely well, and this gave her great pleasure.

Strange that I should not have realized it then, she thought. Of course that was the child. He or she rescued me. I wonder whether it is a boy or a girl. . . . For a moment the chance of Mary's death crossed her mind, but not wishfully so, just as a mere hypothesis. She dismissed it as improbable. And only then did she also dismiss it as too good to be true, telling herself, Good things do not happen to me; if this had happened, it would simply be terrible and nothing else.

It was then that, one by one, in a strange order of increasing unpleasantness, three notes and the letter came back to her mind, and Günther as an appendix to them. Her first thought, upon opening this mental package, was for Crocifisso.

What an imbecile, she thought. If he had only asked me, politely, I would have gone to bed with him and he would have finally known I was a virgin. I might even have liked the experience, or I might not, in any case it would have been a good solution. But thank God he did not. What a swine, and what a fool, a fool, a fool, a fool, a fool, a fool. For all his ugliness,

261

his blond legs and his *Lederhosen,* Günther is a thousand times better.

She was surprised at finding him, suddenly, beautiful. The moral ugliness of the one became physical beauty in the other at once, like water poured from one container into another.

But what about that letter to Günther? What would Crocifisso do with it? Show it to the doctor, of course.

Well, what of it? she told herself reassuringly. If *he* then taxes me with it, I'll simply ignore the whole thing. The letter is not addressed to him, it does not exist. Simple, clear and final. And if he insists, I'll tell him it was all because of him. Every one of these many mistakes was committed to help him. He had better shut up and thank me on his knees. . . . I wonder if it is a boy. But who will have the courage to go out of this room today?

She realized she was still lying on the floor. She undressed and went to bed.

But how well I slept on that carpet. Too bad I cannot use my energy to go out and make merry. May first. So this is a birthday. I wonder whether it is a boy or a girl. It must be early still. Not much light in the lines between the shutters. A cock in the distance. Tasso barking downstairs. I wonder what the children will say. Why don't I get up and go find out, ask, show a little interest? She is my sister, after all. What can happen to me? What can they say? She nothing, in any case. As for him, it is still early; if Crocifisso *has* given him the letters, I don't believe he has had the time to read them. Perhaps I can prevent it if I get there in time. Günther will come—here is a good excuse. I can say, "Don't let me go at this moment. Speak to Günther, make him understand. Give him that letter without reading it, prove to me that you trust me, and I shall prove to you that I am honest, worthy of your trust." Yes, that is the right thing to do.

She jumped out of bed in a hurry and got dressed again. Only then did she realize how tired she was. She staggered to the washstand, staggered back to her bed, staggered from chair to chair, from drawer to drawer, could hardly lift her hands to comb her hair, wished Adalgisa would come, did not dare ring the bell, was afraid of faces from which she might see how much everybody had learned about her during the night. Then she staggered downstairs instead of staggering upstairs, simply because it was easier.

The children were in the dining room. Everything was in perfect order! She remembered the chair; it showed no trace of its fall.

"Aunt Ludmilla, Aunt Ludmilla, the stork has brought a boy! We are all going to see it now."

Adalgisa was feeding them, trying to keep them calm. She threw a glance at Ludmilla which revealed more than a whole written accusation. Ludmilla felt faint again, made a great effort not to lean on the table and closed her eyes.

"I have not eaten since yesterday morning," she said, laughing nervously and most unsuccessfully.

"Here, Miss Ludmilla, here, eat something quickly, it will do you good."

Adalgisa had changed. She was being familiar, she patted Ludmilla on the back. Ludmilla burst into silent sobs.

"You must not cry, Aunt Ludmilla, this is wonderful. A boy!"

"You know," said Sonia, very seriously, "I heard Mama crying terribly during the night. Was she afraid the stork would not bring him here? I thought the stork had let the child fall from the roof, and then I had a dream that the stork had really let the boy fall and the boy had become a cup of tea!" She laughed. "A cup of tea."

Filippo also had his story to tell. "Sonia dreamed the whole thing. Mama never cried. I was awake all night, I know. The stork came through this window. I heard it as the window was being opened, then I heard the stork speak with Papa and then I heard him run upstairs. I really did."

"That is not true," said Sonia. "Storks aren't allowed in

houses. And then, how would a stork open a door? And speak?"

"Storks can do anything they want. They don't have to ask your permission. Are you a director of storks? An engineer of storks? A lawyer of storks? You are nothing."

"*You* are nothing. And a stinker too. Tfu!" Sonia spat into Filippo's face, wetting Ludmilla's face too.

"Shame on you!" shouted Adalgisa, and she slapped Sonia so hard that she cried.

"Storks don't open doors," Sonia kept sobbing in anger. "And storks don't go upstairs."

"They do, too," answered Filippo in that unpleasant tone of the child who plays the role of the baby because someone has protected him by hitting his attacker.

"Here, one for you too," said Adalgisa. "And if you don't behave, the stork will come back and take the boy away!"

They were both terrorized into silence.

"Is it possible?" asked Filippo.

"Anything is possible," answered Ludmilla, relieved by the whole scene.

Now came Kostia, calm, erect, adult in his great seriousness. "I have just seen the baby grow," he announced, before even saying good morning to his aunt. "It has not grown much," he added, "but some."

"Do children make noise when they grow?" asked Sonia.

"Children always make noise," said Kostia. "You cried all the time."

"And I was growing?"

"Of course you were," said Kostia, "but not because you were crying. Crying makes you grow smaller. Every time you cry, you lose an inch or so."

"And what noise do they make when they grow? *Zzzz*, like the flies?"

Everybody laughed.

"No," said Kostia finally, "they make no noise at all. The new boy does not cry."

"Has he not learned yet?" asked Sonia.

"What a fool you are," said Filippo. "You don't have to learn how to cry."

"Sonia cried all the time," said Kostia. "She cried so that nobody could sleep on the same floor of the hotel where she was sleeping."

Sonia was very proud. "Imagine, Aunt Ludmilla, I cried so that nobody could sleep in any of the rooms of the hotel."

"The floor, not the hotel," said Kostia.

"The floor, not the hotel," repeated Sonia. "Think of that, Aunt Ludmilla. Wasn't I stupid?"

"You still are," said Filippo, and he got himself slapped by Adalgisa again. He was about to cry.

"Careful!" said Kostia. "Watch out, you're losing an inch."

Filippo jumped down from his chair to put a hand over his head and say, "I am tall like this. Up to here. Same as yesterday. I have not lost an inch. But Sonia has lost many. If she had not cried she would be as tall as a mountain."

"Liar!" shouted Sonia.

"Come on, Sonia," said Adalgisa, "tell him you prefer it this way. If you were as tall as a mountain you could not live in your house."

"Right," said Kostia. "You could not even see us. You would have to climb down every morning and back up every night. And you would have snow on your head. And catch cold."

"Then I prefer it this way," Sonia said. "Will the new brother grow as tall as a mountain?"

"No," said Kostia, "he will cry, sooner or later. Life is full of sorrow."

There was a great silence, then Sonia said, "Thank God."

And everybody laughed, but Aunt Ludmilla had tears in her eyes.

"Here comes your father," said Adalgisa, and Ludmilla rose from her chair to congratulate him.

"Hurrah!" she said, flinging her arms around his neck and

kissing him three times, then hugging him and hugging him. "I am so happy for you, so immensely happy." She was.

He blushed, smiled, made a very austere face, then smiled again, patted Ludmilla on the back, kissed his children and said, "In a few minutes we will all go upstairs to see the new baby. Too bad that Mama is not well, she will have to stay in bed the whole day."

"May I go to see Mamachen?" asked Ludmilla, speaking to her brother-in-law.

"Of course, you should," he said, with an encouraging smile.

But Kostia said, "No, you may not. No one is allowed to see her unless she calls."

"Nonsense," said the doctor, surprised at this lack of respect on Kostia's part.

"She told me so herself," said Kostia. "Uncle Crocifisso is with her, they have important things to discuss and she does not want to see anybody until she calls."

Ludmilla looked at her hands; they were completely numb. She knew she would not faint. But she receded from the world into a deep sense of unhappiness that made her smile, then stare at everyone as if she had never seen them before.

"I wonder what on earth he is doing there," said the doctor, looking at Ludmilla with concern.

She found it useless to acknowledge his question. Soon enough he would know.

"Did she really say so?" asked the doctor, and Kostia, very seriously: "Yes, Papa, she did."

The next two hours were lived by Ludmilla in the limbo of nonexperience, as the worst form of moral torture she had known. She could say nothing, yet there was much to be said; she smiled when she realized that they thought her indifferent to their affection and their happiness. Indifferent? They would be to her soon; they did not know they were already indifferent because of the way they saw life—in other words, because they were in the right and she was not. She had no legs, no hands, no voice, no logic—only confusion and unhappiness. How well she understood the dead, who stay put and refuse to take part in things they no longer are meant to enjoy. Still, she had to drag herself upstairs to the third floor, with the children and the doctor at her side chatting and shouting excitedly because of the new life that had fallen among them like a blessing. As they passed the closed door to her mother's rooms, she remembered that she was still alive in there, but only for another few minutes.

Are they beheading me or skinning me alive? she asked herself. Or perhaps roasting me on the public spit?

And it surprised her that she felt nothing at all. She had drawn up her case against herself so clearly that she felt she deserved special praise plus a reward from Mary for renouncing those emeralds. She thought, Mary keeps her husband, keeps my part of the inheritance, and has a new child. What more can she ask? And all this just because I tried to be honest with her.

In the baby's room, while everybody else was bending over the crib and making unrestrained noises of delight much too coy for her to endure, she looked deep into the mirror and admired her beauty—all her own work, another aspect of her honest behavior. Here was the patron saint of this day! Had she been only a little less honest, Mary would be crying now instead of rejoicing. She would have completely lost her husband's love. He would be torn between mistress and wife, mistress and baby, mistress and family life, and no one could have done anything to repair the great havoc brought about by Ludmilla's fatal appearance. Because no one could have brought the scandal to the surface. She, Ludmilla, would have played out a comedy of real love with Crocifisso; she could have married him and settled down, perhaps in her own lover's house, and her joy in her love would have provided all the energy she needed to hide it and belie it. And yet she knew that, with all that, she would be much less beautiful than she was now. A few hours of the purest despair had done more for her beauty than all the cosmetics in the world, or even all the happiness in the world, could have done. None of the expressions assumed by her the day before to suit the various jewels had been equal to this. But what purpose had it all served? She was only more hated than ever.

"Aunt Ludmilla, don't you want to see the baby?" asked Sonia, sounding surprised.

Only then did Ludmilla realize that everybody was looking at her.

The one advantage of becoming an outcast, even if only for a short while, is that the worst in us no longer casts a shadow over the best (which must certainly exist, even if only in infinitesimal degree) and we discover to our astonishment that we actually are better than we imagined we were.

That was Ludmilla's discovery when she went to see Mary. With infinite sadness she held Mary in her arms. But she was unable to cry, while Mary, who, God knows, had no reason to cry, was even granted the sweet relief of tears. Ludmilla was sad in a dry, sterile way—without purpose, and with no relief in view. She held Mary in her arms and was surprised to realize that the jealousy dividing them had no deep roots. That it was a fairy tale, a shadow, that it was not true. Only the bond uniting them was true. Even Mary's husband was an outsider.

"Ludmilla, they tell me you are leaving today, that you found another man last night, and that no one knows who he is. They tell me all sorts of things about you that seem meaningless taken one by one, but if I consider them together they all mean that you feel lost and lonely, and I know why. Ludmilla, you too will soon have a husband and children. Forget this episode with Crocifisso, we were all foolish to believe that it could work and to set the trap for you. Please forgive us and stay."

"But there is nothing to forgive."

"Don't say that, Ludmilla."

"And besides, who am I to forgive?"

"What do you mean? Who has suffered more than you from this terrible situation? We have despised Crocifisso since yesterday. And we are glad he's leaving."

Mary was observing her sister closely, and to strengthen the effect of her words she added, "Even if his departure does create a new problem for us—to find a godfather for the boy."

Ludmilla smiled, but said nothing.

"In fact," Mary continued, "we both consider him very indiscreet and not at all a gentleman."

The outcast was beginning to see a chance of crawling back into the world. There was still that closed door and the criminal court in session behind it, but it was taking them a long time to judge her case, and this was a good sign. She should have been called in to receive her death sentence in person or to confront her accuser. Knowing her mother, Ludmilla could not believe that a person so starved for someone to punish would permit such an occasion to pass.

"Ludmilla, why are you brooding so?"

That was when the doctor came in and said, "Ludmilla, they tell me there is a gentleman asking for you downstairs. He has a suitcase with him. You will introduce him to me and then we will decide what to do."

"I was just telling Ludmilla," said Mary, "that she must not be precipitate simply because of this broken engagement. After all, Crocifisso was probably not the right person for her."

"Most certainly not," said the doctor.

Had there been any need of further evidence that the doctor was not in love with her and never would be, it was shown by his cheerfulness as he spoke about Ludmilla's new friend. He stopped halfway down to the hall, in front of a mirror, and began to explain to her that he had not really been angry with her the night before, but simply worried, and that she must not construe his reactions to imply lack of trust in her or disapproval of her going out late.

"Our own situation being so delicate, with the divorce and all that," he said, "we must be very careful as to what people might say about our family and our guests. You were not wearing a hat; this is not done. I hope the servants will not gossip about it. And then, of course, we are still in May, it is cold after sunset, you were not even wearing a warm coat."

He was looking at his own reflection in the mirror and feeling very satisfied with it. She was looking at hers and feeling even more satisfied than he, but quite dissatisfied with his indifference to her. Did he notice how beautiful she was? Not in the least; he was looking at his necktie, his mustache and his beard, at his coat and his waistcoat, his trousers, his shoes— and not a glance at her, not even for the sake of his vanity to see how intently she was looking at him. Oh, she thought, how I wish Günther were beautiful and elegant! That I should give this man the satisfaction of losing me to a monster like Günther is the peak of injustice.

"And of course you understand," said the doctor, who was now concentrating on his leg to make sure that the crease of his trousers suffered no interruption at the knee, "that it would be highly improper for you to leave this house in the company of a man. If you insist on going, you may go, but we must find someone to accompany you. As for this friend of yours, I shall have a look at him, then we can ask the police or the bank to let us know precisely what sort of family he comes from, and if he seems to be the right sort. He may see you here before you leave, and of course he will have to meet your mother too.. How does this strike you as a plan?"

"Oh, very good, very good," she said. "Let us go now. What are we doing here? Are we so very beautiful?"

In broad daylight, and against such a background of opulence, Günther looked even more what he was than in the starlit spring night: a promising adolescent bird-watcher and globetrotter who had kept all his promises except those connected with personal cleanliness. To grant a female to this type, no matter what sort of female and at what point in his life—past, present or future—would be a gross anthropological error. Such a type had no women, it had only books and tools for blazing jungle trails and utensils for cooking vagrant cats on open fires.

The doctor looked at Günther and made a great effort not to laugh in his face. He let an ugly noise escape from his nose; then, without trusting himself to speak, he made a gesture to Ludmilla meaning "Introductions, please." But it might just as clearly have meant "Don't keep me in this predicament or I'll burst."

Günther, distrustful of this strange man in morning coat and striped trousers, as he was of the furniture and everything else, stood there like an explorer who has finally discovered the native cannibals and does not quite want to shoot them down without letting them speak.

Ludmilla did not even greet him. After a first horrified glance she turned her face away and began, "This is . . ." She could think of nothing suitable to say. To mention his name, to state, "This is my fiancé," or even "a friend," would have been like committing herself. What she felt like saying was, "This is what I found at the zoo yesterday. Forgive me, I'll take it back where it belongs." But time was passing, and here she was, breathing hard, finding no words to finish her phrase. She tried again, twice: "This is . . . This is . . ." Then she said, sobbing in Günther's face, "No, this is not . . . this cannot be!"

And Günther, feeling (as he wrote afterward in seven hundred pages) that this was a great moment in his life, allowed his own sobs to make their dramatic entry into the texture of his speech and said, "Oh, my beloved one, please do not cry! I am here, *Gott sei dank*, your beloved one is here at last, to rescue you from this criminal mob!" (The words in German were " . . . *dein Geliebter ist nun endlich hier um Dich von diesem verbrecherlichen Pack zu retten!*")

Ludmilla's own sense of drama was hurt by the vulgarity of this display, and even more so by his utterly Germanic sincerity. She sobered up at once and took refuge on a blue velvet Récamier sofa where Günther could not reach her without crossing the doctor's path. Her only concession to drama was that she put her feet on the couch, and by this act lost the butler's support for the rest of her life. (Bernhard, who had at first let Günther wait for Ludmilla outside the house door, like a beggar, and had hoped that the doctor would not allow him to come in, was watching everything from behind the blue curtain that divided the drawing room from the entrance hall, and Günther's insult to the family had disturbed him much less than Günther's armored mountain boots on the blue Chinese rug. Also, the doctor irritated him by touching the glass top of a coffee table with his fingers; but he had to be careful with the doctor, who, in his estimation, was almost a member of the family. Besides, he counted on the doctor to take action against Günther and had already signaled the chauffeur to stand by in case a stronger hand was needed.)

Unfortunately the doctor's knowledge of German was exclusively medical and philosophical. Current German he understood only when it was spoken very slowly and clearly; German melodrama broken up by sobs was far beyond his grasp.

Günther, unaware of all this, wiped his nose with a handkerchief that was in itself a scandal, and, still sniffing and sobbing, he flung terrible curses at the doctor, his wife and his mother-in-law for making that poor angel Ludmilla cry.

"You are lucky," he went on, "that I have no time to call

the police. We are leaving on the twelve-forty-five express and there is no later connection for Ludwigshafen."

The only words the doctor understood were "police" and "twelve-forty-five express," and he quickly replied in his basic German, "Police in my house? I'll police you out of my house! No Ludmilla twelve forty-five. You twelve forty-five to hell!"

Bernhard thought most imprudently that the time had come for him to make his entrance, and he came in and asked, "Did you call?"

The doctor was about to say, "Yes, kick this fellow out of my house!" when the old lady's voice, that most forbidding, icy, soft and resentful voice, said, "Bernhard, no one asked you to come in here. Please leave us alone and shut the door!"

This was Ludmilla, little Ludmilla herself. No one had ever known she could speak in that voice. Bernhard froze at the sound of it, the doctor looked toward the Récamier sofa to make sure it was Ludmilla herself and not his mother-in-law speaking and then turned to Bernhard as if to repeat the order.

Bernhard melted out of sight, but, as he shut the door, he stayed between the curtain and the door to continue watching. He saw how Ludmilla now settled on the couch even more comfortably than before; her heels, which had only been near the velvet, were now pressed against a cushion, where they would certainly leave marks.

She looked, and felt, like a great Roman lady sitting down to watch the gladiators fight. This was her first experience of having two men struggle over her. Courtship and flattery had always pleased her but left her incredulous, and the moment a man managed to convince her of his admiration was the end of him, because she always concluded, with a phrase heard from Mary and from her mother, "How can any man be such an idiot as to fall for Ludmilla?" This, however, was different, this was like the *Iliad*, her favorite story; and stupid though she considered herself to be, she was enough of a woman to know that when two men exchange insults and blows over a woman, she dwindles to a symbol in their minds and at the same time rises to one in her own. She only wished that they would begin to throw things and wound each other, lightly of course, so that all her crimes of the previous night would be forgotten. She wished also that the doctor would look at her and see how beautiful she was.

But she expected too much. Günther, almost forgetting the train, had embarked upon an extremely well-documented lecture on the freedom of women in our age of enlightenment, their inferior position in Italy, and the obvious designs that these worthless Italians had on the money of rich foreign girls. He went on to insult the opulence of the old lady, the pretensions of the house and the furniture, the ugliness of the paintings, the statues and the art objects, and the ridiculous figure of that man before him with his mustache and his striped trousers and rolling eyes. And the doctor agreed to all this, nodding and saying like a puppet, "Yes, yes, but no police and no twelve forty-five." He was obviously going by the tone of Günther's voice and trying to give the impression that he understood German.

Ludmilla did not know where to interfere or how to take an open stand against Günther without losing the thrill of a real fight, but she was gathering courage to say something when again Bernhard came in, red in the face with indignation, and said to her, "Fräulein Ludmilla, you ought to be ashamed of yourself!" What made him act so imprudently was not only hearing the house and its supreme mistress insulted, but also seeing that, in Günther's excitement, his boots were beginning to touch the white bearskin on the floor and almost crush its red wooden jaws, and that, when he stepped back, the way a lecturer does, he almost sat on another blue velvet couch and soiled it with his greasy leather trousers. This time the doctor understood and tried to save face by telling Bernhard to do exactly what he was about to do on his own—namely, kick this man out of the house.

"Away from me, you ridiculous servant!" shouted Günther, planting his legs wide and putting one foot right on the bear's head. "I am leaving this ridiculous house, I don't want to stay here, and you, Ludmilla, are coming with me. This is no place for you!"

Ludmilla was paralyzed with terror. She had no will of her own and was so used to obeying orders that she feared her own weakness rather more than Günther's strength.

"I am not packed," she said. "I cannot come."

"You can come with what you have on," said Günther.

Bernhard intervened. "Fräulein Ludmilla is not leaving this house without her mother's permission!"

And the doctor again shouted, "No twelve forty-five Ludmilla! Get out of here, you!"

Günther shouted in his turn, "I shall not leave without Ludmilla! Ludmilla, obey and come away at once!"

"Not today," she said. "Tomorrow."

"Tomorrow?" He sneered, and she saw that he had put a hand to his belt, where he kept his camping knife.

"Please, Günther, don't!" she cried, while the doctor, Bernhard and the chauffeur began to push him out of the room.

But he disentangled himself and, while he waved a threatening finger in Ludmilla's face, shouted, "You said tomorrow? All right, you will pay for this. By God, you will! I am going now, going to the station, and if they don't exchange these tickets, you will pay for them! My poor mother has not earned this money with the sweat of her brow for me to throw it away because a stupid rich girl forgets to pack her things!"

And more quickly than the others could push him he ran out of the house. Bernhard made a very serious face in order not to laugh, the chauffeur went out laughing, and Ludmilla laughed so much that the doctor became angry.

"May I ask what has happened?"

At that moment Adalgisa appeared and said to him, "Madame wants you upstairs." And Ludmilla stopped laughing.

275

On his way to his mother-in-law's room, the doctor met his cousin coming downstairs, looking very proud.

"What is it?" the doctor asked, but he was not given the honor of an answer. The other bowed formally, closing his eyes to make it even more evident that this mark of respect was farcical, and disappeared. The doctor caught sight of himself in the mirror and did not like his face. There goes Satan, he thought.

When he entered the old lady's room she was sitting up in bed, pale, her chin trembling, her hands dancing on the blanket.

"Yes?" he said, and sat down. Then he thought, This was a mistake, I should have gone to her as I usually do and taken her pulse. But he had lost all faith in himself. I have it coming to me, he told himself. God knows where this is going to lead us all.

"Yes?" she asked, and he repeated, "Yes. You called me, I think."

"I did. And now I want you to tell me everything about my youngest daughter, Ludmilla. It seems that my trust in you was misplaced. Or was it not?"

"Your—your trust?"

"My trust. Misplaced, I said."

"Oh. No, I don't see why."

"How very strange," she said. But she could not go on in that detached tone.

"You are very pale," he stammered, terrified at his daring and expecting a violent rebuff. "Of course," he went on, as he saw that she was gazing absorbedly at some object behind his back, probably to avoid looking at his face, "of course, what right have I to speak?" Then he remembered that this kind of self-abasement, which always went down so well with the Jesuits, would not go down here at all.

276

"Yes, I am pale," she murmured.

He could not understand. This was like trying to decipher the meaning of a scene at the cinema without having read the caption that preceded it. He opened his mouth several times to ask her to explain what she had said, then decided to turn his head and follow the direction of her eyes. A mirror had been left standing on the mantelpiece. Now he understood. But how could she at such a grave moment in her family life still have thoughts and eyes for herself? This gave him hope and encouraged the liar inside him. It will be my last lie connected with this sordid affair, he decided; and he said aloud, "I was caught unawares. The only reason I failed to come and ask you for advice and help was that you have not been well at all these days."

"I know I am not well, and I hope this will soon help me out of the picture entirely, but that was no reason—I repeat, no reason—to keep me in the dark about these matters. Ludmilla is still my responsibility, not yours. You had no right to—"

Here she coughed, and he waited for the coughing spell to subside. It angered him to be kept in suspense by such a lack of self-control on her part. And he knew it was lack of muscular discipline; Mary did the same thing. Besides, her choice of words in condemning him seemed so inadequate that they sounded cynical and disrespectful to Ludmilla. What did she mean by his having "no right" to flirt with her? Of course he had no right. She should have said, "I am ashamed of you, get out of here and never show your face in this house again." That would have been adequate, not this "You had no right to," preceded by a justification of her taking the thing into her own hands.

The coughing spell continued and he had to do something irreverent for a culprit in front of his judge: pat the judge on the back and say, "Look at the ceiling." If he did not complete the phrase with the suggestion of the little bird up there, it was because he at least did have a sense of her dignity. The cough having subsided, he went back to his chair and she resumed her accusation in a lower key.

"You had no right to keep the things you knew about her to yourself instead of coming to her mother and saying, 'Your daughter has done this, that and that.' We would have been rid of her immoral presence long ago."

So she knew everything. But how, and since when, and in what light? These were the facts that still must be established before he admitted everything and asked her to spare Mary. Because he knew that, with her mania for sincerity, she would have gone to Mary at once, no matter whether this was or was not the right moment.

"May I ask you one question before I speak?" he whispered very humbly.

"Yes." She had fully resumed her solemn role.

"When did you learn the—the facts, and how?"

"This morning, from your cousin."

He decided to say nothing and let his silence be a witness to his profound contrition. But *she* said nothing.

Cleverer than I thought, he concluded, and he stepped out of his role to explore the ground again before he admitted too much.

"But may I ask to be confronted with the whole accusation? I swear to you I intend to conceal nothing. I know I have done wrong."

"You," she said, and her voice was now quivering under the weight of moral indignation, "you were guilty of allowing your cousin to suspect you of the most horrible things. If you had come to me, this would have been avoided."

"What horrible things, may I ask?"

"You know. And if you don't, I am going to tell you. Your cousin thinks that you and Ludmilla . . ." She coughed again and this time he would not have gone to her help if she had choked to death—he felt unworthy. She cleared her throat and

278

went on: ". . . . that you and Ludmilla . . . had something immoral in common."

"The swine. How does he think he can judge such a thing? And why did he come to you instead of asking me?"

"That is exactly what I told him. And I am glad that you have proven to me how wrong he was."

Here the liar made his official statement. "I did not have to prove it to you. My conscience is clear."

"I know. I see, and I never doubted it for a moment. At first I was furious with him for entertaining such base thoughts, but then, when he showed me the evidence, I understood."

"What evidence?"

"You will be given a chance to see it and enjoy it in the next few minutes. Let me finish with him before I give it to you."

"I want to see it now. For I too have my grievances against him." This was added in despair, as a shot in the dark.

"The evidence is here. These letters. He believed what he chose to believe, and it was something awful, unheard of, to believe or even to imagine for a moment, but it would never have come to this had you said to me in the beginning, 'Ludmilla is unworthy of your respect, she has no right to live under this roof or to call herself your daughter.' You chose to help her, you gave her a fair chance to redeem herself by marrying a respectable young man, but she obviously did not want to be saved. She thought she could corrupt even him. Well, I am glad she was wrong. I would warn any man to stay away from her, from my own daughter! Here, read these letters."

She first gave him the unfinished letters to Crocifisso; then she said, "And now listen to this." And she translated word by word Ludmilla's letter to Günther. "Now, if this is not madness, pure unadulterated madness such as can be dealt with only in an insane asylum, I ask you, as a doctor, to tell me what it is."

"May I see that letter in German for a moment?" he asked, and he took it with him to the window, where he could stand with the letter high in front of his face as if to read it better, and let the glow of shame slowly fade from his cheeks and his ears.

"Can you read German script?" asked the old lady, who had always assumed he could not. And in fact he could not, but she was eager to hear him say he could. He knew this from her tone, and he also knew why: she wanted to bestow greater virtues on those who still deserved her love, now that Ludmilla was gone from the world of the living. This sort of redistribution by her of the spoils of love had always saddened him. He chose not to answer her question and to mark his ignorance of German script by sounds of wonder and deception, while in reality he was thanking the Lord, and especially the Holy Virgin, for his narrow escape from danger, and swearing to them that he would never again be caught in such sinful temptations. This while maintaining his utter disbelief in God. It was his form of modesty: Who knows if I am not wrong and they right?

"What a sad day," he concluded aloud after a while. "A child is born, and an adult dies."

"Yes," said the old lady. "When your cousin told me a short while ago that Ludmilla had specifically asked him to live with her without getting married, and to keep this a secret from me, I refused to let him go on and asked him to leave the room at once. He insisted on telling me, he said he was speaking in Ludmilla's interest. I still did not understand why he had not gone to you instead of coming to me. But I let him continue. He said he was sure Ludmilla was trying to involve you too in her intrigue and to ruin you. Then he showed me these letters and I felt I could never recover from my humiliation. And I was right. I never will. This will shorten my life. It has already done so. I may die any moment. But I do not want to see that person again. Never, in any circumstances.

Let her do what she wants. Or perhaps not, because she does not know what she wants. I would have her interned. She is right in one thing: her sister was interned for less than this. It is the only truth I can find in her letter. All the rest is a pathological lie."

There was a long silence in which the doctor tried to decide whether or not to say that it would be a crime to have Ludmilla incarcerated, no matter how immoral she was. But the old lady had more to say.

"And to think that I silently chided Mary for her attitude toward Ludmilla! Now I see how right she was. Poor Mary, I must apologize to her for thinking her ungenerous. What were your grievances against your cousin, by the way?"

"My grievances? Oh, nothing. Indiscretions in front of the servants. But this justifies everything. Women like Ludmilla are fatal to mankind."

"This means," said the old lady, passing from condemnation to self-pity, "that I am fatal to mankind. I bore her, I brought her up. . . . Your cousin says she admitted to him having had intimate relations with countless married men. Countless, he said. Or she did, rather."

"Horrible," said the doctor, thinking of syphilis. "We must get rid of her without delay."

"Send a telegram to Luther asking her to come here, and send another telegram to Katia's doctor in Berlin. We must have her committed. When I think of poor Katia, such an angel . . . She may be insane, of course, but at least she is so for moral reasons, and she does not harm others. I must write to her too. I have been so neglectful of poor Katia lately. Tell me, what is this Günther like? Have you seen him?"

"Yes, a few minutes ago. And I kicked him out of the house."

"Why? What sort of person is he?"

"A German in *Lederhosen*. He wanted to take Ludmilla away with him."

"That might be a good solution. But why should we assist her in her criminal career? Why ruin another decent man? So you kicked him out. Is he going to return?"

"It seems so. Tomorrow, from the little I was able to understand. I shall find out."

"Do. But if he returns tomorrow, you must show him these letters, all of them, and explain everything to him, so that he knows what he is about to wish upon himself."

"I shall take care of everything." The doctor left the room, and this time he avoided his reflection in the mirror. Not that he feared to find his features scarred by hypocrisy, but he offered this sacrifice to the Mother of God—just in case she existed—as the first in a series of acts of contrition.

Ludmilla in the meantime had become optimistic. At least Günther was gone, the fool. Crocifisso would certainly be going, she was back in her room in her own bed, having escaped *Lederhosen* and Ludwigshafen, and the only thing that was still missing to make everything good again was her mother's blessing. Now, to reason logically and without undue fears, her mother's reaction could not be much different from the reaction of the butler. And if her mother had not called her yet, this meant that she was angrier at Crocifisso than at her. Besides, now that she was in bed she could feign a collapse (not a difficult task at that point—she was quite close to one), and time would bring clarification and forgiveness.

An hour passed, then two, then three. No one came. Time was working in her favor. Only one thing made her a bit impatient: that no one should have noticed poor little Ludmilla's disappearance and then come to her room and discovered poor little Ludmilla in bed, all alone and abandoned. She was her mother's daughter, after all, and self-pity was in her blood. Then she recalled the baby. How could she have forgotten him? So many things had taken place in those few hours. The child protected her, no doubt. Then she heard the little birds outside and saw their shadows playing inside the shadow of the big tree filmed by the distant sun on the screen of her curtain. This came to her as good news. Why should she be mistreated on a bright day like this one? It is a brief step from confidence that nothing is wrong to overconfidence that everything is right. She took the step. No one could praise her for those letters, even less for her scheme—it would take a superior intelligence to do so—but they were masterpieces; she regretted, in fact, not having them right there to reread. Like all born liars, she regarded herself as unlucky rather than stupid, and even in her ruin she praised herself for her great cleverness.

More time passed. She was hungry. She had eaten no lunch and no dinner. Gone were the birds, the tree, the sun, and still no one came in. She heard the distant voices of children, dogs barking; obviously no one cared, not even the servants. Or could they have been given orders to let her rot away like a leper? "But we will see who wins," she said, speaking aloud to the closed door that was not for her to open.

Then it did open and the doctor came in and flung himself on her, kissing her lips, her cheeks, her naked shoulders, and in the first moment of rapture she had not even seen that Mary was standing in the doorway. . . . She woke up with a scream; it was dark. Two o'clock in the morning from three clocks: dining room, cathedral, belfry in the hills.

It was a busy first of May, with a new life to be ushered in and a strong adult life to be considered worse than dead and crossed from their minds and hearts.

The doctor knew he could now enter Ludmilla's bedroom without fear for his good name. His conscience was at rest. He despised her and hoped that this could be discreetly inferred from his mournful demeanor and the glance of repressed indignation with which he asked what time it was, whether the children were out with Brigida, whether the new baby's nurse had been relieved by Adalgisa, whether there would be roast or stew for lunch, before he dared ask whether his cousin was back in his room and Miss Ludmilla out of hers. Since the servants knew everything, he wanted them to know a few additional things as well: Ludmilla was no longer a member of the family, and therefore he, his wife and his mother-in-law were to be spared all their malignant remarks. Nothing would have disturbed him more than to be known in the kitchen as cuckolded. In his Mediterranean world, a man whose unmarried sister-in-law had an affair was cuckolded, his wife's reputation suffered from it, his baby daughter would find it difficult to marry into a respectable family. The new cook was from Rome, and even though Rome is well up in the north, the doctor still felt uneasy.

He entered Ludmilla's room, waiting for Adalgisa to pass by before he opened the door, and making sure she noticed the expression of disgust on his face. Ludmilla was snoring, her head under a pillow. He closed the door again from the outside, wiping his hand with a handkerchief as if the knob had been soiled.

XIII

"How right you are," said the old lady in monotonous response to Bernhard's chatter.

And he: "Madame is right, not I. Madame is absolutely, one hundred per cent right." (He loved that new expression, picked up in London banking circles by Pierre, and by Pierre's mother from his letters.) "Madame has seen it with her usual eagle's eye: Fräulein Ludmilla is deranged. Something suddenly went wrong, and her behavior is exactly, but exactly, the same as Fräulein Katia's years ago, when I had just come to Moscow from Germany. But exactly the same behavior. If I only close my eyes when I see Fräulein Ludmilla, and think of Fräulein Katia, then reopen my eyes, I have the impression this is still Fräulein Katia in front of me, but exactly, as I said. Madame is so right! And, if Madame allows me to be impertinent and express an opinion of my own, Madame is also right when she says that the first sign of this mental disease is an exaggerated admiration for her own person. Poor Adalgisa was shocked this morning when she saw Fräulein Ludmilla in the nursery. Fräulein Ludmilla had not yet seen the baby, she had just come upstairs for the first time, the children and the doctor were all looking at that tender little thing in the crib, but not Fräulein Ludmilla. Where was Fräulein Ludmilla? In front of the mirror smiling at herself, exactly like Fräulein Katia before she was interned, but exactly. And I am no doctor of the mind, Madame knows this, I am just a poor butler in Madame's service, but I do have a mind, I reason, and I said to myself when Adalgisa was so flabbergasted, I said to myself in the silence of my modest mind, 'This is not good. This is not like Madame, this is not like Fräulein Mary, this is like Fräulein Katia years ago. But exactly. I did not say so to Adalgisa, because she has been in this house for only a few years, but I could have. Instead I said, 'Adalgisa, this is none of your business, hold your tongue.' I felt I had to be a little harsh because with these Italians one never knows, and besides, there were the cook, the chauffeur and the gardener there, and I thought this was not right that these low people should be allowed to criticize their masters. Even I don't do that, and yet I have seen everything since God knows when and Madame often asks me to say what I think, is that not so, madame? But let us not speak about me, let us speak about Fräulein Ludmilla, who is now in great trouble. Madame is absolutely right when she says that a person like that should be sent to a hospital where she can do no harm. Here she has already harmed a blue cushion, the back of the blue couch in the drawing room, leaving marks with her heels that will never come off. This morning she did this, while she was listening to the worst insults ever flung at this house—and by a German nonentity!"

The old lady smiled. *Nonentity* was one of her words.

"I see that Madame is smiling, but if Madame had heard what was said by that German nonentity downstairs I am sure that Madame would not have smiled. Against the house, against Madame, against Fräulein Mary and especially against the Herr Doktor, the poor Herr Doktor, unable to defend himself. It was all in German and the Herr Doktor understands no German."

"I beg your pardon, the Herr Doktor knows German better than I do."

"I know, madame, but not that German! A fine person does

not learn foreign profanity when he learns a foreign language! The Herr Doktor is far too educated to know those things, but we all know them because we know our own language. And Fräulein Ludmilla just sat there with her feet on the couch and smiled. Again, this tendency she has to mingle with the lowly. Has it ever been heard that a distinguished young lady should have such vulgar friends? It seems that she had promised to marry that young man, and Madame should see what his boots did to the rug, to the white bearskin and to the legs of a chair. And when Fräulein Ludmilla said she could not leave without a suitcase, what did that young man answer? That she would have to pay for the train tickets, because his mother had not earned that money with the sweat of her brow to see him spend it on stupid rich girls. I apologize for repeating this to Madame, but this was exactly what he said. I am almost sure that his mother must be a washerwoman or servant girl in some inn, because only the son of such a low person could be so vulgar."

"Yes," said the doctor to the old lady, "I think you are right. This is an excellent sign. A man who remembers what he owes to his hard-working mother, and has the courage to say so to a rich girl, is a good man. We should not dismiss him, you are right. But neither can we cheat him, and in that you are right, too. We must present him with the full case history, fearlessly, honestly, and if he still wants to marry her after that he may do so at his own risk. We are out of the picture. But where I don't agree with you is that she should be incarcerated."

"And suppose this young man turns her down, what are we to do? Keep her here? A nice example for Sonia. And besides, even in front of the servants . . . Quite apart from the fact that I would not want to live in the same house with such a person. I am not going to live much longer, so that solves the problem as far as I am concerned."

"Nonsense."

"Please, no unwanted encouragement to live. Let's be practical now. What will you do—send her out in the streets to do openly what she has begun to do in secret?"

"I don't know, but I still say she is not insane. I wish she were."

"I have thought very seriously about this. She must be insane. There is no other explanation. How could she, coming from a family like ours, develop such an inordinate taste for lying and deceit?"

"Some people just turn out badly. This happens, as the saying goes, in the best of families."

"You may be right as far as lying, stealing and killing are concerned. But not the other—not promiscuity."

"That too."

"Oh, no. If that were true, I would rather see her dead. I want to help her. We may send her to Vienna. There is a famous doctor there, his name is Freud, and it seems—"

"I know all about that man Freud. He studies dirty things. Now, I am a freethinker and an atheist, and I am passionately interested in psychiatry, but not in filth. Thank God there is a limit, and that limit is established by decency, higher morality, and even the tradition which is upheld by the Catholic Church. And, mark it, I detest the Church and what it stands for, except for certain rules about purity."

"So you would rather let her drift."

"We can pray for her and hope."

"How will you pray if you have no one to pray to?"

"Praying can do no harm. And it may help. One never knows."

"Well, I believe in God, but then, of course, I am a Lutheran. I believe in my conscience as God's instrument, I believe in doing things. Of course, a clean and serious institution such as the one Katia is in seems preferable to any experiment in this dangerous field."

"And I, who don't believe in God, believe that we should add specifically to the words '*sed libera nos a malo*' in the Paternoster a codicil for our protection from the evils of medicine: '*atque a medico.*' You Protestants do not believe in error and redress. Someone who is mistaken is either right, because he is destined to do wrong, therefore he is doing what he should, or else insane, because he fails to see your point. But with all this, we still seem to be getting no further. Let us wait until tomorrow, and after this young man has turned her down we can search for another solution and perhaps find one which the gods do not allow us to see this afternoon."

"Miss Ludmilla has not come downstairs for tea," said Adalgisa. "Shall I call her?"

"No," said the doctor. "Leave her alone. If she wants tea she can either ring or come downstairs."

"And if she is sick?"

"She is not sick. She is . . . she is . . . I believe she is trying to— Well, never mind. She is not sick. That much I know."

"Miss Ludmilla has not called and has not come downstairs for breakfast."

"Very well, Adalgisa, she will either call or come down when she sees fit."

"Should I not—"

"No, you should not. She knows we are here."

Sonia overheard and asked questions so that the doctor lost his patience.

"Out with you, children. I don't want anyone here. Adalgisa will take you to the playhouse in the garden, you will have a picnic there, and—"

"Will Aunt Ludmilla join us?"

"I don't know."

When he saw how sad Sonia looked, he added, "I only know that if you don't behave she will *not* join you."

"And if we do?"

"I don't know."

The doctor's conscience bothered him. That his mother-in-law should be strict in matters of morality he could understand, but that he should have thought of warning Günther, as his own contribution to the great cause of truth, seemed too much even for an Italian who believed in the principle that no man should help a woman deceive another man. He was losing himself in these considerations when he heard the doorbell.

"Ludmilla's last chance," he said. "Either this or the madhouse."

A few minutes passed, then a few more, and he began to wonder.

"Should it take him so long to come up from the gate to the house?"

The bell rang, angrily this time, the rusty cord was being pulled with such violence that he could hear it through the wall. Another few minutes passed; no noise of steps outside, none in the entrance hall. What was Bernhard doing? He looked into the hall. Bernhard was there, looking out into the garden, and down at the gate was the gesticulating shape of Günther.

"Bernhard, why don't you open the gate?"

"Not for that man."

"Open the gate, please, I am expecting that gentleman."

"You are expecting him?"

"Yes, I am. Let him into that room and tell him to wait for me."

"Not in that room."

"Why?"

"He ruins the furniture, he has nails in his boots, his trousers are greasy, his hands are greasy, his hair is greasy, I am responsible to Madame, this is her house."

"I say open that door and let him in. And then leave us alone, please."

"I cannot understand your German," said the doctor, after Günther had finished his first angry speech all in one breath.

Günther, after a brief hesitation, asked, "*Latine loqui?*"

"*Loquor,*" said the doctor, shivering in a momentary doubt as to whether he had used the right tense. He had never expected to be using Latin that day, and especially for a quarrel.

"*Quo usque tandem abutere patientiae nostrae?*" shouted Günther, with true Ciceronian indignation.

"Marcus Tullius Cicero?" asked the doctor with obvious elation. "*Catilinaria?*"

"*Ubi* Ludmilla?" asked Günther, his fists almost in the doctor's face.

The doctor did not want to be tempted into a fight, and all he could find to say was, "*Ne nos inducas in tentationem.*"

Günther smiled and said, "*Non sum Deus, sum Gunterus quidam.*"

But this time the doctor was beginning to realize that his Latin had never been suited for current conversation, and he said so in Italian. To which Günther replied, in a clumsy medieval Italian mixed with Latin, that he had come to get Ludmilla and where was she?

Italian now being established as a possible means for their communication, the doctor said that Ludmilla was not ready but would come in a little while. He then explained that he was very pleased to see Ludmilla engaged to a scholar and asked him to identify himself a little better. What did he do in life and what guarantees could he offer of being a serious man?

Günther pulled out of his shirt a Doctor's degree, summa cum laude, in Greek philology from the University of Heidelberg and another, also summa cum laude, in the history of art; then, almost disrobing to do so, he detached from his shirt the strings of a small bag tied to his back, and out came a few learned publications and articles, all bearing his name, Günther Korn. And now came his life history: something, in German terms, quite similar to the doctor's life history, only more dreary and more scholarly, because Günther was the son of a kitchenmaid in the household of impoverished princelings, and he had taught the classics not only to his master's proud and stupid children, but also to his own humble and intelligent brothers and sisters, all now working as servants or shopkeepers in the small feudal community, but all well read and eager to learn more.

The doctor had to make an effort not to engage Günther at once as his own and his children's tutor. He confessed to his own ignorance, his broken dreams of travel, study and academic achievement, and even his intention of marrying off Ludmilla to a cousin of his, whom he described as a nice person but not much of a scholar. He asked Günther what his plans were for the future and was pleased to learn that he might soon lead a group of his townsfolk on a guided tour of Italy and Greece. He was even more pleased to hear that Günther traveled third class and that Ludmilla would, too.

"Were you able to get a refund on your tickets yesterday?" he asked, noticing to his great shame that tourist German, the international blabber of the rich, was the only German he really knew well.

"Oh, yes," said Günther, "that is why I am so polite today. Besides, I know my Ludmilla."

"And where did you meet your Ludmilla, may I ask?"

"In the flowery realm of poetry."

"Yes, I quite understand, but, speaking in vulgar geographical terms, where?"

"This is a moving story that I can never tell without the balmy irrigation of tears. Unless, of course, I have a good cigar."

"There are plenty of Havana cigars here," said the doctor, opening a box and sniffing at it with delight.

"I have my own." And out of Günther's sack came two Tuscan cigars of a kind famous in Switzerland because they indicated at incredible distances the presence of the poor. They infected trains, wineshops and cheap inns with an acrid smell of urine, horse manure and various chemicals. The doctor knew those cigars only too well—they had been his only luxury in his student years; but he never would have dared smoke one of them now. He accepted one from Günther because he could not very well deny the young man the right to smoke his own cigars.

"Yes," said Günther, emitting the first mephitic cloud and leaning back, kitchen utensils and all, on the blue velvet couch. "Yes. It was my young master, Escarantus von Zittogen Temp, who had met Ludmilla at the school for young girls where she was staying in Switzerland, and he commissioned me to write love letters to her. His love letters, of course; I never saw the lady until after the seventy-ninth letter and the twenty-third sonnet. That is where I developed my taste for epistolary love, the most fruitful kind of love for a scholar—Dante's love, Petrarch's love, the love of those who did all the talking themselves and never let the women talk. When the women talk, a poor scholar is left without time and also loses his inspiration. Yes, I wrote beautiful letters, which inflamed Ludmilla's schoolmistress—the owner of the *pensionnat*—and even more her husband, who was a scholar himself, more than they inflamed Ludmilla, who never even read them until shortly before she met me.

"Prince Escarantus von Zittogen Temp was not a brilliant talker; he only had a great name and was what we call *ebenbürtig*—that is, eligible to marry a sovereign princess. His parents were not at all pleased that he should court a bourgeois girl, even though she was rich and beautiful, and at a certain moment, when they found that they could marry him off to one of the daughters or nieces of one of the ruling kings—I don't even know which one, because these things took place far above my mother's kitchen duties—I was called to the castle and told by the old prince and princess that, unless I stopped writing those letters and sonnets, I would have to stop teaching Latin and Greek to their older children, and my mother would have to stop washing their dishes. This meant losing our home and our livelihood—nine brothers and sisters and a widowed mother. So I stopped writing, and soon Prince Escarantus had to stop courting Ludmilla, not because Ludmilla cared about the letters but because all the letters addressed to her were to be read and censored first by her schoolmistress.

"Prince Escarantus had not made much headway with Ludmilla herself, but he had been invited to have lunch and dinner with her and had been granted many other privileges no outsider is granted in those schools. All this because of my letters. His natural timidity and his good manners had prevented the schoolmistress from realizing that he was hardly literate at all, that he was almost an outright idiot. In fact, his reputation as a scholar and poet had been greatly enhanced by his reputation for modesty. When he left and didn't write another letter for months, the schoolmistress, on her husband's instigation, urged Ludmilla to write love letters to him, which she did because they made her read the letters from me that she had never read before, and they even made her schoolmates learn my sonnets by heart. Some of these sonnets were in Latin; they became texts for translation exercises. But, of course, Prince Escarantus never answered Ludmilla's letters— he could not use my epistolary services without his father's consent. The sovereign princess did not want him after all, because even by her standards he was too unintelligent, and he went to kill lions in Africa, and had killed ninety-one when I left home a year ago. Now perhaps he has reached the two-hundred mark. I know that he was thinking of setting himself up in the lion-skin business in America, which would be a blow to his parents, who believe that all trade is dishonorable for a Prince von Zittogen Temp.

"But very soon the husband of Ludmilla's schoolmistress came to Schloss Zittogen and asked to meet the author of the letters. The old prince, who is a real gentleman, told him the truth and sent him to me. So I found myself suddenly treated as a great scholar and invited to lecture in Ludmilla's school. That is where I met her and fell in love with her. Reasons of honor prevented the schoolmistress from giving me a steady teaching job at her school or letting me court Ludmilla, and I also preferred it this way because Ludmilla made fun of me. This of course was her right, but I knew that my sonnets and letters flattered her very much. The schoolmistress and her husband wanted me to publish the sonnets, but as they were written in the service of young Prince Escarantus, his father, who had the last word in this, forbade me to publish them under my name, and I, of course, refused to have them published under his son's name. So they will remain unpublished until one of us dies and the other can give them a name. In the meantime I too became a victim of my letters, because they had flattered me as much as they had flattered Ludmilla, and I became so unhappy that the schoolmistress decided to pay for my tuition at Heidelberg, and, to prove to them my gratitude, and also to impress Ludmilla, of course, I completed my doctor's dissertation in six months, and another one in another six months, whereupon I received two degrees, both summa cum laude, and enough money to take a trip. I visited Italy and wrote a book on the antiquities in Apulia."

At this point the doctor had tears in his eyes, and it was he who became sentimental. "Apulia?" he said. "My home? And you, a stranger, know more about my home than I do?"

"Oh, perhaps not," said Günther, shaking the ashes of his cigar nonchalantly onto the white bearskin, unnoticed by the doctor. "I am writing a second book on Apulia. It is to be called *Götterwandlungen von Griechenland nach Apulia*. It is all about the metamorphosis of Grecian deities as they crossed the Adriatic."

The doctor was ashamed of himself and his wasted time and his abandoned projects. He had already forgotten about Ludmilla, almost even about his new son. He was back home again, but more intensely so than ever before, through the magic of this Germanic monster in front of him.

"Yes," said Günther, "I hope to study Apulia more thoroughly next time, in a matter of months, if I can help my mother first. Because, you see, my mother lost all her savings to the old prince. When they heard that I was in Switzerland and someone was paying for my studies in Heidelberg, the old prince, who had spent too much money to present his daughter at court in Berlin, thought that I was being kept by Ludmilla's rich mother and felt that if I had become rich I owed him a percentage of my wealth, because I had in a way stolen that wealth from his son. Besides, I had made the connection while in his service. So he asked my mother to lend him some money and she gave him everything. When I came back I asked him to repay her money and we were chased out of the village, homeless. Fortunately for us, one of my brothers is employed in a chemical factory in Ludwigshafen, and that is where my mother lives now. He has bought an old tavern for her and she goes on washing dishes there and serving beer and sausages."

"Enough said, young man." And with these words the doctor hugged Günther and kissed him like a brother, on the lips. "We are brothers," he said, "and, as a brother, I owe you complete loyalty. Nothing would please us more than if you married Ludmilla. But you must know the whole truth about her. You read Italian, here are a few letters she wrote to the man she was engaged to, and here is a letter she wrote to you before writing these three. Read them all, they are the documents of a morally unbalanced personality. You must know what you are getting into. In the meantime, let me go and speak to Ludmilla. And before I forget, please stay for lunch. I also want you to see my newborn son. I am sorry I cannot ask you to become his godfather. In a moment of unfortunate rashness, I asked somebody else. But then, this all depends on your reaction to those letters. So now read and form your judgment. And allow me to suggest that you be lenient. You can do so much for her."

He left the room, and immediately afterward Bernhard, led like a hunting dog all the way from the kitchen by a trace of acrid smell, entered the room and shouted to Günther, "Look at that filthy scum with his boots on the silk chair! Look at the ashes on the bearskin! Look at those filthy iron things on the blue couch! Out of here, back to the gutter where you belong! This is Madame's house, and I am responsible for it!"

Ludmilla had stayed awake from two o'clock until sunrise, then had fallen asleep, because it was too early to call anyone, and she was too weak to get up. Günther's ringing the bell woke her up again, and the birds were singing and their shadows were clear on the white curtain, just as they had been before.

That was yesterday, she thought. It is the second time I have seen the sun come in from there. It must be close to noontime, and no one has come.

She rang the bell and Adalgisa came.

"What time is it? Where is everybody? Why has no one come in for two days? I could have died, in fact I was not well, am not well now, why am I left alone like this?"

Adalgisa was too kind to tell her the truth. "We did look in several times, you were always asleep. The doctor thought you needed a long rest, so he said, 'Don't disturb her, she will call.' So I did what I was told to do. Do you want some breakfast now?"

Ludmilla was very much tempted to say no. She knew this would have been the wisest thing to do, in fact the only thing, but the mere mention of breakfast made her dizzy with hunger.

"I don't know," she said. "I am still much too sick, perhaps I should eat nothing at all." Seeing that Adalgisa was likely to believe her and obey her, she hastened to add, "But then perhaps it would be unwise."

"I personally think you should eat something."

"You are probably right, Adalgisa. But where is everybody?"

"The doctor is downstairs with a gentleman, the children are out with my mother. I was supposed to go out with them, but I wanted to see how you were, so I asked my mother to go in my place. And Madame is upstairs in bed, and the Signora is also in bed, and the baby is with the new nurse. That is all. What shall I bring you—eggs, meat, sausages, coffee, tea, what?"

"Oh . . . I would say a bit of everything. But I don't want to be disturbed while I am eating. So don't tell anybody and don't let them come in."

She blushed because her game was much too obvious, so she made it worse by trying to correct it. "You know how doctors are. If they say you should not eat, then they shout at you when you're eating. So don't tell the doctor I'm eating. As a matter of fact, tell anyone who asks you that I don't want to be disturbed. I am asleep. No, not asleep—not well. That's it, not well."

Adalgisa nodded without changing her expression and left. Those few minutes before she came back with a huge tray full of good things were for Ludmilla the longest she had ever lived. This was her first experiment with self-imposed hunger.

"Lock the door and stay here till I finish," she said. Then, as she was ashamed of being observed in her passion of eating:

298

"Open the window and look outside, see if there are any clouds."

"Not one."

"Flowers in the garden?"

"Many, a great many, the whole alley is in bloom."

"Many birds in the trees?"

"A great many. Can you hear them?"

"I can."

Another gulp, another sip, a sigh, then: "Take this away. I am finished."

And she had finished everything. Not a crumb left. And still a rage to eat more, and more and more, forever.

"Close the window again, it is cold."

She leaned back on the pillow, in a state of drunken delight. We'll see who wins, she thought. They cannot chase a sick woman out of the house.

And she believed that because she was less afraid than she had been the day before, the others should also be less angry.

When the doctor came in, he too was unable to pick up the old threads of his recent indignation and be inspired by them for his new role. And without that emotional premise he had nothing to say; in fact, he almost had to apologize for coming in without permission. This proof of his weakness irked and humiliated him, and these two added emotional weights weakened him even more. But it was late for him to withdraw and make a better entry.

Why did I let my beautiful anger seep through my fingers yesterday? he thought. What a different show that would have been!

But no matter how hard he tried to revive it, he was unsuccessful. He cared too little for his part in this business and was too happy about his new child.

"How are you?" he asked, as he saw Ludmilla rested and indifferent and knew therefore that she would notice all his mistakes. His tone was not even interrogative enough to lend life to the question. Because the question stood for "Are you ready to be judged? Why don't you spare me the effort and give proof of contrition so that I may quickly absolve you and send you away?"

"Very well," she replied, with intentional clumsiness, to suggest an untruth and a will to conceal it.

He took his time examining these words, as if there were a riddle in a fairy tale. He repeated his question: "How are you?"

"Very well."

This was worse than a riddle; it was a closed fortress. One cannot judge a blank wall. So he begged to be let in.

"We did not come for you, because you were always asleep. And besides . . ."

He shrugged his shoulders and began to pace the room, his hands behind his back. This was a triumph for her, but it gave her enough strength to weaken her, because she allowed herself to look at him while he was looking at the birds in the tree filmed on the curtain. She saw how handsome he was, and how little he cared about her.

"He wants to send me away and doesn't know how to go at it."

And while she realized that she had lost her strength, he was gaining new vigor from the sight and the song of the birds. Someone upstairs, someone he had met .yesterday for the first time, was as new to the world as these birds to the season. The doctor sniffed and said, "Smells of fried eggs and coffee—I am glad you had your breakfast. Let's open the window. Do you mind?"

Ludmilla said nothing, but her silence had no power. He pulled the curtain apart, opened the window and said, "Aaaah!" The next minute he was leaning outside, inhaling the perfumes of spring with the snuffling of the just and saying to the birds in the tree, "How can anyone stay in bed on such a morning?"

And Ludmilla said, "Not everyone can leave his room even on such a day."

He leaned out and called, "Adalgisa!"

The maid's voice answered something Ludmilla could not understand, but it was joyful and innocent, because any voice thrown into a bright day in spring picks up flowers and purity like the jeweler's needle feeding pearls to a string.

"Why aren't you in the park with the children?" he asked, and the maid's answer sounded apologetic but innocent again.

"All right," he said, with the voice of forgiveness. And Ludmilla wished those words had been addressed to her, as a closing remark to a conversation which was still to begin.

"Well," said the doctor, leaving the window and coming toward her. His cheeks were pink, his eyes proud, and he looked at the mirror to correct the slant of his necktie and approve of himself as he had approved of the world. "How are you?" This time the question had a different undertone of medical politeness. It sounded like "And how is our patient doing this morning?"

Again Ludmilla said nothing.

"What time is it?" he asked, looking at the watch on her night table. "Eleven-fifteen already?" He pulled out his own watch. "Mine is slow. It can never be trusted." That last word hit the mark solidly. "But," he added, "this is a minor matter." He smiled again, and Ludmilla felt humiliated.

What is he expecting of me now? she wondered. That I approve of this joke?

"May I sit down?" he asked after he had sat down. Now he began to look at her, and she looked at the carpet between them. It was too late to avoid his face, she had seen it already and been bewitched by it. A faint metallic noise made her lift her eyes cautiously to his waistcoat; his hand was playing with the chain and the watch. Her approval of this play took in her mind the form of a confession. She wished it would suffice; words had strayed from the truth in those letters. Her license to speak was withdrawn; his was still good, why did he hesitate to use it?

He made a final effort, swinging the chain around his index finger and unswinging it, then said, "So we are all your beastly persecutors, it seems."

"No, you are not," she said. Her tone would have been adequate only to say, "I love you."

"But not only are we your persecutors, your jailers, your enemies, we are also your friends."

She looked up. This sounded hopeful.

He saw the grateful look and killed it instantly. "This is not my opinion. I am only quoting you. Did you not say to me that I was your only friend? Every single person you meet seems to be your only friend. You are truthful in every direction. What shall we call this, plurisincerity?" He liked his little joke and allowed himself a self-congratulatory chuckle.

She did not have to look into the mirror at this point. She knew she looked like a homely schoolgirl.

"Ludmilla?"

"Yes."

"Ludmilla, tell me."

Her eyes met his, pleading for mercy. "What?"

"Why?" Fearing she might not understand, he repeated and clarified: "Why must you do such ugly things?"

She put both hands on her face to hide it. This movement was too calm and defensive. He wanted more for his taste. She understood this and threw in a few sobs, without crying. Then, artificially diminishing the sobs until she brought them to a standstill, she said, with a spent voice, "Don't ask me."

"Too easy a way out. No, Ludmilla, I am sorry, but I must have an answer to my question."

Now the sobs broke out naturally. "I don't know. If I knew, do you think I would do them?"

"But this is very grave."

"I want to die."

It took him time to identify these words between her sobs, and his answer was cold. "Ludmilla, stop that nonsense. And don't say that you don't know why you do certain things. This might be dangerous for you, were you asked precise questions by people who—" He stopped.

"People who?" She too was cold. This sounded much too strange to admit of comedy, or even to evoke real tears.

"People who might wish to . . . imprison you. Your mother said that she found one correct statement in your letter: 'For less than this, my sister was interned.' Now, Ludmilla, I don't think you should be interned and I don't think you are a bad woman."

This had a false sound, but the words were so good that she preferred not to think of the tone. "Your cousin says I am."

"Who is he to say so? Men are all so conceited; they think they know. Dear Lord, who knows anything of life, even of himself? Know thyself, says the proverb. Who does? No, Ludmilla, you are not a bad woman. You are only a bit stupid. This does not mean that you are unintelligent. You have a quick mind, but when it comes to living you are stupid. You are too independent. You need guidance. Any woman needs guidance. You had too little at home."

He lowered his voice here, as if he did not want to be overheard, because this was like siding openly with Ludmilla against Mary and her mother. Ludmilla became attentive, while remaining mistrustful.

"And no wonder. You simply had no home. Circumstances, your mother's constant travel, she herself being a very lonely woman hard hit by fate—no wonder you were kept in school too long. And in school you knew flattery and had your first success as a woman—but that is not apt to sharpen one's wits. On the contrary, it dampens them. Flattery is dangerous, even for men; imagine what it does to a young girl. A girl needs someone she can trust, not someone she can charm and enslave. She needs a father, who will not flatter her but help her guard herself against her own vanity. You never had that help. That is why you fling yourself at every man."

She shuddered with horror. "Every man?"

"Well, one is enough, if he is not the right person. Two are a multitude. But you can change."

"I cannot change."

"Ludmilla, don't ever let me hear such stupid things. Self-abasement is proof not of humility but of pride: you put yourself on the devil's list and you do so only to humiliate those who had warned you. If Mary Magdalen could change, why can't you?"

"Well, you have placed me rather low."

"Low—here again is your pride. I said Mary Magdalen to quote an example. Don't misconstrue my words. Yes, Ludmilla, I believe you can change. I have, in fact, great confidence in you. I think you are a good creature."

Having now gone so far in the direction of pure moral praise, the doctor felt inflamed by the high motives that were prompting that praise and also felt he could look at his sister-in-law with affection, or, rather, with charity, with hope—hope for her, not for himself. But there is nothing in the arsenals of lust so self-igniting as detachment and charity. The soul groping through the dark for the kindred soul finds the body in its way and embraces it unknowingly, recognizing it later as the body of that soul.

"You are a good child, Ludmilla," he went on, aflame with the sight of her shoulders. "A good child, Ludmilla, a good child."

He drew his chair closer to the bed and threw a terrified glance at the door, and it was now her turn to become frightened. Never before had she known what it meant to want a man. Now she did. What made it all the more dangerous was that she felt no shame. Had her own mother walked in at that moment, she would have thrown the bedsheets off her body, as a warning to her, and said to him, "Come and lie with me; her presence is obscene, ours is pure." What made her say the thing that killed her happiness was the thought of his happiness.

"All your big words," she said, slowly, because of the effort it cost her to lie in this moment of truth, "are only aimed at seducing me. You are a swine."

She regretted at once not having added, "I am a virgin." But she took this failure as just another sign of the fates: it was written that he must not believe it. And she watched her one chance of happiness fade from his eyes.

"Ludmilla," he said, "how can you think such evil thoughts? My impulse was as pure as could be, I swear it on the head of that child upstairs."

He did not have to swear; she knew he was speaking the truth. The only thing that saddened her was the immediate return of his sense of righteousness. He was no longer terrified that someone might walk in.

"I am surprised and shocked," he said. "All I feel for you, and all I felt before you insulted me with your vulgar remark, was, and still is, and will forever be, pure human affection— namely, a desire to give you friendship, to make you feel that you are not alone."

She was beginning to feel tired. The effort had been too great. So she decided to confront him with a different question, one that had to be asked sooner or later, at the risk of appearing cold-blooded again. She rearranged her nightgown, pulled the bedsheet up to her chin and asked, "What do you expect me to do now? What is to be my first step toward salvation?"

"Why," he said, "either marry that German, who seems to be a decent fellow, or—"

"How do you know he is a decent fellow? What proofs have you?"

"I have spoken with him for an hour and a half."

"When? This morning?"

"Yes, he came early, as he had promised."

"Is he still here?"

"Yes, he may even stay for lunch."

"Oh. So he got his refund on those damned tickets after all. And you found him enchanting."

" 'Enchanting' is not quite the word; serious, rather." (She smiled.) "Well read, honest, intelligent, and, above all, devoted to you."

"The father I so needed. A bit young for a father. And if I were allowed to choose, I would choose one a bit cleaner. My own father, whom I vaguely remember, was a great gentleman, presentable, clean-shaven, with long trousers—and no kitchen utensils on his back."

"Ludmilla—Ludmilla dear, dear Ludmilla . . ."

She became frightened again by his tone. "What is it now?"

"Ludmilla, he is your only chance. And you seem to forget: If he . . ."

She caught his meaning at once. "Has he seen that letter?"

"What letter?" The doctor knew what letter, but he was trying not to tell a lie.

"What do you mean, what letter?"

"Of course not."

"Are you sure? Can you swear?"

"Ludmilla, see how your pride gets the better of you all the time. Instead of being humble, you act as if you had a right to judge. Why should I swear? Don't you trust me?"

She weighed her answer for a very long time, then decided to pretend she believed him. But she decided also to make him pay for her pretended confidence.

"I believe you, don't look at me that way. I only said so because I know you very well by now, you Italians. A woman has no right to cheat another man. Even if he's your worst enemy, you owe him loyalty, just in case he might forget to be as fair with you the next time."

"Ludmilla, how can you be so cynical?"

"I am not being cynical, I only want you to understand that I know very well why you did not show him that letter—because you understand that a woman too has her own dignity. Or has she not? I can assure you that if Günther ever saw that letter I wrote in a moment of madness, he might be the handsomest, richest, most intelligent man on earth, I would not want to see his face again, ever, ever."

The doctor felt his ears grow red. "Of course," he said, "of course, that is logical."

"Logical or not, I don't care. I want you to understand my feelings and to agree with them. Or disagree. But say which."

"But, Ludmilla, I have said so already, I don't have to repeat myself. Or do I?"

"No. If you told me the truth you do not. At times, you see, I forget that Ludmilla is the only liar in a house of truthful people."

"What nonsense, Ludmilla. Why always this self-abasement? I have told you already, it is a sign of pride."

"What is so wrong with pride? You have none, I suppose." He seemed annoyed, and she became frantic again. "And suppose I did not want Günther for a husband, what other avenues are open to me now?"

"Your mother thinks you should be committed to an asylum."

"I know. That does not surprise me at all. It is reciprocal. But she can do it to me, while I can't to her. My bad luck."

He gulped that down with difficulty, thinking how much of Ludmilla's reproach was aimed at Mary, and feeling like a coward for not defending her.

"Well, what other chances, you ask? Your mother thinks—"

"I know what she thinks: I should go and live with Luther."

"Right."

"And telegrams have already gone out to everyone concerned or not concerned: the insane asylum in Berlin, Luther, Pierre of course—"

"No."

"Are you sure?"

"Quite sure this time."

"This time? And how about the other time?"

"Oh, Ludmilla, really! I said 'this time' to avoid further questioning."

"All right, all right, I believe you."

Now there came a long silence, and the birds filled it.

Finally Ludmilla decided to speak. "I know only one thing: If you send me to Luther, I am going to kill myself. I'd rather go to a mental hospital."

"What is your wish, then? Tell me honestly, please. I must know."

She listened to the birds now deliberately, then she looked at their shadows, then she sniffed the clean air, thought of the children and felt tears rise in her throat, her nose, her head, and swell her eyes.

"I want to stay here," she mumbled.

"What did you say?"

Whether he had actually heard her or not was unimportant. She knew that it could only hurt him to acknowledge it. She looked at him with love and said, clearly and distinctly, "I want to travel. Go to Italy and Greece, look at paintings and monuments, do excavations and the like."

He was beginning to understand, and he seemed relieved, but not quite trusting yet.

"But how? All by yourself?"

"No, no. Not by myself. With him, helping him in his work."

"Well, at long last! I see. Then—then you love him."

"I don't know." Again there was a pause. He seemed to want it so, and she took pity on him. "Yes, I imagine I do."

Then, having gathered strength for a new lie, the final one, she said timidly, "I love him very much."

Had this been meant for him, the doctor could not have been happier. His joy found a natural outlet in a resumption of his moralizing.

"And now be honest with me, Ludmilla, and tell me, how could you, loving him as you do, write such a base letter?"

Tears were beginning to roll down her cheeks, to expand and fade into the linen of her bedsheet.

"Don't become upset again," he said, patting her hand like a good doctor. "All is well that ends well, and we promise to reform, do we not? Count on my help."

She looked at his movements as he prepared to leave. Another quick glance at the mirror, with another straightening of his necktie; then he discovered that his fingers were dirty from the window sill and asked her permission to wash them. A bit of water in the basin, and she was suddenly reminded of her appendicitis operation, when she lay on the table in terror, and the surgeon, washing his hands of the whole thing, was talking to the nurse and looking at his knives with beastly pleasure.

"Tell Madame that I will see her later," said the doctor to Bernhard, whom he met outside Ludmilla's room.

"But, Herr Doktor, it is about that man who does not want to leave the house. The Herr Doktor should see what he has done to the couch."

"Do as I told you. Tell Madame that I will see her later."

XIV

"WHAT I DON'T UNDERSTAND about these documents," said Günther to the doctor, pointing to Ludmilla's letters on the table, "is that they tell me such horrible things about you and your family. Why did you give them to me? Do you want me to believe that you really kept Ludmilla a prisoner and tried to marry her off to a man she did not like?"

"No, no," said the doctor, realizing that, in his haste to be sincere, he had given Günther the three notes in Italian which were not self-explanatory at all, and the letter in German which was incriminating only for him, not at all for Ludmilla.

"What then?" asked Günther.

"Oh, that was all my mistake. I don't want to tell you the whole story. In fact, I hope you will not tell Ludmilla I gave you that letter. Please destroy it."

"Never," said Günther. "This is the most beautiful love letter I ever received, in fact the only one. And it is so dramatic, so well written! Ludmilla is an extraordinary creature! There is poetry in this letter. Even the other three are good; I like them. Obviously she must have written them to that Italian you wanted her to marry. She was trying to deceive him and to reassure him with regard to her love for me! How truly feminine and how poetic! What inventiveness! If women told the truth, I believe that the world would lose more than half of its drama! Have you noticed how she refers to my ugliness? Charming! I must congratulate her on it!"

"No, please do not. You know . . . I should never have shown you those letters. I did it out of sincerity, to make you aware of Ludmilla's psychological complexity. But I spoke to her a few minutes ago, she knows you are here and she will soon join us for lunch. And she said she would never want to see you again if she knew I had given you these letters."

"Oh, how touching of her! How true to her nature—she is shy, she lacks faith in herself. She should be encouraged, rather than held back. She should be told not to be over-modest. She has a right to live, she is young, she is beautiful, she is a goddess. We are all at her feet. You too, I hope. I wrote a poem in Latin while you kept me waiting here. Two poems, as a matter of fact. One about the stupidity of your butler, who came here to insult me because I was sitting on this couch. And one for Ludmilla, in which I liken her to the breezes of spring, coming and going eternally, combing the trees, listening to themselves in those borrowed vocal organs. I hope she will like it, but I fear that her knowledge of Latin is too faulty. Don't you think it is?"

"Yes," said the doctor, "but all the same, could you help me in this? I—I told her a lie. She was so horrified at the thought that you might have read those letters, I confess I did not have the courage to tell her you had."

"Yes, but I cannot tell her a lie. If she tells lies, that is her right and her charm, but a man telling lies—don't you think that would be rather odd?"

"Yes, I do, but at times, for the sake of peace . . . Life is —I mean the circumstances of life . . . You know what I mean. And of course I don't want you to tell her a lie, only to wait a little with the truth. Could you do this for me?"

Günther looked at him. He clearly understood what had been asked of him, even though it had all been in Italian, and he concluded with a smile, "How true, Italians look like men, but their souls are so feminine."

On any other occasion the doctor would have strangled a man for such a remark. But this time he stood there and whispered, blushing, "That is not true at all. But I *must* ask you, please, not to mention those letters for the moment."

"All right," said Günther, "as you wish. Only may I ask you, why *did* you show them to me?"

"My dear friend," said the doctor, folding his hands as if in prayer, "you want to know too much. Why this, why that, why does it rain, why is there a moon—dear Lord, if we want to know everything, as Dante so appropriately says, there would have been no need for the Virgin Birth." And he quoted from the *Divine Comedy:*

> State contente, umane genti, al quia
> Che, se potuto aveste veder tutto
> Mestier non era partorir Maria.

"Lunch is served," said Adalgisa. "Shall I call Miss Ludmilla?"

Bernhard refused to serve at table that day and it was just as well, because Günther's table manners were not apt to charm. Nor to reassure the doctor, who was looking at Ludmilla all the time while Günther spoke of learned things, and then again while he himself expressed his (to her) very exaggerated admiration for Günther's learning. And yet Günther said beautiful things, each one better than the last, which escaped Ludmilla's appreciation, partly because they were spoken in a mixture of learned Italian and learned German, plus Latin and Greek exemplifications, partly also because of her own affliction. The doctor had never made greater concessions to stupidity and ignorance, or to what seemed a profound lack of interest in classical scholarship. But he felt, and he knew that she felt, that this was not a learned exchange between scholars, but a deal on the slave market, and its resemblance to the ways of antiquity was clear.

"Hear, Ludmilla, hear what our friend Günther just said about the spirit of the dance in ancient Greece. It is a new, a most original, conception of Greek drama and Greek life."

And Günther, making him feel like an illiterate rich man, if not like a rich lady who feigns interest in things that make her eyelids droop in the face of the speaker: "Please, don't exaggerate, my friend, this is not my conception and it is nothing new. Jane Harrison, the English scholar, said this in her first books almost twenty years ago; every beginner knows it."

"I see, I see, how very arresting all the same. And our friend Ludmilla, I am sure, had never heard about it. What a rare privilege. How I envy you, Ludmilla, how I wish I had not given up my interest in these studies." He could not very well invoke his poverty as an excuse, but by the time he thought of that he had already done so and could not contradict himself. "Yes, yes, yes, how fortunate are those who can afford to devote all their time to poetry, archaeology, the contemplation of the past and of beautiful forms. I had to take care of my seven orphan sisters and of my father's impoverished land."

"But you certainly have all the time you would want now," said Günther. "You are richer than I am, no duties hold you back, you travel a great deal, from what you yourself told me, why don't you write poetry, visit museums and read Jane Harrison? I do these things, and yet I own nothing on earth but my rucksack and my cooking pots. I don't even have a library, while you have. I have seen only a few of your books: you even have Jane Harrison's last book, published six years ago, called *Prolegomena to Greek Religion*. It is beautifully bound in red leather and gold, but it shows no sign of having been read. The same could be said of many other English books in your library."

"Oh. Oh, I see. That surprises me. Of course, I don't know English."

"Neither do I, but I read it. Who reads English in this house?"

"Everybody—Ludmilla's mother, my wife, Ludmilla herself."

"I don't live here," said Ludmilla.

"I see," said Günther. "Typical of the rich. They buy more books than they can read, and always seem to buy the books they do not read. The pages of Jane Harrison's books are glued together, probably by humidity or by furniture polish; your butler takes good care of that. He is responsible to Madame for the library too, then, not only for the blue couch, the cushions and the carpets—hahaha."

Ludmilla and the doctor did not laugh.

"Tell Ludmilla about your book on the gods' wanderings from Greece to Apulia. Tell her in German, it will be easier for her to understand you."

"Oh, we shall have plenty of time, plenty of time, when we are married," said Günther, and Ludmilla became very much absorbed in some bread crumbs that seemed to have gone under her plate and could not be dug out without lifting the plate almost up to her face. The doctor could not see her eyes, he was afraid of her tears, and made another effort to attract her attention. He tried to remember a joke he had made a few days earlier, which he knew would have amused her, but could not recall it. Günther took full advantage of the silence to try to amuse both the doctor and Ludmilla with a devilish trick of his own.

"Why is my little Ludmilla so sad?" he asked. "She has no reason to be. Her love is looking at her, and her love is so proud of her."

This promised to take a bad turn. The doctor coughed and asked, "What are your plans about the trip? We seem to have forgotten about it."

"Wait a moment, I want to say something funny: Little Ludmilla should not be sulking, but proud. Any young lady who can write such beautiful letters . . . Hahahaha ha ha ha . . . ha."

Ludmilla did not look at the doctor; she kept her head bent over the dish and just threw a frightened glance at Günther. The doctor did not look at her, but almost imitated her movements. Then Ludmilla lifted her face very high, as if to show only her jawbone and chin, and turned slowly on her chair to get up and leave the room, while the doctor asked Günther in a trembling voice, "What letters?"

Günther apologized. "I am so sorry," he said, "I should not have mentioned them, but they were so well written, so charming . . ."

Slowly the doctor turned his head, and he saw that Ludmilla was about to leave the room. "I told you not to mention this!" He waited for her to be gone. "Now it's the end. No engagement, no marriage, no nothing. I am sorry to have to say you are a fool!" And he ran after Ludmilla.

He found her in the music room, wiping her eyes and smiling.

"It is nothing," she said.

He made eloquent gestures of self-justification, but he could hardly speak. "Ludmilla . . . you see . . . I swear to you I did not know how—"

She interrupted him. "Never mind," she said, "I knew it."

"You knew what?"

"I knew that you had given him those letters."

"You knew it? But I assure you . . . You could not have known it, because I never—"

She put a hand over his mouth. "No, please. I knew it this morning when you told me you had not. But never mind. You are forgiven."

"Ludmilla, I swear to you—"

"No, please, don't swear. I understand. I also understand why you lied to me, because I do it—lie—all the time. You

and I are alike. And don't take from me the pleasure of forgiving you. It is hard always to be the object of forgiveness,
very hard. *You are forgiven.*"

He still stood there, with his hands in the pleading position
typical of defense lawyers in courtrooms, but his face looked
less anguished.

Ludmilla smiled and said, "You may smile, you have nothing
to fear." Then she looked into his eyes with an intensity that
troubled him and said, "I can never begrudge you anything.
You may speak ill of me, you *will*, and nothing will change in
me. Let's go back to the dining room. That poor devil is nice.
In his German way he did the best that could be expected of
a man. He was even tactful, Germanically speaking."

The doctor seemed relieved. "He *is* nice, eh? You *do* find
him an extraordinary person?"

"Oh, yes, very much so. Even if I don't understand half of
the things he says. But he will teach me. I shall become a
femme savante, you'll see."

They went back to the dining room. Günther had finished
all the wine and opened another bottle which had been in the
cupboard: precious, ancient Rhine wine which the doctor drank
in small sips and only on great occasions. And there it was,
high in the water glass, and Günther with red cheeks and
shining eyes and a flower (yes, a flower) behind his ear. And a
stinking cigar in his mouth.

"Ach!" he said, and because he felt at home he did not rise
from his seat. This was his first exercise in marital politeness.
"Here you are friends again, no one would ever think you had
told me and written such awful things against each other!
How poetic! How primitive, how Russian, how Italian, how
much like the *Iliad!* Thank God there are no trains today! Is
there more of this wine in your cellar? I hope so!"

This was a bad beginning for the doctor's next measure,
namely, the ousting of these two from his house as quickly as
possible. Ready as he had been in a moment of madness to

rape Ludmilla, now that his judgment had returned he remembered all the dangers relating to bad women, syphilis first of all, and did not want her to kiss the children before leaving. Also, he did not want the scenes, the tears and the questioning that could not be avoided if the children came back. In case there were no trains, he had made plans to send them to Milan by car, Ludmilla to stay with a Swiss family, Günther at a hotel, expenses paid. He was even prepared to send an old German spinster with them so that no one might say Ludmilla had been alone with a young man.

But Germans are not easy to dislodge, especially when they ascend the mystic clouds of their *Kultur.* Now Günther was examining his soul in the light of his *Pflichtsgefühl,* or sense of duty, and examining Ludmilla in the light of "Dyonisios-Bacchus-Rhenanus," as he called it, or the spirit of Rhine wine, and speaking in blank verse, and speaking a great deal about *Posaunen*—"*die Posaunen der Schönheit,*" or the trumpets of beauty, which, through the "divine plumbing of poetry," inserted their sweet call into his spine and urged him to celebrate the "mystic union" with the "spiritual body of antiquity" as represented by Ludmilla. And yet, and yet . . . he had taken solemn vows, in the deep heart of Mother Night, at a "supreme mystic meeting" two years before at the University of Heidelberg, pledging himself to Chastity in the Service of Learning! Who could release him from those vows if the head of his student fraternity, or *Brüderschaft,* was not there in person? He asked the doctor for advice, and, seeing that the doctor was confused, partly because he had not understood and partly because he could not believe his own ears, Günther repeated the question in Latin: "*Libera nos a castitate, Domine.*"

To which the doctor, not quite knowing what to say, answered, "*Ora pro nobis,*" and was very much ashamed when Günther laughed.

"No," said the old lady, "I cannot see my daughter Ludmilla, because my daughter Ludmilla is dead."

"Very well," said the doctor, "then you will see her ghost."

And the ghost went upstairs and they spoke a great deal about the weather, how nice it was that the birds sang in May and not a word about the trip or the new man in Ludmilla's life. Ghosts have no future.

"This," said the doctor to the chauffeur, "is for the railroad tickets to Germany. You will buy three first-class tickets with sleeper, the two ladies together, the gentleman alone. And the car must be back here tomorrow night."

Ludmilla's twelve suitcases were piled on the roof of the car and tied with ropes.

"Did you say goodbye to Mary?" asked the doctor.

"She was asleep. But how about the children? May I see them? Just for a minute?"

"It would upset them unduly. Better not. Anyway, you will be back before long."

Ludmilla made a last effort and smiled. "Of course," she said. "Very soon."

Günther had to be called in from the garden. He had picked violets and daisies and made himself a garland.

"Bring me two or three old newspapers," said the doctor to the chauffeur. "Hold them for me here. And also—put two bottles of Rhine wine in the car. And now, dear Günther," he said, "may I do something which will prove very useful to you, both in your work and in your less exalted activities?"

Without waiting for an answer, he put his hands behind Günther's ears, unhooked his spectacles, and cleaned them with a small cloth he had put into his pocket for that purpose.

"You will get a much clearer view of things," he said. "The sky, for one, will seem brighter when observed through clean glasses. And don't touch the lenses with greasy fingers. That is

318

what makes them sticky." He placed the glasses back on the scholar's face and said, "Good luck to you both and God bless you."

"God?" asked Günther. "What god?"

"Any old god, provided he be almighty." Then, upon second thought, the doctor added, "And not German."

"What was that again?" asked Günther, blushing.

"I mean, none of that nonsense of Mother Night you mentioned yesterday. As for you," the doctor added to Ludmilla, "write to us and let us know how you are. We may come for the wedding."

"I don't know how to thank you," said Ludmilla with tears in her eyes.

"Just a moment," he said. "Will you please get into the car?"

She got in and sat down in the far corner. The doctor thereupon took the newspapers from the chauffeur and spread them open on the seat next to her.

"This being your mother's car, not mine," he said, "I don't want it soiled. And if it were my car, the same would be true."

Ludmilla felt a great tenderness for him.

"And now, Ludmilla, goodbye. Good luck to you and remember what I told you this morning. There is always hope in life, provided we have faith in ourselves."

She was still hoping for a brotherly kiss, but all she got was a brotherly handshake.

"I don't know how to thank you," she said. "You are my best friend."

"Not that word, please."

"But you are," she said, blushing.

"Nonsense, I am a poor devil like you, struggling to fight against his own weaknesses and to defeat many big devils at once. Or rather, one after the other. God bless you."

The door was closed, the doctor waved his hand for a moment and ran back to the house like a happy little boy before they reached the garden gate. Ludmilla looked for the last time at the door, at the windows, as they shrank in the distance, and finally at the whole house towering high over the grottoes, the alleys and the trees, then looked at her own image in the mirror in front of her and imagined herself in an evening gown with that diadem of emeralds—and this man for a husband. Sobs shook her unadorned bosom as she sank back into the velvet cushions.   *

"*Humectant lacrimae,*" said Günther, taking her hand. "Now we will have all the time needed to work on that poem together. You can mirror yourself in my words."

A few minutes later, when they were past the gate and speeding toward the lake, he saw that Ludmilla was again looking into the mirror to make sure that passers-by would not notice her tears.

"Feminine vanity," he said. "Hahaha, feminine vanity. *Vanitas vanitatum . . .*"

Within five minutes of Ludmilla's declaring him her best friend, he became her worst enemy. Not in his own private view, however. He was discreet by nature and believed that opinions were dangerous in any case, because they lead to political theories that in turn lead to "acts of freethinking," or scandal. He would really have done what his mother-in-law always claimed she was doing and never did: considered moral disapproval the equivalent of death. But how could he not speak about Ludmilla, with those two women eager to justify themselves in their own eyes?

"Ludmilla is her own worst enemy," was their initial theme; "No one can do her greater harm than she has done herself," the first of many variations on that theme.

In his moments of remorse the doctor told himself that since Ludmilla was her own worst enemy, there was no harm in his trailing behind and being almost her best enemy. This was done for her good, not for their idle pleasure. He actually be-

lieved that speaking harshly of her (especially as they all loved
her and were not speaking in public) would in the end reform
her. How, by what secret channels, as she was not there to hear
them, he did not ask himself. But he also believed at the same
time, and without seeing anything contradictory in these two
attitudes, that it was very bad to speak so about an absent person. Still, what point was there in speaking charitably when she
was not there to hear them speak charitably? He consoled himself by saying, or, rather, by secretly thinking, Words come and
words go. What we say against Ludmilla today will be forgotten in a year, so let these women talk, give them a chance to
repent their excesses in a year, or perhaps even earlier, if they
really go too far in their insults. Which they did, and this
caused him to worry: To atone for this nonsense they will
apologize to her, she will feel justified, and next time she will
be worse!

The child was christened in a hurry and named Luca Leonardo Ivan (or Vanka) Aburbio Licurgo Ganidio, the three
latter names being his father's angry inventions, also his only
way of opposing the bishop, who would have preferred names
of saints.

The godmother was the wife of a notary and trumpet player
whom the doctor had cured of pneumonia, and it was never
clearly stated whether she represented Ludmilla or not. After
the christening Crocifisso went south, having given his godchild
a small cross worth not more than a few pennies—for it turned
out that it was brass, not gold. And now the child's grandmother (who had not left her bed of suffering and humiliation) suddenly realized that Ludmilla had not given the child
that famous watch for which she, his grandmother, had sinned.

"This is so typical of Ludmilla," said she, fuming with righteous indignation. "I told her what a burden it was on my conscience to have kept that watch for myself instead of giving it

to one of my brothers or to one of my sons. And she took my confession as an encouragement to sinning."

Ludmilla was suddenly resuscitated from her death to be asked why she had stolen that watch. But Ludmilla never answered the letter. Günther instead wrote endless letters about Ludmilla and the Spirit of Antiquity, Nietzsche and the rebirth of the classical spirit in Germany, Wagner and Greece, archaeology and Apulia, Goethe and Italy. Ludmilla, he said, was still untouched, his vows of chastity having been prolonged by him until after the completion of his next trip to Italy and his next book; in the meantime Ludmilla was helping him, together with ten other students of both sexes who would all go to Italy with him.

What troubled the doctor in those letters that were read to him in translation was that, for all their madness, all their Germanic bad taste, they revealed an erudition of which he would never be capable. He hated Nietzsche, whom he had never read and never would read, and was irked by the sudden discovery that his mother-in-law had read Nietzsche's *Zarathustra* and discussed it with Mary, and that both were exalted by the coming advent of the superman. How they could reconcile him with their worship of Tolstoy he never understood, but to them it seemed easy. Luckily, they agreed with him on his hatred of Wagner, even though they disagreed with him in his worship of Verdi, whom they detested almost as much as he detested Beethoven, Schubert, Mozart, Schumann and Brahms. He hated archaeology while being attracted to it, because he regarded it as a crime against poverty. To dig meant to upturn the fertile soil and ruin farms, wreck villages and homes, cut down olive and almond trees, and also expose to the greed of the north (especially of the Germans) things solemnly consigned by history to oblivion and buried underground where all the *gloria mundi* belongs. He respected the past, all of the past, even the minor, recent, unhistoric past of his immediate ancestors. These were the true descendants of the Greeks, even though they knew nothing about them, and to disturb the ancients in their slumber was a crime against God, regardless of His doubtful existence. As for the superman, that was idolatry of the worst kind. Only God deserved worship, if at all, and then only in the forms of the Catholic faith, which at least made people humble and pure, even though it kept them ignorant and dirty. He had rebelled against that Church, but certainly not to accept the god invented in a wooden Swiss dwelling by a German professor called Nietzsche. As for museums, he hated them, while feeling very much ashamed of not knowing all the things they contained. His attitude to them was exactly the same as toward schoolbooks. One must know them, or, rather, one must prove that one has read them carefully, but long ago and then never again. In isolated instances, namely out of context, he even liked poetry, prose, statues and paintings; but he could never mention them, lest the original sin of his ignorance become known.

The result was a deep, inarticulate hatred of all Germans who had the courage to take trains and go through Italy or to Greece, and who therefore knew his own country better than he did. At this point in his life, with his divorce and situation of bigamy preventing him from going back to Italy, he did not have to acknowledge all these motives behind his resistance to learning and to travel. He could take a short cut through the maze of his feelings and begrudge those like Günther their undeserved good luck.

Someday, he thought, when this divorce is recognized in Italy, we will all go to Florence, to Siena, to Rome—and to Greece! I only hope that Günther will not go to my native district and make himself ridiculous, exposing Ludmilla, too. We have enough enemies as it is.

XV

Now, Mary my love, we are rid of that filthy sister, who even robbed our child of his watch, and we must begin to economize, to cut down on all things that make us appear different from other people, and we must work. As soon as your mother is better, we shall leave this royal palace, this Versailles, this ugly liability which should be housing a regiment, not a small family like ours, and move to a small apartment not far from the hospital, where I shall finally begin to do my work."

"Oh yes, your work, your great scientific work. We shall discover all the laws of biology and psychology, you will become a superman, and I Madame Curie."

"No, no, just a small doctor and his wife. You will look after the children and teach them languages, and I shall cure the sick and pay the family bills. And all the money we save will be used for our trips to Florence, Siena, Pisa, Rome and Greece."

This standard conversation took place at the end of October. The old lady was still more or less dying of humiliation, bitterness and overeating, and most of the big rooms downstairs had been closed. No invitations were being received and none sent out. The children had no friends. But what seemed infinitely worse to them was that they had no aunt. They had behaved so well, so well, so exceptionally well, that day, and yet Aunt Ludmilla had never come back.

"When is she going to arrive? It is so boring here without her."

"How can you say such things when your mother is with you all the time? Do you hate your mother? Do you want her to die?"

After due humiliation and repentance on their part, and after Mary had shed all the tears of which she was capable (and they were many), this other standard conversation was resumed.

"When is Aunt Ludmilla coming back?"

"Aunt Ludmilla is never coming back. She does not love us any more."

"But why? What have we done to her?"

"Nothing, my children, absolutely nothing bad. She never writes, she never asks about her mother or about you. This is all very sad, very sad."

New tears were shed, then came the grand conclusion: "If you expect everybody in the world to be as loving as your mother, you will be greatly disappointed in life."

November first. Sonia would celebrate her birthday on the fourth, and Kostia had been preparing a puppet show for the great event. He worked in the attic, sawing wood and driving nails into a small stage, then oiling it and painting it with thick lacquers and using tinfoil, brass decorations, velvet and silk and cardboard and glue, painting curtains in red and gold, drawing scenes, using up all the discarded toys he could find in the house; and no one except his stepfather was allowed to see how the work was proceeding.

It was proceeding very well, they reported today in the old lady's sitting room, both of them looking proud as well as mysterious. Kostia had unknowingly adopted some of his stepfather's ways, which created a resemblance between them even though they had no features in common. Kostia was typically Russian, blond and of pink complexion, with high cheekbones and eyes that seemed slanted without actually being so; however, he had a cynical cast to his mouth that could be nothing but Roman, and his mother watched it grow with apprehension, as if any resemblance to his father might be fatal to him. His stepfather, on the other hand, was so black and solemn that even when he smiled he seemed to threaten the world with extinction. But a few movements of the hand and of the head and a proud way of walking were sufficient to put all of Kostia's traits under the same un-Roman and uncynical sign as his stepfather's.

"Yes," said the doctor, "everything is almost ready for the big show, which will be given here in this room. Only three days to go. Today is All Saints' Day—although no one has noticed it; but tomorrow is All Souls' Day, the Day of the Dead, and we shall walk to the beautiful cemetery of Massagno which I have just discovered. Too bad that you cannot come with us," he said to his mother-in-law. "If I were close to death," he continued, "I would want to be buried in Massagno."

There was a frightened silence in the room. Even Kostia felt it painfully. Mary rushed out to hide her tears.

"Go tell Mary not to behave like a child," said the old lady to the doctor.

He went out of the room and found her in the upstairs nursery, where the baby was asleep. There she stood in one corner, looking at her child from a distance and crying.

"Your mother does not want you to behave like a baby. She sent me here to tell you."

"And why should *you* behave like one? Only a baby could be so inconsiderate."

"What have I done?"

"What have you done? You wallow in death, you offer my mother a cemetery in which to be buried, you make her feel in every way that she is dead. That is what you do all the time.

You close up more than half the house and cut down on expenses, getting rid of the very things she has always been used to. That is what you are doing."

"But, Mary, please, don't be silly. She never goes into the rooms I have closed up, she has never even seen some of them."

"She knew they were open, she knew they existed."

"No, she did not, I had to remind her of their existence. And I asked her permission every time I made the slightest change in the house."

"Of course you asked her permission, but that was like saying to her, 'You are never going to have a big house any more, you are never going to live as you once lived, you are dying, this is your limited space, these few rooms, and you don't need flowers from the Riviera every morning.'"

"And indeed she does not. They make her sneeze. And that sneeze costs us more than a day's food for sixteen people—breakfast, lunch and dinner plus tea and second breakfast in the morning and all the food that is being stolen in the kitchen. One sneeze of your mother's. Precious flowers arrive from far away, they take two nights and a day to get here, they are put into vases, taken to her room, she sniffs them, then sneezes and says, 'Take them away.' Fifty francs gone. Seven or eight more sneezes for the same price, but it is only the first one she is paying for. And she worries all day because we are not going to have anything to live on after she is gone."

"Who cares what we are going to live on? Do we have to despoil her of her own money?"

"But, my dear, please be reasonable. What do you mean by 'her own money'? She cannot take it with her, and if she has finally come to her senses at the very last minute, don't try to bring her back to the old days of absurdity."

"See? How cruel of you—'the last minute'! How can anyone be so inhuman as to remind a person that this is her last minute?"

"I never did that. The last minute for her money, I said, not for her. In fact, I do this to insure her a long life without discomfort. Would you want her to end her days in poverty?"

"Money is of no consideration."

"That is the hypocrisy of the rich. If you had ever seen people toil for their bread, you would know that money is sacred. And to spend it unwisely is a crime. It is a fact that we must die. That is the first thing we learn about life. 'Don't jump out that window to grab the moon, because the stuff you're made of is not of the best quality. It breaks, it bleeds, it swells, it smells, it leaks, your divine soul is not at home in it; but that is all we are given, so let's keep it in good shape because the shop won't take it back and replace it.' So that's your lesson for today. If your mother gave up her toys when she was ten, that was not a sign of death. And so today, if she gives up her stupid habit of paying for empty rooms and flowers she can't even have in her room, that is a sign not of death but of maturity. And if she thinks of us and of our children, that is another healthy sign. Let's go downstairs."

"A postcard from Aunt Ludmilla!" Sonia's voice. "Two postcards from Aunt Ludmilla! Three! Four! Five! Six!"

She was repeating aloud what Kostia whispered quietly to himself as he counted the cards that had come in with the afternoon mail and placed them on top of the letters, because they seemed to him more important. They were beautiful postcards with views of Florence. Blue skies with towers and red roofs; blue skies with a red cupola and a white-black-green-and-pink-checkered church with round holes for windows; blue skies and a huge fountain with a white man standing naked at the center of many streams of water and surrounded by a number of naked women, all in bronze, comfortably seated at the edge of the fountain and directing the water against him; blue skies with green hills and belfries; blue skies with tall green trees that looked like pencil points; and the last one: a beautiful child in a very rich costume, holding a bird in his hand. One postcard was for Kostia with love and kisses from Aunt Ludmilla and Uncle Günther, one for Sonia, one for Filippo, one for the baby, one for Tasso from his friend Ludmilla alone, and one for Mary, which said:

DEAR MARY,

I hope that you have found that gold watch in my room, I had forgotten all about it, I hope Mamachen is feeling better, we are here with friends. Florence is beautiful, we are going from here to Greece, where Günther is sure he can find ancient jewels for me buried in some strange place he alone knows about. I will look like Madame Schliemann with Helen's jewels, only I hope I will look a bit better than she did. Remember me to your husband with sincere friendship and gratitude.

Your loving
LUDMILLA

The doctor looked at the postcards with seeming indifference, distributed them to the children, pocketed the one with the red cupola which was for the baby and the one with the baby which was for the dog, then looked at the two letters that had come in, both from Rome and both for the old lady.

"Well," he said, walking down the hall and followed by the family, "they could have said a little more. Who cares what treasures they will find in Greece?"

"Will you open these letters, since you are to be in charge of everything quite soon?" asked the old lady, and the doctor protested, but she smiled. "I meant to show you the letters long ago, but never found the courage."

"*These* letters?" he asked, without opening them. "These letters arrived today, a few minutes ago."

"I know, I know. But the same letters have arrived many times before, I can tell you exactly what is in them. And, as I may not be here much longer, I would not want you to be

329

taken by surprise. But wait. Another thing, before you open them: Promise me that you will not let your temper get the better of you. Money is so unimportant in life."

He made an effort not to give her the same lecture he had just given Mary, and began to fumble with the letters. One was from Avvocato Tegolani, as he had already begun to suspect, and it said: "Another two thousand lire, if sent on time, will be sufficient to persuade our enemies to desist from their evil intentions. I have done what I could, I am sorry if I have not been able to do more. Yours in true friendship," and the signature.

"What does this mean?" he asked. "How dare this man still write to you and ask you for money? Have you sent him some? You must have, or he would not speak of 'another two thousand.' How long has this been going on, and why was I not informed?"

"I was quite wrong to let you see this letter. You promised you would not lose your temper, and you did."

"That has nothing to do with the fact that you have allowed this unspeakable criminal to exploit you again after he left you almost penniless."

"Penniless? Don't exaggerate."

"He has cost you a fortune, more than you have right now. He has insulted you, your daughter and me, and here you send him money as if nothing had happened. For what purpose? Who are these 'enemies'? What is their evil plot?"

"A plot to kill you," she said, blushing.

"Nonsense, who on earth could want to kill me?"

"Your wife."

"Mary? Oh, I am sorry, I had forgotten all about my first wife. But what you tell me is pure nonsense—yes, pure nonsense. I apologize for being rude, but the truth itself is rude, especially to those who go to such lengths not to see it. Had you spoken to me when this whole thing started, you would not find me so rude today. Of course you did not want me to be

330

angry. But how can it be avoided? You always say I am the only person in the world you trust, and is this the way you trust me? You pretend you can protect me against imaginary threats, when you cannot even protect yourself against the worst kind of swindler! You are ruining yourself, your daughter, your grandchildren and even me, if I may throw myself into the heap of your victims, since I seem to be the cause of all this. And you dismiss such a crime from your conscience by saying merely that money is *so* unimportant. Is it really unimportant to you? What else would have given you this privacy, this luxury, the travels you seem so to need—"

"Forgive me for interrupting you, but I always hated those things, I hated travel, houses, luxury, everything, I hated life itself, until I had these children—Kostia first, and then yours— to console me in my endless unhappiness. Of which unhappiness you know nothing at all, young man, nothing at all."

"Very good, I know nothing at all and I am not interested in it, since it is a thing of the past. You just said that the children have put an end to your troubles, so let's assume they have. And, being happy for the first time in your life, you can think of nothing better than the willful destruction of your happiness, as if these children were your worst enemies. Two thousand francs are a lot of money, a whole year's livelihood in great luxury for a family of five. And you take this away from the only people you love, to spare me the unpleasantness of reading an idiotic letter made up of false threats? My first wife would never do me such harm, and she at least hates me! God beware of your love!"

He threw the letters on the floor and began to pace the room in a fit of anger. From the bed came in a garbled way the question, "How dare you speak to me like that?" Then sniffing sounds, meaning that she was crying.

"How would I dare *not* speak to you this way? I would feel like a criminal if I dismissed this as a trifle. You could put me into the same category as your friend and adviser Tegolani if I

kept my word not to let my temper get the better of me. It is
not at all a question of tempers here, it is a question of morality
on the most elementary level."

Sobs came from the bed.

"Just a moment," he said, and he went out of the room. He
was wise to do so, because Mary was just coming in to find out
why she had not been called to join them.

"Go downstairs and keep the children quiet," he said.

"What is it?"

"I'll tell you later."

Then he went back into the room and found his mother-in-
law calm and frowning, the true picture of wrath. She was
angry at herself.

"No one has ever spoken to me like that," she said in a slow,
heavy whisper.

"Well," he said, "now that I have, why are you complaining?"

She came out of her closed universe of self-hate to show
amazement. But he was not looking at her. He was looking at
that second unopened letter on the floor and wondering what
surprise it might contain. He picked it up, and when she saw
him she said hastily, "That's nothing. I never paid them. I always sent them to—to Rome."

"You mean to Tegolani again?

"Ah . . . yes."

"And how did this man ever find the effrontery to write to
you again, after what he had done?"

"He never did."

"How was the contact established, then? Did you write to
him first?"

"I—I wrote to him when those first threats arrived, because I
felt that if I forgave him he would welcome a chance to be
helpful. So I asked him to discover who the people were and
how to stop them, or have them arrested. He answered very

kindly and I came to the conclusion that he is not a bad man at all."

"Who wouldn't be good, with a person like you?"

She smiled, taking it for a compliment. "He seemed ashamed of himself, and I must say that he was able to make many things clear to me. He himself had been robbed and cheated. His brother, who is a saintly man, wrote me two letters, too."

"His brother? I thought you kicked him out of your house once."

"I did. But perhaps I was wrong. And—"

He stopped her with a gesture of the hand. "Let me read." He opened the letter. "This is unsigned," he said. "It is a threat to kidnap Kostia. But I thought we were long past that period. And besides, I do not believe that this comes from his father. Do you?"

"I . . . never gave it any thought. I only tried to stop it."

"By sending money."

"Only once. Then I sent the letter to Rome, and . . ."

"And what? Have the threats stopped coming? No. So where is the great help you are getting from your dear lawyer? Let it be understood that under no conditions will that man ever get more money or even a single letter from you!"

He was going to leave the room when a thought came to him. "Does Mary know about this?" A long, long silence. "Does she?"

"Yes."

"Very good. I am not going to mention it to her. I don't want her to make a scene that would last us for three months. Agreed?"

She nodded instead of answering him. It was the first time in her adult life that she had been made to admit she was wrong. And in such a direct manner, without any regard for her age, her poor health, and her tradition of infallibility, broken only by her at times with open confessions that did nothing but confirm it anew— "I infallibly know when I am wrong, but am at least honest enough to admit it." Here no such chance, no public thanksgiving for her consenting to be seen in a state of momentary wrongness, prolonged by her for the benefit of others, with permission to judge her, but only after she had judged herself. And not even a heart attack; the doctor was too close. So she said, "I want to die." Which was the closest she could come to saying, "You are killing me." She expected something in the style of "Never say such a thing, we need you." Instead of which, all she got was:

"I don't see the connection."

"Very clear: I am wrong, I cannot stand this feeling, I must die."

But even now he missed the point. "I cannot understand," he said. "Are you the only person in the world ever to have made a mistake? No. You have made a mistake, all right, don't repeat it, but don't exaggerate your guilt. None of these attitudes can bring back the money that was spent. It was your money, let's forget it. Others too have thrown away their money stupidly."

She shook as if whipped by these words. "That is no comfort to me. I am not a coward, I am not trying to hide behind others. I want to pay for my mistakes."

"Senseless words. Pay again? To whom this time, and with what?"

"With my life, to atone for the havoc I have always created around me. I would much rather die than go on enjoying a life to which I have lost every right."

"In other words, a senseless sacrifice on the altars of pride."

"Yes, of *my* pride. Why not? I have pride."

"Oh, you don't have to tell me that. Your pride is very, very visible, and it prevents you from seeing yourself and the world in correct reciprocal proportions. You can see only yourself, and you cannot believe that a person like you could ever be wrong. But as you are a human being, like everybody else, you are just as frequently wrong as everybody else, and when you are made to admit it, instead of saying to yourself, 'Very well, next time I won't do it,' you want to die. Nonsense, you don't want to die any more than I want to die. You want to be pitied for having been wrong. And that is pride again. Or moral blindness. I must go now. Cheer up. Don't think of it any more."

These last kind words filled her with tenderness. She cried abundantly after he left the room, and pitied herself very much for being blind.

Yes, she thought, I am morally blind, but whose fault is it? No one has ever told me these things. He is the first one, and it hurts. He cannot understand that a person like me has great difficulty in overcoming her pride, at my age and in my weak condition. I must do something for his family now. They will be poor because of me. But why did he wait until today to tell me?

There was a knock at the door.

"Come in!" she called.

No one came. After a while, another knock.

"Come in, I say!" Still no one came.

"Come in!" she shouted, this time in her angriest voice, a voice that the walls of this house had never echoed yet: her voice of Rome, of Naples, Cairo, Moscow, St. Petersburg, Berlin, the whole world she had roamed in a state of constant fury.

Sonia came in, crying, "Look, Grossmamachen, look, Tasso was knocking on your door!"

The dog, who had been lately admitted to that room after years of the strictest prohibition, put his paw on the sheet, expecting a caress, while Sonia threw herself on the bed in a fit of joy.

"Get out of here, you dirty dog! And you, silly child, get down from my bed! Out of here, I say! Leave me alone!"

Mary had heard the first "Come in" from far away while she was clumsily wrapping up the new baby like a salami, an operation that always took a great deal of time and more skill than she possessed, and the frightening familiar sound she had not heard for years made her hands tremble, which slowed down her work. She therefore followed the events without being able to do anything about them; but when she finally heard the last angry shouts, she decided that this crisis was more important than the baby, and she put him back into his crib and began to run downstairs. On the steps she fell heavily and was unable to extricate her legs from the mass of her clothing. Old Bernard came to her assistance, but then fell on her and had difficulty in getting up. Finally a maid came by, assisted them both and helped Mary drag herself to her mother's room, while Bernhard went in search of the doctor.

The sight of a person needing more attention than she did made the old lady furious.

"What is this now? What has happened to you? Why don't you go to bed?"

"I heard your voice and came to see whether you needed me."

"I don't need you, especially in that condition. I don't need anybody, ever. It's you who need help. Why don't you go to bed? What happened to you?"

"I fell down the stairs."

"You would. And then came here to reproach me for being the cause of it all?"

"No, Mamachen. I came here to see whether you needed me."

"Dear Lord, do we have to go through all this again? I need nothing, I want to be left alone, and that is the only favor no one grants me. First the dog, then the children, then you. What do you all want from me?"

"Sorry, Mamachen, I only meant to help you."

"Yes, and so you fall down the stairs like a fool. If you wanted to be helpful, you could have noticed that your mother is sick to death."

"Oh, Mamachen, lie down, please, how are you?"

336

"Very well indeed, and stop asking silly questions. Just go to bed at once. Lie down here. I am going to get up so that I can look after you."

Mary could not understand what her mother was whispering to herself while getting dressed: "Of course she wants to be pitied for having been wrong. Of course."

"Mamachen," she said, "I swear I don't want to be pitied, but I don't know what I have done that was wrong."

"Shut up, you fool, I am not speaking about you, I am speaking about Ludmilla."

Mary was happy. She watched her mother walk about nervously and then go out of the room, and she felt like a child again, protected and yet frightened a bit. This protection might end in a storm any minute, so every moment that passed quietly was a victory, like so much work achieved.

The doctor had gone out for a walk. He was so angry with the old lady he could have strangled her and he was sorry he had concluded his reproach with exactly the kind of thing she had been striving for: indulgence.

They get away with everything, the rich, he thought; and it's always we, the poor, who forgive them. And they consider themselves nobler than we are, because we worship money and they despise it. That is where Mary got her stupid ideas. That is what ruined Ludmilla.

The thought of Ludmilla added to his gloom. He pulled the illustrated postcards of Florence out of his pocket and began to look at them. Here she was traveling, she was going to the places he had always wanted to visit someday in the future; now the future had come, all of the projects of travel had become possible, but they were disappearing, and he was again a poor man, poorer than in his student years, because he was much older, loaded with great responsibilities and without a career, a steady income, a profession—all of this so that he might sit back in the habits of great wealth while the last remnants of this wealth were being squandered stupidly under his very eyes, to protect him from imaginary enemies. And he must still be grateful to that terrible woman for doing this to him, while she had already forgotten her momentary shame and would laugh it off in the light of her great principle that money counts for nothing. He began to hate the big house, the park, the car, the servants, all of them except for dear Brigida and Adalgisa, and to think of Ludmilla and Günther again with growing envy.

There is a real man, he thought, who does not care what he looks like, and I dare give him a lesson on how to clean his glasses! I never thought I had married for money, I still do not believe it, but, looking at it from the outside, I did. I am made to feel it all the time. If only those who believe it realized my problems. How will I earn a living here, in a foreign country, where I am hated on account of *her* wealth?

He walked back into the house like a stranger. The first person he met was Bernhard, in his beautiful uniform which differed from his own suit only because Bernhard had longer tails and gold buttons.

There goes another puppet like myself, all dressed up with her money, he said to himself.

Bernhard had not seen him yet, he was dragging his flat feet under his shaky legs, walking like an old duke, lost in thoughts of historic stupidity.

So there he goes, doing nothing, and my children pay for his idleness!

When Bernhard saw the doctor he approached with a condescending hurry and looked even more aristocratic: glassy blue eyes, a mouth open for speech long before he was close enough to speak, open arms, as if he were welcoming a guest, and an air of false humility that had always irked the doctor.

"Oh, Herr Doktor, Herr Doktor, I was looking for you, looking for you everywhere, looking just everywhere for the last hour. Fräulein Mary needs you, she fell down the stairs, poor thing, and bruised her arm, here, and hurt her foot. Now she is lying on her mother's bed, don't worry, she's all right, but she needs you, of course, she needs you. Go upstairs quickly. Where have you been? I was looking for you and looking and looking . . ."

"All right, I heard you!" cried the doctor. "If you had really looked you would have found me in the garden." And, freezing the old man with a severe glance, he walked past him and went slowly upstairs.

No, he could not afford to be unkind to Mary, and he did not want to be. In fact, he was jealous of her, strangely jealous; jealous, for the first time since he had met her, of that environment which had robbed her of her best qualities and kept her in a state of constant childishness.

Poor Mary, he thought, little does she know how heavily she will have to pay for her mother's generosity. If I go into that room now and find them together, she will hear it from me and there will be a Russian drama. Better stay clear.

To find his equilibrium he ran upstairs to the new nursery. He was afraid of his other children at that moment. Their cheerfulness would anger him, and their questions even more so. The baby at least was still too young to ask questions. He walked into the room and found the child strangling in his own clothing, the little face purple and the tongue sticking out of the mouth in a last attempt to breathe. The doctor grabbed scissors and cut the cloth from around the dying child's neck, then massaged him until he began to cry and could be put back into the crib. Only now that the danger was over did he ring the bell to punish someone.

When Adalgisa told him in tears that the Signora had insisted on tending the baby, he felt a great pity for Mary and decided to say nothing. This was a warning from the gods to take the destiny of his family into his own hands.

339

The old lady had risen from her bed and resumed her activities; the house had felt her presence, it had swelled with her anguish, the walls had become tense and sonorous like the skin of a drum; she could have filled thirty more rooms without entering one of them, by simply being, and by invading the air with her plans for the future, the past and the present.

The first thing she did was to write a long letter to Avvocato Tegolani and tell him that he was a criminal and would soon be made to suffer for his sins. Then she wrote another letter to Pierre, to ask him for the immediate restitution of all the jewels belonging to Katia, and all the money he had received in payment for the sale of the villa, the garden and the lands belonging to his father, as well as the factory in Voznesensk. Unless her claims were satisfied at once, she would resort to legal means. This letter she reinforced with two long telegrams sent ten minutes after the letter had been posted, making further demands the meaning of which would be obscure inasmuch as the letter had not yet been received. Then she wrote to Mr. Schultz and asked him to send her a trustworthy notary for the drafting of a new will. She wanted to surprise her son-in-law with the sudden arrival of so much money and so many jewels, plus a new will bequeathing everything she owned to Mary. At the same time, she wanted him to know that she did not need his help. Every time his hard words came back to her she sprang up from her chair as if stung. She hated him, and yet her innate sense of justice made her see that he was right.

She paced the rooms downstairs, the air was stuffy, everything smelled of silence—there was a dead smell she had almost forgotten since the children were born.

"Open the windows, open all the windows," she ordered, and she was frantic until they were opened, because that smell, that smell, how could one make any plans for the future with that smell killing them?

"What? No flowers in these vases? I want flowers everywhere, flowers from the Italian Riviera. How dare you forget to put them into these rooms?"

"The doctor ordered them stopped last week."

"Oh, yes, oh, yes, I do remember. But never mind, I need them now. Not on my desk, not in my bedroom, but everywhere else in the house."

Bernhard came trotting and panting like a clown who plays the horse on a very small stage, and he repeated what the maids had just told her.

"The Herr Doktor, the Herr Doktor, not I, please believe me, not I, the Herr Doktor said we must economize, yes, save money, madame, can you imagine that?"

Everyone else expected an explosion at this point, but to their surprise her self-assurance fell like the wind—one moment the whole world goes up in a round glass and the gods drink it furiously, the next moment they put down the glass and every tiny leaf resumes its static existence. She sat down in a place where no one ever sat, on a tall, decorative chair in the hallway between two statues. There she sat with the servants in front of her and said nothing.

And that was when the doctor came and asked, "What, you are on your feet? And who gave you permission?"

"No one," she said, blushing. "I—I felt better."

"All right," he said, as if that were a matter of course, "but don't go out, because it is cold."

She had expected a smile, an expression of joy; after all, this was gracious concession on her part—she had never admitted in her life before that she was feeling better. And the servants were equally surprised by his coldness. He had already resumed his solitary walk through the house, when he turned back and shouted from a distance, "Close the windows in these rooms! Who told you to open them?"

There was a moment of the greatest confusion. No one knew whether he had been speaking to her or to her servants. In both cases this was a most unusual procedure, to shout orders in her presence as if she were not there at all, and in the same tone that he had used with her, which was like saying, "Remember, I really meant to be unkind!"

No one moved, they all looked to her for guidance. Then Adalgisa called, "Madame wanted some air."

The doctor returned slowly, with his hands behind his back, still looking displeased, and said to the old lady, "If you need air, one open window will suffice. With all the windows open we may all catch pneumonia. The children will come back in a moment from their walk, they will take off their coats expecting to find the house heated, their perspiration will freeze on their skins. Wear a fur coat when you are in the house with the windows open."

"All right," she said, humbly. "Bernhard, my fur coat, please."

"Send Frieda instead," said the doctor, "send Adalgisa, it will take him a year before he goes and comes back."

She was going to say something, then her self-control took command (it always did when others had lost theirs) and she threw a rapid glance at Bernhard, to make sure he had not heard.

The doctor felt he had gone a bit too far, but could not bring himself to be polite again. He hated her too much. To him all those crimes against poverty, as he called them, were unforgivable. He tried to apologize, but with so many grievances alive and working in him, he could only worsen matters.

"I am sorry I was so harsh to the poor man," he said, "but his presence here irritates me. He does nothing all day, and is paid I don't know how much, but certainly more than I or any of my colleagues at the hospital earn. Do you need him so badly?"

"No, of course not," she said, pleased to have found something he wanted her to do. "I keep him out of habit. He has been with me for years."

"That is no reason. You can no longer afford him."

"You are right. But how am I to send him away? He is old, he does not want to go back to his family."

"Oh, I see, he does have a family."

"Oh, yes, his children are well off, in Germany. I know them. They came to visit him in Rome. Nice people."

"And of course you paid their expenses."

"Why not?"

"Right, but why does he not live with his children now that he can no longer work?"

"I think he deludes himself that he can still work."

"To open doors and receive people. But we have no social life. We are outcasts, we live like criminals in hiding, and it is humiliating, besides being economically unsound, to have a butler who opens doors when nobody comes in. Tell him at least not to wear his stupid uniform, it will make me feel better. Pay him if you must, but let me warn you: you will soon have to engage a day nurse and a night nurse to assist him."

"Please talk to him," she said. "Make him understand that he should go home."

"Very well, I shall do so with great pleasure."

"Then you can also help me get rid of my car. What do I need a car for? And a chauffeur?"

"Why, certainly, leave it to me."

"Also the cook. Why should I have a cook?"

The doctor was delighted. "Nothing could please me more," he said. "In fact, we should leave this villa at once, take a small apartment in town, where you would have your room and also teach the children as you taught your own children when you still lived in poverty with your husband; or, if you prefer, you could travel, visit your other grandchildren and thus keep the family united. The day may come when some of us may need the assistance of the others, you never can tell."

"Yes, yes," she said mechanically, remembering how she had hated to live in poverty when she was young, and how her great romantic love had almost faded in the face of daily chores and the absence of luxury. But her husband at least had been ambitious, while this man here seemed to like the small life and the unambitious wife.

"How are you going to live?" she asked.

"Very well, almost as well as your servants, only with greater dignity and less waste of other people's foods. You should see the amount of food that is wasted every day in your kitchen. And God knows how much they charge you for it, too! Who goes to market with your cook every morning? Who compares the figures in his book with actual prices? No one, of course, and it is we who pay—or, rather, you. Let's get to work."

He walked away, head high, his conscience clear and his plans even clearer. He went downstairs to the kitchen and felt at ease again the moment he left the soft-carpeted stairs to walk on ugly brick floors. The humid air coming in through the door, the smell of horses, leather, grass and varnish, the large kitchen table scarred by knives, made him think of his adolescent years when his mother baked bread and prepared meals for twenty-five members of the family, while he sat and imagined dead epochs of history. From time to time his mother would remind him to keep his eyes on his book, not on the table, and how satisfied she was when she saw his eyes on the book. That was all she could do for his education, for when her eyes fell on books it took her a long time to read, and then an equally long time to understand what she had read.

He looked up and saw many faces staring at him: the German chambermaid Frieda, Bernhard, Brigida, Adalgisa, the gardener, the cook, the chauffeur.

"Oh," he said, mumbling something by way of an apology. "Is everything all right?"

No one knew whether this question was addressed to him; they looked at one another, then at the doctor, and said nothing.

"All right," he said, as if he found their answer satisfactory. "What are we going to have for dinner tonight?"

The cook, a tall, fierce-looking Roman, looked at him impertinently and asked, "Why do you want to know?"

"Why do I want to know?" He chuckled, thinking of the natural answer— "Because I have a right to know."

The cook seemed in no hurry and repeated the question.

"Yes, why do you want to know?"

"Curiosity. Can't a person be curious?"

Now the cook walked away from the table, picked up a cleaver and a few onions, then came back to the table and began to cut the onions until the doctor had tears in his eyes. So he timidly asked again, "Can you tell me what you are going to give us for dinner?"

"Why don't you ask Madame? I take orders from her every morning."

"I happened to be here, so I asked you. Anything wrong in that?"

"Nothing at all, absolutely nothing at all," chanted the cook triumphantly, and the doctor chose to take this as a sign of cordiality rather than a new insult. "Nothing at all," concluded the cook, ending his improvised song in plain conversational tones again. "You are the master here, you have a right to ask." He now burst into song again.

"You have a good voice," said the doctor.

"As a matter of fact, you are not the only one who has told me that. Avvocato Tegolani said years ago that he wanted to introduce me to a great impresario who would take me to Paris where I could become a singer. But I refused. Later I regretted it because I left the Avvocato on bad terms."

"You left him on bad terms? Why?"

"It's a long story. He is an excellent man, a very honest person, a good Christian, but he has one great fault: he always suspects everybody of robbing him. He would come to the kitchen and ask me how much I had spent that day; he insisted on seeing the books—he had no sense of dignity and no respect for the individual."

"That's a very grave fault," said the doctor.

"I agree with you. All you have to do is to look at my face," the cook said, exhibiting his face from different angles (and he looked like a criminal), "to know that this is the face of a good man."

"Yes," said the doctor, who was carried away by such impertinence.

"My only fault," said the cook, "is an excess of honesty. I am always ready to help the other fellow, and completely forgetful of my own interest. Ask anybody in Rome."

"I believe it," said the doctor, who was glad to have found a weak spot in his enemy.

"You do, but not everybody else does. Take, for example, my sense of economy. No one has ever seen me throw away a tomato, a parsley leaf, a slice of bread. I use up everything, because I believe that food should not be treated lightly. The poor don't have it, we should thank God for what we have."

"True."

"I am glad you see things my way. We both know the value of things because we have lived in poverty. I at least have, I don't know about you."

"Oh, you can be sure I have. My father was a well-to-do landowner, but in a very poor country, and when you are surrounded by poverty you feel it, too. Besides, we were eight children at home, and you know what that means."

"We were nineteen, and no money to live on. My father was a cobbler in Viterbo, some of us went to America, some stayed home, both our parents sick and old. I myself have a wife and five children in Rome to support, and I work here in an unfriendly foreign country."

"Why don't you live in Rome? There are jobs for a person of your capacity there."

"Impossible. I have a very delicate situation there."

"Can't you tell me what it is? Perhaps I could help you."

The cook seemed hesitant. He frowned as he looked at the other servants, who were coming and going, then said, "Wouldn't you like to know what we are going to have for dinner tonight? Come here. I'll show you something. I did not want you to see it before because you would consider me extravagant. Put your head into this oven and sniff."

The doctor did so and came out with an expression of delight. "What is it?"

"Pheasant pie, made with leftovers of bread and with the sauce of the pheasant we ate a week ago. That is how I manage to keep Madame's food bill so low. A good cook is one who, with cheap foods, can prepare expensive meals. Anyone can prepare expensive meals with expensive ingredients, that is no great art. Go find another cook like me if you can. Adalgisa, who is a peasant woman and can only prepare chicken feed or pig feed, spends more on her revolting meals than I, to feed your whole family. Not to mention Frieda's cooking. The heavy German soups and cakes with which she clogs the intestines of your children cost more than my refined cooking. And your dear German butler Bernhard has his daily bread baked for him especially in Zurich, because our tasty Italian peasant bread, this bread here that is baked once a week by Brigida's sister up in the mountains, is not good enough for him."

"Quite interesting," said the doctor. "And now tell me, what is it that prevents you from going back to Rome?"

"Just a moment," said the cook, "let me finish. Do you want to see what your German butler does with his own specially baked bread?"

He took the doctor to the other end of the kitchen, where two metal garbage pails stood in a corner, lifted their lids and showed him what was in them: five or six rolls of white bread, a few slices of black bread, almost a loaf of peasant bread. That was enough for the doctor. He picked the various items from

347

the dirt with knowing hands, like a surgeon working on an open wound, blew the coffee grounds from their surfaces and placed them on the table after testing their softness with his fingers. He then summoned everybody to that part of the kitchen and started his investigation.

"Who has thrown away this bread? It is neither stale nor old, and whoever did it does not know the value of bread. Bread is sacred, it is the staff of life. In my country, when a slice of bread falls to the floor we pick it up, kiss it, make the sign of the cross and apologize to the Lord Almighty for the offense. This bread will have to be eaten. It can be disinfected on the fire, toasted if you prefer, but in no circumstances will I tolerate bread being thrown away under my roof. I want to see the baker's bill for the last month, and if we buy too much bread, the thing to do is purchase less. This is an order, and whoever transgresses it need not work in my house. Have I made myself clear?"

He examined the expression on each face for the slightest indication of rebellion. Then, as a last surprise, he found severe words even for the cook.

"You must have known this for some time," he said. "Why did you fail to call my attention to it until now? God knows how much bread has been thrown away in the last three years."

And before he could weaken again he left the kitchen, modifying his expression of anger into one of sadness, so that the culprits would know he was not a bad man. What made him so lenient all of a sudden was the feeling of having accomplished something. He had started on a serious economic reform of the budget and had spoken to people as he had always dreamed of doing. The faces of his audience had given him the certainty that his words had caused a change in human beings. Was not that the whole aim of education?

XVI

THE NEXT DAY was a beautiful day. The sun shone brightly, everybody was weeping in the streets, and those who were not walked in mournful silence. Brigida and Adalgisa, with black veils over their heads and their eyes red with tears, were waiting for the doctor and the children to go with them. Kostia would have liked to stay home and put the finishing touches to the theater and the puppets. The chauffeur, Bernhard and the cook had promised him their help. Bernhard would help him carry the theater to his grandmother's sitting room and hide it there under the table so that it would be ready on the morning of Sonia's birthday; the chauffeur had been helpful with brushes, varnish and other things; and the cook had promised to make sugar puppets exactly like the villains in the play, so that the entire family would punish them by eating them up after the play. How could Kostia take time off to visit the cemetery? But his stepfather would not listen to reason.

"This is a day devoted to the dead, one should not work today."

"But no one has died in our family."

"How about your grandfather? And my parents? And besides, we are all going to die, and if our children cannot come to the place where we are buried, it will be very important for

349

us to have someone sit on our grave and think of us, someone who has never seen us or known our name. This is what we are going to do today for people we don't know."

Before leaving the house, the doctor asked Mary whether she felt well enough to join them.

"Oh, no," she said. "I must cheer up Mamachen, who could be driven to despair by these chimes. I am going to play the piano for her."

"Play the piano? You can't. I think it would do you and your mother a world of good to pay tribute to your dead by tending other people's tombs."

"I cannot stand these chimes," said the old lady. And, pretending not to know what they meant: "Did some important person die? Why are you dressed in black at this hour? Are you going to a funeral?"

"I thought you knew this was All Souls' Day," said the doctor. "We spoke about it yesterday. Won't you join us in the hope that someone else, whose dead are out of reach, will tend your husband's tomb in Berlin?"

She stiffened and said, "I hope no one will dare do such a thing. For us Protestants, sorrow is a private affair. We hate intrusion while we are still alive, why should we permit it when we are dead? We bear our pain with dignity and the world has no right to perceive it, let alone make it an excuse for a manifestation of public hysteria."

"Hysteria? But there is no hysteria in this. No hysteria and no sorrow. It is a holiday, the truest holiday, perhaps, in the whole Latin world. *They* are back with us for a day. Come, it will do you good."

"Thank you," she said, "but it is a matter of principle with me. I know you must be right, there is something, no doubt, to this sharing of sorrows with the crowds, but I am much too rigid for that sort of relief."

He thought of something kind to say, in order to apologize

for the great joy it gave him to be rid of her presence for the day.

"You know," he said, hating himself for saying it, "I don't think you will have to adopt such drastic measures with your household expenses. Things have changed very much since I cut down on waste in the kitchen last night."

With these words he was gone. She looked out the window and there she saw them, flowers and candles in their arms, with their baskets of food for the dead, running out of the garden in a hurry so as not to miss one more second of their holiday.

When they came back at dark, Bernhard was gone. It had been a tragic scene, with tears and solemn speeches.

"Never before have I been forced to eat stale bread from a garbage can. Not even criminals in jail are fed garbage. I have no teeth, and bread is all I eat. I never stole a penny from this house, I have been with you twenty years, and if you must save money, save it on me, I'll work for nothing, but not as long as this man treats you as his slave. I won't say goodbye to Fräulein Mary or to the children, I am heartbroken, I am going home to die."

"Where is Bernhard?" asked Kostia, who was eager to make the last arrangements for Sonia's birthday party.

No one would answer him. In the kitchen his friends were no longer his friends. He went to his grandmother, but she too would not tell him. At dinner she refused to eat. Every time Adalgisa tried to serve her, she recoiled as if a monster of some sort had come near her with a tray full of horrors.

"I cannot understand," said the doctor in whispers to her, "why you should refuse these breaded artichokes. You have not even tried our new bread soup. What are we having for dessert, Adalgisa?"

"Bread pudding, sir."

351

"What an excellent idea! Our cook is a genius! Tell him that, Adalgisa, tell him I think he is a genius." Then he tried to find some fresh bread on the table, but every slice he touched seemed to be as hard as wood. "Now we must hear how Grandmother and Mother have spent this day at home." And without waiting for their answer he went on: "We saw beautiful tombs, we tended three that were abandoned—one of an old man who died seventy years ago, leaving five children and a widow. God knows where they are now. We had sandwiches on the tomb of a widow who died only fifteen years ago, but no one came to see her today. She left three children and seven grandchildren. We brought flowers to a child of three who died just five years ago, but no one came to see him either. I wonder why. Perhaps his parents are abroad. And now let's hear, how did you spend this day at home?"

To his surprise, the old lady pulled her handkerchief out of her purse and hid her face in it. Mary did the same, then left her seat to run to her mother's side. The two women left the room and there was a long silence.

"Why is Grossmamachen crying?" asked Sonia.

"What an idiotic question," said her father. "She is an orphan and a widow, I thought you knew."

The chauffeur was the next to go. He left without taking his salary, also without saying goodbye, without seeing the children, without helping Kostia in his last preparations for Sonia's birthday party. But he left with the car, and with quite a few pieces of silver he had taken from the pantry and the dining room. He just left, early in the morning, no one even heard him leave, and only later in the day was his absence noticed in the kitchen.

"It may please you to know," said the cook to the doctor, "that your chauffeur has left. He has taken the car, so you won't have to find a buyer for it now. It was not yours, you never wanted it, I understand, so the loser is Madame, who did not want it, either."

"But—but wait a moment, what does this all mean?"

"Shall I repeat the story? Very well: Your chauffeur has just vanished from sight and from Switzerland."

"You mean . . ."

"I mean."

"And you can tell me such a thing without seeming at all anxious to get the police?"

"No use, sir. But you may be proud of your work. It was you who made him leave."

"I did?"

"You did. By saving on your bread bill."

"What does bread have to do with a criminal act? I am going to call the police!"

"Listen to me, sir. If you want to save anything, sit down for a moment and listen to me. That chauffeur is no fool. He has been planning this for months, and to be frank with you I knew it all the time."

"You knew it? Are you with him in this?"

"Of course not. But I knew he could not live here any longer. Neither can I. In fact, the next one to abandon you is your cook."

"You? And what do you intend to take away from here, the kitchen stove?"

"No, sir, only the memory of the greatest disappointment in my life."

His tone was so tragic that the doctor forgot his rage for a moment and asked, "What disappointment?"

"Never mind, this means nothing to a person like you."

"I have not been unkind to you," said the doctor. "Why should you speak unkindly to me?"

"You have not been unkind to me? You have treated me like a thief and a fool. This after I had given you evidence of my devotion and my honesty. Had I been a dishonest man, I could have stolen the floor on which you walk and you would not have noticed it. I know you regard Avvocato Tegolani as a criminal; you may have good reasons. I am not interested. I was only his cook and I found him a good man except in two things: he was stingy and he did not trust me. I told you all this yesterday and you agreed. Then I told you in the greatest confidence that your servants were wasteful, and the first thing you did was to accuse them in my presence, looking at me as you spoke. It was then clear to them that you were repeating what you had just heard from me. What is all your education worth if, at your age, you have not even learned elementary rules? Avvocato Tegolani would never have behaved that way, had I been friendly with him as I was with you. He had a sense of honor."

The doctor blushed, his eyes flared with indignation, but he just clenched his fists and said nothing. What he found unbearable was that a cook should give him a lecture.

"I am sorry," said the cook, "but I felt I must tell you the truth."

"Oh, you were right. It is for me to apologize."

"Come, Doctor, don't exaggerate."

"I am not exaggerating at all. I cannot understand how I could have done such a thing, and I promise that this will never happen again."

"I know it will not, because I am leaving."

"Please don't leave."

"I cannot stay here any longer. I have lost face."

"No, you have not. I will explain to the servants that it was all my fault."

"Never mind, I cannot stay. I have my dignity. The trouble is," he added, sighing, "I don't know where to go. I can't go back to Italy."

"Why can't you?"

"It is a delicate matter, and I am so reserved that I can never bring myself to talk about delicate matters. I am too sensitive."

"Make an effort and tell me. Perhaps I can help you."

The doctor was beginning to fear that the man would stay on, and he hated himself already for this new proof of weakness. But the cook seemed reluctant.

"No, no," he said, "not now. Later, perhaps." Then in a strangely cheerful tone: "You know why I was angry with you? Not so much because you betrayed me in front of the servants as because, by behaving that way, you lost your car."

"How is that?"

"Very simple. I had never liked your chauffeur, and I disliked even more the policemen he was constantly associating with."

"Policemen, you said?"

"Yes, policemen. Swiss policemen, the most respectable type of police I have ever seen in my life."

"And what was wrong with them?"

"Nothing at all except for my suspicions. I had a feeling that they and the chauffeur were up to something, but I could not denounce a man on the strength of personal dislike alone. Yesterday when I saw you in the kitchen I thought that if I could only summon enough courage I would warn you. That is why I began to tell on the household—it was a way of approaching the subject. And then you came out with your undignified search of the garbage pails for bread, and frankly—"

"But you had shown me the bread."

"Indeed I had, but I did not suggest that you take it out and place it on the table and make that speech. When I saw you do that, I said to myself, 'This man deserves no confidence. He is capable of accusing the chauffeur without reason and saying where his information comes from. I must protect the chauffeur as well as myself.' And so I did. But you, to rescue a few slices of stale bread from the ashcan, lost an expensive car in the garage. And a few other things with it, I am sure."

There was a painful silence; then the doctor asked, "What can I do now?"

"I don't know. Certainly not tell the police."

"Why? The Swiss police are honest."

"What do you know about that? Have you lived here as a poor immigrant? Have you had them as your enemies? The police are the same everywhere. Do you know what would happen? They would publish the story in the papers, giving your whole identity: a man married in Italy and living here with a woman who is not his wife."

The doctor became pale and decided that this was the moment he would have to do something he had never done before: hit a man in the face. His hands trembled, his voice quivered, as he tried to pronounce insulting words he had never spoken since the age of ten, but all he managed to do was cough and clear his throat.

"Never mind," said the cook, who had kept his composure and was looking at the doctor almost with tenderness. "I mentioned this only to warn you. At least in Italy you always have a friend who has a friend in high place and you're protected. Here there is justice; this is a German country, don't forget. Even if they speak Italian, they are all Germans, and they all hate the Italians, especially those from the south, like us."

"How right you are," said the doctor, relieved.

Now the cook became pensive. "If only I could go back to Italy! I have a feeling that the car has been taken to Italy and may be sold there. Unfortunately I cannot go to Italy."

"Why won't you tell me what prevents you from going back to Italy?"

"Because you cannot help me."

"Never mind, tell me anyway."

"It is a situation like yours. I have two wives. I cannot get a divorce. I am guilty of bigamy. If I could ask my first wife not to denounce me, then nothing would happen. She wants money."

"How much?"

"Oh, never mind. Too much."

356

"But I must know. Even if I cannot afford it, let me know, perhaps we can think of something."

"Well, if you insist—but what is the point of telling you? Two thousand francs."

"Holy Mother of God!" said the doctor, and he made the sign of the cross. "And—and how about having your wife come here with the children?"

"Impossible."

"Let me talk to my lawyer."

"If you want my friendship, don't. My second wife will not leave Italy, her parents are there, the children go to school there, and with my first wife the situation is also quite difficult. Give me your word that you will not talk to your lawyer and you will not talk to Madame about it."

"Why?"

"I know you think me a criminal of some sort who is afraid of lawyers. I can read this in your eyes."

"No, you are wrong. I was thinking that I would not talk to the lawyer, but to Madame I would, because she might help you."

"That is exactly what I don't want. Madame has spent all her money and is now at the end of it. I would rather not see my family again than take a cent from her. So now you know. Do what you will, talk to the lawyer, talk to her, but not to me again. I am leaving tomorrow."

"Please don't do that," said the doctor. "I respect you and want your friendship. But I also want to help you."

"I am grateful to you for this. I shall stay on a few more days or weeks, until you find another cook, but I do not intend to take a cent of your money. Understood?"

"Understood."

They shook hands and were brothers.

357

"What do you mean, keep this a secret from Mamachen?" said Mary. "Impossible. It was her car, she must know."

"But she is not well."

"She is very well, thank God. Besides, that is not the kind of news that would upset her. It would upset her more if she found that we had not told her the truth. I did that once, in Rome, and will never do so again."

"You are right," said the doctor, but he knew that if he told her of the loss he would accuse her too of having been responsible for it. For the first time since he had left the Jesuit college he longed to speak to a confessor.

"Mary," he said, with tears in his voice, "I must admit that I have behaved like a fool. The car has been stolen. It is my fault. Even the chauffeur became annoyed with my interfering in the kitchen and left like Bernhard."

"How dare the cook say such a thing?"

"He is right. And he's a wonderful person. He gave me a lesson I shall never forget."

"That does not impress me in the slightest. How can you be so childish as to think that the chauffeur stole the car because you interfered in the kitchen?"

"He did."

"Look, if that man was a thief, he was one the day before you went into the kitchen, and no amount of consideration on your part would have kept him from doing what he did."

"And so you don't think that your mother will be angry with me?" he asked.

"Angry? What is a damned car anyway?"

This was too much for him. "It is high time for us to become poor," he said, "or I shall lose my mind. But one more thing before we tell her. I believe that it would not be a good idea to denounce this thief to the police. The police mean your name in the papers, and . . ."

"Of course not. Do you think my mother would lower herself to the point of denouncing a thief to the police? Who cares?"

"You are quite wrong," he said. "Criminals should be denounced to the police. In this case not, because our own record is not clean. That is the great disadvantage of going against the law. At any rate, the cook is leaving, too, and he said he would help us find the car again. If he does, we should of course give him something." He was about to mention the cook's problem, but decided to wait. If he asked for two thousand, he will settle for two hundred, he thought.

"I could not be more pleased," said the old lady, sitting up in her bed. "I hate automobiles, and anyone who is stupid enough to steal one may have it. Horrible, vulgar, scientific contraptions which run after nonexistent horses with the speed of ten or twenty horses. How I hate the very word that describes that mechanical horror!"

Mary and her husband could not quite decide whether her sudden emphatic pronouncement was anger in disguise or something else. They understood it when she said, "As a matter of fact, this theft relieves me of a stupid problem which bothered me all last night: if we are to go to Rome now, would it not be much better for us to travel by train than by car? We must economize and learn to travel like gypsies, but just imagine the whole family jammed into one car with all the suitcases on top and a few trunks forwarded by train! We would be awfully crowded in that car, the three of us plus the chauffeur and the chambermaid, would we not? Of course, the chambermaid could go by train. But now, with the car gone, the problem no longer exists."

Mary and her husband exchanged glances. Then Mary said, seeing that her husband was staring into the void, "Mamachen, we could not accompany you on that trip."

"Why?"

"With bigamy and all that, the lawyer said we should be very careful not to move from here."

"Ach, lawyers, lawyers, lawyers, I am beginning to be tired of them. See what happens when you trust one like Tegolani. Of course, the others are much better, but lawyers they still remain."

The doctor cleared his throat and said, with a tired, rattling voice, "Two days ago you were ready to pay thousands upon thousands of francs to Tegolani because you were afraid of fantastic threats, and today you propose that we go to Italy when you know that is the only thing we should not do."

"I know," she said, "life is full of contradictions—but that's the way it is. Now, frankly, I do not believe it would be more dangerous for you to travel than to stay here with this gray sky. It is going to rain any minute, perhaps tomorrow it will snow, and the Swiss are so boring. I was just looking at those cards the children have received from Ludmilla, and it makes me angry when I think of that stupid girl with all the sunshine of Italy and all the beauty of Florence, while we sit here and have nothing at all. And just as frankly, since we all seem to be in a mood for frankness, I don't think you are right when you mistrust your countrymen as you do. I know they are limited in their views, ingenious and deceitful, but they are not wicked, oh, no, not under that blue sky of theirs! If the police come to our train compartment, I will simply say, 'These are my children, and they are not traveling in order to commit bigamy, let them have a bit of your sunshine, they live in Switzerland, poor dears.' I know the Italian policemen would understand me and let you pass. I just know it, and nothing can change this certainty of mine. It is rooted in my heart."

Mary smiled and said to her husband, "I think Mamachen is right. Shall we take the risk?"

"No," he said dryly, without looking at either of them.

"He's right, he's right," said the old lady, taking Mary's hand in her own and caressing it. Then, with a sigh: "There was another reason, too: I have written to Pierre, I have written a few other very important letters, and the answers do not come. I cannot sit here and wait eternally without spoiling my chances of acting cold-bloodedly when the answers do arrive. A little trip would be the right thing."

"When did you write those letters?" asked the doctor.

"Let me see. Yesterday? No, two days ago—three, as a matter of fact. No, two. Either two or three."

"Well? It takes fifteen days for a letter to reach Moscow."

"Not fifteen. Eight or ten."

"All right, eight or ten is not two. Don't expect an answer before a month has passed."

"A month? A whole month? Another whole month waiting for an answer in Switzerland?" She had tears in her eyes. "In another month, less than a month, as a matter of fact, I shall be dead."

November fourth was a very cold day. Mary woke up in tears; she had cried the whole night while her husband was snoring. He, with a clear conscience and a sense of economy, had found his rest after saying the most horrible things, from which it had been clear to her that he wished her mother to die. With what ease, with what joy he had begun to dismantle the world in which she had been living, taking the sacred bedboards down and pulling out the mattress from under her mother's sacred limbs, almost suggesting with his peasant irony that it was a great privilege to sleep on the cold earth, because sooner or later, no matter what one's station in life, one would be stationed under the earth with no chance of waking up. What right had he to speak that way? Was this his house and had it been his money?

He was snoring, having saved so much bread and confessed all his sins and found the sins of others greater than his own. She almost hated him, but that made her suddenly lonelier and sadder. For she loved him so much that she feared he would abandon her the moment he woke up, to punish her for hating him. She therefore cried and imagined the worst, and not even the thought of her children could console her. They meant nothing to her without the two persons she loved, her mother and her husband. So she woke up, and as she knew her husband detested tears in the morning (how uncivilized of him, how Italian, how peasantlike), she left her bed in a great hurry and took her tearful face, like a *soufflé de fromage* right from the oven, to the exacting gourmet who liked tears hot and rich, made to order and plentiful; and in her mother's arms she cried and cried and cried.

"I know, I know, Mamachen, why you refused to come downstairs last night: you miss Bernhard, Adalgisa knows nothing about serving, she pushes the plate under your chin, she touches your cheek with her sleeve, she wears no gloves and her hands smell of garlic. I know—and it is all my fault. I should never have married him. But I love him, he is not a bad man. Please don't leave us again, forgive him, please, he will learn."

At this point, despite all the pleasure of crying, the old lady became angry.

"Mary, I have never heard such stupid talk in my life. You, a happily married woman with a wonderful husband, you, the mother of four beautiful children, can speak that way to your mother? Are you not ashamed? How can I afford to die now, if you have not learned to live?"

The last sentence was meant to reagitate the waters that an excess of wisdom might have cleared for the rest of Mary's life. The old lady knew how easy it is to find normality again round the corner from tragedy, and she especially knew how difficult it is to re-create an atmosphere of drama after it is proven ridiculous. So she proceeded cautiously with her own logic. But that beautiful phrase, "How can I afford to die if you have not learned to live?", threw all logic out of gear, by insinuating that, if Mary learned how to live, her mother would reward her by dying. At the same time, the old lady's logic was perfect: she knew that her death was expected, if not by Mary certainly by Mary's husband, and she knew he was right; in fact, she knew that this feeling was recent in him, and that she always managed to ruin every chance she had to be found indispensable by those she loved. So she must not teach Mary that her husband and children should be her only cares, and that Mamachen after all must be resigned to play the onlooker's role.

"I don't want you to die, Mamachen, I don't want you to die, I do not care if I am happy or not, you are the only thing that counts, you have suffered so much because of me, I don't want you to suffer, I want you to be happy, to live at long last after years of self-sacrifice, to have something from life."

"All right, all right," said the old lady, nodding like an old teacher to whose ear faultless answers in the classroom sound like beautiful music. "I know, darling Mary, I know. You are the only person in the world who *knows*, but you must be resigned to my death as I am. We never get what we deserve in life. Self-sacrifice is worthless if we still hope for a reward. Remember this, my child: Virtue is its own best reward. Self-sacrifice must be complete to be worth anything. You must prepare me for my death, you must give me the feeling that I no longer count, that other people count more, people younger, more active and more useful than I am. You must not cling to me. My death is my own task. Even if we are surrounded by the people who love us, we cannot take them with us, they cannot see us through the door. We die alone, and loneliness begins before that door is reached."

She had performed her painful duty, told the truth, now she could cry over her own unhappiness.

"I have been wrong," she sobbed. "I have always been wrong in whatever I did, and I know it. That is what kills me, that knowledge. . . . Oh, no, it is not true, it is not true!"

"What is not true, Mamachen?" sobbed Mary, who knew that her mother wanted to be asked that question.

"It is not true . . . it is not true . . . that I want to be pitied when I am wrong. I have always, always, asked for atonement. I am too proud, too proud to want pity from anyone. And I don't regret my pride. I am proud I am proud!"

"Yes, Mamachen, so am I. We are a proud people, we are anything but soft. We face everything with courage. But I want to die with you."

The doctor found them together in tears, and he was very angry.

"Cry as much as you like," he said, "since that seems to be a Russian sport—though I don't see why you should cry on a day like this, our daughter's birthday. But if you must, close the windows at least, it is freezing outside."

The German chambermaid Frieda was much too stupid to know how to build a fire. That had been Bernhard's task for years; he knew his fireplaces as a teacher of voice knows his pupils. For him they sang and for others they did not, not even for Brigida, who had spent her whole life making coals in the mountains of Switzerland: an acrid smoke was blown into her face by the wind and made her cough.

"Leave it to me," said the doctor, but he was not much better. The cook had to be called, and he lit a fire in every fireplace in the house before the family was allowed to get up. Mary stayed in her mother's bed and continued her pleading.

"Mamachen, please, Mamachen, listen to me. If you don't swear that you will think of life only, I will die in a few days and that will teach you a lesson. When you are here, everything else becomes important, too, but if you don't want to live I don't care what happens to my children."

"Yes, darling, I promise. I will think of life. In fact, perhaps I will begin to write that book today."

"What book—your memoirs?"

"Yes, my memoirs."

"Oh, good! I am so glad. It will be a great book. And you will write it also a little bit for me, won't you?"

"For you exclusively, my child, you alone count, you alone understand me."

"Thank you, Mamachen. And we will send a telegram to Bernhard asking him to come back."

"Oh, no, darling, we can't. We must save. I have spent far too much."

"Nonsense, you have not spent enough. Think of the money we are saving by not going to Italy."

Her mother thought of it, and it did not take her too long to come to the conclusion that in order to save more money she should call Bernhard back. It was too costly, in terms of time and energy and *joie de vivre*, to adapt oneself to Adalgisa's way of serving at table.

For Sonia this was a very special day. Four years; in one more year she would have a handful of years belonging to her, one for each finger. And she loved being treated with severity that day by her father, just like a punished child: "You stay in bed and don't dare to get up until we tell you. And when you get up, stay in your room until we call you."

The party and Kostia's puppet show were a great success. Even the old lady had a good time. But after she had admired all the toys and seen the play three times and laughed at all the stunts, she began to feel tired, actively tired, irritated, like someone who has spent all his money to purchase the wrong things and wants to forget the occasion, the time and the money wasted.

It was snowing, and the children were anxious to have their first walk in the snow and their first snowball fight. Almost instinctively the doctor thought that this duty would fall to him—he must play in the snow (a thing he hated), he must run and shout and take snapshots (all of which things he hated), while his wife would be staying with her mother, who seemed angry and sad again. He was angry and sad, too; he happened to be in one of those moods, so rare of late, in which he wanted to sit and read a serious book, a book on medicine, and take notes for a lecture he would never deliver. So it was with resentment that he put on his fur cap and fur coat (two things so foreign to his body) and said, "Children, let's go and leave your mother alone."

"No, no," said Mary, "let me go."

"Are you not going to look after your mother?"

"Indeed not. I am going to play with the children. I am their governess today, Mamachen must be left alone, and I wish you would work, too, it would make me feel useful for once: my two geniuses at work and I the guardian of their privacy!"

"Mary, how did you know that I wanted to work?"

"I did not know it, I hoped you would, as I hoped Mamachen would be working again. Thank God she is."

"Is she? I have my doubts. She seems restless to me."

"That is her nature, I know her, but she is really making projects, and God knows what great things may come out of her restlessness—a book, or a solution to our problems."

The doctor looked at Mary incredulously, then shrugged his shoulders, rushed to his bookshelf in the library, picked out one, two, three medical textbooks and went back to the fireplace to enjoy his reading. But the inspiration was as quickly gone as it had come. The first contact with his books always gave him a shock, as if he saw his image in a mirror for the first time after years. He recognized himself, but he no longer recognized the world in which he had been living for six years now. It seemed more and more insane to him.

This is not possible, he thought. One cannot live this way. Why should I always give in to these women? Where is my resolution to teach Mary how to live parsimoniously?

He closed his books and went to see his friend in the kitchen. "I must speak to you," he said to the cook.

"Not now," answered the cook dryly. "I am busy preparing Sonia's birthday cake and the sugar puppets. If you want to come and see them, you may, but do not talk to me, I cannot be disturbed."

The doctor obeyed, and spent the next two hours in the kitchen, like a boy who has shunned his homework and enjoys the sight of other people's activity while he lets his dreams run wild. What a great artist that cook was. He had made puppets exactly like those in Kostia's play. And a birthday cake so big that the doctor asked, "Why so big? Who is going to eat all that?"

"Don't you have other children here today for Sonia's party?"

"No. We don't know any people with children."

"Oh, I see. I had assumed you did. Poor Sonia, so she has no one to play with but her brothers and her parents. Too bad."

"It is not our fault," said the doctor again, feeling he had to justify himself, because the cook seemed to be very shocked. "You understand me, don't you?"

"No, sir, frankly I do not. I think you should have managed better. With the means at your disposal, I don't think you did well at all."

This was said with a grave air that made the doctor feel very small.

"You really think so?"

"I do. No wonder if a man in my position is unable to solve his problems. I am stranded, as I told you, but my difficulties are purely financial. Yours are social. My children have a status, they have friends, no one insults them for being illegitimate, while you live with that fear all the time, you have no friends, and I don't think that your condition is enviable. In fact, I do not envy you. But this is all your fault."

"My fault, you say? My fault? But what should I have done?"

"Ah, don't ask me. Who am I to know? I am just giving you my personal impressions, nothing else. And it seems to me that a man like you should have managed much better."

The doctor was once more impressed with the cook's superiority. "But I assure you," he said pleadingly, "I assure you that this is not my fault. It is no one's fault. The circumstances were against us. For one thing, my mother-in-law does not make things much easier. She shuns people and treats all those we meet in a manner that does not encourage them to become friendly with us. She is very reserved. And besides, she lives far above her means, and the moment she dies we will be ruined. That is the reason I am trying to cut down on expenses."

He was glad he had finally spoken the truth with the one person he could trust. "And how about that car?" he asked. "What can we do to catch the thief?"

"If I could go to Italy, where I am sure he went, I could do a great deal. But the longer we wait, the harder it becomes."

"And you said that unless your wife receives two thousand francs, she will denounce you?"

"I said so, but I also asked you never to mention it again. And you gave me your word."

"But look, I would be doing this for myself and not for you."

"Well, if you insist . . ."

This quick surrender made the doctor become prudent at once. "Do you think that she could be persuaded to desist for a little less? Let's say five hundred?"

There was a long silence; then the cook said, "I was right in not trusting you. I never sought your help and never will. But you insisted on knowing how much I owed, and now you ask for a reduction, as if I were trying to cheat you out of your money! And you call yourself my friend? Thank you very much, but I have no use for such friendship."

And he opened the oven, to shovel another dozen "villains" into it. The doctor felt as if he too belonged in the oven.

Two thousand francs, he kept repeating to himself while he was watching the cook play with the children, who now worshiped him. I don't see why five hundred would not do. I was blackmailed, too, by my first wife, and I always offered less and she was glad to take whatever she could get. I don't see why the wife of a cook should be any different from mine in this. No one expects to get what he asks for.

He did not take part in his children's games that evening; he felt an outcast and was far angrier with himself than with the cook. Much as he hated to be treated harshly by a servant, he could not hate a man his children loved so much, a man who amused them as he had never been able to amuse them, a man who had taught him two lessons; and therefore he decided to plead with himself and get his own permission to spend so much money on the search for that car. For there was in him an economical personality which supervised every one of his actions in terms of financial convenience, or, rather, of advantages obtained, and not a single act of generosity could pass unnoticed and unweighed by this ancestral judge.

He took paper and pencil and began to calculate: Loss of car—question mark. Then he wrote down the monthly salary of the cook and multiplied it by twelve, subtracted from this the salary of Adalgisa, also multiplied by twelve, and decided that he could save a bit of money on her, as she was used to poverty, and what she got in terms of food and board was more than she had ever earned before. And suddenly he remembered that he had saved two thousand francs on Tegolani. But now, considering it as earned money, he became stingy with it, and again he thought, Two thousand francs! If I was clever enough to save it, why should I throw it all away at once? Perhaps I can save half of it. Let's try.

As he rehearsed his speech to the cook, on his way down to the kitchen again, he felt more and more touched by his own goodness. Here a man who had studied Greek, Latin and medicine was gladly going to apologize to a cook for an act which did not constitute an offense. Can an offer of money be regarded as an offense when the sum is so high and the recipient so low that he makes it a practice to accept tips from guests and from his masters?

"I owe you an apology," he said, with a quivering voice, because he was afraid the cook might again become unpleasant. "I was unkind in offering so little when I knew you needed much more. Please do not interrupt me, please let me talk. You have been wonderful to my children, and we all like you, so you must not consider me your enemy. Please don't."

The cook smiled, and the doctor was so grateful that he immediately made a mistake. "Let me give you the whole sum," he said, "but please take my advice before you send it to your wife. Don't give it all to her at once. Try to persuade her to accept less, and keep the rest for yourself and your children. You need it, she does not."

"Yes, of course," said the cook, "but I am afraid she will only get angrier if I try to pay less. I know that woman and I know her family. Terrible people."

"Look," said the doctor, "I had the same fears, and I always paid less than my wife asked me. As a matter of fact, there came a moment when I stopped paying altogether and nothing happened. That was at the time of the legal separation. She gave her consent anyway. So try to do the same. I am going to pay you little by little, that will force you to be prudent with her."

"That won't do. I can give you my word that I will be prudent."

"As you say." The doctor left, cursing himself for his stupidity, and it was only after he had gone upstairs that he realized the cook had not even thanked him for his offer.

As one who wishes to be encouraged to do wrong, because his conscience bothers him, the doctor explained to the old lady that those two thousand francs were well spent, and also that the cook was a good man.

As soon as he left the room she called Mary and said, "I have never seen a man with so many great virtues as your husband. He never asks for anything that he himself might want; but when others are concerned, then he makes the effort. He came here a few minutes ago and said the cook was leaving and that he needed a certain sum because he has two wives, and no divorce—in other words, a situation like yours. I think we ought to give the poor man much more than what he says he needs, which is two thousand francs."

"Of course we should, but what will my husband say?"

"We must not tell him. He grew up in a world of small people, he sees small, even though his soul is great. We, who see great, have smaller souls than he, we are naturally cruel, he is naturally kind. That is the difference between us."

"Oh, Mamachen, I love you. No one but you could have seen the truth so clearly. You help me understand my own husband! What would I do without you?"

XVII

TEN-THIRTY. Another hour to wait before going to the station to meet Malachier. It was very cold outside, and the snowstorm did not abate. It had begun early in the morning, before daybreak, and the whole house seemed to resound with the gusts of wind shaking the doors, the windowpanes and the trees. High notes, as if of sudden orchestras, fell from the glass roof into the hallway below and were followed by brushing, hissing, roaring sounds that beclouded the music again. Little Sonia stood in the hall, holding one of her new puppets by the hand. She looked in every direction, but especially upward at that glass roof now partially darkened by the snow.

Her father opened the dining-room door and called, "Sonia, come here, don't stand there, it is cold."

"But I want to hear the music," she said.

"Come here, I say, it is cold in the hall."

She obeyed reluctantly and sat down on a footstool next to the table. She watched her father's yellow face and yellow eyes; this was a strange thing for her to watch; never before had she seen a yellow man. He in the meantime watched his eyes in one of those ancient mirrors that show nothing but patches of antiquity, and then again he consulted his watch.

Mary came in and said, "She is much better now. She wants to get up and go out."

"What?" asked the doctor. "Does she have to be strapped to her bed?"

"No, no. She promised she would not move from her bed. Only she feels much better, and I am glad. I think this is a good sign."

"Of course," said the doctor, who seemed not at all convinced.

"And how are you feeling?" asked Mary, touching his forehead with the palm of her hand. "You are not going out. We'll send the butler."

"I am," he said. "One cannot invite such an important person from Paris and not meet him at the station. It is not done."

"But you are not well, you have not been out yet, and this weather is awful, no cars can travel and no carriages either. Let me go. I can meet him."

"Oh, no. Not you."

"Come, come," said Mary, smiling, "are you still jealous of him?"

"Of course not, but this is not done. A physician sending his wife to the station to meet a consulting authority in the field?"

"And if the physician is ill with jaundice?"

"Never mind, a physician is never ill. Besides, mine was a very mild attack." He wanted to say more, looked at Sonia and said, "Go back to the nursery, you!"

Sonia was about to cry; she could not understand her father's sudden harshness. Her mother took her by the hand and said, "Come with me, Sonia, we will go to the nursery together." Then she turned to her husband and said, "Please don't move. We will find a solution for the train."

Kostia opened the door at that moment and then, seeing his parents there, started to withdraw. "I am sorry," he said.

"No, no, come in," said Mary. "Do me a favor, Kostia, take Sonia upstairs and play with her for a while. I have to discuss something with your father."

She went back to her husband, and in a motherly voice, which was unusual for her, she said, "Now what is it again? Must you think of those trifles all the time? The past is past and why bother about it?"

"Why bother?" he asked, pacing the room with his hands behind his back. "Why bother, you say? When I think that it was all my fault—that I, who was chiding you and your mother for being dupes of the first swindler you met, should have fallen for the lies of that criminal and called him my friend, and refused to announce the theft of the car to the police . . . ! How he must have laughed at me when he and the thief drove out of here together. And to think that the car had been right here, or only a few miles from here. The police could have found it at once, had I only been less of a fool! How could I, how could I, how could I?" He became more and more anguished; he wrung his hands as he went on: "And to think that I could still have taken back those two thousand when I learned he had received almost twice as much from your mother! All I could do was stammer a few stupid words —it was I who let him go. And then the police in the house, why had I given him money—almost implying that I was his accomplice . . ."

Mary followed him step by step, not knowing what to say, but he seemed not to notice her.

"Yes, all my work, my splendid work. And to think that he was a good man—or, rather, he seemed one. That hurts more than anything else. Did he have to shatter my faith in mankind?"

Mary stopped him to throw her arms around his neck. "Darling, my love," she said, "this is the only regret I allow you to have. He was a good man, he obviously was and still is a good man. What made him throw away this most precious possession on earth, the trust and friendship of an honest man like you, for the dubious advantage of a certain sum of money? People

374

who trust one because of money, says Mamachen, want that money, they are expensive friends to have, and you must be rich to please them. We trusted him because of his soul, which is the safest, rarest form of trust. That he should not have appreciated this is *his* misfortune, not ours. We must pity him. As for the money, it is dirt anyway. He who wants money *deserves* money, nothing but money, for he is very, very poor."

These beautiful words had a magical effect on the doctor. "You are so right," he said. "You are the noblest creature I have ever seen. Still, how are we to protect our ideals from the debasing fears and sights and smells of poverty?"

"Oh, those," she said, shrugging her shoulders with contempt. "One must have faith. We, you and I, and Mamachen most of all, are extraordinary people. See how little joy in life Mamachen has had from her money." Then calmly, though she knew she was speaking of the day when her mother would no longer be alive: "We will work, we will live modestly, sacrificing for our children and for science. You will make great discoveries. This is a blessed age to live in—think of Madame Curie. Would you not want your Mary to be a second Madame Curie? And yourself to be a new Curie, or Pasteur, or—or any of those great discoverers? Would you not? Tell me, now, frankly, would you not?"

"Yes, yes," he said, feeling a bit embarrassed by her childish enthusiasm.

"We will achieve it!" said she. "And now let me take Kostia and walk with him to the station. We are Russians, we love snowstorms, you are not, and besides, you have been sick. Agreed?"

"All right," he said. "But make Malachier understand that we cannot pay him fantastic sums such as he must be used to in Paris. After all, it's your uncle who suggested we call him. Could he not pay for the trip and the consultation?"

"We will see," she said in a hurry. She did not want to be

drawn into these financial talks again. It seemed to her that if she went to meet Malachier with a stingy mind, he would feel it and be stingy with his genius.

She called Kostia and told him to dress for the storm. Kostia proposed that Sonia and Filippo be allowed to come, too, he would drag them on his big sled, but their father forbade it. It seemed highly inappropriate to have Malachier met as a relative by his wife and his children. Secretly, it seemed to him that Malachier would then not be encouraged to do his best as a physician, because he had the friendship of this family in any case, even if the patient were to die.

Sonia and Filippo went back to the nursery, Mary and Kostia disappeared in the snowstorm, followed respectfully by the new butler, and the doctor went down to the kitchen, to make sure that the new cook learned the rules of the house and saved yesterday's bread. It won't be much, considering what we spend here every day, he thought, but at least it is something. And he felt, as he spoke, as if God were within hearing distance, nodding approvingly at this proof of good will.

Death is our first and only birthday present, tied with the umbilical cord and never opened. It may be lost, be opened by mistake or hate or curiosity, or torn open by animals—rats, dogs or microbes—be thrown into the fire, melted by water, so we must keep it hidden; but those of us who pretend that they were glad to receive it are liars. Oh, how I wish I could die laughing! But I cannot, because I never cheated death out of a single moment of life. No one on earth will be able to mourn me as I can mourn myself, because I know that my whole life was useless. Mary and the children will remember my usefulness, my presence, my attachment to life. I was only attached to death, I crossed life clinging to the hand of my governess, and now where is that hand? And who was she? Was I swindled by a shadow that pretended to be Death and was not? Those who go deep into themselves to attract their victims there, to be sought out of love and to be loved exclusively and forever, find that there is no such hiding place and no such person as themselves. Not only will they die alone like everybody else, but they will have lived alone, frightening away their family and their friends, because no one can fill the solitude of others. No one in his sane mind will wish to explore it in order to discover, at the end of the cavern, a lone person in need of light and love. "Light and love are outside, why don't you join us there?" That is what they all say, and they are right. Why don't you join them there? Because you have not joined them there before, and you regret the lost occasions, the lost years.

After the old lady had written this in her journal that morning, she realized that her disease this time was grave and final. She felt her heartbeat in her throat, her breath came heavy and she began to gasp for air. She was afraid of death. She was beginning to discover that what she had believed and what religion taught about the vanity of things human and the frightening presence of God was exactly the truth. Only, she had never believed it and religion had never taught it. So she wrote in a hurry:

There is an austere coquetry in philosophy and even in religion. Everyone recognizes the greatness of those glimpses of truth we are allowed to handle, but when death nears we realize that the God we have known we never knew and that His love was not for us. I am afraid, and I cannot ring the bell, because those two, my daughter and her husband, are liars like myself— and all doctors are liars. No one knows anything. And those who know can only die. Knowledge, in fact, is a symptom of death.

She stopped writing and reread what she had written. This was the truth. She had finally caught it. She now looked at the body of her knowledge, the actual, calligraphic body, and felt pleased with it, as if she had received an invaluable present. This indeed was a reason to live! She did not want to die. She now tested her eyesight: The snow battering the windowpanes was beautiful. She liked it, and in spite of her illness she could smell it. She wrote in her book:

The smell of snow is an extremely delicate affair. Only people from the north can recognize it. By its noble nature it is capable of piercing through the walls of sound and eyesight: one can see it and hear it. But then even our feelings become perfumed with snow. O blessed substance of my fatherland, thank you for visiting me here in this horrible country of cows and chocolate!

Now she knew what she wanted: to get well and go to Russia. Why did I hesitate so long? she thought. Why did I let that beast of a Pierre prevent my going there? What a fool I have been, and how dishonest of him to take advantage of my natural shyness!

She had a coughing spell and spat into her handkerchief. Now she felt better, her lungs were clear, her headache was gone. She got out of her bed, put on her dressing gown, found her slippers and began to pace the room, making plans for her trip. That was the moment when the maid came in.

"Frieda," she called in her feverish voice, "prepare the two big trunks and all the smaller suitcases! We are going to Moscow. You will like it, I know, you will like it!"

Kostia was so excited by the snowstorm that he kept shouting, "Aaah!" and "Oooh!" from the moment he and his mother left the house. Not only had the garden and the street changed absurdly, with the light shining upward from the earth and the sky dropping darkness downward, but the beauty of the snowstorm was in this: that it separated one human being from another. The huge sealskin which represented his mother, who was less than one step away, disappeared with

378

each drift and then reappeared, and her voice too was stolen from her throat and sent elsewhere, far from him. Perhaps his voice too was thrown into the air and could never meet hers, because their ears were still here with them, still attached to their heads.

"You know, Mamachen, Sonia and Filippo are very lucky today not to have come out with us."

"Whaaat?" shouted his mother almost into his ear, and only the wind reached him.

He understood from her position that she was bending over to catch his words, so he repeated them. "Sonia and Filippo are very lucky . . ."

"Yes? Why?"

Another long and violent swirl of snow that they had to take with their eyes closed; then he yelled, "They are lucky not to be here with us. They are inside where it is warm. We can stand it, but they could not. They are too small."

"Whaaat?"

"They are too small."

"Ye-e-es." A big smile seen through the snow showed him that she had understood.

"We are strong, but the wind is strong, too!" Another smile from her. "It is very, very strong!" She nodded, not to speak and expose her teeth to the wind. "And it would have been impossible to pull the sled—"

"Don't talk!" she shouted. "Too cold."

"But look, Mamachen, look at the storm! Could I have dragged the sled in that wind? Impossible, and they would have been lost!" She nodded again. "So they are very fortunate to have stayed indoors."

Then, after another pause, as he could not go on enjoying all that beauty in silence: "In Russia this would be much worse."

"Yes."

"But this is terrible, too. We will tell them when we go

379

back. We are the only ones to go out on such a day! I am glad Sonia and Filippo are in a warm place. Also Gross-mamachen is warm now. For her it would be even worse to be out. And also for Papa. He was very wise to stay home."

This went on until they reached the station. Every now and then the butler, who was walking behind them, would find himself falling upon their shoulders. He would apologize to the wind. They could not hear him.

"I am so glad you have come!" she said to Malachier the moment she saw him on the station platform. "My mother is determined to recover. She is well. Her mind is very clear, it is only her lungs that are not well. Do you think she will recover?"

"We will have to see her first," said Malachier, caressing Kostia's head. "Here is a healthy-looking little boy!" And Mary was annoyed by this easy way out. He was not taking her seriously.

"My mother is very strong. Do you think there is a chance? I don't mean just a chance of recovery, but of quick recovery?"

"Madame," said he, smiling and shaking his head, "if I could tell without seeing her first, there would be no point in my coming all the way from Paris to do so."

"You are right. But you will do everything you can, won't you?"

"Why, most certainly I will," said he, becoming facetious.

When the coachman waiting with his sad horse outside the station refused to drive them uphill to the villa he became suddenly offended, and Mary was afraid that he would not take good care of her mother.

"I am sorry," he said, "but I never walk uphill, not even in fair weather. This is a very bad storm, and I am not equipped for it. You would not want me to catch pneumonia, would you?"

The coachman did not care and said so, which irked Malachier very much. All Mary could do was offer the man three times his usual fare, and now he agreed to the trip on condition that the butler help him on the way by walking with him in front of the horse.

Mary had feared for her mother's life while this discussion was going on, and now she was proud to have saved her again. Timid as she was by nature, the mere sight of the frown on Malachier's face had filled her with terror. She did try to assure herself that he would do his duty in any case, that he was going to be paid a lot of money, and that, as a true Frenchman, he would do his best for that reason—as well as for the sake of his good name—but still, there remained the humiliating fact of illness, which, especially in a person as perfect as her mother, was not devoid of culpability: She is weak, her intelligence is impaired, she will have to undress for the doctor, he cannot have much admiration for her, and if she dies, who will be able to detect at which point in his study of her disease he became less attentive to the symptoms and to her chances of survival than to his town shoes which the snow might have ruined, or to *his* health? His conscience will not bother him. We are in his hands completely, and we must make him work, we must keep him awake and in good spirits.

"You are going to spend the night with us?" she asked in anguish.

"I hope so, madame. Unless there is a good hotel next door to your house. I had a very uncomfortable trip. The train was cold, the bed narrow, the noise unbearable."

"I would not let you go to a hotel for anything on earth."

Instead of thanking her, he froze into silence. Kostia took advantage of it to ask his mother whether he could not join the coachman and the butler and walk in front of the horse.

"Why, certainly, my darling," said Mary.

Kostia jumped down from the carriage and quickly disappeared in the storm, but she could hear his joyous chatter and the coachman's grunts in response. Mary smiled, she wished she could communicate that smile to her son. She was proud of him; he too loved the tempest, this supreme fable of nature which is not made for vulgar souls. One more reason to look after Malachier and cure him of his grave poetic deficiency.

People who don't love nature don't love life, she thought, and they cannot restore others to the enjoyment of something they themselves do not enjoy.

Malachier looked at Mary with a certain contempt, the typical contempt of the man who has given up life to engage in success, punctuating it with such items of pleasure as good cooking and occasional love affairs. He had found Mary attractive the first day he met her, but had detested her the second day on account of her Russian intensity, which made for heaviness. And he disliked her husband even more than he disliked her. The thought of a whole evening in their company and in Switzerland made him utterly despondent.

After a few minutes, however, he decided not to give in to gloom. He concentrated on the thought of her uncle, his best patient in Paris, and said, "I saw your uncle and your aunt the day before yesterday. They are anxious to know how your mother is."

"It all depends on you," said Mary. "We are in your hands."

"We are all in the hands of the Lord," said he, correcting her. "But we'll see, we'll see what we can do. By the way, how is my dear colleague your husband?"

"He could not come to meet you. I forgot to tell you, he had a touch of jaundice, so I made him stay home."

"Jaundice? Well, that's too bad. We'll have a look at him too, but I'm sure it is nothing. However, he was wise not to come to the station in this weather. And how is his scientific work?"

"Oh . . . going well, proceeding steadily."

She knew this was a lie and that it would soon be detected, but she felt impelled to please Malachier and was actually afraid that he might be upset by the news that her husband had done nothing remarkable in his field.

"Well, I am very pleased to hear that, and most anxious to hear more from your husband in person. So in the end he proved right. His instinct was his best adviser: he had to go back to a country where his language was spoken. I regretted it very much when I saw him leave, I had plans for him, as you well remember. And the young man who took his place is now a professor, he is very well known and has written three books. But we seem to be turning. Are we almost there?"

"Yes," said Mary. "It will not be long now."

A sudden shattering noise overhead made the doctor run upstairs. It sounded as if the storm, having settled inside the house, were working on the inner walls and hoping to pierce through them before being dislodged. He never thought this could have happened in the old lady's room, so he first opened every door in every other direction. Finally he met Frieda in the nursery, where she had gone in search of him.

"Where have you been, Doctor, where have you been? Madame is up, she wants to pack her trunks and leave for Russia!"

They both ran to her room now and had great trouble trying to push the door open. When they finally made it, there was snow on the floor, the window was wide open, and the old lady was gone.

"Dear Lord!" cried the maid. "She has jumped out the window!"

They leaned out and saw nothing but snow, more and more snow, coming up, coming down, flying past them in circles and hissing softly into their faces. They ran downstairs again without bothering to close the window at all, and ran out of the house to search the snow for the corpse. An impossible task. The old lady's windows overlooked a closed section of the garden, and the key to the gate could not be found. They looked up at the house in despair—and saw her at the window of her bathroom, in her robe, with a shawl tied over her head.

"What are you looking for?" she called.

"What are you doing there?" shouted the doctor. "Close that window, close it at once and get into bed, you fool!"

She heard him, was so horrified, so angry, that for a moment she felt tempted to jump in order to punish him. But she decided to stay and wait for him.

Frieda arrived first. She grabbed the old lady by the arm, pushed her toward her bedroom, closed the bathroom window, then closed the bedroom window, and when the doctor arrived the old lady was still standing there, baffled but amused too, because she felt she had triumphed over the stupidity of men and the forces of nature.

"This is so wonderful!" she said as he came in. "I feel so well! That was exactly what I needed: my Russian snow, my winter, my storm! Aaaaah!"

"All right," said the doctor, viewing the ruin of the room, snow everywhere on the furniture, with a strange, savage joy. "Do what you want, jump out the window, fly up in the air, I give up. I have no patience with you!" And he left.

The arrival of a stranger has a soothing effect on strained situations. Malachier brought with him an aura of serious work, and of hopes unfulfilled but still attainable, that made the doctor very eager to please him. Mary did not even ask whether her mother was well or not; she trusted science and had two scientists now under her roof contending against only one disease. She was pleased when she heard what her mother had done, as believers in doctors always are when symptoms become graver in the magical presence of the healer.

The first visit to the patient was almost one of pure courtesy, such as a great impresario will pay to a great comedian in prospect of a great play to be staged by them together. The old lady understood that she was going to be asked to play the patient and to submit to whatever definition of illness Malachier might find suitable for her. Mary was also present at this first meeting and found it delightful; she could almost see the battle between knowledge and evil taking shape under her eyes. Had her mother been lying there dead, she would have found the doctor's smile more credible than the cold stare of death. Her husband instead was annoyed and amused at the same time. He sided with the Fates: to him this magician was an indiscreet onlooker whose comedy might be punished with a show of severity on their part.

"I heard that Madame was doing some very foolish things while we were on our way from the station," said Malachier.

"Yes," she said, "I did something foolish—according to your standards, not ours. We Russians need our snow, we must greet it in person. I don't believe that fresh air can have harmed me."

"Unfortunately, madame, medical science does. I believe that in a matter of hours you will have a much higher temperature and feel much worse than you do now."

Mary became anxious and rose from her chair to allow the medical examination to begin, but Malachier said, politely, "Please do not move. We will have plenty of time later. I prefer to face the enemy at its worst—when the fever has set in."

"No higher temperature will set in," he said to the doctor as soon as they were alone together. "I think this is no mystery to you either, my young friend. Had someone else opened the window, she would die. That it was her own doing and that medical science claims she was wrong are sufficient to make her feel better. This is her way of establishing a contact with the world. Apart from that, she is tired. Persons of her type expend so much energy that they die of exhaustion. There is nothing to be done but let her die as she has lived."

The doctor was pleased to hear his own diagnosis expressed in such clear terms, but did not have the courage to say so. To claim professional equality with so brilliant a man as Malachier would have seemed grave immodesty.

"Your wife tells me you have done important scientific work since I last saw you," said Malachier.

Mary felt a cold chill run up and down her spine, and she turned her back to the two men in order not to show her embarrassment. But what she heard surprised her.

" 'Important work' is a merciful lie, but work I have done. I have read a great deal, I have even practiced medicine a bit, and am now seriously thinking of taking up a major work in the very near future—if not here, perhaps . . . elsewhere."

"I see, I see. And where would you continue your work? In Italy?"

"No, not in Italy."

There was a silence. The doctor wanted to say, "France," but could not, for fear that Malachier would discourage him.

"In Germany?"

"I don't think so."

There was another long silence, then Malachier said, "I would not advise you to go to Paris unless you had something definite there—an assistantship, a research project in collaboration with others. But, of course, if you intended merely to settle there as a general practitioner, then the whole picture would change. You might do so at any time. It would not be too easy at the beginning, but the economic problem is not one to you."

When Mary turned her face to Malachier, trying to avoid her husband's eyes, she saw those eyes avoiding hers, and yet searching them, too. The liar was ashamed of himself.

Lunch came as a blessing.

When Malachier finally left, it was the doctor who had caught a bad cold from exposure, while the old lady had recovered. Mary was busy with the children upstairs, and the doctor in his sickbed had time to think of his own future. So many things had been discussed that afternoon—and how well Malachier could pass from one to the other, without letting the main object of his conversation grow dimmer in his mind. Here a scientific subject was spiced with an epigram or a quotation from a poet; there he made an excursion from medicine into sociology, with a knock on the closed doors of politics, just to exchange greetings with the boring people closeted therein; well-being was connected with good cooking, and good cooking made the basis for clear thinking, and not through chemistry or physiology—rather, through the medium of pleasure, because clear thoughts, almost like human beings, liked to be heard and felt where the living was good. Every answer Malachier gave was a small essay of its own, a gem, even though often of no value at all.

Yes, that is the country for me, the doctor said to himself while taking his own pulse. I must not die. This would really be disastrous, now that I have found my way in life.

What pained him still was Malachier's discouraging remarks about the uselessness of his going to Paris to do research work. Gone were his chances in that field. But there remained general practice, and then Paris itself, a constant schooling in all the disciplines together. Go to Paris, oh, yes, Paris, that was the guiding light, salvation from pettiness, from atrophy, from complete humiliation.

To live with a woman like Mary one must be very strong, he concluded. Not rich, but strong and understanding. And to be strong one must be satisfied with one's own work, and I am not. The lie she told about my work shows that she feels it, too. Love is only a condition, not an end in itself.

With these considerations, he allowed himself to fall asleep.

XVIII

THE NEXT MORNING brought a letter from Rome, announcing that the old lady was being sued for twenty thousand francs for slander, then a letter from Pierre saying that the matter discussed was now in his lawyer's hands, and finally a letter from Schultz giving the name of a notary who would come to Lugano from Berlin for the modest sum of one thousand francs plus expenses, to draft the old lady's new will for her.

These letters were brought to the doctor by Mary with a note from her mother, saying: "You have a right to see these things. I have been very foolish again and I am sorry. I know that saying so does not help any of us very much, but sorry I am, believe me, and I wish I were dead. If you want to dismiss the entire household, please do so. I am ready to live in a Swiss inn, and eat Swiss food, to atone for my stupidity."

Together with these letters there was one written in German and addressed to the doctor. The handwriting was almost illegible, and definitely academic, and, of course, masculine. He hesitated for a while before opening it, then decided that all the other letters were far more important and he must take them up with his mother-in-law, without reproaching her and acting as if the course of those few days had aged him twenty years at least. Calmness and resignation, these were the two qualities he needed most. But he was angry again. So he post-poned his conversation with her and in the meantime wrote a note to a notary of his acquaintance, asking him to come over at once. He then drafted a telegram to Schultz thanking him for his offer of the notary from Berlin, but refusing it.

"Translate this into German," he said to Mary, "and send it off, please. This is the way to do business. And now let me wait another few minutes before I see your mother."

"Very good," said Mary. "Will you promise not to be un-kind to her?"

"Of course. No point in it. As a matter of fact, after you have translated that telegram, why don't you read me this let-ter?"

The letter was from Günther in Athens. Mary began to read aloud that Ludmilla, as Günther said, trusted no one else in the world but her brother-in-law. "A good beginning," she said, sneering.

The doctor sneered, too, and said, "Go on."

"Mmm . . . mmm . . . mmm. '. . . How many times has Ludmilla said to me, "No man is better, cleverer, kinder and more affectionate than my brother-in-law." . . . We left the others of our group in Naples, came to Athens alone. . . . You need have no fears, my vows of chastity were interrupted only once. Now they are ended, but you still need have no fears.' "

Mary blushed at this point. "Shall I go on?" she asked. "I don't see why I should be so well informed as to the sexual life of my sister and a German archaeologist."

"I don't, either," said the doctor. "Go on all the same."

"Mmm . . . where was I?"

There was a long pause, then she handed the letter to him, saying, "What language is this?"

"Ancient Greek. Yes. Poetry, too. Must be his own."

And the doctor began to look at it attentively, with great embarrassment because he could not understand it. For the last twenty-two years he had been under the impression that he knew Greek very well, because twenty-two years before he had been an honor student in the language. This was his first meeting with reality, the reality of life that corrodes our proud early knowledge first, then proceeds to corrode our later acquisitions as we leave them unused.

"If this has happened to my Greek, what will happen to my medicine in a few more years of idleness?" he asked. "Let's see. This is something about love and death. Wait. . . . Ah—nothing important. Read on from here."

She began again. " 'I denied myself to her time and again, because I considered it wrong for us to live as man and woman together before I had finished my book. I also wanted to make sure that Ludmilla had eternal reasons to give herself to me. Also, I must . . . openly . . . openly . . . confess that I thus imagined I could tie her to me for eternity, . . . denying her tonight for eternal reasons what she wanted tonight for frivolous reasons . . . and would no longer want tomorrow for eternal reasons—' " Mary interrupted herself and said, "I do not understand this passage, it is very confused."

"Go on."

"Mmm . . . mmm . . . ah—where was I? 'It worked, I confess openly in an honest . . . confession, I mean expression, of my . . . intimate truth. . . . We were very much . . . excited together . . . in museums, . . . and in the classical countryside, . . . in cathedrals—' " She stopped here and smiled. "Isn't that a bit strange?" she asked.

"Read on," he said.

"Mmm. '. . . because the purity of our human-conditioned souls gave us . . . gave us . . .' " She stopped to find the thread of the sentence.

"Gave us what?" he asked.

"Just a moment. German is hard to translate. Oh, yes, I have it: '. . . because the beauty of painting, sculpture and architecture seemed infinitely greater and more lively in the purity of our human-conditioned souls, which sacrifice had liberated from human bonds.' " She looked at him for light.

He only nodded and said, "Go on."

" 'We knew unforgettable moments of philosophical and . . . and'—how do you say *kunsthistorisch?* cultural, no, art-historical—'art-historical joys, . . . and she said to me, "I have learned more from you even than from my brother-in-law; but he is still more of a man than you are." ' " Here Mary frowned. "What can she mean? How does she know?"

"She means it only as an impression. Don't suddenly get suspicious."

"I am not suddenly getting suspicious," she said. "I have been suspicious for a long time. Can she refer to the time you were in the library with her?"

The doctor became angry. "But you forget that we never were in the library together."

"Oh, yes. But still . . ."

"Don't be silly. Go on."

"Mmm . . . mmm . . . 'This is why I am coming to you today . . .' Or, rather: 'This is why today I am addressing myself to the man to ask him, What is virility if not the power of restraint on one's own basest instincts?' Mmm . . . mmm . . . Where was I? Oh, yes: 'A man is one who always keeps his word, never losing his dignity.' "

"Beautiful," said the doctor. "Only he has a strange idea of his dignity. Go on."

"More Greek verses."

"Skip them."

She continued to read:

"*It is not that I repudiate this gift of the gods to the human called Ludmilla [three Greek words] in the true sense of the words, although [five more Greek words] would be infinitely more appropriate to describe her and her virtues; but I would not want her to step down from her pedestal, to leave the temple* which was built to protect the world from the fatal enchantment of her sight more than to protect her from the covetous eyes of the world. I know, I know I have no right [one Greek word] to be the only onlooker and worshiper; I feel as if I had stolen the sun from the world and were keeping it for my pleasure alone, thus neglecting mankind and impairing agriculture. But if she is to be worshiped by others, let these at least be worthy of her. What irks me and wounds me deep down in my bone marrow is when people blind to the best in her, deaf to the most in her, deaf to the most precious tones in her voice, people, in one word, utterly unworthy of coming near her, do come near her, and even dare to give her advice and treat her almost with contempt. She is too good and too pure to distinguish between frankness and vulgarity, so unwillingly she encourages them; and this has caused me and is still causing me great pain, I openly confess.

"Now, there is, for example, a man whose manners and whose wit are beneath anything I have ever seen, a man who has never read a book and who has the greatest contempt for the classics (and no excuse to be so, because he is rich and may even pass for refined on first sight), and this man allows himself to treat her as a stupid little schoolgirl, saying so in these very words, and missing no occasion to remind her of her ugliness! Yes, you may marvel at my words, her ugliness! And she believes him! Then, of course, the task of reassuring her falls to me. Gladly so, I shall openly confess; I have spent hours, days at times, trying to reassure her, to undo the evil work he did in two seconds. The other day I could not stand it any longer and told that so-called gentleman [five Greek words here]. Would you believe it? Ludmilla flung her arms around me and kissed me tenderly, as she had rarely done before; and even later, that same night, she said to me, 'What would I do without you? Who gives me hope? Who restores my self-confidence? You alone.' What a sweet moment that was! I shall never forget it as long as I live!

"Unfortunately, this man not only destroys her self-confidence, he teaches her bad words and she uses them freely, and he constantly makes vulgar jokes and is given to that lowest form of hilarity which consists in double meanings and plain silliness."

Mary interrupted herself here to say, "Ludmilla always was inclined that way. She did not have to learn from him. That is where Günther is mistaken."

"Go on."

"Now, I want you to know that this terrible man has followed us everywhere. I often have asked Ludmilla whether she is in love with him and she has always said no. 'Don't you see how ugly he is?' was her first and constant argument. So I asked her to get rid of him once and for all and she did so, four times. He went to Berlin, or so she said; then, suddenly, before he had time to reach Berlin, back he was in Florence, in Rome, even in Greece. Which means that Ludmilla was telling me lies, a thing I had already understood and discussed with her many times, so why should she go on telling them when she knew this to be unnecessary? I did not have to learn from her that he had never gone to Berlin at all, because I knew it from the way she reacted to art: insensitive to painting and sculpture, absent-minded when I read poetry to her, totally indifferent to nature."

Another pause. Mary could not help commenting on this. "But she has always been indifferent to nature and to art. That is where Günther is mistaken."

"Go on."

"Mmm. '. . . indifferent to nature. But there is more: Here in Athens, Ludmilla met a young French diplomat—' " Mary stopped here to laugh. "I know him!" she said. "Alain de Citoges! He wanted to marry me. That is why Ludmilla tries to win him now! He never liked her."

"Mary," said the doctor, sitting up in bed and staring, "you never told me about this man! Who is he?"

393

Mary was so delighted to be able to mention someone her husband did not know that her voice quivered as she said, "A very, very nice young man from a very good family. Beautiful, strong, witty, wicked—oh, so wicked."

"Mary!" There were tears in the doctor's voice. "Mary, come here, sit down here on my bed. You never told me about him. Had it not been for this letter, I would never have heard of him."

"But, darling," said Mary, regretting her words, "believe me, he never meant anything to me. I always laughed at him. He just amused me, that is all."

"He amused you? Did he ever kiss you?"

"How can you say such a thing?"

"Swear on your children's heads."

"I swear."

That seemed to calm him. "Now tell me another thing: This Alain, did you meet him after you had met me?"

"Let me think. No, before."

He seemed relieved, but she hesitated a bit, then said, "I was mistaken. It must have been after—yes, it was after."

"I see."

There was a long silence. He stared before him, the picture of despair. "So it was after," he said. "After the great love, amusement. Nice."

"Darling, how can you say that?"

"*You* said it. These are your words: 'He amused me.' "

"But, darling, I don't see anything wrong in that. He did, he made me laugh."

"You pretended, and you even wrote down in your notebooks, that no one had been able to distract you from the image of that first love—my image. Am I mistaken?"

"No, you are not. And there is no contradiction between the two things. Even when Alain made me laugh, there was always your image in my heart. Always. I swear."

"Then why did you start when you heard about him, how

did you know he was in Greece now? Has he written to you lately? Do you correspond with him, either directly or indirectly?"

"Darling, how can you imagine my doing such a base thing? Correspond with a man? Are you insane?"

"So you do not."

"Of course I do not. The mere fact of having to say so is insulting. Do you think me a prostitute like my sister?"

He was still staring before him. She repeated the question: "Am I like my sister? Tell me I am, so I can jump out the window and free you of my filthy presence."

"No, do not," he said, holding her arm. "I believe you. Only I still cannot understand your sudden outburst of joy at the mention of his name. And your knowledge of his whereabouts."

"But I don't know his whereabouts, I swear. And perhaps it is not even he Günther mentions in his letter. Let's see." She read on. "Mmm . . . mmm . . . Here we are: '. . . a young French diplomat . . .' Where is it? I must have lost it again. Oh, here it is:

"Here in Athens, Ludmilla met a young French diplomat, a Prince de Brignolles . . ."

She looked at her husband triumphantly. "You see? I was too quick in jumping to conclusions. I just said Alain de Citoges because I remembered how Ludmilla always tried to catch his eye and never succeeded. And I know Ludmilla: she would try again and again, if she had to spend her whole life doing so. And without caring for a man a bit. That's Ludmilla for you."

The doctor beamed and nodded.

"Prince de Brignolles?" she went on, sneering. "There is no such title. The Brignolles are counts, not princes. And I know who this must be: the son of Countess de Brignolles, born

395

Kravatzky-Kravalitzy; she is from St. Petersburg, she is even distantly related to us. But I have never met the young man. This must be one of Ludmilla's lies. She always tries to make her friends appear more important than they are. But let's see what she has done now with this 'prince' of hers. Mmm . . . mmm . . . Here we are:

". . . Prince de Brignolles, a very cultivated person who can write epigrams in classical Greek and has contributed an interesting article to a magazine for which I write, too (the article was translated—he wrote it in French). He was fascinated by Ludmilla the moment he set eyes on her. I must openly confess I was not at all displeased when I noticed that Ludmilla was flattered by this civilized tribute to her beauty . . ."

Mary laughed and laughed and laughed, then went on:

". . . And I gladly gave her permission to go out with him one evening, when I realized that there was no other way of making her happy. My presence would have hampered her: I know I can be quite boring at times, and, au fond—as the French so cleverly say—the notion that my Ludmilla stays with me all the time, that she never abandons me even for one split second, and never betrays me, is quite sufficient for me. I love, and my love is faithful to me: that is my true Ludmilla. The historically conditioned Ludmilla, the Ludmilla omnimode determinata, to use a term from Scholastic philosophy, needs frivolity and champagne, nonsense and mirrors. But I must also openly confess that my heart was set at peace: Ludmilla herself—unsolicited by me—gave me solemn assurance that she would not allow the prince to behave disrespectfully to her. I believed her and gave her my blessing.

"And what happened that evening? I was quietly reading in my room (I had forgotten to tell you that we were staying at the house of some very rich friends of the prince, people who were away for the season) when her suitor, that horrible man, walked in. Without apologizing for his visit, he sat down in my armchair next to the table on which I was working, and began to insult me. He seemed so completely distraught that I paid no attention to his insults and just tried to hear what he had to say, why he had come. Can you believe me? He had come to reproach me for letting Ludmilla go out with the prince! I was going to tell him that Ludmilla was my care and, last but not least, also my future wife. He did not let me. 'You don't know who that man is,' he kept repeating in a fit of anger. 'He is one of the most depraved men in the world.'

"At this point, I must openly confess, I was ready to say something, but I did not know what. I should have said that I knew only one depraved man in the world and that was he, but unfortunately this idea came to me only on the following day. My trouble is, I think, that, when someone talks to me, I always try to take him in, as the Latins so well say—capire, contain, the contrary of answering or ejecting, throwing out. This is true for all answers, but especially for what goes under the name of 'quick answer' or 'answer to the point'—in other words, the so-called brilliant remark, which, in most cases, is but a cheap epigram, based on a double meaning and as such amusing only to the lowest minds. Even in literature I detest this verbal game, and in fact it is the only grievance I have against Shakespeare."

Mary looked at her husband with a bit of malice in her eyes; he had never read Shakespeare and she had read him in two languages, English and German.

"Go on," said her husband.

"But he was in such a state that I took pity on him. Poor devil, I thought, he and I after all suffer for the same person, only I suffer less, because my suffering is of a higher quality, but I should not be proud of this, because he was born vulgar and devoid of that love of the classics which is my greatest fortune.

What he seeks and hopes to obtain is Ludmilla at her worst, so I should work on her and not on him, or, rather, on him too, but then only to better him!

"With these notions to comfort me, I proceeded to comfort him to the best of my knowledge. 'Nothing can have happened to her,' I said, 'you have no reason to worry, you should worry instead when she is in your company, not in other people's company.' He listened to me, it seemed to amuse him for a while; but then his eyes became foggy with images that I ignored or tried to ignore because I had a feeling that they were vulgar. He was restless, he went into the kitchen looking for food, but the servants had gone to sleep and there was nothing, so he began to search the house for wine and found bottles of very fine French champagne, which he proceeded to drink without asking my permission. I told him the bottles did not belong to me. 'Oh, leave me alone!' he answered, and threw a handful of bank notes on the table to pay for them. He was obviously hoping for an indignant reaction on my part, but I pocketed the money, which I later left in an envelope for the owners of the house, whom I did not know, with a full explanation of what had taken place. So now the indignant reaction came from him: 'I did not think you would pocket that money,' he said. And I said, 'Oh, I see! That must be the reason you gave it to me. You were hoping that I would refuse it. But you were wrong. I always pay for what I take, and I had no intention of offering you champagne.' Afterward I was sorry I had spoken that way, because he became sullen and did not speak another word until Ludmilla came back. When she rang the bell I ran to the door and he started after me. 'Stay where you are,' I said, and he sat down again. I don't know who gave me the strength to be so impolite. But I was.

"Ludmilla seemed in good spirits, she hugged me, I knew that her conscience was clear, and I said to her, 'Ludmilla, I must tell you something: That man is here, please send him away and don't sit with him for hours now.' 'He is here?' she said, and

burst into loud laughter, then ran into the study and made such
a scene that I thought he would leave at once. But he just
listened to her, bending low as she spoke (that being the only
sign that he had understood the gravity of her charges), then
said to her, 'You have learned many things from your master,
you do sound like a dusty archaeologist. My compliments. If
you feel that way about me there is no reason you should see
me again. But if you don't want to lose me forever, drop the
prince for all and completely. Which means that if you meet
him on the street, you will not answer his greeting. Agreed?'
She looked at me, looked at him furiously—you should have
seen the struggle in her soul, I was sorry for her—and then,
through her teeth, she said, 'Agreed.' He smiled and ran out
of the house without even saying goodbye to me. Now I must
openly confess that I was really beginning to have enough of
this. So I said to her, imitating his tone, 'May I also make my
conditions known, my friend? Same as his, only that instead of
applying to the prince they apply to him and him only. Agreed?'
And she said, 'No.' I must say I was baffled for a moment. I
could not bring myself to believe that such an answer was
possible, and tried at first to ascribe it to my tactless procedure
(I had given her no time to recover from one blow when I had
administered a second). So I said, 'Please consider what you have
just said. I give you ten minutes to think it over.' (I should
have said, 'I give you until tomorrow.') And she laughed in my
face. Her voice, I am sorry to say, sounded quite vulgar.

"Well, I must now openly admit that during the rest of
that night and the following day I often wished one of us two
were dead. As for my own death, that was an old wish and it
did not surprise me at all; what surprised and horrified me was
that I should wish for Ludmilla to die. But I finally made it: I
persuaded her that I had not really thought of leaving her, and
she forgave me. It makes me laugh when I catch myself speaking
that way. In any other case it would have seemed absurd not to
use a whip, but with Ludmilla it is different: it is she who for-

gives when she is wrong, and she is apt to apologize when she is right. This makes her so endearing to me.

"The next thing I did was to go to the prince and ask him frankly to save Ludmilla from that horrible man. This, I must openly confess, was not an easy task at all. I too am jealous and possessive by nature, though it may not seem so. I knew I was encouraging this man to do what Ludmilla herself had sworn to me she would not let him do. But what choice did I have?

"Ludmilla was taken by surprise. She was preparing to go out when the prince came with a beautiful present for her: a broche of ancient make with a blue stone in the middle (nothing excessively valuable, but the object in itself is a museum piece) and minor stones in other colors on the sides, the whole mounted in ancient gold. I must say I was hurt when he gave it to her in my presence, and I decided to let my feelings run free for once, so I looked at the prince with angry eyes and left, without saying goodbye. What happened now? She accepted the brooch, she accepted the company of the prince, then told him she was busy and went out to see her friend. I had expected to have dinner with her and leave Greece the next day; not at all. Here I waited and waited, and was about to go out and look for her where I thought she might be (and I must openly confess that no thought could be more revolting to me—I hate to spy on people, no matter how good the reasons), when I was met on my doorstep by the prince, who, in despair, was coming to see me. She had snubbed him a few minutes before, and she was not alone. This hit me like a knife in the back. But it was obviously my fault, I had asked for it, now I had to bear all the sad consequences without saying a word.

"The prince came in, he was in a terrible state. His behavior, however, was far more dignified than that of the other man; he did not drink, he did not speak a word against that other man, in fact, he taught me something I myself did not know: that in a case like this, one must try to discover what is good in the person one is jealous of, rather than what is bad, for we have eyes for what is bad, but none for what is good. He had no bitter words for anyone and apologized to me in the most touching terms. I must now openly confess that I never felt closer to any human being than to the prince on that night. However, as I said, he found words of excuse (and very dignified ones) even for his own bad behavior, saying that, after all, he was in love. I tried to console him, told him that I alone could understand his pains and promised I would do my best to help him win her back (by that time, I must openly confess, I was beginning to feel tired of Ludmilla). I even offered to let him stay there until Ludmilla came back, while I would leave with my belongings and go to a hotel. But he said no. He did not want to besiege her. 'That is not done,' he said; 'I wish it were, but unfortunately I can't, because it just is not done.' He left quite early, in fact, and had tears in his eyes. 'Farewell, my friend,' I said, 'and do not despair. True love always wins in the end.'

"Ludmilla came back an hour later. I was tired and angry again, because I thought this was an open insult to me and I should not allow it. 'Sorry I am a bit late,' she said, 'but it was all your fault. I owe you no apology.' 'Could you at least tell me where you have been all day?' I asked. 'Where I have been?' she repeated two or three times, as if to gather courage before saying something cruel. (Even in her worst moments, I must honestly admit, she had regard for me.) Then she said, 'I have betrayed you, my dear friend, betrayed you, for the first time in my life.' I clenched my fists to regain the control I had already lost inside my whole being, then said, 'It surprises me only that it should have been the first time. I never think of these matters, because they are too vulgar, but I had thought without thinking [five Greek words here] that you had already betrayed me long ago.' 'No,' she said, 'I had not. Today was the first time. And you have only yourself to blame for it.' 'As usual,' I replied, trying to smile. 'No,' she replied, 'not as usual, because today you did something you had never done before.

You had two reactions, one after the other, one that I liked because it was spontaneous, and the other that I hated because it was cowardly. You were here when the prince came with his present, and you looked at him with the hate and contempt he deserved. I was glad, I felt suddenly protected. Then, for no reason in the world, you left the field to him, to the man who had dared make a present of jewels to your future wife. So I drew my conclusion and betrayed you with him.' 'Here, in this house?' 'Here in this house first, and then later at his house until now. That is where I have spent the evening.'

"I was beginning to see black. 'You have?' I asked before jumping at her throat. 'I have. And with the prince you trusted so. My other friend was right; he, whom you despise, would never have behaved as this swine did!' I put a hand over her mouth and said, 'Don't soil your mouth more than you have with your lies.' 'Lies?' she yelled, pushing my hand away so that I stumbled and fell. 'Lies? I am telling you the truth.' 'No, you are not,' I said. 'Prove it!' she said, and this was the moment. So I said, 'If you want to know the truth, the prince was here this evening, here on that chair, crying because he had seen you in the street with that man I detest and despise.' 'The prince was here?' she said, stuttering. 'That is impossible, because he was in bed with me. When was he here?' 'When were you with him?' I asked. 'When was he here?' she shouted. 'All evening,' I said. 'He left only a few minutes ago.' I had expected a complete breakdown at this point, but she was calm and smiling now. 'Of course,' she said, 'and, knowing him, that does not surprise me at all. I was with him before.' 'When?' 'Earlier, much earlier. And after that he had the nerve to come here and whine in your company! Stinkers, both of you! I have no respect for either of you!' I grabbed her by the arm and said, smiling, 'Look, Ludmilla. When you came in you said you had spent the whole evening with him, you said you were coming from his house, straight from his house.'

"She saw herself caught in a web of lies, looked at me like a wounded animal, and broke down so completely that I had to console her. She wanted to kill herself, she sobbed in my arms, she said she did not know why she was telling me such lies, she begged me not to leave her alone, she humiliated herself to such a point that I feared for her sanity and—I must openly confess that, without even knowing what I was doing, I broke my vow of chastity, even though I had another hundred pages to go. And I broke it again and again the whole night long."

Mary could not go on. The fire, vice and madness of that episode seemed to be present in their room. They both felt guilty and jealous. They had become occasions and not people; this lascivious story told by a fool who had known his first woman at the tail end of everybody's orgy at his expense had emptied them of their own souls, deprived them of their names and their rights. Did they not know that they were man and wife, and that the laws, the walls, the furniture, the presence of four children in the house, sanctioned and sanctified their love? What was this strange uneasiness invading them?

"That is a dangerous letter," said the doctor. And he quoted from Dante:

> "Galeotto fu il libro e chi lo scrisse
> Quel giorno più non vi leggemmo avante.

"But we must finish reading it, because we are not in sin."
Mary read on:

"I must now openly confess that, in spite of the joys of that first night, it was also fraught with tragedy, because Ludmilla passed constantly from passion to disgust, from self-abasement to reproach, and by the end my only wish was to sleep undisturbed. I wondered at her energy. My mind stops working instantly when I am tired, but hers—oh, hers is set aflame, even in her sleep she will talk and make sense. [One whole page of Greek verse here.]

403

"But of course . . . [another half page of Greek verse, which ends with the comment, 'Is it not?'] Also, I must confess, there was bitterness in me, because I did not like to think that in order to obtain what I was now obtaining I had thrown my treasure to the wolves. Why had I not done wrong a bit earlier? Why only now, and so stupidly now? Thus when she was not torturing me, I was torturing myself. Because I knew she loved me. There were those words of hers about my first 'spontaneous reaction' that she had liked, and she had been glad to feel protected. Obvious proofs of love. And I, the idiot, blinded by my own love, had not seen hers moving in my direction. Love and love do not mingle, therefore [six Greek words here], or, much rather, [three more], because the [one Greek word] is [another Greek word] with [three]. How I hated myself for having been so foolish! Because that was the thing she would never forget: my leaving her alone with the prince. 'I was crying so bitterly that he took advantage of my weakness,' she said. 'And to think that the evening before I had promised never to let him touch me!' I must confess that I was utterly at a loss to remind her that she had done much worse than I, and her lies had been infinitely worse than my one cowardly retreat, or desertion, as she called it. But I could not defend myself, because I was concealing something from her, and that sufficed to give me a bad conscience. [One, two, three, four, five Greek lines here.]

"Finally I broke down and said, 'Ludmilla, my love, will you listen to me? Will you let me defend myself? After all, you were honest with me, even though you became so only when all your lies were spent. Your confession last night was an act of despair, and you cried because I had deprived you of your best toy, your lies.' 'What do you mean?' she said. 'Am I nothing but a liar? For one merciful lie I told you to spare you greater sorrows, you will go on accusing me for the rest of my life. I am not going to accept this. You should thank me for lying to you.' 'Let me finish,' I said; 'that was meant only as a comment on your nature, this is typically feminine, it is, in fact, the reason I love you—you are like a child.' 'And so are you,' she said. 'A child would be more courageous and defend his best toy, admitted that you loved me as a child loves his toy. But you do not. You left me in the hands of that man, and that was why I later went to that other man. I owed him an apology, you forget, I had promised him I would never see the prince again, never even answer his greeting on the street. Why should you be the only one to exact promises from me? I am an honest woman: when I promise something I keep it, while you do not. You had promised to protect me, why did you leave me with that man?'

"So I broke down and made my full, open confession. It was a real [five Greek words], but while making it I realized what a fool I was. She was so indignant that she refused to live in the same house with me. In vain did I plead, cry, batter my head against the wall; she packed all her belongings and went straight to the hotel with that horrible monster. I was going to write to you then, but did not find the strength, or, rather, the [one Greek word] to do so. It was [three Greek words] of [two], as in [two more]. Then I resigned myself to my fate, also because my own Ludmilla was more faithful to me than to herself. The prince came here to relieve me of my promise to help him win her for him, and to tell me that he did not begrudge me my happiness, because I deserved Ludmilla's love more than he did. But when he heard the truth he broke down and did nothing but drink for three days, neglecting his person and his work as well. I had to humor him and bring him back to life.

"He finally left, and for a day it was a great relief to find myself alone again. I rested, I wrote poetry, I took notes for my book, and was perfectly happy when Ludmilla suddenly came back, saying she had seen the lights in my room and had been wondering how I was and whether I needed company. She had never been kinder and more charming. She did things she had never done before: she tidied my room, brushed my clothes, prepared coffee, told me I looked tired and must rest, and while she did these things I let her be as if she were a dream, in order that the dream might go on existing and unfolding in front of me, behind my back, in the next room. [*Five lines of Greek.*] It was not only joy that kept me silent and apparently indifferent, it was the fear that she might suddenly become like a wild beast again. She first took it as [three Greek words], and tried to humor me, then she became like a child alone at night in a dark room. The pity that was in me already overcame me completely and I began to cry, silently at first and then more and more loudly. 'Günther,' she said, 'what is this? Why, if you want your Ludmilla back, don't you fight for her? Ask her whether she likes the man she is living with, thunder against him as you used to do. Come, say something!' 'I would not dare,' said I. 'Who am I to speak, anyway?' 'Oh, nonsense,' she said, 'don't debase yourself, you are a great man, a genius, a poet, and you are a kind man, and also my savior and my guardian and teacher and friend—or are you not my friend? Am I mistaken? Come, be yourself, assert yourself again, fight, I love you when you fight, and I betrayed you only because I love to see you fight, get angry, lose your patience. I don't like the professor in you, he is too German for my taste, too distant, and too boring.' I went on crying as she spoke, I could not help it, this was too much like a dream, so I cried and cried and cried until she started to lose patience and said, 'What am I to do with a person like you?' 'Nothing,' I said. 'I am no good. Go to your friend, he is much better than I. You said so, you must know.' 'Oh,' she said, sighing, 'why should you always believe me so? You are incorrigible, I'm beginning to fear that you will never learn.'

"Then, after giving a few more signs of her growing impatience, which did nothing but paralyze me all the more, she sat down next to me, her elbows on the table and her hands under her chin, like a teacher in school, and began to recite the lesson I was supposed to know by heart. 'All right,' she said, 'it is a bit silly for me to be answering questions that have never been asked, but I shall answer you as if you had asked me

whether I like living with that man. Well, to be frank, I do not.
He is unkind, he is even a bit of a faker, intellectually speaking.
Stupid? Oh, no, not at all, not the least bit. An organizer, yes.
In fact, a man of genius in the handling of money. He needs
money, makes plenty of it and cares little about the methods
employed. What are these methods? Would you not want to
know? Well, so would I, but I don't think I ever will. How do
rich men make money? Does anyone know except themselves?
At times I wonder whether they do themselves. Take my eldest
brother, Pierre. He has something in common with this man. He
too has mistresses, but does not divorce his wife. As a matter of
fact, though, I think he will now. That American dancer he is
showering with jewels, that's the one who will make him divorce
his wife. And I am the woman who could make this man divorce
his wife, if I insisted. But I shall not insist. I am not in love
with him. I respect him; in fact, I respect him so much that
I would never marry him without really loving him. If a woman
like me marries a man like him, she stays faithful to him
for the rest of her life, and I don't know . . . Suppose I
met you, Günther, in a museum, where I found myself all
alone, or, still worse than alone, with him. I would just come
to you and say, "Günther, the way you can speak about
paintings and sculpture teaches me so much that I want
to stay with you until I have learned all I want to know,
and that means probably years, all my life. He does not
care, he sees nothing, he knows nothing, except how he can use
other people, even people like you, to make money. I am tired
of that, Günther." This I would say, and in a matter of hours
perhaps you would have become my lover and he would either
kill me or kill you. Or follow me and pester me as he has done
during this trip of ours, until I went back to him. And again it
would be all your fault, because you would not fight enough to
keep me. You would prefer to sell me to another stupid prince,
I would resent it, and back I would be with this man. So you
see, what is the point? Tell me, what is the point?' These were

407

her words, I have been able to transcribe them as if she had dictated them to me, because, I must now openly confess, I had never imagined that a divine creature like Ludmilla could be so profoundly confused in her thinking."

Mary interrupted herself here and said, with hate in her voice, "She is a prostitute! And he is a fool!"

"Right," said the doctor, "she is a prostitute. But he is not a fool. He is an honest man. Go on."

Mary sighed, cleared her throat and went on:

"A great feeling of pity prevented me from speaking for a long time. Then I said to her, 'My poor, abandoned child! Why don't you marry him and make an effort to stay faithful to him? I would never agree to betray him with you.' She seemed hurt. 'That is typical of you,' she said. Then, upon noticing my tears —a bit late, I must say—she began to caress me and to kiss my hair, and I cried more and more, and finally she said, 'I'll tell you why. Not only because I don't love him enough, but because he is not quite distinguished enough. I would never be able to introduce him to my family. There are certain minor things that I could not explain to you, because you don't know him at all, but I know him quite well, I have studied him completely, like a book. And there are certain things I could never accept. I am very much like my mother in this . . .' "

Mary shook as if struck by lightning, threw the letter on the floor and shouted, "No, no and a million times no! That is too much! To soil Mamachen's name that way—oh, no! In what is Ludmilla like Mamachen?" Tears of indignation were rolling down her cheeks.

"You are right," said the doctor. "How dare she?"

He did not feel like going on with the reading, but it was Mary this time who picked up the letter and read on with excitement, as if she had finally found what she wanted.

" '. . . I am very much like my mother in this, I cannot stand provincial people, and he is one and will forever be one, no matter how much money he makes. My father too was a very simple man, had received no education, but he was a born gentleman, and my grandfather, who hated him because he had taken his daughter away from her husband, never found anything to say about his manners. He was really a born gentleman. . . .' "

Mary again interrupted herself and said cheerfully, "She must insult even the memory of the dead! Oh, what an awful creature! And have you heard about Pierre and a mistress? That was news to me, too. Ludmilla and Pierre are really the limit!"

She giggled joyfully and went on:

" '. . . a born gentleman. He never boasted about money. This man does!' These were Ludmilla's very words!

"I must now openly confess that I was listening to her, but also losing interest, I was becoming numb, and she noticed it and asked, 'What is it? I am telling you these things because you are my only friend and I want your advice, but you seem to have lost interest. I am all alone here.' She noticed that I was becoming soft again, because even a change in the tone of her voice will bring about the miracle, and she smoothed my hair and asked me, 'Is it true that I am all alone in the world? Who is my only friend? Tell me, who is he?' 'Your brother-in-law,' I said. She became very serious and said, 'Yes, you are right. But he is far away and he despises me. Oh, he would give me advice, why haven't I thought of him sooner? Why?' There was real pathos in her voice, and then she began to speak of your children and of her mother whom she had treated so badly and whom she wished she could see again before her death. She had tears in her eyes, and I consoled her a bit.

"Then, as usual, unexpectedly, she was cold and reasoning

again and said, 'I know, I know now what I need. I need a home,
but not a home in which I am the mistress; not for the moment,
at least. I want to be a good family girl, in a respectable household, with no responsibilities, no difficult choices to make, such
as those I should make now among three men. I love my little
nephews and my niece, I love them so, and they love me. And
then I love my mother, and I have never had a chance to stay
with her since I was nine. Never. Always in boarding schools
or with people like Pierre and his wife, who had their social life
and left me alone with their children as if I were another child.
I was too young to appreciate children then, and besides, their
children were not as nice as Mary's children. Oh, I want to see
them again, to run wild in the garden and play with the dog,
oh, how I love that dog!' So she went on talking about you
and your children and the dog, and your beautiful house and her
dear mother and her dear sister who—she claims—dislikes
her, and she admitted that it had been the fault of both, because each had been prejudiced against the other, but that now
perhaps if they lived together again they might get to know
each other."

Mary lifted her head from the letter and said joyfully, "See
the trick now? Wait, don't say anything, listen to this." And
she read now in a tone so ironical that it began to irritate her
husband (it was hard to understand what came to him already
censored and condemned to disbelief):

"So I said, 'Ludmilla, why don't you go home to your mother?'
'How can I,' she said, 'if I don't go with you? What shall I tell
them? I don't want them to know our secrets. They might think
we have quarreled.' So I said, 'I can write to your brother-in-law
and explain to him that it was my idea, not yours.' 'Oh, thank
you, my friend,' she said. 'You are the only friend I have on
earth, apart from my brother-in-law. This will allow me to leave
without angering my other friend, the one you hate so much.'

'Your friend? I thought you disliked him,' I said. 'Oh, yes, I do,' she said. 'He is not a kind person like you.' 'Then why don't you come back and stay with me until you leave?' I asked, and she said, 'I could not do it. I gave him my word I would go back tonight.' 'Does he know you are here?' 'Oh, yes, he does. I never tell him a lie. He would not like that. It would be the end.' 'How about me?' I asked. 'Do you think I like lies?' 'Oh, with you it is different. You are a civilized person, and if I lie to you it is only because I love you too much.' This, I must openly confess, left me quite speechless for a while, because it seemed to me that the logical structure of her argument was weak. And I committed the mistake of calling this to her attention. Oh, how I wish I never had! But to go back to my fatal mistake, I laughed and said, 'You love me too much to tell me the truth, but not enough to live truthfully.'

"I saw her wrath rise like a flame from the depths of her soul and shoot upward, straight into her head, I saw the flames through her beautiful eyes, and they reminded me of the windows through which I had seen my father's body burn in the Ludwigshafen crematorium, except that here I was watching my own dead body eaten up by the flames. And this is not my image, for she said so. 'You have spoken the truth,' she said. 'You have built your own funeral pyre and lit it. This is the end of our love.' In vain did I plead, 'Ludmilla, don't take me seriously. I did not really mean it.' 'That does not interest me,' she said. 'I do. For I know you are right. Obviously I do not love you enough, or I would find the strength to be faithful to you. But your love, too, is not worth much. You love only yourself. You used me only as a model for poetry, as a term of comparison, or as an audience for your lectures on art.' What could I say? There was, alas, a great deal of truth in these words. And she went on: 'You don't deserve that I be honest with you. Have I not come here on my own today and been truthful to you? Yes, but you could not see this, because you love only yourself and your work, which is your spiritual boudoir. You and your mirror of writing! Who could hope to be noticed by you when you are busy making yourself up in order to be worshiped by posterity? Where am I in your life? What have you asked me today? To stay with you. Did you bother to ask me whether I was with child? Oh, no. That thought never crossed your mind. It crossed the mind of the man you despise. He asked me and I said no. I would have said yes to you. At any rate, three men may claim this child, and if it is allowed to come to life at all it will reveal the father's name, perhaps not for years, when a resemblance unfolds. So here again I am answering questions you never thought of asking. Why I should go on doing this I don't know, so goodbye.'

" 'Will you come again?' I asked, and she said, 'No, you must work.' 'What shall I write your brother-in-law?' She said, 'Whatever comes into your mind.' 'And when an answer comes, how will I let you know?' She thought a while, then answered, 'I don't know. I shall probably write to my brother-in-law myself —or no, I don't know now. I am a bit confused.' 'But how about the child?' 'I don't know, it is too early to tell. At any rate, I can take care of myself.' 'But if I want to know how you are, where shall I write?' She was pensive again for a while, then said, 'The prince.' 'Are you going to stay with him?' 'Why should I stay with him? I am probably going to say goodbye to him. He is the only friend I have.' 'But why should he know where you are and I be kept in the dark?' 'Because you are an egotist and he is not.' With these words she was gone.

"And to think that if I had refrained from making that last stupid remark she would never have come to the conclusion that she did not love me enough, and now perhaps she would be back with me. How I regret all my mistakes, how I wish she would let me prove to her I no longer care about my work, I care only about her! Where is she now? Is she with you? I doubt it. The prince told me she had been with him for two days, but he was very reserved. Perhaps this had to do with the fact that I was (and still am) in this house as his guest, or the guest of his friends. I had forgotten that detail. I am now seriously think-ing of moving from here at once—that is, as soon as I have finished my chapter on the funeral vases in the Athens museum. I should also finish a poem I have begun (in Greek, but not in ancient Greek this time; I am trying my hand at Demotiki, with results that seem hopeful), and of course it would be a grave mistake for me to change environment, it might kill my inspiration.

"But to go back to my Ludmilla: The prince said she might be on her way to Lausanne with his sister and the Duchess d'Escarande, a friend of Ludmilla's mother's. Please find her for me and tell her that wherever she is, no matter how many mis-takes she has made since I last saw her, I want her back, and I shall never be too logical with her again, or make silly remarks like the one that hurt her so. I hope she has forgiven me, and it may help to let her know that I have finally understood. Weeks of solitude and suffering have opened my eyes to the truth: I am nothing but an egotist, except in my love for Ludmilla, for whom I would sacrifice everything, even the poem I have written about her since she left."

Mary lifted her eyes for a moment, then said, "There is a postscript:

"Ludmilla may need money. She had none when she left, so please send her some. I will be glad to repay you as soon as I get some from Germany. My mother promised she would send me some soon.

"Yours with a brother-in-law's devotion,

"GÜNTHER"

There was a long silence. Mary was still standing by the window, holding the letter in her hand and staring at her husband. He seemed more tired than disgusted.

"And do you want to know who the Duchess d'Escarande is?" she asked.

"No," he said. "Why? Who is she?"

"A *whore*." It was the first time she had used such a word.

He said nothing, looked at his watch. "We have been two hours with this letter," he said. "And your mother has been waiting for us all this time. Go tell her I am coming."

"Shall I show her the letter?"

"No. Not for the moment, at least. We'll decide later." Then, to humor her, he added, "I must now openly confess . . ."

Mary laughed with gratitude as she ran out of the room.

XIX

THIS HAD NEVER HAPPENED BEFORE, that Mary should stay away from her mother for two hours, especially when an important letter had arrived. And it was not two hours her mother waited, it was countless times a few minutes—two, three, five minutes at the maximum, namely the normal time it takes a normal daughter to stay away from a very sick mother who is terribly worried and has no one to confide in.

Even the first two minutes were too long, because the old lady had specifically said to Mary, upon giving her the note she had scribbled in a hurry for her son-in-law, "Come back immediately." And Mary had begun by not coming back immediately. When her mother realized this, she repressed her indignation and decided that in view of the gravity of the letters, and in spite of everything else (her sickness, her old age), she would say nothing. Two minutes later she was still of the same opinion, and as she watched the tiny gold needle under the larger hand of her watch enter the domain of the third minute, she was certain that Mary would be made to spring out automatically from any of those segments which seemed to prolong the needle for a fraction of each second. A whole minute passed that way, and Mary still did not open the door, and the silence outside gave no promise that she would open it in the next second or two.

Much against all her principles, the old lady lied to herself and pretended to be utterly indifferent to what was being discussed between her daughter and her son-in-law—concerning everything that was important to her. She looked for a suitable substitute to those important matters, but nothing seemed more important than everything, and a fruitless search for substitutes again made her aware that everything, not just this or that thing, was being decided now. She thereupon decided to use up a little time in self-reproach, for not having been clear in her recommendation: I should not have said, "Come back immediately." I should have said, "Come back *im-mee-diately!*" Mary is so used to my impatience that she takes it as a matter of course. I will have to remind her of that, but gently so.

Again, before looking at the watch this time, she decided to be very lenient, and also took some time to praise herself for her patience. Then she followed a noise in the distance, and only after it had hopelessly died away without materializing into steps and the opening of her door did she look at her watch again, to realize with a pang of real pain in her heart that ten minutes had passed and Mary was still absent. This dealt a blow to the nobility of her purpose, and she decided that instead of being *very* lenient, she would only be lenient, and then, after everything had been calmly discussed, she would, leniently and gently, but quite firmly, tell Mary that it had not been too considerate of her to behave as she had, letting her mother wait more than ten minutes.

"Had I not told you to come back immediately?"

"Yes, Mamachen, but—"

"There is nothing to add. I asked you to answer just that one question, and I asked you for a specific reason: to check on my own memory, not yours. You are young; that your memory is good goes without saying. In fact, it would surprise me greatly if I were to discover that you had forgotten, while it would not surprise me at all to discover that I had only imagined and not actually said to you, 'Come back immediately.' I am an old and sick woman, my child, and at my age memory plays strange tricks."

This imagined conversation pleased the old lady very much, because in it she found a chance to exercise what she had always admired so much about herself: that stringent, icy logic which imposes itself by its mere force, like God. Oh, how she wished she had been a man and a lawyer! How she still felt she could destroy any opponent by the strength of her arguments, so clearly and simply stated, and so wittily too! And how stupid of her to waste this logic on people like her children, who, even when intelligent and sensitive, were apt to consider her logic a very normal quality, and at times even to disregard it or be irked by it. Mary was a good case in point. What Mary needs is a bit of my death, she thought; that would teach her a lesson . . . But there again, unfortunately, death could not be given in small doses. To cure unawareness, disrespect and lack of love, one had to give the real thing, not just the fear of it. And the real thing cannot be taken back. How many times she had wished she could die and return after a day or so, when everybody she had left had learned a lesson and become more attentive, more affectionate, more grateful!

This again brought her back to the thought of logic. Why had she never taken her talent more seriously and written novels, philosophical treatises or books on law? Now she was old, and not even her daughter was aware of her greatness. As for her son-in-law, that was another story. Why had he never been enthusiastic about her notes on pyschology? That he admired her she knew, but he was so restrained in his praise. And he had never discussed medical problems with her since their first conversation years, oh, years and years before. Yet everybody else had said that she was great and that those notes were highly original. Rudolf Eucken, a noted philosopher, had written her long letters and encouraged her to write on, even though he had critized her philosophical approach. Tolstoy had answered her long letters in great detail, and so had

Théodule Ribot. All of them had accepted her as their equal, except for her own son-in-law, who had only found harsh words for her, whose praise of her writings concerned only those cynical notes she had written about Roman society and Italian religion.

Now she looked at her watch again: thirty minutes had passed. This was a shock. All thoughts about herself disappeared to make room for her worries. What could those two be doing together with those letters? And why did they not come and tell her what they thought? And if her son-in-law was still ill and could not move, why did Mary not come and tell her so? Or was he dead and had Mary fainted at his bedside? No, because Mary would certainly have screamed before fainting, and someone would have heard—she herself from her room would have heard it. So that hypothesis had no foundation. But, all the same, why should they let her worry? This was unkind, more than unkind—inhuman. And her logic began to work:

"But Mary, my dear child, this is *in-hu-man*, one simply does not do such things. That you should fail to see it is bad enough, but that your husband, a doctor, should allow a sick person like myself to worry for more than thirty minutes, this is indeed quite surprising."

What irritated her was that she should feel well enough to get up and find out for herself. She thought, He is probably angry and thinks that because I was able to stand almost naked in the snowstorm while I was ill, and nothing happened to me, I might as well get up now and go to his room, after what I have done to his family. In a way he is right. I had no business writing to Tegolani again after he had told me not to. He does not care now whether I live or die. But how about Mary? Can she have the same feelings about me? Are they against me together after this? Or have they taken my note of this morning as a definite answer and are they now busy dismissing the servants and preparing to move to a small apartment in town? (That possibility frightened her more than anything else.) And now that even Malachier has been proven wrong by me, and his disastrous diagnosis of disaster given the lie by my recovery, how can I expect him to worry over my health?

Another fifteen minutes passed, and still no sign of Mary. Voices outside in the snow: the children playing. Could Mary be with them? Impossible. Then why this unusual delay? The old lady jumped out of her bed with a swiftness her muscles had not known for years and put on her fur coat, while her feet felt the carpet for her slippers. But a noise in the hall made her take off the coat in a hurry and jump back into bed, in order to look sick and dignified—still lenient, but at the end of her moral resistance. The steps neared—and they passed by the door to go on and pass by the next door and so on and on until they melted with the noises outside. And only three more minutes had passed.

If she had not been interrupted by those steps, she could have slowly opened the door and seen who was passing and explored the vast spaces of the halls to evoke Mary's arrival, to extract her from the unknown by the strength of her anger. Now, of course, it was too late for that, because Mary could not fail to appear and to apologize. And would she appear alone or in her husband's company? Would they come arm in arm, side by side, or one after the other? She first or he first? Aware or unaware of the effects of their negligence? In a spirit of reproach, taking her health for granted, or humbly, as they should? The image she preferred, namely that of their humility, corresponded to her own spirit of humility in front of her past actions and the future disaster that would follow. Tears came into her eyes and she was glad. This allowed her indeed to be lenient and to forgive them fully; those tears took charge of expressing reproach in terms beyond all logic.

She quickly arranged the bedsheet in front of her, on her bosom, then shook her arms so as to allow the embroidered sleeves of her nightgown to reach down to her wrists and leave her pale, long, beautiful hands abandoned there, as two more proofs of her abandonment, then waited, sipping the tears that rolled down her cheeks and making a great effort not to scratch her nose and her chin; continued waiting and waiting, but no one came. She remained petrified in that position for a while, judging it unwise to change it for another which, in her state of ignorance and anguished curiosity as to what those two had decided, could be less successful—and more dangerous! Any evidence of energy might be taken by the doctor as a sign that she could easily get out of bed and start keeping her word as expressed in that note. Oh, no, not Adalgisa again serving at table! So she stayed pitiful as long as she could stand it, then looked at the watch again: an hour and ten minutes! She grabbed it from the night table and held it close to her eyes, staring into it as if to discuss the reasons for the long delay, shifted her glance to the door and back to the watch again, comparing one white surface with the other, and looking very, but *very*, surprised. This was a good expression to adopt now. Of course it was not lenient, but it was not encouraging in terms of her ability to get up and start packing.

And if I rang the bell? she thought. Oh, no. Then Mary would feel that I am well taken care of by the maid and do not need her presence. Besides, if the maid came when Mary appeared, it would not be possible to be sincere with Mary.

She looked at her watch again: only two more minutes gone by. It was unbearable. Now she suddenly felt a great urge to use the *chaise percée*, preceded by strange rumblings and displacements of masses in her lower intestines; but she decided at once this was the worst possible thing to do at the present moment. First of all it took time, then more time, for the maid to come and empty the receptacle, bring it back, open the window and use the perfume atomizer to remove all traces of bad odors from the air. And if Mary or her husband arrived in the meantime, how could any reproach insert itself successfully into this embarrassing routine? She decided to wait, and in order not to look at her watch again she placed it on her stomach, face down, and closed her eyes. Now the masses inside her intestines became more and more menacing and painful. She lay still as long as she could, then engaged in a real battle with her body, to retain her position until Mary had come to notice it and feel sorry. She even thought of a good line: "Oh, you? It is not you I want, it is the *chaise percée*. At least it serves some purpose. Push it close to the bed and leave me alone."

This had Shakespearean greatness to it. She repeated it loudly, several times, always hoping that Mary would come in and hear at least part of it, to be frightened by the fact that her mother was talking aloud to herself.

"What is it, Mamachen?"

She modified the tone, to give it that touch of delirium which is always so effective: "Oh—you? It is not you I want, it is the *chaise percée*." A pause here; then (she was undecided still) either "At least it is helpful" or "It serves a good purpose." Then, after a sigh: "Push it . . . push it . . . closer . . . and leave me alone." Mary would now certainly insist on remaining, but she would have to obey. The tone here must be pleading and weak: "Leave me alone, I say. . . . Leave me alone. . . ."

What a beautiful scene! And what a lesson! No mention of the time and (she looked again), dear Lord, *ninety-two minutes* she had waited! Only the pain and the desire to be left alone, alone, *alone* . . . Now the masses went upward, finding no outlet; and this, from the strategic point of view, was a victory, but what pain, oh, God, what pain! Her face contracted, and she knew from inside her physiognomic mask that it must look frightening. "This is good, this is good," she kept saying to herself. But the pain was not good. Her breath came thin, she made it more so and the heart began to beat faster and faster. Why did Mary not come in at this point? Oh, why? "Aaaah . . . ouch . . . oooh . . . oy, oy, oy . . ." This was all new, it had never appeared in her repertory of clinical blackmail and was very much approved by her. But the pain, oooh, the pain!

She now looked at her watch and it was night. One second

before it had still been the middle of the morning, and the watch itself had been visible like any other object in the room, but the moment she tried to find its two hands and the Roman numerals around it, and the smaller inside dial served only by one needle, she saw nothing but a milky-white surface with no hands and no numerals and nothing. But from under the watch, in fact from the cup of her hand that held it tight, a darkness spread and covered everyhing. So now, using the watch as a portable moon, she directed it toward the *chaise percée* and rolled painfully out of her bed. When she found herself on the carpet, with the portable moon still in her hand, she lifted herself on her hands and knees, then climbed back onto the bed, turned and found herself seated on its edge. Now she rose with great pains in her intestines and dragged herself to the *chaise percée*, used it, closed it again and crawled back into bed. But she did not feel better.

She woke up with a pain in her head, her eyelids and the back of her neck, just as Mary was saying, "She is resting."

"No, I am not," she said, and realized that her cheeks must be burning.

The doctor stood there, too, he looked as if he did not care —but because he was sad, not because he was angry or disgusted with her.

"Your watch was on the carpet," said Mary, replacing it on the night table.

These words gave the old lady a sudden gust of nausea. It took her some time to realize that she had not been up at all and had not used the *chaise percée*. But she no longer felt like using it. Nausea seemed to have replaced her other urge.

She cleared her throat and asked, "Where are the letters?"

"Here on the desk," said the doctor.

"Have you read my note?" she asked, without actually caring, only remembering how much she had cared.

"Yes, yes," he said, "no reason to worry. Everything goes to the lawyer."

"And Pierre's letter?"

"Unimportant," he said. "The usual nonsense."

"I am not feeling well," she said. "I want to vomit."

"To vomit?" he asked. Then, with an air of perfunctory reproach: "Something you ate, of course, or perhaps you sat in a draft. Take her temperature, Mary, I will be back." And he went out.

"Is he angry with me?" the old lady asked, as Mary came back with a porcelain basin, a towel and a bottle of Eau de Cologne.

"No, not at all," said Mary, who also seemed absent in thought.

This changed the constellation of her symptoms at once. The nausea grew weaker, almost disappeared, to be replaced by a much stronger headache and by pains in the legs, shoulders and hands.

"Has anything happened?" she asked.

"No," said Mary. "Why should anything have happened?"

"You were away so long. I waited and waited—ouch. I think. . . . Ouch."

"Do you want to . . . use that thing?"

"Yes. But you leave the room."

"No, Mamachen. Why should I? Let me help you."

"Please, I don't like it."

Mary insisted and helped her, but she felt so disgusted with herself for being weak and suffering that her bowels did not function, and the back of her neck hurt now so much that she had to be supported back to her bed.

"Hold my neck tight," she said. "Here, very tight. It hurts."

Mary did as she was told. She looked concerned, and her mother was suffering more than she had ever suffered in her life, but still the old lady had a feeling that Mary was not present in spirit.

"Something has happened, I know it, you must tell me."

"But no, Mamachen, nothing has happened. Let me take your temperature."

While Mary was waiting for the thermometer to saturate itself with her mother's temperature, the old lady kept repeating the last words she had spoken. They had lost all meaning in her mind, only the sound remained attached to her memory, with a vague feeling of connection between it and Mary's attention: "Something has happened, I know it, you must tell me."

Mary was beginning to fear now that her mother would die in her arms. She rang the bell, and when the maid appeared she said, "Call the doctor at once."

The temperature was over forty-one degrees centigrade. The old lady's face was swollen, her tongue stuck out, her eyes were haggard, she seemed blind, and horrid sounds with horrid smells exploded every few seconds from her mouth. This was not Mary's mother, Mary could not accept this, and all she could do was to cry, "No, no, no!" as if to correct a mistake that the Lord had permitted, and He must, He must be warned in time.

A mass of vomit blinded Mary. That was the last thing she could recall.

"Exactly thirty-seven—no fever. You may get up in a short while, when the halls have become warm again. Now the windows are open, they are sweeping the staircase, it would not be prudent for you to go out of this room."

The doctor turned his back on Mary and began to pace the room. Mary followed him with anguished eyes from her bed and repeated the question she had already asked several times in the last twenty minutes: "And Mamachen is better, you say?"

"Much better. In fact, perfectly well. Cheerful, even hungry. No fever either. I keep telling you these things and you do not believe me."

"I do, I do, but you should have seen her yesterday morning."

"I did see her. It must have been something she ate."

"Oh, no. It was my fault. I stayed out of the room too long.

It was that stupid letter. I had promised to go back to her room at once. She worried, and it almost killed her. And what actually did all the harm was my reticence. She noticed there was something we were hiding from her. Mamachen is so sensitive, she cannot stand a lie; she is so clear, so pure, that falsehood in her presence is impossible."

He now turned like a soldier obeying a sudden order while marching, clicked his heels and said, "Mary, if this means that you want to show her that letter, I say no. Günther was a damned fool to write it in the first place, but I can understand his plight, poor devil. He was also a damned fool to write it in German, and in that German script I will never be able to decipher, and I was a damned fool to let you read it to me."

"Why?" said Mary resentfully.

"Because that was not a letter for a woman to read. I am ashamed of it."

"But, darling, we have no secrets, you and I."

"All right, we have no secrets; but all the same, that was a letter from a man to a man, not to a woman. Don't be afraid for me, I have told you a thousand times I detest Ludmilla, she is a prostitute, she deserves nothing good; but she is your sister, after all, and you should not be exposed to her vulgarity. Useless to talk about it now, it is too late. But as for showing that letter to your mother, no and a thousand times no."

"But why, since she knows we are concealing something from her?"

"Because it could upset her too much. If you want to know the truth, your mother is not sick at all, she is emotionally exhausted. Emotions can revive her, they could almost keep her going without her breathing or eating; but they can kill her, too. And if waiting for you upset her to that point, as you claim, one more reason not to give her that letter to read. Besides, if Ludmilla suddenly asked to come back, we should not make it harder for either of them. She has a right to see her mother if she wants to."

425

"After what she has done?"

"Unfortunately, yes. After what she has done. Not even a criminal should be denied the right to see his mother. Nor a prostitute either. We are responsible for the sins of our children."

"How can you speak that way about Mamachen?"

"I only say that our children may err, but it is not for us to judge them severely. That the sins of the fathers should not be visited upon the sons does not imply that the sins of the sons may not be visited upon the parents. We brought them up. And we brought them up badly, or not at all; these are responsibilities that no one else can take, for they belong to us. Your mother is too old and too rigid to change her outlook now. But she must see her children if they come back to her—just see them and be kind to them."

He looked at his watch and said, "We have been here for six minutes without seeing her. Let me go and stay with her. You may get up in ten minutes. Put on this warm robe and this fur coat, here they are, and come straight to her room."

He left, as a preacher might leave the pulpit after delivering his sermon. The reason he had spoken so well was that he did not believe a single word of what he was saying. He was, in fact, speaking against himself, he being at the same time the giver and the taker of wisdom; there is no better recipe for truthful preaching.

That letter had upset him too much. No other worry but Ludmilla found a place in his mind now. He did not even care to save on bread and bread crumbs, let alone what remained of the capital (the real amount of which he still did not know). And whatever temptation Ludmilla had represented for him until then had been killed by the notion that Ludmilla was not pure any more. Had she belonged to one man only, and legally, and especially to a man he did not envy as a man— namely, a man less handsome than himself—and had he been just as obsessed by notions of the impurity of sex, he would not

have despised her; on the contrary, he would have felt like a
conqueror, and would have tried to conquer her only to give
her back to Günther. But those two other men had debased
her, because they belonged to a cynical world in which even a
prostitute is treated like a lady and a lady is taught things that
only a prostitute should know. Upon mentally examining these
two sinister figures, he found, to his surprise, that he was not
so jealous of the prince, because the prince was a man of great
tact—he would not slander Ludmilla or despise her sister who
was guilty of divorce. He was, besides, a man of learning. Love of
the classics was, in the doctor's opinion, as good as salvation—
in fact, better. But that other man, oh, that upstart, who had
studied neither Latin nor Greek, who knew nothing of history,
philosophy and poetry, who drank champagne, who gambled,
who taught Ludmilla dirty words, oh, what horror to think
that such a man had the right to say of Mary, "Oh, yes, that
divorced woman living in sin with that doctor? She must be
like her sister, who has been my mistress for some time."

Why had Günther failed to specify in his letter where this
man came from? Let's hope he is not an Italian, the doctor
thought; and if he is, that he is not from Naples or (God forbid!) from Apulia. For if this were the case, how could I let
him live? He would have to either marry Ludmilla at once or
pay with his blood for the offense to my honor.

Günther could well afford to be grand about these matters,
but not he, with a wife and a daughter to defend. Even as a
little child he had been very sensitive to matters of honor. It is
true that he did not live in Italy now, but all his sisters did,
and both his parents were buried there. He had accepted many
strange new ways, and he believed himself an ultramodern
man by now. He allowed Mary to write letters to lawyers without
showing them to him, and he knew that she began those letters
with "Dear Friend"; he forbade her closing with "affectionate
greetings," but the "Dear Friend" remained. He even allowed
Mary to converse with men at parties without calling him to her

side so that he might hear what she said; but he trusted her to repeat to him exactly what she had been told and what she had replied. His ideal for Mary's behavior would have been for her to flee into hiding at the sight of a man, so that it would be abundantly clear to everyone how she hated adultery. Mary was much too "Nordic" and too "Protestant" for such behavior. However, she showed, by her jealousy, that she was safe and faithful. It is true that this jealousy had proven a great burden to him, but how he blessed it now since Günther's letter had arrived! "How lucky I am! How incredibly lucky!" he kept saying to himself every so many minutes.

What still disturbed him very much, since that letter had come, was his own guilt. Who but he had pushed Ludmilla down the slippery path? And who but he could help her now? And if he himself did not have enough confidence in her, or despised her too much to listen to her lies—let alone give her advice—could he deny her the right at least to see her own mother again? Ah, here began the trouble. He could not; and yet, could he allow her to be friendly with the children, to take Sonia on her sinful knee, and to kiss the child with her lascivious lips? Those were very grave matters. Apparently the right to see her mother was not as simple as he had thought. It included the right to see everyone else, even the dog. And, knowing Ludmilla, her playful nature and her success with the children, he knew that once she came it would be impossible to get rid of her without making the children very unhappy. And it is so easy with children, so easy to corrupt them. A smile will suffice to transform a serious matter into a joke, and once the fear of punishment is gone who will tell them where to stop?

But it was not for him to deny that ill-advised, foolish girl the right to see her mother. So he relied on Mary's weakness, feeling sure she would never be able to obey his order not to tell her mother about that letter, especially when the danger of Ludmilla's return was in sight. He had his own way of communicating with Ludmilla and telling her how much he dis-approved of her (and how much he still cared): his Catholic upbringing had developed in him the habit of speaking to God as if he were in His presence; God no longer existed in his mind, but the habit remained, with absent persons now as his interlocutors—in this case, Ludmilla. His severe words in the mental conversation he now proceeded to hold with her almost moved him to tears, because the Ludmilla of his thoughts—that same Eternal Ludmilla who in Günther's opinion was more faithful to him than to her lovers—had been able to hear them.

But ten days later Ludmilla had not yet given any sign of having heard them, while, to his great surprise, his words to his wife *had* been heeded: Mary was actually keeping a secret from her mother; she had not told the old lady about the letter.

That morning he went to the library in a hurry, telling himself he was going to the library in a hurry to look up the *Larousse Médical*; but then, with the *Larousse Médical* spread open on his desk, he noticed a certain disappointment and a tendency to keep looking out the window. He tried to tell himself that what really attracted him was a large snowdrift by the gate, but when the postman came he knew he had been looking for him and was disgusted with himself.

When the mail was brought in and there was nothing but bills and letters from uninteresting people, he noticed again with disgust that he was rather disappointed, but immediately afterward noted in himself a symptom of recovery from all unworthy feelings of resentment because Ludmilla had not written. My moral health is good, he thought. To hell with Ludmilla, let her go her own way. I have other things to think of. Mary is a saintly person, and when that devil of a mother of hers dies, her saintliness will all emerge. There is only one thorn

in my heart: the doubt about the nationality of that lover.
Let us hope he is a German, and if he *must* be an Italian, *let
him be from anyplace north of Naples*. Then he corrected
himself: No, north of *Rome*. *Florence*, in fact. The emphasis
of the last sentence was another symptom he at once recognized as a lapse into his adolescent habit of praying. If God
had not been mentioned, it was only out of respect for Him: He
knows I am not a believer, so, if He does exist, He will at least
not think me a hypocrite.

The bell rang, someone knocked at the door.

"A lift boy from the Grand Hotel," said the butler.

"What does he want? Let him in," the doctor said, noticing
with anger that he had expected a telegram. But he was
pleased to see the owner of his last "independent" suit. "How
are you, young man? How is my suit? How is your father?
Come, warm your hands at the fire. You look cold in that
light uniform of yours. Don't you have an overcoat?"

"No, sir, but I am used to this. The manager sent me to tell
you that there is an Italian countess who needs a doctor this
afternoon after three."

"An Italian countess? I don't know a single Italian countess.
And why would she want a doctor after three? And why come
to me when the town is full of doctors who need money and
could very well use some rich patients?"

"I don't know, sir, but this countess asked for you."

"And why did you have to come all the way up here in the
storm to call me? They could have telephoned."

"The telephones are broken, sir, on account of the storm."

"Very well, go downstairs to the kitchen, you will find your
friend the cook of the Grand Hotel and he will feed you. Then
we will walk down to the hotel together."

He went upstairs to give Mary the good news, thinking
proudly, I am becoming famous, I might soon become rich if
this goes on.

But Mary had good news of her own to give him. Not only
had she not mentioned Günther's letter to her mother, but

she had almost persuaded the old lady that Ludmilla was good.
"And you know, when Ludmilla writes there is a chance that
she may ask her to come here and live with us again."

"Mary, you are wasting your time. Ludmilla will never write
and it is all for the better if she stays out of our lives. As for
her staying with us, no. Can you imagine her kissing the
children, after she has had God knows how many syphilitic
lovers? No. But now hear my good news: A rich Italian countess
who is staying at the Grand Hotel wants a doctor. Think how
much money I could make if we lived in town!"

"Who is this Italian countess? What is her name?"

"I don't know."

"I know—this is your wife in disguise who has come to kill
you. Don't go!"

"Nonsense. My wife has no money to stay at the Grand
Hotel. And besides, you don't do these things yourself. You send
a man to do them for you. In France, perhaps, or in Russia,
women kill their husbands personally; but in Italy, unless a
woman has no one to serve her, she finds a relative, a friend,
she hires someone."

"She may have sent an enchantress. Or this may be a bad
woman who is going to make you forget me and the children."

"What nonsense again! This is the beginning of a brilliant
career for me!"

"And how about your scientific work? If you begin with
general practice for vulgar reasons of greed, you are lost as a
scientist."

"My scientific work can well afford a minor interruption of
a vulgar type. Never mind. And don't become hysterical. The
hotel manager is an old friend, he will not allow anyone to
harm me. He knows our situation, I can even ask him to be on
hand just in case. There is only one thing that still bothers
me."

"What?"

"How can we learn the nationality of that man?"

"What man?"

431

"Ludmilla's lover."

"Oh. German, of course. Why?"

"Are you sure? Because if he were Italian he should be killed. I could not do it myself, I would not even think of doing it, but I would formulate a solemn wish that he be killed."

Before leaving the house the doctor did an untypical thing—he went to his dressing room and chose one of his winter coats for the lift boy. His usual stinginess did not stop him here, his thought being that this was a propitiatory gesture: If I can lose Rolls-Royces and silverware to save on a few bread crumbs, I might as well sacrifice something of much less value to gain a few clients.

Mary's behavior immediately after he had left was also far from typical.

When she returned to her mother's room, the old lady's first words were: "Mary, you were right. I have been very unjust to Ludmilla. I want you to write to her."

"Thank you, Mamachen, thank you," said Mary, kissing her mother's hands and feeling proud of her achievement.

But the old lady went on: "Yes, write and ask her to come back. As a matter of fact, send a telegram. Ask her to come with her young man. I want to see him too."

That was a moment Mary was never to forget. It was her first great victory (and probably her only one) over her jealous nature, which told her she was giving up everything she had—her mother and her husband. For a brief moment she was tempted to say, "Ludmilla is now living with Marie d'Escarande. She has had three lovers." But she clenched her fists and told herself that she knew her husband much too well to be afraid of Ludmilla's rivalry. So she said only, "I don't know where they are, but my husband will know. He is out now, when he comes home we can discuss it with him." And again she felt proud of herself.

"Have the children gone out, too?" asked her mother, looking at the snow, which was coming down heavily.

"No, Mamachen, they are somewhere about with the new governess."

"I want them to have tea with me. I also want the dog."

"Yes, Mamachen, I will get them," said Mary, and she went to look for them.

As usual, the old lady passed in a matter of minutes from complete indifference to extreme impatience. Ludmilla, poor Ludmilla, abandoned by her mother, exposed to all sorts of perils, must be helped, must be comforted, hugged, welcomed home and given a hot bath.

She rang the bell, and when Frieda appeared she said, "Prepare the blue guest room at once for Miss Ludmilla, and one of the guest rooms upstairs for a gentleman who will come with her. Make sure that there are towels and hot water so that she can take a hot bath, because she comes from a long trip."

"Very well, madame. Will it be for tonight?"

"No, probably not, but be ready, no one can tell when she will come. Perhaps even tonight."

A little later she felt tender in her heart even for Pierre and rang the bell again to send a few telegrams. Mary was still not back, ten minutes had passed, the children had not been heard, she began to worry about them, and, in order to keep herself calm, she started a long telegram to Pierre, asking him to come with his wife at once because she needed his advice concerning Ludmilla. She was happy to feel that she was being good again, and tears streamed down her face as she rewrote the telegram three times to make it even more affectionate and urgent. Then she stopped and began to think that perhaps it would be better for the whole family to take a trip to Russia and spend Christmas with Pierre in his big house. Quickly she drafted a list of the most important presents and other items to be bought for the trip, then put away her notebook, because she heard the children on the stairs, and tidied herself to receive them. It is good to be good, she thought, laughing with childish joy. It is much better to be good than to be bad. I must always remember this!

433

X X

⧜⧜

A<small>T THE</small> G<small>RAND</small> H<small>OTEL</small> the doctor was greeted by the whole
management like an old friend when he arrived with the
lift boy, after a long walk in the snow. Everybody felt sick or
remembered some recent symptoms to avail himself of the
services of their dear doctor. For some time he did not even
bother to inquire the name of the patient who had called him,
because he was engaged in lecturing the manager, the clerks
and a few of the porters and maids on the importance of hy-
giene, both physical and moral, as against medicine and medicines, which are the curse of people's health and of their
purses.

He refused payment for his many consultations, saying,
"These rich people upstairs will pay for you. Who are they, by
the way?"

"A Countess di San Pronto with her husband and daughter.
The daughter must be ill—she came in yesterday all wrapped
up as if she had the mumps or a toothache. They live in your
old apartment."

He knocked on the door of what had been his sitting room,
and a man's voice, a deep broken voice, answered, "Come in,
sit down and wait!"

As he entered he had a glimpse of a pink robe disappearing

434

into his former bedroom just before the door was slammed with a noise he remembered only too well. Other familiar noises followed: the heavy and squeaking door to the boudoir, the bathroom door, various drawers, the switch of the big lamp in the middle room, and the bell to call the maid. He waited and waited and finally decided to sit down in that comfortable armchair on which he had taken the first embarrassed afternoon naps of his married life, much to Mary's amusement, because that was a habit utterly unknown and morally inadmissible in civilized countries. And what with habit, the long lecture, the long walk, the cold air outside and the excessive heat inside, before he knew it he had fallen asleep.

What aroused him was his first snore, and he opened his eyes to see red, scarlet and pink, in a dazzling confusion of velvets, silks and skin. After blinking a bit he realized this was a red-haired woman in a red negligee, her naked arms lifted above her head and fumbling there with hairpins, and her breasts showing. She was not young, as he could tell from her dry hands, her wrists and the lines on her neck, but the rest was still good, and she had something strange and very vital which attracted him instantly. She was smoking through a long cigarette holder which she held like a trumpet aimed at him, firm in her teeth while she coughed, and she seemed to be coughing with her breasts, with her shoulders, with her eyes, and coughing deeply, like a sick old man.

"You are a handsome animal," she said. "They told me about you, but I never believe these women's tales. I must say that for once I was wrong. Quite, quite wrong," she said, making a half-tour of the doctor's chair. He was so completely under her spell that he forgot to get up and greet her the way a gentleman should. She spoke Italian in a way unknown to him, with no trace of an accent, but it sounded like a foreign language, perhaps because this was the language of a person used only to giving orders. An immoral empress, like Theodora of Byzantium, wife of Justinian—this was his first thought. And he kept listening, fascinated also by that masculine voice which was nevertheless powerfully feminine. Some words sounded Neapolitan, others Tuscan, still others Venetian. And the *r*'s were all French.

"So, they tell me you're a doctor, young man. A doctor, eh? Now, really, handsome, if you want my opinion, there should be a law, yes, a very strict law against handsome doctors. They should not be permitted to exercise their profession."

Her hands finally came down and quickly drew the curtain in front of her breasts.

"Madame," said the doctor, who was at the same time excited and irritated, curious and frightened, "are you the Countess di San Pronto who sent for me?"

"Oh, how angry you seem. Well, yes, and I have a patient here whose patience seems as strained as my own. But don't talk that way! And don't look at me with those eyes—I haven't done anything to you. Sooner or later one has to undress for a doctor, or are you even a prude professionally? What is it? You still look at me disapprovingly. Are you impressionable? All right, I shall keep all my symptoms to myself, strictly to myself, young man. Send me a doctor who looks more like a doctor and who does not stare at me that way. Or is that the clinical eye of which one hears so much these days?"

The doctor could not speak. A most violent heartbeat made it impossible for him to open his mouth without moaning. He had never been so taken by a woman; in fact, he had never seen such a wonder on earth. For all her vulgarity, the charm was irresistible. He was ready to fling himself at her feet and say, "You are an angel, let me spend the rest of my life with you."

All this in cold blood, knowing he could never love a woman of that type. She felt it, smiled at him and winked. This is the sign, he thought, and he tried not to think where he was: in the room where his children had played, next to the room

436

where they had been conceived and born. She drew closer and put an arm on his arm, and he was sorry that his heavy coat stood between his skin and hers. A strong perfume—which, to make things worse, was exactly that which Mary used—came to him from the folds of her robe with a strange warm undercurrent of body smells. She was completely naked under her negligee.

"No, my dear," she said, "better be careful now. My husband is in the next room."

The door opened and a tall, gray-haired man with a very narrow face and a long nose emerged and looked at them with small purple eyes that seemed no eyes at all—the impression the doctor had was of two spots made with a purple pencil on a fold in the skin of a white face.

The doctor rose from his chair and started toward the other door.

"Stop, stop," said the man, with a voice that seemed to come from a closed wooden box. "I hope I am not disturbing you."

The doctor stopped and turned his head without turning his body. The woman came to rescue him, took him gently by the hand, leaving the front of her robe quite open, and pulled him toward her.

"Come, meet my husband."

At this point the doctor decided he was the victim of a conspiracy, something connected with his first wife, and he instantly knew he was right when he noticed the cold smile on the woman's face.

"I don't want to meet anybody," he said, and looked at the door from which he had come in, expecting the police to appear. To his surprise the husband seemed far more embarrassed than he.

"Oh, I am sorry," were the only words that came from the closed box: and the tall man went out into the corridor, closing the door behind him.

437

"Now, was that nice of you?" said the woman. "My husband will think that you dislike him, this will make him unhappy for hours. I hope you will be here when he comes back and be kind to him. You should apologize, you should really apologize—but do as you like. Only I don't want you to be unkind to my husband again. It is not for you to criticize him. He is an excellent man. A better man than you. Look, look at you! What big eyes! Are you going to devour me or will you say something nice? I swear I am not here to harm you. I called you because I needed you."

While saying this she caressed his face and his chin, but gently, as if he were a child, so that his secret calculations were upset.

Should I or should I not? he asked himself.

"Come," she said, "come with me into my bedroom."

He followed her with his heart beating against his eyes, his ears, his throat. She opened the door to the bedroom, then to the next room, which had been the nursery, always dragging him by the hand, and stopped in front of that open door with her body showing more clearly than ever through the folds of her robe—the tips of her breasts actually pushing the robe open.

"I want you to say something nice to me before you come into this room," she said languidly.

He put both hands on those breasts, kissed them, then kissed her face; but she withdrew.

"No, no, no," she said, "you are either too cordial or too cold. You may check on the resiliency of my breasts later, but now I have someone else here who is probably watching us. Doctor, meet your patient, please."

She showed him in, stepping aside to let him enter, then closed the door behind him, and he found himself alone in the presence of Ludmilla.

Ludmilla laughed and flung her arms around his neck, almost choking him with kisses, of which one almost went on

438

his lips. Again he was mute, and very much excited. Save that in this case his feeling was different. Ludmilla was a world he knew, she was first of all, at this moment, proof that this was not a strange conspiracy to catch him in sin; and secondly, she looked like Mary, only infinitely younger, less plump, more vital—and less beautiful. Her Tartar face and pug nose combined in a beauty so strange that nothing compared with it. And she was suntanned, which made her look savage. And then she was Ludmilla.

"Never mind that woman, she is a bit crazy but she has a heart of gold. I don't know what I would do without her."

"But who is she?"

"You haven't met her yet, of course. That is an old friend of the family, Marie d'Escarande. She gave another name, one of the many her husband has, because she did not want Mamachen or Mary to find out."

"So that is the famous whore."

"Darling, don't say such things. Of course at home they call her that, but I wish you would not. What she does with her body is no concern of ours. What counts is what she does with other people's souls: She is the kindest, most generous person I know. There isn't a thing she would not do for her friends."

"I swear to you, Ludmilla, I was ashamed. I still am. I never, never in my life . . ."

"Come, come, let's not talk about that. She did it because she has her theories about me."

"Theories about you? Ludmilla, please leave this place at once and come home. What theories can such a person have but those she seems to apply to the first comer?"

Ludmilla smiled and shook her head. "I won't hear any talk against Marie," she said. "She is the most loyal, generous, self-sacrificing friend I have. She is, in fact, the only friend I have."

The doctor smiled. He was not angry at all, and yet this was the kind of thing that usually made him angry. "There was a time," he said, "when you called me your only friend. And Günther too."

"Günther?" she said. "Oh, my God, I had forgotten all about him. But tell me, how is everybody? How is Mamachen? How is Mary, how is my darling Sonia?"

"Very well. Come home with me and you will see them all."

While he said this he was afraid she might accept, and he was greatly relieved when she said, "No, not through the back door, and not unless I know they want me back."

"But they do, Mary has been wonderful about this. She loves you, she wants you back, she even tries to insist with Mamachen that you be allowed to come back."

"No, no, no. I wish I could; but, first of all, here they would never let me."

"Who? That woman? What right has she? What is she to you? We are your family. I don't want you to stay with these people. Let me tell you precisely what I have in mind to do. I agree with you that perhaps you should not come home to-night. Let me prepare the ground, but tomorrow or the day after you will come home and leave these people forever. Then, in due course of time, you will go back to Günther, who is the man for you."

"Günther? *Günther,* you say? Never."

"But why?"

"Let's not even talk about it. Not after what he has made me suffer. You may say what you wish against Marie, I know that if she had not rescued me from Günther I would have gone mad or committed suicide."

"Be calm," he said, but it was as if he were speaking to himself, because all the bad things he had known about Ludmilla seemed to have faded into nothing at the sound of her voice and the signs of her beauty, both so new and so free from the stamp of any man's ownership that he feared for his safety unless she promised to go back to the only man he was willing to accept as a rival.

"Be calm, Ludmilla, and tell me what Günther has done to you." His hands were on her arms, holding her away from him in self-defense, and she was gravitating toward him. Her eyes became veiled.

"Ludmilla . . . please, Ludmilla, did you hear what I said? Answer me and be precise: What has Günther done to you that you should hate him so?"

"Why force me to remember? You can be so stupid at times —not you in particular, all men with their insistence on precision."

She began to pace the room with her hands behind her back, not like a woman at all. But the tone was that of two women, Mary and her mother.

"What has he *done* to me? Any number of things. His shirts lying around, rancid with perspiration, his *Lederhosen* caked with mud, tomato sauce and oil, his manuscripts, his books, and those fried eggs for breakfast! Isn't that more than any man should do?"

The doctor blushed. Fried eggs for breakfast had become almost an obsession in his life these days. He had not eaten them for years, and it seemed to him at times as if Mary had divorced her first husband only because he ate fried eggs for breakfast.

"Ludmilla, be reasonable, is it a crime to like fried eggs for breakfast? If you hate them, tell him so."

"I don't, I never did, I never hated him either. Now I hate both. And his adoration, and his arrogance! He made me feel either too stupid or too intelligent, or both at the same time, and too weak and too strong. Oh, no, he is not a man at all."

"What is he, then?"

"A scholar, a professor. Even his archaeology is a fraud. He brings back to the light something that was buried for thousands of years, and buries it again in his knowledge. I don't know how to put it. I am ignorant, but he makes everything seem German, deep, important, scholarly. Even fried eggs, even the dirty socks which he leaves absent-mindedly on the dining-room table next to his dirty plates (for me to wash, in his German expectation)—even those become part of his work. You feel that they must be some kind of footnote. And his worship of me? Another fraud. If I don't listen to my praise in verse, I am guilty of irreverence toward him. So where am I in this? I have tried everything. I have even gone back to him; he does not understand, he does not care, he does not fight to win me again."

The doctor at this point became uneasy, like a hunter in ambush with the prey sitting on his gun. Making a very stupid face, he asked, "He does not fight to win you back? From whom?"

"From no one—but I mean, had there been anybody, he would have lost me. A woman must be made to feel that a man wants her back and is ready to kill—"

"Of course, of course. And so you went to Marie d'Escarande . . ."

"Well, no—yes—that is a long story and it would not amuse you. I met her and she said, 'Come away with me,' and I said— Oh, but let me tell you something else, another of his disgusting habits: he always takes advantage of people. This was in Athens. We had lived there for a while in a filthy hotel when people I knew offered us a house belonging to some Greeks, friends of the Schliemanns'—a most beautiful house full of statues and books. These people were away, they are always away. We moved into their house for a week or ten days. That was the extent of the invitation. But he must still be living there, as far as I know. And the people through whom we had obtained the house are no longer our friends—I mean, no longer Günther's friends. Now, is that honest? Is that good taste?"

This was the doctor's chance. He decided to say, "I know of other things that are just as dishonest and in just as bad taste, such as . . ." But he hesitated.

She noticed it and asked, panic-stricken, "Did he . . . write to you?"

This was his second chance. And again he was hesitant. In that split second she had taken the offensive, and the prey shot the hunter with his own gun.

"Don't tell me anything! I don't want to look into that cesspool of filth! Spare me the stench! Oh, the swine, the snake, the worm! He knows you are my only friend, and he writes to you. I imagine he must have told you everything, our most intimate problems, or what he considers to be our problems. His alone—*I* never had any problems in common with him. And the lies, oh, the lies! No, no, no! And you, you who knew this and came here without warning me—why did you do this? To spy on me? Is that your friendship? If that's your opinion of me, why did you come at all? And I, the fool, let myself go and talk about matters that are none of your business! No, leave this room at once! I cannot see you any more! A man who treats a woman as you have treated me is not my friend, does not deserve to be my friend! No, I have no one in the world but my honest Marie and her darling husband. That is *my* family! Get out of here, I cannot stand the sight of you! Get out or I will call the hotel manager and have you kicked out of my room!"

There was no way of stopping her. "Ludmilla, for God's sake don't shout!"

"I will shout as I goddam please, the whole city must hear me, I will open the window, I shall call the police! This is a plot! A dirty plot! And you are all a pack of swine!"

He sank on his knees. "Ludmilla, for heaven's sake, Ludmilla, be calm, hit me, but do not shout. And listen to me, I beseech you, please listen to me!" A mixture of disgust and fear made her attentive. "Ludmilla," he moaned, "I swear, I swear to you that I never believed a single word of what he wrote! Ludmilla, why don't you trust your friend?"

She was now curled up in a corner of the sofa, biting her

443

fingernails, her fingers and her hands, and then groaning and trembling, and staring at the carpet, and then showing the whites of her eyes. At moments she seemed dead, then a new gust of shame shook her like an electric current and sent waves of hot blood to her cheeks.

"Ludmilla, my dear little Ludmilla," he said, getting up to touch her arm.

"Don't touch me!" she screamed.

"All right, I won't but please listen to me. Please believe me. On my word of honor, no one thinks badly of you, and no one ever did. Not even Günther." She seemed calmer, so he insisted on this point. "In fact, now that I think of it, all he wrote was a hymn to your beauty and perfection."

There was a long silence, then she murmured, "That is what a woman gets for being considerate and kind to a man. Marie is right: one should treat them like dogs. For that is what they all are, all of them, none excepted."

He became confident. It was a good sign that she should murmur things instead of yell, and above all that she should let him stay. After another pause, in which she shook a little less and pulled her hair over her face, he heard a sneer from behind that black curtain.

"Nice," she said. "First you did not believe a word of what he wrote and then he wrote only good things. Which of these lies should I believe?" He said nothing. Another sneer from her. "I would like to see that letter."

"Of course, you will."

After another pause: "And in what language was it written? Not in Italian, I suppose."

He could not speak.

"Did you hear me? Not in Italian, I said."

"No."

"And so Mary had to read it to you."

He waited a long time and then whispered, "I had never

444

seen his handwriting before. When the letter arrived, I thought
it was from . . . I don't know . . ."

"And so Mary read it aloud, did she not?"

"It was written in German script—"

"And you both had a good time with the lies of that snake,
that worm, that criminal."

He was regaining strength. These insults were no longer
for him. So he said rather firmly, "No."

She giggled. "No? As if I did not know my sister. Even if
you did not, she did, she did, I know she did."

She was on her way to louder tones again, and he again
looked at the door.

"Of course she did," Ludmilla shouted now at the top of her
voice. "Tell me she did, tell me the truth for once!"

"But she did not, I swear to you."

"You swear to me. You swear to me, that is all you can do.
But you kept it secret from me and were asking me questions,
to check—and now you swear to me. And Mary, feeling superior, went to her dear Mamachen with that letter . . ."

"No," he cried in a very firm tone, "she did not! That I can
swear on the heads of my children."

She laughed, she even showed her face for a moment. "Oh,
I see. That you can swear on the heads of your children, while
the other you can only swear, no heads involved. As if I had not
known it all along. Why did I have to ask? I knew it, oh, I knew
it. I could even repeat the words she said, I know Mary so well,
oh, so well. Of course she did not show it to her mother, this
is a new refinement. Or did it come from you?"

She looked at him, and her glance seemed clear and cheerful, even teasing for a second, which was like heaven to him.
He said nothing.

"I know, I know," she said. "It came from you. You must
have said, 'Mary, let's not lower ourselves to Ludmilla's level.
She is a prostitute, but we are pure, we are superior, we are ex-

ceptional people, so let's be noble on this occasion too. If Ludmilla wants to come home and see her mother again, she has a right to do so. The sins of the fathers must not be visited upon the sons, but the sins of the sons—"

"Who told you that?" he asked, in a fit of admiration.

"No one told me, I knew it because that would be your natural reaction. You are my mother's only true son and her only true husband—in fact, you are only out on loan to her only true daughter. And then you said to Mary, 'Mary, I forbid you to show that letter to your mother. It might kill her.' And perhaps in your heart you were hoping she would, so that you would be rid of me forever."

"That is a lie! That is the damnedest lie I have heard so far!"

"First of all," she said, "you don't call that a lie, but a wrong guess; and secondly, it is not a wrong guess, because it is the right one. And so Mary, having received such a strict order from you, could not resist the temptation to tell, because she has never concealed anything from her dear mother."

"No," he said. "She did not show the letter. Had I wanted her mother to read it, nothing prevented me from showing it to her myself. As a matter of fact, Mary was just telling me before I left the house today that she was proud she had not said one word to her mother about it."

"That is it: she was proud! How well I knew it! Well, and then let me tell you I am sorry she did not. I would rather she had. At least my mother has a right to be stupid, proud or indignant about it. She is my mother and from her I accept it, even if I don't like it. Not from my sister, however. Oh no! She has no more business to protect me and forgive me than she has to denounce and condemn me. Now I am certain that I shall never set foot in that house again!" After another pause she said cheerfully, "No. I had better stay away from happy people. I am not good for them."

446

He wanted to say something, did not know what, and a knock on the door cut his last hope.

"Come in!" said Ludmilla, and Marie's head made its appearance, as on stage, with movements of curiosity made more evident by pouting, blinking, and rolling of the eyes in every direction. Ludmilla laughed joyfully.

"Are you two in agreement now?" asked Marie. "I heard ominous tones before that promised nothing good, and I was on the point of coming in to defend you, my child. Then I thought I had better stay out. One never knows—what sounds like a quarrel at times ends in a love scene, and I would not want to be the one responsible for breaking up such a fortunate turn." How he wished she had been right!

"Nonsense," said Ludmilla. "Come in, Marie."

And Marie made her entry in brown velvet, with a beautiful set of emeralds, necklace and earrings, that the doctor recognized at once.

"This," Marie said, noticing his look, "is a copy of the one you have at home. You recognized it, I know. Years ago my idiot of a grandfather (I am also an Escarande) sold two necklaces and parures to pay his debts, and they were bought by your late father-in-law for his wife. Ludmilla tells me no one knows where one of these is now. She has received or will receive the other one, I hear. My husband had this one remade from the portrait of Anne d'Escarande in the Louvre. Beautiful, eh?"

"Yes," said the doctor, like a beaten dog.

"Sit down," Marie said, and he sat down. "So, tell me now, you live with your mother-in-law, do you? How is she?"

"Very well. That is, she has *not* been well lately, she is at the end of her forces."

"That she has always been. She loves to destroy herself, after destroying others. I know her very well, I am only a few years younger than she. But I never had a conscience and she

447

has one, eating away at her heart and her liver; that is why
she looks older and I look younger. And I feel younger, too,
thank God. I like your mother-in-law. She has imagination, she
is even a good woman, in spite of what people say about her.
You must have noticed it, too."

"Yes."

"But she does not like me. And neither does your wife like
me. Poor Mary, she must have had a hard time with her mother
all these years. She should grow up and be more generous
with her brothers and sisters. Ludmilla loves her, you know,
Ludmilla loves her mother too, but Ludmilla has always
been hated or neglected. I hope you don't mind my frankness. I have always been that way. That is why I can tell you
that I don't think you did the right thing for this child when
you pushed her into the arms of that idiot of a Günther. Had
I been there at the time I would have insisted that Ludmilla
be allowed to stay with her mother and would have worked on
Mary, rather than on Ludmilla. Don't interrupt me, please. I
know I am saying many things I should not say. I also understand that you should be defending Mary. She is your wife, you
love her, and that is good. But you must have been in love with
Ludmilla at that time, or you would never have found such a
terrible man for her."

There was a gasp, a cough. The doctor felt that he must
speak, and this made him gasp and cough again. Marie put a
hand on his knee and patted it.

"Come, come," she said, "don't take it so badly. These
things happen in the best of families, and you did not behave
worse than any other man in your position would have. And
Ludmilla, like any other woman, could not have behaved any
better. She accepted your solution, to be out of your way. Because Ludmilla must have loved you, too. And I cannot blame
her, looking at you. So you both did the wrong thing—she for
good reasons, you for bad ones. And you are both forgiven.
What I cannot forgive is those two women who let her go

without caring what would happen to her. I know the whole story, you don't have to tell me anything: for her mother it was either the insane asylum or that cousin of yours. I have some understanding for Mary, but only when she is jealous of her husband, not when she is jealous of her mother. Mary is no longer a child, but she behaves like one. With the result that everybody else behaves like one. Ludmilla too behaves like a child where her mother is concerned. Now she wants to go back to her, or at least she wanted to before you came. She insisted on seeing you, she thought you could help her. I said, 'No, he is a prisoner, and he probably would not help you if he could.' I trust she has come to her senses now. But even if she has not, I will not let her go. I am glad she came to me. I am no angel of purity, as you may have heard if my name was ever mentioned by your women. But they both envy me. From which I may conclude that being right is not what people want. However, if I am no angel I am no judge either. When a person is in trouble, I try to be of help. I saw that Ludmilla was in trouble, I helped her get rid of that other silly man who wanted her for snobbish reasons, I helped her get rid of a French diplomat who is a bore and whom she did not love anyway, she had got rid of your German professor herself, and now I shall help her get rid of her mother. Because I know exactly what will happen if she goes back. Ludmilla will become a little girl again. She will not succeed in satisfying her mother, because her mother knows the difference between a real little girl and a false one, but she will succeed in wrecking her own life again by acting like a little girl with men.

"No," she went on, "I have a man Ludmilla might marry if she wants to. He is neither a genius nor a moneymaker—but, after all, she has intelligence and money, so there will be no competition there—he is a landed gentleman, half Hungarian, half Prussian, with an estate in Pomerania and an estate in Hungary, both worth nothing at all but with two pleasant houses and good hunting grounds. She may fill those two houses with

children until there is not a safe spot in the forest for the deer
to hide in. She may then take a lover; all the husband will do
is add another name to the guest list and another plate at his
table. No drama, no killings, no hurt honor, no compulsory
boredom such as you have in your country, my friend. She
claims she would not want children immediately; she is not
quite sure whether she loves the man or not, but I say this is
nonsense. What happens in the small space between our eyebrows and the lining of our scalp we do not know, but what
happens below the eyebrows and all the way down to our toes
we do know and we'd better let it happen without interference from that small and confused region above. She says she
would want little Sonia with her for a while. I think that a
very good idea. You could let her have Sonia for a few
months."

"What do you mean?" asked the doctor, who was speechless
again with indignation. "My daughter?"

Ludmilla stiffened, then blushed. "I am sorry," she said. "I
did not know you had such a low opinion of me."

"It is not that at all," he said, feeling he had given himself
away too quickly. "There is Mary to be considered. She is Sonia's
mother."

Ludmilla was embarrassed. "He is right," she said to Marie.

"I know, I know," said Marie. "The idea was mine. I wanted
to save Sonia from that madhouse. You will forgive me again for
being so frank. We know each other by now, this should not
surprise you. And then, with you I feel I can talk. You are not
only devilishly handsome, but also wise, understanding—
strange for an Italian, especially one from your part of the
country."

He felt uneasy again, and at the same time attracted to
that woman.

"I am afraid I have to go," he said, looking at his watch.
"They are waiting for me."

"Oh, please don't leave so soon," said Marie. "You must have

450

tea with us and meet my husband. You owe him an apology, and I shall punish you by insisting you stay for tea. Ludmilla, you will hold him by the tails of his coat if he threatens to leave, won't you?"

Marie left the room in a hurry, and Ludmilla at once began to fill the air with words, as if nothing had happened. The doctor was sitting like one who meditates a quick escape; he passed his hands over his knees and looked sidewise at her.

"Marie won't keep you much longer, don't be impatient. Henri will be here in a second. And you must meet him. He is very different from her, but nice, and a genius of a sort. Do you know that he is interested in medicine? I don't think he made any serious attempt to gain recognition for his ideas, but they say that he is remarkably good."

"Is he?"

"Oh, extraordinarily so," said Ludmilla. "Of course, I don't know anything about medicine, but he has a theory that certain parts of the brain do only certain things and certain others only certain other things. It sounds silly when I say it, because I don't know what it means, but—"

"I know," said the doctor. "Phrenology."

"Is that what it is called?" she asked, hoping to make him forget their quarrel by arousing his scientific interest. "He has also invented an electric belt that you tie around your waist. It gives you energy for the whole day."

"Ah, is he the inventor of that?" asked the doctor. "I had wondered for some time. It takes genius to be able to fool so many people."

At that moment the Duke d'Escarande came in and apologized for interrupting a medical consultation. "Is everybody all right?" he asked the doctor.

His wife briefed him: "I have told you a hundred times it is not a consultation. This is Ludmilla's brother-in-law."

"Ah. Of course, of course, Ludmilla's brother-in-law. How are you, Doctor? Are you well?"

Marie laughed. "This is the first time I've ever heard anyone ask a doctor how he is!"

"Why not?" said her husband. "Doctors have their health to worry about, too. Am I not right, Doctor?"

"Yes," said the doctor.

"See?" said the duke. "He says yes. Now tell me: Apropos of illness and good health, two subjects—or, rather, one subject with two sides to it (like all subjects, I should say)—which you must be discussing all day long, have you ever heard of an invention called the Energo-belt?"

"Yes, Ludmilla and I were just speaking about it. Your invention, I hear."

The duke smiled and bowed deeply. "You are much too kind to call it that. A very, very small contribution, not even a contribution, just a layman's attempt at doing his bit for the health of mankind. And, since you were so kind as to call it an invention, may I say that it is mine. But what I should have invented and never did (and I doubt very much that it will ever be invented) is a machine to keep men from behaving badly toward their fellow human beings. The Energo-belt was stolen from me, and now the thief is making money and I am not. Do you think that is fair?"

"Of course not, it is unfair."

"Did you hear that, Marie? It is unfair, he says! Why, I could not be more grateful to you for putting things so clearly. Because it *was* unfair. And this is not the first such instance I have suffered in my lifetime. At one time, many, many years ago, I invented a machine for the automatic distribution of chocolate bars and cigarettes at railroad stations. You may see it at all stations now, but who reaps the benefits? Not I. Someone else, someone who is a thief. I was not upset so much by this theft (although my wife says we have lost millions that way), and the reason is that it was a purely commercial enterprise, not a service to humanity, while the Energo-belt is indeed a great service to mankind. Have you ever tried it, Doctor?"

"No."

"Oh, but you should. How can you prescribe it to your patients if you have not tried it yourself? Let me tell you just one simple fact. As you know, happiness is not of this world. That is what the sages of old said. Also, the Gospels say it. But there was no electricity in those days. Now there is, and here we have the Energo-belt, and also happiness, because in fact the Energo-belt makes you feel extremely well. The first idea came to me from science. Let me tell how. It happened as I was asleep. I had a dream, and in this dream I kept saying, 'Why don't we charge our bodies as we charge batteries?' When I woke up I said to myself that it was not a stupid idea at all, and so I studied a little anatomy to find where the regenerating electricity should be applied and found that the best place was the abdomen, because not only do we keep all the food there before it becomes blood, but also because we grow layers of fat there, which the Energo-belt quickly reduces to nothing. So the Energo-belt does two things: it gives new energy and takes away the fat, which is detrimental to health. And you know who told me I was right? Dr. Malachier, a famous professor who is our family doctor."

"I know him. He was here a few weeks ago to see my mother-in-law."

"Ah, is that so? I am glad he came, I am sure your mother-in-law felt better immediately after he had left."

"That did happen," said the doctor.

"I am glad to hear it. I hear it all the time, but every new confirmation pleases me. Malachier is a very great man, one of the greatest we have in medicine. He is, in fact, our family doctor—as I think I told you before."

The doctor took advantage of this lull in the monologue to say, "I must leave now."

But the duke had already conceived another thought and wished to express it. "It is so pleasant to sit with you and hear your opinions," he said. "How did you find my wife?"

453

Marie made a gesture of impatience and shouted as if he were deaf, "Henri, I have told you a dozen times already, it is not I who am ill, nobody is ill. This is Ludmilla's brother-in-law."

He turned to her with a glance of severe reproach. "I must contradict you, someone *is* ill, you just heard mention of Malachier's coming here to cure the doctor's mother-in-law. Am I not right, Doctor?"

"Yes," said the doctor, "and that is another reason I must go now. She is still not well . . ."

"Just a moment, Doctor, just a moment. Tell me something. . . . Now, what was I trying to say? Dear Lord, what was I trying to say? Oh, yes. Tell me, if you have a mother-in-law and you are Ludmilla's brother-in-law, would you not be the husband of one of her sisters? Wait, don't interrupt me, I have it: If you are the husband of one of her sisters, it can only be Mary, because Katia is in the hospital in Berlin and I already know Olga's husband."

The doctor nodded all through this and now said, "Yes, I am Mary's husband, and she is waiting for me because her mother is not well."

"Ah, so you are! I guessed right. But why did you not bring her with you? We know your wife. We know her very well. We even know your mother-in-law—in fact, we know her better than we know your wife, because she is our own age. How is she? You said she was ill. I am sorry to hear that."

"Yes, she is ill, I must go to see her now."

"I understand, I understand, but did you not also say that she felt better after Malachier had seen her? Why don't you call him again? And why haven't we seen your wife here?"

Marie shook his arm and said, "Are you asleep today? What is happening to you? Don't you know about Ludmilla? She has been with us for weeks, and you still ask silly questions."

"Oh. I see. Of course, of course, my memory plays tricks on me these days. But . . . isn't it too bad we no longer are

454

friendly with Sophie? She had such delightful conversation, such wit—and such a great interest in medicine, as you probably know, Doctor. What a rare person she is! What an excellent hostess, and what a gourmet herself. Did you know that famous chef of hers in Rome, Monsieur Morin? Well, he served as a young cook in my brother's house, then went to Sophie, and I remember well how he behaved. He would not allow her to be given any letter that came from Moscow, because her Pierre, her elder son, was always writing alarmingly or unpleasantly. I do not care for Pierre. But I recall how Mary tried to fight off the cook, who, she felt, had too great an influence over her mother. Mary, I recall, was a bit jealous of her mother. Yes. She was. Is she still? And how many children do you have? And your painting, is it proceeding now? I remember your telling me about your problems. Was this before you married Mary, or after?"

Marie pulled his sleeve again, seeing that the doctor was growing pale and nervous, and again she shouted, "Henri! Are you living in a dream, or what? This is Mary's *second* husband. The *first* one was a painter."

"Oh—you are right. The famous divorce case, with the same lawyer who was engaged by Louise of Saxony. What ever happened to her? Is she still with her Italian songwriter Toselli? Have you ever met that other romantic couple, the Queen of Saxony and Monsieur Toselli?"

"No," said the doctor, "we have nothing in common with them."

"Of course not, of course not—and yet, a divorce . . . That is a great deal to have in common. People are so stupid that they are apt to shun the company of anyone who is divorced. Thus a divorce unites people more strongly than marriage. I know of two such cases in Westphalia, where everybody is Catholic and where no one divorces. They have lovers and mistresses. Now, these two cases I was speaking of are both related to us through the German branch of my family—in fact, they are closer relations of my wife's than of mine, because my wife, being an Escarande de Bagnolles, is also of course a Cormoloy de Citoges. Indeed, she has no right to the name Escarande, while I have no right to Cormoloy; but we both add the other name to our own because of old historic resonances in these two names combined. As I was saying, these divorced cousins of my wife became friendly with all the divorced couples in England, France and Italy, where they met the Queen of Saxony; and all they talked about was their divorces and how badly their friends behaved toward them afterward. This may explain to you why I asked whether you had met them. You have not, that is quite understandable. In fact, perhaps you have developed a revulsion against other divorced couples because they talk too much about their divorces. To which of these two categories do you belong, Doctor?"

"To neither. I must go now . . ."

"Ha ha ha! That, that, that indeed is a clever answer. Which means that you will either talk or not talk about your divorce and that you either like or dislike those who do—or who don't. You are clever, I must say! To neither! Ha ha ha, to neither! Haha . . . ha . . . ha. To neither, he says, to neither. I will have to remember that. But tell me, before you go—so my wife is doing well, is she? Oh, forgive me! I keep forgetting she is not ill this time. But why haven't we seen Mary? Dear little Mary, she was beginning to grow too fat the last time we saw her. I believe that in spite of her hate for Monsieur Morin she enjoyed his cooking. Oh, yes, oh, yes, don't tell me anything, I recall now that we have not been on good terms with Sophie for many years. But why is that? I have never found anything even vaguely irritating in her ideas, and I recall that they were quite original, quite daring, quite modern. Was she not a Socialist of some sort and a believer in free love? I personally am a good Catholic, but I agree with her I find the Church boring. Well, my wife had some differences with Sophie and thus a good friendship went to pieces. It is so rare that one

456

finds intelligent people, people with an interest in medicine. But you know, Doctor, you know what I say? I say this: that when women are too intelligent their husbands suffer, because suddenly this dinner partner or that whist player, or that philosopher, or a musician you have known for years, is no longer on the guest list and he no longer has you on his guest list. That is the only reproach I have to make to my wife after thirty-nine years of married life. Should I consider myself fortunate or unfortunate?

"But now," he said, "before I let you go, tell me, why can't we discuss Ludmilla's plans with Sophie before we leave Lugano? When my wife and Ludmilla told me all those horrible things poor Ludmilla had been subjected to, I failed to connect her mother's name with the many pleasant memories I have of our friendship (or with the name of Monsieur Morin) and I said, 'By all means we must fight off these two terrible creatures, Sophie and Mary.' And today, all of a sudden, here you are and— How was it that name Morin came up? Or was it something else that opened the closed treasure chest of those beautiful images of Rome, of Moscow, of Baden-Baden, of Ouchy, and the perfumes of foods, and the taste of those sauces Monsieur Morin prepared with such art? What was it that unchained all the ghosts of that age when we were younger and better able to enjoy the good things of life? Be it as it may, the moment I was in that world again I felt it a stupid thing to oppose Sophie and Mary and keep Ludmilla away from them. They are so good, so kind, so understanding—I really don't see, Ludmilla, what you have against them."

Ludmilla stiffened, crossed her legs, picked a long cigarette holder from the table, rolled herself a cigarette, and began to smoke it angrily, her leg shaking the while.

Henri looked at her and laughed, then touched her ankle and said, "You would have made a good dancer, Ludmilla. You have beautiful ankles, I am sure that your legs must be even more beautiful." Then he turned to the doctor and said, "I

457

know why Ludmilla is so reluctant. We found her with a terrible German archaeologist who had her in his custody, like a child in the hands of her governess. And it seems that her brother-in-law, with whom she must have had—"

Marie put a hand over his mouth and said, "Henri, you are tired today, you have been talking for an hour without interruption and inventing things you must have seen in your dreams. Go to bed and don't show up again until you have had a good rest."

He laughed and laughed, then shook hands with the doctor and said, "I am being ordered to bed. I have a very strict doctor, as you can see. Well, goodbye, my friend. And I do hope that we will soon have a pleasant reunion with Sophie and Mary, either here or at your house. Goodbye. My love to both those delightful women! Goodbye. Are you warmly dressed? It is cold outside today, put a scarf in front of your mouth as you go out. Goodbye. Goodbye."

He kissed his wife's hand, patted Ludmilla's ankle again, pinched her cheek and was gone.

"Now I have no excuse," said the doctor. "It is very late for me."

Ludmilla kissed him again with disturbing affection.

Then Marie said, "And do I get a kiss, too?" She grabbed his head and kissed him on the mouth. "If you want to write to us and let us know what happens, we shall be in Milan, at the Continental. Goodbye." She pushed him out and closed the door.

As the doctor walked, almost ran, down the wide staircase, everything on that staircase seemed unchanged and good. The same smells came up from the entrance hall—a mixture of clean linen from the dining room, clean carpets, clean door-knobs, freshly painted doors and traces of perfume from the passage of elegant people. Suddenly he saw something extremely familiar which he himself had brought back to this place: his image in the mirror. Oh, that mirror, that mirror in which his first expensive English clothes had shown him to himself as a completely new person—how many memories were connected with that mirror! His children shrieking with joy upon seeing more children like themselves move exactly as they did and come toward them wearing their own clothes and their own friendly faces. What purity in those memories, and how much filth he was leaving behind!

He crossed the lobby, and the hotel manager, the lift boy, the whole personnel busy with arrivals, sent him their smiles from beyond a thick curtain of hotel courtesy aimed at new clients. He was their friend and they were his friends, he liked them all, they were solidly Swiss, and in spite of what Mary said against them they were more like her than Ludmilla. Good, clean, moral people, he thought. How dignified they are in their show of servility! In fact, how clumsy their servility, because it is aimed not at pleasing others but at defending themselves from the intrusion of standards which do not belong in Switzerland! Oh, how he loved them.

The snowstorm had become fiercer. As he stood in front of the hotel everything seemed to reproach him for his idleness. The four granite figures of giants protruding from the façade of the hotel and holding up the weight of the balcony with their heads and their hands—the first mythological figures in his children's experience—were now partly disfigured by the formation of ice and snow on their eyes and shoulders; and yet they kept holding that balcony, his children's balcony, as bravely and silently as they had for years, even after his children had left. They were even more solid than the Swiss with their honesty and lack of refinement. "What did you do up there above our heads while we were working for you?" And the trees along the lake shore, naked and blackened by humidity, with a coating of ice weighing them down, were working hard to keep their shape and their place. Some branches hung, broken but not detached, the white of the wood looking like torn flesh. He could hear the noise of the battle: thousands of glass beads beaten together in the wind and shedding splinters, each with a sample of wood encased in it, like relics that the faithful contemplate under glass, imagining the body of the saint whose bones or clothes they were. The tall mountain range across the lake had been cut to the level of the water and consumed in the storm; it was one with the wind and the snow. The lake itself, still fighting here and there to shake off ice, had been almost completely paved with irregular gravestones of all sizes. In the few open areas, smaller pieces of the unfinished jigsaw puzzle were already floating about, waiting to be put into place. The missing pieces were being formed under his eyes: thinner layers of ice that the waves broke every second, but they kept coming together and forming thicker parts, which the very resistance of the medium helped weld together.

He stood there for a while in thought. Then he walked home in the snow, thinking and thinking.

At first he felt that Ludmilla and her friends had been polite with him, then he slowly decided that they had kicked him out—with kisses and compliments, but still he *had* been kicked out and insulted. In his provincial world, which he carried with him and exuded as a body exudes warmth, only complete insanity could have justified such a quick passage from tragedy to social conversation, from sexual frenzy to a lesson in morals. And what a lesson, and pronounced in what beautiful style from the throne, as it were, by a queen, indeed an empress of all empresses on earth. That politeness had confused him. He had seen prostitutes before, had felt the heavy atmosphere of sin and the violent instincts it awoke in his blood, but always all in its typical setting of vulgarity—which is a moral guarantee, something that keeps that world distinguished from the world of politeness, of principles, of poetry, of wives, mothers and sisters. No such distinction here: a declared whore who was also a great lady, wise as a peasant woman, kind as a mother, pure as an angel.

And that idiot? He had seen idiots in his village, idiots in Naples, idiots in hospitals, all of them pitiful and helpless, and his reactions to them had always been the same: a sense of superiority, a desire to shelter them from the cynical attitude of those more fortunate than they. Here the idiot himself had the cynical attitude, he was articulate, self-critical, even intelligent at moments, yet always an idiot, and a wonderful idiot who could say to a stranger, "Put a scarf over your mouth or you might catch cold." The doctor could have kissed him for those words. But then this man speaking of Mary as "little Mary" and of her mother as "Sophie" made him feel an outsider. Could that idiot be like them or they like him?

And what was Ludmilla? Was she pure? Was she beautiful? Was she above reproach? Yes, she was all these things, and he had been a coward to suspect her. But now suddenly something became clear to him: she had insulted him only because he had been hesitant, and for admitting without comment that he had received a certain letter. But she herself had asked Günther to send it and given him permission to write anything he wanted. Then, after that scene, Ludmilla had crossed her legs and smoked a cigarette. If that was not evidence of complete moral corruption, what was it? And now everything was finished. He had lost all his dignity, and also lost his chance to be in the company of that beautiful woman.

He reached his house in a state of complete self-contempt, saying to himself, I had not enough courage to be good, I had not enough courage to be bad. What sort of man am I?

XXI

IT IS TYPICAL of well-brought-up children to be impatient for
either punishment or praise, with the result that whatever
they do becomes a source of anguish to them. They are impatient to be punished in order to be able to return to their
games or their duties, because the limbo in which they live
before their crimes are punished is far worse than the punishment itself. And when they behave well, they cannot just rely
on the notion that virtue is its own reward, because if this
were true, then vice would also be its own punishment. Later
in life these calculating children become heroes whose every
act of courage on the battlefield is sure to be rewarded with a
medal and a detailed description beautifully handwritten on
parchment.

Mary had done something good only a few minutes after her
husband went down to the Grand Hotel that afternoon. She
had to be rewarded by her husband, and her impatience in
this case prevented her for hours from worrying over his health
or fearing for his life in the snowstorm. When, hours later,
she began to realize that she had failed to worry for so long,
the intense resentment she had felt until then was instantly
transferred, like a bureaucratic file transferred from one desk to
another. He had been classified until then as "unwilling to turn

up"; now he was classified as "prevented from turning up." Who could be detaining him? Ludmilla, of course.

She felt suddenly that Ludmilla was very near. And yet she had no reason to believe it. Neither Ludmilla nor Günther had been heard from for ten days, perhaps Ludmilla was in Paris with Marie—thus she tried to reassure herself that the danger was not imminent. But she knew it was. This is the last good afternoon I am spending with Mamachen, she thought instinctively. And at once her feeling that Ludmilla had lost every chance with her husband was gone. Her hands were cold, but the course she must take was clear.

She went to her mother and said, "Mamachen, now that Ludmilla is forgiven, I feel I must tell you something which has been on my conscience for some time."

"What is it? Have you concealed something from me again?"

"No, Mamachen . . ."

"Then what? If it is something I know already, it cannot be on your conscience."

Mary became frightened by her mother's logic. Again, even before she began to do the right thing, her mother proved to her that she was wrong.

"Well, Mary? Why this silence?"

"I was just thinking . . ."

"Speak up: What were you thinking?"

"Just a moment, Mamachen, I think I hear my husband, he can explain these things better than I."

"You don't have to call him. You don't even have to tell me what it is. I know everything. Ludmilla is here."

"No, Mamachen, it is not that."

"Ludmilla is here, and she has done something wrong, and you helped her hide from me until you were sure I had forgiven her."

"Oh, no, Mamachen. I would never do that, and neither would my husband. We haven't heard from Ludmilla for a very long time. We were waiting to hear from her before we told you."

"Told me what? Something you knew about her? Has she left that German and gone away with another man? I know she has. It would be just like her. She imagines that way she is like me or like you. She too must have her true love and her divorce. But don't keep me guessing. Tell me."

"Mamachen, will you promise not to be angry?"

"I cannot promise anything to a person who has no confidence in me. You have not been loyal to me—for the third time in your life."

"Mamachen, I don't want you not to be angry with me. But please be angry only with me. I did not have the courage to harm you and to harm Ludmilla. I am sorry."

"All right, be sorry, but confess too. What is this mystery? Can't you see I am suffering? Does it amuse you to torture me?"

"No—of course not."

"I like your answer. So I may now infer that it does not amuse you to torture me. But then speak up, I say, speak up!"

"Mamachen, you were right. She left that man, had two lovers and is now living with . . ."

"Go on, with whom?"

"With—Marie d'Escarande."

"Oh. That indeed I had never expected. Ludmilla is cleverer than I thought. She can surprise even me. Tell me everything. And, first of all, why did you keep this from me and when did you first learn about it? I know when: That morning when those letters came there was also a letter in German for your husband. That was what kept you away from me for hours, until I had a crisis that almost killed me. And still, after I asked you repeatedly whether you were concealing something from me, you said no and no and no. How can I trust you? Tell me how."

Mary found nothing to say. She saw her happiness destroyed; all the long effort to prove to her husband that she was free of jealousy had been useless. Now she would lose him, he would never forgive her, he would see Ludmilla in secret, because Ludmilla was nearby, and she would never know. Would it not have been better to keep everything quiet and let Ludmilla come back, and control all her movements in the house?

"Well?" asked her mother. "Are you sifting lies from truth so as to give me only what a sick old person may take without peril to her health? You don't have to. My health is gone. I have only a few more days to live."

"Mamachen, I am sorry . . ."

"Speak first, then we shall see whether you deserve to be forgiven so easily. All you want is to be free of remorse. That is typical of you. When you choose the path of evil, do so at least with courage, don't try to hold the roof over your head while you escape from home. Leave the roof with the house, to protect those who remain loyal to the house."

"I will show you the letter," said Mary, and she went to get it.

She came back with Günther's letter and gave it to her mother, murmuring, "I did it only to help Ludmilla, and I want to be punished as I deserve."

Her mother grabbed the letter and said, "My lorgnon. I left it there on the dresser."

Mary found the lorgnon, then left the room. Now she was anxious for her husband's return so that she could tell him it was all his fault. And why was he so long? She was about to turn again from aggressive defense to passive anguish when she saw him come in, covered with snow. She was so pleased that she immediately took up her self-defense by appearing more anguished than she really was.

"Where have you been all this time? With Ludmilla?"

He had just begun to take off his scarf and had not yet put down his hat when he realized what she was saying and dropped both hat and scarf on the floor, standing motionless like one struck by a blow.

"How—how do you know?" he asked.

Now it was her turn to be struck. She had to lean against the wall. "So I was right. You were with Ludmilla."

"Who told you?"

"Never mind. I have my ways of knowing things. You cannot hide the truth from me. Tell me everything."

"I was going to tell you, but you did not give me time. Who—whoever can have told you such a thing?"

"I am not going to answer that question now. Why were you away so long and where is she and did you know she was in this city before you left the house?"

"I swear to God I knew nothing. I was taken by surprise."

"You must have known where you were going."

"I went to the hotel. First I saw the manager's family and everbody else, and then the mysterious client asked whether I had arrived and—"

"And it was Ludmilla."

"No. Let me talk. It was a Countess di San Pronto—"

"Of course, Marie d'Escarande, that is one of her titles."

"So I learned, when she told me."

"And Ludmilla was with her."

"No."

"Where was she?"

"Let me tell you."

"You were alone with Marie in her bedroom."

"No, I was not."

"In her sitting room."

"Let me talk."

"You were, and it took you all this time to discuss whatever you discussed with her. Where did you see Ludmilla, and how long were you alone with Marie? I want to know everything, even if I do know it already."

"What do you mean, you know it already? If you do and if you don't let me talk, I won't talk."

466

"You must talk. That is the least you can do. And you must tell me everything, leaving out no detail. You have been hours with them. And let me tell you another thing: If you think that *your* Ludmilla will ever set foot in this house again, you are mistaken. Mamachen is just reading Günther's letter. And she is furious with me for having kept it from her for so long. Who made me keep the secret but you? And for what purpose but that of allowing your love to come back? What a fool I have been not to see through your dirty schemes for so long! But now you are going to tell me everything, this very minute!"

Seeing that the apologetic method did him no good, the doctor tried to adopt the method of parallel aggressiveness and compete with his wife in her attacks on Ludmilla.

"Indeed I am!" he shouted, with a pretense of joyfulness. "I have been afraid you would still want your sister here, and I am glad, I am immensely happy that you have shown that letter to your mother. I was a fool to prevent you from doing so before! Ludmilla is finished as far as I am concerned, I don't want her near my children. She still thinks she may come, but no, oh no! Not after what I have seen!"

"What have you seen?"

"What have I seen? Ha! First of all that Marie d'Escarande, and then Ludmilla, smoking cigarettes with a cigarette holder as long as this. And Ludmilla crossing her legs like a man!" He sneered and added, "I have never seen such a person as Marie d'Escarande! It seems to me as if I have been down in hell. I really had a glimpse of the worst!"

Mary smiled, then became somber and said, "It was an awfully long glimpse you had! Four hours for a glimpse is a good deal."

"It was not four hours. I was almost an hour with those other people."

"That makes it three. What did you do there in three hours?"

"I was horrified. I—heard what they had to say, made it clear to them that the answer was no, and came away."

"Why did you bother to listen? When I say something you don't like, you know it before I even begin to talk. But there you had to listen to everything. One does not give such people a chance to talk. How long were you alone with Marie?"

"Not very long."

"Did she receive you in her nightgown?"

"How do you know?"

"She always does with those she wants to seduce. She even seduced our cook, Monsieur Morin."

"How awful! Her husband mentioned Monsieur Morin."

"Was he there, too?"

"Yes, all the time."

"All the time? Are you sure?"

"Well, he left for a few minutes, then came back."

"And in the meantime?"

"In the meantime she talked, then Ludmilla talked—"

"Did Ludmilla embrace you?"

"Why, of course, just normally."

"How?"

"Just as you would embrace a relative."

"And how about Marie?"

"What an idea!"

"Did she or did she not?"

"Of course not. What do you think I am?"

"A man, a handsome man. Did she say that?"

"No. I don't remember. I was not listening."

"What were you doing, then?"

"Nothing. I was just listening—I mean, I was there, disgusted by what I saw, and trying to find a chance to say goodbye and leave."

"One doesn't have to find a chance, one just leaves and says goodbye while leaving. Is that so difficult? And what did Ludmilla have to say? How did she manage not to be recognized by the hotel people? And how did she justify the whole comedy with you? Did you tell her about the letter?"

"Give me time, give me time. I shall answer every one of your questions, but give me time. Yes, I did mention the letter."

"And how did she take it?"

"Oh, she was furious. She made a scene, she threatened to call the hotel manager and have me kicked out."

"That was what she had to say about her behavior? She just repeated the performance as Günther had described it in his letter. And of course you apologized and said, 'Please, Ludmilla, please don't call the manager, I will be good.' "

"What nonsense! I did nothing of the sort!"

"I don't believe it! Knowing you and the constant fear you have of scandal, I am absolutely certain that you must have asked her not to call anyone. Tell me the truth: Did you or did you not?"

He blushed and said, "I did, but not in the tone you imagine. I just said, 'Please, Ludmilla, don't do that, let's talk about it.' "

"Oh no. You did not say, 'Let's talk about it,' for you knew she would have made even more of a scene. You promised instead that you would never talk about it again. Be honest, now —that is what you said, or is it not?"

"In a way, but not exactly so. I beg you to consider—"

"Don't beg me to consider anything, otherwise you will force me to consider that you were fooled all along like a little boy. You had enough information against her to make her kneel in front of you and apologize, and you managed to apologize yourself, perhaps even on your knees, what do I know about it, I wasn't there to watch you, and you left without having the pleasure of hearing one word of explanation about her evil doings with those men in Athens. Not a word."

There was a long silence, then the doctor said, "Mary, you are right. I had not thought of that. I guess I am just a damned fool. Forgive me."

She was pleased, but again her triumph was of short duration. A new gust of uncontrollable jealousy took hold of her.

"Too easy, to apologize to me for apologizing to her. Three hours for that! I wonder if you are telling me the truth. A man like you, who sees a woman smoking a cigarette and crossing her legs, and sees that woman in the company of a prostitute who receives him in her nightgown, and does not slap that woman or both women in the face—what sort of man is that?"

"She was not smoking when I saw her. She smoked afterward, while Henri was there."

"Henri you call him. That degree of intimacy! A good sign indeed! You must have made a conquest of him—that is, of her, because all her new lovers graduate to the honor of calling him Henri."

"I did not call him anything. I say Henri now because I hate titles and you know it. They said Henri to him, so I repeat Henri speaking of him to you. I felt sorry for him. He is a complete idiot, but he is better than his wife."

Mary became pensive for a moment. She seemed to have quieted down. "Yes," she said. "He is not a bad man, and, were it not for her, we would have stayed friends with him. I personally liked him very much."

"He spoke very kindly of you and of Mamachen. Very kindly."

"Did he also mention Monsieur Morin?"

"He did, several times."

A timid smile appeared on the doctor's face. Mary smiled back, they kissed and were happy.

"Let's go upstairs and see Mamachen," said Mary. "And you explain it all to her."

The old lady seemed to have become immensely patient. She was experiencing one of those states of mind that egocentrics use as evidence of their wonderful character when they say, "I am not like the rest of mankind. I can be frantic over little things, but when something big happens I am calm and self-contained. In fact, I am the only one who displays courage." The truth of it being that liberation from the jail of their nothingness, the boredom of their lifelong resentments, is a great pleasure, even if the occasion is unpleasant, as it always is. Love does not free these people of their shackles. They cannot give themselves, because they don't exist, or, rather, what exists of them they detest, and they cannot imagine how anyone can like them. Thus no amount of love may soothe them, while the slightest unpleasantness, by first hitting them hard, makes them forget their own problems and they find themselves dwarfed by the presence of something bigger than they. Modesty, so rare in them, is their momentary relaxation. If this can be obtained only through sorrow, it does not mean that they love sorrow; but one concentrated dose of objective sorrow is a good antidote to a sea of subjective, stale and undefinable sorrow. It is said that the prisoners at Auschwitz who were freed to clean the ovens and bury the dead enjoyed their work, even though they were burying their families and would themselves be buried the same way by other prisoners. This is not true. They were enjoying the exercise and the heat from the ovens. And what the doctor saw, as he entered the room where the old lady sat in bed, was a prisoner who had just been released from her chains to bury her own dead.

He mistook her serenity for an extreme situation of *lèse majesté*. "Forgive me," he said, "it was all my fault. Mary suffered the pains of hell, she would have given her life to show you that letter. I forbade her to do so, I said to her it might endanger your health. She obeyed me reluctantly . . ."

"Never mind, you were probably right. There was and still is little to be done as long as Ludmilla does not write. I don't know where that awful woman Marie lives, and I would never write to her. All we can do now is wait and make plans to rescue the poor child from her new governess."

Mary became frozen with terror as she realized that her mother was not at all impressed by Ludmilla's misbehavior.

"But Mamachen, Ludmilla has—"

"Be quiet, Mary. Idle talk as to who is responsible will not show us the way out of this horror. It was probably my fault, but what good will it do if I wallow in remorse? We must do something here, and the first thing of all is to find Marie d'Escarande and take Ludmilla away from her. She is a terrible woman, because she can exercise a strange charm. Even I fell under it for a short time and regarded her as my best counselor. Yes, Mary, I did. I never spoke about it, no use now. Later sometime I'll tell you the whole story; but right now I must help Ludmilla and get her to come back."

"Ludmilla is back," said the doctor. "But she cannot be rescued, I fear."

"Back? Ludmilla back? Here in the house?"

"Oh, no, not here. Back in Lugano, at the Grand Hotel, in our former apartment, with Marie d'Escarande and her husband. I tried to rescue her, and for a while I even thought I had succeeded—until she did something in my presence that revealed to me how low she has stooped. I doubt that it will ever be possible to call her back."

"What did she do?"

"In my presence, and in the presence of Marie's husband, she crossed her legs and lit a cigarette."

Instinctively, the old lady covered her face with both hands. She shook her head to deny the reality of what she had heard, then looked at the doctor and asked, "Ludmilla? You mean Ludmilla did that?"

"Yes, Ludmilla did that."

"And she probably laughed, or smiled. She must have been proud of her new style."

"She is. She was. She smiled impertinently and looked— well, vulgar, almost like one of those . . ."

Mary was sternly supervising the effect of these words on her mother, ready (so it seemed to her husband) to reprimand her if she did not react with enough indignation.

The old lady lifted her eyes to the ceiling while tears

formed in them and in her nose. She wiped her nose, sniffed, then said with sobs in her voice, "And to think that Pierre, a man of forty, would not dare light a cigarette in my presence! Nor cross his legs. And yet he could. Men do today—and I have become modern, too. When I said to him, 'Pierre, don't you want to smoke?' he looked at me as if I had forgotten who I was and said, 'Mamachen, how dare you?' And now my youngest daughter must do that, in the presence of two men! What have I done to deserve such punishment? I had so hoped that we could still rescue her, in spite of everything. All the bad things I have read in this letter are nothing, they can happen to anyone, they are only a sign of confusion. But smoking—oh, smoking is so deliberate, such a willful flaunting of vulgarity! Worse, much worse than spitting into people's faces. That gesture symbolizing contempt: *Pfffff*, smoke into your eyes. *Quelle horreur!*"

"I told you that she crossed her legs too, didn't I? Well, the duke, if I am to use that stupid appellative, touched her ankles and spoke of her legs and said she would have made a great dancer."

To his surprise, the old lady laughed. "He is not a bad man. In fact, I like him very much. He is amusing, he is kind, he is a great gentleman. And then, he is so devoted to medicine. It is rare to find such great devotion to science, to mankind, especially in a member of his idle and corrupt class."

This brief parenthesis of social levity opened the doctor's eyes. He now understood how Ludmilla could have fallen so easily, without noticing it. Her own mother took the occasion of a tragic discovery to converse pleasantly about people she knew. Oh, there was something corrupt about wealth, and he swore to himself that if he were to receive some of her money he would make it a point to live in poverty, so as not to be tempted to become frivolous.

"All right," said the old lady, "I thought we could rescue her and make her see what she was doing to herself, but if she smokes and crosses her legs there is only one solution: put her into a mental hospital. Not for long, just until she recovers. And then find her a husband, someone who does not love her too much, as this poor fool does."

"I had forgotten to tell you," said the doctor, "that Marie has found a husband for her. A landowner, partly Hungarian, partly Prussian, with estates in Pomerania."

"Has she? Some former lover of hers, I imagine. Who could that be? Let's see. . . . Dora's son? No, Dora is French, he would be partly French. Tatyana's son? He would be partly Russian. Inge's son? He is married already. Did she say whether he was married or single?"

"Single."

The old lady pondered for another few seconds, then said, "Can't be. Unless he is some provincial nonentity. No respectable youngster, single, half Hungarian and half Prussian, with estates in Pomerania, is known to us. Well, we shall stop her. Call the police and have them arrest Ludmilla."

"What? The police? But it will be a scandal! And then, arrest her on what grounds?"

"Disobedience."

"She has received no orders—she was free to do whatever she pleased. Not even Günther may have her arrested, because she was not married to him. And that too may come out and it would be a very great scandal."

"Then have Marie arrested for keeping her a prisoner."

"Impossible."

"Why?"

"Ludmilla will refuse to come here. She will say—and it is true—that it was she who went to Marie."

"We must do something. How long will they be here?"

"They may have left already. They were going to Milan."

"Do you have their address?"

"Hotel Continental."

"Very good. Pen and paper. I shall write to my daughter."

474

XXII

THREE NIGHTS BEFORE CHRISTMAS. The old lady was writing in her notebook, and her hand holding the pen made huge shadows on the ceiling. It was very late, and it was snowing again; she could tell from the tone of the train whistle in the distance. She wrote:

There are stars of which they say that they disappeared thousands of centuries ago, but their light, their last light, like a ribbon detached at one end, keeps coming our way and falling into our eyes and being folded up into our memories. Though its source is dead, that light will be seen by generations of men, who will believe what they see. The past of those dead stars will be our future long after our future is dead. In a small way that is what happens to us with our feelings. We write letters, we write them truthfully, we shed our feelings; because we have said everything, nothing of those feelings remains in us.

I have been doing this all my life. Last week I wrote a letter to Ludmilla. I expressed my feelings about her in it, she has read it and believed it and she will not be back. Yet a few hours after it had been posted, I was feeling that even if she smoked and crossed her legs I would want her back. How I wish I had never learned how to write!

She had now come to a point in her life when she regretted everything she had done or failed to do, and her one wish was that her children might forget what she had taught them, all the sternness and the haughtiness and the constant resentment against everything and everyone, but she feared that in this she had been too good a teacher. They would fight and keep fighting over her spoils and in her honor. She was beginning to believe in the hereafter. This was a foretaste of the punishment she would witness from on high, longing in vain for her old limitations and her blindness, as she had longed during her life for omnipresence and omniscience.

The only thing man cannot be with any great hope of success is an egotist [she wrote]. *If we were really vain, we would lead saintly lives, in order to be able to watch ourselves with admiration from the Heavens. O my children, don't fight over what I leave after my death. The children of the Virtuous walk freely and lightly as if they were dead already. Their lives are not a spectacle, and their eyes are not tied to the ground: they watch the sky. And their dead parents can afford to forget them, because they are the sky, and by watching the Spectacle of Infinity they find themselves together with their children. Amen.*

She dated this "5.43 A.M., December 23, 1908."

Then she put down her book, her pen and her glasses, turned off the light and arranged a pillow between shoulder and cheek. She felt extremely well. She had once more given logical form to her feelings; they had now become a thought worth quoting, perhaps even worth publishing. In fact, she was tempted to turn on the light again and reread it; the wording of those images did not come back to her mind, she wondered how she had said that about dead parents and living children meeting by looking at the same thing. Had she spoken of "parallel interests" or not? She was sure she had not. Perhaps she should.

Her emotion was great; it always was when she reached

that supreme form of liberation which consists of verbal expression. In fact, it was so great that she could hear her heart
beat through the bedsheets and she felt almost as if the floor
under her bed was trembling. Could it be an earthquake? No,
it must be her heart. I must not read it again, or I will never
sleep, she thought. But the joy of achievement was too great.
So she applied what she believed to be her own invention, not
knowing that it had always been the mental trick of all writers
on earth: I have it, she repeated to herself, it is mine, the
words are mine, the images are mine; now I can think the
opposite, to give my mind a rest. And like a little girl who
runs out of the classroom for recess, she stepped down from
the pedestal of morals and, for the first time in her life, began
to evoke images of a woman in sin—Ludmilla being the subject.

The first discovery she made about that unknown universe
was that Ludmilla must have unbuttoned her blouse and taken
off her shoes and stockings in the presence of a man who was
not her husband. She never went beyond that image; it hit
her with such violence that she felt it in her chest, like a
stone thrown at her from a dark corner of the room. Her left
arm became stiff with pain, her breath became a knife tearing
away from her throat to her stomach, and it was only after a
while that she could think, Her father too was not my husband
when I did this in his presence. But she had not done it for
her first husband, and the frightening memory of that night
in which the man she had married at her father's injunction
had tried to pull her clothes from her came back to her memory
so vividly that she felt his fist hit her again and again in her
chest, three, four, five times, until she tried to scream because
she could not breathe. But even screaming was impossible.

The pain finally quieted down and now she saw herself
throwing things at the man, as she had done that night, and
seeing his face bleed from a wide gash in his cheek made by a
glass she had thrown at him. She recalled now, for the first time

in her life, how she had locked the door in his face after pushing him out of the bedroom, and how she had refused to see him the next day, and the next night and for many nights. And then her flight with her young love (not yet her lover), a long uncomfortable ride by stagecoach, and the arrival in St. Petersburg, and the first night in a very poor house belonging to his mother, and the horror of that first night too, because of the illegality of it all. She had never dared remember that sad period in her life; in fact, it had sunk into nothingness, dragging with it even the first good night of unrestrained enjoyment. Which had come, she now recalled, long after Katia's birth . . . and Pierre's birth . . . and Ivan's birth, and Mary's, and Olga's and Ludmilla's. It had come. . . it had come . . . When had it come? Yes, once, in Egypt, *on the night before he died,* and after a long scene of jealousy because he had dared to look at his day nurse with tenderness. And after that a life of sorrow and solitude and unspeakable anguish, caused by want of . . .

The shock of this sudden awareness made her blush in the dark, so that again she could not breathe. Instinctively she covered her face with her arm, then pulled her nightcap down over her eyes. And still this did not seem enough. She hid under the blankets, but there again she could not breathe. "Am I also one of those—women?" she asked herself, and decided at once that she was not, because she had denied herself such coarse pleasures all through the years of her married life. Respectable love, true love, shuns all coarseness; it kisses a mouth, but the lips must not part, out of respect for the kissed person. Now she recalled that she had caught herself experiencing pleasant sensations elsewhere, but had dutifully strengthened herself against such horrors and successfully disciplined her body not to debase her love. And now this past experience, suddenly thrust into her face as her own, and she forced to recognize it as her own . . .

In the slumber that followed she saw herself besieged by a

478

number of policemen who were holding her chauffeur and her cook and also, strangely enough, Luther and Bernhard, and asking her, "Are these really your servants?"

"Yes, why?"

"Because they have stolen your underwear, your monogrammed underwear, and here it is. Do you recognize it?"

And she had to say, "Yes," because she never told a lie. Then she was asked to unbutton her blouse and her shoes, to prove that she was not telling a lie, and she screamed, oh, how she screamed this time. But the scream ended in a moan; the pain started again and the knife worked while she slowly resumed breathing.

"What is it, Mamachen, what is it? Are you in pain?"

Mary was nearby in her nightgown. But she remained invisible.

The old lady was going to say, "No, I am not," because the objective situation would speak for her, but she said, "Yes, I have a pain, I have a . . ."

And suddenly the pain subsided and she realized that the light had been on and Mary was visible. The lights inside her had been out. This frightened her; she could hear herself breathing through her throat with a faint hissing sound, like a train out there in the snow.

"Mamachen, you look ill!"

The doctor pushed Mary aside and approached with his stethoscope. But the old lady, who had never before acted so stupidly, became frantic and stammered, "No . . . no. I cannot . . . I cannot . . . No, please no!"

"But I can unbutton your nightgown. Let me," he said.

"No . . . no . . . no . . . no . . . no . . ." And she clasped his hand in hers, breathing with pain.

"All right," he said, while Mary watched the scene with a very stern face, as if she were witnessing a crime. "We can wait until you feel better. But I really should do it, you know. Let me give you an injection."

479

"N-n-n-n-no . . . no . . ."

"But what is this now? You have had injections before, it will do you no harm. On the contrary. This is camphor, it will soothe you at once. It is a new thing . . ."

"No. . . . I feel better—ouch—it is only in my arm. . . . I leaned on it too long while I was writing."

"It is not your arm, let me assure you."

"No . . . here . . I am now feeling . . . better." Then, falling back on the pillows like a dead body, she whispered, "Ludmilla. Her fault." And she began to sob.

"Mamachen, oh, Mamachen," cried Mary, "we should never have told you—I should never have told you. It is my fault. Mamachen, forgive me."

The old lady smiled and said, "Nothing . . . to forgive. . . . Better . . . to know . . . than . . . not to know. My father's blood must be in her veins. My mother was not one of . . . those women."

"Mamachen, what a thought! Of course she was not."

Mary had never in her life heard her mother speak ill of her saintlike grandfather. This was the first time. And rarely, very rarely, had she heard her grandmother mentioned at all. She looked at her husband, and he nodded as if to say, "Didn't I tell you not to speak?"

She bent her head and whispered inaudibly, "I did not know . . ."

"Mary, come here," said her mother. "Here . . . closer. Give me your hand."

"Yes, Mamachen, here is my hand. Don't cry, Mamachen, what is it, Mamachen?"

"Nothing. . . . It feels good to hold a clean hand and to know . . . this child has not betrayed me . . . not insulted our name, not . . . unbuttoned her blouse and taken off— Ouch . . . ouch, it hurts. . . ." The old lady lost consciousness.

It was daytime when she realized that she had been given an injection and was not to leave her bed. Mary and her husband looked worn, and this pleased her.

"What is the weather like?" she asked, smiling.

"A most terrible snowstorm. You should see the garden," said Mary, speaking against the windowpane, so that she had to wipe it clear with her hand. "It is hardly any more visible through a clean window than through a foggy one."

"Is it?" said her mother, enjoying this clean conversation after the horrors of the night. "I want to see it."

"No, you may not," said the doctor, looking at her severely.

She was pleased by this too. Everything helped bring her back to normality, and she especially liked being treated like a child.

"Now we will give you a light breakfast," he said. "Then you must try to sleep for an hour or two, because you had a bad night."

Her weakness was so great that she mistook it for strength and sat back, motionless and smiling. It was morning, there was activity in the house, her mind was crystal clear, and she was forced to stay in bed, so her conscience was clear, too.

She closed her eyes before breakfast, and did not know that she had closed them, for her waking situation was already one of dreams. She continued to watch the same scene she had watched with her eyes open, and would probably never have inserted into it any absurd image had the noise of the breakfast table and the tinkling of cups and spoon, plus Mary's whisper to the butler, not asked to be placed somewhere in that scene.

At first she recognized the breakfast table, and Mary going, "Shh, make no noise, leave everything here," and the butler trying not to cough and finally doing so into his handkerchief. She could even smell fresh bread, the tea, the soft-boiled eggs, the toast, and was going to say, "I am not asleep, give me my breakfast, I am hungry this morning." But then she thought, They must see me, why don't they say to me, "You are awake, eat your breakfast now"? What are they waiting for? She had forgotten how to open her eyes. In spite of her efforts they stayed closed. After a while this became anguishing, but she did not want to scream, because she knew that then there would be pain in her left arm.

She spoke. She said, "Mary, bring me my breakfast." But Mary stood there, with that finger on her lips, staring at her mother as if to suggest to her that *she* should make no noise because *she* was asleep. "Mary," she said, "I am not asleep. Do I have the right to keep my eyes closed or is that a reason not to be given breakfast? I am hungry, Mary, I am very hungry." But Mary would not move. "Mary, I know you cannot see me if I keep my eyes closed, but you should at least be able to hear me." Still no reply. "Mary, I don't want to scream, because of my arm, can you understand that?"

At this moment the doctor came in and said, "Was I not right? Don't throw away the bread crumbs!" And she laughed.

Mary did not laugh, she continued to stand there, blocking the window from her mother. Sunshine streamed into the room. The rays of light looked like worms and soapsuds, then soapbubbles, and finally she recognized them as her jewels. The bracelets, the necklaces, the earrings and the parures became more and more agitated. They rose upward like snakes, then fell upon themselves, making the noise of the Chopin Sonata Number Two that she had played so many times and Mary had played so many times. But Mary would not stir. Her finger on her lips and her whole face were now darkened by the sunshine they blocked, and the faint shushing sound she had been making became the pleasant noise of the wind combing the fir trees in the Russian forest. Mary had become a tree. The breeze came from her and hit her mother in the chest.

"Mary, stop it, I am cold."

And the doctor said, "You are right. Silence is cold. That is why the dead are cold. They don't speak."

At that moment Ludmilla came in and she was naked. "Ludmilla," said her mother, "what are you doing? Get dressed, the children might be here any moment!"

But the doctor said, "When you begin to unbutton your blouse, this is what happens."

Ludmilla's body became rounder and softer in the sunshine, and now also Marie d'Escarande was in the room, but she was Ludmilla, and was not Ludmilla at all, she was Mary and then also their mother, and Marie was now pulling her left arm and saying, "Get up, you liar, lazy child, get up and join us in our games."

She resisted and the arm began to hurt again. Now Ludmilla, who was Sonia, took the emeralds from the breakfast table and put them on her shoulder, tied the necklaces to her breasts, hung the earrings on her nipples and said to Sonia, who was herself, "Sip here the milk of elegance that stems from me. This is Chopin—tuberculosis."

And her grandmother said, faintly, "Don't drink it. Chopin is contagious, he wrote the Funeral March."

But Ludmilla went on. Then Marie d'Escarande took the large emerald parure and said, "This belongs to my family. We can play with it."

"No, no!" shouted the old lady. "My husband bought it for me with the money he had earned. I was never able to wear it, because he died."

"Who was your husband, anyway?" said Marie with a sneer.

"My husband was an honest man!" she shouted, and Marie laughed.

"These jewels are for prostitutes. Anne d'Escarande was a prostitute, I am one, Ludmilla is one. They are not for trees like you and Mary."

"Give them back to Mary!" she shouted, and Marie began

to hang them on the tree and they turned black and fell off, making the noise of a stone in a well.

And the doctor, who seemed indifferent to all this, said, "Mary is a family tree."

And suddenly Mary's children were hanging on that tree, hanging by their necks like dead bodies. The old lady was frightened but said nothing, because the doctor seemed to find it normal, and with doctors one never knows what is normal and what is not.

"This is education," he said. "Your children did not hang properly, that is why you lost them."

Suddenly all the jewels were gone, but for one diamond on Ludmilla's pregnant abdomen. There were three men in the room, but they were not visible. They were all Marie d'Escarande, and yet they were three men. And the diamond seemed to melt and it spread as it melted and it became a stain of glue left by the passage of a worm on Ludmilla's white skin.

"Ludmilla, what is this?" asked her mother. And Marie said, "Who will recognize in this the portrait of these men? Until the picture is developed, no one will know."

The old lady tried to close her eyes, but she knew she could not, because this was all happening under her eyelids. She made a last effort and opened them.

The room was empty, no one had been there at all, the breakfast table had been taken away. It took the old lady a long time to realize this. She could still hear the echo of all those voices and see the shadow of Mary's tree in front of her, and she wondered how they had all managed to slip out of the room so quickly. In fact, she knew that what had roused her from her dream was the great silence of the room, the fact that they had finished speaking. She reviewed the whole scene, and was very much relieved to realize that it had never actually taken place. What remained of it was that pain in her left arm and the absolute certainty that Ludmilla must not have her jewels, which she might use to attract men.

"Mary," she called, faintly, because each word passed through her arm. She never thought Mary could hear that faint call, but she had not observed that the door to the next room was open.

"Yes, Mamachen?" said Mary's tender voice, and now Mary was near her. "Did you have a good rest, Mamachen?"

"Yes, thank you. I am hungry."

"We did not give you your breakfast because you were sleeping so deeply that you could not even hear my call."

"Was I?" she asked. Then: "Mary, yes, bring me something to eat and also ask your husband whether that notary he once recommended could come today. I want to modify my will."

"Nonsense, Mamachen. You can think of these things twenty years from now."

"No, no, I must do it today. Please don't contradict me."

Oh, what a tragic mistake it had been to write Ludmilla such a letter! But could she write another one now, without making herself ridiculous and confirming what Marie had most certainly said about her character? Marie knew far too much about her past: a past of jealousy, of intolerable moods that had driven her husband to despair—had, in fact, probably killed him. She had atoned in silence for her "faults" and "mistakes" of those years by tormenting herself day after day, and had slowly transformed her remorse into a feeling of self-pity that had covered up everything in that far province of her life, like a permanent fog that never lifts. Now that fog was gone; not only could the whole world see what a tyrant and beast she had been, but she herself could, and no matter how bad Marie's personal morals, she was right: Marie had never been a hypocrite or a coward, she had sinned in the face of the world; and Ludmilla was intelligent enough to recognize it and also to recognize her mother's true features in the person Marie

485

would describe, with her infinite skill as a comedian. Ludmilla and Marie had this in common: they could destroy a person by the strength of their wit alone, without altering anything, just by telling the facts and quoting what that person had said. She, with her righteousness, with her immense hypocrisy, had always found it necessary to distort and dismember the truth before she could afford to write about it; and she had never written anything but fragments, moralistic tracts and worthless philosophical essays. Even in recent years she had copied Marie d'Escarande, stolen from her the best tricks in her writing, confident that Marie would never cross her path again. Ludmilla now would recognize the source of her mother's witticisms by just hearing Marie talk. And Marie would see to it that Ludmilla judged her mother as the heavy, stupid and pretentious person she was.

Far back in her youth, Ludmilla's mother had clung to Marie as a disciple to his master, and she had been only too glad to see her slip and lose ground in society—knowing, however, all the time, that Marie was much better than the people who judged her. But she had pushed Marie further down into the pit of sin by adding all sorts of details to the stories they told about her love affairs, to amuse their guests. And Marie had retorted by accepting their slander as a challenge and saying, "I am accused of this, that and the other. There is not a word of truth in these accusations, but there soon will be. I don't like lies." There was also, in Marie d'Escarande, a certain reverence for truly honest people that these people themselves found ridiculous (and Marie suffered very much from their contempt); but Mary's mother was not among these. One of them was her niece Mary Tempi, the daughter of her elder sister who had been picked up by the Russian grand duke in the night club in St. Petersburg. Mary Tempi detested her aunt as she had detested her mother, while she worshiped her "father," Mr. Schultz, whom Marie despised. Of Mary Tempi Marie said she was narrow-minded, blinded by her desperate passion for Mr. Schultz, and even more blinded by her narrow-minded religion; but she would have done anything to be regarded as a friend by her, while she had given up taking Ludmilla's mother seriously after she had discovered how possessive and insincere she was.

To think that such a woman as Marie now had Ludmilla in her hands was almost more than the old lady could bear. In vain she repeated to herself what she had known for years: that Marie was a prostitute. I am not even that, she concluded, with the simplicity that people acquire when death nears. But from this to acknowledge that she must now write to Marie and apologize—that step seemed too difficult to take.

Several times in the course of the day, while the children were showing her their toys and their stunts with the dog, she had asked for pen and paper and made little drawings on one sheet after another, much to the children's delight. Every now and then she stopped and said to them, "Just a moment, let me think of something else I want to draw." And she then recalled the details of that terrible dream, blushing with shame because the children were so close and might have been in that same room during the dream—an absurd thing to imagine, but upsetting all the same.

She regretted the will she had just written, signed and sealed, and she could not understand the ancient urge that made her still do what she did not want, either to spite herself or to spite others. Then she retraced the course of events and saw that it had been the doctor's fault; he had given Ludmilla to Günther. Had Ludmilla stayed home, nothing would have happened. Yet she felt no grudge against him. He was an instrument of destiny, he meant well, he did not know. She even saw through Mary's jealousy; but here again, there was pity rather than resentment in her heart, and also a sense of guilt. I have made Mary what she is, she thought. She will be my true follower, my living punishment, my monument. . . . Her shame was now so great that she became afraid of it and tried

487

—this time not out of cowardice, but out of sheer respect for the people who loved her—not to feel it too much, because she knew that it might kill her. In fact, she felt it as a physical burden on her chest. And in her arm.

The children were still waiting for her drawings. She smiled at them and said, in a faint voice, "Grandmother must write now, leave her alone. When she has finished writing, she will make a new drawing for you."

She took her notebook from the night table and wrote, under the "thought" of the preceding morning:

Last privilege on earth: to hide, not to be seen, which means not to see those we have harmed. But afterward we shall see them all the time, so what is liberty for others will be prison for us who have done wrong. And no escape in suicide. Oh, my children, don't punish me; forget me and let me go. Be free so that I may be free.

She dated this "December 23, 1908, 4:29 P.M.," closed the book and called the children to her bed again. She felt better because of the new thought she had formulated. In fact, she felt so well that she no longer wished to hide from those she had harmed.

"Children, be patient. Grandmother cannot make a drawing now. She must write a letter, but it will not take long."

Sonia was on the verge of tears. "You always promise you will play with us, then you don't keep your promise. That is not nice."

"Sonia," said Kostia, "how dare you say such a thing to Grossmamachen?"

But Grossmamachen was not angry. She was ashamed. "Soniushka," she said, "don't be angry. This is a very important letter. I must write to Aunt Ludmilla so that she will come even sooner than expected."

Sonia's eyes became luminous with joy. "Good, good, write

to Aunt Ludmilla, tell her we want her today and she must never never leave us again."

"I will."

Mary came in at that moment, followed by her husband. She held two letters in her hand. "Mamachen, this is from Ludmilla and this from Pierre. I hesitate to give them to you, but as I would never open them myself . . ."

"Of course you should not open them yourself. Give them to me."

The old lady opened Ludmilla's envelope first, then began to breathe heavily, put a hand to her throat and gulped several times.

"Mamachen, you are not well." Mary turned to the children and said, "Out of here, you!"

Her mother smiled, then said, "It is nothing. Don't be alarmed." She put down Ludmilla's letter, opened Pierre's and began to read it in silence, then said cheerfully, "Listen to this, it is so typical. First of all, there is neither 'Dear Mother' nor 'Mamachen' nor anything. It might be addressed to his kitchenmaid, no one would know. And here is what he has to say:

"This letter, I imagine, will reach you by Christmas or shortly before, so I might as well begin it with the usual Christmas greetings. After which I might as well thank you for announcing your forthcoming visit to Moscow accompanied by daughter, son-in-law, grandchildren and (I suppose) your personal French cook.

"Having discharged these filial duties, let me add that I do not believe in your visit, and neither do I believe in your reconciliation with Ludmilla. In fact, what worries me is that your letter contradicting the last one and agreeing in full with the one preceding it should not have reached me as yet. Are you not well, or have you lost all sense of inconsistency? Please confirm your delayed contradiction, for we are all quite worried here. Were you still on good terms with Ludmilla and with us, I would advise that you postpone your departure for at least another twelve hours. It would be somewhat inconvenient for you to reach a new (and of course final) decision while on your way here. International express trains do not stop at small stations for the whims of their passengers, even when they are as illustrious as you, and if you made up your mind in some long stretch through the German forests or the Polish plains, it would be inconvenient to be let off the train in a completely uninhabited, wintry landscape infested by wolves. Your cook might find it irksome and leave your service at once. If, however, as I rather suspect, your change of mood was due to my threat of a lawsuit to counteract the one you were threatening me with, let me tell you that this is unnecessary. I am not going to sue you; it would cost me too much money, and, as you seem to have used up the fortune rightfully inherited by you from your hardworking husband, it would give me less expense and greater moral satisfaction to send you half such potential legal fees for your personal whims and for the salary of your cook.

"I hear that you have found a new governess for Ludmilla in the person of Marie d'Escarande. What an excellent idea! How many things she will learn in that household that she would never have been able to learn in her own mother's home, thank God. Congratulations on having become so modern in your educational system. You were much stricter with me, if I recall correctly.

"Merry Christmas again and a Happy New Year from your old-fashioned, obedient son,

"PIERRE"

There was a moment of deep silence, then the old lady said, "All right. I tried my best. I behaved like a good Christian, and as such I accept the humiliation in silence. He will be sorry when I die. To hell with him." She then took the letter out of Ludmilla's envelope and looked at it with great sus-

picion. "This is not Ludmilla's writing," she said, and looked
into the envelope to see if a letter from Ludmilla was still in
it. The envelope was empty. She seemed still incredulous, then
began to read aloud: " 'It is with great reluctance that I . . .' "
She blushed, went on reading silently, her hand trembling, her
face twitching nervously, then she passed the letter to Mary
without a word.

Mary and her husband read it to themselves:

*It is with great reluctance that I break a silence of years to
write you a letter. Believe me, please, I am doing this only to
help Ludmilla, and on Ludmilla's repeated insistence. I have
tried to make it clear to her that this is not the correct thing
to do, but the poor child is so much upset by the cruel things
you said in your letter that she seems to have lost her mind.
I again apologize for reading that letter, but she insisted so that
I could not refuse—since I have become what your son Pierre
calls "her new governess" (although I would rather call myself
her friend).*

*I can quite understand that you must have been upset by the
news of her doings, which not even I, with my rather free views,
can find commendable. But was it necessary to add to her burden your own sorrow, your illness, your disappointment and your
eternal condemnation? Ludmilla is too sensitive and too inexperienced to bear so much all at once. If you had in mind to
ruin her forever, you could not have devised a better plan. I
find it quite surprising that a person of high principles such as
you are should know so little about the ABC's of Christian
charity. A person hard hit by the effects of her own foolishness
(for which foolishness you, as her mother, are at least partly responsible) needs first of all affection and a home—not contempt
and a preacher. I shall make no comment on the things you say
about me in your letter, because it was not meant for me to
read; but I shall ask you a simple, objective question in your own
interest: If you have such hard words for those who give Lud-*

milla shelter and friendship, why don't you try to compete with them in these two things that Ludmilla needs at this moment? You have not sent Ludmilla enough money to flee from that "terrible woman" and come back to you. In fact, you make no mention of either your desire or your readiness to receive her in your house if she should choose to take refuge there. (Which, by the way, she would never think of doing since receiving your letter. And if she wanted to, I would not let her at this point.) She wrote to Pierre when she joined us in Athens, and Pierre has at least sent her money; not much, but enough for her to go to Moscow. (She will not go; his letter was not very encouraging, either. Pierre sounds exactly like you. It is strange that a person like you should beget either victims or victimizers, but no normal, civilized, undangerous people.)

Ludmilla still feels it her duty to come listen to your sermons and let herself be confused by your guidance, or, rather, by the absence of guidance she would find in your house. I have taken the responsibility of saying no to her, unless you first recapture her affection and her confidence. Write to her like a mother, not like an executioner who cannot wait to get his hatchet on the victim's neck. Be simple, be human; and, first of all, think of her for once, if you can, and not constantly and hugely and resentfully of yourself, as you have always done since I first knew you. You have remained alone, you say. You asked for it, and you will die alone if you don't mend your ways. It is never too late.

My husband sends his greetings.

MARIE

As soon as Mary lifted her eyes from the letter her mother said, with violence, "How dare she say I have not made it clear to Ludmilla that she should come back here? I said it in so many words, I quite clearly remember, and if I must first explain to a stranger like this woman what I intend to say to my own child, then there is no point in anything any more.

How dare she? And how dare she censor my letters and tell me what I should write to regain Ludmilla's affection? This is unheard of! I was just about to write an affectionate letter to Ludmilla when you came in with this one. Now, of course, I cannot dream of writing it any more. It would sound like giving in to this impertinent request, this imposition! And she wants money, too! How French of her! If I had someone as my guest (and Ludmilla with her is more than just a guest, she is a prisoner), I would never mention money at all. The French are all alike! And I should let Ludmilla be influenced by that . . . unspeakable woman?"

She sneered, stared before her and said, "I want to get up."

"Get up?" said the doctor. "But you are ill."

"I am not ill at all. I am well and I want to get up!"

"To do what?"

"That I have not decided yet. But I want to get up. Later, perhaps, I may go to Milan."

"To Milan? Insane! You cannot leave the house."

"I can and I will, if I so decide. I have not decided yet."

Twenty minutes later she was dressed, combed, healthy and determined. To do what, she did not know; but she was determined, and with determined steps she paced the rooms from one end of the house to the other. She looked at the same wintry view of ice and snow from every window, almost injecting her doubts into it, disappointed that the ice remained icy and her doubts painful. Then she sat at her writing desk and wrote, "Dear Ludmilla," but the thought that she was doing this for Marie made her stop. She found nothing else to say. She tried writing a telegram, with the same result. And again she paced the rooms, the halls and the stairway. Not a trace of pain in her arm; it was all in her forehead, in the form of determined indecision. Mary was delighted again: this was a sign of health. The only thing that pained her was that phrase in Marie's letter, "You have remained alone, you say."

"Mamachen, you have not remained alone. Mamachen, please, tell me you have not."

"What is it, Mary?" Before Mary could repeat the question, she had understood. "Oh, no, no, of course not." Then, with mounting anger: "I never wrote that! Do you believe me?"

"Yes, Mamachen, I do," said Mary, and her mother sneered again for a second, thinking, Why should she? Does not everybody know I tell lies?

"So you believe me. Well, this is it: Marie tells lies in the face of written evidence to the contrary. A detestable person. But there is no word strong enough to define her. And the cruelty, to say, 'You will die alone, if you don't mend your ways'! *She* should tell me that! How about her own ways? Oh, no, this is too much. I must do something to stop her. I must!"

She presided over the dinner table as in the old days, and there was silence in the room. Her face looked ominous, so charged with hate that the butler could not serve without running the risk of upsetting the plates. His hands were trembling.

"Children," said the old lady with energy, "why don't you talk? Why don't you laugh?"

Sonia looked at her and asked, "Is Aunt Ludmilla coming for Christmas?"

"No," she said, "but I can swear to you that she will be here before the year ends."

Everybody looked at her and was frightened by her great, silent anger.

After dinner the children went to bed and their parents prepared the Christmas tree in the music room. The doctor felt and acted like the butler during dinner: he kept looking at his mother-in-law and doing the wrong thing, while her angry eyes pierced him and passed through him to go straight to Milan. Mary was crying and trying to conceal it. And the old lady stood there, like a judge, saying nothing. Suddenly there was a noise at the door and Tasso came in, hesitant. She stared at him, then said, "Come here, dog." She sat down on a chair and summoned him with a gesture of her hand. Tasso came to her, she patted him on the head and said, "You are a good dog." Mary burst into tears, and her mother looked at her, then tears began to roll down her cheeks too, and she said, "It was all my fault. I know. Marie is right. She is right! But I cannot, oh, I cannot write that letter if she is to read it first."

"Mamachen, you should not, and she is wrong. Let's not think of it. Tomorrow is Christmas Eve and we must try to be cheerful." Whereupon Mary cried much more desperately.

Finally her husband cleared his throat and said, "Where shall I put this big star? Here on top?"

Mary looked and said, "Yes . . . yes . . ." Then she covered her face and ran out of the room.

"I *know*," repeated the old lady.

"Look," said the doctor, "there is no point in making this an obsession. I am just as responsible as you are, if not more; but I reproached myself in silence, once, this afternoon—or was it yesterday morning? No, two days ago—as a matter of fact, two weeks ago, when that letter arrived. And then not again."

She laughed, and as this was against her whole dramatic plan, she laughed even more, and Mary came in and looked at the two, not knowing what to say. Finally her mother said, "You do have a fine sense of comedy, you Italians! But when I said, 'I *know*,' it was something else I meant. I knew I was hungry and was going to say so. You interrupted me."

"Hungry?" the doctor asked, coming down from the ladder with the star in his hand. "But we have just eaten the most sumptuous meal."

"Still, I am hungry. I must eat something immediately."

"All right. Then I will cook for you. I hate to have the servants get up from bed and work for us again. You wait for me here, I'll be back with a dish of the best spaghetti you ever ate in your life."

Mary was pleased and so was her mother. The doctor went downstairs and the two women continued preparing the presents under the Christmas tree. But the mere thought that she had found something to do, something on which to work, something to transform, through mincing and destruction, into something unknown (food, mastication and new bodily strength), made the old lady so frantic that she regarded it as a stupid delay that the doctor, who had just left the room to go downstairs, should not be back already with the dish of spaghetti.

"How long do you think it will take him?" she asked, and Mary said, "I have no idea, probably an hour."

"What? An hour without eating? But I am hungry now, I have not eaten for three days, with all these worries."

This was not true at all, but the daughter had such faith in her mother's truthful nature that when the old lady told a lie, or, rather, when her statements happened to be clearly inexact, Mary chose to believe that she herself had failed to interpret correctly what she had seen; and thus now she preferred to think herself wrong in believing that her mother had gulped down most of a pheasant at dinner plus a small hill of mashed potatoes on the side, plus a creamed soup, and fish and mushrooms with a thick yellow sauce, and cheese and salad and three slices of cake and an apple and countless candied fruits and chocolates plus bread and butter on the side between courses and during them.

"How stupid of me not to have noticed it, Mamachen. I believed you had eaten tonight."

"What do you mean? Do I have to prove to you that I am not telling a lie? Why should I tell a lie? Since when do I have to justify the amount of food I eat? Am I surrounded by spies in my own house? As if it were not enough to have my daughter taken prisoner by a prostitute, and my words read and sifted by a prostitute, and my most sacred feelings ridiculed by my elder son—I must also render account of my

496

hunger on those rare occasions when I want to eat something. That was not eating, what I did during dinner. That was good discipline—willful concealment of my sorrow, my horror, my disgust with the world and with all of you who have always taken advantage of me! Do you think I enjoyed what I 'ate' at *your* table tonight? Stones on my stomach, gravestones on my hopes and illusions, that is what I tossed down my throat tonight, this morning, yesterday, and I imagine you must also have observed how much I ate this morning, yesterday, the day before—or haven't you kept record of everything? Very bad, very bad."

Mary was so shaken by sobs that she sank to her knees, putting her head on her mother's lap.

"Now, now, Mary, you are really oversensitive. One cannot even converse with you any more. Don't become like Katia, please. After all, what have I said? That I was hungry. Is that such a tragic occurrence? It can happen in the best of families. Come, you ought to be happy that your mother feels well enough to want to eat something instead of allowing her sorrows to kill her. Or do you prefer to see her die, eaten up by repressed pain? Do you really? Answer, please."

"Oh, no, Mamachen, I do not."

"Well, then, don't cry like a stupid little goose, or you will make me cry, too, and the Lord knows I have better reasons than you."

Mary lifted her head, but she was still sobbing abundantly, and when her mother's soft hands began to hold her face and stare into it with that frightening look of endless sorrow, she had another fit of convulsive sobs and began to slip onto the carpet.

"Mary! *Mary!* I order you to control your nerves! You are a Russian woman, remember, not a Swiss cow. Russian women do not cry—they take action! They dominate, they *do* something! Come, now, you must stop crying, you need strength first of all, this has weakened you, and to what end? Ask yourself like a true Russian woman: to what end? Do our enemies change and become more humane because we suffer? No, indeed; they only feel encouraged in their cruelty. Come, eat one of those sugar snow men on the Christmas tree! It will do you good. Here it is."

And she rose from her chair, pulling Mary from the floor with unexpected strength, and dragged her to the tree, then tore one of the little sugar snow men from it and pushed it into Mary's mouth, while Mary was still crying. Mary tried not to open her mouth, but the snow man was already past her teeth. This made her smile. She chewed the thing and liked it.

"Good," said her mother. "My little Mary is eating like an obedient child."

"It is you who must eat. You were hungry, I was not. I ate plenty at dinner."

"I? Oh, no. Not I. I was hungry, but you have made me lose my appetite with your tears. You know I cannot stand tears. When one has so many reasons to shed them, and one is disciplined enough not to yield, the sight of tears in others— especially of silly tears—makes one lose everything: appetite first and then also the strength to conceal one's real sorrow from the others."

Now it was Mary's turn to feed her mother, take her head in her hands and look into her eyes with infinite sorrow. When the doctor came up with his plate of spaghetti and knocked on the door of the music room with his foot, the two women were munching the last cooky star on the tree. They opened the door and their eyes grew wide with appetite as they saw the luscious mass on the large tray. Steam and promising odors of tomatoes, meat and butter, herbs and cheese came from that plate. But what the doctor saw filled him with sadness.

"You have destroyed your appetite!" he announced. "You have devoured the whole tree!"

"Never mind," said the old lady. "This can easily be corrected with a touch of caviar and a glass of champagne. I am only just beginning to be able to enjoy it. I was much too weak before."

He was still incredulous. "Had I known that you were going to eat sweets before this," he said, "I would never have cooked two kilos of spaghetti. Who will eat it tomorrow? I can't eat anything at this late hour." He marched to the dining room, put the tray on the table and said, "Let me run downstairs for caviar and champagne before this becomes inedible."

Mary put two plates on the table and found forks and napkins, and when the doctor came back the spaghetti was gone. Then they ate all the caviar and drank the champagne, and after this the old lady said she had to have a bite of something sweet. Again the doctor ran to the kitchen to find the remains of the cake they had eaten at dinner, and she finished it all by herself and went upstairs with a large loaf of bread in her right hand, tearing away at it with her strong teeth, as if the loaf were Marie d'Escarande and she Marie's personal devil in hell.

She fell asleep and was met with a beautiful dream which seemed to have been waiting for her. It began even before she was asleep: Ludmilla was in bed, the way she was when she was a very little girl, plump, ugly and suspicious, wanting her mother all for herself; and her mother was glad that she had finally recaptured that old chance to give Ludmilla the affection she needed.

"Yes, Ludmilla, I was too grieved over my father's death that day, I remember quite well. I could not give you anything, your presence irritated me, I did not want to be without my father, and I had just begun to understand how much harm I had done him. I was the cause of his death. How could I think of you or anyone else? But now you understand. I am so glad you have gone back to your childhood to find me. The next time you grow up, don't let these ugly things happen to you, and avoid such people as Marie d'Escarande. If you knew how frightened I was when you had grown up the first time, and she had taken you a prisoner and wanted me to write you only such letters as she would approve! Yes, you are still too young to understand, but all you have to do is to stay close to me and never let anyone come near you unless I first approve. Tomorrow is Christmas Eve, you will play with Mary's children, they will be pleased to find an aunt so young."

And Ludmilla cried because she had not had time to prepare a Christmas present for her mother. Then Pierre came and he was jealous of Ludmilla, he also wanted to be in his mother's arms and be forgiven, for he too had not prepared a Christmas present. He was kissed and forgiven, and the dream was interrupted by the doctor's voice.

"Are you in pain?" he asked.

"No," she said, waking up.

She could not sleep for the rest of the night. The urge to take action was in her again, running all through her body. She left her bed, cautiously like a child, and listened to the sounds in the next room; there was snoring in two tones— Mary and her husband were fast asleep. She opened her bedroom door, tiptoed out into the hall, went downstairs, turned on the light in the dining room and looked for food. There was none left. She descended to the basement, where she had never been, had difficulty finding the lights, but finally did so and found herself in the kitchen. There was a pot on the stove with the rest of the tomato sauce; she found another loaf of bread and ate that with the sauce, then looked for more food and found none. In despair she started back to her room. As she was crossing the entrance hall she heard a sigh, as of a person in pain. Her heart beat so intensely that she had to sit down, and the pain in her arm began again. Another sigh— and Tasso came to her, wagging his big white tail.

"Good, dear dog," she said.

After a while, shivering, she went back to her room, the dog following her. She got into bed.

"Come here, dog," she said, and Tasso jumped up beside her.

Thus she spent the few hours that separated her from the Great Test—the arrival of the morning mail. Would Ludmilla write, or telegraph? And would Pierre, repentant, do the same? She was too cold to get up again and find a shawl, so she shivered but stayed exposed in order to be able to caress the dear dog.

When the doctor woke up and came in he found her there, trembling, purple in the face and arms.

"What are you doing like this?" he asked. "And why is the dog here? Get out of here, Tasso."

"I let him in," she said. "He was out in the hall, I let him in, he is kind to me, please allow him to stay."

"But you are cold. This is insane."

"This?" she asked. "This alone?"

When breakfast was brought in, she refused it. Mary was worried.

"Mamachen, are you ill? Why don't you eat?"

"How can I, with this anguish devouring me?"

XXIII

AND IN TWO HOURS the Great Test. Her first precautionary measure was to turn the clock away from the bed, so that she would not see it. Her appetite for action having now been awakened, there were many more things that appeared necessary to her. Why stay in bed, where she had received no letters lately? She jumped out of bed, but her legs would not give her support, she stumbled twice, then fell backward onto the bed again.

Mary saw her, ran to her and said, "Mamachen, you are weak. Don't get up, please."

"You too, Mary? You too want to betray me? Do you want me to feel I was right when I wrote I was alone?"

Mary said, "So it is true. You did write it."

"Oh, nonsense, Mary, of course I never did. I was only quoting that prostitute who accused me of writing it."

But Mary did not seem satisfied.

"Mary, now, really, do you believe Marie d'Escarande more than you do your own mother? You too?"

"No, I do not."

"Mary, give me my black evening gown."

"Your black evening gown?"

"Yes, and quickly, too, for God's sake!"

Such expressions were rare. Mary was frightened. She rang the bell and asked Frieda for the black evening gown, while her mother was shivering in her nightgown and holding onto the back of a chair.

"But that evening gown is being altered," said Frieda. "It is all taken apart and the seamstress is still asleep."

"My green velvet *tailleur*, then. Quick!" shouted the old lady.

"But that has been put away with the summer things."

"My Russian costume, then!"

"Y-yes, madame, I'll be back in a minute."

"Mamachen, why that costume?"

"Because I said so." She had suddenly remembered that she had not put on that costume since she had been photographed in it with Ludmilla on her knees, and all the other children around her, and her husband standing next to her.

"Mamachen, are you sure it will not be too—too tight?"

"Never mind, we can open the seams, I must put it on at once!"

Mary looked at her mother, whose eyes were feverish.

"You are not well, Mamachen. How about the thermometer?"

"That won't keep me warm. Do you want me to get dressed in a thermometer?"

The costume was brought in, it was old, it smelled of moth balls. At that moment the doctor came in with a few letters in his hand. The old lady sat down in her chair and looked through the mail. No letter from Ludmilla, none from Pierre. She stood up, pushing Mary away, and said, "Prepare the bed for me."

"Here is the costume, Mamachen."

"Costume, hell, you fool."

"What have I done?"

"Nothing. You are an instrument of destiny, that's all. Leave me alone."

503

The doctor had remained close to the door; now he came forward and said, "You are very ill today. I order you to stay in bed."

"You order me? Nonsense. It is I who don't want to get up. Ever again."

With nervous gestures she tore open the envelopes from which she expected nothing, sneeringly read the various letters to confirm her opinion, then threw them to the doctor, who looked at them with almost a clinical eye. There were greetings from Günther for the family of his "dear Ludmilla," there was a letter from Luther which the old lady tore up without reading, and a few other unimportant items of Christmas hypocrisy.

The doctor held her wrist, pulled out his watch and counted the pulsations, then said, "Why should this clock be turned away?" He turned it toward the bed again and she closed her eyes so as not to see it.

She now allowed the symptoms of her illness to come into her body from all sides and take their clinically appointed places and functions, thus dismembering the picture of her principal worries and her personal resentments. This made her feel better. She was now driven to her death by a hundred horses, no longer doing the job all by herself and to spite people who were either unable to help her (Mary and her husband) or absent or unwilling to bother (Ludmilla, Pierre, everyone else, including Marie). Her only hope now was to sleep without dreams. Happiness was her new disease; hopes thrown like seeds into the open fields of dreams flourish too quickly and it is painful to lose them upon the blaring order of a bell, a fly, or sunshine trumpeted into the face.

"The dog, please. Send the dog here, and the children."

"No, you must sleep."

"But I can sleep when they are here, in fact I sleep much better if I know that I have no chance of dreaming."

"I'll give you a sedative."

"No. Give me something to live for, that is what I need."

Suddenly, before the doctor could find a trite answer to this (which she would be careful not to hear), she remembered that her role was still an active one; telegrams too could arrive, even after the postman had proven a failure.

"I must get up," she said, "and I must have that costume on. Don't ask me why, I am too tired to answer. I promise I shall sit in that corner with a thick blanket over my knees and a shawl over my shoulders—but not the one I always have, another one, a new one, or an old."

"Mary," he called, "Mary, do as your mother tells you and just see that she stays quiet and sheltered from the draft."

He was going to leave. She stopped him.

"Tell me the truth," she asked in a whisper, hoping that Mary would not hear. "Do I have syphilis?"

"What?"

"Do I have syphilis?"

"How can you have such an idiotic thought?"

"Then I have not?"

"Of course not; but how can such a stupid idea come into your head?"

"I read that letter yesterday and did not wash my hands. Marie must have it."

"First of all, you don't catch it this way; and then, how do you know she has?"

"A sinful woman like Marie? And do you think Ludmilla has it?"

His mute indignation pleased her, but she still wanted to justify herself.

"It is not for my own sake that I am worrying, it is for the children. But if you are sure, I can only be glad that I was wrong."

"Why have you made me think of it?" he asked. His own fears had been aroused and it was difficult to put them back to sleep. The prostitutes, the French, the aristocrats—what more to worry a man of principles, and especially a doctor?

"I was right, then," she said. "Now you know why I worry so much." This was not true at all. The idea of syphilis was a refinement added to her worries in a recent moment. "Do you think she has not written because she is ill and cannot confess it?"

"Nonsense."

"Then she might have been busy."

"She was waiting for your letter."

"Yes, but why not send me a telegram for Christmas?"

"It may still come."

"You really think so? Then let me get up at once."

"It will be brought to you instantly if it comes. Why don't you stay in bed?"

"No, please don't insist. Tell me another thing: Could you go to Milan?"

"What for?"

"To rescue her."

"No."

"Then you would rather let her stay there? People like Marie are never idle. Every minute that passes, Ludmilla sinks deeper into mud."

He said nothing.

"And besides," she said, "I would not want her to get into the habit of neglecting her mother at Christmas."

"Send her a telegram."

"You think I should?"

"Why not?"

"And . . . Marie?"

"She will give it to her."

"Are you sure?"

"I am."

"What reason do you have to believe it?"

"None, but I don't think that she is a beast."

The costume did not quite fit, but it was ripped open here and there and she sat in a chair next to the window, with a small writing table next to her, a cushion behind her head, a blanket on her knees, and her eyes glued to the white road beyond the gate.

"I don't want the children here," she said, "only the dog."

She began to draft telegram after telegram, throwing them all away because they said either too little or too much. She first wrote, "Merry Christmas"; then she thought that she should sound sarcastic, so she added, "You could at least let me know how you are." Then she remembered Marie and was afraid that she would not let that pass. So she wrote, "Merry Christmas in spite of everything." Then she was visited by an impulse of charity and wrote, "Merry Christmas to you and to your friends." Now came resentment for their failure to answer her impulse of charity, so she wrote, "Extremely anxious exact immediate detailed news your health wish you Merry Christmas please answer at once Mamachen." Mary came back with her husband and the dog, the various telegrams were read, and the last one was approved.

"I shall send it myself from the station," said the doctor. "Kostia and perhaps the other two will accompany me. It will be a pleasant change for them, especially since they are not allowed in the drawing room or the music room because of the presents. Do you want to come with us, Mary?" he asked.

Mary refused.

Tasso looked up and understood. He was impatient to go out, he jumped, he barked, he howled.

"Take him with you," said Mary, and soon she and her mother saw from the window the group of black coats, red gloves, brown fur caps and white woolen caps—plus the sled and the dog—all deformed by the bulk of excessive warm underwear, and shortened by the masses of snow into which they plunged at every step. Through the closed windows came the laughter, the barking, the calls to discipline, and the metallic noise of the sled runners as they hit a stone. Beyond the gate, the steep descent toward the station looked like the curvature of the globe, bordering on nothing. There were moments of sunshine on the lake, but the lake could not be seen except for vines of sparks through snowy clouds. And there was a strange semblance of activity beyond the garden walls of other villas, when the weight of the snow finally defeated the resistance of the treetops and produced a new snowfall in miniature, brief but complete with thump and clouds and dust.

Mary stood by her mother and looked on as long as her husband was still trying to assemble the children and the dog in marching order, but as soon as they disappeared she withdrew from the window, as if that were her mother's personal horizon. She sat on the bed and from there tried to have as much of a glimpse of the road as she could with her mother's profile concealing most of it. She had often seen her mother besiege landscapes, roads or city streets without waiting for anyone in particular, like a highway robber of a selective kind who does not have to kill or rob in order to survive, but who still cannot survive unless he pretends to these sad necessities. And, now for the first time, she saw her waiting for the demonstration that a whole life of blackmail had not been rendered void by a few weeks of common sense. It was the supreme test of the romantic way against the cynical way—Mary's test, too, for that reason. She was studying her mother for what was to become her own way of dealing with reality: by besieging the world until it yielded what she expected of it in recognition of the intensity of her worry, or what she called her "altruism."

The pulsations of fever could be seen, black against white, in the profile of her mother's cheek and double chin, and the voice registered it, too. "I am going to write to Tolstoy," she said. "He will tell me what to do, but I believe he will say we must be charitable with Marie."

After another pause she said, "I must rewrite that telegram."

"But it must have been sent by now."

"I'll write another one."

"Wait, perhaps an answering telegram is going to come."

"I shall wait another twenty minutes."

Mary was so anxious for her mother to receive a telegram that she kept craning her neck to see all the shadows that passed in the snow, coming up from the end of the world; and, realizing that by doing this she aroused her mother's expectations, she felt guilty, as she always felt when her mother was sad. Thus she felt guilty for Ludmilla's misbehavior, for Marie's cruelty, for Günther's idiocy, for the doctor's mistakes, but most particularly for the things that made her enviable: her husband and her children.

"You have a wonderful husband and four beautiful, healthy, intelligent children," said her mother.

"Oh, no," said Mary instinctively.

"What do you mean, 'Oh, no'? Mary, you worry me. You too?"

"What do you mean, Mamachen, by 'You too'?"

"I mean you are like your sisters—insane or possessed by that strange urge for . . . new things."

"No, Mamachen, no, please don't believe that. What I meant by 'Oh, no' was that nothing counts for me but your happiness."

"My happiness? Waiting for a silly telegram of Christmas greetings on the eve of my death—that is what you call my happiness? You, who have at least real happiness, should know better than to speak lightly about it."

Mary felt even guiltier, she was ready to apologize and say, "I did not mean to be happy, Mamachen, forgive me."

"Yes," her mother went on, scouting the horizon, "you should be happy, in fact you should have gone out with your family and left me here alone with my old grudges. You should be more of an egotist than to waste your time with someone like me. And if you think I regard this as happiness, waiting and waiting for Christmas greetings that are not even handwritten, you must think me very stupid. What makes me wait is only an impulse of altruism. I would not want Ludmilla to feel that she has left her mother without a telegram on the last Christmas of her life. That would be a terrible remorse for her to have."

Mary began to sob and made her usual gesture of sinking onto her knees. But her mother stopped her with a forbidding gesture. "No, my child, no. Don't worship faulty human beings. Only God deserves worship."

"Oh, no, Mamachen, you do, you more than anyone. You, not I, should be more of an egotist, and you should have had an easier life. Even when you are ill, you think only of others. I shall never, never be worthy of your example, Mamachen."

Her mother's attention became absorbed in a shadow at the gate. But it turned out to be a messenger with packages, probably from some shop. She turned to Mary and said, "Perhaps you are right. I should have been more of an egotist, my children would have respected me more. They have become too accustomed to the thought that they can spit on me, because I exact nothing in return for what I give. I am their moral washerwoman. They sin, I wash and rinse their souls and hang them out to dry. Now they can sin again in peace. What will they do when the washerwoman dies?"

"You must never die, Mamachen. You must live only for yourself from now on."

"From now on? With these sick limbs and this weak heart? Don't be ridiculous! Don't offend me, don't laugh at me, Mary! It is really not generous of you. From now on, she says! From now on, flowers and prayers for you, and worms for me, and the black earth, in an abandoned grave."

A knock on the door prevented Mary from playing her usual melodramatic role again. "Come in," she said, and the butler came in with six packages, all of them from Milan, all addressed to the family, all in Ludmilla's writing.

"But this is it," said Mary with a triumphant laugh that sounded a bit false. "She thought of us, she sent presents—

that is better than telegrams. Let's open the big one first."

And as she looked for scissors she said dreamily, "I wonder who has given her the money. Not Marie certainly, she complains because Ludmilla has received none from us."

The first package contained a beautiful doll with a small note in Ludmilla's hand: "This doll is for my darling little Sonia from her loving Aunt Ludmilla." Mary observed the doll from every side, undressed her, looked at the glue under her hair and said, "Italian toys are very bad. This will break after three days. She could have bought a real doll in Nuremberg, where we buy toys for the children. But she obviously thought of it at the last minute."

And she passed it on to her mother, who said, in her feverish voice, "Ludmilla *would* aim for bigness. This is horrible. I can only hope Sonia will not notice it."

"Oh," said Mary, throwing away the box and beginning to cut the strings of another package, "Sonia is not so stupid. She knows everything about dolls. Unfortunately, she does not know everything about Aunt Ludmilla yet."

"*Unfortunately*, you say?"

"I am sorry, Mamachen. I meant fortunately, of course. It is *un*fortunate that she should worship her aunt. That probably results from Ludmilla's skill as a clown. Children like clowns."

"Real clowns are wonderful people," said her mother, looking at the gate again. "Do you remember that clown in the Italian opera *Pagliacci*? Wasn't that a moving story? And so true."

"Yes, Mamachen, and I also remember the clowns in Russian fairy tales, and the ones in Andersen."

"Right. And Ludmilla is certainly not that kind of clown."

The next package contained a toy pistol, a pocketknife and a round hat in black oilcloth with a large rose of green cock feathers applied to it.

"What is this?" asked Mary, and she proceeded to read the enclosed note. " 'To my dear nephew Filippo, a soldier's hat from the glorious Italian regiment of the Bersaglieri, who fought in the conquest of Libya, a pocketknife like those of American pioneers who blaze trails in the Wild West, and a pistol to shoot down brigands and Australians, from the great Brigand Leader Aunt Ludmilla.' "

"None of these things, of course, will be touched by the child," said Mary. "A soldier's hat? From Libya? Must my son be mixed up in colonial wars? If that is not corruption of minors, what is it?"

"Don't touch the hat," said her mother.

"But I did already."

"Then wash your hands immediately and disinfect them. Soldiers have syphilis. This is Marie's idea. Ludmilla is too much of a snob to look at soldiers, but Marie will take anything: soldiers, chauffeurs, cooks. And the American pocketknife—to a five-year-old child! And the pistol—Mary, go wash your hands, please."

"I will, I will," said Mary, taking the pistol in her hand, and suddenly there was a frightening explosion and a spark, followed by acrid smoke. The old lady was so shaken that for a long time afterward she could not calm down. Her left arm hurt.

Mary was too confused to realize what had happened. The butler and Frieda came running in and she cried, "Help, help, take away these terrible things, throw them away at once, but be careful, the pistol is loaded and the hat is infected."

They brought smelling salts for the old lady, and iodine for Mary, who held her hands apart. The butler browned them with iodine, then washed them with Eau de Cologne and finally wrapped them in two clean handkerchiefs. While doing this he tried to cheer the two women by saying the pistol was a toy, he himself had always played with such pistols, could he have it for his nephew if Filippo was not supposed to have it.

"You too?" asked Mary, horrified. "You played with implements of war? And you want your nephew to receive that dangerous weapon? Oh no, these will be thrown away and so will that awful hat that has belonged to some dirty soldier."

"But, madame," said the butler, "that is a child's hat, it cannot have belonged to anyone, it is new."

"Don't touch it, I said. It is infected!"

"No, madame, it is not. The doctor will tell you that, too. It is brand new, it is a toy."

"And is there a country where implements of war and soldier's hats are regarded as toys?"

"They can be found even in Switzerland, madame."

"What a horrible thing. I thought this was a civilized country."

The doctor came back at that moment, preceded by the dog and the children.

"Aaaah!" yelled Sonia, seeing the doll. "A present from Aunt Ludmilla, I'm sure!"

"Out! Out!" cried Mary, and the children were pushed out at once, but Filippo had seen the hat and the pistol and he shouted, "I saw a soldier's hat and a pistol and I know they're for me!"

Kostia, who had pushed the others out, was still there, trying to make himself invisible, but his mother said, "Kostia, please, you go with them, there must be a present for you too in these packages and you must not see it. And do me a favor: Don't tell the others there are presents for them."

"But they have seen them."

"All right, but Sonia must not think the doll is for her. We must have it washed and disinfected, and it is not such a good doll anyway. Besides, even if she is to have it, it must be a surprise."

"Very well, Mamachen, I will not tell."

"And Filippo will not get the hat and pistol. Those are implements of war. They are dangerous. We almost killed ourselves, the pistol exploded."

"But pistols do, Mamachen. I have seen such toy pistols myself."

"You have? Where? Who ever showed them to you?"

"No one, but I have seen them in shop windows."

"Here in Switzerland?"

"Yes, Mamachen, in the windows of a toyshop on the square."

"The world is going mad," said the old lady indignantly. "Kostia, you may have seen them, but remember, these are not toys, these are very sad things that only criminals can like."

"Very well, Grossmama," said Kostia, and he left.

The doctor seemed concerned. He put a hand on the old lady's forehead, then took her chin in his hand and turned her head slowly, asking, "Does it hurt?"

"No," she said. "Why?"

"Nothing. I just wanted to see your cheekbones in the light."

One of them was quite red, the other was not. "You may have a higher temperature," he said. "I must ask you to put this thermometer in your armpit."

She did so while he looked away. "I know I have no fever," she said.

"That is what I hope, too, but it seems all very odd. As a matter of fact, one never knows with you. I have never seen a more baffling physiology."

"Let's open the other packages," she said.

The next package contained a small fireman's helmet in cheap brass and a very small fire engine, perfect, with rubber on the wheels and every detail exact.

"What?" said Mary. "She goes in not only for colonial wars but also for setting fires! This must be for Kostia, her darling little arsonist. What a cheap helmet this is! And look at the engine." She could not help being enchanted by that toy, so she kept silent for a moment while she handled it. The doctor and the old lady were interested, too.

"I think I know that toy," said the old lady. "Give it to me." She took it and began to look at it from all sides, with a strange dreamy expression that soon became focused into a smile. "This toy," she said, "was in my hands when I was small. It may well have been the first toy of its kind, and it was given to Marie's brother, the one who died. It was given to him when he was nine or ten. He was my age. I said I would marry him to have that toy, and everybody laughed at me."

She found the key to the small engine and began to wind it up. "Try it on the floor," she said to the doctor, and the doctor placed the toy on the floor, where it began to run.

"I wonder," said the old lady, casting another glance at the gate, "how Marie can have had this with her in a hotel in Milan. Let me see, don't they have a villa near Milan? They have so many villas, but there was one near Milan which belonged to her family. Yes, the boy lived there for a while. And that is also where he died, if I am not mistaken." Her face grew somber. "Let's wash and disinfect our hands, we have touched that toy . . ." she began, but the doctor, who was usually so much of an alarmist in these matters, said, "No, there can be no danger." And he went on playing with the toy for a few minutes.

Mary seemed disappointed. "Still, the helmet is utterly out of place and I don't think we should give it to Kostia. Let us see what she says." The note attached to it said: "To my future engineer Kostia, his Aunt Ludmilla."

The next package contained a celluloid ball for the baby, with no note from Ludmilla, and Mary commented, "She might have sent him back that watch she stole."

"That was not stolen by her," said the doctor. "The chauffeur took it."

"Ah."

And now the last two packages. One contained a Milanese panettone with a note: "This is so good that only a doctor can distribute it without letting the gluttons eat too much." No signature.

There was a silence. Finally Mary said, "How very, very stupid. Is she trying to be witty?"

No one answered these words. There was too much curiosity about the package obviously meant for Mamachen. Mary was red with anger and had tears in her eyes. She unwrapped the package and out came a red rubber ball with a note attached to it: "To Tasso, who will run for this ball and always bring it back to Ludmilla."

Mary's anger instantly became righteous. "Is that all?" she asked, looking at her mother.

"I don't know," said her mother, looking at the maze of paper on the floor and on the bed. "Was there no other package?"

"No. There were six of them. We two have been left out, it seems."

"I don't think she would do such a thing to her mother on the last Christmas of her life."

"It is not the last Christmas of your life, Mamachen, it definitely is not. But I hope it will be the last Christmas Ludmilla receives a telegram from you. This is preposterous!"

The doctor and the old lady were silent. They both looked at the gate once more, then the old lady said, "I might as well stop waiting. And I shall not write to Tolstoy. With his views on war I know what he would say about a person like Ludmilla. And if he heard of this he would refuse to believe it. All right. This is part of my cross. I asked for it. I should have been more of an egotist, as you so rightly said. And to think that I put on this costume remembering my little Ludmilla as a child, and in the hope that it would help me get a kind word from her—just a word!" She put both hands before her face and cried like a sick child.

She did not want to eat.

"But you haven't even had breakfast," said Mary. "You must strengthen yourself, you cannot starve."

"I cannot eat and I don't want to eat. If I ate anything, I would vomit."

"Why don't you take off this uncomfortable costume, then, and go to bed and sleep?" said Mary, as if speaking to a child.

"I am too weak to take it off," her mother said. "As for sleeping—as if I could sleep after this! It will be weeks before I find any rest."

The doctor intervened: "I propose that you sit down again and wait another hour or so. Perhaps the telegram will come after all. Mary—I mean Ludmilla—must have found it very embarrassing to choose a present for you. And she is probably tormenting herself."

"How do you know?" asked the old lady.

And Mary added angrily, "Must you always defend Ludmilla?"

"All right, all right," he said. "I was only trying to be helpful." Then, to the old lady: "We are going to eat something with the children. I don't think we can afford to be late, because they are hungry and tonight they will stay up until late with the excitement of the tree and the presents. I would like everybody to have a nap this afternoon. We'll leave you, then. We shall be back here in less than an hour."

But Mary shook her head and said, "I am going to stay here. I don't want to eat, either."

"You must eat," said her husband. "You have no excuse."

The old lady said nothing. She seemed hurt rather than sick. She sat back again and let them cover her knees with the blanket, did not thank them, did not answer them when they took their leave.

"You must not act this way," said the doctor to Mary as they were going down the stairs. "Your mother is quite ill. She has pneumonia."

"How do you know?"

"I know. She will have an extremely high temperature in a matter of minutes."

"Is she in danger?"

"Yes—although, of course, one never knows with her."

They sat down to eat in a mournful atmosphere which the children picked up from the air, almost as if it were a germ. Mary could not bring herself to eat. She shook her head when the soup was placed in front of her, and a severe glance from her husband made things worse. It confirmed her fear that there was nothing to do but wait for the worst.

"Make an effort," he said, and he put an extra slice of bread into her soup, on the theory that she would eat one slice in order not to be forced to eat two.

"What are you doing?" she asked. "I could not eat two slices of bread. I could not even eat one."

He tried to be cheerful. "This is the system of the Russian folk tale," he said, to re-establish contact with the children too. "You remember the story of the peasant who could not sleep because his mother-in-law in the next room snored? The priest ordered him to take a pig into his own room at night. He complained even more and was ordered to put a cow there, then a donkey, then a hen. He was now going mad, so the priest ordered him to take out the hen first, then the cow, and he began to find it bearable; then, when the pig too was removed, he said he had never had such silence and could no longer hear the snoring old woman in the next room. If you can't eat two slices I will give you a third one, then a fourth one, and you will eat two without noticing them."

Kostia and Sonia were beginning to smile, but Mary lost her patience. "Try these systems with the children, not with me," she said. "I am going upstairs to see how she is."

An aura of tragedy was present now. Kostia and Sonia dropped their spoons, and it was obvious that they too could not eat their soup after this. Filippo imitated them instinctively; the butler became pensive, the governess aloof. Mary knew that she should have made an effort to bring back at least a semblance of normality (if not of festivity) to this sad Christmas Eve lunch, but she could not control herself and did not really care to do so. In the face of real tragedy (she knew that her mother was dying) she behaved like a child, blackmailing God in order to obtain what she wanted: If you let my mother die, I shall be cruel to my children and it will be your fault. Is that nice for a God, to make innocents suffer and to lose a good soul to the devil? She also felt superior to those who did not blackmail God. Self-control and resignation were, to her, proofs of indifference. There was, behind all this, a feeling of her own unimportance in the world, the one thing she could not bear. If she herself were to die, would they accept it as easily as all that? Therefore, tragedy must be.

"Mary," said her husband, looking at her pleadingly. She was almost at the door, she stopped for a moment, hesitating between good and evil.

"Mary," he repeated, "your mother would not like this. If she felt even slightly better she would be here with us and would eat."

Mary hesitated for another second, then her pride got the upper hand. She saw herself being treated like a child in the presence of her children, and she stiffened. She said, imitating her mother's voice, "I am not used to being treated like a child. When I don't feel like eating I don't eat." Then, realizing how sad and upsetting this was for everyone, she went on in a very severe tone, which sounded absurd after her proud remark. "I am just going upstairs to see if she needs anything. I'll be back for the next course."

On her way to her mother's room she was undergoing that very complex process of adaptation to bad news which, in activists of her type, takes on the form of a struggle between mortals and immortals, and results in a series of unwritten plays and fairy tales that keep the mortals busy and unaware of the complete inanity of that busyness. Having acted her part of the Bereaved One who is unable to eat (a part that in her husband's world was reserved for the after-death comedy), she had shaken it off and was through with the worst, even before it had happened. Thus now she was trying to recapture her sorrow in order not to be found out by her mother. And she repeated to herself aloud, as if she were God Himself threatening her with disaster if she did not cry at once, "She has pneumonia, she is going to die! But you do not care! You have no heart!"

"Who has no heart?"

These words were spoken from above; they frightened her so that for a moment she could not recognize their origin and the voice that had spoken them. She looked up and there It stood —her mother's ghost, ready to leave, with fur coat and white gloves and little fur bonnet tied under the chin. Mary's shriek was heard all through the house. Everybody ran in her direction and found her with her back to the wall, on the landing, eyes big and blinded by terror, and one step from her, equally pale, the ghost. Finally the ghost spoke, and it became clear that it was nothing but the old lady herself, who was on her way out.

"I was going for a walk," she said, fully aware of the unhoped-for success of her stunt. "That room stank with lost hopes. I could not stand it any more!"

There was a great silence, then Mary flung herself into her mother's arms and whispered, "Mamachen, Mamachen . . ."

The doctor looked annoyed. "I hope you are not going out. Or, rather, I am telling you that you are not allowed to go out."

"And why not?"

"Because you have pneumonia."

"Nonsense. I never felt better in my life."

He was at a loss. "You—you can't. You haven't even eaten anything today."

"Have you eaten?" she asked everybody.

"We were eating," said the doctor. "Mary refused to eat."

"She did? All right. I will have to sacrifice myself again. Not that I care to eat, but I will, to set her a good example."

She did not even sit at her place, which had been kept empty out of tradition and with no plate because she was not there.

She sat on her own right, where Mary always sat, and she did this not for any symbolic reason, only because Mary's soup was still there, cold by now. She did not give the butler a chance to take it away; she had finished the soup and eaten the two slices of bread before his hand touched the plate.

"Sit here, Mary, at my place," she said when she realized that Mary was still standing and waiting for her to move to the head of the table.

Mary sat down like a frightened child and said nothing. She kept watching her mother and was suddenly transported back to Rome at the time of her secret correspondence with Pierre, when her mother had blackmailed her with exhibitionistic eating.

"What comes next?" asked the old lady, almost choking with bread in her mouth. Everybody was back at the table and trying not to look at her, except for Sonia, who was trembling.

"Sonia," said the doctor reproachfully, "eat, don't stare at your grandmother."

Sonia looked at her plate and there was nothing on it, so she grabbed a slice of bread and, imitating her grandmother, gulped it down almost without chewing, so that she had to spit it out again with a great deal of coughing and other ugly noises. Even Filippo knew better than to look. But the old lady seemed not to have noticed anything; she was waiting for the second course, glassy-eyed with appetite. When it came, she swept more than half of the meat onto her plate without noticing that a few slices of meat and a great deal of sauce fell on the tablecloth and into the three glasses in front of her plate. She seemed only to see what came up toward her mouth on the tines of her fork. And when the butler, helped by Mary, picked all the slices from the tablecloth and tried to conceal the sauce stains with a clean napkin, she took some of the slices back from the serving plate and put them onto her own, then lifted the clean napkin and began to blot up the sauce with fresh bread, which she ate without any restraint, licking her fingers with obscene noises that made even the doctor shudder.

She looked at him without noticing anything, smiled and said, "Learn. I mean, tell Mary to learn. I am doing this for her." Then she turned to the butler and said, "Bernhard!" The butler, who bore no resemblance to Bernhard, looked inquiringly at the doctor, and the doctor gave him no help. "Bernhard," called the old lady again, "Bernhard, tell Monsieur Morin that I am eating, tell him, and tell him also that his roast is excellent."

"Yes, madame," said the butler, and hurried out.

Kostia was crying into his plate. The only person who kept strangely calm was Mary, whose face seemed almost as insane as her mother's. Mary was happy. This was normality, this was health, this meant that everything would go on as it had in the past: the "exceptional energy," the "indomitable spirit" were the full, living, working personality of her darling Mamachen, whose immortality was now an established fact. The doctor caught a glimpse of Mary's face and recoiled: she was more of a baby than her own baby upstairs. In fact, she had forgotten that baby, together with the rest of the family; only these two existed and they existed only for each other—the rest of the world was beclouded.

"Children," said the doctor, "we will have no dessert for lunch today, because tonight, under the Christmas tree, there will be not only presents, but guess what?"

Six pairs of eyes in varying degrees of innocence looked at him.

"Guess what?" he asked again. Slowly the eyes that had kept wandering back and forth between him and the other leading actors focused on him, as if to find a safe refuge from what they had been forced to see. "Guess what?" he asked again, with feigned impatience.

"Panettone," said Filippo, and his eyes smiled at the image of the dessert he liked best.

"Panettone," said Sonia, still oscillating between the two centers of attention.

"I said it first, you cannot say it first."

"Sonia is not saying it first," said Kostia, who could not fall for his stepfather's trick but was tired and frightened.

"All right," said the doctor, "there will be panettone and many, many other things of which you have not the faintest idea. But we must keep our appetite for those. Let's all get up and go back to the nursery, and no one shall come out of it until I signal with the little silver bell. Agreed?"

The children nodded and slipped down from their chairs, going to their grandmother to thank her for the meal. She shook hands with them, smiling formally as if they were important guests, and they left in good order, followed by the governess and the doctor, while the two actors were still playing their scene—which was suddenly interrupted by the doorbell.

"A telegram!" said the old lady, "I know, this can only be a telegram!"

It was, but not from Ludmilla. It came from Moscow, from the least interesting of her forgotten children—Ivan. She read it, threw it on her plate, wiped her hands with a napkin and said, "This is the limit. Even that imbecile of an Ivan sends a telegram—but nothing from Milan. Well, she has ruined my appetite once more. Let's go."

"Why don't you take a nap, Mamachen?" asked Mary.

"What was that word again? A nap? Since when have you seen me take naps like an Italian priest or an Italian lawyer?" She was aware of having said something unkind, so she added, "Some Italians must take naps, because they get up too early; but not I, not a Russian woman. Let's take a walk in the snow, that is more like us. Will you come with me?"

"Mamachen, please, Mamachen, think of the long, beautiful walks we can take in a few days if—if you are well and we all go to Moscow."

"Moscow? Oh, yes, Moscow. This is not our Russian snow. Very well, I shall wait. But no afternoon nap, oh no. Not in the winter, and not even in the summer, of course. . . . I want to see the Christmas tree."

She walked haughtily through all the rooms, entered the music room, sat on the sofa and closed her eyes. When the doctor came in to see what she was doing she was asleep, snoring so heavily that the small tinfoil bells on the tree began to move and the angel hair parted slowly in the dry air.

Mary smiled tenderly. This was another proof that her mother would live. But the doctor was worried. He recognized in that strange sound the beginning of coma.

"Mary," he said, "you go upstairs and take a nap. I prefer to sit here and read a book."

"May I stay, too?"

"Please don't insist."

"But . . . is she all right?"

"As you can see, she could not be better. When she wakes up I'll call you."

Mary left on tiptoe. He took the old lady's pulse and counted, watch in hand, then shook his head in disappointment. "Hours, in any case," he whispered. "And why here, of all places? What are we to do?" He looked at her, then at the Christmas tree. One of the two must go, but which one was more cumbersome? He sat down on a small tabouret next to the sofa, as if he were a visitor, and did something he had never done in the old lady's presence: he lit a cigarette. He smoked it slowly, looking at her with a clinical eye, watching the road map of her face for the message he expected, much as she had watched the horizon from her window for that telegram which never came.

"A nice Christmas for the children," he said, shaking his head. "You *would* come here to deliver your present." He shook the cigarette ashes into a flowerpot and asked, in a tone of despair, "Shall we remove the Christmas tree or the family tree?"

The snoring became heavier, disturbing in its ugliness. The old lady was drooling. He took his handkerchief, wiped her chin and lips, then, seeing that he would have to repeat the same gesture many times, applied the handkerchief to her mouth and afterward spread it like a bib under her chin. He smoked another cigarette, made a tour of the room, came back, sat down and said, looking at her, "When you have finished delivering your present to the family, I shall marry your daughter. If you let me."

He gave her all the time to snore back at him and said, "What a strange person you are. How many qualities, how many useless qualities. What great intelligence, what little wisdom. Is everybody as strange as you in your big country out there, where the snow is much whiter than our snow, and the soul is much bigger, wider, deeper than our soul? I would so like to know. If you had only been more stupid, your children could afford to be less stupid. My mother was stupid—that is, if you compare her mind to yours. I don't know. . . . I don't know. . . ."

He stuck the second cigarette into the humid topsoil of the flowerpot and looked at her again. "Whether He exists or not, the Lord have mercy on you." He yawned, then added, putting a hand in front of his mouth, "My nap is gone."

An hour later he made up his mind to go and prepare Mary, a terrible task.

"Mary," he said, shaking her out of her sleep. "Mary, listen to me. The time has come to be strong and responsible, worthy in this too of your mother's example."

Mary understood at once. "Mamachen is dying," she said. He looked away, saying nothing. "I knew it," she said quietly.

He took her by the hand and they walked downstairs. The snoring could be heard from the entrance hall, five rooms away. Mary began to run, he stayed behind. When he entered the room, Mary was speaking to her mother.

"Mamachen . . . Mamachen . . . are you asleep?"

"Nonsense," said the old lady, "I never sleep. I am not an Italian!"

525

XXIV

ON THE AFTERNOON of Christmas Eve, before the tree is lit and the presents distributed, in those empty no man's hours when it would be so important to have something to do, children find it impossible to play with last year's toys, because they have been demoted. Kostia, Sonia and Filippo were proud of having to endure a few hours of boredom in the nursery with their hated old toys, and they were exercising their first snobbery on the poor newcomer who thought that this confinement was a holiday because so many brothers were assembled for so long in his room. They were his toys, his living toys, this was his Christmas; and his ignorance amused them even more than his happiness.

"Look at him, Sonia," said Filippo, "he does not even know that this is boring! Here," he said, throwing a tiny wooden horse into the crib, "do you want this?" The baby grabbed the horse and tried at once to eat it. "Look! He does not even know that a horse is not for eating!" Filippo tried to take his horse back, but the baby would not give it to him. "Look! Sonia! Kostia! Look! He thinks I care about that horse—he thinks it is a *new* horse. How stupid he is! He does not know that tonight we are going to get *new* toys!" Then, to the baby: "Keep that horse if you want it! I don't care for it! It's old!"

The baby nodded, laughing. "But look! He likes an *old* toy! He must be very stupid!"

Sonia was also fascinated by the stupidity of her younger brother and began to look at him as one looks at an animal at the zoo. Then she threw one of her old dolls to him and he seemed delighted, which made her laugh at him, and that also delighted him. "He does not know that we are laughing at him!" she said.

At this point the governess intervened to explain to Sonia and Filippo that they too had been just as "stupid" when they were small, but that stupidity was not the word for it. "Oh, I remember very well," Sonia said, and Kostia at this point also had something to say. He said that no one could have informed the baby that one day was different from the others.

"I see," said Sonia. "He knows nothing. He has always lived in Switzerland. This is a country for cows and watches and chocolates."

"You must not say such things," Kostia retorted, looking at the governess, who was half Swiss. "You too have always lived in Switzerland."

"Oh, but I know that there are other countries. He does not."

"That is right. He does not. And so he cannot know that you don't like the toys you liked yesterday."

"Yesterday? A year ago, not yesterday. Why don't you give him your old toys?"

"Because I still like them."

"Then you don't want new ones?"

"Yes, I do, but I want intelligent toys now, while before I wanted stupid toys."

"What intelligent toys do you want?"

"Fire engines that work, automobiles, trains, books . . ."

"Boring books?"

"What do you mean by boring books?"

"Books with only words in them and no pictures?"

"Yes, but they are very interesting."

Sonia became pensive. "You must be very old. Only old people like boring books." Then she thought again for a moment and said, "The other day I saw a boring book and I looked at it and I think I was beginning to like it. I am becoming old."

"Yes," he said with a smile, like an old man.

At this moment there was a noise behind them and they saw their grandmother standing there. She took Kostia's head with one hand and pressed it against her fur coat with infinite love. She smiled at the other two, then went near the crib and smiled at the baby without touching him. After this she went out again. The three wanted to follow her.

"Oh, no," she said. "There is still plenty of time. After dark. You will hear the bell."

They stood there, waiting for the darkness and the bell.

"Where is she now?" asked the doctor as he saw Mary come back to the music room, where he was unpacking toys and placing them under the tree.

"I left her in her room, she said she was going to have a rest."

"To sleep, you mean?"

"She did not say so, but I think she may."

The doctor said nothing. He was still too angry at having believed those deceiving symptoms, and too grateful to the old lady for not dying in the music room. He had lost hope. Not that he wanted her to die, but this was neither life nor death, this was a game of hide-and-seek with God, which destroyed everyone but her and God.

"Ludmilla's presents," he asked. "Where are they?"

"Oh no. Not those, after what she has done."

A noise was heard in the next room, and Ludmilla's voice resounded strangely in the words, "Why not Ludmilla's presents?"

They were both paralyzed for a moment, then they saw the old lady at the door.

"You scared us so," said Mary. "You had Ludmilla's voice."

"Did I? How strange."

"Yes," said the doctor, still trembling. "You did. Why are you not upstairs in your room?"

"I have been upstairs. I visited the children."

"You should not do these things, you are not well."

"My illness is not catching."

"I never meant that."

"Tell me, rather, why not Ludmilla's presents?"

Mary said, "But they have not been washed. And then, I think she does not deserve the honor."

"Why not, Mary? She loves the children and they love her. Let us be Christian on this day at least." The old lady sat down on the sofa where she had been sitting before, and the doctor looked at her with apprehension.

"We are ready," he said. "Let's light the candles."

He lit the candles, and at once the smell of country fireplaces and childhood enveloped the two ladies and disposed them to tears and sentimental song. The doctor liked the smell, too, but to him it was only a resinous scent; fireplaces in his memory had the smell of jasmine thyme that seems to be part of all burning wood in Mediterranean countries.

They exchanged the traditional three kisses, and the old lady took out of her purse a huge gold watch with a chain to match, saying to the doctor, "This was my husband's watch. It is for you now."

"Thank you," he said, annoyed by the weight and opulence of the object. "But I think that this should go to Pierre."

"I do with it what I please."

He thanked her again, then said, "Unfortunately I have not even thought of buying you a present—with your money."

She stiffened, Mary stiffened, and he went on: "Not even for you, Mary, do I have a present. I don't believe in Christmas, not even in God, to be quite frank."

"Must you always bring up unpleasant subjects at the wrong

moment?" asked Mary, and she handed him a gold cigarette case.

He thanked her, saying, "With an object like this in my pocket, I shall have to stop smoking. Futility encased in heavy gold—what sense is there to it? I thought you had made me a Christmas present already in May: our new child."

He stopped, seeing that he was really offending their sense of the sacredness of Christmas, and said, "We are ready now. Shall I ring the bell?"

Mary sat at the piano and played "Stille Nacht, Heilige Nacht," and both she and her mother sang, with Germanic heaviness and repressed tears. From the top of the stairs came the procession; Kostia, Sonia and Filippo in their best clothes, as stiff as soldiers on parade, followed by their governess, who also sang and had tears in her voice. From the kitchen came, also in stiff marching order, the cook, the butler and the chambermaid, Frieda, followed by Adalgisa and Brigida, who looked embarrassed. All the women received presents from the old lady's hands and the traditional three kisses, even if they were not traditional for them but only for the giver. The men received gifts and handshakes, while the children were allowed to find their presents under the Christmas tree.

The usual shrieks of joy and disappointment began, calling for the good offices of a peacemaker who could not exercise his full powers without bringing offense to the spirit of Christmas, but who reminded the children that the day after Christmas was just another day, and that whatever punishment had not been meted out on Christmas was not for that reason called off. Filippo had received beautiful presents from his grandmother—a whole village in varnished wood, with trees and people and even horses and carriages, a work of art such as only German toymakers could produce; but he was very unhappy. He searched the whole area under the tree, upsetting many stars and silver chains and running the risk of burning his hair. No loving reminders could deter him. He stepped on Sonia's toys, for which offense she hit him with one of his toys and broke it. He cried, his father spanked him gently, then jokingly "unspanked" him by going through the motions of a faked spanking, and finally had to warn him that a new, real spanking would be served him the day after tomorrow, when, Christ having been taken home, unruly little children would receive no protection from the Holy Child. Filippo had been trying to find his pistol, his pocketknife and the black-and-green soldier's hat. Other toys were offered him in Aunt Ludmilla's name, but he wanted those. Sonia was envious of his village and asked for it as indemnity for the breaking of a doll's finger and the soiling of a doll's dress. Filippo did not want to let her have the village, and this strife between them was something so new, so unexpected, so irreverent, that everybody except the old lady felt at fault—while she reveled in her sadness.

"This is the picture of what will happen to my children when I am gone," she murmured, without even losing patience any more.

Mary went to the piano and played "O Tannenbaum," which no one sang at first, then everyone sang, except for the doctor, who had begun to notice something strange in the behavior of the dog and was anxious to discover whether his fears were justified. He had noticed that Tasso—who on all such previous occasions had been in the way, sitting heavily on picture books the children were looking at, licking their faces and mistaking their gestures of dismissal for the act of throwing something he would have to pick up and bring back—was now possessed of a strange terror and throwing rather sinister glances at the Christmas tree and the children. Incubation of rabies, was the doctor's first thought. I'll send the butler upstairs for my pistol, take Tasso out of the house, go with him to the end of the park and shoot him there, then bury him late at night.

He did not like animals, did not believe in the existence of a soul behind the clever make-believe of animal behavior. And what irked him so much in the Protestant spirit of Christmas was exactly this willful confusion between levels of culture. All that kissing of kitchenmaids and chambermaids, all those brotherly handshakes with cooks and butlers, and their admission to the drawing room on the most intimate occasion of the year, led to the logical conclusion that levels of humanity were marked only by differences in wealth. Had the butler been only more ambitious, and had he worked as a weaver in the family cotton mills near Moscow, or as a messenger boy in the family banking house, he might by now become Ludmilla's husband or Pierre's associate. The butler did in fact look like Mary's grandfather; and his utterly uninteresting remarks, which, if made while he was serving at table, would have caused the old lady and Mary to frown, were today accepted by them as subjects for polite conversation. And his patronizing way of reminding the children that they must not quarrel tonight because the Holy Child would not like it was also more than the doctor could bear.

In a landowning family down in Apulia, first of all there would have been no tree, no candles and no presents, and then no trespassing of levels by inferiors. Kisses between mistress and maid, handshakes between mistress and menservants, perhaps; but no boldness on the part of the maids or the menservants. An accentuated clumsiness, a faked embarrassment, on the contrary, would have been offered by the inferiors and expected by the superiors in a tacit agreement that this was but a ritual, exactly as when a person offers to share his meal with a stranger or to give him his house. Even a person as illiterate as his own late mother would not have listened too seriously to the "thoughts" of a manservant—not, indeed, because she regarded herself as a learned woman, but because she was not. Here, instead, the old lady seemed to be learning from the butler, and thus encouraged him to go on with his stupid remarks.

All of these thoughts and dispositions had been simmering in the back of the doctor's mind for a long time, and if they remained secret there was a reason: He had for a long time firmly believed that the old lady's death was imminent; only now was he beginning to understand that she would outlive him, Mary and probably all of his children, after ruining all of them financially and mentally. Already the gulf between him and his wife, him and his work, was too great to be filled.

"Come here," he said to the butler, in a tone such as no one had ever used in that house with a servant. "I must speak to you."

The butler, who had just begun to explain to the old lady that unless we forgive all our enemies on Christmas Eve we are sure to call upon ourselves the curse of God's wrath for a number of generations to come, did not like to be interrupted at such a moment, and said, "Yes, yes, I'm coming," then asked the old lady almost in a tone of command, "Do you understand me correctly? Do you see what I mean? And this goes for you too!"

Without losing sight of the dog, the doctor came closer to see how far this lack of respect in his servant would go. The butler noticed this and nodded as if to repeat his assurance that he would soon come, then went on speaking to the old lady. "Jesus said it, too," he warned now, with his finger in the air. "Jesus said it very clearly: '*Omina bona mea mecum porto,*' which means 'My good men I take along with Me.' And he added, '*Bonis voluntatibus,*' which means that they must be men of good will, do you understand what I mean?" And the old lady nodded, lost in thought and feeling very small before this great scholar.

The doctor was furious. "I told you I had to speak to you," he repeated, looking at the butler without the slightest Christmas spirit in his eyes.

The old lady noticed this and ascribed it to the same strange, complex mentality that had made him, years previously, refuse Brigida as a godmother for his son. "This man knows so much," she said, looking sternly at the doctor and indicating the butler. The gesture was almost Biblical. "He answers my most anguished question!"

The butler was beginning to feel uneasy. "Nothing new," he said. "It is in all the books. It's Latin, after all. The greatest philosophers have known it for a long time."

The doctor preferred to address himself to the old lady and said, "I have to speak to him for a moment, if I may."

"We will continue later," said the old lady to the butler with a sweet smile. Then, to the doctor: "Do you think that my telegram has been received in Milan?"

"I don't know."

"I hope it has. I only wish it had been more explicit. In fact, I think I'd like to send another one tonight."

"Tonight? For what purpose? There is no urgent reason. And besides, who would go to the station at this hour?"

"I would," said the butler, "especially to do a good deed. I always know, especially on Christmas Eve, if a person intends to do something in the spirit of Jesus, and that is why I have taken the liberty of offering my services—because I wanted you to see how my soul functions. That is the law of God." He blushed, bowed, and followed the doctor through the room.

It seemed to him as if the doctor were in his service. This became clear from the way he bent over, like a great man lending a friendly ear to a smaller man's opinion.

"What were you saying, Doctor?"

"First of all, let me tell you that it is *Omnia bona mea*, and that *omnia* means 'all,' neuter, the feminine form being *omnae* and the masculine *omni*, and it is *fero* and not *porto*, and the whole thing means 'I carry all my belongings with me.' Which has absolutely nothing to do with the saying 'Peace on earth, good will toward men.' But this is not the place or the moment for such theological and grammatical discussions. What I called you for is my pistol. You know where it is—in my dressing room together with my hunting rifle and my field glasses."

534

The butler had to gulp twice before he could swallow his pride, his Latin, his theology and his un-Christian feelings of rebellion; then he said, in a broken voice, "I did not quite understand you. What was it you wanted from your dressing room?"

"My pistol. My revolver, you know?"

"Your pistol? For—excuse me—what reason?"

"For the dog."

"Tasso? You are not going to shoot Tasso?"

"I am sorry if this upsets you, but it has to be done. The dog has rabies. Look at him. We must take him out of the house and be rid of him at once. It will be better for him also."

"But Tasso hasn't rabies," the butler said, answering the doctor's whispers in a loud voice that could be overheard by everyone. The children ran to the dog and started playing with him.

"Away! Away!" shouted the doctor. "He has rabies!"

"I know dogs," said the cook, who had been speaking with the governess. "That dog is healthier than all of us!"

And now Brigida and Adalgisa, who had known dogs, rabid and otherwise, ran to the scene, and the dog at once became cheerful. He was licking the children's faces and putting his big paws on their shoulders; the doctor had to tear them away from him. He opened the door and let the dog out. Everyone but the children, Mary and the old lady went out into the hall and watched the dog, who became playful and watched now this, now that hand in the group, waiting as usual for the ball to be thrown.

"How can you say such a thing, Doctor?" asked Brigida. "Look at him, he is so good. He wants a Christmas present, too!"

The butler laughed and ran back to the music room saying, "Nothing wrong with our Tasso! He was feeling neglected because no one has given him a Christmas present!"

"How right you are, my friend!" cried the old lady. "Bring him back here, we do have a present for him! Mary, give me that ball Ludmilla sent to the dog. Indeed, the Lord has eyes for *everything*. And He has spoken to us twice through you this evening," she said, squeezing the butler's hand.

The children were impatient to go out and bring back the dog. But the butler went out first and held the door closed from the outside. By that time even the doctor seemed reassured, although he felt misgivings which had nothing to do with the dog's health. Once more he had been proven wrong.

Mary and her mother were now staging the comedy of giving Tasso his Christmas present. "Poor Tasso, come, get your present. . . . Look at it. Do you like it?"

But again Tasso behaved strangely. He was terrified of that ball, tried to disentangle himself from the butler's grip and threatened to bite his hand. The butler gently tapped him on the nose, and Tasso began to howl and to froth at the mouth.

"I told you he was sick," yelled the doctor. "Shut him up in the stable! This is the incubation period, he is dangerous already, he must not be let free."

"Can't I pat him?" asked Kostia, with tears in his eyes.

"No," said the butler, pushing him away. "He is going to bite you."

The boy ran to his grandmother and began to sob in her lap. Sonia and Filippo did the same, and Mary, whose usual crying place had been usurped by her children, had one more reason to cry.

"Nothing will happen to your dog," said the old lady. "I shall go with him to the stable and see that he has a warm bed and his present to play with."

"You will not," said the doctor. "This is the most dangerous thing to do. Please do not interfere."

"And you, please, do not contradict me. I will intervene on behalf of my friend." She followed the butler, who was holding the dog by the collar and was already at the end of the hall. "Here," she said, throwing the ball. "Give him this and wait for me."

536

The dog pulled free, ran after the ball and brought it back to the butler. There was a general sigh of relief after a moment of mute fright.

"I was right," said the butler, "there is nothing wrong with this dog!" And again he threw the ball, which the dog brought back immediately. The butler gave it to the old lady and said, "You throw it now."

She walked toward the dog with the ball in her hand, and Tasso began to run away from her. She followed him, cornered him, he remained for one moment in front of her, head low, trembling in every limb, then dashed away from her and ran to the opposite end of the hall, where the others were standing.

It was clear to everyone that he was afraid only of the old lady.

"Tasso," she cried, "you too?"

XXV

~~~~~~

A N HOUR LATER the children were tucked into their beds,
clasping their toys to their hearts and feeling happy that
their dog was not doomed. The butler, in his coat and galoshes,
was standing in front of the library desk and waiting while the
doctor wrote.

"Here is one. See if you can read it," said the doctor.

The butler read, " 'Mother gravely ill please come at once
signed Mary.' "

The doctor handed him two more and said, "The first one
goes to Milan, one to Paris, and the others to Moscow. We
may be mistaken about dogs, but dogs never are about us. Two
days before my father died his hunting dogs began to shun him
and he shot them that same night to protect himself and his
family. He believed they were sick, they knew he was; and they
were right. I had forgotten this until I saw what happened in
the hall tonight. Take a lantern with you, and a stick against
dogs. And God be with you," he added, by way of apology for
all the unpleasant things he had said before.

The butler felt reinstated in his rights. He nodded gravely
and said, after giving the matter a great deal of thought, "Such
is life."

The doctor let him out as a guest, opening both the glass

door and the heavy house door for him, then he slowly went upstairs.

In front of the old lady's room he stopped and listened to her voice. "Oh, no," she was saying, "I have no reason to go on living. Even the dog now avoids me. Marie was right: I lived alone and I shall die alone."

The doctor felt a sudden rage. He wanted to go inside and shout, "You are not going to die alone, we are all here, and stop tempting the Lord even in the last days of your life." But he returned downstairs.

It was almost midnight. Time for High Mass at home. And here? This ugly tree, further deformed by tinfoil stars, silver apples and candles, artificial snow, paper dolls and paper chains. He was about to turn away from all this when the doubt hit him, Did the butler remember to take the house keys with him? Can I leave him outside in the cold night? But why should I think of these things? Because I am master now, this house belongs to me. He is my butler, I should not treat him like a slave. . . . Then he recalled his recent anger because the butler had been treated too much as an equal by Mary and by her mother, and he thought, What a heap of contradictions I am! Next he remembered the cook, his recent friend. And again he felt lonely, like a child in the forest; all these large paintings, all the vases and lamps and candlesticks, and the tables, the armchairs, the sofas and the china, and the bronzes, the statues, even the books, were a forest of things inimical to him. He would sell everything and save for his children. Suddenly his eyes fell on the lamps. So many of them and so excessively bright, and to what purpose? I can wait in the dark, I know the place, he thought. He turned off all the lights and steered himself a safe course between tables and chairs in his blind wandering from room to room.

Gone was his enemy; the old woman representing waste of time, waste of money, waste of food, waste of filial devotion, would no longer be wasting his time and his food and his money and the feelings of his wife. Now he would have to come forward with his own values and ideas. How comfortable it had been all these years to postpone the beginning of his work because this woman was a tyrant. The ashes in the fireplace had slowly become sources of light, like bread crumbs that in times of famine become breakfast, lunch and dinner. He saw his image in the mirror with the shadows reversed: light in his nostrils, light under his chin, and his forehead invisible. How right the Italian language was in describing the wicked as "captive." Poor woman, she had been captive of so many inane things; she had never grown up, she had been choked in her crib and bloated into a big balloon, and this balloon had now been punctured and deflated.

But thank God Mary can grow up, he told himself. This must be a complete funeral. No corpses rotting in the house, haunting the nursery and infecting the air. We shall have all the flowers of the world and all the music; barrels of tears to be poured on her grave, and then nothing. Life will be normal and cheerful, with a purpose ahead of us and no tired remorse over forgotten sins.

Having now settled these postmortal affairs, he found himself confronted with moral fears: If God does not exist, divine justice exists, and I am wishing for the death of a person who is to my wife what my wife is to Sonia. If such a thing can go unpunished, then indeed there is no justice on earth!

How he missed Mary, how natural it would have been for him to open up his soul to her, as he had done after the theft of the car. Who else could listen to him and absolve him? He walked out into the hall and heard a sigh in the dark. He turned on the lights and saw Brigida, all wrapped up in her shawl.

"Brigida, what are you doing here at this hour?"

"I cannot sleep, sir."

He realized suddenly that to absolve Brigida for wishing death to a person she worshiped would be a bit strange. Yet his sense of high masculine and cultural superiority made it imperative that his confession take on the form of an act of forgiveness.

"Brigida, when we wish death to someone who is constantly in our way, we never really think of that person's life as a whole . . ."

"What did you say, sir?"

"I was saying that when we wish death to someone, we never really think of that person's life, but only of that part of it which happens to interfere with ours. Do you understand me, Brigida?"

Brigida understood that she was not supposed to understand, only to agree. "Oh, yes, oh, yes, I understand."

"That is good. So, as I was saying, we never really think of life as a whole. And that is why death comes to us as much—how shall I put it?—as much bigger merchandise than we had ever thought of purchasing."

"I know, I know, sir. When my poor husband died, we had to purchase the coffin we bought. When it comes to big things such as death or disease or a wedding, we only buy purchased things. But they are more expensive than the others. All the things that have to do with God are expensive."

He felt lonely again, this time because he wanted someone to laugh with him. Also because he was in possession of an excellent argument against religion, and it was a great pity that no one would hear it. So for the sake of this nonexistent but appreciative audience, he completed his thought. "Which, you see, Brigida, is one more proof that God knows little about the world, and those who say that God does not exist are being kinder to Him than those who try to justify His doings. Even His favors are a punishment!"

"Punishment for our sins."

"Yes," he said, "in a way. Think of Madame, a very good case in point."

"Madame is so good, she will go straight to heaven."

541

"I hope so, but now consider, Brigida: God might have changed her character, opened her eyes, made her a little more patient, a little more capable of enjoying what she had, instead of keeping her so long in the dark and then taking her away, still in the same state of ignorance."

"Amen. But Madame is not going to die. Madame is very strong."

"Don't tell me that, Brigida. I have already telegraphed to her sons, to her daughter."

"What's wrong with that? She will be very glad to see them and they will be glad to see that there is nothing wrong with their mother."

He was becoming impatient. "Brigida, if you were a rich woman I would bet you anything that in less than a week she will no longer be with us. But you are poor, so all I can say is, remember my words."

"No, sir. Don't worry, she will never die. She is going to see the day when your children are married. And God bless her and keep her with us for another hundred years."

Brigida walked away like a witch in a fairy tale, and he began to think, What have I done? And how will Mary take it? I used her name. I should have learned that whatever I do is bound to be wrong!

The task of telling Mary was so unpleasant that he forgot his fears about the butler and the keys and went upstairs, first to the old lady's room, hoping to find her in coma. He turned out the lights in her sitting room, then opened the door slowly and put his ear to the darkness inside, to hear only a normal breathing sound. At one point there was a sigh and he knew that she was looking at him.

"Are you awake?" he asked.

"Yes."

"May I turn on the light?"

"Yes."

She looked well, was sitting up as if she had been in that

posture for some time. With a very troubled conscience he came closer and put his hand to her forehead.

"No fever. Any complaints?"

"None, thank you."

Why had she said "thank you"? He was ready for the usual diatribe, which he would accept in Mary's place almost with pleasure; but she seemed to have nothing to say.

"Do you want tea or something to eat?"

"No, thank you. I have eaten too much these last days. I am tired."

She had not said "tired of life," just "tired." Very strange.

"Have you been awake all this time?"

"No, I must have slept an hour or more, but I think I should make an effort and go back to sleep."

She was beginning to make sense. This was a sign of death. Wisdom was nearing.

"Let's hope that Ludmilla's telegram will come in the morning," he said, to further test her state of health. But she said nothing.

He went back to her sitting room and sat in an armchair, feeling that this was a dishonest thing to do, worse perhaps even than wishing for her death. He justified it to himself: If she has a heart attack, I am here, on hand. But then he saw through his self-deceit and blushed, and whispered to himself, Here I am, blushing in the dark. The radiators were cold, the fireplace was full of ashes and black stumps, he wanted to go get his fur coat but thought, She might think I am gone. If she hears me go now and then come back, she might suspect me of looking for her will or trying to read her letters. These fears had never come to him before. They were ramifications of his feeling of guilt. After a while he felt so cold that he decided to leave through the hallway and go to bed. Tomorrow morning, he thought, I will find it much easier to explain everything. And besides, what does Brigida know? This woman cannot live much longer; what has not happened yet may happen any day in the near future. Mary has no right to complain. She will be grateful instead that I called for Pierre and Ludmilla.

This gave him courage. It took him another while to overcome the torpor in his legs, which (How unwise of my legs, he thought; even in parts the body is stupid) seemed to prefer the painful cold that ran all over them to losing a small area of warmth between the cushions of the armchair and the sides of his thighs. "Let's go," he ordered. And then, speaking to the muscles in that warm area: "You, who are warm, must sacrifice what you are hoarding to the general good of the whole body." But his legs did not obey him and he continued sitting there, sitting. . . .

He even found the courage to pass through the patient's room. The dry smell of face powder, Eau de Cologne and camphorated alcohol which ruled in that room, superseding other smells of sofas, silks and polished furniture, was now imbued with rotten glue and a mixture of vinegar and sugar. This cannot be, he thought, cupping his hand over his nose; it takes longer than that. But there it was. He uncovered his nose again and sniffed the darkness like a dog. Yes, this was it, the final smell in which all individual differences drown. He covered his nose again, and again he searched the darkness with his ear to identify the stream of life, but could not find it.

No harm in turning on the light, he thought, and felt the wall behind him for the switch. The light went on and there she was, staring at her own room from just outside the world. The mouth was open as if she had just cried or were now crying.

He knelt next to her bed, made the sign of the cross and thought, This is not more absurd than taking off your hat. The good manners of death. And again he crossed himself, folded his hands and whispered, *"Requiescat in pace."* Other prayers came to him and he whispered these too.

Now he could also speak to her, because she understood. So he said to her, "You, who have always treated others like things, to better possess them, have now yourself become a thing and no one can possess you. Was it worth it, to let others rot away during their lives by not allowing them to have souls of their own? See what happens to you when your soul is not with you? This oversized body of yours, and the body of your habits which continually inflated it with rotten winds, always stood like a cloud between us and the sun, between you and yourself. And was that worth it, too? What good was achieved? Now you know many things. You also know that I was fond of you and yet was wishing for your death, and you also know why: because Mary was rotting in your shadow. Help her, while there is still a little hope to prepare her for life. Don't make her spend her days in noisome vanity, like a moral hyena, loving only herself, seeing only her own image in the pool of her tears. That is what you have always done, you Narcissa of the north, female and fearful counterpart of our gentle Narcissus of the south. We barbarians from Greater Greece, who are half non-Christian and half nonheathen, often sin like Narcissus, by falling in love with our own image, while we are young and still capable of pleasure. But when we leave the forest we also leave the brook. You have made your own brook with the stream of your tears, and here you are, having seen nothing of the world but your own face, and not for pleasure, because it was no pleasurable sight. Yet you forced everyone to watch his own image in the pool of his tears and of yours, because you wanted company. Now take your old mistakes away from us and see that Mary is freed forever from the spell of her own image aping yours. Allow her at long last to be my wife. You promised her to me but never let her leave the house. . . ."

Mary interrupted him. "Mamachen is not well and you don't even wake me up? Why did you sleep here on this chair all night? She heard you snoring, called you several times, got out of bed and came here twice, but did not have the courage to disturb you."

"I am sorry," he said. "She should have shaken me. Doctors are there to be roused from their sleep, she has done that with me for the last six or seven years, why all of a sudden should she be so considerate?"

He straightened his necktie in the mirror and it took him a long time because he was angry.

"Are you ready?" sobbed Mary.

"Yes!" he shouted.

"Not so loud," she begged, clenching her fists.

He walked into the old lady's room, where Frieda had just opened the window and a breath of clean air was still chasing the stale air back into the curtains, the blankets, the bottles and their throats, while the white glare of snow was washing off the shadows from areas not reached by artificial lights. Before looking at the patient he looked at the light in the middle of the ceiling which he had lit in his dream, and turned it off. Then only did he look at the patient and see that she was very ill. He said, "Thank God—" and then stopped in time before saying, "this is it." And while putting his hand on the patient's forehead he corrected his statement as best he could: "This is less bad than I had feared." Then he took out his watch to count her pulse and give himself time for a further correction of that first statement.

"However," he said, speaking to the patient, "now I want you to realize that you are very ill. You are not desperately ill, not in danger, but ill enough to behave wisely for once and do only what I tell you. No wandering about the house, you will obey my orders or I will have to tie you to your bed. Understand?" This last word spoken softly. The harshness of his first remarks was a reminder to his medical conscience and the last word a resumption of the speech in his dream, inserted, as it were, in an earlier chapter God had allowed him to rewrite.

The patient's voice came as a voice in a crowd of shouting people—feeble and broken. "Yes. Yes."

"Do you hear noises in your ears?" he asked.

The patient nodded.

"It's the fever," he said. "How are you feeling?"

"Very well."

"Better stay quiet. Do you want a little tea?"

"No," she said. "Nothing."

It was with great relief that he told Mary, "I had seen it coming, but was not sure. In any event, I sent off a few telegrams, signing them with your name. But, as I said before, thank God it is not so bad as you had led me to think."

"You really think it is not grave?"

He did not hesitate; the fear of facing her despair was stronger than his strivings for honesty. "No," he said, "definitely not. But I cannot be certain. That is why, almost as a form of superstition, I sent those telegrams."

Mary was strangely indifferent to the telegrams. He had expected her to inquire about the wording of them, but she stood there, frowning and pensive. "Now let me tell you what I think," she said. "I know that she is not going to live. This is the end."

His fatigue fell upon him like a hail of big stones. Every part of his body was aching. All he could bring himself to do was put both hands on her shoulders and say, "Please, Mary, be strong. Think only of her, not of yourself."

She disentangled herself. "You need not tell me. I have never been so strong and so quiet. I was going to ask you, in fact, whether we should not telegraph Ludmilla and Pierre,

and Uncle Jules in Paris. And of course Olga. Have you telegraphed Olga?"

"No, but I will."

By lunchtime Christmas Day the patient seemed a little
better. Her fever had responded to a new miracle drug called
aspirin and had gone down two degrees.

"But this is wonderful," said Mary.

"Of course it is," he answered. "But before we rejoice I
want to be sure. You go downstairs and have lunch with the
children; I'll take a second reading of the temperature."

She left, and a few minutes later someone knocked on the
door. It was Brigida with a calling card in her hand.

"What is this?"

"This will chase away the fever. I prayed to it all night."

"Oh, I see. Thank you." It actually was a calling card of
some Swiss priest, with the name erased and with the words
"Pray to Saint Anthony for recovery from severe colds, fevers of
the lungs, and arthritis."

"That's very nice, Brigida, but you should keep this."

"No, no, sir, Madame needs it today. Put it under her pillow
and you will see what happens. Three people have used it in
the neighborhood and it helped them a great deal."

He took it, thanked her again, and went back to his patient
with a certain apprehension. But the reading was higher this
time, and he again felt a great tenderness for his mother-in-law
and had tears in his eyes when he asked her how she was.

"Not well," she answered feebly, "but it will pass."

"Of course it will," he said, "have courage, we are all here
to help you."

"There is something so moving about the faith of these
simple peasant folk," said Mary, almost to plead for good news
as she came back. She noticed her husband looked less worried
again but preferred not to play her last card by asking for a

definite answer. "I think one must have faith," she said, "and prayer counts, no matter where it comes from. Superstition is one thing, and the great mystery beyond us something else."

"Yes, yes."

She began to observe her mother with an inquisitive eye and whispered, "She does look less flushed."

But he said nothing.

"Well, and that reading? Has the temperature gone down completely?"

"The first reading," he said, pausing here for a sigh, "must have been somewhat wrong."

By four o'clock the inflammation had spread to the left lung, the temperature had risen to 40.6 degrees centigrade, and the patient's pulse could clearly be seen and counted in the sacks under her eyes, in the eyelids themselves that blinked. It could also be heard in a light hissing sound that might have come from anywhere outside the house but actually came from the throat of the patient. The physiognomic lines were broken here and there by swelling of the face. There were coughing spells, drooling, glassy eyes, and delirium. Her sheets were so hot that they smelled like fresh ironing, and Mary's hands felt almost scalded when she touched them. Blankets and sheets were constantly thrown off the patient's body, and so was her nightgown. Mary found it difficult covering her up again without looking. All sense of dignity having been lost by the patient, Mary herself became her mother's dignity, and she refused to let the maids come in lest they hear, see or smell the growing evidence of moral and organic decay. And thus she and her husband learned how to make a bed and how to use a mop and a broom, and they were isolated from the rest of the house except for brief periods of respite that became shorter each time.

By ten o'clock that night, to the hissing of strenuous respiration was added a faint sound in two notes, as when a child calls his mother from a very great distance.

"Ring the bell and ask for ice," said the doctor. "I should

have thought of this before. She must have a headache."

The patient nodded almost imperceptibly and went on calling, now so faintly that she seemed to be humming a lullaby. There was no ice in the house.

"Silly fool," said the doctor when he heard this being whispered at the door. "Tell her to go out and make snowballs, wrap them in towels and bring them here."

The patient made an effort, gulped several times, then spoke her first connected words since morning, but so feebly that the doctor could not understand them.

She was gulping again and collecting her forces to repeat what she had tried to say. This time he listened more carefully, but again he missed the meaning. Her speech was garbled. Mary in the meantime had come back from the door, but she also could not understand the words.

"I cannot tell what she is saying," he said. "But what is that stupid maid doing? Why should it take her hours to come back with a bit of snow? Lack of imagination is the worst trait in these damned Germans. If Adalgisa were not busy upstairs, she would have understood without asking me."

Then he turned to the patient and, waving his finger in her face, said, "I shall open the window now to gather snow from the window sill. Don't throw off the blankets. Understand?"

He ordered Mary to stay close to the bed and hold her mother, then went to the window and opened it. The night smelled clean. He gathered enough snow to make a very tight snowball, wrapped it in a towel and called Mary to take it while he closed the window again and pulled the heavy curtains in front of it.

"Now," he said, coming toward the bed, "this will relieve your headache more quickly than all the medicines in this world."

"Shh," said Mary. "She was speaking again and I could not hear."

"Oh, I'm sorry," he said, and went on describing the virtues of icepacks against headaches. Now the patient was trying to speak again and they both became attentive. Mary knelt next to her mother and came so close that her ear almost touched her mother's lips. Then she lifted herself and whispered to her husband. "She says, 'Don't shout.'"

By three in the morning the temperature had reached 41.1 degrees centigrade. The two notes now came more quickly and loudly, in a vibrating voice; they sounded like a parody of opera. Strange postures of the head helped convey that illusion. The doctor observed all this as a reminder to himself that medicine is also a parody. All it can do is approve of recovery or approve of death.

If we do not believe in the powers that be, he thought, we must believe in our own powers; but the agnostic position—which alone expresses modesty, and is therefore religious—cannot be kept for more than a few seconds at a time. What I normally consider my agnostic position is only a digestive position, for it induces somnolence. Here the task itself is so actively asking us to understand, that every gesture of the suffering body is a challenge. And I sink deeper into silence like a boy shamed by his teacher for not knowing the lesson. The boy engages in some minimal semblance of activity, such as scratching his hands, fumbling with buttons, doodling, calculating in his mind the length or the weight of the blackboard, and I, here, do anything rather than concentrate on this task and hear these ranting questions that expose me in front of myself. I rearrange the pillow, wipe off the drooling from her chin and neck, use violence with her to give her clean sheets.

He gave her clean sheets, wiped off her drooling and rearranged her pillow.

Before daybreak the singing came to a stop, the patient's temperature remaining the same. But the two notes were either hissed or grunted, and in this latter case they suggested the pains of constipation. Eyes glassy and blinking indicated a beginning of mental derangement. At moments the old lady seemed puzzled, then indignant, then terrified, assuming statuary postures as if in imitation of famous works of art. Now she reclined like Madame Récamier, now she held her hand to her breast like Titian's Cleopatra, now she got out of bed and stood naked, face up in a tragic expression, like Niobe. Mary and her husband could do nothing but play a countergame to prevent her from leaving the room, to push her back into bed, to calm her down, and they did this in silence, panting, too, from the effort, so that the whole scene was insane: three persons wrestling in slow motion without coming to grips, because the patient was not aiming her movements at anything or anyone, she was just trying to escape from some inner grip which always overtook her if she stayed in one posture for more than a few seconds.

After twenty-five minutes of this fighting she became tired and fell back onto her bed, but continued to fight there; the fingers of one hand wrestled with the fingers of the other, while the toes of both feet scratched at the footboard.

At nine Adalgisa tried to enter the room. Mary let her come in without protesting. The patient was being given an injection of morphine.

"Why don't you both go to bed while I stay here?" Adalgisa suggested.

"I think we should," said the doctor. "Mary, let's go downstairs and have something to eat."

He noticed a great change in the way she said "Enough" when the butler poured coffee into her cup. And it was not the result of sleeplessness and the experience of horrors.

"You are here," he said, putting his hand on hers, as soon as the butler was gone.

He let another minute pass, then said, "Medical science has only just begun to experiment with blood transfusions. What I have been witnessing since Christmas Day is even more miraculous: a blood transfusion without surgery. Your mother's strength is now becoming yours. Put it to a good use, such as the education of our children, and the attainment of limited goals. Supernatural goals, such as making of me a great scientist, are an excuse not to advance from here to here." And he marked with his hands the distance between the sugar bowl and the marmalade jar.

The first telegram to arrive was from Paris. It said:

DESOLATE BUT UNABLE COME STOP ARE KEPT HOME BY COLD WITH BRONCHIAL COMPLICATIONS STOP DOCTOR CATEGORICALLY PROHIBITS ANY DISPLACEMENT BY RAILWAY OWING UNFAVORABLE METEOROLOGICAL CONDITIONS WOULD DECLINE ALL RESPONSIBILITY IN CASE OF OUR INFRACTION HIS ORDERS STOP WE PRAY FERVENTLY FOR SOPHIE'S RECOVERY BUT STRONGLY ADVISE YOU ASK INTERVENTION MALACHIER STOP MALACHIER CANCELS ALL IMPORTANT ENGAGEMENTS AWAITING YOUR INSTRUCTIONS PLEASE TELEGRAPH HIM IMMEDIATELY 15 RUE CIRQUE PARIS STOP ANXIOUSLY AWAITING NEWS SOPHIE STOP OUR BEST WISHES BUT INSIST MIRACULOUS INTERVENTION MALACHIER STOP AFFECTION

UNCLAUNT

The doctor read this while Mary was not looking and then left the room. He did not want Mary to misunderstand her uncle's intentions, and even less, to understand them; in either case it would have been a disaster. Wrongly interpreted, the message would have brought Malachier back to the house at her expense; rightly interpreted, it would have dealt a severe blow to her myth of family unity and her hopes for the future in Paris.

Knaves and fools, he kept saying to himself as he ran down the stairs to the library. Do they really believe that people cannot read between the lines of such a vulgar document? For all their great refinement, they have less education than my stableboy at home! Am I not a doctor, too? If they believe in

Malachier more than in God, why don't they send him here at their expense again? The fact is that they don't take us seriously any more, they don't believe she will ever die. And if she does, they will drop us at once and for good. This leaves Paris out of our calculations. We can count only on ourselves —that is, on me.

He drafted six or seven answers in French, but was not quite sure of his style or his grammar. And every time he reread that long telegram he discovered new things that irritated him, especially the waste of words, so much so that he tried to redraft it imagining how much money he would have made them save that way. Then he thought of Malachier, who had been living on their imaginary diseases for years, and felt such hate for him that he decided not to send him a telegram at all.

They can inform him, he decided. And I will show them how one can write a concise telegram without using that ugly word 'stop' all the time.

In a fit of inspiration he wrote: "Grateful prayers Godalone canwork miracles Bestwishes Nephewniece."

When he came back upstairs the patient was beginning to be restless again, but she was still wrapped in a painful lethargy as in a cobweb of invisible tubes from which steam petered out in whistles and deep, baggy noises. Mary was anxious to shake her from her unnatural sleep, but did not quite dare.

"Is there anything we can do?" she asked. "Do you think that if we called in Malachier . . . he and you perhaps . . . a consultation?"

Instantly the doctor regretted the telegram he had just sent. He should at least have consulted Mary before snubbing her uncle and Malachier. Now how could he explain?

Overwhelmed with guilt, he said, "Yes, why not? Let me wire him at once." And he ran downstairs, hoping to catch the butler and change the telegram, but the butler had gone. Too late anyway, he remembered; she is in coma. Besides, I did not actually refuse Malachier in that wire. He may interpret it as consent and come anyway. Let's wait. Meanwhile I can get Cappelli.

He called Dr. Cappelli at the hospital, then went back upstairs. But on the way he thought again of that telegram to Uncle Jules, and now he feared what he had hoped for a few minutes before. Suppose Malachier does take it for consent, he thought. He cannot arrive before tomorrow night, and we will have spent all that money to have him tell us authoritatively that she is dead. Can I stop him?

The best thing to do was to see how the patient behaved in the next hour or so. Perhaps she was dead already, while he stood there trying to decide.

He did notice a change for the worse on the patient's face. It seemed almost purple, there could be no doubt that this was the end.

"Why not give her oxygen?" was the first thing Dr. Cappelli said.

"Let's order it at once," said Mary. "Do you think that a consultation with Dr. Malachier might be of use?"

"One moment. Let me ask your husband a few questions."

The two doctors stood now in front of the patient and looked at each other.

"It is entirely up to you," said Dr. Cappelli. "You can afford it, and if it gives your wife any satisfaction, go ahead; but I am afraid that when he arrives it will be too late."

"That's exactly what I fear. I shall send him a telegram and ask him not to come."

"No, don't do that, if you have asked him already. He might still arrive in time."

Mary heard these last words. "Yes," she said, "let him come. If you asked him, it means there is still hope. What do you think, Dr. Cappelli?"

Dr. Cappelli shrugged his shoulders, closed his eyes in sign of resignation and shook his head, meaning, "Yes, no, perhaps, God only knows."

Those oxygen balloons not only filled the lungs of the patient, they filled Mary's ears and eyes and hands, they amplified the image of her mother, they made it into an abstract thing, they modernized it and displaced it to a far region in which even the air was received like a telegram or a pneumatic letter.

Early in the morning of the twenty-eighth the temperature fell and the patient's face cleared. "She is well again," said Mary, and the doctor did not know what to think. He had spent that whole night wishing for Malachier to come and wishing for him not to come, hoping for the patient to die and not to die. Now he was only tired.

Mary tended her sleeping mother like a doll, combing her hair, holding the hairpins between her teeth and appraising her work from time to time. Her husband watched her. His steps took him toward the bed from the window, then he turned stiffly like a sentinel and watched the snow which was turning to rain and lashing the panes from right to left, from top to bottom.

"Ludmilla?" The patient's eyes were still closed, but she had spoken clearly.

"Mamachen?" asked Mary.

After a long silence, first a twitching of the face, then the eyes opening wide, taking in everything but without any clear perception. Then, again the same whisper, "Ludmilla?"

"Ludmilla is coming, Mamachen. Can you hear me? Ludmilla is coming."

The patient looked at the doctor and again asked, "Ludmilla?"

"Ludmilla is coming," he said, too, and she turned her eyes slowly toward the door, which had just been opened softly by Frieda with a telegram.

"This must be a telegram from her," said the doctor, opening it and reading: "ARRIVING TOMORROW MORNING LUDMILLA." He showed it to her, but her eyes did not follow the yellow sheet of paper; she kept looking at Frieda and calling her "Ludmilla."

The doctor summoned Frieda with a gesture and took her by the arm. "This is Ludmilla," he said. The patient smiled, made a weak gesture with both hands as if to embrace Ludmilla, but was too weak to lift her arms. The new Ludmilla came closer and hesitantly presented her forehead for a kiss.

Tears were in those wide eyes that saw only the thought and the wish. "Ludmilla," she said, "your blouse."

"Yes," said Mary, without even trying to understand. "Yes, Mamachen, Ludmilla's blouse. Isn't it pretty?"

"Ludmilla's birthday," said the patient, very slowly.

"Yes, Mamachen, Ludmilla's birthday."

Frieda was kneeling next to the bed and weeping, her face deep in the blankets, while her "mother's" white hand rested on her neck. A gust of wind shut the door with a bang. The patient turned her head in that direction again and said, "Pierre?"

"Yes," said the doctor, greeting an invisible Pierre, for he knew that those eyes could see nothing by now.

"Pierre with the bear!" said the patient, giggling feebly. "Pierre's present for Ludmilla!"

"Yes," said Mary, remembering. "Pierre's present for Ludmilla's ninth birthday!"

"Pierre's present for Ludmilla!" said the patient again, very slowly, as if learning that lesson. "The bear!" And she laughed, but her laugh soon became a violent cough, which in one second caused her face to swell and turn purple. Mary came with a towel, Frieda held the patient's head, and after a short while the face cleared even more completely and a strange, childish expression made her look very much like Sonia.

"The bear dances!" she said, and started laughing again.

"You must not laugh, Mamachen, or we will send the bear away!"

She stopped laughing immediately and became somber. "Ivan?" she asked, and the doctor greeted Ivan, who "spoke" to his mother for a few seconds while she listened so intently that she seemed to have forgotten the others in the room. "Yes, Ivan, yes, Ivan, yes, I know," she said gravely. Then Ivan was forgotten. "Olga?" she asked, and Olga was produced from the window. She stared at Olga and said nothing, then asked, "Where is your father?"

"Here," said the doctor. "Can't you see him? How are you?" he asked, and Mary called, "Papa, come and say good morning to Mamachen."

The patient seemed delighted. Her husband was close to her bed, she kept smiling and nodding. Suddenly she mistook Mary's arrival with the usual towel, aimed at her chin, for some frightening appearance. "Oh," she said, panting. "Oh! Not that man!" Mary withdrew and waited. "Papa!" shouted the patient. "I did not mean to make you die of shame! I had to divorce him. He was impossible! Papa, forgive me!"

There was a solemn silence in the room. Mary knelt next to her mother's bed. Frieda had started to withdraw, but Mary called her back with a gesture and the two women now knelt there. The doctor left the room and came back with a silver crucifix he had taken down from the wall over his bed, the crucifix his parents had kissed with their last breath. He put it against the patient's lips, then on her chest, and put her hands over it. She kept looking at him while he was doing this, and suddenly she took a deep, long breath which seemed to pull all the life out of her fingers. They stiffened. Then came a snoring noise with the emission of air, which lasted much longer than the first breath, then nothing for a while, then another still stronger intake of oxygen, followed by a long, vibrating, symphonic snore, then again nothing, but for a very long while, so long in fact that both Mary and the maid lifted their heads to stare at the patient's half-closed eyelids in a face all contracted by suffering; and now an even longer intake, which was so strong that both feet stiffened and jumped up slightly under the covers. At the peak of this intake, a weak sound, muffled but still quite audible: "Mamachen."

Mary knew that the word had been taken up to heaven, it had gone back to the ancestors, where it would stay. Never, in all the years she had lived close to her mother, had she heard that word pronounced by her or that person described.

The room seemed empty, Ludmilla, Pierre, Ivan and Olga were gone, there remained only the doctor, Mary and the chambermaid, the three of them kneeling and crying while—strange for that time of year—a violent thunderstorm was beginning to rage over the garden and the house. Lightning flashes lit the room, flickering on the empty eyes of the dead woman, grumbling furiously with all the wrath of the Protestant Lord to Whom she had addressed so many volumes of impertinent letters during the sixty-five tormented years of her existence.

XXVI

WHEN THE DAY BROKE and the strange thunderstorm died down, that room, the center of all life in that house for so long, had become a veranda. The door shook, receiving wind and snow from the outside; the old lady was dressed up and proud—she had never been seen by anyone in that position, like a statue which rests on the square before being lifted onto its pedestal.

People were beginning to arrive, and they gathered in the music room, where the neglected Christmas tree was still proclaiming its old message of new life. To the doctor, the very presence of these sharks, big and small, with varying degrees of dangerousness, was a new lesson. Looking at them, he knew what great impediments there are for the rich before they can feel loved. She was right to despise money as she did, he thought. And who was I to come and teach her a lesson?

These visitors were for the most part underlings, hotel owners and merchants. But there were some rich people among them, who had never seen the old lady and would never have accepted her friendship, but who had taken a special pleasure in adding her name to their lists of benefactors, donors, endowers, builders, reformers. They were united today in their financial grief; the cow was dead, no longer would they know where to ask for large sums without having to explain, to plead, to make a point. Before, they had always counted on her (and always repaid her with contempt for her generous response).

Who had told them of her death? Had they been waiting on the road beyond the garden walls, almost in ambush, to come out with their message of grief the moment she no longer needed their love?

Here was Countess Etruscoli di Torretrusca. The doctor knew her name because she had a villa in the neighborhood and her servants were Adalgisa's friends. Also because she had spread many rumors about his illegal situation and his failure to go to church. Why had she come? And so early in the morning?

She ran toward him and said, "Our dear benefactress is no more!" Then she took both his hands in her own and looked into his eyes. "I see that you more than anyone else are aware of the loss that has befallen your dear wife and your children. We must be strong, very, very strong, and try to be worthy of her. What a generous soul! The bishop said last night, speaking of her, 'Almost a Catholic—in fact, a better Catholic than many of us.' The bishop wishes to be remembered to you and to Madame. He offers his prayers, his most fervent prayers."

The doctor knew this to be a lie, but he not only accepted it, he responded with tears. "Mary is unable to come downstairs," he said. "She has been wonderful, she has had not one minute of rest since Christmas Eve, and it was only when . . . this happened that she broke down. You know, she was very close to her mother."

"Oh, don't I know? Everybody in town admires your wife for this. But no wonder. With such a mother, how could a daughter not be attached to her?"

The doctor wondered how much this evil woman knew, and he said severely, "She was a most generous person. Many people have taken advantage of her."

"How true, how profoundly true, and how sad. But it must be a great consolation to you that some at least have become better human beings by the mere fact of accepting her generosity *as a lesson.*"

He was through with her and beginning to scan the horizon of black coats and frowning faces, all ready to come up to him with more of the same nonsense.

"I don't want to keep you much longer," she said, "and besides, there is so little one can do on such occasions. I only wish to add that the orphans of Milan are sending her a floral tribute. What else could they offer, poor dears? And their prayers, of course, those count far more." With these words she was gone, as if escaping from her own comedy.

He observed her as she left, saw in her way of walking down the garden path the eagerness with which she would now go and spread more poisonous gossip about him and his family. A peasant with a huge wreath over his shoulders passed her and she turned back to see if the black ribbon with the gold lettering on it was from her little orphans of Milan.

We paid for this too, thought the doctor, as he saw the wreath walk into the house all by itself—only the puffing betrayed the presence of a human being behind it.

A few more handshakes and a few more assurances that Life Cannot End Here. He was beginning to wonder whether they were all making fun of him, when someone added to the usual nonsense the remark that perhaps one hundred thousand people had been killed that same night in southern Italy.

Then he saw the newspaper that some visitors had brought with them, and it said that an earthquake of cosmic proportions had destroyed half of Sicily and Calabria, killing entire populations and wiping out whole cities. Apulia was not touched, except by lighter tremors that had caused a great deal of panic and made the church bells in the region ring for hours. Further details were unobtainable, communications had been disrupted, trains were carrying anguished relatives and regiments to exhume the dead, rescue the wounded, feed and house the homeless and protect the whole region from thieves.

He became completely absorbed in the news. He knew he must take the first train and go home, even if his own region was not touched. This called for his presence, not only as a relative but as a doctor—all the doctors of Italy who could go south were asked by the papers to offer their assistance. His first impulse was to send telegrams to all his relatives and ask for news, then he remembered what he had just read: communications were disrupted. Again the difference between his world and the world of the rich was flung at him. Even in death the rich had their privileges and were served with private tears, while the poor had no tears for the immensity of their plight.

I am not needed here, he thought. Mary will understand. This is the first installment of the price we must pay.

Now all the objects in the house, and all those that had arrived because of this funeral (such as that wreath walking along by itself) and every garment on the back of a visitor became a symbol of money. He could no longer stand it. He saw figures and bank notes everywhere. And he felt it his duty to steal everything, or, rather, to steal back what had been stolen, even down to his own English suit, his shirt, his necktie and his pearl tiepin, and the rings on his fingers—everything must go.

Mary will understand, he thought again as in a trance. Mary will understand.

He was already on his way upstairs when he saw a commotion in the crowd and heard a noise of wheels and horses on the gravel outside. The house door was flung open by the butler and everyone looked at him, it was his duty to receive the guests.

The noise had been a fiacre so charged with suitcases and trunks that it seemed as if the old lady herself were back from one of her long trips. But when the old lady herself actually stepped out of the fiacre, the doctor knew that this was a hallucination, and he made a great effort not to lose his self-control. He closed his eyes to cancel the mistaken impression, then opened them again—but there she was again.

She threw herself into his arms and sobbed, "Mamachen, oh, Mamachen!" The voice alone was Ludmilla's.

The two sisters met at the top of the stairs. Mary had just come out of her mother's room for a moment of respite when she saw her mother coming upstairs and recognized her. In contrast to her husband's behavior, she did not try to keep her hold on reality, she was glad to be frightened. But she soon realized who it was.

"Ludmilla!" she cried. "Ludmilla, what have you done?" There was horror in her voice.

Ludmilla understood it and for that reason became even more like her mother. She took Mary's head between her hands, with a great gesture typical of her mother's most detestable moments of high melodrama, and said, using the sacred words over which she had fought with Mary in early childhood, "Mops, Kindchen, komm zu mir."

This did it. Both sisters were now back in their childhood, and since their mother was no more, their feud had no scope now, and over these things they cried. Finally Mary took Ludmilla into the room and showed her to the pale corpse, as if to ask, "Which of you two should wear these clothes? Decide, Mamachen, please decide." But as Mamachen continued to stay dead, the tear stream found new channels and could flow past the dry lands of used-up images.

The sisters cried until they had forgotten why they cried and Mary found the strength to say, "Ludmilla, please go to my room and take anything you find in my closets, anything, but please don't wear what you are wearing now."

Ludmilla, who had been looking for fresh tears, applied them to the corpse at once, as she screamed at her sister, "What have I done to you? Must you, even today? Why don't you leave me alone?"

And Mary cried in answer, with fresh tears of her own, "Can't you understand?"

"No, I can't. I can't, I can't!"

"Haven't you even a little respect?"

"You, rather, have no respect at all. What is wrong with this dress? Would you want me to wear pink, or white? I had this made expressly in Milan. Such an ordeal—first with the seamstress, now with you. What do you want of me? Leave me alone!"

Mary wept out of resignation now. "You are right. Forgive me, I spoke only because it reminded me too much of . . . of . . ." And her hand showed the door beyond which no one now cared even if they ate each other alive. And because no one cared, they pretended someone did, and for the first time in their lives they made peace, undictated, unthreatened by Mamachen, and swore solemnly that they would never fight again. But Mary noticed that her sister kept looking at the mirror and that even her tears were now directed at the mirror, no longer at the corpse. She noticed it and swore to herself never to forget it as long as she lived. Ludmilla for her part observed that Mary could never have dressed up as she had and made the impression she made.

Mary is not like Mamachen at all, she thought. I alone am her successor.

Mary did not have the time to grasp the meaning of the earthquake; or, rather, she did, but only in terms of her own tragedy. At first she was taken aback by the sight of a newspaper in her husband's hands. How could he still be interested in the world when the worst thing in the world had taken place under his roof?

"Here, look at this," he said. She looked at him instead, as if he had committed sacrilege; then she decided to look at the paper, hoping to find an explanation for his behavior.

"GIGANTIC EARTHQUAKE DESTROYS MESSINA, ENTIRE POPULATION KILLED," she read.

She threw a glance at the first lines of the report to see if by any chance the hours coincided and was satisfied to see they did.

"Of course," she said, with a sigh of relief. "During that thunderstorm. How terrible." She might have said, "How wonderful," it would have sounded more sincere. "How really frightful!" She was discovering more things she liked. "Unbe-liev-able! Good God! One hundred thousand victims—and this is only the first estimate! Poor, poor Sicilians. How I understand them! How close I feel to them!" She nodded in approval. God had seen fit to split open the earth and make the sea recede for miles before it lifted its white crest sky-high and beat the burning city and killed whoever had not been already killed by fire and earthquake—all this to give the world a pale idea of what she and her family had lost. "It is the end of everything," she said, now feeling proud, as if her mother had achieved it all by simply abandoning the world to its fate. "I knew the world could not go on without Mamachen." She was not crying now.

"This is not all," said the doctor. "Read down here."

"What?" she said joyfully. "More earthquakes? Don't tell me!"

"No, but it seems—"

The butler interrupted him. "Two cars are at the gate, but they cannot come uphill."

Pierre had arrived with his personal valet, his secretary and his light luggage, which consisted of fifteen suitcases and five steel-bound trunks. The cabs he had taken, one for himself and two for his servants, were so overloaded that they couldn't make the steep grade, and so the luggage had to be unloaded at the foot of the hill and carried up piece by piece, and the trunks were thin and long, they had to be carried like coffins, every one of them by four men, two in front, two in back—the pallbearers of wealth.

This was a funeral in reverse, only that out of one funeral he had made five. Pierre waited for the whole thing to be over, even though he was anguished and impatient to see his dying mother. He knew nothing of her death, but he detested all interference by either objects or servants who carried them.

As he approached the house, Mary became frightened again. He too looked like his mother now. And his first words were a stab in her heart. That was her voice, her arrogance, the worst of her.

He did not have to ask. He understood and, as he kissed Mary, blinked in a vain effort to shed tears.

Even upstairs he could not cry. He looked at his dead mother in silence, frowning exactly as he had always frowned in expectation of the storm that always came after a first moment of silence. Thus it was only after the first moment had passed that their reciprocal behavior showed the presence of death. The usual play had come to a stop. No storm exploded from her eyes and lips, no counterstorm began to gather in his eyes and on his countenance. He had not been received. This was no meeting, only a juxtaposition of dead images.

Mary was watching him and stiffening in an expression of indignant curiosity. Does he really feel nothing? she thought. Ludmilla was watching them both and taking her eyes off them every few seconds for a quick glance at the door (but the doctor did not come), and soon it was clear to them that their mother was stronger in her silence than she had ever been before. They were losing the race. Imperceptible noises from their noses, their throats, their knuckles or their shoes disqualified them for the competition in muteness. Even the windows came alive in the wind, and the wreaths and the flowerpots crowding the space between the windows and the bed were also alive with the clatter of leaves. There was the sound of wheels on the gravel, the steps of horses, the loud voice of a coachman and the squeaking of brakes. Someone else had arrived. Mary slipped out of the room.

Ludmilla and Pierre stayed, alone together. Pierre looked at her as if he had not noticed her attire a few minutes before when—blinking nervously, again without results—he had kissed her. He looked at her and looked at her, more and more angrily, then walked sidewise as people do in church so as not to turn their backs to the altar; and when he was close to her he said, "Must you be an actress even on such occasions? I for one find it in bad taste. Go change your clothes."

Ludmilla stared at her mother, her lips quivering, and the tears for which he envied her so much came back to her and she let them roll freely down her cheeks, as a reproach to him. He frowned, blinked uselessly for the third time, turned his back to his mother and walked out.

Ivan had arrived, with his wife and one suitcase. He too had expected to find his mother still alive, and he too looked like her, but in her best and weakest moments. When he and Pierre stood facing each other, they looked like two versions of the same basic theme of egotism and shyness. Pierre took it out on the world; Ivan, on himself, with the result that he looked somber and subdued. Tears came easily to him; he always cried over himself, and had plenty to cry about. Which angered Pierre even more, as he went on blinking, still with no effect.

Then Mr. Schultz arrived. He had not come to stay, had brought no suitcase, had arrived walking in the rain and had forgotten his galoshes. He alone carried with him as he entered the house some of that same earth to which the old lady had returned.

"I am sorry," he said, watching his shoes intently as he wiped them on the mat in the entrance hall, "the road is simply buried in mud." Then he lifted his face to see if his unfortunate wording had been noticed—and it had. Mary, the

568

doctor, Ivan and his wife were all crying. Should I apologize? he wondered, then decided to let time pass over this wound; but he knew it would always stick in their memories, even years afterward. He decided to atone for this frightful *faux pas* by making an exception to the rule and exhibiting some of his grief. He knew the hysterical habits of the family and disliked them, as he disliked all unrestrained displays of feelings, so much so that his grief, which had almost exploded into sobs as he was walking up the hill in the rain, disappeared now at once, as if he did not know who the dead person was or who these people were. Mary felt it at once and began to observe him with that slight impoliteness which is possible only in the presence of death.

"My daughter and her husband were so grieved," he said, knowing perfectly well that this was the wrong thing to say, because no one could care, "that they did not find the strength to come or to send flowers."

"That is kind of them," said Mary, smiling sadly. "How are they?"

"Oh, very, very well."

Only then did it occur to her how unkind it had been of the Marchesa Tempi and her husband not to send flowers or a telegram if they did not feel like coming. "Everybody is being so nice to us," she said, crying without restraint.

Mr. Schultz looked at her intently and nodded in his usual manner, as if he were listening to some business report. He also blinked like Pierre—Mary noticed it. But his eyes remained dry.

"Up this way," said the doctor, feeling profoundly ashamed of his gesture, which he feared might be interpreted to mean "Come and see what I did in my capacity as a doctor."

Mr. Schultz began to climb the stairs. Pierre met them on the landing. He was just leaving his room and trying to pass off his boredom as deep sorrow. A quick glance in the mirror proved to him that he had not quite succeeded, so he rearranged his frown to appear more tragic. When he saw Mr. Schultz, whom he had last seen (without speaking to him) at his club in London three years before, he decided to ignore him again. This was his right, he was here the First Mourner, as his mother's first son.

"Pierre," said Mr. Schultz, closing his eyes and stretching out his hands.

"Frightfully sorry, sir," said Pierre in English, "my name is Pierre Vladimirovitch von Randen." And almost but not quite moved to tears by his cruel behavior, which his mother would never have condoned, Pierre slowly walked downstairs, regretting that he had not done more to finally provoke those tears.

Mr. Schultz had the same sentimental near miss and the same afterthought as he stood there on the landing, shaking his head in silent disapproval and feeling absolutely indifferent. The doctor noticed it. He knew these states of negative volition or emotional impotence; he had, in fact, begun to study them in the book of the German psychologist Wundt, *Diseases of the Will.*

"In here," he whispered, slowly lowering the handle of the door to the death chamber, and thinking of the earthquake again to give his voice a more natural pathos.

Mr. Schultz nodded as he entered the room and looked at the face of his friend, who seemed as tired of her role as he was of his. He was frowning so terribly that the doctor took pity on him and touched him on the shoulder, indicating a chair next to the bed. But Mr. Schultz refused it, with obvious disapproval. And having made that first gesture of "No," he went on with it as if it were the theme he had been looking for. "No and no and no. This is not possible." It slowly became clear to him that no action was expected, so his prudent advice was useless.

Now he nodded again, beginning to realize that his friend was really dead. Never before had she remained so indifferent to his approval or his disapproval. And he finally succeeded in crying. Tears formed under his eyelids, and as soon as they fell he showed them to the doctor and was sorry that Mary was not present to witness them, too. He won't bother to tell her, he said to himself. This thought restored the inner balance that had been upset with such difficulty, and there he stood, nodding again, disapproving again, to no avail. His eyes were not even a bit red.

Never had the old lady's authority been more supreme. All these arrivals, all these efforts to show grief, were exactly what she had always wanted and exactly in the style she had imagined for them. In fact, they did a great deal to restore the feeling of her presence in the house.

Mary had remained upstairs, she had entered the death chamber again just in time to observe Mr. Schultz emerge from it completely untouched by what he had seen. And he had wandered a great deal along the halls, stopping in front of every window and trying very hard, with the help of the rain and the desolate garden scene, to refill his old heart with some of the sadness that had seemed so unbearable on his way there from town. The others had all gathered in the dining room some time ago and were confronted now with grave decisions. Who should be first to admit his burning interest in material things? Here the butler had come with a huge tureen of soup and was standing next to it, spoon in hand, and questioning every one of the faces that came up to him. The mourners walked all around the table with their hands behind their backs or their arms folded, they looked at him, looked at the soup and noticed that it was slowly getting cold—but no one dared.

The doctor, who was really not interested in food at all, suddenly sniffed the flavor of the soup and said, in an authoritative voice, "Let's all sit down and eat. Mary will join us later."

He sat down, staring at his plate, and when a bowl of soup was placed on it he acknowledged its presence by unfolding

571

his napkin, taking a spoon and lowering it into the steaming liquid. The others waited a bit longer, hoping that someone would insist, almost force them, and they regretted it, because the doctor ate his soup in peace, then looked at them and, when he noticed Ludmilla seated in her mother's chair and again looking so much like her, said angrily, "Get up from there. Take any other chair, not that one. Quickly, now, before Mary comes."

Ludmilla obeyed like a child, and there was, in the way she suddenly shunned contact with that chair, something of the sacred horror of death in her. But Pierre took all this as a personal insult to him. Who was this man to give orders to his sister in their own house, where he had been only a guest? He looked at the doctor with growing indignation, but before anyone knew what he was going to say he bowed his head on the table and cried like a child, pushing glasses and dishes away from him, upsetting his own and his neighbor's soup bowl and a bottle of white wine. Everyone else cried with him, and this was, they all felt, what their mother would have wanted. Now they could force one another to eat—because she would have wanted them to eat. When Mr. Schultz arrived like the next candidate for death, having managed to look tragic just because he did not feel so, the others were already in that state of grieved attention which follows the first violent outburst of tears and precedes a good meal.

"Is there any Veuve Clicquot Ponsardin?" asked Pierre, speaking to both the butler and his brother-in-law. "My mother used to have some famous wines, and I drink only champagne with my meals."

The butler bowed and went to satisfy Pierre's wishes, and the doctor did not seem to take offense. He was, in fact, relieved and almost touched that Pierre felt at home.

With a whole bottle of champagne down his throat, and another one coming in a hurry, Pierre began to feel affectionate.

"But why is it," he asked, "that you refused to let Malachier come, once Uncle Jules had arranged it?"

The doctor flushed and said, "It was too late." He hastened to add, "But Dr. Cappelli came, he is a very good physician."

Pierre stared for a long while at his champagne. "Oh, well," he said finally, "one doctor is as good as another."

"How right you are. And all of us put together are worth nothing at all. Believe me, I know it well. What can medicine do? What can anyone do when the big hour strikes?"

"You are probably right," said Pierre. "Uncle Jules has a blind faith in Malachier, but then Uncle Jules is a damned fool. Malachier lost five days of consultations, but to hell with Malachier. He will send you his bill. I promised you would pay him. I said, 'Send him the bill. If money is all you want, you can have it.' "

"Right," said the doctor, and it was now his turn to grieve.

Pierre finally ate something, forgiving every teaspoonful of caviar, every slice of black bread, every bite of chicken, roast beef, every potato, every glass of champagne, before they were admitted to his mouth, as if these things had betrayed his trust in them for years and were now given a new chance to tell him the truth.

Ludmilla, Ivan—and his silent wife—and Mr. Schultz were showing a more charitable attitude toward their food. They humbly chose from the many dishes and trays on the table and picked this or that thing with a truly Samaritan fork. But every now and then the bulk of food coming in through their mouths met with bolts of burning pain coming up from their hearts (a fragment of dear memories wrecked in a sea of tears), and the two fought like dogs in a dark alley. Down came the fork, down came the glass, and the hands of the mourner covered his face.

The doctor was not eating at all now, he was mentally saving to pay Malachier for his mistakes. So he patted the mourners on the back and said, "Life must go on. Eat, it's good for you."

573

Pierre must have guessed his thoughts, because he smiled and said, "Why don't you eat, too, as long as there is something in the house? Or are you saving on bread crumbs again as you have saved on cooks and chauffeurs and Rolls-Royces?"

The doctor looked at him, and from then on until he died many years later he never understood why at that moment, instead of hating Pierre for his vulgar remark, he loved him like a god. "How do you know?" he asked, and Pierre laughed.

"My dear fellow," he said, "you are famous. Your economic theories have been discussed in the London Stock Exchange, in Berlin banking circles, in Moscow, even in New York. Come, now, eat something as long as there is food on the table. Make yourself at home, perhaps this is the last time you will be eating a good meal."

And again the doctor felt an urge to worship Pierre, kneeling in front of him, and again this left him very much confused; he did not know what to think of himself. He hated him a minute later, but only when he noticed that there was nothing left to eat or drink.

"Wasn't I right?" said Pierre, loudly enough to be heard by the others too. "You always come too late." Then, turning to the butler: "Is there still something in the kitchen? Bring also a few more bottles of champagne."

"Thank you," said the doctor, and his voice was unsteady. The next minute he found himself gagged in black velvet. Ludmilla's arms were holding his head from behind.

"You are a good man," she said. "Let me bring you something to eat."

And she ran out of the room, to come back a few minutes later with a tray in her hands, like a servant. The butler walked behind her with two bottles. Pierre and Ivan were laughing. Mr. Schultz was looking on with glassy eyes. He had not followed the discussion and seemed lost in his own thoughts.

The doctor ate like a good child, while Ludmilla sat beside him, filling his glass and even, at one moment, feeding him

574

when he began to cry. Pierre was amused by the spectacle and smoked a cigar. But soon he too was unamused and cried into his champagne glass for a moment, before he became as absent and looked on as stupidly as Mr. Schultz. That was the moment Ludmilla lost interest in the doctor and went over to Pierre. She whispered something in Russian and the two of them left the room, arm in arm. They crossed the various rooms until they reached the Christmas tree, then they turned back and Pierre called his brother. Ivan joined them, and the three of them walked back and forth, from the dining-room table to the Christmas tree, from one end of the house to the dining-room table, through different periods of furniture, paintings, porcelains and fabrics, while the doctor, Mr. Schultz and Ivan's wife watched them in silence, feeling like intruders, with no way of expressing their opinions because they had nothing in common. The first two or three times the walking group seemed very close, as if their grief had welded them together for the rest of their lives. They did not even look at the rooms they were crossing. Then they began to observe what was around them and disappeared from sight as they examined this or that object to the right or left of their path, appraising everything—but still only on the basis of sentimental values. Each object reminded them of their dead mother, their dead father, their dead childhood illusions. However, they soon disentangled themselves, each with arms folded, thoughts active, an isolated being poisoned by greed.

What with hunger, fatigue and the cold air, Mary had fallen asleep in her chair next to her mother's body.

"Where do you think you are?" asked Pierre, shaking her brutally. "If you have no feelings, at least show some respect for us who have."

"I am sorry," said Mary.

"Not so loud," said Pierre, who had now lost all his capacity for crying and was furious. Mary left the room in tears. He ran after her, and Ludmilla, who was angry at Pierre, joined them in the hall.

"I don't know how it happened," said Mary, "but you must understand, I have not slept for weeks."

"As if we had been having a good time," said Pierre, feeling tender again at the thought of his sacrifice. "You were here all the time. I—I never saw her again." The flow was re-established.

"No one prevented you from coming earlier," said Mary.

"Mary . . . Pierre," said Ludmilla in sobs. "Please—please remember . . ."

Mary took refuge in her sister's arms. "I am sorry. I never meant to say such a terrible thing, but he made me. Pierre forgets how many times I asked him to come, how often *she* hoped he would come—he forgets everything. To reproach me for this!"

Pierre burst into loud sobs and beat his head against the wall. "No one told me she was dying," he said.

"You knew it for years," cried Mary, cold with hate. "And all you did was write her angry letters. Do you think those helped her live longer?"

Pierre crouched on the floor. Mary now knelt next to him and implored him to forgive her. The whole house came alive with their sobs, as if their mother had just died at that moment; and they finally dragged themselves back to her room, that being the natural place for their discharge of sorrow.

The doctor had gone out of the house before this happened. When he returned they were still crying audibly. He was not alone. The undertaker and an employee of the Swiss Railways were with him.

"I cannot let you see her," said the doctor. "The whole family is upstairs."

"But we must have a look at the freight," said the railroad man.

"I would suggest," said the undertaker, "that you use more respectful language. And that you leave everything to me."

"It is the language of the regulation," said the employee, "and I am not employed by you. I know my duty, and if you don't use more respectful language yourself with the employees of the Federal Railways, you can take your corpse to Berlin by your own means. No freight service for you."

"I am sorry," said the undertaker. "I did not mean to offend you."

"But you did and you are still trying to interfere with our services. I have to see the freight and to take measurements."

"Sorry," said the undertaker, "but that is my job. I make the coffins."

"Gentlemen," said the doctor, "no one has to take measurements. A coffin is not like a dress, which must fit."

"But you don't even know how tall she is."

"Very tall. Make it a big coffin, the biggest you can find."

"No, sir, we are not in the habit of doing our business sloppily. There are coffins and coffins. I refuse to provide a coffin that is not satisfactory."

"Satisfactory to whom, may I ask?"

"To our client."

"I am the client in this case. You cannot serve an object, or what the gentleman here calls 'freight.' "

"All the same, sir, all the same, I must see the . . . person."

"And so must I," said the railroad employee. "If you want to take the express to Berlin tomorrow night, I have to file a complete statement by tonight."

"Very well. Will you wait here for a moment, until I get the family out of that room and we can go upstairs?"

The doctor went up to the bedroom. The sobbing had now died down to occasional sniffing and sighing. It was almost four o'clock. Somewhere behind the clouds the first sunset of death was taking place, colorless, unnoticed but for a paler quality in the light. Someone had closed the window; the

577

sweetish smell of organic decay was mixing with the perfume of flowers and candles. One candle had been lit already and more were being inserted into the silver candelabra Adalgisa had polished and brought from the dining room. No one was looking at them yet, but the doctor was certain that the moment someone did new tears of envy would be offered in tribute to the powerless corpse.

He touched Mary on the shoulder; she looked at him, said no with her head, then whispered, "Thank you. I am not hungry."

Ludmilla was watching them. He made a sign to her and walked out of the room.

"Ludmilla," he said, after closing the door behind them, "can you do me a favor? I have to get you all out of this room— you know why. I have the men downstairs, and this must be done now or we won't be allowed to leave tomorrow. Mary has had no sleep, no food, for the last I don't know how many hours. Will you see to it that she leaves and has something to eat?"

Ludmilla nodded without speaking a word and went back into the room. Less than a minute later she and Mary, arm in arm, were going downstairs, followed by Pierre and Ivan.

Even the samovar was shedding poison now. It had acquired a "sentimental value." Mary felt it as she was pouring tea. Pierre looked at it from above the newspaper he was reading. He was waiting for something—certainly not for tea, because he had a bottle of Napoleon brandy open in front of him and was drinking frequently from a large glass which was also shedding poison, together with the dozens of matching glasses that were part of a precious old service. And so were all the cups and the spoons shedding poison, and the sugarbowl and the small napkins and the tablecloth, because on every one of these items of property there was the old lady's monogram.

"I have never learned Italian, yet I can read it very well," said Pierre.

"Can you, really?" asked Mary.

"Yes. I can translate while reading: 'One hundred thousand victims in a gigantic earthquake in Sicily . . . tidal waves of untold proportions . . . all of southern Italy affected . . . Never before, since the Lisbon earthquake in the seventeenth century, which caused the church bells of Amsterdam to ring, has one of this gravity been experienced.' But isn't that the region your husband comes from? He must be very worried."

Mary frowned, she looked at the door, hoping that the doctor would come in, and Pierre went on reading: " 'All the doctors in Italy are rushing to the scene to bring their help. . . . The King of Italy was among the very first to leave for Messina. The Government of the French Republic is sending medicines and medical assistance. The Emperor of Russia has telegraphed his heartfelt condolences. His Majesty William the Second, Emperor of Germany and King of Prussia . . . His Majesty George the Fifth, King of England and Emperor of India . . .' Shall I go on?"

"No, thank you," said Mary. "One or two lumps, Ivan?"

"Why isn't your husband going?" asked Pierre.

Mary was about to answer when Mr. Schultz opened the door into the room, then, seeing Pierre, withdrew and closed the door.

"Mr. Schultz!" called Mary. "Mr. Schultz!"

The door opened again, Mr. Schultz appeared briefly and made a sign to her meaning "Come out here, I must talk to you privately."

Pierre could not see him, he had turned his back to the door, and when Ivan looked, Mr. Schultz had already disappeared again.

"May I be excused for a moment?" said Mary, and she rose from her chair.

"Where are you going?" asked Pierre.

"I'll be back in a second, don't move, please."

This sounded like an order and her gesture was clear as she

579

turned back from the door before leaving the room. "One second," she said, lifting a finger to mean "one" and also "Don't you dare."

Out in the hall Mr. Schultz was asking the butler for his overcoat and hat.

"Dear Mary," he said, "it is better for me and for you if I leave. I don't care to see Pierre again, but I don't want to make a scene or to provoke him. It is unfortunate that he should have such a bad character. I pity him, I am not really angry at him, but there is nothing I can do. So I had better go to my hotel. I shall come back when you return from Berlin. I am leaving for Italy tomorrow, you know that I have large investments in Southern Italian Railways and Tramways, there has been a most frightful earthquake and I must go there to have a look at the situation and also to bring help to the homeless. It is one of the moral obligations that a man like myself cannot neglect. And you don't need me here."

"But we do need you here. Do you have to go now? Can't you stay until dinnertime at least? Or spend the night? Please don't go."

At that moment Pierre appeared from the dining room and said, "Mary is right, Mr. Schultz, we need you here, you must stay on."

This was the occasion Mr. Schultz had tried to avoid. His conversation with Mary had been in Russian, Pierre had also spoken Russian to him, but he now answered in his best English. "Oh, I hear you speak Russian. Isn't your name Pierre Vladimirovitch von Randen?" Pierre's face became livid with anger. Mr. Schultz went on, his tone still aggressive. "I only wanted to make sure," he said, "that this was the same *gentleman* I met on the stairs as I arrived this morning."

"I am," said Pierre, in a shrill voice which was unnatural to him, "and I am also the same gentleman you met five years ago in the London Stock Exchange and did not recognize."

Mr. Schultz opened his arms in a sad gesture of apology,

which was also a reproach. "Young man," he said, "the occasion then was different, less grave, and I may have been wrong at that time, I am ready to admit it. But the difference in age between us was the same then as it is now. I happen to have been a junior partner in your grandfather's firm, and a lifelong adviser, almost a father, to your poor mother. My reactions must be excused in the light of my old-fashioned upbringing. I have never been able to accept the modern principle that a young man, no matter how intelligent, has a right to treat his mother as you did in those days. But you were spoiled by too much praise—especially by her praise, for she worshiped you, as you probably know. However, let us forget the past. Here is my hand."

Pierre shook hands with him, but an expression of disgust was on his lips. Then, in the coldest tone, he said, "You are the executor. We are leaving tomorrow and cannot come back here to read the will."

"I know, I know. But I am not in possession of the most recent will. I know nothing about it."

"Who does? Who has it?"

"I don't know. I was asked to give the name of a reliable notary and I gave it, but my suggestion was turned down by telegram. Your mother had found someone here who was just as trustworthy and of course less expensive. She was right."

The doctor was just coming downstairs with two men. He showed them to the door, then joined the group.

"Did you advise Mamachen in the rewriting of her will?" asked Pierre very coldly, in French.

"No," he said, "of course not."

"But you do know that she rewrote it."

"Yes, I do, but that is all I know."

"Well, that will is not valid. Mr. Schultz is her executor, and if he has no evidence of a new will, the only legal one is the one he still has in his possession. I hope, Mr. Schultz, you still have it?"

"I have, but I also have your mother's letter and telegram referring to her intention of drafting an entirely new will."

"Well, it is not valid. She was sick when she wrote it—or was made to write it."

"What do you mean?" asked Mary in a very loud voice that brought Ivan, his wife and Ludmilla out of the dining room.

"Exactly what I said."

"Let's not discuss these matters here," said Mr. Schultz, and they all moved to the blue drawing room next to the entrance hall, the room so familiar to Ludmilla.

"Let's sit down," said Mr. Schultz.

"Thank you for the invitation," said Pierre. "I happen to be in my own house, in *our* house, I should say, *our mother's* house. And I choose to stand up. Now, you, there," he said to the doctor, "you are familiar with the matter. You advised her, you provided her with a notary of your choosing, one you trusted, I suppose."

"Of course one I trusted. I certainly would not have recommended one I did not trust."

"You were not her executor, it was none of your business. Mr. Schultz had provided her with one he trusted, why did you have to meddle in her private affairs? This is all highly illegal."

"I am sorry," said the doctor. "I merely suggested a solution less expensive than the one she had in mind."

"You had no right to suggest anything at all."

"Pierre, please, Pierre," said Mr. Schultz. "One notary is as good as another."

"That is what I say," said the doctor.

"Like doctors, I suppose," said Pierre.

"What is this about doctors?" asked Mary.

"Be quiet, Mary," said the doctor.

"Oh, you don't know?" said Pierre. "Well, let me explain. Malachier was supposed to come here and see Mamachen when she was ill. Uncle Jules arranged it all, and your husband refused him, because in this case too he had a doctor he alone trusted, one of those slimy Italian country doctors who know nothing at all."

"I beg your pardon, Pierre, Italian doctors are as good as a hundred Malachiers put together, and it was not Uncle Jules who arranged for Malachier to come, it was my husband."

"That is a lie. I saw the telegram, I spoke to Malachier myself and saw your husband's telegram to Uncle Jules, and his reply."

"False. Uncle Jules never answered our telegram."

"But I told you I was there when he answered it."

"You were with Uncle Jules?"

"I was with Uncle Jules, even if this displeases you. His guest, to be more precise. I saw the two telegrams. No matter now. Malachier was kept idle for five days because your husband probably wanted to save on doctors and on telegrams—his usual way. That is all a thing of the past. Malachier will send you the bill for five days of idleness. At the rate of one thousand francs an hour that makes a pretty good sum you will pay out of your pocket, not out of ours. Enough of this. Let's see the will for whatever it is worth."

"But I swear to you I don't know where it is."

"Let's find it."

"Where?"

"Wherever it is most likely to be. Not in the kitchen stove, I suppose."

"Do we have to do it now?"

"I cannot very well come back from Moscow for the purpose. We can discuss it in Berlin if you prefer, but we must have it with us, and we might as well look at it once we have it, to see if it is legal."

"I refuse to open Mamachen's desk," said Mary, sobbing again.

"All right," said Pierre coldly. "I can open it for you."

"No. I refuse to let anyone open it. Not so long as she is here."

"Where is that notary? May we see him?"

The doctor tried to say, "Yes, I shall send for him at once," but all he managed was to cough and blink and blush and bow to Pierre like a butler, and then leave the room.

Pierre was ashamed of himself and angry that he was ashamed. He would have wished to be angrier—in fact, so angry that he would not notice the enormity of his behavior. Ivan and Ludmilla, who were just as concerned about the will as he was, were behaving like traitors. They stayed closer to Mary than to him, they tried to comfort her, they shook their heads in disapproval and avoided his glance.

"What is this?" he asked. "Don't you all agree with me? Or don't you care? Ludmilla, Ivan, I am speaking to you: Do you care or don't you care whether your mother has left something to you?"

The two just looked at him severely, in an effort to stop him.

"What is all this hypocrisy? May I have a clear answer? This is the third time I have asked you."

Mr. Schultz now left the room in a rage. Mary saw him, wiped her tears and called him back.

"I want you to be here when I answer my brother," she said. Then, turning to Pierre: "For your information, I am never afraid to lose money or material possessions. I could not despise them more."

"Nonsense," he said, "you have never lived without them. Ask your husband. He must know what it means to live in poverty; as a matter of fact, he has shown a remarkable attachment to our money and possessions. Bernhard and Luther told us!"

"Pierre!" said Ludmilla. "Pierre, please!"

The doctor was just coming back like a slave eager to be beaten when Mary exploded, after looking at him with great severity. He thought for a moment that she was going to accuse him suddenly of murdering her mother and dismiss him like an unfaithful servant; but she was speaking in his name, which made things even worse for him.

"You will soon see, Pierre von Randen, how much I care for material possessions and money and whether I am unable to face poverty rather than your base insults to my dignity! If I have never lived in poverty, even less have you! And long before my husband lived in poverty our father was born penniless. Easily done, to invest on the strength of a name that was not made by you! Much credit would you have in your damned London Stock Exchange and in your snobbish clubs, had your father not toiled as he did, and saved, yes, saved every penny he made!"

There was a solemn silence for a moment. As in all family scenes involving money matters, everyone thought that by not moving from his place and not changing his facial expression he could consider himself superior to the others. But Mr. Schultz, who had no interest to defend and did not care about knowing how he would behave in Pierre's place, thought it wise to avoid direct questions by humiliating Pierre.

"Shame on you," he said. "Less than twenty-four hours after your mother's death!"

The doctor at this point, having forgotten his inferior position, pulled out the big gold watch he had received for Christmas from his mother-in-law and corrected Mr. Schultz. "Less than sixteen, Mr. Schultz, less than sixteen!"

"Oh. Oh, sixteen?" asked Mr. Schultz, blushing and not quite knowing what to say. "All right, less than sixteen, then. That makes it infinitely worse. Less than sixteen."

Mary made such big eyes that the doctor felt pulverized, and Pierre burst into a loud laugh. Then, dwarfing the poor doctor with his height and putting his huge hand on the small hand that held the watch, he said, "You are a remarkable fellow, my little man. I must say you Italians are exceedingly funny at times. Nice watch you have there. It used to belong to my father. Who gave it to you?"

Had the whole world come down upon him, the doctor could not have been more crushed. How can Mary forgive me for my lies and stinginess even in the face of death? he thought. She had defended him, but only to spite Pierre, and no matter how much she pretended to hate Pierre he remained her ideal of a man whose decisions are wise because he is a success. Even his cruelty was a reason for her to admire him. No one could laugh at Pierre, no one could call him an amusing little fellow, because he was an unamusing giant; and how the doctor wished he could be like him for a second. Why, too, had he missed his chance to teach Pierre a lesson by giving him the watch and saying, "Here, you may have it, I don't like it anyway—it is too vulgar for my taste." What a great gesture that might have been! Instead of which, everybody had looked at him with contempt as he left the room like a thief.

And those thousands upon thousands upon thousands of francs that Malachier would ask—who was ever going to find them? And there was no way of refusing to pay; Mary's pride was involved. Oh, if only the money were to be given to the victims of the earthquake, what a difference that would make! He was heavy with shame, heavy with grief, heavy with panic fears of poverty. He could not even think of going upstairs to the children, whom he had not seen for almost two days (an eternity to him). And so he too, with his false reasons, did what the others had done with theirs: he offered them in tribute to the source and recipient of all tears.

Twelve candles were lit in the old lady's room. Adalgisa had brought up the silver candelabra from the dining room, after she and Brigida had polished them to the point of being worn away—by rubbing them as they rubbed pots and pans in the kitchen, with sand and laundry soap. The old lady would have found it offensive to place beside a corpse these candlesticks which were used on her dinner table. "Is that a roast of beef or a dead body?" she would have asked in the arrogant tone Pierre imitated so well. ("Nice watch you have there. It used to belong to my father. Who gave it to you?")

Brigida and Adalgisa were kneeling in a corner, whispering their prayers. They were practically motionless; when the doctor came in, their black shapes moved as little as the thick curtains in front of the open window and the palm leaves in the vases they had brought upstairs. In the short time he had spent downstairs witnessing a revival of the old lady's worst traits, these two good peasant women had transformed the dead woman into an object of worship of their own. One might have said this was a wealthy Catholic peasant who had died, giving precise instructions as to what should be done to present her to God. With a few paper flowers and silver ribbons at her feet, and more flowers at the back of her head, a whole lifetime of austere international elegance and expensive simplicity had been annulled. The newcomer to the court of the Protestant Lord was not likely to be admitted there; she was more likely to be referred to the same half-pagan god who had received the doctor's own mother in that barbaric world "down there." Every one of these things, the candelabra, the paper flowers, the ribbons, was a bearer of new evidence that she was truly dead—because she accepted all so patiently.

You alone could explain that I was right in not wanting Malachier, he thought, looking at those white, sagging cheeks that had been red and bulging only the evening before. But with you gone, Mary will not forgive me, ever. And you alone could say, "Bury me here in that small cemetery back of the garden, where it will cost nothing to carry me, instead of taking me by train to a distant foreign country." I cannot say these things.

He heard Mary's footsteps. She came in and he froze with shame and apprehension, not daring to look at her, but knowing how horrified she would be by this masquerade of flowers and ribbons.

Mary stopped near the door, and it took her a few minutes to appraise what had been done to her mother. Then she walked slowly to the end of the room where the two peasant women were kneeling, kissed them both and cried in their arms; they were her family.

The doctor did not move. The scene filled him with hope: Mary was entering his world and leaving hers. He understood what had been wrong with her; it was more than her education and her unhealthy attachment to her mother, it was also the absence of women friends who could receive her nonsense, give her theirs, serve as a bridge between him and his wife, and, in a way, even protect her against him. She was not only a woman but a whole foreign world, and he had no smooth path to reach it. Women, in the tradition of his world, must have their chambers, and whatever they say to other women is guarded even more jealously from their men than what they say to their men is from those other women. This has nothing to do with faithfulness, and, in fact, it does not become the object of male jealousy, for it would be beneath men's dignity to look into that world.

"Don't cry," said Brigida to Mary. "Look what a beautiful mother you have. When the Lord sees her come looking so beautiful, He will call the Holy Virgin and all the angels of heaven to greet her, He will take her in His arms and seat her in a star all to herself right over this house so that she can see you as if she were just outside the window here. You should be pleased instead of crying. Or don't you want your mother to be in such good company?"

"You are right, you are right," said Mary between sobs. "I am pleased." And what they had done became beautiful now because of the kind thought behind it. "We'll leave her just as she is, we won't let anyone change anything."

"Oh, but why should they? Isn't she much more beautiful this way?" And Brigida began to find resemblances between the old lady and a mountain madonna of her acquaintance.

"You know what she looks like? The Madonna of Tesserete."

"Why, of course," said Adalgisa. "They must be related."

Ludmilla appeared and broke the silence with an angry voice: "Who has done this?"

"Shhhh," said Brigida, lifting both arms.

Ludmilla turned to Mary. "We are expected downstairs, all of us."

"Downstairs?" said Mary. "I am not hungry."

"Pierre wants us downstairs."

Mary frowned with disgust and said, "Tell them we are coming." Then she looked at her husband to see if he had understood. He had.

Brigida had gone back to her prayers. Mary touched her on the shoulder and said, "We are going downstairs for a moment." Brigida nodded, meaning that she would defend the Holy Image against sacrilege.

The whole family was assembled in the room that was always called the old lady's writing room, and there was also a stranger: the notary, who seemed so happy to be the center of attention in such a gathering of fabulous-looking people, all interested in him, that he could hardly control himself and was rather pitiful, having no companions in his happiness. When Mary and her husband came in, feeling hated already for having kept everyone waiting, the notary went up to them and kissed Mary's hand, then kissed the doctor on both cheeks and whispered uncontrollably cheerful words of condolence, before sitting at the large desk again—not where the old lady had always sat, but on the opposite side, where the inkstand and the penholders stood, so that he could face his audience. He had not removed these encumbering objects, and this lessened his dignity a bit; but no one dared, he least of all, to change the position of anything on that sacred desk.

He held the will in his hands and repeated, for Mary's benefit, what he had said before to keep the others from becoming impatient. "Ladies and gentlemen, it is a sad occasion for me to be here, but then life, as we all know, ends inevitably in death, and we must all be resigned to the decrees of Divine Providence. It was a great honor for me to receive from the mouth of your dear mother the expression of her last will. She was a most remarkable person, as you all undoubtedly know, and . . ."

Pierre's twitching and the nervous agitation of his legs made the poor notary lose the thread of his speech.

". . . and . . . as I was saying . . . You will forgive me if I am so inconsiderate as to just read the document to you without saying all I wanted to about your dear mother. Because she did speak to me as if I were a friend, more than just a humble notary. And that was a great honor for me, the greatest honor I have ever . . . ah . . . received—been awarded, I mean. She treated me as a real friend and she said, 'I want my children to realize how much I love them and how much I have suffered for them.' "

He looked up, hoping to see the effect of his words in tears, the equivalent of applause, and was appalled by the tenseness, the impatience, almost the anger that surrounded him. "I am sorry," he said. "Perhaps I talk too much."

Another glance at those faces, and one more apology. "I am sorry. You must all be in a hurry. Well, now, here we go." He cleared his throat and read, in German: " 'A wise son maketh a glad father, but a foolish son is the heaviness of his mother. . . .' "

"Whatever is that nonsense you are reading?" asked Pierre, getting up and marching toward the notary with the obvious intention of crushing him between his finger tips like an insect.

The man rose from his seat and retreated backward as far as the window. "This is how the will begins," he said.

"Pierre," said Mr. Schultz very quietly, and Pierre sat down on another chair rather close to the desk.

"Go on," he said.

The notary returned and went on, again from the beginning: " 'A wise son maketh a glad father, but a foolish son is the heaviness of his mother. Treasures of wickedness profit nothing, but righteousness delivereth from death.' " He looked up again and defended himself timidly by asking, "Isn't that wonderful? I believe it's from the Bible. But perhaps it is hers, I don't know. She was—"

"Will you please read?" said Pierre.

"Yes yes yes yes, of course. 'He becometh poor that dealeth with a slack hand: but the hand of the diligent maketh rich. . . .' "

Mary was beaming, almost exalted, but the doctor was not. In the Swiss accent of the notary the meaning of the German words did not come through to him.

" 'He that troubleth his own house shall inherit the wind . . .' "

The word "inherit" made everyone shudder, and Pierre became red in the face; but he said nothing. Mary looked at Pierre, Ludmilla and Ivan, and these in turn looked at her, as if to say, "This was for you."

The notary went on: " 'And the foolish shall be servant to the wise of heart. . . .' "

"Are we through with the Proverbs?" asked Pierre.

"Proverbs? Ah—yes, almost." And the poor man went on: " 'Whosoever loveth correction loveth knowledge: but he that hateth reproof is brutish. . . .' "

Again glances were exchanged between Mary and the others, this time with sneers.

" 'There is that maketh himself rich, yet hath nothing: there is that maketh himself poor, yet hath great wealth. . . .' "

"She was very, very sick, that is all I can say," said Pierre, looking at Ludmilla and Ivan for approval.

"She was not," said Mr. Schultz in a slightly higher tone.

591

" 'Poverty and shame shall be to him that refuseth correction: but he that regardeth reproof shall be honored. . . .' "

Another glance between Mary and the others.

" 'A good man leaveth an inheritance to his children's children: and the wealth of the sinner is laid up for the righteous. . . .' "

"Are we through with the service?" asked Pierre, and now everybody looked indignant, so he lowered his head in shame.

" 'He that spareth his rod hateth his son: but he that loveth him chasteneth him betimes. . . .' "

Pierre cleared his throat.

"One more," said the notary. " 'A wise son maketh a glad father . . .' "

"We have heard that before, twice," said Pierre.

"No, no, this is different. '. . . . But a foolish man despiseth his mother.' "

"Thank you very much for a fine sermon," said Pierre, stretching his big hand across the desk, "but may I read the rest?"

"Hm. I don't think you may," said the notary, and he went on: " 'My dear children, these are some of the things I say to you and wish you never to forget. Because, as the Bible so well puts it, "There is gold, and abundance of rubies: but the lips of knowledge are a precious jewel." . . .' "

It was Ludmilla this time who looked as if she were going to do something about it. But she only straightened herself and looked so much like her mother that Mary cast her glance to the floor and shuddered.

" 'I beseech you, my children, do not quarrel over worthless material possessions. . . .' "

"Over what shall we fight, then?" asked Pierre between his teeth.

Everyone looked at him severely, and the notary went on reading, " 'The few things I still own have been justly distributed by me with the help and advice of Mr. Schultz, whom I consider as my second father and my most trusted friend. To the document now in his hands I wish to bring the following modifications: All of my jewels, none excepted, go to Mary. . . .' "

Everyone looked at Mary, and Mary said, "This is irrelevant. Mamachen's will is all contained in the beautiful words we heard before. These are the worthless possessions she was speaking of."

"Be clear," said Pierre. "What you mean is that this new will is not valid."

Mary was going to answer, but her husband gave her such a jab with his elbow that she asked him innocently, "What do you want?"

Pierre sneered, Ludmilla blushed and looked intently at the floor, and the doctor, scarlet with embarrassment, said, "Mary has no more right to attack the validity of this will than you have."

"I spoke to my sister, not to you," said Pierre in a voice shaky with anger.

"May I interrupt both of you?" said Mr. Schultz. "What you said was exactly what I was going to say. This is not Mary's will, it is her mother's will. How Mary will interpret it is an entirely different matter, and there is plenty of time for that."

"Of course," said Mary, blushing and smiling as she tried to attract Pierre's eyes. Again her husband tried to jab his elbow into her side, but she withdrew and everybody saw the elbow detach itself from the doctor's body and search for its target without finding it, while the doctor himself presented a most innocent face to the audience.

Ludmilla, whose face was red with anger, could not help smiling bitterly.

"Go on," said Mr. Schultz, and the notary went on: " 'Every object in this house, every piece of furniture, every painting, carpet, tapestry, in one word, everything, even the smallest object, goes to Mary. . . .' "

This time no one moved, but there was heaviness in the air.

" 'All the shares in the bank and in the factory that are still in my name go to Mary. . . .' "

"I looked into that when I received those last threatening letters," said Pierre. "Mary gets fifty-four rubles, I can pay her right now out of my pocket." He made a gesture to reach for his wallet, but Ludmilla stopped his hand and the reading went on:

" 'Mary has suffered more than the others and I have been a burden to her with my constant evil temper. My other children have forsaken me, they are well off, I need not bother about them. Mary shall continue to live in this house if she cares to.' "

"Are you satisfied?" asked Pierre, looking at Mary.

"How can you say that?" answered Mary, in tears.

"Oh," he said, "you are not? What else do you want to take from us?"

"Nothing!" she cried. "And I will prove to you—" But again she was forced to stop, this time because her arm was being pinched so hard she had to bite her lip.

"Who gets the house?" asked Pierre.

"I don't know," said the notary. "This is all."

"Very good. I am going to prove that this will is not valid. Let's have a look at your document, Mr. Schultz."

Mr. Schultz rose from his seat and moved slowly toward the table, sat down in front of it, turning his back to the notary, and pulled out of his pocket a large envelope, which he unsealed and spread on his knees before putting on his glasses.

He read to himself for a while, then said, "The house goes to some organization for the care of orphans in Milan, represented here by one Countess Etruscoli di Torretrusca. Mary may live in it as long as she pleases, paying rent to this lady through her lawyer in Rome whose name is . . . Here it is: Pio Tegolani."

The doctor gasped and lost control. "That criminal!" he said. "This cannot be! The man stole everything we had—he is a known thief!"

Pierre sneered. "You mean this will is not valid, either. We shall see. It can become an interesting fight." He turned to Mr. Schultz and said, "My mother must have thought she had the right to leave everything in this house to Mary. But there are things here that belong to me and were lent by me to my mother—carpets and other possessions I had inherited directly from my grandfather. I have come with special trunks to take them back."

"I know nothing about this," said Mr. Schultz.

"I do," said Mary, "and I would never dream of depriving you of your belongings, Pierre. You too, Ludmilla, must have faith in your sister. We will settle everything. Mamachen does not want us to fight."

Pierre withdrew from Mary to avoid being embraced by her and said coldly to Mr. Schultz, "And how about the money? What is left and how is it distributed?"

Mr. Schultz read: " 'I have made it a point not to leave any money to my sons, because they should earn their own money as their father earned his. I am bequeathing fifty thousand francs to Mary, fifty thousand to Olga, and fifty thousand to Ludmilla, and it will be their duty to provide, together with their brothers, for the living expenses and medical care needed by their elder sister, Katia. I am also bequeathing five thousand francs to my butler, Bernhard, five thousand to the children's governess, Gertrud Luther, five thousand to my cook so that he may get a divorce from his wife and bring his children to Switzerland—' "

"No!" shouted the doctor. "That man was a thief and has stolen more than five thousand francs already. Not a cent for him!"

"All these things may be discussed later," said Mr. Schultz dryly. He went on: " 'Five thousand to my chauffeur—' "

"Never, as long as I live!" shouted the doctor. "That man was a thief, too, and stole our car among other things."

"May I ask you to be patient for another few minutes?"

"All right."

And Mr. Schultz read on: " 'Five thousand to the Lutheran church of Baden-Baden, five thousand to the Russian church of Geneva, two thousand five hundred to the personnel of the Grand Hotel in Lugano . . .' "

"I am not interested," said Pierre. Then he looked at his brother, who during all this time had remained silent, like a huge sulking bear, biting his fingernails and yawning every now and then. This seemed to amuse Pierre very much. "Here is one who will never fight for material possessions, and yet look at him, he is hurt because his mother left him nothing, she did not even bother to anger him with her remarks."

This was enough to make Ivan feel sorry for himself, and he burst into loud sobs that were silently accepted by the others as evidence of his filial devotion.

By midnight everybody was snoring except the old lady. No one dared go to his room. They were all caught by sleep wherever they still happened to be, seated in front of an empty champagne bottle in the dining room (head back or forward), slumped in an armchair in the hall, crouched on a sofa in the library—all unconsciously avoiding the horizontal posture because that was the posture of death, and to let oneself lapse, in a state of forgetfulness, into the posture of death might have looked like the expression of a wish to "keep Mamachen company." They remembered her words only too well.

The doctor heard his father's voice calling him from the fields on a very damp night long before daybreak. "Either

596

you join my farmhands here and till the soil, or get up, wash your face and do your homework; but you cannot stay idle at this late hour."

He stretched his arms, his legs, rubbed his eyes and yawned, and only then realized, from the strong smell of cold cigar smoke and cold furniture polish, that he had fallen asleep in the library. It distressed him to see that he had left all the lights in the house still burning, then he remembered that he owned fifty thousand francs and all the jewels and the furniture, but not the house itself, and knew he was anxious to leave it, sell the furniture and the jewels, and put all that good money in the bank. But still he felt an agitation in his chest which seemed out of proportion to these wishes and plans.

He rose from the couch, beat the cushions into shape again, loosened his necktie and unbuttoned his stiff collar; but still he felt uneasy, and it was clear to him that this could not be ascribed to the expenses of the funeral or the presence of those people in the house. Perhaps the children, he thought. But he knew that the children were well; this was not one of those familiar forebodings warning that one of them would be ill the next day. Perhaps I need a shave and a hot bath, he concluded. But even that did not relieve his heart.

He walked into the dining room, where Pierre and Ivan sat in front of their bottles, one with his nose in the air and his mouth open, the other with his chin on his necktie, slowly drooling into his vest. He examined them as if he were in a museum, then went out into the hall, where he found Ludmilla, another statue to be studied with care, then to the library, where Ivan's wife and Mary seemed to be playing some guessing game, with their heads hidden under cushions; and he studied them too, but his mind was still busy with the unknown causes of his misery.

He went upstairs, locked himself in the bathroom and lit the gas heater to prepare himself a hot bath—and in the flame he recognized the source of his anguish: fires raging from the earth, fires caused by broken gas mains, consuming everything, people homeless, corpses buried under ruins, tidal waves, icy winds and heavy rains. . . .

He turned off the heater and decided to wash in cold water— This is the least I can do to be closer to them.

While Mary was upstairs washing and dressing, Ludmilla was trying to put her ruffled hair back into shape without having to comb it. Adalgisa was helping her, holding a fur coat to protect her against the morning chill and the eyes of the family.

Pierre now appeared in the entrance hall, unshaven, pale, and unpresentable, but he did not seem to care. "Ludmilla," he said, yawning and stretching, "I must talk to you at once."

Ludmilla joined him in the dining room, where the butler was setting the breakfast table, and where Ivan was still snoring.

"Wake up, Ivan," said Pierre, shaking him roughly. Ivan grumbled and said, "Yes," without opening his eyes.

"Let's leave him here," said Pierre. "Come into the drawing room."

Ludmilla followed him, he grabbed her by the arm and said, "If that slimy, dirty little Italian does not get out of our way this very morning, I shall murder him with my own hands. Let him go and take care of his savages down in Sicily. He has engineered all this, and if he stays here Mary will never come to her senses."

"You are wrong," said Ludmilla. "It is Mary who has engineered it all, against his will."

"What do you mean? Haven't you seen him pinch her and push her every time she was about to make concessions?"

"Yes, I have, but it is Mary, I tell you."

"No, Ludmilla, Mary is one of us, she cannot be so cunning. I am beginning to suspect that this whole story of the lawyer from Rome who stole so many precious things is a fraud. And also the theft of the car. This man is an Italian, don't forget. How can you trust an Italian?"

"Pierre, you are not serious, I hope."

"Of course I am."

"Nonsense. I refuse to listen to you. If he has a fault it is that he is too honest, too gullible."

"Are you trying to defend an Italian against your own sister?"

"And you, since when have you developed all this great faith in your sister?"

"I haven't, but now that I am the head of the family, knowing my sister's innate weakness and her natural preference for criminals, I feel that I ought to protect her. I shall have the whole situation investigated by the police. Before our name is dragged in the mud let us discover the truth and take Mary back to Russia with her children, leaving this man to his own criminal exploits. But not before he has given back all he has stolen from us."

"Pierre, you are insane. How can you say such things? I know all the facts and I am completely ready to defend this man."

"You are in love with him."

"Nonsense, I do not think of him as a man."

Pierre was watching his sister carefully. She was blushing.

"I see," he said. "You are lying to me. There is a vast intrigue here of which I alone am the victim. Either you tell me the whole truth at once, or I am going to tell Mary."

Ludmilla looked at her brother in amazement. She had stopped being frightened. Only a second before the thought that Mary might be told would have made her do anything—give up her claims on those emeralds, or return them to Mary after having received them—and now, all of a sudden, here she was, looking at her brother. She knew what had taken place in him and how undangerous he was with all his threats. He needed company, deep down in the void of his heart, and not just company, but company in conspiracy, to know that he did not have to be ashamed of his greed. He knew that Katia's jewels were as much in Ludmilla's mind (and had been for some time) as Mary's jewels; and years before he had taken those "to protect Katia against her insane squandering habits." Now he could not afford to let Mary be more generous with Ludmilla than he was—also, because she might stop there and decide not to be generous with him at all, and then what would he do? How would he justify his claims without first relinquishing some of Katia's possessions? Ludmilla and Mary were left with only fifty thousand francs each—a considerable fortune, but not by Pierre's standards, and he knew that they knew it. Therefore the first thing he must do now was tie Ludmilla to himself by any means, and this idea of defending the family against a foreign thief had a special attraction for him. It was, in fact, a continuation of the plots he had frequently invented in his childhood to scare his little sisters and appear a great hero. Except that in his childhood he had believed in those plots only to the extent that they served the purpose of his game, and for the short duration of that game, but now that he was a grown person he believed them in earnest and considered this progress beyond the figments of a childish mind. Ludmilla knew the comedy was Pierre's way of dressing up like his mother. He felt like her, Ludmilla only looked like her. She also knew, as a born slave, that when the master dies and the son of the master takes over, he has more imagination and more strength in his arm, he wants new whips and is not used to the screams of the victims which had long ceased to amuse his father.

"Pierre," she said, giving him just the kind of intelligent smile he wanted, "between us, this is nonsense. I am not going to ask for Katia's jewels or miniatures, because my peace with you is dearer to me than they are; but neither are you going to play this game. Mary has not forgotten Katia's jewels, and she mentioned the miniatures the last time I was here. I don't

care about Italians, and besides, I am not the kind of person
to do such a thing to my sister. But I trust this man and I assure you that he can be our best ally, if we know how to
manage him. I don't trust Mary, especially when she makes
promises, because she withdraws them easily the moment she
sees they may be accepted. He at least can be pinned down to
his word. Let me handle the matter and don't interfere. I am
your only ally, but the pact between us must be clear."

Pierre's feelings were hurt. Not only was he being denied
the assurance he needed, but his honesty was being questioned,
and still more his intelligence, his tact, his knowledge of the
world and its ways. And by whom? By a silly little girl who
had already made many mistakes and would probably make
more, now that she no longer feared her mother's authority.

"What a fool I have been to speak in my usual straight-
forward way," he said, as if talking to himself. Then he looked
at Ludmilla very closely, trying to read in the center of her
eyes how much falsehood there was behind her words. "What
do I know about you?" he asked, and immediately answered
for her: "Nothing at all. You may be in on all this against
your sister, nothing proves to me that you are not. And I, the
fool, trying to warn you against that man who is closer to you
than I am! Now, don't think I will stand for this sort of dirty
business behind my back for one more minute! I have always
hated dishonesty and cunning—and that is all I seem to get
from those I try to help."

Tears choked him now. He sounded like his mother. A feeling of doom, unknown to him until that moment, weighed
on him like a hand from above; this was his punishment. He
would be cheated by his sister exactly as she and he and everybody else had always cheated their mother. Now he knew it.
And he overplayed his role, not only to hurt Ludmilla and
produce in her the kind of humiliation that would make her
confess and repent, but to commemorate his sin, to fix it in
his heart and to be punished for it. Oh, how lonely he felt,

and how invested with the task of defending the purity of his house!

"Ludmilla," he said, "be honest with me, tell me the whole truth and you will be forgiven!" His passion for the truth, or, rather, his fear of being cheated, made him suddenly generous. "Look," he said softly, "I am generous. I shall say nothing about your low insinuations concerning Katia's things, which I have simply kept and shall keep for her, to return the day she recovers and is able to live a normal life again. I know there is something deceptive in all this, I know that you must have discussed these matters with someone here, and I know *you*, oh, I know you very well. I know you are concealing something from me, and that it is connected with this man. Now, as long as our mother was alive I could afford to disregard all this, because it was none of my business—or at least so I thought, and I regret it now. But I am not going to stand for dishonesty and treason in this house after our poor mother has gone. She is watching us, she knows everything we do or think. We must remain united, and if there is anything we did while she was still alive that is wrong, we must confess it to each other. I am the head of the family. And all I want is honesty. You must repent your sins and be truthful with me. And this, Ludmilla, regardless of what Mary does. I am quite willing to let you have all my part of the heirlooms, provided you tell me the truth."

Ludmilla stood there in despair. She, who had thought that it sufficed to imitate her mother's voice and way of dressing in order to become like her, was now pushed back into her former position of a total slave by the insane moods of this man who spoke of purity when everybody knew that he traveled with his mistress and spent far more on her than on his family. But she did not dare say anything. Mamachen knew, Mamachen understood, and Pierre was probably right—not, indeed, in suspecting the doctor, but in suspecting her. She herself had not known it until then, but now she knew that her plan was to obtain those emeralds by any means and let Mary cheat Pierre if she so pleased. How could she now deny the truth?

"Ludmilla, I am waiting," said Pierre—and this too was Mamachen, her very words—"I am waiting for the truth, not for the lie you are preparing in your mind. You ought to thank God on your knees a thousand times a day that you still have someone to guide you through life. What would you do without me? So don't misuse this God-given opportunity to tell the truth and be given the truth. Come, Ludmilla, quickly, speak, I am waiting."

"I swear," she said, and she understood for the first time in her life how close the truth is to the lie, over the tenuous bridge of promises, "I swear that there is nothing, not the slightest feeling in my heart of which I ought to be ashamed. Pierre, you must believe me. I was only going to plead your case with this man, which is also my case, because I too have been cheated by Mary. And I too would rather give everything to you than let her keep it unjustly. Not because of the objects themselves, but because Mamachen gave me those emeralds, and I want to have something to remember her by. If they were glass beads I would have the same feeling about them. I don't hate Mary, I know that she will understand, but only if we approach her tactfully and through her husband. I swear to you he is a most excellent man, devoted to her, honest and kind. You are wrong to suspect him as you do."

Pierre seemed unconvinced, because the truth sounded so easy and, as a man of action, he distrusted solutions that did not challenge his intelligence. (The truth must be earned, like everything in life.)

"Are you sure, Ludmilla? Are you absolutely certain? Your conscience does not trouble you?"

"No," said Ludmilla, but her voice seemed unsteady again.

"Hmm. You said 'No' in a way that I do not quite like. And there are too many things against this man. I have dozens of letters from Bernhard, and from Luther before that, proving that he was maneuvering to get our mother on his side against Mary's strongest efforts. And there is this notary, whose wife is his child's godmother—in your place, by the way. I don't like to be cheated. I hate baseness more than anything else. A man who takes advantage of a sick person, of a woman, to obtain without working what it took honest men years of hard work to make is a low creature. I prefer a real swindler who is able to swindle because he is more intelligent than I. But a little, slimy Italian who saves on servants' salaries and watches what they eat—Ludmilla, that is not style. And I am right when I refuse to take his word. How do you know that he is not a thief? Are you so clever? Have you so much experience of the world of beggars and tricksters?"

"No, but I have sworn to you, Pierre, and you must believe me. Besides, he is Mary's husband and she loves him. He is devoted to the children—"

"Any dog is devoted to its pups. As for Mary, it is better if she opens her eyes before it is too late. I don't trust Mary's wisdom at all. She is very much like Katia, more and more so every day. She should be helped. The children would remain with her, these things can always be arranged, it is only a matter of money. She kept her first child, she can easily keep the other three. We can take her to Russia, and if she needs assistance there are always good clinics in Berlin, as we all know. I am for action, and action means prevention. What are we waiting for? If I could only have some clue on which to act. I am sure there is plenty that is being kept hidden from me. And from you too, Ludmilla. Don't forget, we are the dupes, we come from a world where cheating is unknown."

He began to pace the room. He was already feeling better, and this made him certain that his mission was holy.

"I owe this to my mother," he said, looking up at the ceiling, his face exalted. "I have been much too soft, too indifferent, I have neglected my responsibilities and let this household go to the dogs out of pride and stupidity. How I regret it,

Ludmilla. And do you think I want to go on in the wrong path and do nothing to correct my mistakes? Oh no. Not Pierre von Randen. I shall see through this mess, even if it takes me another trip to Switzerland and a disastrous neglect of my own business. I feel a great responsibility and I am not the man to shirk it—certainly not because an inexperienced, silly girl like you says I should. If I were derelict in my duty, I would never be able to look at my face in the mirror again without spitting at it in contempt! In fact, I must not waste my time speaking to you about my decision. What am I, after all—a man, or a weak woman who goes to another woman for advice? My self-respect alone would prevent me from letting this thing continue, if my filial devotion and my duty as the head of the family did not suffice to make me act. A man who does not act is not a man, Ludmilla, and no one can respect him."

Ludmilla was terrified. She too was now beyond the reach of tears. What could be done to stop this madman?

"Yes, Ludmilla, and I know I am right, because already I feel much cleaner. This is always a sign that I am doing the right thing. For I too have a conscience."

He stopped to think of his mistress, and a new piece of useful reasoning was yielded by this seemingly negative thought, which might have paralyzed any other man into shame and inaction. His secret logic ran as follows: If I were in Ludmilla's place and a person who had the right to ask me tried to make me admit that I had traveled with my mistress almost to the house where my mother had just died, would I tell the truth or not? And the answer he gave himself was, No, I would not. Which means that Ludmilla is lying. He looked at her and knew.

"Ludmilla," he said, "I understand your terror of the truth. We all fear our own consciences more than the devil himself. I am not going to be content with what you have told me. I must investigate, because this is my duty; and if I find that you have told me a lie, I promise I won't punish you. In **fact,** I shall forgive you, because I understand. I too have things to hide, and I know how it feels to be confronted with one's judges."

He looked at Ludmilla again and the sight of her terror was all he needed to be certain he was right. She tried to say something, but at this moment the doctor came in to tell them breakfast was ready. The others were in the dining room.

"Please let us finish our discussion," said Pierre dryly, and he shut the door. "Well?" he said, smiling proudly. "What do you think of your brother as a detective?"

Ludmilla could do nothing but stammer, "What—what are you going to do now?"

"I don't know, but something—and very soon, before we leave this house for Berlin. Of course, this must remain our secret. I don't want to upset Mary, I remember only too well how terrible it was when Katia resorted to hysteria in order not to be taken to the hospital. And that was during a normal situation, which this is not. We are all badly hit by what has happened. So I am going to be very prudent. However, this does not mean that I am going to be careless. In fact, I think the little man must not be allowed to leave for Sicily. I want him close at hand, where I can watch his every step."

Ludmilla nodded. She too had made her plans. And her mother could look at her and listen in; Ludmilla had nothing to be ashamed of. Pierre was insane and Pierre must be stopped.

Mr. Schultz had spent the night mostly in the death chamber, with brief stops in the old lady's sitting room, where he had tried without success to sleep more openly. First he had fallen asleep while sitting next to his dead friend, and had been aroused by the noise of his own snoring. Ashamed of this, he had gone to the sitting room, and there all sorts of thoughts had kept him awake. First of all his dislike of the doctor. Never before had he seen or heard anyone so incapable of the most elementary self-control. He blushed with shame at the thought of that scene during the reading of the will, when the doctor had pinched Mary's arm to prevent her from making any promises. And he too now suspected something strange, if not outright unclean, about that second will and that notary whose wife was the godmother of Mary's last child. Disgusted as he was, he preferred not to give vent to his suspicion, because he realized that Mary was quite happy with the Italian and that he was a most excellent father, but he felt sorry for Mary and very much worried about Ludmilla. What sort of guardian would the undisciplined doctor be for her, a virgin? Was she even safe in the household of a brother-in-law who gave in so easily to his passion? Should Mr. Schultz tell Mary of his apprehensions, or would this make her suffer too much? Ludmilla was now an orphan, and someone must look after her. Mr. Schultz did not like the thought of Pierre's being entrusted with the task, because Pierre had a mistress who was well known in banking circles for having already collected from the estates of two rich men whose deathbeds she had made for them with her charms in her London apartment. With all this, Mr. Schultz preferred Pierre to the doctor, because he had respect for Pierre's energy and exceptional financial acumen. Besides, Pierre was so much the descendant of his frightful but wonderful grandfather that Mr. Schultz had to make a great effort, every time he treated him harshly, not to look into his eyes—for there he saw the expression of the man to whom he owed his whole career.

Back to the death chamber now, as there was nothing he could do to help Ludmilla or correct Pierre or educate the doctor. And the calm of that room, the smell of all those flowers and the soporific whisper of Brigida's prayers made him fall asleep at once. The third or fourth time he woke up and went back to the sitting room he decided to turn on the light and look at the old lady's papers, as this was his duty now, not

merely his right. And at once he came upon the Marie d'Escarande letter and Günther's famous letter to the doctor.

It took him several readings to believe what he saw. To him
(as to his wife's daughter) the very name Escarande was a
source of such physical disgust that it would have made him
throw up if he had not been extremely careful to control his
reactions. And here he found Ludmilla in the clutches of that
prostitute, a lost woman already, with no hope of redemption.
Now he knew who had killed the poor woman in the neighbor-
ing room. And Ludmilla dressing up like her mother, imitating
her voice and her ways—what a disgusting comedy, what
sacrilege, what moral and physical murder!

A painful oppressive feeling of heaviness came over the old
man, making it hard for him to breathe; his lungs seemed
unable to lift the weight of the whole world that lay upon his
chest.

"Mr. Schultz," Ludmilla said, "may I talk to you about
something very urgent?"

She had come to her mother's sitting room looking for him.
She had her plan: to tell him frankly about her brother and
plead with him to ask Mary to be generous with Pierre. She
was so much afraid of Pierre's plans that she was determined not
to want anything for herself any more.

Mr. Schultz had only just begun to breathe again, but was
still much too weak to move, and Ludmilla's voice hit him
deep in his chest. She saw him gasp for air and crumple some
papers with both hands, and she realized what they were:
Günther's letter, Marie's letter. Never before had she felt any
real shame. Now no hiding place was far or deep enough for
her. She thought of all the forests in the world, all the holes
in the earth, all the explosions and cataclysms of nature, and
none would have sufficed to protect her from this shame. Her
self-contempt was such that she did not even feel worthy of

helping the poor man, who was about to fall like a tree cut at the base. This was no longer Mr. Schultz, this was an episode in the drama of her own punishment.

The doctor walked in at that moment and saw him. "Mr. Schultz!" he cried. "Mr. Schultz! Are you ill?"

But Mr. Schultz was unable to speak. His eyes pleaded for help. Ludmilla was closer to him than the doctor; she saw him fall and did nothing.

Because he had made all his plans to ruin her and get back at least one part of what he felt should have been left to him, Pierre took no precautions against Mary (which precautions would have consisted of reminders to himself to hate her), and Mary won him over with a smile and a few minor presents. He was quite well aware of this while it was happening and made mental notes of how she was taking advantage of his goodness, and for years afterward reproached her and hated her, magnifying the episode—in the good family tradition—to the point where nobody could believe it; but that morning, while the doctor was trying to revive Mr. Schultz, Mary walked into the drawing room and found Pierre so happy and so sure of himself that she mistook it all for benevolence and paid him back in the same currency. She had armed herself mentally to meet with a resentful, gloomy Pierre, and this was a relief.

"Pierre," she said, "I cannot stand the feeling of suspicion which existed here last night. Please, Pierre, tell me what the objects are that you would like to take with you, and I shall give them to you with joy."

Pierre's reaction was one of aloofness. He wanted nothing this way, he wanted everything his own way. "I don't want to *take* anything from you, Mary," he said.

"Forgive me if I used the wrong word. I just want you to know that this is said in a brotherly spirit—more than just said, it is *meant* in that spirit."

"This is very kind of you, Mary, but please don't deprive yourself and your family of the things you have *rightly* inherited."

"My God, Pierre, what are you saying? Who can claim he has rightly inherited anything but his duty to be generous and fearless?"

This was going too far. Generosity and fearlessness were two aspects of greatness that Pierre would not give up for anything on earth. Whether in point of fact he had ever had either of these qualities he did not even ask himself. What he cared for was the reputation. People must always think, when they pronounced his name, "Pierre von Randen, that fearless, generous, great gentleman."

So he said, very much against his will, "Mary, you know me well, I hope you don't imagine that I care."

She looked at him, as if waiting for more, and this made him say more, because he could not stand a cold reception to his words.

"In fact," he said, "I am very much surprised by your assumption. I am at present—and I apologize for saying such a thing, but you know me well enough not to think that I'm bragging—a very rich man, and if I said something last night about those few objects I own here, it was only because of their sentimental value. So please don't think I am here to *deprive* you of anything."

"Pierre, I don't know how to tell you this, but I really and truly don't care. I'd rather give up everything and live in poverty than have you think that I am greedy or ungenerous. I have a great many faults, but not that fault."

It was he now who looked at her as if waiting for more, and this made her say more; if he could not stand being doubted, neither could she.

"All the harsh words exchanged between us in the past are long forgiven, but the one thing I never could accept was your saying that I had only one aim in mind—namely, to get the inheritance all for myself. No, Pierre, I am not like that, and you are not like that. We have a great many faults, but they all stem from an excess of pride, of generosity, of greatness."

She had tears in her eyes, as she did every time she said the opposite of what she really thought; it was like being redefined and purified, not by herself, but by God.

"Yes, Pierre, we are all a bit insane, but we are generous and good at heart. I know it is extremely hard for you to accept a present from me, but do it as a favor to me. What can I give you here to take away in your trunks?"

This annoyed him very much. "Mary, you speak of those trunks as if I had come here to fill them with your belongings."

"With yours, Pierre, with yours."

"Mary, now I am really beginning to lose my patience."

"But you said so yourself."

"Because I said something, you must immediately elaborate on it and come to the strangest conclusions. See how suspicious you are? I said so, yes, what of it? One says so many things."

"Pierre, I am sorry I hurt your feelings. I was wrong and I apologize. But please let me ask you once more to relieve me of a few of these burdens that may have to be sold. You would not want to hear that things you might have liked to see in your own home, things to which you had a right, have been sold. We cannot go on living in this house, it is too big for us, and too expensive."

"All right, if that is what you want, I can buy a few objects from you."

"Pierre, really, now it is my turn to lose my patience. Since when have money matters entered our relationship?"

"As you say, Mary, but I can promise nothing. Let me just see the things you have in mind to give me."

Thus began their inspection tour. The cabinet they had been leaning against, the very chairs on which they had been sitting were abandoned in haste to be silently asked with worried eyes, "Whose cabinet, whose chair are you? With whom would you prefer to stay?"

"Do you want this cabinet? It is real Boule."

"Very beautiful."

"Do you want it?"

"No, no. Keep it."

"But I really don't care."

"No, no. I'd better not."

"Katia had one like it."

"Yes—I have it. I am keeping it for her."

"Why not take this one too?"

"No, no. Thank you."

"But why not?"

"No, no. Really not."

He seemed hesitant, his eye wandered from the carpet to a certain French tapestry and from there to a smaller cabinet full of Greek statuettes and Egyptian cats and Pharaohs, some in blue terra cotta, others in ancient gold, and pieces of Chinese jade and other such objects. Mary pretended not to see what seemed to attract him there and continued to look with a certain intensity at the Boule cabinet and the chairs next to it, hoping that he would join her in their contemplation. He did not. After a while they seemed like two strangers in a museum who are so much interested in the things they are studying that they believe themselves alone.

It was finally Pierre who went over to his sister and challenged her to prove to him that what attracted her was better than what attracted him.

"You really love that cabinet," he said, and she was caught by surprise.

"No," she said, then corrected herself at once: "That is, yes, very much, but it is too precious for the kind of life we are going to lead from now on. It belongs in a much bigger house, it calls for a more splendid *train de vie*, such as yours.

I can see it in your house in Moscow. It would be in its right place there."

"I cannot see it there at all. In fact, I have a feeling that I never will."

"Why be so pessimistic, Pierre? I offered it to you. Or did I not make myself clear enough?"

"You did, you most certainly did, but now come here and look at these things in that cabinet, please. Those, it seems to me, are more apt to give a certain distinction to a large house. And they fit so well with the carpet and with that beautiful French tapestry. Don't you think so, Mary?"

"Why, of course, Pierre, I agree that the carpet perhaps might look all right, provided there were only a little light in the room, because in a strong light its weak points would show, and that would make a bad effect on your guests; but all in all, it is a pretty grandiose carpet—or, rather, it was one, long ago. And I also agree with you that the Gobelin might be an addition to a large and stately house; but do you *really* think that those tiny Greek Tanagra things and those poor fragments of Egyptian objects that were once beautiful would be at all appreciated by the kind of people you see in Moscow?"

"What do you mean, the kind of people I see in Moscow? Are they any different from the kind of people our grandfather saw when he acquired them?"

"Our grandfather did not acquire them all, he only got the Tanagra statuettes from Schliemann."

"Well, speaking of those, for example, wasn't Schliemann also one of those people?"

"Schliemann was an exception, Pierre."

"He was also a banker, and our grandfather was one, and those objects were very much admired in his house. I cannot understand your ideas."

"There is little to understand, Pierre. I was only suggesting that perhaps those smaller objects would yield more of their beauty to a person who lived in seclusion, surrounded by his books, than to a brilliant man of the world. And besides, they seem to belong in a more Mediterranean climate than Moscow."

"As you say, Mary, as you say, but here again I note your absurdity. What difference can the climate make to things that are kept in a cabinet anyway and that were buried in mud for thousands of years?"

"Pierre, if by this you mean that you want them, go ahead, choose from among them and I shall give you some; but it seems to me that, in a way, those objects are less in your style than some of the others."

"You are wrong, Mary. You seem to have the strangest idea of what my style should be. But, just to follow your way of thinking, which other things?"

"Oh, well, the big carpets, for example."

"Those that were stolen in Rome?"

"No, those of course were yours. But Mamachen bought others here, at an auction. They are beautiful, and very big, much too big for our needs."

"Well, let's have a look at them."

They were in the writing room and in the entrance hall, and one was in the sitting room upstairs. Pierre looked at the two downstairs and said dryly, "I'll take those to relieve you of the burden, and because you lost the ones I owned."

"We did not lose them, they were stolen. Together with the best pieces of the Greek collection."

"Not the Egyptian collection."

"No. That was bought in Egypt for me."

"They are yours?"

"Yes, they are mine."

There was a long silence. Then Mary said cheerfully, as if emerging from a deep meditation, "But I want to give one of those pieces to your wife—a gold brooch dating back to the time of Rameses the Second."

And she opened a drawer in her mother's writing desk, chose

from a bunch of keys, opened the cabinet and took out a small gold object which immediately made Pierre look gloomy as he compared it with the many other objects of the same type which were larger and heavier. In fact, he was so angry as he felt it in his hands, lighter than the lightest paper, that he was about to refuse it with bitter words.

The closing of the cabinet, with Pierre's eyes looking so intently at every object in it, gave Mary such a fright that she surrendered on another field.

"Now that I think of it," she said, "the Gobelin might also look quite nice in Moscow, in your dining room perhaps."

"Why, of course it would," said Pierre, and from his promptness Mary knew that she had given up too much.

"Unless you want another one of these Egyptian objects," she added.

"No, no, you are quite right, they are better for people who have time to read and like to sit at home alone and look at their possessions. The Gobelin will do. I'll take it with me."

"I am so glad you like it. It has always had for me a very special sentimental value. I used to sit here and watch it for hours while Mamachen was playing the piano." She had to wipe her eyes and make an effort not to break down. "It is . . . a living part of her, a whole period of my life."

"I also remember it," said Pierre.

"Oh, no, you can't," she said. "You were never with her, never, never. In fact, it reminds me of the days when she was waiting for your letters and they never arrived. And when they did . . ."

This time she broke down and he too, against his will, began to sniff. He made an effort and said, "How about the jewels? Do those too remind you of something?"

"Not really," she said, with a smile between her tears. "In fact, when Katia got the pink sapphires for her wedding, I could not understand why she should be so proud. Do you like those pink sapphires very much?"

"I never look at them. They are in the bank. Katia can have them back when she leaves the asylum. Any time."

Mary nodded, then said in a soft voice, "I am going to give something to Ludmilla too. Jewels, I mean. Don't you think I am right?"

"I agree that you should," said Pierre, staring at her.

"Why don't you let her wear some of Katia's jewels for the time being?"

"I have no right to. Suppose Katia recovered quickly, from one day to the next, what would she say? And how would Ludmilla accept the idea of returning them to their rightful owner?"

"I had not thought of that. Why, is there really hope for Katia to recover so quickly?"

"One never knows."

"I thought one did. I had believed she was ill for life. But of course, if you have better reports from the doctors, I am glad, very glad. I wish you had told us before." Then, seeing that her words had hit the mark, she added sadly, "I really wish you had. It is so rare that one gets pleasant news. Mama-chen would have liked to hear that there is hope for Katia. It would have made things easier for her. She might still . . . be with us." And she broke down completely.

The tin-lined wooden coffin was brought into the upstairs sitting room because Adalgisa had made a mistake and shown the men in through that door, not the bedroom door; and when Mr. Schultz, who was lying on the sofa in the throes of a second heart attack, saw it, he tried to lift himself on his elbows. The doctor stopped him and said, "Don't move. You must lie down and remain very quiet if you want to get up again at all."

Mr. Schultz obeyed and followed the coffin with haggard eyes, breathing with great difficulty. After the horrid object was gone and the door safely closed behind it, he tried to say something; but the doctor again stopped him and said, "Be quiet. Not a word, not a move, nothing." He then turned to Ludmilla, who was still standing there, far from the sofa so as not to be seen by Mr. Schultz, and said, "Have someone call the hospital for oxygen at once, and . . ." He hesitated for a moment, then said, "That's all. Just have them send the oxygen."

Ludmilla slipped out of the room, and the doctor sat down on the edge of the couch to have a closer view of the patient's face.

"It will come very soon. Don't think of anything, don't be afraid, everything will be all right if you let nature take its course."

From the next room came the voices of those who were lifting the corpse and placing it in the coffin.

"Wait a moment," said the doctor, and Mr. Schultz smiled sadly at the absurdity of this recommendation. The doctor left the room and went into the bedroom, where he locked the door to the hallway from the inside, so as to prevent Mary from going in. Then he came back to the sitting room and resumed his place near the patient.

Pierre and Mary walked in, followed by Ludmilla. The doctor made a sign to them that they should ask no questions, and this irritated Pierre. He came to Mr. Schultz and asked him, "How are you? Do you need a good doctor?"

Mr. Schultz lifted his finger in the direction of the doctor and said nothing.

"A specialist?" said Pierre.

Mr. Schultz opened his mouth and, in spite of the doctor's severe glance, said, "Best doctor on earth."

Pierre did not understand. "What was that?" he asked.

Mr. Schultz touched his heart and frowned a bit, to indicate that it was dangerous for him to speak.

And now it was time for the body to be sealed into its casket for the journey to Berlin.

For a person who had traveled all her life, to have become a package, a trunk, was worse than an insult, it was utter absurdity, and—one of the many aspects of death—an instance of the fact that she had now become a thing. Also, it seemed absurd that she should change expression—as she had—and still keep that stubborn silence which had so easily been broken by entreaties during her life. Gases had swelled up her stomach and she seemed to exhibit it as a reason for looking angry in her sleep. It was not for her to speak. "What do *you* have to say about this?" she seemed to imply. As an alternative to this interpretation, one could see her as a person intent on trying to remember a name or date or some other detail by which to prove to her family that they were wrong as usual. And they were all willing to be proven wrong, if only she would say it. But there exists no friendship between the living and the dead.

"See? I have nothing, I let myself be put into a trunk, I laugh at your old-fashioned way of living, and you don't follow my example. Do what you wish, I'll stain these clothes, I'll spit on them, I'll rot in them; close the lid and spare yourself the expression of my will. Take, take my poor belongings, fight over them, be done."

In an aura of reproach beyond words, the inner lid was closed with great sizzling of lead along the edges of the tin box; and then the tin box, not their mother, was nailed into a beautiful oak box, like a present of gigantic cigars.

Pierre was completely destroyed. The lesson, finally, had penetrated his mind. His mother was no more. He came into the room where Mr. Schultz was lying as one would come to an apple tree, waiting for the apples to fall. Would the old man yield his fat business and his many connections together with his body now, and dismiss his banking soul like a dishonest employee, for failure to perform its duties? Pierre knew that he would inherit most of Mr. Schultz's business, because, in spite of the old man's ostentatious dislike of his character and ways, he still represented Mr. Schultz's only link with a family he worshiped. He was right. Mr. Schultz opened his eyes and spoke to him in Russian, and the doctor was linguistically kicked out of the room.

"Pierre," he said, "I don't have long to live. I trust your great intelligence and am devoted to your name, as you know. But I must warn you of one thing: If you go against your mother's will, I shall use my last energies to destroy your position in New York and in London. And that would take only a few words about your private life. Coming from me, they would suffice. Give me your hand."

How right are those who say life is a school. More than just a school, it is a special tutoring class for retarded children, where the teachers are trained to repeat the same thing with dozens of examples, in the vain hope of having it enter once, if for only a few minutes, into the slow minds of their pupils.

Mary had just seen her mother sealed and nailed into her trunk with all the things she would forever need, and yet the moment she herself was to decide what she might need on that trip to Berlin, she repeated the same old phrase to Frieda, "I don't know, ask . . ." as if her mother were still there, in the next room. But instead of correcting her mistake and trying to decide for herself, as she now must, she refused to decide, as if she could that way blackmail the Lord into returning to her the person He had just called to His kingdom. Frieda, who had been her mother's maid, was just as helpless to decide. She could not even tell which suitcases or trunks and how many of them were to be filled with what.

The doctor found them still undecided hours later, and it

was he who patiently, if a bit clumsily, took Mary's dresses and other personal belongings out of closets and drawers, placed them on beds and armchairs before making his choice, selected just one suitcase out of the dozens that were piled up in the attic and decided upon that one. It was at this point that the two women came out of their inaction to criticize him and fill seven more suitcases with all sorts of unnecessary things for a trip that was to last not more than five days.

Should Mary wear her mother's mourning dress or should she borrow only a few veils and other bits for a makeshift attire, pending more lasting work by a seamstress after she had returned? The question became anguishing, Mary feared she might be delaying the whole trip. This was not very likely to happen. There had been a delay already, of which the doctor had not seen fit to inform the family lest they criticize him; and this worried him greatly. He had told the Swiss Railway representative who had witnessed the sealing of the casket that in view of Mr. Schultz's attack they could not leave that night, and the railroad man had made arrangements by telephone to have the party (consisting of two railroad cars—a sleeping car and a weeping car with the casket in the middle) transferred to an early-morning train. Thus, while he did everything with his usual efficiency and in the shortest time, because that was his habit, the doctor seemed rather to encourage Mary's hesitancy by saying, "Take your time, make up your mind, have Frieda help you, Adalgisa can help, too, with the sewing machine. She is very good."

"But what nonsense, there are only a few hours, how can you speak that way?"

"We may have to postpone the trip until tomorrow if Mr. Schultz is unable to leave. I am waiting for Cappelli to decide. Mr. Schultz does not want to call his daughter, he wants to leave here, but he probably can't."

"But then let Pierre make arrangements for another train."

"No no no, I'll do that, if necessary."

"But you must do it immediately. You cannot hope to find another train at the last minute."

"Leave it to me."

His usual fear of asserting himself in any other way than by just doing things, without speaking about them, made it harder and harder for him to tell the truth. But Mary was so strengthened against her despair by this practical problem, which, although it was centered upon the very cause of her despair, buried it in a net of calculations which had nothing to do with human feelings, that she seized upon it as a drowning person seizes upon any solid object floating about.

"Let me tell Pierre, he knows best, he always travels, he may get a train at the last moment as a personal favor, even in Switzerland."

The doctor could do nothing to stop her. She had found another reason to be pleased with this new problem: it allowed her to decide without deciding; she ordered both her mother's mourning dress and an everyday black dress of her own packed together, thus postponing the choice until after they arrived in Berlin. The doctor now saw no hope of making her responsible for missing the night train. He went back to his patient and found him sitting up, weak but determined to go back to his hotel.

"I had not realized you were to leave tonight," he said. "Or, rather, I had known it all the time but somehow the connection between here and today seemed to be broken. I must have been quite ill."

"Don't talk," said the doctor, "and above all don't sit up. Lie down again and wait until I give you permission to move. I'm waiting for a friend and colleague of mine who will probably come with the ambulance, but he will take you back only if he finds you well enough."

"I cannot stay here. You are all going to Berlin tonight, and I shall leave before you."

They were interrupted by Dr. Cappelli's arrival.

"What is this?" asked Pierre, coming into the sitting room, where the two doctors were still talking about the patient. "Mary makes me go to the station in a hurry to see if we can count on a morning train and they tell me this has already been arranged by you several hours ago. Why the mystery? And why should not even Mary be informed about it?"

The doctor did not know what to answer. Pierre began to speak to Mr. Schultz in Russian, and his voice became more and more excited. His hands trembled, his whole face was distorted by anger. It was clear to the doctor that he was being accused again, this time for good reason, and he wished he could disappear underground, but as this was not possible he savored all the shame, all the hatred of himself for having let a minor matter grow into a major scandal. The immediate result of this was a feeling of solitude which nothing could relieve. He did not even speak to the other doctor (whose presence made things worse), but walked slowly out of the room, to take refuge in the death chamber, where solitude was so vividly expressed. He knelt down in a corner and, looking at the brown coffin through his tears, asked himself aloud, "Why must I always be so weak?"

He heard a sob behind him and before he could turn and see who was crying there a hand was on his head. "We are all like that," said Mary. "She was that way, too. But now we can be different. She will show us the way."

He wished he could remain in that dark room forever, with his head under Mary's hands, and never have to face the world again. But the world must be faced. They were looking for him. Dr. Cappelli was still waiting, and so was Mr. Schultz.

After the patient had been put into the ambulance, he found himself alone with Pierre in the entrance hall. He did not know how this had happened. A heavy silence made his anguish almost unbearable. Pierre seemed unwilling either to speak or to walk away and leave him. The doctor looked at him almost imploringly. Pierre still said nothing and seemed utterly inimical. The doctor cleared his throat; then, knowing very well he would regret it afterward, he unbuttoned his jacket, took his gold watch from his vest, chain and all, and handed them to Pierre, saying, "This is yours, I believe."

Pierre was still staring at him with an air of contempt. He simply took these objects and, without speaking a word, put them into his trousers pocket and walked away. A minute or two later the doctor saw him in the dining-room pouring himself a huge glass of cognac and drinking it as if it were water.

"You could have said thank you at least," he murmured, imagining himself in the act of shouting these words to Pierre. As a matter of fact, his face did show defiance and courage. After this he went back to the death chamber like a little boy who goes to complain that his best toy has been taken away from him. But Ivan and Ludmilla were there. He withdrew and closed the door. Back in his bedroom he found Mary sorting the necklaces and earrings she had decided to give Ludmilla.

"Come and help me decide which ones I should give her," she said.

"Nothing," he said, in a fit of indignation. "Absolutely nothing. Not one pin."

Mary was so surprised that she just stared at him.

"And I'll tell you why," he said. "Do you know that your dear brother has accepted my watch, the one you gave me for Christmas, without even saying thank you?"

"My Christmas present? Mamachen's Christmas present?"

"Yes. Exactly. And not a word of thanks. As if I were a thief and he were doing me a favor by not calling the police. But I told him."

"You did?"

"I did. I said, 'You could have said thank you at least.' I said it politely, but I said it."

"And he?"

"And he, can you imagine what he did? He poured himself a huge glass of cognac and drank it like water."

"What?"

"Yes. As if he had not heard."

And again, for the tenth, twentieth time in two days, the mute corpse celebrated everyone's weakness, everyone's basest feelings.

The second night was coming: one more night away from beds and still not getting anywhere. Forgiven and consoled though he was, the doctor felt uncomfortable even under Mary's protection. He sneaked out of his room to reach the servant's quarters where the children were confined.

At the end of the hall he met Ludmilla. He was so sure of the contempt he had deserved from her more than from all the others that he hoped she would pass by without looking at him.

"Darling," she said, putting her hands on his shoulders, "may I see the children for a moment?"

That word was no longer a term of endearment to him, it was a form of social promotion, almost a decree knighting him.

"Why, of course you may," he said. "How kind of you to think of it."

"How silly of you to use such words. Why on earth should I do it out of kindness? They are my own children, I adore them, you know that."

They walked together into the more modest section of the hall and took the narrow servants' staircase to the third floor.

"You are such a good man," she said, "and I know you so well. I know that if it were up to you, there would never be any strife in the family. And I don't mean to criticize my sister. We are all evil creatures in our family. You are the only one who is clean and generous and honest."

"Oh, don't say that. You don't know me."

"I know you so well I even know why you answer me the way you do. Because you at least had the courage to show what my sister had decided—but it was her decision, and your acting upon it proves you a good, devoted husband. You are wonderful."

"But I assure you . . ." He did not dare go on.

They had arrived.

Whatever Sonia said was repeated by Filippo in the same tone.

"I never want to leave Aunt Ludmilla."

"I never want to leave Aunt Ludmilla."

"Aunt Ludmilla is my aunt."

"Aunt Ludmilla is *my* aunt."

And there was strife already, for the right to climb into her lap. Then came the questions: Where was Mamachen, where was Grossmamachen? And then the whole comedy of their feeling superior to the little one, whose ways and habits were so different from theirs that they could not help laughing at him; but he laughed with them, because everything to him was still a holiday.

The duty to feign cheerfulness proved easier to perform than the opposite duty in the opposite wing of the house. Ludmilla was her old clownish self again, and the doctor felt very much tempted to run back to his room, call Mary and have her come here with the necklace of emeralds for her sister. But he mastered his impulse. And then he began to worry about Ludmilla's kissing the children and staying with them so long. He was anxious to wash and disinfect them. Let's not forget what she has done, he kept repeating to himself.

The door to the next room opened slowly, and Kostia's pale face made its appearance.

"Kostia, my child!" cried Ludmilla, disentangling herself to be able to take him in her arms. But Kostia did not want to be greeted that way, any more than he wanted to be spared the sad news. They had spared him so well that they had ousted him from their lives. This was partly the fault of the servants, who knew of no better way to defend themselves against his questions than to treat him a bit harshly—but it was mainly his stepfather's fault, because he had insisted at once that all the children be removed from the scene.

"Where is my mother?" Kostia asked, withdrawing from his aunt, who, in spite of her efforts, had been unable to get rid of the other children.

"Where is my mother?" yelled Sonia, and Filippo repeated, "Where is my mother?" Then they both repeated it in their own language: "Where is Mamachen?"

"In her room," said Ludmilla. "Now be quiet and let me go to Kostia's room for a moment."

Kostia had gone back to his room and closed the door behind him. His stepfather entered first and saw him crouched next to his bed as if it were a deathbed. Sobs were shaking him.

"Kostia," he said, patting him on the head, "Kostia, what is it?"

The boy looked up, and his eyes met those of Ludmilla, who had just come in and was bending over him. "Grossmama-chen is dead," he said, unashamed of his tears now that they had heard him sob.

Ludmilla's eyes were also full of tears, but she tried to keep up the pretense. "How do you know this?" she asked. "I don't believe . . ." But she broke down, still shaking her head in denial.

"Kostia," said the doctor, drawing the boy to him and sitting at the desk, "Kostia, I must tell you the truth." He hesitated. "I must tell you the truth: She has been very ill, really very ill, and so . . . This, you see, my boy, is the process of life. It ends in—in the separation of body and soul. But the soul does not die, I can assure you, and we all know it. This is a fact, and a consoling fact. Imagine, would it not be terrible if the soul too were to become extinct? Eh? Answer me, think of it, be logical. And behave like a man, a little man."

The boy hid his face on his stepfather's shoulder and wept there silently, while the children laughed in the next room.

What Pierre found infinitely more insulting than the will itself was the presence of that boy who had lost his grandmother while his own sons had not lost theirs. Kostia's tears were Mary's tears, they made her cry with greater pain, but neither Pierre nor his brother could cry during that night. They were sleepless and angry and paced the halls, the rooms downstairs and those upstairs, like two lions in a cage. Ivan's wife was the only one to have broken the spell and gone to bed. Ludmilla was also crying, torn as she was between her love of the children and her hatred of their mother, who had given her nothing the while Pierre had reaped at least a few rugs and that beautiful gold watch.

It was decided that Kostia would also go to Berlin. The idea of the trip and the presence of the relatives in the house had helped him find his calm again. He was sent to bed. And before sunrise, when Mary went to wake him and help him get into his best dark suit, she also spent some time watching her other children in their cribs. This gave her much strength. The coffin in the meantime was being taken out, and when she appeared with Kostia to have breakfast there was nothing upstairs and no reason for her to see that room again. Suitcases and fur coats, hats and shawls, everything was piled up in the small library downstairs. Kostia clung to his mother like a child. The only other person for whom he had eyes was his stepfather.

XXVII

W HY SHOULD THE TRUMPETERS of such a foreign city as
Berlin blow so hard into their heavy trumpets on such
a cold day for someone who had died so far away from there?

These were the doctor's thoughts as he followed the hearse
to the tune of Chopin's Funeral March. In front of him walked
Mary with Kostia, Ludmilla, Olga, Ivan and his wife and
Pierre, all in one line. The doctor had been in line with them,
but he had slowly dropped behind, where he had Bernhard on
his left and Fräulein Luther on his right, together with a few
other former servants and distant relatives who did not dare go
near those huge veiled orphans and that poor sobbing boy in
the blue suit. The doctor kept looking at Kostia's bare head and
worrying because it was too cold and the boy's hair too short.
He would die of pneumonia. But nothing could be done
about it. Twice he had tried to put a scarf over the child's
head, and both times Kostia had reacted with violence, tearing
it away and letting it hang loosely over his shoulder. Now,
of course, he would lose it, and the doctor kept an anguished
eye on it, then looked sidewise and watched the passers-by take
off their hats, and behind their backs saw in the shop windows
the fat trumpeters, the black horses, the hearse and the mourners. Bernhard and Luther were watching him with contempt;
he saw their faces, too.

How much snow everywhere, and what a dirty city it was. The doctor could not help thinking of Prussia as Austria's ally against Italian independence and hating everything about these Nordic barbarians.

He recognized the tomb: there it stood with the huge naked angel hovering over the marble effigy of his father-in-law. But the whole monument was blackened by the dirty air of Berlin, and it looked smaller than in the many photographs at home.

After the reading of the prayers in German the coffin was lowered into the marble cubicle and the lid with the inscription placed over it.

The trumpeters had left, the horses and the hearse had left, there remained only the mourners and the minister. It was snowing and windy.

"Kostia," the doctor said, "put on your hat."

But still the boy remained hatless, clinging to his mother and sobbing. The doctor was attracted by Olga, and felt that she was looking at him, too, with a friendly curiosity despite her grief and despite the good reasons she had for hating him. He had never sent that cable, and she had learned about her mother's death from the papers in Dresden where she lived, and from Luther. She looked less like her mother than the others, and to him this was a good recommendation. She did not look like Mary, either, she was very oriental in type and very beautiful. He was somewhat ashamed of his curiosity, and worried lest her husband become jealous. The husband also looked at him with great interest. Perhaps they hate me, thought the doctor, and he wished he had not made arrangements to go home that same night.

Pierre detached himself from the group and came to shake hands. "We shall part here," he said. "I am going back to Russia now. Goodbye and thank you for everything. I am sorry I did not see my godchild before leaving Lugano. But I want you to know that if your son needs a career he can always count on me to give him work as a cook or a farmhand on my estate."

The doctor was so stunned by this remark that it took him some time before he recognized it as an insult (the mere fact of Pierre's having spoken to him had seemed at first so much of an honor).

"Thank you very much," he said at length, "but the boy will study Greek and Latin and become a breadwinner in some honorable if modest profession."

Mary had overheard the exchange, and she detached herself from the group to answer Pierre. "My son will become a scientist like his father, never a cook or a farmhand, and certainly not a banker."

"Oh, oh," said Pierre, imitating his mother so that Mary and the others shuddered. "I see, I see. Mopsie is becoming proud. Well, Mopsie, if your son Kostia needs my help, he can become my personal chauffeur. You can count on me, Mary, I always keep my word."

Before she could answer him, he was turning his back to her and shaking hands with the Lutheran minister, who had overheard everything and seemed very much absorbed in that handshake. She looked to the others for help: they, too, seemed interested only in the minister and waiting to shake hands with him.

"Now, Kostia, put your hat on!" said the doctor, and walked over to the minister, his hand outstretched. Pierre saw that hand and slowly pushed the minister in the direction of the others, without letting go of him. Ivan caught a glimpse of Mary coming in his direction, and he brushed her aside as if he had not seen her, to go after his brother. His wife tried to follow him, but Mary was too close, so she kissed her and said, "Goodbye, Mary, goodbye."

"But we will see you again," said Mary, sobbing in her arms.

"I don't know, Mary, I don't know. Come here, Kostia, give a kiss to your aunt. You are a good boy." After this she grabbed the doctor by the arm, to prevent him from following the others, and kissed him on both cheeks, with many tears.

"But we are not leaving yet," said Mary. "We are all go-

ing back to the hotel, are we not? Our train leaves only at
seven. . . ." And she held on to her sister-in-law as to a hostage.

"All right, Mary, don't cry. Think of our dear Mamachen. We
shall meet at the hotel in a few minutes. Goodbye." And she
left them alone, almost running away from them to join the
others.

Mary stood there alone for a moment, then came back to her
husband and child, sobbing. "I have no family any more! So,
this is how they are, all of them!"

"Mary," said the doctor severely, "Mary, for God's sake,
what are you saying? And what are *we?*" He clung to her and to
Kostia, and thus they walked to the cemetery gate, looking at
every tomb along their way, and almost greeting in those horrible monuments the silent neighbors of their poor, abandoned
mother.

At the gate they met the minister, who shook hands with them
at long last, and this consoled them very much, but they soon
realized that he was keeping them as if on purpose, and in fact
they were missing a chance to be seen by the others who were
there, at a few steps from them, climbing into Pierre's limousine.
As the minister chatted and chatted stupidly about God, death
and resignation, they saw there were two cars, both obviously at
Pierre's orders, and in the second car they saw Luther and
Bernhard, and the other seats empty. Both cars left, and when
they tried to find a taxi or a cabbie, there were none for miles on
end. It was snowing, it was late, they began to fear for their
train, and when they finally reached the hotel frozen and tired,
they were told that the others had left and were expected back
late that same night.

Only a few hours from Berlin they were almost alone in the
third-class compartment, because Mary's mourning had moved
the hearts of the other passengers; thus Kostia was able to lie
down on the hard bench, with his stepfather's coat for a mattress, and Mary found room to put her feet on the opposite seat,
next to Kostia.

"See the advantage of being in mourning?" said the doctor to humor her. "We have saved on the expensive first-class ticket plus the sleeper, and we travel like kings because we have so many cushions and shawls that we don't feel the hard benches."

Mary smiled gratefully and said, "You are right. And when I think of poor Mamachen . . . What did she get from all the money she spent? Nothing at all. Or, rather, sadness and solitude. And a great deal of both." And she cried over her mother's life more than over her death. Then she began to speak of Pierre's last remarks. But the doctor stopped her.

"He belongs in the past, let's think of the future only, our own at long last."

And they decided to live in closer contact with their children, banning that terrible Germanic discipline which was responsible for all the worst misunderstandings in the family.

"This is the spirit of Mamachen's last recommendation to us," said Mary. "I am only sorry I did not give at least one of the necklaces to Ludmilla."

"Never mind," said the doctor. "Ludmilla is alone, she is rich, and she knows how to live by her wits. We have four children and will probably have more. There are so many debts to pay that before we can settle in that smaller apartment in town little will be left of what your mother has left us. And we shall need every penny."

After a while he added, "Only now can I say that I am married to you and not to your family bank, to your family factory, and to your old family feuds."

When they finally reached the station of Lugano, after a journey of three days and three nights, their clothes were so heavily impregnated with the odor of tobacco, rancid fats and all the smells of German third-class railroad cars, and so thick with greasy coal dust, that they no longer looked like civilized people. For the first half hour after stepping out of their traveling jail they could not get accustomed to the clean air of Lugano and the absence of that drumming in their ears, in their whole bodies.

"Aaaah," said the doctor, stretching his arms and feeling his whole body with his hands, "aaaaaah, what a relief." And he began to tell the porter about their trip.

"Never again," said Mary, wiping her smudged face with her black fingers, leaving dark marks where an even layer of coal dust had existed before.

"Of course, never again," said the doctor. "First of all, it is to be hoped that there will never be another reason for a trip of this sort. And then, never shall we go to Berlin for such sad purposes. If I were to die now, all you would have to do—"

"Now, please," said Mary, seeing that Kostia was beginning to cry in spite of his dull fatigue.

"All right, all right, I just wanted to mention it because we should consider ourselves fortunate for two reasons: one, that we are alive, and two, that we have a clean cemetery here at a stone's throw from the house. But even down in that part of the city where I think we may find an economical house, there is a most beautiful cemetery one may reach on foot."

"I hope," said Mary, smiling, "that your parsimonious spirit does not make you plan to avoid paying for normal transportation to such a place."

"Of course not. But note the effect on you: we are able to talk serenely about a matter that we would never have had the heart to approach had we traveled first class with plenty of comfort and time to torment ourselves."

Sonia and Filippo had been told that they must ask no questions, because their grandmother had gone to a hospital and their parents did not want to talk about it. Other precautions had been taken on the doctor's instructions: The whole wing where the "catastrophe" had taken place was closed, and Mary's personal belongings had been placed in the dressing room next to the room formerly occupied by Ludmilla. Most of the dining-room furniture and paintings had already been crated and piled up in a corner, and the dining-room table had been set in the music room, from which the Christmas tree had been removed—although this would never have been done before January thirteenth in normal days, that being the Russian New Year's Day. Mary was pleasantly surprised to find herself spared painful reminders of a life that could never be resumed. And when she saw that a hot bath had been prepared for her, she was so happy that she let herself go with expressions of joy which a first-class trip with private drawing room would not have evoked.

The next morning, while Mary was still sleeping, the doctor dashed out of the villa and down to the city, where he looked up his new landlady in the person of that Countess Etruscoli di Torretrusca who had managed so well in depriving his family of their house. He was received by her administrator, who said yes, they could live in the house as long as they pleased, and named a rent which was so appallingly high that the doctor found no adequate expression for his anger.

"Don't you realize," he said, "that we cannot afford such a rent?"

"I have no means of knowing what your budget is, Doctor," said the man with a smile. "But of course you are free to live elsewhere if you prefer. We are in no special hurry. You may pay by the month if you so please."

"I don't think I should pay at all if I promise to leave within a month or so."

"That," said the administrator, "is not for me to say. If the countess agrees to have you there as her guest, that is her privilege. But I doubt that she can, unless she is willing to pay the orphanage in Milan out of her own pocket for the rent they would be losing."

"Look," said the doctor, "my mother-in-law drafted this will at a time when she still thought that her lawyer in Rome, that bastard, that thief, that criminal of an Avvocato Tegolani—"

The administrator interrupted him coldly. "I am in no position to discuss the validity of the will. But I would advise you against using such words when you speak of the man who happens to be our adviser and benefactor in Rome. It so happens that I know Avvocato Tegolani personally, and—"

"Let me show you the evidence."

"No, sir. I must ask you to leave. I cannot allow anyone—"

"All right, I'm leaving. But I am leaving that house, too. I am quite determined not to pay such a fantastic sum, not even for one month."

"That, sir, will have to be discussed between you and the countess in person."

"To hell with her," muttered the doctor as he left; and when he reached the house again he said to Mary, "Ah, but I told him."

To dismantle a big house, dispose of all the furniture, choosing only the things one may need for an entirely different kind of life, is not a matter to be dealt with in the space of a single month. And then the servants, and the bills, and the many unknown threads that still bind a dead person to her house and keep coming to the surface—all this was a strain for both the doctor and Mary. Seeing how upset she was, he had asked his friend the notary to speak to the countess, and they had come to an understanding (which was that they could afford to propose a lower rent for as long as the family cared to remain) that seemed generous to them, and entirely feasible— though not to the doctor, and even less so to Mary.

"No," she said, with a sweet smile. "Never. I am through with big houses and servants. All I want is a small nest for us two and our children. I shall be their teacher, I shall keep house and cook for you. Perhaps we may allow ourselves a maid, but I want to live as you have always wanted to live. And the money we still have we'll spend on travel and in scientific work."

They therefore accepted the offer of the countess only for a short while, to give themselves a little time. An apartment in town had been found, some of the furniture had been sold and some was to be stored, the servants had been told that they must leave as soon as they had found other employment, and finally the day came when the old lady's rooms had to be opened again for inspection, to decide what was to be kept and what sold.

"Let me do this alone," said Mary, and she went upstairs with her fists clenched, murmuring secret prayers as she mounted the stairs.

She had not noticed that Tasso was following her. When she opened the door to her mother's sitting room and turned on the light, the first thing she noticed was that there were no flowers on the mantelpiece, nor on the desk, nor on the small round table, none in front of the portrait of her father and none in front of the oval pastel representing her grandfather. This hurt her more than the sight of the room. She heard a noise, thought it was Adalgisa coming for instructions, and when she saw it was Tasso she had a sudden impulse of hate such as her mother had once had when the dog had been "knocking" on her door.

"Out of here!" she cried at the top of her voice. But the big dog jumped on her mother's chair and tried to hide there behind the bulk of her writing desk. "Get out of here, you dirty animal!" she cried. "How dare you!"

Her voice produced a strange effect on her. In that large room, from the four corners of that high vaulted ceiling, her mother's voice had resounded again. Mary gasped, felt faint, slumped into a chair, then, ashamed of her weakness, rose and again shouted to the dog, "Out of here, you dirty animal!"

The door opened and Sonia appeared.

"What do you want in here?" asked Mary, now profoundly ashamed of her hysterical reaction.

Sonia asked, "Is Grossmamachen back? I heard her voice."

A bolt of burning pain went straight to Mary's heart. She gasped, then cried, more and more in her mother's voice, "Who asked you to come in here, anyway? Get out!"

As Sonia burst into tears and slowly made for the door, Mary almost ran after her and took her in her arms, to protect the child from her demonic self. But pride had the upper hand. She slammed the door and ran to her mother's bedroom. There too what struck her was the lack of flowers. Of the scene she had witnessed there only a short while before, and of the total transformation of that room into a chapel, not the slightest trace. But of the normal days before that, how many signs, and how strong and how lively; and must she disregard those in favor of a scene she could call back to her memory only by a gigantic effort, and even then not successfully? Besides, had she not just heard her mother's voice in the next room? Of course she was aware that it had come from her own throat, but could it go unheeded? She murmured her own name: "Mary . . . Mary, come here. Mary Mops . . . Mary . . ." She spoke a bit louder: "Mary?"

The door opened, a dark form came in, and it was Adalgisa, and to be caught in that insane and intimate mistake made her so angry that she screamed, "Who asked you to come in here?" Adalgisa was frightened, exclaimed something, and the next moment she was gone. Mary now realized what she had done; but her anger was alive and she must find an outlet for it.

Again the door opened, and a carpenter walked in. This was one of the men who had been working in the drawing room downstairs, crating the paintings. He was impudent enough to ask, "Should we begin to crate the furniture in here? What is it you have decided to sell in this room?"

"Sell?" Mary shouted. "Sell this room? Are you insane? Who authorized you to come here? Go to hell, all of you! Out of here, out! Nothing must be touched in this room. Nothing, ever! Do you understand?"

She now opened the door to the hallway and screamed, "Why are there no flowers in this room?"

Adalgisa appeared again, in tears. This angered Mary all the more.

"I want fresh flowers here, the same fresh flowers I am used to seeing here. Why have they not been brought?"

Kostia showed up from nowhere, holding Filippo by the hand and followed by the dog.

"That dog again? And the children? What are the children doing here? Who allowed them to come in here, anyway?"

The voice, the voice, how it resounded, louder and louder.

Mary was sobbing as she paced her mother's rooms and the hallway, and then the rooms again, as if chasing after her mother's ghost; and between sobs she was screaming, "How dare they? No one must touch these rooms. . . . I want flowers from San Remo every morning, every morning, every single morning. . . ."

The doctor had been busy with the carpenters and with a hundred other chores. He heard that voice and shuddered; then, mastering his feelings, he went into the entrance hall and called from the bottom of the stairs, "It was my fault. Please take your time—"

"What?" she shouted. "Take my time? We are not going to leave. This is my mother's house and nobody is to live here after her . . . after us."

She no longer knew what she was saying, and at each word the wound grew deeper in her heart and her sobs grew louder.

The doctor hesitated for a moment, then began to run upstairs, and when he saw her he was suddenly struck by her physical resemblance to her mother. He was holding a hammer in one hand and a nail in the other. He let them fall, and, bringing both hands to his face, he asked with anguish, "You too, Mary?"

638